ERIK VALEUR

THE SEVENTH CHILD

ERIK VALEUR
TRANSLATED BY K. E. SEMMEL

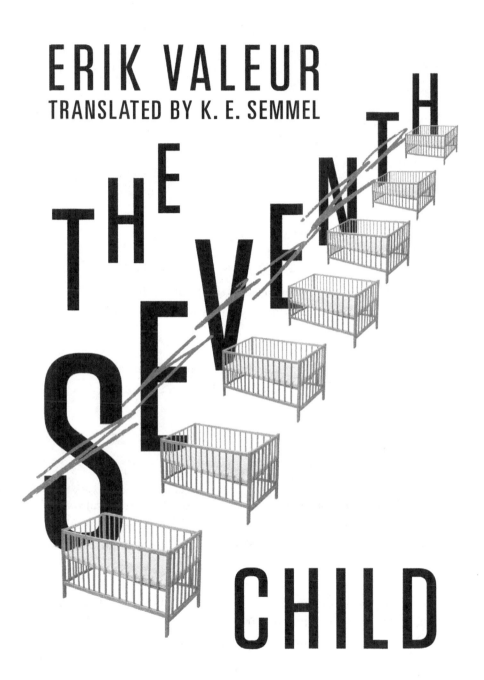

THE SEVENTH CHILD

PUBLISHED BY
amazon crossing

Text copyright © 2011 Erik Valeur and JP/Politikens Forlagshus A/S
Translation copyright © 2014 K. E. Semmel

The Seventh Child was first published in 2011 by JP/Politikens Forlaghus A/S as *Det syvende barn*. Translated from Danish by K. E. Semmel. First published in English by AmazonCrossing in 2014.

ISBN-13: 9781477849804
ISBN-10: 1477849807
Library of Congress Control Number: 2013915843

Prologue

It must remain a secret how I uncovered the new and hitherto unknown information in the case that became known as the Kongslund Affair.

I made that promise as solemnly as possible, considering that it's rather silly to make oaths; the truth can never be suppressed when Fate has other plans. And it always does.

In any case I will try to report, as simply and objectively as possible, the strange events that for a brief time held an entire nation in thrall. I hesitate to side with either camp regarding these events, which only a merciful God of the most forgiving kind will be able to regard with mild eyes. And I can almost hear the famous matron at Kongslund sneer at these thoughts, because what does God have to do with any of this?

In her world, which for sixty years was inhabited by tens of thousands of orphaned children, there was no merciful God—certainly *not* one resembling an absentminded, silver-haired, elderly gentleman inclined to forgive human beings by day's end.

In that world, there was only the stubborn will of the formidable governesses to mitigate the sins and the arrogance of previous generations, and from the very beginning, that doomed project had been subject to a dark and unmanageable Fate that operated outside the reach of both religion and reason. Creating obstacles was Fate's favorite pastime; shocks and sudden blows its areas of expertise.

"Fate is the only power of any significance, and it knocks over the children of humankind as it pleases," she would say with that contagious enthusiasm that was her trademark; then she would laugh so hard the walls trembled and she would add, "Here at Kongslund, we've needed the help of neither God nor the Devil!"

I can still recall the rumble that rose from her bosom after she uttered such statements. They caused us children to hold our breaths in equal parts delight and terror. Even today, all these years later, I am inclined to agree with her.

Like the main characters of this book, I spent the first years of my life at the Infant Orphanage Kongslund, and I have returned there several times since, driven by forces I have never fully understood. It must have been what enabled Marie to finally locate me.

I base my retelling of the Kongslund Affair on her detailed notes— especially those concerning the lives of the six children with whom she spent the first months of her existence at Kongslund and who became such an obsession for her—combined with my own investigation of those events for which she was unable to provide an accounting.

The mystery of the seventh child is, as I see it, also a story of Marie's longing. I think the psychologists at Kongslund would agree with this interpretation, as they study the world's damaged beings through gleaming glasses, while smoking their pipes.

We can only hope that Marie and Fate, in spite of everything, can reach an accord here at curtain call.

If that wish is granted, her journey has not been in vain. She will be sitting somewhere in the shade of the beech trees—the very same ones that once sheltered Denmark's last absolute monarch—singing the song she sang as a child, night after night, the one about the blue elephants.

And this time, I don't think she'll stop until she has reached the final verse.

April 30, 2011

If you find a friend, you've got a chance.
If you find none, you will succumb.
—Magdalene, 1969

THE WOMAN ON THE BEACH

September 11, 2001

The woman was found approximately halfway between the Skodsborg Beach Hotel and Bellevue Beach in the early morning of September 11, 2001.

Just a few hours later the world would be altered forever. This strange coincidence determined the course of events in this peculiar case, and one can only conclude that Fate thought it amusing to put two such unusual occurrences on the same day.

The less significant event was soon forgotten, though for the first few hours the police considered it with utmost gravity, describing it in much detail in their initial reports. The alarm sounded at 6:32 a.m. The dead woman was lying close to the edge of the water with her face pressed into a gray sludge of sand, as though she'd tried to devour Copenhageners' favorite beach in a single, greedy mouthful. Her arms were bent backward, her hands open, and there were small patterns of sand in her palms. This discovery prompted investigators to momentarily speculate that a ritual murder had been committed by some depraved individual. But of course, as one detective noted, before the sun rose over Øresund, the eastern wind might have simply whirled the sand across the body, and it had come to rest in the dead woman's palms.

It was a dog walker from one of the tony suburban mansions on nearby Tårbæk Strandvej who, terrified, called the police. Investigators had no doubt the woman in the sand was dead the moment she hit the ground. There was a cone-shaped crater in her forehead. Blood had seeped into her hair and soaked the sand beside her temples.

Technicians found light-gray hair on the sharp rock that had pierced her skull, but most of the blood had been washed to sea by the tide long before the body was discovered. The dead woman carried no identification, though her clothes and wristwatch led the police to believe she was from Australia (or possibly New Zealand). But by the time investigators arrived at that conclusion, it was too late; no one was paying attention to a dead woman on a beach in Denmark.

No doubt, someone would have dug deeper into the case had the world not been turned upside down during these very hours—and this was a coincidence that no one at the alleged crime scene could have anticipated. As technicians combed the sand around and under the woman for critical leads, two hijacked airplanes flew into New York City air space, and all activity on God's green earth lost significance. In the days that followed, only one image burned through the airwaves and into the Danish consciousness: the smoking towers and the charred bodies that fell and fell and fell, down and down and down, toward the concrete.

If the case of the dead woman ever had a chance of making it to the front pages of the Danish newspapers, that chance was now lost. Most media never mentioned her. Two smaller dailies printed a few lines, and a few weeks later, one reported the police decision to close the case, labeling it an "accident."

After that, the dead woman literally sank into oblivion.

The police had been unable to identify her. At their Copenhagen headquarters, homicide detectives concluded that, since there hadn't been a single call about her or any missing person who matched her description, no one was looking for the woman. Repeated INTERPOL searches yielded nothing, and no one came forward to identify the dead woman from the macabre photo of her that had been widely circulated. The police had no leads and no good ideas. And not a single registry or database provided any information that could break the deadlock.

In this way Fate outplayed the efforts of mortals—simply to amuse itself, one might think. But, to tell the truth, the police had no serious qualms about dropping the case; after all, there were more important things to worry about.

* * *

And yet.

A few years later, the chief inspector who'd led the investigation was interviewed for a series of newspaper articles on the subject of unresolved murder cases.

In the middle of the interview, he suddenly mentioned the woman on the beach between Skodsborg and Bellevue, a case that by that point had been completely forgotten. Several things that morning had always puzzled him—small but peculiar details—and now the retired chief inspector spontaneously found words for his unease.

"If it really *was* murder, I fear it was the act of a very sick individual," he said. "In fact, during those first few days, we suspected we might be dealing with the first Danish serial killer." The aging inspector delivered this statement in a rather gloomy tone that he otherwise abhorred, because he considered it unprofessional to show any emotion regarding his cases.

The reporter pricked up his ears. He couldn't recall having heard of a murder near Bellevue.

On the other side of the table, the chief inspector closed his eyes, as though imagining that popular stretch of beach, recalling items the technicians had marked and photographed in the sand. Then he said, in that same grave tone of voice, "At first we thought it a little strange that she would fall onto the only big rock on that beach. The *only* big rock. It was quite a coincidence. But it was a possibility . . . and we couldn't prove otherwise."

The reporter nodded and found his digital recorder, laying it gently on the table.

"Of course we were surprised that her one eye was so badly *damaged* while the other eye was entirely unharmed, as if simply closed in peaceful sleep. The damaged eye hung halfway out of the socket, and we couldn't see how the rock could have inflicted that kind of injury—at least not at once—or even if she'd fallen twice. But then again . . . it *could* have happened. Or she could have been injured elsewhere some time earlier." The chief inspector opened his eyes. "Maybe she had fallen before . . . earlier that night." He formulated his hypothesis in such a doubtful tone that the reporter dared only a subtle nod, not wanting to impede the eerie suspicion that seemed to be emerging.

Then the chief inspector came to the mysterious discoveries, and his voice sank even lower. "Maybe they had nothing to do with the crime," he said. "But close to the body we found four objects that we honestly thought were . . . were without any logical connection to what people do on any ordinary Danish beach—sunbathe, relax. Yet the objects lay almost in a circle around the woman's body, close enough that they *could* be connected, and that made us really nervous."

To capture every single word that followed, the reporter turned on his small digital recorder.

"To her right—to the south, that is—was a small book, just five or six feet away. Maybe it had nothing to do with her. But it wasn't your typical book, certainly not the kind you'd expect beachgoers to be reading. It was written by a twentieth-century astronomer . . . Fred Hoyle . . . *The Black Cloud*, published in 1957. An old science-fiction novel. You'd have to be an astrophysicist to find it interesting. I read it myself."

He shook his head, almost apologetically.

The reporter hadn't heard of the book, or the author.

"But there was another thing," the old inspector said. "Due west of the body, a little ways up the beach, we found the branch of a linden tree. The peculiar thing is that no linden trees grow anywhere near that spot. So why was it there?" He shook his head once more, as if to deny a miracle of natural history, and then repeated the reservations any officer worth his salt would have. "Of course, some kid could have brought it there and tossed it . . . it just seemed so . . . implausible."

Again he sat motionless, trapped in the past.

"But what *really* puzzled us was that it had been sawed off with a chainsaw—the branch, I mean. And then . . ." He fell silent, closing his eyes again, as if to revisit that beach again, where the body lay face down in the sand and the technicians crept about on their hands and knees.

The reporter nudged the recorder discreetly toward the inspector, but remained silent, aware of the man's unease. Sawed-off branches that thick aren't carried about in the beaks of doves.

"It was very old," the chief inspector finally said, the despair in his voice even more pronounced now. "When we had it examined, it turned out to be *really* old." He shook his head a third time. "That branch wasn't picked up on any forest floor nearby—it had been indoors for many years—and who the *hell* takes a very, very old branch outside to leave on a beach? Why would anyone do that?"

Unable to answer any of the questions, the reporter simply waited quietly.

"And then a little to the east, in the direction of the water, a few feet from her head, we found a small piece of rope. But it wasn't an ordinary rope. It was a relatively thick rope fashioned into a little noose. And that made us really nervous, because given its placement next to the deceased's head, it seemed to symbolize some kind of hanging . . . but the worst part . . ."—he hesitated before continuing—"the very worst was of course the bird."

He pronounced the last word in a near whisper.

"The bird?"

"Yes. A small bird was due north of the body—near her left hand. She was on her stomach, remember. The bird's neck was broken, and given its proximity to the body we asked the medical examiner to determine time of death. It had died that same night. That's why we sent a description of the crime scene to FBI specialists in Washington—the ones who search for serial killers. But, because of the attacks on the Twin Towers, it took them a long time to get back to us. They had enough to do. When they sent us the results of their analyses, they tried to reassure us. They didn't believe we had a serial killer on our hands. Yet, if there was a connection between the dead woman and the objects we found on the beach that day, they couldn't explain it. The FBI had never seen a pattern that even remotely resembled what we'd found that morning on Bellevue. If it was a pattern, that is."

The inspector fell silent again.

"So they told you it was most likely a coincidence?" The reporter's question carried a hint of disappointment.

"Yes, that's right. By all accounts, it was a set of coincidences, odd coincidences, but still. 'Don't worry,' they said. But we did. Or at least I did. And I still do. That little bird is always in my mind's eye."

The reporter put his finger on the recorder's "Off" button and said, "But there's nothing peculiar about a dead bird on a beach. A cat could have broken its neck and dragged it there before being chased off."

The chief inspector stared at the young interviewer for a long moment. "Yes, of course. It is all entirely possible. But it wasn't a baby seagull or a blackbird gone astray. Wasn't even a damned *sparrow* . . ." Anger flashed in his eyes. "It was a bird that never would've flown off to die on some damned beach in the middle of the night, and *that* was the problem."

Once more the older man's gaze returned to that morning on the beach, to details only he could see. The reporter lifted his recorder off the table to catch the inspector's concluding remarks.

Later, in the newsroom, the assembled journalists could hear those remarks as clearly as when they were spoken just inches from the microphone. The old chief's words didn't sway the editor, though. He rejected the story with an irritable snort.

"We can't print that kind of nonsense! Readers will think we've lost our minds."

"It was a small golden canary," the chief inspector had said into the microphone. The speaker crackled a moment. "Understand?"

The reporter was silent.

And for quite some time, the chief inspector had remained quiet too.

"That was the problem," he finally said. "Have you ever heard of a canary flying to a beach in the middle of the night, landing at the very edge of the sea, and breaking its own neck? That's goddamned impossible."

In the next instant, a scraping noise could be heard from the speaker as the inspector rose from his chair.

"That woman was murdered. I am convinced of that. And it's the sickest crime I've ever encountered."

But, as noted, his statement was never published. And the editorial staff forgot, as they are wont to do, everything about the story they found too far-fetched to print.

PART I

THE BEGINNING

1

THE FOUNDLING

May 1961

When I lean forward, I can see directly into the orphanage's garden, and if I stand on my toes and open the window a little, I can catch a glimpse, as if in a dream, of the white-clothed, authoritative governesses who for a generation ruled over Kongslund and all the creatures brought there. They would be sitting on the patio with a view of Øresund, and even today, so many years later, I can still smell the aroma of newly ironed linens and freshly baked bread that seemed to emanate from them, scents that easily drifted all the way up under the roof, making me dizzy and forcing me to lean my crooked shoulder against the wall so as not to fall to my knees.

Ms. Ladegaard would be sitting right there, and over there Ms. Nielsen and Ms. Jensen, and a bit farther down, all the way by the water's edge, I am standing with my little blue Japanese pull-along elephant on its rusted chain, looking at the distant outlines of the island of Hven, where several centuries ago the scientist and pioneer Tycho Brahe built Stjerneborg. Of course, back then, I knew nothing of the scientific significance of that island. At that age and with a pull-along elephant as my only companion, that blue stripe of land symbolized, from as early as I can recall, the secret target of my persistent escape fantasies.

During those years, Kongslund received a never-ending stream of chil-
dren who had been born out of wedlock and were therefore given up for
adoption. They were welcomed into the high-ceilinged rooms by the strong
and straight-backed governesses who made only one promise: to find them
a new home and a new family as quickly as possible.

I was moved out of the Elephant Room in my second year at Kongslund,
and when Ms. Ladegaard became my foster mother, she put me gently but
firmly in the room she considered the most beautiful. "Have a look around,
Marie," she said. "Because this room was designed and decorated by a king
of the people."

Obediently, I twirled on my heels—three full turns—and then I was
once again by myself. I sat down by the window, my gaze returning to
Øresund and the distant island. At least once a day, I would curl my fingers
together and put them to my eyes so that it looked exactly as though I were
staring toward the object of my dreams through a long and tremendously
sturdy pair of binoculars.

* * *

The scream seemed to ricochet from wall to wall as it made its relentless
way through the long corridors of the Rigshospital, and it carried with it
so much rage against darkness and perdition that no one within earshot
would ever forget it. After what seemed like an eternity, it slowly faded,
leaving only a low murmur in the minds of those who'd heard it.

The strange thing was that the scream arrived many hours after the
actual delivery—at the very moment of birth, the young mother had
maintained a surprising and entirely unnatural silence. The little baby
entered this world under such peculiar circumstances that each of the
individuals present on the obstetrics ward would remember the details
of that night—and what had happened immediately before—nearly half
a century later.

Several people remembered both the prelude and the young woman's mysterious disappearance three days later; one even remembered
the delivery itself. But their recollections could be confirmed by only a
few handwritten notes that had collected dust for decades, and that did
not answer two central questions: Who was she and where did she come
from?

No one had the slightest idea where she'd gone following the birth. And no one had any information about the child, not even its gender, since it had been removed from the delivery room according to the hospital's custom during those decades, when thousands of illegitimate children were born in Denmark.

The three people who could shed light on the mystery of that night in 1961 have all passed away: the supervising midwife who delivered the baby; the nurse who watched over the infant during its first hours; and the chief medical doctor who had ordered everyone to refrain from discussing the events. Many years later, a midwife—then a student—who had been on the floor that night told a reporter that the child was retrieved on the third day, as the doctor had predicted, and that in all probability its first home was the famous Infant Orphanage Kongslund.

The midwife, now retired, was only too happy to tell the story to her attentive audience, for she had always felt sorry for the young women who, during the postwar decades, passed in a continuous stream through the Rigshospital, delivering girls and boys who were then given up for adoption.

The first oddity occurred when the chief medical doctor called during the nightly marine weather broadcast, barely an hour before the young woman's arrival.

It was a brief and somewhat formal conversation, which the young midwifery student overheard as she sat across from the on-call nurse, drinking tea. Later she could recall in detail how the chief medical doctor had emphasized how very special this arrival was—*a special delivery*, he had remarked drily (and perhaps with a trace of disapproval).

"She will be brought to Obstetric Ward B by car. She will give birth *alone*. There will be no next of kin present," he'd said. "If she wishes to see the child when she is on the ward, don't let her. No matter what, the child will be put up for adoption."

He had underscored the irreversibility of the decision, and that wasn't typical, either. From time to time, the young women regretted the most difficult decision of their lives, and they were allowed to stop the adoption process. But that wasn't going to happen in this case.

"In three days the woman will be picked up, at the same time of day. The matron of Kongslund, Ms. Ladegaard, will pick up the child."

The latter was standard procedure. But the short notice and the chief medical doctor's involvement were not.

The next peculiar deviation from routine was the woman's arrival. She was brought to the hospital by private car, which at the time was entirely uncommon.

At least three of those present would later recall that the car was dark and rather large, and that it turned into the hospital's entrance on Juliane Maries Road. The engine was still running when the chauffeur, dressed in black, climbed out and helped the young woman from the backseat.

Two midwifery students who had observed the scene from behind semi-closed blinds joked with one another: "Here comes Cruella de Vil," the older one said.

The new arrival was indeed wearing a long, dark coat and a black wide-brimmed hat. But that was the extent of the comparison. The woman on the hospital doorstep was quite young, with short blond hair and dark, narrow eyes, as though she hadn't slept in a very long time. She was approximately the same age as the youngest midwifery student.

Normally, a woman in labor would bring a note from Mother's Aid Society, the national organization that assists women, containing the necessary information. Mother's Aid Society would have already prepared and sent a report to the hospital's social worker. And the social worker would have marked the file with a capital *A* to inform everyone involved that the mother wished to put the child up for adoption.

The delivery would then be handled according to the custom of the time—discreetly, in awkward silence, and with a generous dose of laughing gas. And in the very moment of birth, the medical professionals would do something that would puzzle subsequent generations of more liberated women, because it seemed like an invocation of a very special curse: they would place a white cloth over the laboring woman's face to prevent her from catching the tiniest glimpse of her child. This had become standard practice, a way of easing the separation with the baby, who, until that moment, had been part of the woman's body. The mother would not see the umbilical cord cut, would not see the child's hands searching for its mother; instead, the midwife would wheel the infant out of the delivery room to a waiting bassinet.

Later that evening, when the older of the two midwifery students hesitantly asked for the girl's medical record, the head nurse, blushing, admitted that no record existed.

The younger student, Carla, curiously eyeing the soon-to-be mother, held out her hand. "What's your name?" she asked.

But the girl did not respond. She merely put her coat on a chair and supported herself against it. A persistent whir rose from her chest, as though she were restraining a cough or suppressing a shudder in her slender shoulders.

More than twenty-five years later, the two students remembered this very detail. They ascribed that sound to anxiety, but the retired midwife later realized it might have been something else entirely.

As though the girl knew it was better to get it over with as quickly as possible—that there was no way around her shame—powerful contractions seized her half an hour later. In a sense, putting a child up for adoption was a more heretical act than an illegal abortion, because it condemned the child to begin life in utter loneliness. All these years later, the now aging midwife still recalled the silence that surrounded the fallen young women.

Carla had returned to the delivery room with a little metal canister containing sterile cotton tampons, and when there was a pause in the contractions, she had approached the laboring woman's bed, trying to make contact with her for the second time. "You are doing very well," she said.

Carla wanted to show compassion, to ask about the contractions, maybe even hold the girl's hand—after all, they were almost the same age. During her first few months at the hospital, she had made a concerted effort to provide the suffering girls more than the professional assistance she was taught. "Carla is very attentive to the patients," the head midwife had remarked. But before Carla reached her, the girl suddenly turned and opened her eyes, staring at Carla with a look she would never forget.

The girl's irises had been green and blurry, first shiny with pain and fear, then suddenly clear and cold, glaring up as if from a shaft inside the earth. A moment later they lit up in rage, the likes of which Carla had never seen and the reason she still remembered the girl and this delivery a lifetime later.

From this moment on, the labor progressed quickly, and that too was rather bizarre. After only an hour, the girl's face was as white as the sheet under her sweaty body, and yet she didn't cry. She closed and opened her eyes again and again. Her body seemed to grow stiff, as though the blood had ceased to flow; sweat seeped from her pores, and the crinkled bedsheets became soaked. And yet she made no sound. When the contractions rolled over her, her lean white shoulders trembled. Carla remembered the heat and dampness in the room, the blond hair sticking to the pillow, the smell of shame invariably surrounding the women whose file bore the capital *A*.

Only much later, when she became a mother herself and she had a long life to gaze back on, did Carla realize that her compassion was part of this shame. The realization shocked her, but she shared it with no one until, in retirement, she recalled the mysterious birth. She considered compassion the highest virtue, but that night on Obstetric Ward B, it had had a twin sister whose face was invisible to Carla. The suffering woman, however, had recognized it immediately: condemnation.

The chief medical doctor arrived a few minutes before the delivery and asked Carla to leave the room. But she knew what was about to happen. To complete the curse—that's how she thought of it years later—the girl would give birth behind the white cloth and (according to the midwife) without uttering a single scream, and in the minutes that followed, the child would be taken away, the whole matter concluded.

The young woman was wheeled to the postnatal ward, where the newborn would be sent as far from the mother as possible so she could not hear it cry. (The nurses knew the abandoned children woke more frequently and therefore cried more than the babies whose mothers slept close by, and nobody wanted a desperate mother to start looking for her little one.)

On the third day—a few hours before she was scheduled to leave—the young woman raised her head from the pillow and asked for the head midwife. She wanted to revoke her decision to put the child up for adoption. She wanted to see her child.

The head midwife contacted a nurse who called the head nurse, who in turn got hold of a doctor, who then alerted the chief medical doctor, who restated his command: under no circumstance was the girl to see the child.

In this particular birth, there would be no exceptions.

About an hour passed before the order circled back to the head midwife. She went straight to the young girl's bed and, in a soft voice, rejected her request. No doubt, she thought, the decision was in the child's best interest. "I'm afraid it's too late. The child is already gone," she said.

You could hear the young woman's scream in the delivery rooms on the opposite side of the building; it embodied a mixture of grief, fear, and unrestrained fury, and it slammed against the walls like a torrent of water in a sealed tunnel.

Everyone bowed, closing their eyes tightly, as if only darkness could erase the visions released by that sound.

When at long last silence descended on the corridors, the midwife called Carla into her office, offering her a cup of jasmine tea. "I realize seeing what that girl . . . the one who gave birth on Tuesday . . . went through must have made a strong impression on you," she said, placing a reassuring hand on Carla's arm.

Head bowed, Carla listened to her superior, whom she knew was childless and lived alone.

"I know it's *shocking* for a woman to see another woman reject her child like that. But it's also shocking for the child." The midwife lowered her voice to a whisper. "You feel so distinctly the child's need to nestle against someone—it feels the exact same needs we do, perhaps even more powerfully. The warmth of another body . . ."

She let her last sentence hang in the air, offering no further explanation, and years later Carla still recalled the light tremble of the woman's fingers on her wrist.

Then, as if to drive away the evil that had just passed through their usually life-affirming world, she clutched at Carla more fiercely. "But we can't do anything about it, Carla. When Fate has so decreed, it is best the mother not see her child at all. That's why we do it."

Carla nodded silently.

After her shift the following day, she walked up to the postnatal ward, where a couple of nursing mothers pointed her to the right room. But the bed was empty, the young woman gone. Almost as though it had all been a dream.

Then she heard steps behind her, and a deep voice. "Hello."

This was the final detail she could clearly recall all these years later. In the middle of the room stood a woman with a baby in her arms; she was so tall that Carla only reached her chin.

Confused, Carla curtsied.

"I haven't seen you before," the tall woman said. "What's your name?"

Carla saw a tiny face bundled in the woman's wide embrace, eyes shut tightly. "Oh," she replied, "I am just a midwifery student here on Ward B."

"Not *just*, my dear. No woman is *just* anything . . . and certainly not *just* a midwife. You are the very welcoming committee of life!" The woman's booming laughter caused the baby in her arms to shake.

Carla blushed. "No, I just meant . . ." She forgot what she was going to say.

"You wanted to see if the child you brought into this world was still here," the tall woman said, serious once more. "It is. And now we are going to find a good home for it. The best home it could possibly have. I can promise you that. My name is Ms. Ladegaard. I am the matron of Kongslund, the orphanage run by Mother's Aid Society in Skodsborg." And then the tall woman added, as though talking to the baby, "The children call me Magna."

Carla recalled the faint scent of sweet flowers, mixed with a sharper smell of something she perceived to be cigar or cheroot smoke.

The matron smiled and turned toward the door.

The little child, snug in her arms, puckered its lips. A tiny, almost invisible, rosy red slit in a sleeping white face. Then they were gone.

* * *

A week later, a few miles to the north, the city is about to awaken. The woman has turned on a single lamp in her apartment, but it barely illuminates the room. She's a little older than the girl from the Rigshospital, but her child was also born there, only a few days earlier.

She has invited her visitor to take a seat on the sofa and wait until she has woken the baby in the bassinet. But her guest remains standing by the window, as though the sight of Østerbrogade—between the apartment and the Svanemøllen train station—is the real purpose of her visit.

There are no trams on the street. It's too early.

Then her guest turns. "I brought some new clothes," she says authoritatively, leaving no room for discussion. She is thin, with a pale, narrow face that reveals no hint of what is to occur.

She places a white paper bag on the dining table.

The woman nods. When it comes down to it, what does it matter to her? The agreement has been made, and she will get what she wants. There will be no evidence of the mistake she has made. Life can go on— and no one will ever know.

That is all she really wants.

"I see," the woman stammers; her voice conveys her hesitation. It's her child, after all, at least for another few minutes. But she is exhausted after the hardest few days of her life.

Her guest approaches and hands her a small bonnet and a bright red romper, which isn't very thick. Though spring has warmed the air, it seems strange to put away the woolies—they will not be going with her. Instead, the woman helps her visitor put the baby's arms into the sleeves of a jacket; they exchange no words.

For the last time, the woman considers her decision. Two weeks have elapsed since she first made contact, and she has considered the peculiar method—and the possible risk—time and time again. She has gone over it countless times, because she realizes that something could go wrong, something unsaid, something she hasn't anticipated. But no matter how long she thinks about it, she cannot put her finger on anything. Regardless, it's no longer her responsibility. This is what she tells herself, because this is how it must be.

In the end, she puts the child into the small blue carry-cot herself and carefully tucks the duvet into the sides, placing a pink blanket on top, all without looking at the little one.

The visitor carries the cot into the hallway. "I'll be leaving then," she says, and with her free hand, she opens the front door.

The woman nods. "Well, thank you," she says, absurdly, as though the woman has done her a personal favor. She can't rid herself of the feeling that it's the other way around.

For a few minutes, she stands gazing toward Svanemøllen Station to see if the woman appears with the child. But there's no movement down there. It's as though they've disappeared into thin air.

* * *

A few miles to the north, in the houses on Strandvejen, merchants and executives, chief medical doctors and high-court justices enjoy their well-deserved slumber in beds so soft that only an earthquake—or possibly the pea from the fairy tale—could disturb their dreams.

No one is stirring except for the woman with the blue carry-cot. Moving sideways, she makes her way down the slope by Skodsborg Hill, concealed by the half light of the trees' shadows. At the bottom of the slope, the trees and bushes become few and far between, giving way to a narrow wedge of grass, which the woman, bent low, crosses in short, fast, soundless steps.

Near the shore is a large brown villa. She crosses the villa's driveway. If the thick layer of gravel crunches underfoot, only she can hear it. Then she edges carefully along the wall of the house, holding the cot away from her body.

Though thin, she is evidently strong; despite the cot's weight, her hand does not tremble. She steps up to the house and sets the little cot on the front stoop. Then she stands, straight and motionless. Slowly, she turns in a full circle, inspecting each direction before she withdraws, soundlessly, disappearing within the shadow of the beech trees.

Less than three minutes is all it took.

Had the light been a little brighter, the woman with the carry-cot might have seen the old path between the broom bushes at the foot of the slope, and maybe she would have thought to follow it through the beech forest and up the hill to the neighboring house, with its white northwest-facing façade.

But it likely wouldn't have caught her attention, because the house didn't seem to be surrounded by anything except dense shrubbery, nettles, and low-hanging branches. And even if someone had seen her, the distance would have been more than 150 feet, much too far for anyone to register details or facial features.

Only a dreamer would think that Fate could camouflage its presence so perfectly and leave its canopy bed so early in the morning to notice such an insignificant occurrence.

For a second, the thin woman imagines she sees a shadow between the tree trunks. But maybe it's merely a bird hiding under the bushes. A moment later, it seems as though no one has walked that slope for centuries.

PART II

THE HUNT

2

THE LETTER

May 5, 2008

In my foster mother's world, only one task was really important: to protect the abandoned beings arriving at Kongslund until the ten-member Adoption Council in Vesterbro found them a new family.

"Kongslund is their home, Marie," she said before adding an almost mystical declaration, "And remember: all the best homes are by the water."

When the children departed, she would sing the old song with its seemingly endless string of verses: "One elephant goes a marching now, two elephants go a marching now, then three, then four, then five, then six" until at last I would fall asleep "as they marched off across the spider's fine web."

And then silence again, until it was replaced with the nestling sounds of new children, which would be replaced by another silence. And so the seasons changed, and all the children around me left, one by one, until one day it became clear to me that I was the only one who would be staying.

* * *

The Danish prime minister was seized by a terrible coughing fit. In just a few months, his face had grown more gaunt and pale than anyone would have thought possible. Before long it would hang suspended in the air, like a narrow slip of white paper fluttering in a wind blowing from the slightly puckered lips of Death. For a moment he sat with his head bowed like Hamlet: afflicted by a deadly ailment that might have been tuberculosis had the land he'd ruled for fifteen years not been declared free of that contagion.

Ole Almind-Enevold, the minister of national affairs, was the only other person present in the nation's most powerful office. He cleared his throat uncomfortably.

When the prime minister looked up, he tried to smile at the sole minister in the nation's government he more or less trusted. Not unconditionally, and not naively—there wasn't room for naïveté in the strata where illusions about ideas and principles could destroy a career in the time it took to broadcast a news segment—but rather because he knew the fingers of Death were drumming on his throat, and wouldn't abate.

The premier placed a light-blue handkerchief to his mouth, and Ole half expected blood to seep through, as though on clean, heavy blotting paper.

Slowly, the premier's persistent cough ebbed. The handkerchief remained unblemished. The conversation resumed.

"They think I'll survive a year," the prime minister declared in a surprisingly strong voice.

The desk he sat behind wasn't large, but it was a treasure from his childhood home, constructed in fumed German oak, lavishly ornamented with dark carvings. In front of him was a copy of *Independent Weekend*. He read aloud from the front page, his voice once again dry and raspy: "Ministry sources anticipate that the prime minister will step down within a year. The official announcement may come as soon as the Party Congress convenes this fall. Due to health concerns, the prime minister and his advisors are discussing his possible successor."

The prime minister accepted this statement without batting an eyelash; he even tried to laugh. But that brought his cough back, and he doubled over so far in the upholstered chair that Ole feared the nation's leader might capsize.

Once the fit had subsided, he resumed reading aloud: "Since the successor appears to have been found already, a power struggle leading up to the congress is not anticipated. In spite of his advancing age, it is expected that Ole Almind-Enevold, the experienced minister of national affairs and a true patriot, will be tapped. He enjoys unparalleled, nonpartisan public support."

The prime minister eyed his friend and colleague of many years. "You've already been elected," he said.

Ole didn't know how to interpret his tone. It was well-known how exacting a boss the prime minister was; he didn't forgive colleagues their mistakes. Quite a few had been deceived by his seemingly friendly smile and bowed confidentiality. This was no doubt still the case, in spite of his weakened condition.

"Unless you screw up, it's a done deal," he said, adding, "But you don't make mistakes, do you?"

His meaning was clear. The prime minister was loath to hand over his scepter to a man who'd bring shame upon it. That would, no doubt, disturb his eternal slumber.

"You never had any children . . ." he said, as if in simple observation, but the questions were implied: *Any skeletons in the closet that I should know about? Mistresses, love nests . . . ?*

All the minister of national affairs could do was smile reassuringly.

"You didn't want to adopt—many people do that." The prime minister already knew the reason for this decision, but he continued, "I understand your wife never liked the idea of adopting a child, so . . . well . . . yes, not much to be done about that."

The prime minister was clearly trying to provoke his subject. Everyone knew that the leader of his country would never have kowtowed to a woman—only four served in his entire administration—nor would he expect any different from his cabinet members. He suffered the women's presence, reporters joked, merely to placate the electorate.

The premier tossed the newspaper onto his desk and suppressed another cough. "In this office—and at your age—it is likely only an advantage . . ." he concluded, referring to the man's childlessness, his voice dwindling to a whisper. "You will have to maneuver the actual successor into place . . . the next generation. That will be your task. To bring the party into the next great era."

There was nothing left to say.

The two men shook hands. And it was a handshake they both knew committed them unto death.

* * *

That morning—just a few feet from the dying prime minister's office—the so-called Kongslund Affair began, though it revolved less around the house that was identified as the scandal's point of origin than it did around a group of individuals: high-ranking politicians, career officials, and media personalities.

The day was May 5, 2008—the sixty-third anniversary of Liberation Day.

The letter had arrived at the Ministry of National Affairs, or National Ministry as it was called for short, by regular mail in the wee hours of the morning. The long blue envelope was placed in the stack of mail in the enormous reception room, which since olden days (back when the National Ministry was still called the Ministry of the Interior) had been known as the Palace. And there it remained until 7:30 a.m. when the office manager arrived.

She didn't have long to consider the letter's peculiar appearance—it bulged, as though a piece of cloth or a deflated ball were inside—because her boss, the chief of staff, was already turning on all the machines in the office.

Orla Berntsen usually began his mornings with a few moments of meditation, breathing calmly in the half-awake ministry. The office manager wondered if this ritual was simply a way for him to catch his breath after bicycling through Copenhagen traffic—or perhaps because he was thinking of his wife and two daughters whom he'd not seen for nearly two months. But because he never talked about himself, no one knew.

The guard at the gate had informed him that morning that the minister of national affairs was at the Ministry of State but that, as always, he would assume his place at the table at precisely 9:00 a.m. As usual, the chief of staff dropped his bike clips in the round ashtray that bore the ministry's monogram, and, wetting his fingertips, flattened the creases of his pants before sitting down.

He wasn't a morning person, and he wasn't an athlete: his obsession with cycling was a result of the government's environmental PR scheme meticulously designed by the Witch Doctor (the nickname given the newly minted PR chief in the afterglow of the unexpected and legendary 2001 election). "We need to demonstrate our concern for the earth's climate and for the Danish environment in concrete ways!" he had said. And within a few months, the fervor gripped every top politician and high-ranking official, whether voluntarily or not. Throughout the spring of 2008, the faint odor of sweat and deodorant hung in the air, especially early in the morning, and, in the case of the chief of staff, especially around his shoulders and neck.

As evident by Orla Berntsen's rare media appearances—rare because he detested such appearances—he was cut from a large, square gray cloth. Thickset, wearing a gray suit and a gray checkered tie, he wasn't much to look at when hunched over his vast Brazilian rosewood desk. Out his window he had a view of a gorgeously landscaped courtyard in which the gardener had erected a small fountain. A beautifully carved snake rose impressively from the fountain's center in the shape of the letter *S*, spouting a blue cloud of water into the sky. In calm weather, the column of water reached so high that it caught the rays of the sun and formed a rainbow spanning several rooftops, and gave the illusion that the various wings of the ministry were connected via a colorful bridge.

The chief of staff turned away from the window. The view reminded him of days he didn't care to think about now, days sitting under the rain-drenched trees in the neighborhood he'd hated as a child.

Instead he turned to the stack of mail that had been placed on his desk. On the top of the pile was the odd blue envelope that would come to cause so much harm. The moment his fingers touched the envelope he sniffled involuntarily, as though anticipating events impossible to imagine.

Given the acts of terror unleashed on New York, Madrid, and London, the letter probably should have been handed over to a bomb squad. But in its ongoing confrontation with the many terrorist and fundamentalist forces threatening Denmark, the administration had constructed an important and effective image of fearlessness.

For seven years, the National Ministry had efficiently enforced refugee and immigration policies, in addition to upholding its mission to preserve Danish identity and the national character. It was in this same spirit that the office manager decided to perform a cursory inspection of the strange envelope before placing it on her boss's desk. She'd held it up to the light, assuring herself that it contained neither explosives nor the flattened body of a rat—the latter having actually happened to a former minister (the symbolism self-evident).

The envelope bore none of the stickers or slogans generally favored by critics of the administration. According to the date stamp, the letter had been mailed in Copenhagen on May 2, 2008 from the post office in Østerbro. With his letter opener, he flipped the envelope over—found no return address—and then flipped it back again.

Cautiously, he pressed the bulge. It was soft, giving a bit at his touch.

He turned his attention away from the envelope for a moment and poured coffee into the mug his daughter had given him for his forty-sixth birthday, their last celebration together. On the mug were the words WORLD'S BEST DAD. He used it only when he was alone.

Most likely, he thought, the envelope contained an angry message from a concerned Dane fearful of all the foreigners streaming into the country; in exchange for the electoral victories in 2001 and 2005, the National Ministry had pledged to keep immigration under control.

That's the kind of letter it could have been. And were it not for one little detail—the address—that's what he certainly would have thought.

The address hadn't been written in pen or typed with a computer. Instead, the sender had gone to the trouble of cutting letters from an old magazine or newspaper—one by one, in different sizes but from the same cheap gray-white paper—neatly affixing them to the envelope, letter by letter, without wasting any glue. For a long time, he stared at the impressive handiwork, before pressing a button to call the Fly—she'd earned her nickname at a Christmas revue for buzzing about completing her tasks. As a personal secretary and office manager, though, she was unmatched.

As she settled in a seat behind him, he felt a puff of air. He handed her the blue envelope. Her lips moved, and he realized she was counting each of the letters. He'd done the same thing. There were sixty letters all in all. A few of them were red, but most were black, and some of those were bordered in white, including the *l* in Orla and the *l* in Pil.

Orla Pil Berntsen,
Slotsholmen,
Christiansborg Slotsplads, Copenhagen K.

Three lines. Very melodramatic in their multicolored layout.

"I don't know what's in it . . ." he said, hesitating. Seeing his middle name made him nervous. He hadn't used that name officially in many years.

Carefully, the Fly shook the envelope, as though chasing away the worst possibilities. "Maybe it's just a dead mouse," she said softly.

"A dead *mouse*?" Orla Berntsen blanched in fright.

"Or animal feces . . ." Her pointy nose twitched as if to sniff out the rot in the mysterious correspondence. Her sweating boss gave off a sweet, slightly nauseating odor. The Fly flew to the window and opened it wide.

If the letter didn't have this strange aura around it, he would've considered it a joke. Instead he felt fear creep in, a tickling feeling in his nostrils—which he recognized from the world of his childhood. He knew a headache would descend on him in a matter of minutes.

"Maybe we should let the mail room open it after all," the Fly said in a near whisper.

He imagined the headline in *Independent Weekend*: "Top Official Lets Innocent Officers Face the Music."

"It's probably nothing dangerous," he said, grabbing the letter opener.

The Fly emitted a little squeal and eased away from him.

"I'm sure it'll be a dud, and they—whoever they are—will just get a lot of free publicity." Once again, he sniffled.

Then he used the fine, arched letter opener that Lucilla had given him as a wedding present in 2001; he hesitated only a second before emptying the contents onto his desk. He had no idea who'd sent the letter, or whose fingers had painstakingly folded two pieces of paper around the contents. He blinked rapidly, as though finding himself in bright sunlight, as he held up one of the cloth balls, studying it curiously through his eyeglasses.

"What on earth . . . is that?"

Soundlessly, ever loyal, the Fly mimed his question behind his back. He could almost feel her tremulous breath against his skin as she drew closer.

To his surprise, he was holding a pair of delicately crocheted baby socks.

He stared uncomprehendingly at the peculiar item. He sniffled once, then again, much too loudly, before turning halfway around, relieved to find the Fly still standing there, now more than three feet away and thus unable to determine the envelope's contents. *A pair of baby socks?* For a moment his mind went blank, and then it registered the remaining contents. With fingers that, to his irritation, trembled as if cold, he quickly picked up one of the sheets of paper, turned it away from his secretary's gaze, and studied it.

What he saw looked like a copy of two magazine pages. On the left side of the page was a round circle resembling an old-fashioned picture frame, inside of which was a photograph of an old mansion with rust-brown walls. It appeared to be floating in a gray mist that hid both the sky and the foundation of the building, as though it had never been anchored in earthly soil.

No less than seven white chimneys—three on each end and one in the middle—rose from the steeply pitched roof above ivy-clad walls, underscoring the fairy-tale character of the rendering. The tiles gleamed, suggesting the photo had been taken early in the morning, before the sun had evaporated the dew.

On the right side of the page, the anonymous sender had placed another photo, one that resembled a black-and-white reproduction of an old amateur photo: under a Christmas tree that extended to the ceiling, a small group of children sat on a carpet, staring up at the photographer. They were all wearing elf hats. A couple of the children smiled, while others looked solemn, as if unsettled by the scrutiny of the person behind the camera.

Above the photograph, in block letters, were three words: "THE SEVEN DWARVES."

Under the old photograph was the only text accompanying the two-page spread: *The seven dwarves—five boys and two girls—live in the Elephant Room and are all ready to find a good home in the new year!*

The chief of staff wrinkled his forehead involuntarily—avoiding the Fly's attention—and continued reading: *Because the biological parents' identity can be protected, they choose adoption rather than illegal abortion. It is rumored that famous Danes, whose names and reputations would be damaged beyond repair by prying eyes, have benefitted from the discretion of Mother's Aid Society. In these cases, it is essential that the names of the biological parents are kept secret.*

"It's nothing," he said without being asked a question. He could feel the Fly behind him, curiously trying to see what he was looking at. He covered the two photographs with his arms. "I'll take it from here."

Her disappointment was palpable. She whirled toward the door and then stopped.

"It's nothing," he repeated, a little louder. "I'll handle it."

The Fly—Fanny was her real name—lingered stubbornly in the doorway for a moment before reluctantly leaving; a gust of air followed as the door slammed shut.

He breathed deeply and stared once more at the letter. If she had been there, Lucilla would have warned him about the fear now tightening its grip on him.

Though the pictures revealed nothing—except what was repeated in the short text—he understood their meaning immediately, and he knew what they were of.

Taking a deep breath, he turned to the second piece of paper, which was thicker—entirely white and stiff—and crinkled softly as he unfolded it. He'd almost expected another photograph (perhaps even of himself), but what he held in his hands contained no images. It was a copy of a form or official record—the kind the authorities had used since Gutenberg's time.

There were traces of a hole punch on the left side of the page, and he guessed the original had been removed from a three-ring binder before being copied.

He leaned closer to the paper and began to read. The year 1961 appeared in the top left corner, nothing else. He drew a quick breath as his eyes scanned down a dozen or so narrow fields: *Name. Date of birth. Place of birth. Current address.*

There were other fields for more nontraditional information: *Biological mother. Name. Current address.* Below that: *Biological father. Name. Current address.*

At the bottom of the form, the unnamed authority had included a spacious category for *Name and address of adoptive family.*

It was an adoption form intended for families who'd applied to foster one of that era's unwanted children. He'd seen such forms before, of course.

Only one of the boxes had been filled in, the very first one. Someone, presumably long ago, had written a single, still fully legible name: *John Bjergstrand.*

The name meant absolutely nothing to Orla Berntsen, but he thought it sounded a bit strange. A small space was left between the first and last names, and beside it the official had added, almost as an afterthought, *Infant Room.*

He could feel perspiration forming on the bridge of his nose, under his glasses. He turned the paper over and glanced at the back of the page. Blank.

Then he sniffled again and squinted. What was a forty-six-year-old, soon-to-be-separated public official to do with an old form that barely contained any information? He sensed that he ought to know the answer, but he didn't.

It wasn't the name itself that was so upsetting—that might have baffled him for a day or two before he forgot about it—but rather something else. A droplet of sweat fell from the tip of his nose onto the handwritten name at the top of the form. Carefully he dabbed at it with a tissue, as though he'd forgotten it was a copy and the ink wouldn't smear.

He stood and turned toward the window, gazing at the rainbow gleaming in the air above the snake's mouth. He felt more than heard the gurgle of panic that arose from his chest. It sounded as though a prehistoric creature had sought refuge inside his body, much as he had once sought sanctuary from his persecutors in the wetlands.

If anyone had been able to read his mind at that moment, they would have noticed that Orla Berntsen did not ask the most obvious question— the question other recipients of such a strange letter would have asked themselves: *Why did I get this?*

* * *

After the election victory in 2005, the office of the minister of national affairs had been expanded to almost double its previous size. The country's second-most powerful man had practically demanded a throne room as a reward for his role in the frenzied election.

Only those in the exclusive inner circle—individuals handpicked by the minister—set foot in his office. They were members of CRL, an association the minister had formed early in his career, though only in recent years had he acknowledged his leading role in it.

CRL was an acronym for Children's Right to Life.

During the 2005 election, CRL had been a real drawing card for the party, since it advocated for the rights of unborn Danish children, and it reintroduced the position that abortion be restricted to cases in which the mother's life was at risk or the child would die anyway. Fertility rates had sunk too low and the nation lacked healthy Danish children, conditions that resulted in a burdened social security system and disturbingly low numbers of young people. Increasingly, the labor market was forced to import workers from distant parts of the world. A growing contingent of Danes therefore supported this commonsense approach—which combined practical economics and Christian morality—not least because they felt that increasing the ethnic-Danish population would strengthen the nation against the growing ranks of newcomers. Danes risked becoming a minority in their own country—both the party and the opposition had conjured up this frightening scenario during the campaign—but the party had held the trump card: the minister of national affairs.

* * *

Ole Almind-Enevold set the tone for an informal meeting with an uncharacteristic, "Have a seat—and Happy Liberation Day!"

The Witch Doctor appeared in the doorway. He slipped along the wall to a vacant chair; being late and out of breath seemed to be an integral part of the PR director's image.

"What's this business about the Tamil boy?" the minister asked, brandishing a thick green folder. With exasperated precision, he tossed it across the table to the department head, whom staff called Bog Man; the hue of his bluish-green skin reminded them of the famous prehistoric man discovered in a bog near Silkeborg.

"What do I need to know?" the minister continued.

Orla Berntsen was relieved that he'd not presented the case to the minister himself but had delegated it to the department head, who didn't dare sit on it lest it blow up in his face. The national minister hated troublesome cases, and he'd always had a straightforward approach to them: clear them away or bury them so deep no one will ever unearth them.

Some reporters (and officials) called him the Almighty One—a play on his surname, Enevold, which means "king" in Danish—and most found his systematic efficiency intimidating.

Bog Man held out his hands apologetically. "It's *only* for your orientation, and *only* if you should run into a reporter from *Independent Weekend* today. They are the *only* ones who care about the case. So far."

Orla noted how he'd used the word "only" three times.

"You can't possibly think that an eleven-year-old Tamil boy could become a sensation?" the Almighty One asked.

"He might," Bog Man replied cautiously. "He'll be the litmus test for the ministry's decision to expel juvenile refugees who don't have families. That's why he's all alone in a cell at Asylum Center North at this very moment . . ." He fell silent, which was unusual for him.

Ole Almind-Enevold shook his head vigorously. "I doubt anyone will care about his case for more than a day or two."

The subject matter was closed for now. Orla Berntsen studied the photograph the guard at the asylum center had sent the ministry. It showed a small boy with an innocent face, thick black hair, and clear brown probing eyes—just a tiny snowflake in the universe. Berntsen nodded to Bog Man. They were in agreement that the case could explode at any moment. Quite a few Danes were still uncomfortable at the sight of a crying child in state custody. They would have to discuss it later.

"It's May fifth," the minister cheerfully reminded the group. The anniversary of Denmark's liberation from the Nazis was the natural starting point in the story Ole Almind-Enevold starred in—a narrative that wove together the Ministry of National Affairs and his own altruistic efforts during the Second World War.

The intervening years hadn't diminished the story's power in the least, and no one dared question it either. According to myth, the minister had thrown himself into the resistance movement in 1943, while still a young boy, hardly able to lift the sacks of dynamite he transported to and from older saboteurs. Because of his broad area of operation and his unrelenting stamina for cycling and running, he'd acquired the cover name "the Runner." As the story goes, he was only thirteen when he helped liquidate a snitch near Svanemøllen Station. The snitch had threatened an older saboteur with a gun, but Ole had leapt forward and seized the weapon. The snitch and the boy tumbled to the ground together and the gun went off, leaving the traitor dead—a bullet between his eyes.

The story proved to have immense popular appeal. "Still running errands for the nation," read the Witch Doctor's powerful slogan in newspapers and on campaign posters during the nerve-wracking election in November of 2001—in the wake of 9/11. During the 2005 election, he introduced a triumphant addition to the winning slogan: "Defending Danish democracy."

In Orla Berntsen's universe, a bureaucrat to the core, patriotism was not a particular virtue. Every one of his enemies was Danish, and his mother hadn't wasted a single opportunity to remind him of the distinctive brand of Danish hypocrisy that had haunted their lives together during his childhood in the row-house section of town, near the wetlands. In those years, during the 1960s, to avoid shame and condemnation, thousands of single young women relinquished their newborn children to complete strangers. Those who refused to do so were barely tolerated in their communities. A boy like Orla, without a father, was viewed as an illegitimate child, a bastard, and the national virtues of community and unity (or *solidarity* as it was quaintly stated in the party program) meant nothing. And it was for this reason that Orla considered hypocrisy the true mark of the Danish national character, though he never admitted as much to others, and certainly not to those in the ministry, where he served as the right hand of the successful minister.

In public, Berntsen fought the invasion of bogus asylum-seekers and economic refugees in a cold and calculated way. But in his personal life, he didn't believe there was any real difference between people—whether black or white, from one culture or religion or another—he was beyond such distinctions.

* * *

Orla Berntsen had almost forgotten the blue envelope he'd left under the mug that reminded him of his wife and daughters.

Once again he looked at the photo of the seven babies in their elf hats. He scrutinized the other photo as well: the majestic villa with its dark, gleaming roof. Not only did he recognize the house, but also he knew why the magazine had included the golden border around it. His mother had had the exact same picture on their living-room wall. Very few people would know that. His mother's voice was a weak buzzing in his head, but he couldn't make out the words. After her death she had developed a habit of whispering to him, but the messages rarely made sense, consisting mainly of fragments of conversations they'd once had.

He stretched his fingers, shaking them a bit, as though sending a discreet signal to an invisible guest in the office.

"I took three calls from *Independent Weekend* while you were out," the Fly suddenly whispered from behind him.

For a second he couldn't place where the voice was coming from. Then she walked around his desk and repeated the message, more loudly, adding a distressing detail: "It was that journalist . . . Knud Taasing."

The Fly understood how this name affected her boss.

He could smell his own sweat mixed with the optimistic scent of the ministry. "Just tell him I'm at a meeting."

"He said it was important . . . something about an anonymous letter." She hissed the final two words between her thin lips.

"Okay. Well, put him through if he calls back. It would be worse to avoid him," he replied, softly sniffling.

Berntsen studied the form again. *John Bjergstrand.* The name meant nothing to him, but apparently someone had felt it important enough to send a copy to the minister's oldest enemy, the reporter at *Independent Weekend*. It was the only possible explanation. As if on cue, the intercom buzzed.

The speaker clicked. "I'll put him through." She didn't have to repeat the name.

For a moment he sat silently, feeling the presence of the other man, and then he said loudly, "Orla Berntsen speaking."

"Taasing." The voice was muted and nasally. It hadn't changed since the day they'd first met, and that had to have been ten years ago, maybe more.

"Yes?" he said.

Taasing spoke with the same preternatural calm as he had the morning he'd become Orla's sworn enemy. Back then the telephone rested on the desk in the Ministry of Justice, and when the old party organ (then in its heyday) had uncovered a scandal that could bring down the minister and his closest allies, the reporter called, not to ask questions, but to inform Orla that the paper planned to print a devastating article the following day—with or without his blessing.

Orla had told him to get lost.

The article was published.

It had nearly destroyed Berntsen's career. Shortly afterward, Knud Taasing himself was disgraced by a fatal mistake grown epic in size, destroying his reputation in less than a day. At the ministry, they had celebrated this fantastic good fortune, raised a toast to it. It was a miracle the man even had a job today.

"You need another number to talk to the minister," Orla said, instinctively searching for an exit strategy.

"I don't want to talk to the Almighty One, at least not yet. But give him my regards anyway," Taasing replied sarcastically. "For now, I just want to talk to you."

Orla Berntsen reflexively covered the word DAD on his empty mug.

"We received a letter here at the paper. It's somewhat, how can I put it, *mysterious*," the reporter said.

The chief of staff gazed at the mug in front of him and thought of his daughters whom he'd abandoned when he'd returned to his childhood home in Søborg.

"I've got a copy right here. It's actually a magazine article, I think, with a photo of a house and some children and a kind of cryptic caption. But at the very bottom there's a note I don't understand: *Copy sent to Orla Pil Berntsen, chief of staff to Minister of National Affairs Ole Almind-Enevold.* That would be you—and your honorable boss. That makes me think you received the same letter. Blue envelope. Rectangular. Red and black letters, all cut from an old glossy, it looks like." He paused. "Very melodramatic. Like something from an Agatha Christie novel."

Orla was silent.

"Are you still there, Berntsen?"

"What does it say?" he asked. Practically an admission.

"It's a short piece on children adopted to new families. I think the pictures may have appeared in a magazine to accompany a larger article on the topic. It hints at something devious, though: that certain children were adopted in secrecy to spare the biological parents from being identified. But the envelope also contains two items"—the reporter hesitated for a second—"some sort of form with a name on it, and then a tiny pair of white woolen socks. Baby socks it looks like. That's what seems most peculiar."

Whatever one might say about Taasing, his descriptions were succinct and precise. The powerful chief of staff heard a muffled rustling of paper on the other end of the line.

"So what do you say?" his tormenter asked.

"This was sent to *you* . . . ?" Orla heard himself say. It was dangerous to lie, and so far the content of the letter was too bizarre and inexplicable to pose an immediate threat. He doubted anyone would be able to make heads or tails of it. It was all so long ago that there was really no connection to his present career or life.

"Actually"—Orla Berntsen heard the reporter shuffling papers again—"it was sent both to me and to Nils Viggo Jensen. He's my photographer on big assignments."

It was a wonder that Knud Taasing was still writing for a national paper (though *Independent Weekend* had been forced to amend its moniker in recent years, as it could no longer sustain a large enough daily readership). A small one to be sure, Orla thought, but still. For years, the topics Taasing covered had been insignificant. If he hadn't had such a glorious past, he'd have penned his last article that fateful day nearly ten years ago.

"Yes, Berntsen," the voice was teasing now. "You're getting it . . . The old circus horse has scented a big story. If not a big story, then at least something to entertain the crowds. I'll admit as much, between you and me. And now it's your turn. I think you received the same mysterious epistle."

"Yes," Orla confessed. There was no point in lying.

His response was met with silence.

"But," the chief of staff continued, "I have no idea what it means."

"You also received . . . a pair of socks . . . and the strange form?"

"Yes," Orla admitted.

"John Bjergstrand?"

"Yes."

"Who is he?"

A soft sniffle. "I've no idea."

"You got the photo of the children too? And the peculiar text?"

"Yes."

"And I suppose you can't tell me who they are?"

"No."

"Or what it all means?"

"No. I don't have faintest idea," he said, deciding to lie after all.

"You have *no idea* what this letter is about?"

"That's right. I have no clue. I've never met anyone named John Bjergstrand. Look him up in the phone book."

"Ha," his nemesis exclaimed.

Orla could hear the reporter breathing heavily on the other end of the line.

"Inside the circle on one of the pages is a photo of a house," Knud Taasing said, changing the subject. "Do you know the house?"

"Well, it's not mine." Orla sniffled again.

"That much I know." Back when it couldn't be avoided, Taasing was one of the few reporters ever to visit Orla Berntsen's residence. But nowadays, Berntsen's private life was as concealed as his emotions, perhaps even more so. The official story was that he was married, had two daughters, and resided on Gisselfeld Boulevard in the wealthy suburb of Gentofte. Journalists also knew that his wife was Cuban. The most critical among them had joked about how Orla—then the chief of the Department of Immigration—had stopped issuing humanitarian visas for refugees after he himself married a foreigner—a citizen of one of the last remaining Communist countries in the world to boot. Those same journalists wondered if this was the reason he was now getting divorced.

"Why would the sender go to the trouble to indicate that the letter was also sent to you—the chief of staff to the minister of national affairs—and why mention *his* name explicitly?"

"I have no idea."

"Is this connected in some way to Enevold?"

"You can't take this nonsense seriously, Taasing," Orla said with a little more vigor in his voice. "The minister hasn't even seen the letter."

"Where is that house?" The sharp tone again.

Berntsen hesitated. The case didn't need to appear more mysterious than it was, and the truth would solve that problem. On the other hand, he couldn't just give away his biggest secret. Not to a reporter. And certainly not to Knud Taasing.

"You know what . . . what I feel and think about my private correspondence, or what I know about it, is nobody's business."

He knew it sounded arrogant.

"Actually it is the public's business, Pil Berntsen. The letter was sent to the *public* as well. Remember that."

Taasing's words held an implicit threat—he could demand access to documents.

"Yes, but it was sent by some maniac!" He could hear his own breath now. This wasn't good; he needed to calm down. He lowered his shoulders and put his hands on the desk. "Listen, Taasing. I'm actually busy. I'm attending a reception at the Ministry of State to commemorate the Liberation."

"Yes, your secretary told me. But I have to tell you, if you don't give me any details about this house—at the very least an address—then I'll be forced to publish the photo and the letter, as well as a transcript of our conversation. And if we don't post a reward for information on the matter, we certainly will ask the public to help us play detective. We *will* get to the bottom of this."

Orla Berntsen wasn't sure a reporter in Taasing's reduced position could really follow through on this threat. Air whooshed behind him, and he felt, more than heard, his mother whisper from the Other Side: *What harm could it do, Orla? Let the truth come out.*

"The house is at Skodsborg Strandvej. It's an orphanage. And now I've got to run." He hung up.

He stood and walked to the window. The snake continued to spray water on the rainbow it had created. He sneezed.

Goddamnit.

Closing his eyes, he sank into the mustard-yellow couch where he sometimes catnapped, never more than five or six minutes and always with his legs dangling over the edge.

Half-asleep on this couch he'd been able to probe the contours of the biggest problems in his career, lay out new paths, and find ways to escape the sticky situations he sometimes landed in. Here he'd earned his reputation as a problem solver, the very quality that had made him a sought-after advisor whenever the administration faced a crisis. At the end of the day, he always found a way. He was a ruthless strategist and a hardened adversary.

During the first fifteen years of his life, he'd weathered the bullying of the other boys, whose impenetrable circle he'd orbited like a tireless insect, persisting solely through his alertness and an uncanny ability to rebuff humiliations. Grinning like an idiot, his square, freckled nose sniffling as if in spite, his light-blue eyes anticipating where the fists would land. That well-honed façade and a flair for lightning quick evasion had remained in the man, long after his expression ceased to reveal his thoughts and the goofy grin of childhood had disappeared.

If any of the boys from the street saw him today, they would only recognize the watchful eyes, the frequent sniffle, and the subtle shift of his eyes behind his glasses.

For once, Orla Berntsen didn't know what to do. He stood. The letter rested on his desk. Had the minister seen it? He didn't think so, because the Fly surely would have mentioned it to him. Triumphantly.

He sank into the chair once again. His large glasses were slightly steamed, his half-closed eyelids thick and taut, his lashes short and blond. Should he inform his boss? There was good reason to. Still he hesitated.

There is no goal that can't be achieved, the minister had told him long ago. *Except by those who hesitate.* (The words had offended Severin, a friend from his youth, but of course Severin hadn't amounted to much.)

Orla had loved the aphorisms Ole Almind-Enevold had impressed upon him during their first meetings following his appointment; they were all about making the right call in any situation—about the determination each extolled, about the will to find the most efficient solution for any given situation.

He who wants to rule the world must react when it changes.

Orla Berntsen had smiled at the obviousness of that one.

He who prioritizes compassion before resolve loses his ability to make decisions.

The minister had never lost his resolve.

He who acts with leniency rather than consequence will be left behind.

This was perhaps the most advanced insight—the very secret: the ability to unleash one's anger without remorse.

He who dares not kill when called upon to do so will perish, Orla Berntsen's boss had said about his efforts during the Resistance—and the entire nation had applauded.

The chief of staff put down his mug. The knitted white socks lay on the desk before him. For a moment he sat in silence, and then he dialed a number on his private line. After a moment, a woman answered in a soft voice: "Attorneys' office."

"I'd like to speak to Søren Severin Nielsen," he said.

It had been more than ten years since they'd last spoken. The rift had been caused by Orla's refusal to extend humanitarian asylum to a Syrian refugee; the media had blown it out of proportion. As the legal representative of the female defendant, Severin had been furious, but Orla had upheld his decision despite their former friendship. A few days later the woman was taken to Kastrup Airport, and no one had heard from her since.

Now his old friend was defending the eleven-year-old Tamil boy who was facing deportation—and, of course, that was a problem, but that wasn't the reason for his call.

"Søren Nielsen is at court," the woman replied.

He left his private number with the secretary and a short, clear message: "Severin, call me. It's urgent."

* * *

A few miles away, the reporter made a ninety-degree turn in his battered swivel chair and tossed his cell phone on the desk.

"Skodsborg," he said triumphantly. "There's only one orphanage in Skodsborg, and that's a very singular one—*Kongslund*—the pride of the entire nation!"

The excitement in Knud Taasing's voice was unmistakable. He pulled his laptop closer. "For many years the administration has given preferential treatment to Kongslund—with special appropriations—and who do you think has been its protector and benefactor since the war?"

He didn't have to say the name, and his companion didn't have to respond. Nils Jensen was a taciturn man.

"And who do you think took part in the Resistance alongside the young Kongslund governesses who were working in total secrecy with the most famous saboteur group in the nation?" Knud Taasing turned on his computer and said the name out loud. "Ole Almind-Enevold, minister of national affairs and soon-to-be prime minister—if death does its duty, that is, and puts our leader out of his misery soon."

Still the photographer didn't reply.

The reporter typed nine letters into the search engine. The stuffing in his rickety chair's cushion flaked off as he shifted his weight, leaving small particles of orange foam on his pant leg. "Kongslund," he said again, almost absentmindedly, to the thin figure in the office's only other chair. "The Infant Orphanage Kongslund. There must be a reason we've received these letters."

"Or maybe there isn't," the photographer finally replied, breaking his silence.

Knud Taasing looked mildly at the man who in some sense had become his friend—the only one who remained after eight long years in the humiliating twilight of his journalistic career.

Nils Jensen put four batteries into a flash nearly as big as the camera in his lap. "An *infant orphanage*?" he said, making the innocent words sound strangely suspicious.

"Yes. And not just any orphanage . . . Kongslund." The reporter waved the blue envelope so vigorously an onlooker might expect the colored letters in the address to come loose and scatter to the floor. "The story is pretty clear as far as I can see. In 1961, a boy by the name of John Bjergstrand was given up for adoption by unknown parents. This boy was one of those who for God's sake—or rather, for the sake of a particular family—had to be fast-tracked . . . his whole existence erased. Presumably because his parents were either very famous or very powerful, or perhaps both."

"Sounds like nonsense to me," Nils Jensen said, spinning the flash in his hands disapprovingly.

Knud Taasing didn't respond. As he'd often noted, it was one of the last remaining privileges of the working class: the right to be contrarian. And Nils had been born to the bottom rung of society. Though, for some inscrutable reason, his parents had given him a camera as a confirmation gift. A fact that was particularly odd to Knud, since the father, a night watchman, was practically never awake during daylight hours. In the late 1970s, Nils Jensen had photographed the massive demonstrations against the Black Square tenement demolition, and he'd sold the pictures to the city's grassroots newspapers. He'd made a name for himself with a close-up of a plainclothes officer beating a demonstrator in a back alley on Blaagaardsgade. The photo was distributed across the country. Three days later, the police officer hanged himself with a short rope attached to a hook he'd drilled into the ceiling of his living room. His wife and colleagues had lowered his dead body themselves. The young photographer never blamed himself, not for a second. As he'd told others in the media quite openly, he'd merely done his duty in the service of documentation.

That statement, and that photograph, had made him a public figure. When, in the late 1990s, the small opposition paper merged with the last remaining organ of the government and became *Independent Weekend*, Knud Taasing had persuaded his editor to hire Nils Jensen as a freelance photographer. They had worked together ever since. Mostly in silence, because the photographer was a man of few if any words.

"There are no John Bjergstrands listed in Krak's Directory or in the white pages," the reporter said.

Taasing typed another twelve letters into the computer database. A few seconds passed before the electronic archive supplied him with the titles of twenty-four articles. "Only four profiles. That's not much," he said.

As expected, the profiles contained no personal information—except that the chief of staff had once lived in Gentofte but had moved from that address, and that he had two daughters—one twenty-three, the other seven.

"They'd had quite a surprise baby. And now they're getting divorced. The wife's alone in the house. But where the hell does he live?"

Nils Jensen was predictably silent.

Taasing found no information about Berntsen's current residence. There were unsubstantiated rumors swirling about his childhood. An anonymous source claimed the chief of staff had been raised by a single mother who, according to another (or possibly the same) anonymous source, had locked him up and beaten him with a coat hanger (this always seemed to be the preferred instrument of punishment in those days, when the indulgence bred by a wave of prosperity collided with the petty bourgeoisie's penchant for old-fashioned discipline). According to these rumors, his upbringing had tortured his mind and soul and made him the person he was: a snarling dog. A national gatekeeper no one passed by in one piece.

Very few people knew the man behind the façade.

According to a tabloid article, he'd earned several pejorative nicknames among the ministry's case officers—the most noteworthy being the Sociopath.

This was what officials called him on those rare occasions when they felt they were at a safe distance in the ministry's narrow hallways. It was a brutal assessment, even for a brutal ministry. *What was the origin of such stories?* Taasing wondered.

Knud Taasing looked quizzically at the photographer, who only shook his head in silence. As usual.

3

KONGSLUND

May 6, 2008

She looked like Cinderella in the fairy tale my adoptive mother read to me when I was a child. She arrived in a dress as green as the beeches on the hill, and none of the governesses ever said a peep about her peculiar background.

"This is my daughter Marie," my adoptive mother told her in a tone of voice that, more than anything, sounded like a warning to the sensitive concerning my oddness. But the woman in green didn't notice. She curtsied to me like a little girl—at once polite and spiteful—and now that she'd become a part of Kongslund's identity (and had been for almost twenty years), I couldn't imagine my life without her.

The business with the anonymous letters would affect her, of course— as it would everyone—but it couldn't be helped. I heard the clatter of the cups in the sunroom and knew guests had arrived at Kongslund, just as Fate had long ago intended.

What looked like a coincidence had never been a coincidence.

* * *

Nils found Knud Taasing wedged between three moving boxes in the corner of his office at the Press Building near the harbor front. He was just waking from what seemed a fitful slumber.

Always a loner, Knud Taasing was born in 1961 to a full-blown hippie, flowing robes and all (before most even knew the hippie age was dawning). His mother had joined the first protest march against nuclear power—from Holbæk to Copenhagen—shortly after giving birth and still somewhat swollen from the difficult labor. Despite the after pains she was suffering, she abandoned her son as easily as a tumbleweed blowing in the wind and had wandered south with a handsome Spaniard (as women did back then). She traveled more than 1,200 miles south through Europe to a large commune in Andalusia, leaving Knud to his factory-worker father who lived in a small row house in a Copenhagen suburb.

Later father and son returned to the island from which the family derived its name, Taasinge, and where relatives had settled more than a century earlier. Knud, Nils had noticed, never spoke of his time there. Not that he asked about it—he didn't.

Knud had evidently spent the night scanning old articles until he'd finally slouched onto an overturned green plastic wastebasket, where he had fallen asleep. When the first and only guest of the day edged his way through the labyrinthine stacks of paper, books, and ring binders to his uncomfortable bed, his eyes were still half-shut.

With some difficulty, Knud got to his feet, mumbling a greeting to the effect of "Is it morning already?" He smelled vaguely of alcohol and oil—strangely enough—as though he, in the middle of his nighttime reading, had gone for a refreshing dip in the slick black water of the harbor basin. A single weekly magazine rested on the table. Stapled to it was a receipt from the Green Messengers.

Nils Jensen stepped closer. The magazine was a forty-seven-year-old issue of *Billed Bladet*, and had cost just seventy-five øre a copy back then. The cover text was set in the same blocky red letters the magazine employed today, nearly a half a century later. It was dated December 27, 1961.

Nils leaned in. The black-and-white cover showed a boy with big, frightened eyes and tightly closed lips. Across the child's striped shirt, the graphic designer had chosen a cursive font characteristic of the time for the four simple but strongly appealing words: *Who will adopt me?*

"I found a reference to this article on the Association for Adopted Children's website," Knud said, one eye half-open. "And voilà, look what I discovered . . ." He lifted the magazine and then let it fall dramatically on the table.

The two photos the anonymous sender had copied and mailed to the Ministry of National Affairs and *Independent Weekend* appeared in the centerfold of the magazine. The beautiful brown villa in the golden circle filled the entire left page. On the right—under the words "The Seven Dwarves"—the magazine had printed the photo that had fascinated Knud for hours the day before.

In the black-and-white reproduction, the seven small babies were assembled on duvets and blankets under a towering Christmas tree. The caption was the same as the one they'd read in the anonymous letter: *The seven dwarves—five boys and two girls—live in the Elephant Room and are all ready to find a good home in the new year!*

This was followed by the statement Knud considered so intriguing: *Because the biological parents' identity can be protected, they choose adoption rather than illegal abortion. It is rumored that famous Danes, whose names and reputations would be damaged beyond repair by prying eyes, have benefitted from the discretion of Mother's Aid Society. In these cases, it is essential that the identities of the biological parents are kept secret.*

No names were provided for the children in the photograph, nor was any other information given about them. The allusion to Walt Disney's beloved dwarves was due, of course, to the fact that the children were all wearing elf hats.

Knud was surprisingly alert despite the fact he'd spent a long night in an uncomfortable position and hadn't even had his first cigarette yet. "If you knew how many children were put up for adoption in this country during those . . . thousands and thousands . . . whole battalions of healthy Danish babies given away. And it wasn't even that long ago," he scoffed and then snatched the magazine from the table.

Including the centerfold, the article was six pages long. The italicized headline on the first page of the feature was nearly identical to the one on the cover: "*Who Will Adopt Us?*"

An explanatory caption accompanied every single photo in the spread. Under the image of a sad, crying child: *Per (in checkered overalls) is a willful little man of 17 months.*

Under the image of a chubby, melancholy girl sitting on a polar bear rug: *What do you think of Dorthe in her pretty white blouse?*

The next showed a cheerless girl in a floral dress: *Lise looks quite down. She is only 18 months and cross-eyed, but that can be fixed.*

The largest photo showed a dark-haired boy in a white bed. Behind him the wallpaper was decorated with odd little round elephants drawn in a childlike fashion. The graininess of the spread made it hard to decipher the elephants' curved tusks and tails, and their raised trunks.

Under this photo was the caption: *One elephant marched along . . . but where is it going? When you're only 9 days old, you don't know much about the future.*

"This is the original article—the mother article if you will—of the excerpt that was included in the anonymous package," Knud said, though it was obvious to Nils.

"It's from the same year as the form," he continued. "Whoever sent it to us has this magazine—and something he wants to share—and he's telling us where to start looking. At the Kongslund orphanage. In 1961."

Again he slumped onto the battered wastebasket.

"That's the year I was born." It was the first time Nils had spoken.

"Yeah—me too. In fact, it was one of the biggest baby-boom years in Danish history."

Knud closed the magazine and tossed it aside. "Next week the orphanage will celebrate the retired matron's anniversary—the famous Ms. Ladegaard, who back in the day was simply called Magna—and on that occasion, they'll bring all the old experts on early childhood education to Skodsborg. Plenty of politicians and famous people will be there, as you might expect given all the talk lately about childrearing, stress, and institutionalization."

The two men headed outside through the empty editorial office and climbed into Nils's beige Mercedes.

"In 1989, Magna was succeeded by an equally formidable woman," Knud said. "Susanne Ingemann."

Nils silently noted the journalist's strange tone of voice as they drove along the harbor toward Kongens Nytorv.

"While everyone else was celebrating Liberation Day last night, a crisis meeting was held at the Ministry of National Affairs," Knud said after a long pause. "I know this from my source in the ministry. Do you know why?"

As usual, Nils said nothing—there was no reason to—the reporter would answer his own question as he always did.

"Because of the anonymous letter that Orla Berntsen received. My source wasn't at the meeting, but they discussed the mysterious letter for at least an hour—and then decided to seek the assistance of an expert . . . a former assistant chief of police in Copenhagen."

Nils sped up through the soft curve near Sølyst and Emiliekilde. It was a gray but mild spring day. The morning's first sailboats were already making their way across Øresund, dozens of them.

"He's one of the minister's old acquaintances, and he runs his own company, does security consulting, that sort of thing. He's been hired by the ministry to serve as security advisor. They want him to find whoever sent this package, and they are giving him free rein to do so. You might remember him from that time you snapped pictures on the barricades in Nørrebro. His name is Carl Malle. He's become a big dog since leaving the force, someone you *only* hire when the shit's burning so close to you that your ass is on fire."

Nils made no comment on this peculiar analogy.

"And it's a very fitting name, Malle," said Knud, who still smelled like oil. "He's malevolent as all hell. But of course, it's terrible timing for them. In a week everyone who knows what's what will be at Kongslund to honor the famous matron. In addition, the minister of national affairs, who has been the spiritual and material protector of the orphanage, is about to make the biggest leap in his career—to the nation's highest office. Ever since the Great War, the party has supported and financed Kongslund, deemed it the shining example of the Danes' compassionate attitude toward the weakest members of society, and party bosses will resist any attempt to shatter this piece of Danish history. Naturally, they can't stand an article surfacing all these years later that suggests that Kongslund's past—and therefore also its present—is in any way unseemly; that the orphanage, in return for the party's support, helped powerful citizens avoid scandals and erased the identities of its little charges so completely that they could never be reconstructed."

The blue envelope that was the root of Knud's confidence rested in his lap; it represented, possibly, *Independent Weekend*'s final chance to secure a prize-winning story. At a crisis meeting held just a month earlier, the marketing team had informed the last band of reporters that only 7 percent of the country was even aware of their newspaper's existence, and that only a sensational scoop could save the paper from the disease that was slowly but surely killing it.

Nils cast a sidelong glance at the neatly cut red, white, and black letters on the envelope, before turning his gaze toward Sweden. The water in Øresund was steel gray, and he briefly recalled his father, who during school holidays had brought him along on his rounds as a night watchman in Nørrebro—perhaps in the hope that he would end up in the same occupation.

They passed Bellevue, with its white sand and small tufts of grass, Copenhageners' preferred beach for more than 150 years. "The name itself . . . John Bjergstrand," Knud said, breaking the silence. "That, of course, is the key piece of information. A boy born in all discretion and adopted out in secrecy—with a new name that we don't know. A bastard child who could completely destroy an otherwise glorious career. And that's exactly what happened, I think . . . a very powerful person had an extramarital affair, but he pulled some strings and covered up every trace of his exploits."

With satisfaction he leaned back in his seat. "Except for one. Which our letter sender found," he said, before adding, "Our anonymous sender doesn't know the parents' identities. But he thinks we'll be able to find out who they are and believes *Independent Weekend* has the guts to go public with the story."

Nils remained silent as they passed Strandmølle Inn and the Jægersborg forest.

"We know it made Berntsen nervous, and we know he's aware of the orphanage. And we know that a silly little piece of paper startled the entire Ministry of National Affairs to the point where it held crisis meetings rather than attending the administration's Liberation Day celebration."

The one meeting, Nils noted, had now grown to many.

"I think the party is involved in some way or another, and the letter writer knows it. In the fifties and sixties tens of thousands of illegitimate children were given up for adoption. That figure didn't drop until abortion was legalized in 1973." He clucked his tongue at the unfortunate if necessary national triumph.

"Yesterday I spoke with a retired social worker from Mother's Aid Society. She visited Kongslund frequently back in the day. She told me that the children were often given nicknames of famous people whom the nurses thought they resembled, such as the actor Ebbe Rode or the writer

Poul Henningsen . . . at one point there was actually a black-haired girl they called *Jackie* . . . after Jacqueline Kennedy!" Knud chuckled briefly, as though the name of the former president's widow was a particularly interesting detail. "There was also a bald baby called Khrushchev. Anyway, the naming was quite innocent, though once in a while it was rumored that this practice was more significant than simple likeness. And those rumors persisted during all the years she visited Kongslund."

They drove under the crowns of tall trees, the road gently curving away from the sound. Enormous mansions stood on each side of Skodsborg Strandvej, right up to the road.

"My source in Mother's Aid Society also mentioned something else . . . in 1966, the old matron adopted a child herself. Or rather, she kept an orphaned girl as her foster daughter. The girl was born the same year, 1961. Later, when she retired, the matron—Ms. Ladegaard—moved to an apartment in Skodsborg, but her foster daughter, who must now be in her late forties, remains at the orphanage." He paused briefly.

"Strange, don't you think?"

Nils didn't think it particularly odd; he'd lived at home until his midtwenties. He signaled a right turn and angled the vehicle down a steep, winding gravel road and toward the water.

At first they saw nothing, and Knud suspected they might have made a wrong turn. Then a dark shadow appeared between the trees, and they glimpsed the outline of the house. It rose up like the giant brown hull of a ship pitching on a sea of green beech trees. Seconds later they saw the seven white chimneys and a towerlike annex that faced south, and finally the whole villa.

Nils braked, overwhelmed at the sight, and then cut the engine.

For a moment both men sat motionless, silent. In a strange way the orphanage resembled an impenetrable fortress within the budding green, as unapproachable as an English country manor—not as big, perhaps, but with the same ceremonial aura emanating from every pillar, cornice, and turret.

After a minute or so, Knud spoke, softly, as though he were seated in a movie theater and didn't want to disturb those around him. "Look at that place, Nils. Fifty thousand Danes were once put up for adoption here, remember. This house was the beginning of their stories."

Breathing deeply, he opened the car door. Nils followed him.

Though it was early May, Nils shivered. It was an unfamiliar and puzzling sensation. With his father he'd patrolled hundreds of backyards, and he was used to the darkness and the cold. Fear, his father had taught him, wasn't something you brought into the bat's domain.

The surroundings—with the house under the shade of rich green foliage—were as idyllic as the magazine article depicted. Yet he felt at that moment that they were being watched; he turned slowly, glancing at the treetops, and heard Knud laugh at his obvious unease. In the midst of his laughter, Knud was seized with a fit of coughing, and he doubled over, a hand on each knee. For a few moments this hacking sound was all they heard.

Only later did Nils recall (with a touch of embarrassment) what he thought he'd seen on the hill: a small figure that withdrew into the bushes before disappearing in the direction of an old white mansion nearby. An absurd thought, of course, clearly an optical illusion. That white house was obviously empty; even at a distance it looked decrepit. There were no curtains, no plants in the sills—no signs of life whatsoever. *You can always tell the difference between an abandoned house and an inhabited one*, he thought. His father had showed him that.

Knud stood to his full height and spit in the gravel. A large black car was parked at the far end of the driveway, but Nils could easily make out the license plate, even at a distance: MAL 12.

"Hello."

Knud spun around, startled by the unfamiliar voice.

She'd approached them without making a peep. "My name is Susanne Ingemann. You're earlier than expected."

She wore a beautiful green dress that fell nearly to her ankles. Nils grasped how lovely she was faster than his shutter could capture her image: tanned feet in light-brown sandals; dark-brown hair with a reddish sheen, gathered in a tight bun with a black clip. She greeted them with a small, deprecating gesture—gracious but reserved—without any effort to make physical contact, not even a handshake. "Welcome to . . . Kongslund."

Nils noted her hesitation at the name Kongslund. *And had she actually curtsied?*

"Let's go inside," she suggested. Before they could reply, their hostess was halfway to the door.

The entry hall had very high ceilings paneled in tall, dark mahogany. Behind the sandstone fireplace that looked as though it hadn't been used in decades, the wall was covered with black-and-white photographs in small, square black and brown frames. Several hundred of them in fact, all of children: tiny faces shining in the light of those old flashcubes they used to use.

Standing motionless, Nils stared at the photographs, which for some reason reminded him of his childhood home, though he couldn't say why. Where he'd grown up the only sentimentality on display was in the golden romances he'd read—with their damsels in distress—or from Bjørn Tidmand's love songs that played on the radio. He looked away, and his eyes fell on a broad staircase that wound its way over the main entrance and rose into the darkness. On the wall high above the staircase was a tall painting of a woman wearing a wide-brimmed hat and standing in an idyllic clearing. Like Susanne, she wore a deep-green dress with long sleeves and flounces. The abundant fabric stretched to the ground, cascading in folds at her feet.

"N.V. Dorph painted that," the matron said, interrupting the two men from their thoughts once more. "Presumably it's Countess Danner, the commoner wife of King Frederik VII."

Knud was suddenly seized with another coughing fit.

Susanne politely ignored him and simply raised her voice. "Dorph furnished the house for the old sea captain who lived here before Mother's Aid Society, and he painted the pictures," she said. "Or at least some of them. So it would be appropriate to begin with a tour, wouldn't it?"

She let them go ahead of her on the broad staircase, and when she followed, Nils heard the green fabric of her dress rustle softly. The beautiful matron had an eerie resemblance to the woman in the painting.

"The house was built between 1847 and 1850 by a famous architect," she said, "by all accounts in consultation with the last absolute ruler, King Frederik VII, during the same period when the Constitution was written."

Knud coughed as if to indicate his skepticism on such a peculiar and cryptic statement.

They were in a long, dark corridor now with three or four closed doors. "This is where the governesses lived, and the matron. Staff resided at the orphanage among the children, which was completely natural." She stood motionless with her back to the enormous painting. "The architect loved this place so much he couldn't bear to leave it, so he built a home for himself next door—on the southern slope—the decrepit white house you might have seen when you drove in. He lived there with his wife and son, and later on the son lived there with his wife . . . and their daughter."

She'd added the last three words after a strange pause that Nils didn't understand.

"The daughter had cerebral palsy," she said, as if by way of explanation.

"Kongslund itself was passed down for generations before Mother's Aid Society bought it in 1936." Susanne Ingemann stopped to open a door. After several minutes in the dark hallway, the light was blinding. The room could've been part of a royal palace, the private apartment of a queen. Even though toy cars were strewn on the mahogany table by the window and small dolls with blond, red, and brown hair lay in the chairs, there was something ancient and proud about the room. It had a kind of emptiness you sense in halls that have been admired but not lived in for decades. Fine golden wallpaper decorated the walls, and on two deep, antique sofas were stacks of pillows of black-green silk, embroidered with rose-colored bouquets. Through the window was a view of a spacious green lawn and a narrow white beach. Between the yard and the beach was a wire fence with two gates, presumably to prevent the children from running into the water should an adult momentarily turn her attention elsewhere.

"This was the private room of the former matron. She lived here for more than half a century," Susanne Ingemann said. "We've left it the way it was." Stepping back into the corridor, she said, "The office is at the end of the hallway, but there is nothing to see there."

The door was open to the office, and Nils glanced into the room. There was a large, empty birdcage on the windowsill.

"We once kept three canaries," she said, noticing where his attention was. "But they've been dead a long time. Let's go downstairs and have a cup of tea."

The peasant is granted access to the very holiest of places, Nils thought. Maybe that had been a test run for the tour that would be given in a few days to the visiting luminaries. Except for Susanne, they hadn't met a single person yet. Perhaps the children had been moved to another part of the house for the occasion. These vulnerable creatures, he gathered, were not to be disturbed by strangers.

She gestured for them to take seats at a low coffee table in a vast room with two tall windows facing the lawn and the water. "During the war, the governesses had their hands full," she said, taking a seat on a small sofa next to the window and offering them tea and cookies. "They were amazing. They took care of orphans as well as children whose parents were in trouble—and during the last years of the war, they worked closely with the Resistance. But perhaps you already know this."

They did, but for a second Nils could hear the pride in her voice, so he said nothing.

"Magna rarely talks about this time."

"Magna?" To his surprise he heard his own voice articulate the question—in a single word.

"Yes, Magna. Ms. Ladegaard. The children always called her Magna. I'm not sure why she doesn't mention this era, perhaps she doesn't want to be described as a hero, a rare characteristic today. She became the matron at Kongslund on May 13, 1948, exactly twelve years after the orphanage was founded, and that's the date we're celebrating Tuesday, her sixtieth anniversary. Although she retired a long time ago, she has meant everything to Kongslund."

She sounded strangely formal.

After a moment of silence, Knud mumbled, "Let the little children come to me . . ." His voice was still hoarse, and Susanne Ingemann blanched as though she found the phrase inappropriate.

The reporter cleared his throat and then asked his first real question since they arrived. "Back in the forties and fifties, I gather there were many children put up for adoption?"

"That's correct," Susanne Ingemann said in the voice of a teacher responding to an especially bright student.

Nils grabbed his camera and snapped it on. Either he was imagining things, or their hostess had become suddenly more wary than she'd been during the tour.

"That lasted into the sixties," she said. "But today, very few Danish children are relinquished—and those who are, well, they live with us. These are children who cannot remain with their parents due to unique circumstances. Abuse . . . illness . . . I became matron in 1989, when Ms. Ladegaard retired."

"But back then," Knud interrupted, "in the fifties and sixties, they were otherwise normal children who were simply *unwanted*?"

"Yes, if you want to put it like that. Often the fathers had left the mothers in the lurch, and in many cases the fathers' identities were unknown. The mothers were alone and typically quite young."

"And they stayed here . . . in the same rooms as today?"

"Yes." Then she added, in a rather arrogant tone, "Where else?"

Knud leaned forward and in a clear voice asked, "Can we have a look at the infant room?"

Susanne Ingemann's teacup hovered an inch from her lips. It wasn't this sudden pause in motion so much as the very atmosphere in the room that abruptly changed at this request.

"The infant room?" she repeated very slowly.

"Yes."

In that instant, Nils understood the provocation. Knud had informed her that he possessed information that hadn't been made public in five decades of enthusiastic magazine coverage. No random visitor could know of the infant room, and neither should Knud.

Of course, he'd learned of it from the form included in the strange blue envelope, but she wouldn't know about that.

It was then the two men realized they weren't alone. They heard him before they saw him. He must have been sitting in a chair behind the white pillar separating the sunroom from the dark living room. He suddenly stepped up to the table, into the light from the east-facing windows. Nils and Knud were speechless, unable to conceal their shock.

"Meet Carl Malle," Susanne Ingemann said. "He's visiting us . . . as a representative of the Ministry of National Affairs."

To Nils it sounded as though she pronounced the word *representative* with a hint of sarcasm.

"Yes." The huge man nodded as though in greeting, but he didn't extend his hand. "I'm the security advisor for the ministry. I'm sure you take no offense at me listening in?" Without waiting for an answer, he sat beside the director. He was almost a head taller than she, Nils noticed.

"Actually, we do . . ." Knud began. When he couldn't come up with a good excuse to boot a stranger out of someone else's home—which he himself was a guest in—he fell silent.

"Consider it a press conference," the man said. "An official one. You are here on business, right?"

"There's usually more than one reporter at a press conference," Knud replied, regaining his voice, but still struggling to take command of the situation.

"Then consider me a communications representative . . . for both the ministry and Kongslund, which, as you know, is funded by the national budget and therefore receives very exclusive support from the ministry. As a matter of fact, it has been my job for many years to protect Kongslund's reputation." Carl Malle allowed a little smile. "Few people know that, but Susanne can confirm it . . . if it matters. But the infamous Knud Taasing isn't exactly known for checking the details, is he?"

The insult was a subtle reference to the misfortune that had nearly ended the reporter's career seven years earlier. It was elegant and cruel, and it hit its mark.

"That's what I thought . . . I don't suppose you reminded Susanne of that affair when you scheduled your visit here yesterday." The security advisor nudged the teapot aside and set a newspaper clipping in front of them. It was a letter to the editor, divided into three columns, from one of the big morning dailies; the date had been inked on the paper in thick red pen under the dramatic headline: "When The Media Destroys People."

Nils didn't recognize the article, but Knud looked like a man staring at a noose.

It was from May 2001, and one particular passage was printed in bold type: **"Six women were raped, and now the Palestinian man who'd been convicted of the crimes has been acquitted. But what if, despite the fact that skilled (male) reporters have raised questions about the technical evidence, he is guilty after all? What if, despite the fact that the skilled (male) judges of the appeals court acquitted him, he is guilty after all? And what if, despite the support of all these skilled (male) media people, he lied after all?"**

Susanne Ingemann's name appeared right below the headline, in italics. She sat silently for a moment, as though relishing the time she'd attacked Knud Taasing directly—and had been proven eerily correct. Without looking at the large man sitting next to her, she said, "What does an old newspaper clipping have to do with all this?"

Carl Malle shrugged. More was needed to throw him off balance. "Nothing besides the fact that the reporter you once so accurately skewered . . ." he spoke slowly, almost lovingly, "is the man sitting across from you. And he has hardly come to preserve the reputation of Kongslund. Or to do any good for any of us."

Closing his eyes, Nils felt an even stronger sense of unease than when he'd seen the figure in the driveway. The letter to the editor had been published three days after the Special Court of Appeals had acquitted the Palestinian. Soon after his acquittal, the disaster occurred that swept the successful reporter off his feet, along with all the editors who'd assisted him. He'd freed a guilty man—a "poor Palestinian" all the bleeding hearts had believed was innocent. Not three months later, that "innocent" foreigner kidnapped two boys from a playground in Herlev, shot them at a rest area in North Zealand, and then killed himself. In his suicide note, he confessed to the rapes he'd been acquitted of and mocked the man who'd won him his freedom, a man who had no idea that the very deeds we consider our most altruistic can feed hatred.

"But that's not what we're discussing today," Knud said softly, his gaze fastened on the clipping. More than anything, this feeble response revealed how shaken he was.

The security advisor didn't respond.

"Yes. She was right," Knud said. "You were all right. The police were right. But I couldn't have done it differently . . ." His words came out thickly, as though he would have preferred to not articulate them. Then, like the matron, he fell silent.

After nearly a full minute of awkward silence, Susanne Ingemann leaned forward, returning to the present. "You were talking about the infant room," she said. Nils couldn't decode the expression in her green eyes, but they contained no anger.

"Yes . . . that's what it was called back then, right?" Knud's question sounded both surprised and naive.

"Yes, that's what it was called. Still is by those of us who remember those days."

A bizarre thing to say, Nils thought, registering the peculiarity of her tone. He could see a faint shimmer behind Knud's eyeglasses.

In spite of Carl Malle's malicious attempts at interrupting the conversation, the charge of the anonymous letter sender had been weighed, discreetly and elegantly, against the phrase *the infant room*—and no longer stuck.

"Of course we still say the infant room, but among us the room has never been referred to as anything but . . ."—and here Susanne Ingemann smiled, looking directly at Knud—"the Elephant Room."

Nils's camera slipped through his fingers and crashed to the floor. The image had come to him at once. The plump little pachyderms on the wall behind the child in the old magazine photo, and the evocative words that flickered through the caption: *One elephant marched along . . .*

Knud ignored Nils's response and leaned forward to clutch at this piece of information, his face revealing a certain involuntary astonishment. "But why do you call it that . . . the Elephant Room?"

"Because one of the governesses painted small figures on all the walls," Susanne Ingemann said, staring at Knud, oblivious to Nils's and Carl Malle's presence. "When Magna was matron, her right hand, Gerda—who is also retired now—decorated the walls from floor to ceiling with small blue elephants. It's actually quite a marvelous sight. They are still there, everywhere. There's another room with yellow giraffes and an even larger room with miniature gray hedgehogs. The one with giraffes is called the Giraffe Room; the one with hedgehogs is, of course, the Hedgehog Room. That's all there is to it. The older children live in these other rooms."

Knud abruptly switched topics. "I've had some time to do a little research . . . very little admittedly." He peered over the rim of his glasses, "But through the nurses' union, I located a former midwife at Rigshospital. During the period we're discussing, the fifties and sixties, she was a student on Obstetric Ward B." Knud studied a sheet of paper he had snatched from his folder. "Carla was her name."

Susanne Ingemann said nothing. The name of the reporter's primary source didn't seem to faze her.

Knud glanced at his paper once more. "She recalls a girl who was, at most, sixteen or seventeen. This girl gave birth to a baby. But, according to the midwife, she was in such anguish at having to relinquish the child, it was as though she'd been condemned to the fires of hell by the Devil himself. She believes it was in April or May of 1961. The girl never saw her baby before she was discharged, before she disappeared—and it was the matron herself who picked the child up."

"That was lucky. Kongslund was the best orphanage in the kingdom. Other children were sent to far inferior places, like Sølund or

Ellinge Lyng, where they were left alone without any contact with adults."

"Yes, so I have heard." Again Knud studied the director over the rim of his glasses, and then he flipped the paper on the table. The balance in the room had shifted in his favor. Carl Malle leaned across the table, trying to read Knud's notes. Susanne Ingemann's hands rested in her lap. Light from the sky above Øresund formed a reddish aureole around her hair.

"There were quite a few rumors back then," Knud continued in a lower voice. "Unconfirmed, but still. Rumors suggesting that the matron of Kongslund, in very special cases and under great discretion, helped certain men—fathers-to-be that is—out of their trouble. Out of very embarrassing situations."

Susanne Ingemann's silence, to Nils Jensen, seemed to signal a wait-and-see approach.

Knud coughed, and this time it sounded feigned. He continued, "Legal abortions were not an option back then, and while the sexual revolution was a few years away, sexual appetites were the same . . ." He smiled faintly. "And from time to time someone famous or powerful, a politician or a CEO or an actor, strayed from home and fathered a so-called illegitimate child. As a result of an extramarital affair, I mean."

"A child born out of wedlock, yes." Susanne Ingemann's voice was as neutral as Knud's.

"And every now and then, for various reasons—maybe because people couldn't or wouldn't visit some quack doctor—these unwanted children were born."

"That's right. Abortion was then called 'illegal termination of pregnancy.'"

"These pregnancies presented an extremely embarrassing problem, perhaps especially for the rich and famous, who couldn't risk exposure. My sources tell me . . ."

Nils noted how one source had become multiple sources.

"That Kongslund often entered the picture. In extraordinary cases, and in all discretion, the orphanage could arrange for an off-the-record birth, and to conveniently find a new home for the embarrassing love child." He lowered his voice. "And then forget everything about the matter."

Susanne Ingemann didn't respond.

"The matron—and that must have been Magna—simply deleted every trace."

Her green eyes studied him.

"Interesting, isn't it?"

No reaction.

"She must have held some kind of power." His voice was more muted now, almost nasal. Knud slumped in his tattered sweater.

"Yes," said Susanne Ingemann. "If it were true."

"Indeed. But that's what the sources say—not to mention the rumors many recall, even all these years later."

"The sources of these rumors—which are probably just that—are from a distant past."

Absentmindedly, Knud scooped up the last cookie from the plate. "But could Kongslund have been able to command the most expensive piece of shorefront in Denmark without enormous goodwill from the highest places?"

He put the cookie back. "Isn't that how it worked? A house full of *bastards* in the midst of the wealthiest and the finest dignitaries? This area was built by kings and admired throughout the gilded age. Kongslund couldn't have been popular. Until they realized a deal could be struck. The rich and the powerful got something in return. Isn't that right?"

Susanne Ingemann leaned back and closed her eyes, disregarding the provocation.

"We're in possession of a letter that was sent to the Ministry of National Affairs yesterday, a letter that more than suggests that Kongslund is responsible for hiding certain children. Here, for example . . ." Knud handed the two sheets of paper to Susanne Ingemann, along with the magazine article and the adoption form. Nils thought she seemed slightly uneasy, but he couldn't tell for sure.

She studied the papers without raising her eyes. Malle leaned over her left shoulder.

"Who is John Bjergstrand?" asked Knud.

No reaction. He repeated the question.

"John Bjergstrand. I really have no idea. Who is he?"

"I think he was an orphan here, in the infant room," Knud said, hesitantly. Her response seemed genuine.

"Well, in that case it was long before my time, and I've never heard the name before." She smiled and for a moment looked almost cheerful, in spite of the serious allegations Knud had leveled against Kongslund. Then she said, "Are you sure your *source* isn't mistaken? Perhaps he or she is confusing Kongslund with another orphanage. After all, there were more than fifty in Denmark at the time." She smiled again. "Denmark was filled with homes that were in turn filled with abandoned children. The little one you mentioned, he could have been anywhere."

"The letter was sent to the chief of staff at the ministry, Orla Pil Berntsen. What is his connection to Kongslund?"

"There's no connection." *Her response came a little too rapidly*, Nils thought.

"We believe he was a child here." Knud was exaggerating again, presenting his own theory as though he had corroborators.

"Orla Berntsen's private life is nobody's business but his own," she replied, enunciating the official's name in a way that left no doubt: she knew him, and he was connected to Kongslund.

"What I'm asking about must be available to the public, given that Kongslund is run with public funds and has been supported by the state—as Malle himself pointed out earlier." His last point carried a vicious undertone, Nils observed.

"In that case, I think you should ask him yourself," she said—again a tad too quickly—and then shrugged. "Besides, we'd like to continue to receive support from the ministry. If you know what I mean." She glanced at Carl Malle, and again Nils noted an air of hostility between them.

"Is the ministry putting pressure on you? Why was he even invited to this conversation?"

Susanne Ingemann stood and then walked a few paces to the window. For nearly a full minute, she stared at the blue waters of Øresund, keeping her back to the three men. Finally she turned and said without hesitation, "Yes, Orla Berntsen was here as an infant." She shrugged as if to minimize the importance of this piece of information. "But that, of course, is confidential. He wasn't put up for adoption, but he was here for a short time because his mother was going through a difficult period. Mother's Aid Society helped her. Later on, he visited the governesses at least once a year—with his mother—and that is the only reason I know about it. The ministry also knows. We're included in the national budget. The ministry supports us, and the minister is a board member. There's nothing covert about it. And none of this has anything to do with him."

It sounded as though she knew him better than she wanted to admit.

"He didn't have it easy," she said, in a strangely detached way.

Knud leaned forward but did not ask the question on his mind: *Why?*

She returned to the sofa but made no effort to sit—perhaps because she wanted to avoid the security advisor. Nils wondered if she would respond to Knud's unspoken question, and then she did, "At one point . . . it's an awful story."

Carl Malle started to stand but changed his mind.

She didn't look in Malle's direction, and even with the sunlight in his eyes, Nils saw the dim, spiteful glow in her eyes as she continued. "It was said that he once witnessed—or was involved in—another man's death. But that may have been a mistake. He was just a boy, after all. All I know is that Magna arranged for regular contact with a psychologist here—Kongslund has always had an established team—and there might have been other arrangements that I'm not familiar with. Of course this isn't something you can print in your paper. I'm only telling you so that you can see that I am being quite honest . . . that we're not trying to hide anything. There's nothing of interest to anyone in this, including *Independent Weekend.*"

All the same, she had given Knud and Nils significant information that would've taken them months to dig up.

"What other arrangements?" Knud asked.

Carl Malle pounded his fist on the table, sending three teaspoons clattering to the floor. "That's enough! That is private information, which this journalist has a record of mismanaging. People have died as a result!" The security advisor began to rise.

Knud collected the adoption form and the other papers and stuffed them in his folder. "Thank you for your kindness," he told his hostess. "We'll return in a week, for the anniversary." He stood. "And on that occasion we'll restrict ourselves to applause."

She watched from the stoop as the two men walked to their car. Carl Malle stayed inside, his assignment apparently complete.

Suddenly Knud halted midstride and turned. He looked at the beautiful matron. "Doesn't it matter anymore . . . that old issue . . . the two young boys . . . since you . . . ?"

She seemed to understand his incoherent question right away.

"Yes," she said.

Nils held his breath.

"And what do you think about it now?"

"I think that . . . it's in the past. Everything becomes history if you are patient enough. And if you don't dig everything up again."

He nodded slightly. Her meaning was clear: let Kongslund's past rest in peace. Then the world—and Carl Malle—will let your demons rest.

"The old matron has a foster daughter, right?"

For a moment he got no response, and then at last came the confirmation, "Yes, she has a foster daughter. Inger Marie. That's the name she was given when she arrived in 1961. But we just call her Marie. She's my assistant, and always has been."

Five short sentences, delivered like wreckage on the shore.

In a single glance, Susanne anticipated his next question. "Yes, it's true: she lives here. In a very beautiful room. The most beautiful in the house. We call it the King's Room because the architect designed it according to the careful instructions of King Frederik VII. It has always been her room."

She waved a slender hand at the roof. "It's the nicest spot in the house, with a fantastic view of the sound and the island of Hven. But she's not here today." She fell silent. "So if you want to speak with her, it'll have to be another day."

She gave two quick nods. Green eyes, auburn hair, shades of gold-red.

Lies, Nils thought. *She's here, but we're not allowed to see her.*

* * *

"I'm troubled by how Carl Malle managed to insert himself into that conversation. And she just let him do it." Knud lit a menthol cigarette with shaky fingers.

Nils turned the large Mercedes onto Strandvejen and headed for Copenhagen.

"It was creepy," Knud added. He appeared paler than usual.

Nils said nothing.

"We couldn't get anywhere with her. But, damn, I would've liked to meet Inger Marie. She would have been able to tell us something about those years, I'm sure." Knud shook his head. "Maybe we should have insisted . . . It wasn't our best performance. We didn't get access to the infant room, didn't meet the foster daughter, didn't get anything on little John Bjergstrand—if he ever existed." There was an uncharacteristic tone of resignation in his voice.

They passed Strandmølle Inn again.

"She was very beautiful, very capable, and very, very much on guard," Knud said more to himself than his companion. Still, it was probably the highest compliment he had ever paid anyone, at least that Nils knew of.

"Did you notice the atmosphere in the house?" Knud said.

Of course I noticed the atmosphere, Nils thought.

"It was very peculiar." Knud rolled down his window and lit another cigarette.

They passed Bellevue and Charlottenlund Fort.

"The place is rich with history, that goes without saying, including the bit with Frederik VII and his mistress."

Knud's sense of the past was about as sketchy as you might expect from someone in a profession suspicious of history (since it didn't sell newspapers). He'd been orphaned when he was twelve or thirteen years old—that was about all Nils knew. His father had died suddenly, and Knud had been shipped off to his aunt and uncle's place on the island of Ærø. Not exactly the kind of home where you'd slog through thick volumes of Danish history.

"He was one of our most beloved kings," Nils said, aware of how pedantic he sounded. "The mistress was Countess Danner, the former Miss Louise Rasmussen."

"I see," Knud said, with a touch of sarcasm. "Some *Miss* she was. Maybe the old matron is related to her. In any event, if we are to believe the many newspaper articles written about her, Magna seems to have had a certain power over men—and Kongslund."

Nils kept his hands planted on the steering wheel, thinking about the woman he had photographed. After a short while, Knud guessed what was on his mind. "Like I said, she's an *interesting* woman. Beautiful. Careful. There's a third thing I can't quite put my finger on . . ." He nodded, yawned, and flicked his cigarette out the window. "Keep her out of your head," he suddenly warned.

Nils recalled how she stood before the painting of the countess—half-turned, her green eyes staring at some point above his head. Then he remembered the shadow he'd seen—or hadn't seen—halfway up the hill. A figure crouched among the trees, nearly hidden in the lush foliage, observing everything that went on down below.

"Son of a bitch," Knud mumbled. "I wish I could've met the foster daughter—I would really like to know what's actually going on in that place." Before long, his head lolled onto his shoulder and he was snoring in rhythm with the rattletrap old Mercedes.

They passed Svanemøllen, and Nils Jensen accelerated.

4

THE ELEPHANT ROOM

May 6, 2008

We feel her presence before we see her—a scent of freesia and a rustle of freshly ironed linen as she glides from bed to bed.

We reach out for her, but we don't complain. We are disciplined creatures who don't exaggerate our yearning. We have come into this world without the slightest demand or expectation.

From the very beginning, we acquired the skills that would protect us from evil: humbleness, obedience, gratefulness. And we passed the message from bed to bed, because we knew that only perfect balance would bring us safely through to the end.

The finest web, the most cautious gait . . .

* * *

The two men in the driveway bowed humbly (I was hiding behind the curtain in the southern annex, above the stoop where I'd literally entered the world) and took awkward leave of their hostess, as men visiting Kongslund tend to do.

I knew it was a passing paralysis, evoked by Susanne Ingemann's beauty and sudden arrogance whenever she—and Magna's kingdom—was threatened.

Standing on the front steps, she curtsied and waved. And they would drive away without knowing whether that little gesture was a holdover from her childhood—an exquisite and studied politeness—or an elaborately disparaging gesture.

I drew back. I'd anticipated their visit but was nonetheless concerned about the journalist's acuity. This Knud Taasing would return with additional questions—for me too—and that meant I'd have to cancel my part in Magna's anniversary celebration. There was no way around it. My reclusiveness was well-known (among the few who knew me), and my absence surely wouldn't cause suspicion or grief—except for my foster mother, perhaps. At her tribute I was supposed to appear on the patio before all the guests, like some sort of Cinderella, and for the umpteenth time play my role as the greatest miracle in the history of Kongslund: the small foundling that awoke to the world on a stoop, and, thanks to Fate's most ingenious string-pulling, found a home at this proud orphanage.

They would have to do without this performance, and my foster mother wouldn't care for that, but that's how things stood. Susanne was uneasy. She'd lied—she had told me she would have to—and I think she recognized a pattern in the events unfolding over the last few days, a pattern beyond her control and comprehension.

For over half a century, my home had been described as the best of the best, a golden lagoon in the nation's cultural heritage, a testimony to the kindness and charity of a people increasingly accused of the exact opposite, and Kongslund's official history up to now had confirmed it.

The grand mansion had been erected at the foot of the hill more than 150 years ago, placed like a rune between the sound and Strandvejen, just below the notch of land that curves around the northern part of Skodsborg Hill.

From May to September, the area teems with green-gold foliage; during these summer months, it lies in a shaded pocket of time and could have remained that way, invisible for hundreds of years, had it not been for the kindhearted emissaries from Mother's Aid Society: the stiff-backed governesses whose single vision was to save the nation's abandoned children.

The story of my arrival is oft told, and scores of magazine articles have documented it, one of the most sensational events to transpire in the early years of Denmark's welfare society.

It happened on the very day that Kongslund celebrated its twenty-fifth anniversary, the morning of May 13, 1961. Perhaps it was symbolic, or perhaps it was merely the kind of coincidence that seems like a sign from higher powers.

The night before the anniversary, the assistants had put flowers in every windowsill. The profusion of flowers blocked nearly all light and filled the air with a thick, sweet fragrance. The children observed the preparations with amazement. For a tot no more than a couple of feet tall, the desire to touch and bend the delicate corollas, to knead and break them, must have been overwhelming. But no one dared give into the temptation; they knew well the force of Magna's wrath.

Very early in the morning on the day of the anniversary, the governesses had heard a loud shout coming from the stairs in the southern annex. It was one of the caretakers: "Something's down there! Something's down there!"

"Something's down there," she said again, this time the note of wonder in her voice was clear.

When the other women reached the source of the noise, they found plump Agnes, staring directly at the blue carry-cot, the little white duvet bulging beneath a pink blanket like a delicious cream puff. She repeated her words without realizing that they would become her hallmark. In the following decades she would repeat them endlessly, speaking to newspapers and magazines and annual reviews, then to her own children and grandchildren, and then finally to her great-grandchildren. Perhaps she would even ask the pastor to shout those redeeming words into her grave when she departed this world, so that she could bring them to the Other Side.

"I found the child in a blue carry-cot outside the door. It was almost like Moses!" *Billed Bladet* quoted her as saying on May 19, 1961. The author of the article had excitedly informed his readers: "The young caretaker who'd first spotted the little orphan was Agnes Olson, 21."

The caption, *ARE YOU MY MOTHER?*, was printed in all caps underneath the photograph of a small baby with squinting, shiny eyes staring directly at the reader. "Take a look: a little girl with an unknowable future. Except for one thing—she will be given away," the article began. The story of the little foundling was laid out in minute detail, next to advertisements for Heart Yarn and Lion Yarn paid for by the Council of Knitting Fashion.

For weeks, newspapers and magazines followed the story, and collections were taken. There was much speculation about how it would turn out—all of it enthusiastic, as though this tragedy was a cause for celebration, and, to this day, illustrates the especially optimistic nature of the Danish character.

In this national spectacle, the Famous Foundling from Kongslund appeared out of nowhere, acquired a duvet and bed, and some years later, a mother.

* * *

It wasn't a normal beginning, but few tracked my fate after these frenzied first days, in large part because over the next couple of years, Magna didn't present me to the public. Only much later did I understand why.

Ugly was the only appropriate term for the creature the anonymous envoy had left on the stoop of the orphanage.

At first no one suspected anything was amiss, because when they found me I was firmly wrapped in a blanket. Agnes Olsen had barely called for help before Magna descended upon her, grabbed the cot, and disappeared into a bathroom. You can imagine her surprise when she set her eyes on my naked body and saw the packaging that the Lord had delivered me in: I was twisted from my right shoulder to my lower back, as though I had slammed sideways into a concrete slab; I was stocky, stooped, and had dangling, flabby limbs, which the amazed doctors from Mother's Aid Society discovered could rotate nearly 360 degrees without resistance. The only positive thing the doctors had to report from those first days was that the defects were relatively symmetrical: if there was a defect on the right side of my body, you were certain to find the same defect on the left side. Only my face reflected the lopsidedness of my back: my cheekbones and the right eye seemed to hang slightly lower, which, combined with my dark, coarse hair, gave me a somewhat exotic look that would later diminish my initial ugliness. As the years passed, my left shoulder sank lower than my right, but for the most part, I could hide it with a slight twist of my body.

"You looked like a little Peruvian whose head had shrunk on one side," Magna laughed. This was how she handled disappointments: by retelling them in a way that allowed her to chuckle, as she gave the unfortunate subject a thump on the back. Like so many champions of justice, she possessed empathy in the abstract, but sometimes fell short when confronted with the flesh-and-blood reality.

"The doctors found it incredibly interesting to study a body that the Lord had equipped with so many idiosyncratic features," she laughed, blowing the warm, life-giving ashes from her cheroot into the laps of those closest to her.

On the third day, the specialists noted another peculiarity about me, something they had missed the first time around: the two middle fingers were visibly shorter than the pinkies. In addition, from the wondrous mold of life, two bizarre thumbs had emerged, wide stumps that seemed to disappear into my hands. It might not sound all that awful—I was still able to clutch things with the deformed digits—but for a child, such a deformity can be immensely embarrassing. I learned to hide my hands in various ways: in the folds of my clothing, in my shirt sleeves, under the table and the seat of my chair, squeezed under my thighs—I almost always sat on my hands, hoping that one day they would be miraculously healed.

My feet, however, were the most peculiar. "A thoroughly abnormal construction," the Mother's Aid Society doctor had jotted in his report.

"Oh my! They're backward!" the children's orthopedic surgeon enthusiastically exclaimed before trying to assume an appropriately dismayed mien. Magna, meanwhile, with signature amusement told her colleagues in the all-embracing Mother's Aid Society about my fantastic design: "And as if that isn't enough, God has, in his outrageous daring, given her a little toe that is bigger and sturdier than each of her big toes."

To cure this defect, my feet and the lower half of my legs were wrapped in foam strips and thick bandages until my toes and instep reluctantly straightened. I was approved for lifelong disability before I even left my cradle; but, for the sake of normalcy, I was put in an infant room bed as soon as the specialists grudgingly departed Kongslund, taking all their notes with them.

Around the same time, during the summer months of 1961, the doctors in departments A and B at the Rigshospital delivered a handful of perfect little boys, and one girl, all of whom were transferred to Kongslund within a few weeks of each other.

By Christmas 1961 there were seven of us, and I'm not exaggerating when I say that what later became known as the Kongslund Affair began with us, though of course no one was aware of that at the time.

In Magna's photo album from that year, there's a picture of us sitting under a Christmas tree, staring up at the photographer. All seven of us are wearing elf hats, and we resemble the seven dwarves in the Brothers Grimm fairy tale. There's Asger, who even then had long, pale limbs and a nose so pointy and elongated that you'd think it was anticipating the heavy, horn-rimmed glasses it would later support. There's Orla, known as the Merchant for his stocky features, in his collared pajamas with the glimmering buttons, his gaze so guarded as to suggest that he already knew of the traps Fate would place in his way. Severin is next to him, looking wounded even then (perhaps this is why he, as an adult, attracts down-and-outs from near and far). Closest to the camera, Peter lies on a duvet with a floral design, reaching for a golden cornet hanging from the lowest branch of the tree. His eyes are like two shiny beads of glass (are these really the same eyes that stare at tens of thousands of viewers every day?). The last two children, those beside me, are in the shadow of a heavy branch of the Christmas tree, and their faces are difficult to make out in the black-and-white photograph.

Kongslund's records show that each of these children—with the exception of me—was adopted between February and June of 1962. Under normal circumstances this separation would be definitive, and any reunion would, at best, take place on the Other Side. Around the time the others left, restlessness must have settled into my soul. The small, crooked legs must have trembled some, and then steadied, preparing for the inevitable.

I wasn't going anywhere.

Every morning during those years, Magna put me on the little Japanese pull-along elephant (donated to Kongslund by an admiring delegation from Tokyo) and called encouragingly to me when I clung to the funnel-shaped ears that had little holes for my fingers. Terrified, I would stare over the curved trunk that stretched nearly all the way to the wide, gray elephant feet attached to four ramshackle wheels. In time, I grasped the symbolism: the elephant's feet resembled my own.

Ugly, I thought at a very early age, because children sense these things quite clearly.

"*Ugly*," the mirror on the wall told me whenever I asked. Through the years, I'd asked that question so frequently that the tedious conversation could take up a whole chapter in a fairy tale.

Ugly, the other kids sneered as soon as they were able to comprehend the oddness of my shape.

At that time, with a stream of healthy, adoption-ready Danish children filling the nation's orphanages, I wasn't in demand. If anyone ever fell for my strange appearance—without being disgusted by the lopsidedness they risked having to live with for years to come—they never succeeded in winning Magna's approval, or that of the Mother's Aid Society adoption council, which was led by the imposing Mrs. Ellen Krantz.

The strong women who controlled my life felt that, precisely because I was so peculiarly pieced together, I was to be adopted only by an exceptionally normal family. And Magna's tacit message was clear from the beginning: *The others will be leaving, but you will be staying.*

Kongslund is your home.

It was in her scent, and it was affirmed in her embrace.

The children around me all left. One day they would be at the dinner table, eating open-faced sandwiches with pâté; the next day they would leave their seats and disappear behind the house, into the flowing folds of strangers' coats, into the arms of their new parents who had come from afar and had only one wish: to take them far, far away from the slope, the sound, and their past.

In the following years my nightmare would be repeated each week—because, like never before, childless Denmark could select from a cornucopia of beings streaming out of hospitals and birth clinics. New children arrived—then exited—and were replaced by others, who would also leave. And soon I held the national record in good-byes (no child had witnessed more departures than I).

One of the black-and-white photos in the hall shows me standing at the very end of the bathing pier, waving to the camera. My body stoops slightly to one side, my left arm limp, and if you take a close look—the shot is taken at a distance of some fifty feet—you can see that my hand is clenched into a fist, a dark little shadow under the edge of my coat. My mouth is dark and round and appears to be emitting a hollow, sad note, like wind in a deep ravine . . . *don't go . . . don't go . . . don't go . . . don't go . . . don't go . . . don't go . . . don't go . . . don't go!* . . . it wails in a fit of madness. "But they must go now," Magna says, smiling to yet another happy couple come to save a Kongslund orphan.

"Come, Marie, let's go over and wave!" she laughs, calling for me.

But I back away from the coat folds and the slamming car doors. I feel a deadening buzz in my arms. I'm only six years old, but I've waved more than any queen.

"Come now, Marie, this is a joyous occasion—the best day Butte and her new family have ever known!" Although the April sun peeks through the clouds, she has dressed me in a hooded red jacket. "Come now, Marie, let's go wish Butte all the best in her new home!"

But I end up at the pier, half-turned like a bent branch that has lost its sprigs. I can still hear Magna shouting: "Wave, Marie, wave! Wave-wave-wave!" The happy couple honks their horn as they pull between the Chinese stone pillars at the end of the driveway and turn onto Strandvejen. Then it is quiet once more.

This was how I met Magdalene—on the old pier, one spring day when I was alone. Suddenly she was beside me like in a vision, this old woman in a wheelchair.

"Marie, look at me!" she whispered.

I'd known of the mysterious old crippled woman who lived in the white house up the hill, but until then I'd only seen her at a distance. Day after day, she sat—curved and hunched—on her front porch, holding what appeared to be a long telescope in front of one eye, gazing across the sound.

Now she was sitting right where the boards of the pier touched land—and she knew my name.

"Marie, don't think any more about it!"

I stood frozen on the pier, staring at her.

Slowly she approached, and in one terrifying instant I perceived the strangeness of her body, how it hung over her wheelchair's armrest—a body more frightening than mine. I saw the black ballpoint pen dangling from a string around her neck, and the little blue notebook in her lap—which seemed even stranger for a woman in her condition.

"Marie!"

But I was unable to respond.

"Marie!" she repeated, more intensely now.

A moment later, something odd happened. A sound pushed its way through my skull, as though the sea behind me had squeezed through a tiny slit in a rock wall: a hiss, a sizzle, a moment of certainty before the water poured through, gushing in cascades so thick and powerful they nearly knocked me down. I will never forget that moment. For several days I sat in Magdalene's living room in the white villa and talked about my life at Kongslund: the Darkness, the children, the green lamp, the blue elephants, the yellow freesia. And the water flowed everywhere, trickling onto the coffee table, onto her wheelchair, down her white, convulsive fingers, onto the footstool where her feet—which were every bit as strange as mine—had found their place. I was like a drowning person who had only just discovered the sea, and now it threatened to swallow us both.

Maybe she understood how inexhaustible this source was. Hatred must have been one of the few survivors. It puffed its chest, drew breath, and crawled, unseen, from the depths into my soul through an unknown backdoor. It shook itself off, glanced around, and found a suitable residence where it could live discreetly and be left alone to grow. Magdalene didn't see it—it must have remained hidden from her—but she was the one who released that part of me. A very skilled psychologist might have been able to explain why Hatred's arrival coincided with the love that Magdalene and I found for each other. Perhaps love and hatred are much closer associates than we assume, but any explanation will remain an academic theory that would have pleased Magna and the Kongslund psychologists much more than those of us who experienced it.

In the beginning I visited my new friend in the white villa nearly every afternoon, and when I returned to Kongslund, Magna looked at me inquisitively, as if she wanted to say, "Don't tire old Magdalene. She's had a hard life." But she didn't say anything.

Magdalene told me the story of the home I would never leave. Her great-grandfather built Kongslund—and later the villa next door for himself—but both he and Magdalene's parents had died, and she lived alone. She came from a family of pastors who'd been closely connected to the old writer of psalms, Nicolai Frederik Severin Grundtvig, and for that reason the family's daughter had been given the practically biblical name of Ane Marie Magdalene Rasmussen. I laughed when she told me. Her cerebral palsy was severe, and yet she was so vital that everyone who met her felt a breeze from Heaven, as if the Lord himself breathed onto the world through her. Even though her body was completely contorted and had been since birth, she radiated a strength that delighted everyone—whether she rattled or snorted or sat in her wheelchair by a window, completely still, reading aloud from one of her favorite fairy tales: *Thumbelina, The Ugly Duckling, The Nightingale, The Girl Who Trod on the Loaf.* From her very first days onward, she'd been surrounded by trees and water and birds and especially children—all those who had passed through Kongslund.

Because of her paralysis, speaking in an intelligible fashion was agonizingly difficult, but over the years she'd trained her throat and vocal cords to shape the words she wanted to use. She told me—and it was quite true—that King Frederik VII bequeathed his old telescope to Magdalene's paternal grandfather, who passed it on to his grandchild who could then, at a distance, observe the world she would never really enter.

When she was roughly twenty-five, she made a decision so incredible that word of mouth carried it all along Strandvejen: she intended to learn to write. Her parents eventually gave in to their stubborn daughter's absurd wish and bought her a slim, black fountain pen with her initials engraved in tiny, thin gold letters. And all summer and winter, the young woman could be seen at her table before the window with a view of the beeches, bent over her notebook, shaping the tricky little letters into words, one by one.

The following summer, when she sat on the patio connecting her letters, her parents saw the furious flash of both God and the Devil in her half-closed eyes.

During the third summer she looped her words together. With a patience no one comprehended, she pushed them onto the paper, line by line, arch by arch, sometimes only ten or twelve a day, sometimes a complete sentence—and this is how life began for her on the neat white paper in her lap. For this body that would never give birth or be loved by anyone besides her family, the words were presumably the only way to realize her dream of telling her own story, of living on when she was dead and gone. Magdalene wrote about the area around Kongslund and about Skodsborg Hill and the people she observed. One page a month—and in a year or eighteen months, she would fill half a notebook (back when she was young and energetic). In her whole life, she managed to fill twelve diminutive volumes—just as many as there were beech trees on the slope by her house—and in her diaries, I found the genesis of the majestic mansion, with its seven chimneys, that was my home. I read about Magna's arrival—right before the war—and about the mystery of Kongslund.

There are children who are born in darkness and are unwanted, she wrote in May 1961, in the aftermath of the discovery of the foundling.

The following summer she added six lines: *The six children who were in the infant room have now all been adopted. Only the seventh child, the one who went through so many surgeries, remains. It is a girl: she is physically defective, but she is beautiful nonetheless.*

This was the beginning of our bond, though I didn't know it then.

She had followed my life year after year, regularly making notes—some of which I would recognize as I grew older. When I was seven I was given, with much fanfare, my own apartment directly above the infant room. This was two years after Magna officially became my foster mother. The governesses filled my new home with a carpet of flowers for the occasion, and the scent lingered in the house for weeks. Magna put my little wooden bed in the room, along with a wicker chair (a present from a Norwegian delegation). By all accounts, it was a great solution. "Marie is so excited about her new home!" Magna's voice echoed throughout the high-ceilinged rooms.

Yet one day after returning from a visit with Magdalene, I nonetheless asked: "Why was I never adopted?" It was, perhaps, the most fundamental question in my life.

My foster mother looked directly at me for a long moment, and I felt disapproval piercing her love. She smelled of the yellow freesia whose stems she'd crushed to bits with a hammer so they would survive longer. Her thick fingers were stained yellow-green.

At last she leaned forward and hugged me tightly. "Oh, but Marie, your hinges were a little crooked when you arrived," she said. "That's why we decided that even families who were capable of adopting such a child needed to be extraordinarily well suited. We couldn't risk having them tire of the trouble after a few years and simply return you."

Return me.

"Was I that much trouble?" I asked.

Along with the freesia, I could now smell peppermint lozenges and cheroot smoke.

I waited for the answer, holding my breath.

"Most wanted children who were one hundred percent healthy, Marie, even if that meant waiting a couple years." She took my hand. " 'She looks cute, but she's sewn together a little oddly.' That's what they'd say." Magna sighed deeply. "And if there were other kids in their circle of friends, well, you could be a little frightening because of your unusual . . ."—she sighed even deeper—"because of your unusual facial features."

"Did they have other children then?"

Early on, Magna and I developed a habit of talking past one another. But it didn't seem to bother her, because she was always able to stick to her train of thought.

"There were a few who fell for you, Marie," she said. "But by the time they had gone through the extended interviews and home visits . . ." She let go of my hand. "When the social workers investigated their background . . ." She looked out over the sound and Hven. "Well, it could be a very prolonged ordeal."

She sighed for the third and final time.

"I've never seen a real bedroom," I said, on the verge of tears.

"But you *have* a real bedroom," she said. "You've got the best room of all—the king himself designed it for us!"

"Was he my dad?"

"We gave you the best home we could find. Here, with us," she said solemnly, wrapping her bear arms reassuringly around my crooked shoulder. "You know all the best homes are by the water." She squeezed me tight. I said nothing more.

Days passed. I shuffled endlessly along the long corridors where I often whispered to myself like some ghost, steadily dragging the Japanese pull-along elephant after me on the short, rusty chain I'd found in the basement and cinched around its neck; it wasn't going anywhere. At night I got up from bed and walked over to the mirror, which was cut from the most beautiful mahogany and embellished with gold. Maybe if I stared into the damn thing long enough, the lopsided cheekbones, the fallen cheek, and the lone staring eye would transform. But these kinds of miracles are the stuff of dreams. In reality, the mirror soon felt a little put out by all the attention and finally asked the burning question that had always passed between us: "Who is the ugliest of them all?"

I remained silent, and it responded: *You are!*

"Is the king my father?" I asked, stupidly.

The mirror and I also talked past one another.

Many nights I sat at my desk for hours staring toward Hven. Since the King's Room projected over the ridge of the roof—indeed over the entire patio—I pretended it was the bridge of a ship that had rolled gently to port after an adventurous expedition. And in the dark I climbed onto my desk, took my position on the bridge, and steered the ship clear of the Swedish coast: my fingers were graceful, my face concentrated, my figure ramrod stiff in the captain's uniform. Often I was so exhausted when morning came that I stayed in bed with bloodshot eyes and a chest so still that the orphanage's doctor had to lean in to ensure that I was still breathing.

I flunked the first school readiness test, but I didn't mind because I had no desire for any bookish knowledge that went beyond the walls of Kongslund. Magna's right hand, Gerda Jensen, tutored me in the sunroom during the first years. My curiosity about the real world went no further than the Chinese stone pillars on Strandvejen that marked the steep driveway down to Kongslund. No further than that. Here in my home only two things had real value: the fulfillment of longing and the erasure of want. But I wouldn't discover that until much later.

One of the last times I visited Magdalene, she said, "Even though you're nobody's child, you can have children of your own someday, Marie. It was the exact opposite for me." The words bubbled up and down in a peculiar hiss, as though she were crying or laughing, or both. When everyone else gave up making sense of her speech, I understood every word. My eyes would find hers and read the message without any difficulty whatsoever (the way only children can). She had never been embraced, had never kissed a man's lips.

"You're right, Marie, I haven't," she said reading my mind, without ever looking up. "I would have liked to."

"Do you want to be my mother?" I asked her.

She laughed, and the noise whistled through her nostrils. Her body twisted into an almost impossibly awkward position. I loved her. I rose from the sand and pushed her wheelchair up the slope, through the grove, and all the way to the king's old lookout.

"Marie, don't push me so fast," she said, laughing again.

I think she would have preferred being spared from understanding all the physical signals one hopes the world will notice and reward with caresses. It's the body and its longing that bends the mind and teaches the eye to calculate the distance to one's desires so often out of reach. The words in her diaries were the lifeline that helped her pass her days.

"Maybe it was because I was so deteriorated to begin with, Marie!" She chuffed the last few words though her nose. "It could hardly get any worse!" The blue notebooks fell off her lap into the grass, and I picked them up as usual. She kept her fountain pen on a string around her neck.

"I want you to have my dairies when I pass away, because it won't be long until you can read them yourself," she said on one of the last days of her life. It was July 1969. She was working on her twelfth notebook.

"Maybe you'll write yourself when you're older," she said, stroking my hair.

I said nothing.

"Write about what occupies your mind. Write about everything you wish to understand."

And then she added, "Who wouldn't like to die having lived a full life?" A week passed before she concluded the thought—much as how time passed when she wrote. "I will die without experiencing love, the love between a man and a woman, and that is the hardest thing."

If God truly existed, he must have been present there, right at that moment. But of course I knew that neither God nor the Devil ever approached Kongslund, because they did everything in their power to avoid such irreparable creatures.

Only Fate could separate—and reunite—us.

* * *

I have Magdalene's final diary.

It's a sky-blue notebook that's slightly curled along the edges, as though someone had splashed water on it and then left it on the radiator to dry. Perhaps she'd taken it to the beach once. I don't remember.

On the second to last page, she wrote: *I have a recurring dream about my beloved Marie. In it she has traveled far from here and lives in a distant country on the other side of the globe; maybe it's Africa, because in the dream I see the blue elephants she always told me about. They are alive, and they are marching with her in an endless row. It's possible that her dreams will come true one day.*

In her fine web of letters I can see everything; her deteriorating hand and her concentration. Some of the letters resemble long-dead spiders—half-erased, with hooked gray legs—and yet they are strangely beautiful.

On the very last page, she wrote: *When mankind takes its first step on the moon, I will know whether my telescope is worthy of a king. I will point it upward—toward the future—and see whether this message is true . . .*

The dots are hers. She would never write again.

She died on the morning of July 21. Something woke me very early that day. Maybe I had a premonition of the marvelous and dreadful things that had happened.

The night before, all the governesses had gathered around the small television in the living room and watched the Americans landing on the moon, and I was excited to see how my friend would react. Probably, she was already describing the landmark feat—imagine flying through space, high above the clouds . . . imagine that . . . what we've always dreamed of, Marie . . . *just imagine it . . .*

I pushed open the door to her white villa.

Because she was not afraid of uninvited guests, she never locked it.

I stepped into the house and walked easily from room to room. To allow her movement throughout the house, the doorsills had been removed long before. There was a very narrow bed on which she slept, but she wasn't in it.

A nurse from Gentofte County Hospital visited her once a week to change her sheets, I knew, and she would roll her around in her wheelchair. But the bed appeared not to have been touched in centuries. I knew something was wrong.

I also knew it was too late.

She was sitting outside, near the corner of the house, her back to her beloved Strandvejen. She was facing the sound. The prize telescope, rigged to a tripod attached to the wheelchair's armrest, was directed at the sky, toward where the spacecraft was supposed to travel on its return to Earth. Her head had dropped onto her chest.

My foster mother and her assistants must have been quite shaken to find me there, me being so young, only eight, and it being so late, and long after they'd begun their search. Magdalene's was the last place they'd thought to look.

I sat curled by the footrest of her wheelchair, where her slender feet had been for decades. Though she was dead, I'd put my head in her lap.

I remember waking when Magna made a strange, frightened noise I'd never heard before.

I didn't speak for the rest of July and most of August. This was the year that I became strange, that strangeness became a part of my soul.

Magna and I never talked about what had happened; she didn't understand my grief. The soul is not, as many believe, a compact mass: a little ball of light between heart and liver. Nor is it, as the bold claim, a void that fills the living body and deftly floats away between the fingers of Death, ensuring eternal life for the spirit. No, the soul is a narrow ledge on which the faithful must balance in their search for consolation. If they make one misstep, they'll never find their footing again, and if they search for Light further afield, all they will see is Darkness. That's what I discovered that last summer with Magdalene. Like space, the soul is not an expression of eternal constancy but of constant change, and this motion has but one purpose: to continue forward, on the narrow ledge, in the absurd hope that you can escape the Darkness.

At night I hide her twelve notebooks inside a secret cubby in the teak bureau that the old sea captain Olbers, the man who bought the home from the royal family, brought home from one of his numerous expeditions to the Dark Continent (he'd been a ship's boy on the frigate *Gefion* and later spent his entire life in the commercial fleet). In a drawer with a fake bottom are my own diaries, which I began to write the same year that Magdalene died. Contained in them you'll find the beginning of the narrative she and I set into motion.

In another of the captain's furnishings, this one a nearly seven-foot-tall cabinet, in a secret compartment behind elaborate carvings of lemon trees, you'll also find a description of our first encounters following her magnificent funeral, the details of our concerns, the notes on our decisions—and, consequently, to my horror—what those decisions led to.

5

MAGNA

May 7, 2008

Of course Magna suspected that Magdalene never truly departed Kongslund, though death had removed her from the physical universe.

At some point, it became clear to me that my foster mother had found and read the twelve diaries hidden in the bureau. Naturally, we never talked about it.

Viewed from the outside, relations between the matron and her foster daughter seemed hunky dory, and in time I was considered her true daughter. To the outside world, Kongslund epitomized the genuine, unfailing kindheartedness that aided even the ostracized and the illegitimate. For here were the sniffling castoffs staring into emptiness, steeling themselves against the traumas that psychologists and professors would write books about for decades.

None of them actually understood the nature of our terror, Magdalene told me, rocking from side to side in her old chair. Abandonment has nothing to do with what you leave behind. Abandonment is where you go. You don't find longing behind you: you find it in front of you.

The psychologists and the prim ladies from Mother's Aid Society were all convinced that our defects could be repaired with fresh sea air and end- less patience. Because that's how it had always been done.

We remained silent, letting them keep their unshakeable conviction.

* * *

My foster mother had remained the undisputed mistress of Kongslund. Even long after her retirement, she continued to hold monthly meetings with her successor, Susanne Ingemann, to discuss the management of the orphanage.

She was the reason that Kongslund's self-governance fund received a generous donation each year from the Ministry of National Affairs' Office of Special Matters (there was no doubt that what was "special" about this office was the considerable sum distributed to Kongslund).

* * *

On a morning in May, Magna cancelled a meeting with Susanne for the first time, offering no explanation. Then she dialed another number. She could feel her otherwise steady fingers trembling slightly. She spoke for a few minutes and then waited.

There were wax stumps in each of the five silver candleholders in the window—one for each of the Five Dark Years. She had lit the candles a few evenings before, at the exact hour when, sixty-three years earlier, the voice from London had announced the end of the war: "We are getting reports . . ."

That Hitler, the son of a bitch, has been defeated.

She'd noticed the uneasiness on the other end of the line, the pause, and the implicit question: *What the hell is going on there?*

But she didn't know anything.

I'm coming over.

She sat and waited. The source of the article in *Independent Weekend* was a mystery to her. How had the anonymous information come to light? She didn't know what else the journalist might have discovered (he had called asking for an interview, but she'd declined, explaining that due to arthritis pain she was bedridden).

After she'd regained some of her composure, she reread the article. Then she stood and found her scrapbooks in the cabinet—three brown, three red, and three white. The brown ones contained photographs, the red ones postcards and letters, and the white ones yellowed newspaper articles collected during the seven decades since the orphanage's founding in 1936. There had never been an article like this one.

She opened *Independent Weekend* and forced herself to examine the heading: "Famous Orphanage Accused of Hiding Thousands of Children." All that was missing was an exclamation point.

To a large extent, the article was based on unsubstantiated accusations. Rumors. Anonymous voices. Unknown sources reported gossip that behind the scenes the orphanage had been a tool for the rich and powerful who'd had extramarital affairs. For decades, their unwanted, illegitimate children had been gathered up discreetly and effectively from hospitals and given new identities, after which no mortal power could ever locate their mothers or fathers.

With a look of disgust, she studied the headline as though it were made of crushed insects, before turning to page six, where she found a longer article and two photos, one archive photo of her and another, larger one of the orphanage. "In the Service of Forgotten Children." *By Knud Taasing. Photos: Nils V. Jensen.*

After she'd read the article three times, she knew the introduction by heart: "On Tuesday, May 13, a celebration will honor a very special woman and the thousands of children who called her 'mother' until they found their own way and their own families."

Magna sighed, puckering her lips as though she were going to spit one of the dead insects onto the carpet. For the occasion, she was dressed in dark blue and wore the earrings that she usually reserved for visits to the theater and funerals (the latter outnumbering the former these days).

"Now approaching ninety, Ms. Ladegaard has been known simply as Magna among the thousands of children she 'fostered' at the home on Strandvejen. She became matron at Kongslund in 1948, and she is still connected to the orphanage, which is located in a great patrician villa near Øresund. From the beginning, Kongslund was famous for offering shelter to the weakest of the weak—the children whose parents wanted nothing to do with them."

She closed her eyes and felt anger stirring. *The weakest of the weak.* She would never refer to her children that way.

Magna hated seeing her name in print. She was baptized Martha Magnolia Louise Ladegaard—an impressive series of names she'd never quite lived down, and which perhaps, in the end, had driven her away from home at a young age. The first middle name, Magnolia, came as a whim to the pastor who'd held her over the baptismal font, the man who also happened to be her father. Though her mother had leaped from her seat in surprise, the God-inspired name could not be changed. That day the church had been festooned with delicate, dried flowers—in addition to magnolia, there were freesia, poppy, harebell, meadow anemone, and prairie clover. It could have been much worse, Magna's mother used to tell her daughter reassuringly. Every time the other kids in the village school teased Martha Magnolia about her flowery middle name, her mother repeated these comforting words: "Well, would you rather have been named Anemone? Or Harebell!"

At age sixteen, she was a tall, rather sturdily built girl with wavy brown hair and a deep, melodic voice. One spring day she traveled to Copenhagen to become a nurse's aide. It was during those weeks that Mother's Aid Society purchased Kongslund and transformed the beautiful villa into an infant orphanage, furnishing the high-ceilinged rooms with the practical sense of strong women. Magna often thought the old king—who'd been so brutally cut off from his biological mother, the promiscuous princess Charlotte Frederikke—would have been delighted by the turn in the home's fortunes. As punishment for her unfaithfulness, his mother had been deprived access to her son. (There was no doubt that a motherless childhood had made him so strange that anger and longing had rendered him infertile. After that the lineage died out. *Suitable retribution*, Magna thought, *for a family who denied a boy his mother.*

The newly furnished orphanage opened on May 13, 1936. That was also Save the Children Day in Copenhagen, and the women of the city used the occasion to call attention to the children's charity. Some 1,600 women with 1,600 flag-decorated prams and 1,629 children—including two pairs of triplets and twenty-five pairs of twins—marched in the bright sunlight from Rosenborg Castle to Tivoli.

Young Martha Magnolia had never seen anything like it. What she witnessed was nothing less than Danish women marching into the future, mothers asserting their worth, defending newborns, striving for basic care—and expressing their right to speak collectively as women.

When the procession ended, a speaker from Mother's Aid Society described the new orphanage that had been inaugurated that very day in Skodsborg—and the young nurse's aide knew instantly which path her life ought to follow.

The orphanage on Skodsborg Hill grew year after year. Tricycles, shovels, buckets, and soapbox cars appeared on the lawn facing the sea, and young women in white caps with bundled babies in their arms could be seen coming and going from the great house. On Sundays childless couples visited, nervously shuffling their feet and clutching their approval letters from the adoption agency. They would take home the child who radiated the fragility and need for love that they themselves were searching for.

When the matron took ill in 1947, she immediately appointed Magna as acting director. A year later Magna became the institution's second matron.

"Being a single mother without a husband was considered shameful in all levels of society," the article stated. "Perhaps it was an even greater scandal for families higher up the social ladder. Several sources confirm *Independent Weekend*'s assertion that potentially controversial adoption cases were handled with unusual discretion by the respected orphanage."

Magna lowered the newspaper for a moment before forcing herself to continue reading.

"They could have been politicians, public officials, or actors who hadn't wanted to risk their reputations and careers because of some extramarital affair, our sources tell us. They could show up at Skodsborg Strandvej, and be confident that the matron now celebrating her anniversary would solve their problems to their full satisfaction. *Independent Weekend* has come into the possession of a confidential document from one of the biggest adoption years (1961), a document suggesting that one such boy's case was to be handled outside the usual protocol. The boy's name was John Bjergstrand."

Magna stared at the white scrapbooks in front of her. There had never been an article critical of Kongslund. This newspaper seemed to suggest that the service offered might have also had a commercial purpose. The journalist continued in the same vein—one that Magna assumed helped sell newspapers.

"Perhaps a current high-ranking official or politician in all secrecy put his unwanted child up for adoption to avoid a scandal. That's what the story suggests. Does the now grown man know his own storm-tossed narrative? And what goes through the mind of a father who, out of regard for his own career, gives up his own child? This man may be a public figure who fears disclosure and therefore keeps quiet. Due to health concerns the main figure in the anniversary celebration, a woman who served as matron from 1948 to 1989, declined to be interviewed for this article. Many questions thus remain."

The newspaper had dedicated a lot of space to the article, which appeared under the headline "In the Service of Forgotten Children." It had even shoved the story of an eleven-year-old Tamil boy facing deportation to the back of section one.

One particular detail worried the retired matron more than any other: A small sign that the journalist knew much more than what was actually printed in the article's five long columns. A knowledge she couldn't think of a reasonable explanation for, and which therefore frightened her. She needed to share the potential consequences with a person she would normally never invite inside her home.

Once again she studied the names above the article: Knud Taasing and Nils V. Jensen. It was bizarre. She folded the newspaper and lit one of her thick cheroots. Possibly, it was a coincidence—but if it was, it seemed almost supernatural. For two days she'd felt nauseated; she knew it must be fear. This wasn't like her.

Although she'd been anticipating the doorbell's chime, she flinched when she heard it.

"Hello!" he said in a lightly ironic tone, giving her a peck on the cheek. Just like in the old days.

He brought his own copy. With a red pen he'd drawn a circle around the front-page story.

"If there is a dark secret behind this mysterious story, the anonymous letter will likely not be the last. The Ministry of National Affairs does not wish to comment on whether one of the letters was also delivered to Ole Almind-Enevold, as has been indicated to *Independent Weekend*. Several sources confirm that Orla Berntsen stayed at Kongslund for an undisclosed length of time during the first year of his life, officially the result of his mother's depression. The chief of staff has declined to comment on this information."

"Can you find out *who* . . . ?" She had poured the coffee, and now the question hung in the air between them.

"Who has given them this information?" He slid the small sugar bowl toward his cup. "Yes, I can, and I'm already on it." He fingered six or seven cubes, just as he used to. Magna counted the pieces with the same disapproval she felt whenever children bought lollipops at the corner store.

He glanced up and for a long moment stared at her. Instantly she felt pain in her lower back, the pain that presaged thunder and lightning and early autumn storms. Bile rose so forcefully in her throat that she had to put down her cup and lean back in her seat.

"Could we be in any danger?" Her question sounded childish.

"Of course," he said. "There's somebody out there—somebody's got ahold of something—and our friend certainly is angry. And scared." He almost looked satisfied—though that was absurd—and then he quietly stirred his coffee with the little silver spoon. He had filled out over the years, and the dark curly hair had gone gray. He laid his coat over the newspaper as if he didn't want to be reminded of it. For a former assistant chief of police, he was appropriately dressed: dark-blue trousers, light-blue shirt, and a blue checkered tie. Nowadays his business card read *Carl Malle, Senior Consultant, Security and Protection Specialist*.

It was almost funny. She'd always felt extremely unsafe in Carl Malle's presence.

"Given that your anniversary is right around the corner, this is most unfortunate," he said. "The spotlight will be on you and the orphanage for at least another week. I think the anonymous letter writer has taken that into account. But thankfully, the journalist at *Independent Weekend* was thoroughly discredited a few years ago, so it's doubtful that anyone will take his information seriously today." Carl Malle smiled. "And certainly not if he were to somehow discover the utterly improbable truth, don't you agree?"

"This is hardly the time to be joking." She sounded curt, even a little fearful. She'd always felt that way in his company.

"I mean it quite seriously, my dear Magna. The truth is so bizarre that no one will actually print the story without confirmation from the primary sources. And that includes only three of us. Unless you think of anyone else from that time . . . and in any case, the person you and I are both thinking of can't even document her own story. That door closed a long time ago, and she hasn't returned. She wasn't the one who wrote the damn letter to that asshole Taasing."

"But did you notice who Taasing referred to?"

"It's a coincidence, Magna. Nothing more. And I keep a leash on Orla of course." Carl Malle's laughter rose from deep within his throat and rattled just like the mechanical clowns banging their drums on the sunroom floor on Christmas Eve. "The minister has asked the head of the department to open the gates of hell to locate the anonymous writer. And hell—that's me. But I'm sure you recall . . . our shared war?" Malle laughed again.

And she did remember the seventeen-year-old resistance fighter whom she'd admired for a few months before she saw his true self.

"We go way back, Magna, but even so, maybe there's an ugly little secret I don't know about? We both mastered those, didn't we? We'll have to flip the barrel upside down and shake it, hope something turns up. I *have* to find that letter writer before anyone else does."

He lit his Norwell pipe and, for a long moment, concentrated on the bowl as if he wished to burn the entire problem up with his tobacco. For a man of his ilk, the occupation by Nazi Germany had been a gift: dark, dangerous, threatening, and full of excitement. Magna had always understood this. Along with two of his school chums, he'd formed a resistance group in Jutland in 1943. They'd been as reckless as only very young men can be, girded as they were by firm conviction in their own immortality. They stole German guns, hand grenades, and explosives; they obstructed train rails with thick oak trees they'd felled in the woods between Vejle and Horsens. They didn't know the purpose of the trains—or what they were transporting—but in the shrubbery where they were hiding, they would hoot with excitement whenever the rails exploded and the freight cars capsized.

They sabotaged like dogs of hell, blowing up practically everything in their path: parked cars, clothes, warehouses filled with military underwear, factories, ammunition depots, and bakeries that sold morning rolls to officers in the Danish Hilfspolizei. As the months passed, Carl became more reckless and erratic, and he made other members of the movement nervous. When the cooperation agreement between the Danish government and the occupying power finally broke down in August 1943, and the Danish Jews faced the same Final Solution as other European Jews, a resistance leader managed to persuade Carl and his two henchmen to carry out the greatest possible heroic act. Thousands of Jews were to be hidden and then smuggled to Sweden over the coming months, and the base of operations would be in the nation's capital. The Devil made a pact with God, and it's debatable whether Denmark would have saved as many Jews and placed itself on the just side of the war had it not been for Carl Malle's arrival in the city.

By then Magna had become a trusted assistant at the orphanage in Skodsborg, and when on September 29, 1943, Danes learned that the Germans were making plans to arrest and deport thousands of Jews only two days later, Magna went downtown with Gerda. They took the tram to a small tavern near the Kalkbrænderi Harbor, which they knew to be frequented by resistance fighters, and there they met Carl, newly arrived from Jutland, sitting at a small corner table. The tall man from Horsens explained the problem to Magna: the Jews had to be located, hidden, and smuggled out. While the resistance fighters organized the escape routes to Sweden, they needed safe homes.

That night, Carl and Magna slept together in her little apartment at the orphanage; afterward, they crawled through a trapdoor in her bedroom and inspected the attic: except for a few boxes with extra toys, it was completely empty. A perfect hiding place.

Then they climbed back down and made love again. He was seventeen, she twenty-three. There was never any doubt that it was his hands, and his will, that determined the rhythm of their lovemaking, the pace, and the time of their climax; she let her head drop and screamed, hoping the nursing students asleep in the annex would think it was only a baby crying somewhere in the house.

Carl was her first—and last—man.

He sat there smoking his pipe as if he could read her mind. No doubt he could. "There was a time, Magna, when we weren't afraid of anything. But that was a long time ago."

"Yes. The five cursed years . . ." The comment was clearly aimed at him.

The Jews had arrived at Kongslund after dark and in small clusters. Men, women, and children with rucksacks and suitcases, no more than what they could carry across the sound to Sweden. Carl Malle and his pals in the Resistance had coaxed, threatened, and bribed their way to seaworthy vessels of any kind. "As long as it floats," Carl would say, towering over the nervous fishermen who didn't dare refuse. There was no boat or coffin ship that he didn't manage to put to sea during those months, and Carl himself would stand in the sunroom whenever another group was about to set sail. "Carry only what's important so you can let it go if you need to run," he instructed them. "If you have to swim, forget your luggage." She recalled how he would laugh out loud each time—and the refugees would look at him apprehensively, as if they couldn't quite determine who posed the greater threat.

As the weeks passed, the governesses grew less nervous. No one had shown the least interest in the orphanage—maybe because thousands of Jews were hiding along the coast, from Gilleleje in the north to the island of Falster in the south.

Until one night.

Two black cars from the Gestapo turned into the driveway and parked. In all, there were seven men and an officer—and no way out, it seemed.

Gerda Jensen, the woman who had painted the blue elephants in the infant room, met them on the front steps, and they halted. She'd wrapped a green crocheted shawl around her shoulders, and she seemed so small that the house behind her appeared enormous. The German commandant showed her his order to search the premises thoroughly. Gerda curtsied.

"*Bitte, stören sie nicht die Kinder,*" she said in a voice so mild. "Please, do not disturb the children." She was so convincing that the German automatically averted his gaze, as though he'd been caught doing something sinful. Ironically, he could have just asked what he wanted to know, because Gerda Jensen had never been able to lie to any living soul. Not even a German officer. But of course the commandant would never have dreamed of this. As it happened, the Germans never made it past the ground floor, where they stood awkwardly—in their long coats and boots—between the beds in the room that would later become known as the Elephant Room.

Gerda approached the commandant. She came up only to his chest. "These children are very frail," she said in Danish. "They are all alone in this world"—she glanced into his face and let him meet a gaze that reflected centuries of storms and breakers along Jutland's rugged west coast—"and they'll never meet their parents." The eight men looked suddenly very ill at ease; a sense of peril filled the air, which none of them could later explain. The tiny woman certainly posed no threat.

"*Fräulein,*" the major said, careful not to look at the sleeping bundles under the small duvets, "*danke schön.*" He turned on his heels and asked to be shown out. The sound of their tires on the gravel road could be heard again, less than ten minutes from when they first arrived.

Not long afterward, liberation arrived, and the Germans surrendered without a fight. They wandered down Strandvejen into Skodsborg, past Kongslund, across Copenhagen, and through Zealand toward their devastated homeland. During the final months of the war, Carl had been very active in the liquidation of Danish collaborators, a necessary evil that was said to mark the resistance fighters for life.

But had it marked him? She didn't think so.

"Soon Knud Taasing will zoom in on the five boys from the Elephant Room in 1961," Carl Malle said to Magna. "After all, he's not stupid."

She was silent.

"If they discover the connection—even if it's unlikely"—he clinked the silver teaspoon against the edge of the sugar bowl—"they will ask about the *father*. They'll ask about him and demand to know where he is today."

"And of course I will tell them that we often don't know the names of the fathers, which is true." She'd regained some of her self-confidence. In contrast to Gerda, she was perfectly capable of lying when it was necessary.

"But why all this secrecy? Why this irregular adoption form? As if you'd attempted to hide every trace. What will you say if they ask about that?"

"I don't remember anymore. There were so many children . . . and thousands of people came to Kongslund. They can't force me, Carl. They're not *barbarians*, are they?"

He ignored the insult. Their lives were intertwined in ways that couldn't be unknotted. He pushed his coat off the newspaper, and she knew what was coming.

"I think Marie might've sent the letter," he said.

Magna didn't react.

"I saw her in Søborg . . . when she was a child . . . creeping about, spying on Orla and Severin. That wasn't normal. And she's had access . . . to information." His last words were strange, ambiguous.

The retired matron remained silent. They'd entered dangerous territory.

"She's always been strange. It's no wonder you couldn't find her a home."

"I did find her a home. The best one," she replied bitingly.

He stood, and the teaspoon clattered to the floor. "If only we knew why it's happening now."

She looked at him. "Yes, but just about anybody could have found that form and kept it, could have sniffed out some of what happened. A visitor . . . a former governess."

"Of course, what our friend fears more than anything else is that it's the boy himself," Malle broke in. "He might have found that form at his adoptive parents' home, and now he's trying to figure out what it means."

Magna noticed her skin was the same color as the ashes in the little crystal bowl set before her. She fell silent.

"Did you erase *every* trace?" he asked.

"Yes—of course I did."

"It's your fault—and *his*—that we're in this pickle."

It was a peculiar, old-fashioned expression. But he was right. Carl Malle had merely been an instrument.

"And what happens if our beloved TV star Peter gets involved? Him and his TV station? It's a distinct possibility, isn't it?"

It didn't sound like a question to Magna.

"Maybe he, too, received a similar letter."

She didn't need to respond to this terrifying prediction. They had to seal off the past, regardless of who had broken through, before it was too late.

"Is Orla really the son of the single woman he grew up with in Søborg?" The question came out of nowhere.

She responded without hesitation. "You'd know best." He'd given himself away. "Didn't you follow him more closely than anyone?"

"A single mother would be the perfect cover. Isn't that right, Magna?"

She didn't reply.

"He'd had a frightening childhood. Interesting but frightening. Such ferocity. Almost as though something had been passed down to him. To kill a man, and at such a young age."

She was no match for him. But she couldn't leave the accusation unchallenged. "He didn't kill him. I talked to the psychologist . . ." She stopped. She didn't want him to know anything more than that.

"The psychologist was scared out of his wits, my dear Magna. You must know that. I spoke to Orla right after . . . after the incident. It wasn't normal. You know that."

"They never proved it."

"No, and why do you think? Because I . . . because *we* . . . protected him."

"How about you, Carl? How many people have you killed?" For the first time she uttered his name, hatred providing them with a shared intimacy.

"Yes, I've killed people, Magna—but at war. Orla wasn't at war," he said. "A fool in the Søborg wetlands is hardly an enemy you have to kill. And certainly not like that."

Silence filled the room for some time.

"I don't understand how this started," he finally said, as if posing his question differently would produce an answer.

Then he left, slamming the front door as he did.

She lit another cheroot and stared at the blue smoke. In her dreams, their staring eyes buried her: children in straight rows, ten thousand at a time. She knew it was too late to escape. Darkness had opened up beneath her.

The small blue elephants would march along the fine web, and she wouldn't see it come apart before she fell, down, down, down. The web that was supposed to withstand everything would break. Darkness would be her grave.

She could reconcile herself with that. There wasn't a single song that lasted forever, in spite of what she'd told the little ones.

She just didn't want it to happen yet.

* * *

Turning toward Ole Almind-Enevold, Orla Berntsen saw for the first time, just beneath the surface, a coarseness in the smooth, almost feminine features of his boss's face.

Recent revelations had induced a sense of shock as forceful as a stranger's embrace, and it had generated a curious awkwardness between them. Fear had arrived at the Ministry of National Affairs—delivered, so to speak, with the daily mail, and it had crawled under the skin of the big man and changed his appearance, indeed, his whole comportment.

The other man's fear induced anger in Orla Berntsen that he found difficult to conceal, even though he understood everything they'd discussed with the Witch Doctor just minutes before. If Kongslund was embroiled in a scandal like the one suggested by *Independent Weekend,* then the ministry would be exposed to a wave of fanatical persecution by a press that still believed public extermination was the preferred entertainment of the Danish population.

Why did the administration support Kongslund for so many years? Was there a connection between the ministry and these allegations? And, if not, how could its longtime patron, the minister himself, have missed such a deception?

How much of the taxpayers' money had been pumped into the institution?

Hadn't the compelling story of Kongslund, and the nation's vulnerable children, been a significant factor in securing the administration's election in 2005?

Followed by the question that Knud Taasing would never let go of: *What does the party think about the fact that the highly esteemed orphanage, outwardly protecting the weakest, most vulnerable members of society, secretly aided the strong and powerful?*

The symbolism could not be missed. It would topple the nation's second-in-command just as he was standing on the final step to the throne.

They were a mismatched pair. Orla's fellow students had thought so even twenty years ago: the taciturn student and his older supervisor, the former minister of justice in an ailing administration recently removed from power. Orla couldn't have cared less. In the older man he'd recognized himself, and he'd not hesitated to pay the price of admission to the chambers of power.

It cost him the only friendship he'd ever known though. Two young lawyers who had once dreamed of opening a practice together. Søren Severin Nielsen had instead chosen a path that would inevitably lead him to lock horns with state officials. As an advocate for asylum seekers, he defended a flood of darker and darker strangers, with a doggedness that earned him the status of the nation's leading immigration lawyer. A consummate idealist, he gave voice to anyone able to offer a heartbreaking story of fear, torture, and persecution. Orla Berntsen, meanwhile, followed his own stellar career trajectory, rising straight through the Justice Department and the Ministry of National Affairs, where he defended the prevailing bulwark of the Danish legal system, one that kept out every fraudulent refugee, soldier of fortune, and imposter. The latest case— the decision to deport an eleven-year-old Tamil boy—marked another milestone. Next year, they would be as young as ten when they were driven to the gate at Kastrup Airport and sent home.

"There's a reason I sent for you." The minister's voice was barely audible in his high-ceilinged office.

Here, too, the odor of sweat and deodorant filled his nostrils. Soundlessly Orla Berntsen stretched his fingers behind his back. His hands were tingling, and his newly discovered anger at the man behind the desk pricked like pins on his skin. "If this is about Søren Severin Nielsen's attempt to stir the press over the expulsion of that Tamil boy, the Witch . . . the PR chief has given them so many legal clauses to support the decision that their heads will spin, when—"

Ole waved his hand dismissively, and Orla fell silent.

The minister didn't care about Tamil children. "Carl Malle paid a visit to Magna," he said quietly. "She had . . . *nothing* to report."

Orla was silent.

"Naturally, Kongslund is innocent of the charge. I assume you understand that." His words sounded old-fashioned.

Though it wasn't a question, Orla replied, just as quietly, "Yes."

"Do you know anything?"

An echo of the voices he'd heard throughout his childhood. *Do you know anything?*

As always, he answered, "No. Nothing." He'd never really known anything. His mother would sit in the same blue armchair that had once belonged to her father, never uttering a word about the past. About his father who'd disappeared. When she'd been silent long enough, he would escape to the wetlands, where he'd squat by the banks of the creek. It was there, one summer night, that he defeated the strongest enemy he'd ever encountered, throwing his evil eye out among the lily pads. In his mind's eye he could still see it lying in green slime on a sorrel leaf, resembling an illustration from the fiction magazine *Horror*. He felt no remorse. It was the same evil eye that he'd fantasized had transformed his father into a rock. Oddly, he found it divested of its power by the water (an observation that would have been of interest to the bearded confessors at Kongslund).

"Well, that's all then," the minister said, interrupting his bizarre recollection. Like rigid tin soldiers, these few words marched across the vast no man's land between them.

The chief inspector had retired from the homicide department at Copenhagen Police headquarters on the very day Denmark entered the Iraq War: March 21, 2003. That gave him exactly eight months, one week, and four days to take all the overtime hours he'd earned as compensatory leave before the end of the year. He spent the first week watching Saddam Hussein's retreat on television.

More than five years later, he was still sitting there—in his favorite chair—watching Channel DK, known for its unambiguous support of law and order and a strong police force. He'd left very few unresolved cases behind, but the few that had been shelved had followed him into retirement. He thought about them almost every day.

His wife had often told their only child—a daughter—that he was *obsessed*, and he had merely nodded in agreement.

He was *obsessed* with patterns that hadn't been exposed and explained.

He'd perused the newspaper on the morning of May 7, and with growing interest, read about the case concerning the anonymous letters that had been sent to both the Ministry of National Affairs and *Independent Weekend*. Something he saw troubled him.

Rereading the article, he studied the photograph that had been used to illustrate the story. He furrowed his now nearly white brow as he scrutinized the big old villa in the picture, the tall windows, the ivy-clad walls, the magnificent corner towers, and the black roof with its seven chimneys.

It suddenly occurred to him what had vexed him all these years. He now realized he'd made an unforgivable mistake in September 2001, when they found that dead woman on the beach at Bellevue. In his mind's eye, he inspected the woman's body once more, as it lay in the morning mist by the water's edge. And for the umpteenth time, he saw the props—he'd never stopped calling them that, even after the FBI's experts had assured him there was no pattern in the finding.

As always, and with the same intensity as before, he sensed the ominous presence of an invisible opponent.

And again he felt a disquieting unease: though the case had been filed an accident, something really had been wrong.

The eye. The book. The branch. The rope. The bird. Had he missed anything?

He closed his eyes, seeing it all again.

The poor little bird had a broken neck and white sand in its eyes. Its beak was half-open.

That image haunted him almost more than any other. He'd never understood how it happened.

But there was another prop they'd never told anyone about, and that's the one he recognized when he opened the newspaper. *The photograph.*

They had found no identification on the dead woman, but they had found an old photo. They had assumed that it originated from the part of the world where the technical examination had suggested she was from.

For that reason they'd never tried to publish the image, and anyway, it would have hardly gotten any coverage during those hectic days. So no one had seen the photo of the house with seven chimneys—the very same one printed in *Independent Weekend.*

They had sent it to the police in Australia and New Zealand, along with a photo of the dead woman, hoping that someone would recognize the exotic villa. No one had, of course, and now he knew why. He'd made a critical error.

The motive lay a few hundred yards up the Øresund coast. The chief inspector was certain of it: the mansion in the photograph—the only personal item on the dead woman—was Kongslund, the orphanage that had now become the center of a mystery involving an adopted boy whom the newspapers claimed might just be the tip of the iceberg in a very deep and dark secret in the nation's soul.

The child of an unknown woman. A deep secret.

Was he overinterpreting, he wondered. His sense of duty overruled his feelings of doubt, as always. When he mentioned the revelation to his wife, she looked at him with alarm (she would much prefer he stayed put in his chair). He ignored her protests and called police headquarters.

He was patched through to his successor and explained his suspicions—that the two mysterious events were connected. The successor, out of politeness and respect for a man who'd devoted many years of his life serving the state, let him finish before he said, "We no longer have the case here. The ministry has asked Carl Malle to continue the investigation."

There was nothing more to be said. The retired homicide chief hung up the phone.

Under no circumstances would he approach the man everyone at headquarters had feared right up until that day when he'd retired. Of course, Malle never really retired, he set up his own private security consulting business instead, utilizing his contacts with top officials and politicians that had made him the de facto ruler at headquarters for two decades. People were aware of his power, and they fell silent in his presence; where Carl Malle was, fear reigned. And neither the retired chief inspector nor his wife, who obsessed about nothing other than their daughter and the flowers in her garden, wanted to reawaken this fear.

The mystery of the dead woman would have to remain buried in the sand.

6

MAGDALENE

May 7, 2008

Of course Carl Malle had to visit Magna, his old ally. I had no doubt he would.

But even if they'd talked all through the evening they'd still be at wit's end. They can't stop the chain of events the letters have set in motion.

If anyone recognizes the name—John Bjergstrand—they'll get in touch with the newspaper and later with the TV stations, of this I am certain. And they will follow up on the case (with its strong undertone of sex and scandalous deception). Danes like to gossip, and the country is, as Knud Taasing had already written in his paper, quite small. If anybody or anything stood out, it will attract attention.

During these first few days, all signs indicate that he will be proven right.

* * *

Fate had its own plans—as always—and perhaps it was my love for Magdalene that started it all.

I was only eight years old when she died, and I cried for eight days; we had only two years together, and that's too few when you're that young. Seventy-two years separated us, and she left me—at least in the physical world—the night humankind first set foot on another celestial body; it was peculiar. I've always had a feeling that the two events were somehow connected.

I sat on my foster mother's lap in Søllerød Church as we sang for the dead. I believe the pastor sensed that this ceremony was something extraordinary. The impressive Mrs. Krantz from Mother's Aid Society was there, as were the governesses and assistants, and so too the new psychologist. My foster mother, Magna, sang the verses of Brorson's Psalm 15—"Rise up, all things that God has made"—so boisterously that you could almost imagine the words flying over the altar, bumping into the thick, whitewashed walls, and echoing back to the congregation, as though Jesus were out there in the Nothingness, rapping on the church spire with his divine walking cane that made even the blind see.

"How shall I praise the evening sky, the many stars there blinking?" the psalm resounded. And in this good company it really was no question, not to this star parade of Good Women.

I thought of Magdalene and her fears, not of death but of everything else that was about to happen. Her passage into the Land of the Dead, for which she naturally had a plan. "I gather they don't have wheelchair ramps," she spluttered a few days prior to the moon landing, before she'd cackled and draped herself over her armrest as though struck by a horrible cramp.

During her final year, she had grown more and more certain that her deformed body wouldn't fit into a normal coffin, and for that reason she'd taken precautions to avoid such humiliation. On a piece of loose-leaf paper she'd folded up her funeral wishes and filed them in her oak hutch. The same hutch that held her notebooks and the telescope that had belonged to King Frederik VII.

When I am dead, I want to be buried under the Great Beech next to my parents. But don't put me in a coffin, because that would be embarrassing to all parties, not least to the person writing these words. If my eternally deformed body has to be squeezed into one of those narrow things they sell at the funeral home in Skodsborg, I prefer cremation.

And for good measure, she'd added: *I don't want people to feel ashamed for me in death. I don't want any stories to be told about how they had to tuck my arms close to my body and dislocate my knees to make me fit.*

Magdalene always thought of others.

I assume they'll be able to maneuver me into the oven the way I am. In any case, it would be a shame (and an expense) to burn a perfectly good and spacious coffin, she wrote, and underscored the last seven words: *They can just leave the wheelchair outside.* She had always been surprisingly practical, and even those basic guidelines must have taken her about a month to write.

Magna, who as the matron of an orphanage was as practical as the deceased, got the wheelchair from the undertaker following the cremation; you never knew when a child might need such an aid. I found it in the janitorial closet and brought it to my room. Every time I felt overwhelmed in missing my friend, I would sit in it. Curiously, every time I sat in it over the years, my longing grew; in the end I spent more time in this sunken monstrosity than in my own mahogany chair made by Thomas Chippendale himself.

People must have thought I was growing stranger. Lonely children develop an ability to make themselves invisible in almost every situation and place. During the years after Magdalene's death, I became more and more taciturn and practically unnoticeable to adult eyes. For children with the ability, this power is easily invoked, and it resembles the condition of a mirage. You come and go as you please. To many adults, such semi-invisible children can be very disturbing, because they have access to a world they themselves are afraid to visit—and in my case, it was even worse, because no one knew where I came from or where I was going. When visible, I would suddenly enter a room where Magna was hosting fine company and instantly draw all attention to me. I'd stand on the rya, all five feet four of me, like a crooked stem in a mound of soil, with my dark, peculiar aura. I think I knew what they feared when they saw a small child like that.

Magna would laugh aloud to alleviate the tension. "Here at Kongslund we're in the unique situation of being wholly uninformed about *both ends* of our lives," she said by way of explanation for the strange child in the doorway. She who could trace her lineage from Børkop through Gauerlund, Gårslev, and Smidstrup parishes, for more than three centuries and eight generations; she, who for a lifetime had been Denmark's most famous and renowned orphanage director, was unable to under-stand the most fundamental longing of the lonely child.

What happened after the moon landing and Magdalene's funeral was therefore quite natural. I have never thought of it as a miracle or a wonder—or as a sign from God or the Devil, both of whom had been ban-ished from this place anyway. My friend simply awakened and returned to me, as though she'd never left. Only she stepped into my life gracefully this time, as though she'd never suffered any deformity.

I simply assume that she, after being happily released from her earthly body and getting well-deserved rest in Heaven, relished the joy of speaking with her alter ego—the orphan Marie at Kongslund.

* * *

Don't worry about me, Marie. I am with the King of the People, the one who built your home, and we're dancing under the heavenly beeches, due west of the Andromeda Galaxy. There is no place in the universe more beautiful than this!

Andromeda. I cried. I was that happy for her.

In the beginning she merely listened to my worries, however large or small, and advised me to avoid the children up at Strandvejen who bul-lied me about my crooked shoulders and called me the Eskimo because of my cockeyed face under the dark, bristly hair (though it had become lighter over the years).

For they know not what they are doing, my best friend whispered conciliatorily and with such new and rich wisdom from the Other Side that even I, at age eight, envied her death. *Renounce them and forget them, disappear into yourself.*

It was ancient advice and more of a relief than anyone could imagine.

Soon she was with me everywhere as I plodded along with the old elephant on its chain. And I am sure she deliberately led me to those places that she'd long ago decided I should see.

Of course what had to happen did, what we together decided. One day when I stepped into my foster mother's living room—once again silencing the visitors until they became insecure and lowered their gazes—there was, to my surprise, a little boy in one of Magna's antique canapés. We studied one another for a while (without any direct eye con-tact, of course); the living room was practically void of air, and several of the adults had violent coughing fits. With great effort, Magna broke the spell. "Say hello to Orla," she said, looking directly at me and pointing at the squat little boy with freckles on his nose. "He lived here once. Here at Kongslund, with you. You were in the Elephant Room together." Then she roared with laughter that sounded like rolling thunder at midsummer. The boy didn't even blink. Clearly he was one of ours.

In that exact moment I knew he felt the same way I did, and that we both carried silence as a shield when we were among adults. We understood each other's thoughts perfectly, as though we were shouting with the full force of our voices. And on the occasion of our future reunion, we would form the sentence that all children at Kongslund have learned: *Dear God! Don't leave us here! For Heaven's sake!*

When I turned nine a few days later, Magdalene discreetly reminded me of her journals, which I had hidden in my bureau—because now I was old enough to read them thoroughly and in order. It was time, she decided, that I gained insight into the world of which I'd become a part.

She had observed thirty-four cohorts of Kongslund children in her time. As I read, she sat in the empty wheelchair by the window and answered all of my questions.

In her words, I saw myself for the first time, standing outside on the past's steep entrance.

Once again Marie has been down by the water and scolded by Ms. Ladegaard. She seems both willful and stubborn. I think she resembles me, she wrote in a notebook covering the years 1961 through 1964.

I turned a couple of pages back: *How innocent they are! Today is Constitution Day and there is a flag parade on the lawn. Marie is standing next to Putte and Jønne. Ms. Jensen is holding her hand.*

From the previous year, I found one of the more rare autumn notes. November 1963: *President Kennedy has been assassinated. Oh to be a child and know nothing of such wicked times.*

Finally I flicked all the way back to the date that was central to my and Kongslund's story—May 13, 1961. Here she'd written: *Sometimes in life you see something you don't understand and you have no one to share it with.*

Even with these few words, I sensed that she'd witnessed something very extraordinary, and that's how I read them: *I had awoken early and heard steps in the gravel.*

Without a doubt, she was the only living witness to the arrival of the tiny foundling.

I'm not ashamed to admit that I followed the incident through the king's telescope. If only my curiosity could sometimes be less strong. It was a messenger, and not a mother. I saw that right away. She simply placed the little one on the steps; there was no farewell, no grief.

She described the arrival of the woman with the carry-cot and her dash back across the slope, and explained how the blockheaded governess, Agnes, had stepped outside a short time later and called for help. How Magna had come running, grabbed the cot, and disappeared into the big villa. And a few weeks later, she concluded with the simple observation that summed up my first weeks at Kongslund: *Some children are born in Darkness and wanted by no one.*

In that moment, I heard her voice as clearly as if she'd been sitting right there in the wheelchair, hanging crookedly over the armrest like she used to.

Of course you have to find out what happened to them!

She laughed and grabbed my hands.

By that point, she'd been dead for more than a year.

Of course you have to find the children who have left Kongslund. Not your parents, who are irrevocably lost, but the children who left and now have their own families. Of course you should make certain there is a home and a bed at the other end. Like here.

I went up to the King's Room and studied the photo of the seven children in the Elephant Room at Christmas 1961: Orla with his silent, piercing eyes, Asger smiling at the sky, Peter under the branch with his drum, where he had been taught to sit . . .

Of course you should.

That day I dragged my Japanese pull-along elephant onto the pier and unhitched its rusty chain, letting it roll by itself into the sea. I stared into the bubbling water where it had disappeared and felt nothing. Then rage filled me, and I turned away from the water and the distant island.

I'd finally found my courage.

* * *

In the beginning my sources for locating the children in the photo included Magna's scrapbooks full of newspaper clippings and postcards, and my discreet conversations with governesses and assistants—especially Gerda Jensen, who sensed that I was moving into dangerous (and surely forbidden) territory but doubtlessly found an element of her own strength in my tenacity. I was a precocious child.

One day she happened to casually reveal where Magna kept her spare key for the office that contained all Kongslund's old records, and it was such a precious and astonishing confidence that we instinctively lowered our voices to a whisper and kept them at that level for several minutes. It's a secret I have never shared with anyone because the records contain information about thousands of adoptive families and the children, information that no outsider ought to have.

I let myself into the office, and on the shelves over the desk were the documents held in ring binders: blue for Danish children, green for the Greenlandic children (who arrived in the 1960s and 1970s), yellow for the Korean children and children of other nationalities (they arrived in the 1970s and 1980s), and brown for the children now residing in the home.

I was interested in the blue binders, which provided a curious person with the children's original names: what they were called before their mother gave them up; what they were called when they were here; and finally what Magna had recorded when they had a new family. Of course most had changed names, because many adoptive parents have a strong desire to erase the past—not least the memory of the biological parents—as efficiently as possible. Many years later, those adopted children could try to locate their roots by using the official records, but from time to time the papers were missing, or their biological source had disappeared. And in those cases, they would only be able to track them down using the details Magna had so carefully recorded in her binders, which she didn't dare hand over to Mother's Aid Society.

This treasure trove stood on the shelves in her office next to a chrome statue of Sir Winston Churchill, a distinction awarded to the orphanage in recognition of its effort during the Resistance. I locked the door and began my long-lasting and systematic search, guided by Magdalene's soft whisper. In the beginning she had spoken to me with the same lisp she'd had when alive, but for some reason that I didn't understand it had nearly vanished by the end of the first year after the funeral.

My search focused on seven stories, or, rather, six, since I knew my own.

I climbed onto a chair and lifted the big blue binders from the shelves. I put them on my lap and turned the pages patiently, the way that children who have learned patience are able to. For hours, I sat in Magna's elegant antique birch-tree sofa with the gray silk upholstery, studying my findings. When I found one of the children I was searching for (and who could be traced to the infant room, Christmas 1961), I wrote the name on a pad along with the words from the adjacent columns in the records. Later, Magdalene helped me interpret the information from her heavenly perch. We would whisper eagerly back and forth, but fall silent whenever we heard creaking in the old house. Magna moved about as though she knew I was up to something. But her sound and familiar scent of freesia and cheroot smoke always gave her away.

This first part of the hunt lasted over a year—and my tension grew to palpable nervousness. It was only because my foster mother's workload had ballooned during that time that she didn't discover what was going on. Whenever she took the bus to Mother's Aid Society in Copenhagen, I locked myself in her office and continued my investigation. Fortunately these were long days away for Magna. Mother's Aid Society in its undisputed wisdom determined the outcome of the many adoption cases that were placed on its table. On those visits Magna would sit at one end of the table and the almighty Mrs. Krantz at the other.

One time, my foster mother had mistaken the meeting date—Easter Monday—and had to leave Mother's Aid Society empty-handed. She'd insisted, of course, that the other nine members of the council had made the mistake (as far as she was concerned, they'd all noted the wrong date in their calendars). I only just managed to put the two binders back on the shelf, lock the door from the inside, and jump behind the heavy mahogany reading chair that was Magna's pride and had belonged to Captain Olbers (upholstered in light-blue buffalo skin brought from the Congo) before I heard her on the stairs.

The chair hid me completely. For close to three hours, I lay huddled up awkwardly and deathly silent while she worked at her desk. This was not a particularly difficult feat for a child who had spent many years lying still and staring into complete darkness, waiting for morning to arrive.

My investigation picked up speed during the fall of 1971—two years after Magdalene's funeral—and it grew more intense as time passed. After I'd exhausted the records, I moved on to Magna's letters, which were by the window in the tall hutch whose drawers opened and closed easily and soundlessly. After that I began studying her notes and listening in on her conversations. The door to her office was almost always open. Now and then I picked up relevant information, because she still used the children's nicknames whenever she contacted the families that had adopted them: Tønde, Butte, and Marilyn (after the actress), de Gaulle, Khrushchev, and Little Gagarin (after the Russian cosmonaut). There was even one called Prince Knud because he was so slow and such a terrible walker, just as the queen's Uncle Knud had supposedly been.

Some of the adoptive parents who'd told their children about the orphanage in Skodsborg regularly visited the home. Orla Berntsen was one of these children. For over a year I'd had a duplicate of his journal in a ring binder of my own, which I hid with the other notes in the tall cabinet, behind the lemon-tree carvings, in the secret compartment Magna never found.

* * *

Later, I sat in my old friend's wheelchair staring out at the sound toward the Swedish coast.

What's on your mind, Marie? she asked from up above, as patiently as when she'd been alive. Often she comforted me with long stories about the King of the People, who had always fascinated her and who she'd finally located on the Other Side.

"More than anything I want to know how they live," I said, staring into the mirror, wishing I could melt into her on the Other Side. I knew she'd understand; we hated our shared ugliness. I think the mirror sensed our joint strength and kept quiet for once.

Well, I understand that, my friend said.

"Maybe I could . . . ?"

Of course you can, Marie. But you'll have to be careful and keep a distance. Don't reveal who you are, because they don't remember Kongslund—and maybe their parents never told them about us.

"Yes, of course," I said impatiently. "I get it," I added in a weak attempt to convince her that I wouldn't do anything rash.

We talked every night, after Kongslund had settled, about my investigations and about our careful notes and our expectations for the discoveries that lay ahead of us—and I was finally ready.

Early one morning, I got up and unfastened the telescope from the brass mounting plate that held it to the wheelchair, put it into a gray shoulder bag, and took the bus to the Town Hall Square. From there I went to Emdrup Square and then Søborg Square, where I changed to line 168 that dropped me off at the corner of Gladsaxevej and Maglegaards Boulevard, and then followed the street signs to the red brownstones I was searching for.

Everything was as I had imagined from the few scraps of information I'd gleaned from Magna's secret journals. This became my favorite trip during the first summer of my new life, and I repeated it time and time again without telling anyone but Magdalene, who I knew would keep quiet regardless of how her new world was put together. She wouldn't even tell the King of the People (whom for some reason, I was sure she was courting).

Orla was the first one that I sought because he was the one I remembered the best when he visited Kongslund as a child with his mother. On a piece of paper in a ring binder containing medical notes, someone had written: *Psychologist dispatched to Søborg again, Orla Pil Berntsen. A grave case, urgent.*

To me, it seemed very dramatic and it stretched my curiosity to the limit.

From my hiding place in the wetlands, I spied through Magdalene's telescope, Orla crouching on a boulder. There he sat, dreaming and nervously sniffling at all the troubles that awaited him back at home—and in the distant future. Children sense these kinds of things. If anyone had ever predicted then he would ascend to the second-most important position at the Ministry of National Affairs, no one would have believed it.

At night I returned home and wrote down all the details, keeping long, painstaking journals the way my foster mother had always done.

While all the other children sat in their comfortable playrooms with their Meccano construction sets, I struggled to put together all the screws and joints of the life I had spied on. My increasing absence was never really noticed because in those years, after the legalization of abortion made it necessary to adopt children from ever more distant parts of the globe, Magna ruled her orphanage with an incredible energy. The way she saw it, I was fully repaired and able to take care of myself. And just to assure her of that, I sometimes told her I was going for a walk in Jægersborg Deer Park with a friend named Lise (who didn't exist except in some old children's song). Absurd as it was, she must have accepted it, because she never even asked me where this Lise lived.

During those months, I went off to meet the world I'd always known existed out there. And what I discovered was that I envied and feared the life I found with a force nobody had warned me about. Maybe, in her supernatural state, Magdalene couldn't see the danger. She had already once failed to see the demons that lived so deep in the core of my being.

Or maybe she simply understood that no warning would have stopped me.

7

ORLA

1961–1974

The first night after her death, Magdalene underscored the point that applies to every child, which I would never forget: If you find a friend, you've got a chance. If you find none, you will succumb. Nobody knew this better than she.

Orla's short and brutal childhood is, as I see it, the story of parents who thoughtlessly repeated the sins of their fathers and mothers, and this includes most parents.

In some children the fear grows unobserved, and the adults who ought to be closest discover nothing; perhaps they hear a sound behind a wall one night when everything is supposed to be quiet but think nothing of it—and therefore continue the destruction.

I always thought of him as Orla the Lonely because he fled through the row-house subdivision as though he had entire regiments of demons nipping at his heels, and nobody intervened. I know that some of the psychologists at Kongslund were scared of him outright, not least after the killing of the Fool in the wetlands.

* * *

Hidden behind a hawthorn early one spring, I observed Orla Berntsen. His middle name, Pil, derived from a father he'd never known and, strictly speaking, couldn't prove existed.

There he was, eleven years old, in the shade behind the garages in the Glee Court subdivision, with thick lips and a freckled nose smack in the middle of his pear-shaped face, all of it surrounded by the bristly, blond hair that he never really combed. A short, stocky boy who exaggerated his innate clumsiness to play the role of the clown to his mates and who always tried his hand at breakneck performances; always laughing a little too loudly and speaking a little too fast, running some twenty-five feet behind the other boys; always the last in the line when teams were picked for soccer games in the wetlands. There he stood at the conclusion of the game—unchosen, unwanted, laughing at himself—because what else could he do?

The other boys terrified him with stories of the wetlands' infamous child molester and ran hooting through the woods as they fled haunting spirits and demons, leaving him standing on the wrong side of the bridge—in the little grove to the east of the creek—with fantasies so menacing that his knees trembled and his freckled nose sniffled from sheer horror.

As if anyone in his wildest imagination would ever consider kidnapping little Orla Pil Berntsen, the illegitimate child of Gurli Berntsen, single mother and office mouse, barely tolerated in their petit bourgeois suburb.

It was a preposterous thought.

His mother was respectable, no doubt about that, but she'd become so too late, many thought, and Orla was proof of that. He was an illegitimate child at the tail end of an era when those who weren't part of an unbreakable family were considered alien, and the one held responsible for this sin (and who was therefore the target of all condemnation) was always the woman who raised the child on her own.

His childhood neighborhood consisted of two short streets and three low townhouses inhabited by office workers, civil servants, school teachers, and, all the way down by the garages, a retired tobacconist who owned two white poodles. One beautiful spring day, a tall, stooped pianist moved into No. 14 with his wife and two sons. He would fold his long body over the grand black piano and pour onto the keys all the melancholy of this Copenhagen suburb, concluding with a bass tone that reverberated in the walls long after he'd closed the instrument. One sunny Sunday, the piano tones drifted out the open patio door, over the hedges, and across the lawns from patio to patio where fathers, weeding their gardens, growled as they grudgingly tolerated these exercises. After all, the man did play on National Radio between reports from Vietnam and Suez and news of street riots in Copenhagen and Paris. His keystrokes were so powerful that they blew the evil away, leaving only a soft clatter from the silver spoons on the cake trays under the sunshades.

One day something strange happened, something that nobody was really able to explain. As the music gained strength, the pianist's two sons would always run back and forth in the yard as though whipped by an invisible baton, and on this particular afternoon they ran ever faster up and down the long, narrow patch of grass, like two crazy notes in an insane score, up and down and up and down, until the tempo had reached its climax and they managed the impossible: to fall at the same spot within seconds of each other and bite off the tips of their tongues with identical precision. Both were taken by ambulance to the emergency room at Bispebjerg Hospital where doctors performed two small, parallel miracles as they stitched the two tongue tips back on.

In this newly constructed suburban neighborhood where everybody sort of knew everybody yet knew nothing for sure, this bizarre coincidence made both children and adults wonder whether there might be a higher power up there—a shared destiny connecting people and controlling life's chain of events. For Orla Berntsen, who watched the ambulances arrive and depart, the episode signified something altogether different and much more mundane. In the end, the younger brother had fallen first, and as a single child, Orla understood that the older brother had known and accepted his fate ever since he'd first seen his brother in the crib. To fall and bite off his tongue a few seconds later was just a small part of his universal duty, an example of the unconditional love that Orla knew existed but had never experienced himself: the love of a brother, the loyalty of a friend, an unbreakable camaraderie, knowing that one is contained inside another regardless of what happens.

Without a doubt, I was the only one who heard his weeping as he walked home, alone, as always.

* * *

Very quickly I understood that Orla Berntsen's problems were of a completely different nature than two bitten-off tongues, and unlike those tongues they couldn't be reattached with some surgical thread and the sincere efforts of a good doctor. Sometimes he didn't leave the house for days, and no one knew why. Then he showed up again, a little more hunched than normal, paler, nervously sniffling, his clear brown eyes like glass and his mop of hair sticking out as though he'd just arisen from a gravel heap. There were rumors that his mother beat him, but no one could prove it (and, besides, it was their own business, people at Glee Court thought).

Every afternoon when Gurli Berntsen returned from the office, she sat down in a blue armchair by the west-facing window and read *Billed Bladet*, exploring the parallel universe where her dreams lived. From a distance, I tried to figure out what she was seeing and what she was longing for, but I never succeeded. And it has occurred to me since that her silence, as she was sitting there, was one of the main forces that drove Orla toward the wetlands and the creek where his life's worst disaster occurred.

So maybe she should have told him everything before it was too late.

About her pregnancy and her shame.

About the man who disappeared. About the smell of damp, unclean carpets and study rooms. About the view to the garden where she'd grown up, and the feeling on her skin of the red kimono that had belonged to her mother and her grandmother before that, and which had lain on her flat, shiny stomach when she'd committed her irrevocable sin.

About her father who sat in the wing chair, rubbing his strong thumbs on the armrest, in eternally circling movements, round and round and round, traveling across the ridges in the cloth where the blue plush had once been, as though this is all that remained of the grand and mighty life force that was ebbing away.

For this kind of retirement, reproach is like a gift; he didn't even have to look at his daughter, all he had to do was fix his gaze on the naked wall above her head and keep quiet as his fingers did the talking, speaking to her across generations through the threadbare cloth, letting her know that sin had arrived in the life of a reckless woman, the greatest sin of all: to give birth to a fatherless child.

During those years, no one could escape so egregious a sin. No one would forget it. Reproach would be present at every single moment and in every single thought for the rest of her life. No motherly or fatherly love was strong enough to erase it.

When Gurli Berntsen realized this truth, she swallowed a whole bottle of the strongest sleeping pills she could find and slept for three days before waking and throwing up for another three days. Two days later she slid down into the harbor basin by Svanemøllen Station, but she was discovered by a passerby and dragged out.

The hospital reported the incident to her parents in Jutland; her father reacted—as men of his type do in that situation—with anger. Naturally. But in the end, there are stronger forces in the world than male rage, as Magda and her girls had always demonstrated (if Kongslund symbolized anything, that was it), and on the third day after the second suicide attempt, Gurli's mother withdrew the family's entire savings and bought No. 12 in the newly built townhouse subdivision, with the long and narrow backyards and the sheltering hedges. Shortly thereafter, Orla was born.

The young woman gave birth to her son at Obstetric Ward B at Rigshospital, and she begged the young nurses to take her child away, away from her belly, away from her shame. But her mother, Orla's grandmother, had the brand new baby baptized in the hospital church, and in a prescient moment, gave him her husband's middle name so the little one came to carry his grandfather's name—a decision that demonstrated the insight of such women into issues of masculine self-esteem.

Reluctantly, the new grandfather entered the church and for a moment let his fingers rest on the hard armrest of the pew as he growled something that might have been interpreted as an "amen." Quite surprisingly, his hands were calm throughout the ceremony, as though filled with heavenly peace.

Little Orla had finally found a family.

The next day he lost it again—for a while at any rate—when he was driven by taxi to Kongslund. Here the strong governesses of Mother's Aid Society would take care of him until his mother recovered (much to her father's surprise, given all the support he felt she had gotten, she had become depressed) and could set up her new home. This account, which Orla later stitched together from his mother's rare confidences and his annual visits with Magna, was made of something altogether different than the stories of the adopted children; that much he understood, even at an age when you're supposed to be too young to understand. His mother had deliberately condemned him to the orphanage while she considered whether he was worth living for—and more than anything to protect herself.

Because of her indecisiveness, he had been at the infant room, in the dark, much too long and had himself become part of the endless span of time that filled Kongslund's children with such terror. Even the psychologists at the institution didn't understand it.

When he finally came home, Gurli showed him his room, put him to bed, and sat down in the blue wingback chair she'd inherited from her father who had died the year before. She would put her restless fingers on the armrest, and they would quiver every time she thought of the man who'd been her father, whom she'd buried with a feeling she was afraid to confide to anyone.

After a few nights, when she thought she could hear her son whimpering behind the wall, she gave him the photo of a smiling man throwing an orange beach ball into the air (she had cut it out of a magazine). The man stood in the sun laughing to the little boy on the beach, and the ball floated upward, almost infinitely, into the sky. She told her son that his father's name was Pil, and therefore it had become Orla's middle name.

Unfortunately, she told Orla, his father had gone abroad to find a place where the three of them could live together, and he hadn't yet returned.

Over the following years Orla read about men like him in his collection of illustrated classics: *The Deer Slayer, Ivanhoe,* and *Captain Grant*—who left behind their children as they struggled their way across glaciers and over mountain passes. And as time passed, he began to understand that happy endings were inevitable in such fairy tales only if you waited long enough. Granted, Fate had led his father away from him, but only for a while. One day he would return to Orla.

* * *

One thing made Orla stand out from everyone else on his street and in the neighborhood where he grew up: he had only ever lived with women. First, all the misses and governesses at the orphanage, then his own mother who never (as far as anyone knew) brought a man inside her home at Glee Court.

But even though Orla Berntsen measured up with most girls when it came to intuition and empathy, his feminine side was strangely lacking the character traits one might expect: tenderness, compassion, gentleness.

"There's something broken inside him," the psychologists at Kongslund would have said. With a demonstratively regretful shrug of the shoulders, they would have added another piece of paper to the unfortunate child's ever-thickening record. But they didn't, because he didn't tell anyone about the visions that tormented him during those early years.

For that reason, his first experience with the opposite sex was an unfortunate one—and it was the only time he reached out spontaneously to another human being, summoning all the confidence he could muster.

The boy raised by so many women met a girl raised by two men (both the aging, unskilled laborer Sørensen and his son worked at the big shipyard in the central city). For some reason she still wet her pants at age eight, and one day as they stood by themselves on the road staring at yet another ominous puddle at her feet, Orla pulled out a bag of licorice candies from the pocket of his anorak. He extended it to her, but she just stared at him with her inscrutable gaze, no hint of delight or thankfulness could be seen in her eyes. Orla, age eleven, stepped close to the girl and whispered, "I'll teach you a game that nobody else knows . . ." he promised, making his voice sharp and sly. "It'll make us sweethearts, or it'll *kill* us."

She looked at him, saying nothing.

"It goes like this," he said. "I line up eight candies, and if you haven't given me a kiss before I eat the last one—the *blue* one—then I die. Because that one's *poisonous*."

Orla assembled the colored candies on the curb, and they squatted down. He now sensed her gaze in a way he didn't understand; it wasn't a worried or mild look as he expected—it was rapt, hopeful. First he ate a yellow candy, then white, red, and orange, then another white, then a green and a brown, and then suddenly the only one left was the blue one. Her eyes were shining as if they were full of tears or she was overcome with fever. *How could she let him eat the blue one? She couldn't let him eat it when she knew he would die from it, could she? She'd have to follow his plan and give him the kiss that would save his life.* Instead, she cocked her head and looked at him with filmy eyes; the little tip of her tongue appeared in the space between her front teeth, nestled there, waiting.

That's how Orla Pil Berntsen discovered that he was merely a tiny flake in an enormous universe; that he was just a little boy with freckles, a pig nose, and a dirty hand frozen halfway to his mouth, who suddenly faced his own death, forced to it by his life's first and only love.

Right then she said the words that no boy or man would ever forget: "Can't I kiss you *and* watch you eat the blue one?" (I think this question was the first inkling of the impending women's liberation movement, but Orla Berntsen was too young to understand its significance.)

The shock didn't hit him in earnest until that night, when he lay in his dark bedroom.

What should he have said?

This was the spring that Fate knocked down the last remaining bulwarks Orla the Lonely had so painstakingly constructed around himself— with a single incident that, more than anything, seemed coincidental.

When the evening bells sounded in Søborg Church, the front door opened, and Orla stepped out with a tin bucket in his hand, a searching and cautious glare in his eyes. The bucket was a light-yellow color, dented, maybe fifteen inches tall. As usual, Orla trudged down to the boarding house at Maglegårds Boulevard, walked to the back of the house where the kitchen was, and said hello to the cook, who jovially tousled his coarse hair and filled his bucket. Then he walked back home under the streetlights until his curiosity got the best of him; he lifted the lid and stuck a finger into the thick gravy filled with Cumberland sausages, rissole, meatballs, and steamed potatoes—all of it glinting white in the brown sauce. He stood for a bit in the shade of a tree licking the gravy off his fingers. Lost in his thoughts—which I would understand only much later—the food grew cold.

Catastrophes sometimes have peculiar, innocent entry points. If he understood the game of which he was part, he would have regretted the evening he worked up the courage to ask Erik, the most popular boy on Glee Court, to join him as he carried the yellow bucket to the boarding house.

On the way home, Orla bent over and raised the lid and stuck a finger into the steaming brown liquid so that his friend could see for himself the delights that awaited Orla and his mother.

"Yuck," said Erik. "Gross meatballs." He was already full, and in his home, meatballs weren't served in a yellow bucket but in a cozy kitchen, with a clatter of pots and pans, his mother humming as she stirred; the meatballs were ladled from a beautiful glass serving dish onto his plate, and his mother would hold onto the dish with thick, sky-blue gloves she'd crocheted herself.

"Yuck," he repeated, as Orla licked the gravy off his index finger. "Look, you've got a *wart* on your finger!"

The focus shifted abruptly and brutally, and Fate awoke with a start. It was true. There really was a big gray-brown growth right below the knuckle on his right index finger, and the gravy made it shine.

He reacted swiftly, and the reaction proved disastrous. "Did you know that if you pop a wart you can make a wish for anything in the world?"

Erik looked at him skeptically but was so fascinated by the brown growth on the dirty finger that he stood motionless. Then Orla squeezed the wart, rubbing it hard between his index finger and thumb and let this recklessness take control of the most decisive moment of his childhood; up to this point, he could have stopped, he could have admitted that he had no secret, had never had one, and maybe then everything would have been different. Maybe his life would have been like his mother's—from youth to old age—a quiet commute from the house to an anonymous office, cloaked in a gray shadow, slipping in and out of an anonymous front door. But it was too late.

His new friend leaned close, having completely forgotten his earlier skepticism, and Orla sensed his disgust mutate into fascination. He felt his warmth and his breath, heard air pushing through his nose and sucking in through concentrated lips, and he felt his friend's body close to his; it was the most wonderful moment he'd ever experienced: they were buddies; everything was suddenly so oddly intimate as if Erik was his brother. He squeezed with all his might, squeezed harder than he'd ever squeezed anything or anyone before, and . . .

Then the wart burst, and Erik let out a loud, desperate shriek.

A long squirt from the pierced growth struck him right in one eye, and a foul yellow fluid stained his left cheek. He danced around on the sidewalk as if in a convulsion of insanity, holding both hands to his face, shielding his eyes, screaming.

"Now we get to make a wish!" Orla shouted to drown him out. But his friend made no wish, none at all, just sobbed.

"I want a big red bus so we can all go to Bellevue for a swim!" Orla shouted. "A London double-decker!"

But Erik had started running, at full speed, toward home. Orla ran after him, the food in the yellow bucket sloshing so much the lid came off. He didn't notice.

"I want a Bluebird car so we can go five hundred miles an hour ... and you can have it!" he shouted. This was his second wish, and it was the best thing he could come up with.

"You're ... a freaking idiot ... stupid idiot!" Erik shouted in between loud, gasping sobs. "I'll grow warts in my eyes ... I'll go blind!"

Orla saw it in his mind's eye: how the contagious fluid penetrated Erik's skin, how a brownish, shapeless mass grew out of his beautiful blue eye and covered half of his face—a boy who would always have to hide behind a mask or wear a hood over his head. He felt the earth and the flagstones slide from under his feet, nausea bubbling from his trembling gut, and then Erik disappeared around the corner by the garages. A moment later, Orla heard the front door slam, and the wailing subsided. His forlorn friend had made it home.

Only then did he discover that gravy, meatballs, and steamed potatoes had splashed out of the bucket while he was running. There was no food left, and his mother would go to bed hungry. In a few minutes, his little misstep had become a complete disaster. He left the bucket on the flagstone by the front door and ran, as fast as he could, to the wetlands. He fled into the darkness he had always known. This was how most children from Kongslund reacted when they felt trapped. I knew it better than anyone.

Here he crouched behind a thorny bush on the opposite side of the creek, near the bridge; he put his shaking, disfigured finger—which now bled and stung—into his mouth, closed his eyes, and felt fear grow in his belly. It rose up and dribbled down his chin like a warm, seeping fluid. It wasn't like blood from an Allied commando at the Siege of Tobruk (that kind of blood would have portended an honorable death). But blood mixed with boarding-house gravy and gall and acidic yellow fear—because he knew what was about to happen: from now on, the other boys—Palle, Bo, Henrik, and Jens—would torment him more than ever.

They would *never* stop, they would chase him wherever he went; they would never talk to him again.

The rain began around midnight, as his mother was going from door to door on Glee Court, the yellow bucket in her hand, asking for her son with a slightly tremulous voice; and in so doing, losing the last shred of respect she'd garnered from the other boys' parents. (*What kind of home is it when a mother can't control her child?*)

Resigned, the fathers got up—anything else would be too insensitive, after all—found their flashlights, and walked in a line toward the creek.

Just before the men burst through the bushes, Orla heard a voice in the darkness, no louder than the rustling of the wind in the leaves, a whisper that repeated itself again and again as if it were inside his head: *I wish I were a star.* Orla thought it was a sentence from a world that had existed long before the flashlight beam shined on him ("Here he is, the little idiot!"), long before his terrible decision to squeeze his wart into the face of the boy who had been his friend for a short, almost unreal instant.

With closed eyes, he stood, the hand with the wart jammed into his mouth as he concentrated deeply on his third and final wish. The men with their flashlights never knew what he was thinking about in that moment—but I think I know what he wished for.

From that day on, rage was the only fixed point in Orla's life. He lay awake in the dark after his mother had gone to bed, thinking about the enemy, the only name he had for his troubles. The enemy was faceless and merciless, and during his twelfth year, Orla developed a taste for violence that followed him many years into the future.

Something drew him time and time again to the garages where his neighborhood ended, and which were built into a hill covered by a giant hawthorn hedge. On the other side of that hedge, yellow tenements rose six stories into the blue sky. This is where the families who couldn't afford their own homes (even a row house) lived. Over the years, the hedge had grown so tall and so wild that you couldn't look over it any longer. At least once a week, the children from the low red houses showered the other side with rocks in an attempt to hit their invisible foes from the tenements, and during those months, no one threw more rocks, or threw them harder, than Orla. It was as though a mighty and fearless rage had taken hold of his squat body, making him jump higher than anyone else as he hurled rocks toward the sounds and voices behind the hedge. When a throw was rewarded with cries and the pounding of running feet, he laughed in a way that almost frightened his allies more than his adversaries; they were on his side of the hedge, after all.

Now, a year or so before puberty set in, there might have been a way to save someone as peculiar as Orla, or so the psychologists at Kongslund would've no doubt claimed.

They would defend the theory, based on careful research, that even the most serious damages could be contained, perhaps even alleviated and concealed.

"Orla was a healthy boy," they would have said. "He was teased some, to be sure, but he never failed to get back up. He always bounced back!" And they would light their pipes and nod to one another encouragingly over the shining frames of their glasses.

Of course that was all complete nonsense.

* * *

One week after the episode with the wart, Orla took the final step on the road that ended his childhood so abruptly: he hurled a ball high up over the garage roof and the hedge.

Spontaneously, he leaped up, grabbed hold of the garage gutter, and put his hand into the excrement left by a stray dog.

I didn't need Magdalene's telescope to see the terror in his eyes. Sitting behind the hedge, I witnessed his life's support columns tumble down; small, seemingly insignificant events can be the most destructive.

For the rest of the day and the rest of his short childhood on Glee Court, this new nickname would become the bane of his existence: *Orla Turd-Hand Orla Turd-Hand Orla Turd-Hand.* The boy I had somehow come to understand ran home as fast as his sturdy legs could carry him and put both his hands under scalding water in the bathroom sink. A moment later he threw up, gasping and sobbing, as his tears mixed with the brown water, as if his insides had overflowed and would never again be able to shut off the stream of brackish water. He ran to the wetlands—where else?—but this time nobody came to fetch him. For a moment he thought he heard his mother's plaintive call, but it was merely the wind in the trees.

The next day he heaved a very large rock over the hedge, toward the boys from the yellow tenements—and this time he didn't just hear screaming, but police and ambulance sirens—and the loud voices on the other side of the hedge wheezed and shouted at the same time. Rumor had it that a boy ended up in the emergency room with a terrible gash in his forehead. "He might die," an adversary on the other side of the hedge yelled, but for some reason there was never any investigation. The two adversaries, whose worlds were separated by the hedge, didn't even know each other's names.

A few days later, the lady from No. 16 knocked on her kitchen window and waved at Orla, who was sitting on the curb staring into a puddle.

She invited him in and served him bread with blood-red marmalade and hot cocoa. At the end of the kitchen table sat her husband, a man known as Mr. Malle. Every day he walked home in a black police uniform carrying a brown briefcase. Orla thought he might bring up the episode with the boy from the yellow tenements, but Mr. Malle merely smiled at him; and in the subsequent months, Orla was the only one on the street to whom the big man said hello.

Maybe his friendship with the police officer made him reckless, because he was unprepared for what happened when he wandered between Lauggaard's Boulevard and Gladsaxe Road—on the outskirts of the yellow tenements—scanning for his enemies. Carl Malle stood in a doorway with his hand on a thin boy's shoulder. The boy's head was wrapped in a thick bright-white bandage (he looked like Lawrence of Arabia, which Orla had seen at the Søborg Theater). The policeman wasn't in uniform, but he'd put one of his black berets on the wounded boy's head, and there it sat, nesting proudly on the white gauze.

Orla would have normally called out to his friend, but not a single word passed his lips.

Instead he turned on his heels and ran to the wetlands, where he stayed until nightfall. Something inside him had ruptured, and he didn't understand what it was. In his thirteenth year, Orla spent most of his time in the wetlands. He wandered about on the big lawns between Grønnemose Boulevard, Horse Hill, and Hareskovvejen, up and down the creek, far into the woods.

Inside a little clearing was a granite boulder that only the strongest boys could climb. One night, sitting there with his eyes tightly shut so they wouldn't run over with brackish water, he thought of his father who had never returned. His mother had once told him a story (and here all the psychologists at Kongslund ought to lean close and take careful notes) about a man who had been transformed into a boulder by the cruel gaze of a giant. And I watched him stroke the boulder exactly as though it were a long lost beloved. I watched him put frogs and insects on it—even butterflies whose wings he'd clipped—piercing their bodies with splinters of glass he'd found on the path; he did it so absent-mindedly, as if his thoughts were somewhere else. At day's end, he would cleanse his sacrificial site of butterfly wings, spider legs, frog's eyes, and once again tenderly stroke the boulder with a soft, dirty hand. It was a peculiar sight, and I would go home to Magdalene and cry until the visions faded.

This was how Orla Pil Berntsen spent the last few months of his childhood, in an ever more desperate loneliness that no one bothered to understand. Between a foggy fantasy of his petrified, vanished father and the all-too-real visage of Gurli sitting in the high-back blue chair looking at the wall above his head as her fingers slowly trembled and shook and glided across the armrest in fine circles.

It all ended early one evening as the sun was setting over the high-rises at Bellahøj, casting a long shadow over the wetlands. He heard the pop of an air gun down by the creek and warily crept closer.

Two boys stood in a clearing watching a wounded sparrow spin, like a fly on a needle, on the forest floor. Leaves swirled about. The boys howled at the trees in laughter.

This is how Orla met real evil: Karsten, thickset, square, with a crew cut; and Poul with his blue, blue eyes that were mean as all hell. They introduced him to Benny, their odd friend: a six-foot-eight dullard who wandered about restlessly in the wetlands. For the most part, Benny hid in the woods on the slopes along the river, where his thick voice ricocheted between tree trunks (the people in the neighborhood had grown used to him—they called him the Fool—and Orla had often seen him, just a shadow in the evening dusk).

Benny had one amazing talent. With a few dangerous twists and jerks of his head—and with his index finger and thumb bent like claws—he could pull his left eye out of its socket, letting it hang halfway down his cheek, dangling off sinews and nerve threads, and then he would swiftly put it back. It was a remarkable trick that awed even hardened bullies like Karsten and Poul. When they asked if he could see with his eye hanging on his cheek, he nodded cheerfully and shouted, "Yeah! Yeah!" But Poul didn't believe him. To him, lying was the worst thing anyone could do (he knew everything about lying from his besotted dad at home on

Søborg's Main Street). Orla shuddered at the sight of those small light-blue eyes—like fiery steel balls—observing the big man; at times they glowed with such malice that Orla felt feverish, and one night, when they were sitting as usual staring at Benny, something happened that no one in the neighborhood would ever forget.

Karsten had gone off to pee on a tree, and Poul was poking a stick in the ground—or so it seemed—and the Fool was between them, humming merrily, proud of his trick and glad to have company, his eye hanging on his cheek, when a blackbird suddenly shot out of darkness and swooped down on his little white eyeball bundled in blood-red nerve threads. Immediately he understood what was happening and the abyss that had opened. "Noooooooooooo," he screamed, desperately clutching at his tormentor's muscular lower arm. But it was too late.

With a snap, the strong boy's hand tore Benny's hated eye from his head and tossed it high into the air; it flew over the creek in a low arc and landed with a little plop in the water, barely audible unless you listened for it. And there it sunk.

Orla, Poul, and Karsten bolted through the wetlands, shoulder to shoulder, cackling like the demons they had finally become. Behind them, Orla could hear the distressed giant's screams—which were drowned out only by Poul's snickering whenever they stopped to catch their breath—and it sounded as though he was splashing about in the creek. Then it was quiet. The three boys looked at one another and then circled back to the site, reluctantly leaving the shadows of the tall trees and creeping closer to the creek bank. From there they saw the Fool's one-eyed face in the water, floating within a cluster of lily pads. The eye socket resembled a black hole. "He's dead, you moron!" Karsten whispered. Poul and Orla glanced at each other without responding.

One of the giant's arms lay motionless, like a broken stick. It was stretched out as if he'd tried to hold on to life. They stood in silence for a few minutes, staring at the Fool peacefully floating in the water.

"Stay here . . . I'm gonna go get something," Orla whispered.

Five minutes later he returned with a little bundle in his hand. "This is Erik's hat. He always hangs it on the handrail of the staircase."

The others stepped closer, and Orla saw their eyes shining in the light from the lamppost on the other side of the creek. They all hated Erik Goody Two-Shoes.

"Look, he put his name in it."

Many years later, Orla would remember only this one image from the creek: the giant in the water and his two friends, standing like gun-fighters in a Western playing at the Søborg Theater. But the enemy was already dead. In dreams he saw Benny sitting there, smiling and goofing around with his dangling eye, still alive; he saw the furious shadow rush forward and downward toward its prey, and he glimpsed the hatred behind the movement leading to the catastrophe—but he can't see the face behind the hand; he feels nothing at all.

They left the hat in the grass, right where the dead giant's sleeve had caught a tree root that jutted from the ground. Later that night they drank Wiibroe beer on the Søborg Square and broke into Orla's school, stealing a slide projector and an Eltra tape recorder, and listened to Jim Morrison sing "Light My Fire" until dawn.

Two days later the police picked up Erik. For hours he sat with his dirty blue-knitted cap on the policeman's desk and cried. In a way his fate was worse than Orla's, because although his parents swore that he was at home in bed by 10:00 p.m., a shadow of doubt would always cling to him; he couldn't explain how his hat had ended up beside the dead man. Nor could the police explain what had happened to Benny. Perhaps he'd simply drowned (and a fish or toad had nipped out his eye); certainly, the officers found it hard to believe that the trembling, sniveling pup before them could have overpowered and murdered the Fool, then brutally removed his eye and set it on a lily pad to stare up at the sky (which is how they found it). In the end, they let the boy go.

In his bed in the darkness beneath the photo of the man and the boy with the orange beach ball, Orla felt the heat from Erik's body like a physical touch and almost sensed his breath against his cheeks and forehead. He skipped school and fled into the wetlands; he sat on the granite boulder and rocked back and forth; he went to the creek and got on his knees and stared at his reflection in the water, like the pixie in the old song . . . and the reflection asked him: *How is it possible that you are so ugly?* He didn't look like anyone he knew: his nose, his hair, his eyes that always watered whenever he leaned forward. He knew nothing about himself. In the picture, his father smiled at the beautiful boy with the sea in the background.

Was his mother's story about the Rigshospital and Kongslund even true?

"What are you thinking about?"

Orla flinched.

"A thirteen-year-old boy studying himself in the creek, daydreaming. It's got to be about something good. A girl is it?" Carl Malle winked, teasingly. He wasn't in uniform. He'd never shown up in the wetlands before.

"Nah . . . I'm just thinking . . . not really about anything." *Had Malle been sent to fetch him?*

"I'm just checking up on you. You look like someone I once knew. It takes a lot to knock you down." There was a peculiar sense of pride in the policeman's words.

Orla slipped off the boulder. "I've gotta go pick up our food."

"No, you don't. Your mother ate with us tonight—and we talked about your future."

Never before had his mother eaten at anyone's house; she'd never eaten anything but the contents of the yellow bucket. Orla was shocked.

"Don't worry. We have a solution."

Orla stood on the soft grass, swaying a bit. *A solution.* Were they going to send him to prison?

"You need to get away from this neighborhood," the policeman said. "Away from these boys. We found you a boarding school on Sjællands Odde."

A few days later, Carl Malle had sorted out the paperwork, and his mother took him to Copenhagen Central Station in silence. She had loved her son with the nagging anxiety that all mothers possessed, but she'd kept that affection hidden behind tightly sealed lips.

"I'll see you," she said.

Orla was silent.

He left his home sure that he was all alone in the world. He disappeared, as it were, from his childhood without a sound, and without anyone really taking notice: the son of Gurli Berntsen, insignificant office worker, tolerated but barely.

A murderer . . . he didn't even know it himself. In the following months a pipe-smoking man from Kongslund visited him and spoke about Orla's childhood in Glee Court (and once about the Fool in the wetlands, and the brutal incident that he'd otherwise put behind him), but the small man didn't ask any questions that Orla felt compelled to answer.

* * *

Where does it come from, this immense rage that fills some people? And why does it afflict some children like a pile driver from Hell, while others seem to go free?

I followed Orla's childhood from my hiding place behind the hawthorn, and studied the slow dissolution that no one tried to stop. In this way a deformity grows in the soul as inexorably as a skull develops its curvature or a nose its angle—without anyone reacting. Orla's humiliation was sent by neither God nor the Devil, but had been passed on to him from the human being who should have protected him, as Magdalene would have said with a lisp: his own mother.

It was this rage deep inside the half-grown Orla that frightened adults, an anger that threatened to explode long before he could build a career and advance to a position where he could overcome the hardships of everyday life.

Magdalene didn't think there was any real difference between the boy who went to Sjællands Odde and the man who, four decades later, processed case after case in the Ministry of National Affairs with a cool, impervious efficiency.

Late one afternoon, Carl Malle visited him at the boarding school. "Do you miss your old neighborhood?" he asked.

Orla didn't respond. The only thing he really missed was the photo on the wall, the one with the man and the boy and the orange beach ball.

Carl Malle would never understand.

"Why did you give the boy from the yellow tenements your policeman's cap?" Orla said.

"The boy from the yellow tenements?"

"The one I hit with the brick. The one with the white bandage. I saw you give him your cap."

"I don't know anyone from the yellow tenements," Malle lied.

Orla recognized the lie, and he lowered his gaze to hide his rage.

The day Orla returned to Glee Court—three years later—Magdalene visited me. She sat rocking back and forth in her flimsy chair, almost like in the old days, and lisping as thickly as she did back then.

Marie, she said, between a series of snorts and spastic movements. *Mark my words. The sins of the fathers and mothers are rarely atoned by children like Orla. One day he'll be sitting in the same chair his mother sat in, and his fingers will slide into the same groove as his mother's and grandfather's and their parents' before them, and because he doesn't understand it, he himself will become part of the Darkness—in the end, he will even become the Darkness itself.*

Sometimes, Magdalene's heavenly predictions were uttered like a curse.

Then she jerked sideways over the left armrest until her wheelchair nearly tipped over, snorted one last time, and disappeared.

8

FEAR

May 8, 2008

My foster mother knocks on the door and waits for me to invite her in. Though I don't respond to her knocking, she nonetheless steps into the room she has given me and sits on my bed. I am seated at my desk with a view of the sound and Hven.

"You're reading those journals," she says, and I can sense the fear in this remark, which she has made time and time again since Magdalene's death. She is convinced that the journals I have inherited from my invalid friend reveal secrets that no child can bear, and she has always protected her herd from anything threatening, anything from the outside.

Today, now that she has long since retired, Kongslund has become the center of a case that may reveal an embarrassing and secretive past, which, according to the newspapers and to the gossip no one can control, involves the Ministry of National Affairs.

* * *

Bog Man had never had such a haggard expression as the day Carl Malle arrived at the ministry. The Kongslund Affair had drained from his skin what little color he possessed.

The department head looked as though he had stared directly into the face of death—even though he had no concrete knowledge of the case and hadn't been present during the intense phone conversations between Malle and the Almighty Enevold.

"Our visitor is *not* a retired police officer but a former assistant chief of police," the irate minister clarified. The atmosphere in the ministry was tense, the humidity high.

The former assistant chief of police spent his retirement in the same place he'd spent his youth—and most of his life: in the quiet brownstone neighborhood of Søborg. From here he'd assembled a handful of his former colleagues and formed a private security firm that offered distinctive expertise to large businesses. His exclusive firm wasn't listed in the yellow pages; only those who knew someone worth knowing would be able to contact them.

Ole Almind-Enevold had known Carl Malle since the Second World War.

The minister had asked his chief of staff to be present for the meeting.

"You're familiar with Carl Malle and everything he represents?" he asked, repeating almost verbatim his message from the crisis meeting three days earlier. "We need him now. We cannot tolerate anonymous threats to this ministry. Even if we can't figure out what the letter writer wants, we have to help Carl Malle as much as we can."

"But that letter has no substance whatsoever," Orla Berntsen balked.

The minister gave his protégé a hard stare. "Regardless of what you think, you have to understand one thing: at any moment, the Captain might become gravely ill. So ill that we . . . that I will have to assume leadership of the country, with all of the complications that entails." It was a name Almind-Enevold only used in private: *the Captain.* "We can't have such a matter hanging over us. It's practically been insinuated that people in the party live a double life. And besides, Kongslund is about to celebrate a very important anniversary in a few days, and under no circumstances do I want the festivities tainted by such a . . . such a madman."

Under normal conditions, Orla would have repeated his conviction that there was nothing to worry about; he knew his words carried weight with the older man who had become his protector. But there was something in the minister's tone of voice that caused him to simply fold his hands and listen. The minister was obviously more nervous than usual.

"What I need right now is a distraction . . ." the minister said, breaking the silence that had filled the air between them.

"A distraction?" Orla repeated, although he knew perfectly well what the minister meant.

"We need something to draw attention away from all of this. In case Knud Taasing's gossipy tabloid intends to pursue the matter. This is Malle's suggestion."

"How about the Tamil boy?" The proposition fell from Orla Berntsen's lips before he'd even considered it. It was logical. "Several newspapers have already contacted us about it," he said. "Maybe we could . . ." He paused.

"Deport him to divert their attention?" The minister furrowed his brow for a moment, then lit up. "Yes. Why the hell not . . . ? That might very well do the trick. The media love maudlin stories . . . assaults . . . abuse . . . *power grabs.*"

There was a knock on the door and the secretary showed in the other two top officials. The Witch Doctor took a seat next to Orla, while Bog Man stood by the window, his eyes drooping further down his cheeks than normal. The department head was near retirement, and it was clear he feared being blindsided in the eleventh hour.

The minister pressed a button on his intercom and raised his voice: "Has Carl arrived? Well, send him in then!"

He met the security advisor halfway between the desk and the door, embracing him and then slapping his back. "How's it going?"

The tall man shrugged his shoulders, as though this was an unnecessary question. "And you?" Malle replied. "Your wife, Lykke?"

"No problems . . . except for the one you're here to solve."

The security advisor greeted the three other officials gravely, holding Orla's hand in a firm grip. His eyes were dark and brown and, combined with the deep creases near his mouth and the curly graying hair, gave his face a Mediterranean look, an impression underscored by his casual demeanor.

"It's been a long time," Malle said to Orla. He didn't ask about his health, and certainly not about his wife and daughters, which made it clear that he was up-to-date on the details of Orla's capsized private life. "I understand you're the happy recipient of"—the security advisor paused for a moment as he sat on the sofa across from the chief of staff— "a mysterious package sent by some insane individual."

"We need to find that man," the minister declared from behind his desk.

"Or woman," Malle replied. "I'd like to speak to Orla privately after we're done here."

"Yes, of course," Almind-Enevold replied.

Malle leaned in. "But first, tell me everything. Has anyone in the ministry seen any suspicious persons in the hallways? In the courtyard or the stairs? Has anyone seen anything strange here at all these last few months? This has been planned for a *very* long time—there is no doubt about that."

Bog Man stared at Malle with evident alarm.

"We're looking into it," Enevold said.

"I need to know everything. Without exception. Anything out of the ordinary. I want to see every meeting and guest list since the New Year. The person we're chasing may be now or has been inside the ministry in order to glean a general understanding of things ahead of time, or maybe out of simple curiosity."

"Of course, Carl," the minister replied.

"And these two gentlemen?" Malle fastened an inquiring gaze on the beleaguered Bog Man and the Witch Doctor with the little goatee that made him look like a painter from the 1960s. Malle's internal radar had already determined that these two were of no use, possibly even detrimental to the case.

"They're here for the sake of *coordination*," the minister said, almost apologetically. "If you need any assistance."

"I've got my own men, Ole. I don't want my hands tied. You know that. And no publicity."

The minister nodded at the two men. The Witch Doctor stood, bowing slightly, and with a characteristic swoosh of his expensive clothing, left the room. Bog Man hesitated momentarily, but then he too made his exit. When he shut the door behind him, the three men left in the room didn't even hear the click.

* * *

Knud Taasing set two shiny folders before his friend. "We're on the right track. Our orphanage has been a favorite destination for a *very* long time. I examined 1961 issues first, of course."

He studied Nils Jensen over the rim of his thin reading glasses and lit another menthol cigarette. "I've got pictures from the orphanage's twenty-fifth anniversary celebration, and it appears as though something peculiar happened that day."

Taasing braced one of his slender legs against a big brown cardboard box and began to stretch. The anonymous letter lay on the floor beside the box where he must have tossed it.

Nils, who had sat in a vacant chair near the window, noticed how the box didn't budge. It probably contained reports and exposés from Taasing's glory days, back when he consistently produced the kind of articles that reverberated across the nation—like the story of the Palestinian man who'd been sentenced for rape, causing Ole Almind-Enevold, then the minister of justice, to issue a blanket condemnation of all foreigners. After the scandal and the man's shooting of the two boys at a rest area, the presumptive minister of national affairs relentlessly used the story as fuel for his personal sainthood campaign during the 2001 elections.

After that, Knud had lowered his head and accepted defeat, broken by the knowledge that his persistent articles had helped acquit the man. He left his wife, rented a small apartment in Christianshavn, and spent five discouraging years struggling as a freelancer before being offered the job at *Independent Weekend*—in spite of protests from the Ministry of National Affairs. Every morning he bicycled to the newspaper building on the harbor front, stopped to shop at the co-op on the way home, and passed his weekends in front of the television. He never discussed his feelings about the lunatic who'd lied to him so phenomenally, or about the two boys the Palestinian had murdered. As far as Nils knew, he'd never visited their graves or tried to contact their parents, and perhaps there was nothing to say anyway.

"I've been through every single issue of *Billed Bladet, Home,* and *Family Magazine* since 1961, and in the May 19, 1961 edition of *Billed Bladet,* I found this article." Knud handed three large photocopies to the photographer. "It's about the Kongslund foundling Inger Marie Ladegaard."

"Foundling Discovered at Doorstep on Orphanage's Anniversary," the somewhat clumsy headline read above a photo of a young woman with a white nursing cap atop blond curls.

"Yes, she exists, but we already knew that. And it's hardly a scandal."

The journalist ignored Nils's typically sullen reply. "I've been digging deeper into the name Bjergstrand," he continued. "But I can't find anyone with that name on the Internet, nor in any telephone books from 1990 through 2007. So we'll have to go back further, and to do that we'll need to check different records and browse through old telephone books. We'll have to go back to 1961, perhaps even further."

The photographer didn't respond.

"Unfortunately, the clippings on the envelope don't match those in our *Billed Bladet* from 1961, as I'd hoped they would. For now, what's important is that the letters are multicolored, because that eliminates most magazines of the time. For example, *Danish Family Magazine* used almost exclusively black type in their headlines. *Ladies Magazine*, oddly enough, was much more progressive in terms of color in both articles and headlines. Same goes *for Billed Bladet*. But I still need to check *Home*, *Family Magazine*, *Out and About*, and several others."

Knud stood. He navigated a path to the window between the piles of paper. "But we have a third lead. A simple question: What was it about that letter that frightened the ministry so badly?" He returned to his desk and slammed his palm on the headline from that day's lead story in *Independent Weekend*: "The Kongslund Affair: What Is the Orphanage Hiding?"

A photo of the old matron, Ms. Ladegaard, was featured below these provocative words. She wore a dark-blue dress with an amethyst brooch and smiled into the camera, standing next to a little girl with blond curls.

Denmark's Mother, the caption read.

On the front page of the second section, the newspaper had replaced Ms. Ladegaard with a younger woman in green, Susanne Ingemann, standing on the stairwell before the painting of the lady in the idyllic forest glade alongside the headline: "A Secret Past?"

Susanne Ingemann will be furious, Nils thought.

"It's begun," Knud said, glancing at the paper. "In fact, I've already gotten some interesting calls." He awoke his monitor by tapping the mouse. "One of them was from that big, new TV station whose director I know, or *used* to know in days gone by."

He stared at an e-mail Nils couldn't see.

"Peter Trøst is a doer, brutally so, you might say. At any rate, you know how famous he has become in our little TV nation. If anyone can shed light on the matter, it's him. And that's fine with me—as long as we solve the mystery first."

The photographer remained silent.

"We need to go to that anniversary event. In the meantime I'm going to try and track down people from back then. First and foremost the governess, Agnes Olsen." Knud tapped the image of the capped young woman who'd discovered the foundling on the stairs. "It probably won't be easy with such a common name. It's as though everyone had an ordinary name back then."

* * *

Orla Berntsen imagined how the two men's faces would abruptly change the second he closed the door.

He had left the minister's office as soon as Almind-Enevold had signaled that he'd like to speak to his old friend and ally in private.

Nevertheless, he thought he could hear their voices through the thick ministry walls, even through the anteroom where the Fly desperately tried to follow him.

What the hell is going on, Carl?

Damned if I know.

Well, you're going to have to put a bloody lid on it!

That's how it would be in there, he was certain. Orla sat down to wait for Malle. It was possible his investigation was nothing more than a precautionary measure, but the minister was remarkably nervous, and Malle's grave warnings suggested that he felt the same.

What did they know? What did they fear?

Orla glanced at the door. A narrow beam of light filtered in, forming a pattern on the floor like a bent sword; it reminded him of the place he'd grown up: the row house near the wetlands. He always thought of doors as highly reassuring, whether tall or short, narrow or wide—and preferably as many as possible. They represented the circulation of air and light, and, above all else, escape routes. Of course the letter had been addressed correctly, and both the security advisor and the minister knew as much, but he couldn't work out what the connection was.

Why was all of this so important to them?

Orla stared at his white forearms. His pulse was normal, his hands calm. He cast a sidelong glance at the door separating him from the Fly's domain. It was a secret that very few knew about. The chief of staff's office—like those of the minister and the department head—had more than one exit, just in case. Officially, there was the one that led to the grand room they called the Palace, but partially concealed behind a floor-to-ceiling curtain was another narrower door that went mostly unnoticed. If you opened it, you'd find a tight staircase winding three floors down to a dilapidated stone floor—and there, deep under the parliament building, a low corridor connected the ministry directly to a network of hallways. Using hushed voices, officials called these hallways *the catacombs*. Only the janitorial staff, as far as anyone knew, had the right to enter them; this group, which consisted mainly of Tamil, Iraqis, Afghans, and Sudanese, had slipped through the needle's eye of the Danish asylum system and been rewarded with permanent, minimum-wage jobs. Their locker rooms and break rooms were located in these hallways. The ministry, despite accusations of racism and cynicism by its foes, invited the very luckiest ones in. Of course, the catacombs might seem rather cold at night, especially to people from the southern hemisphere.

"You look like the lost boy from the wetlands." Malle had entered Orla's office without making a sound.

Startled, Orla's thoughts of escape vanished.

The security advisor didn't seem to notice. He came straight to the point: "Be honest now. Do you have any idea why that anonymous letter was sent directly to you?"

"No," he replied, wondering why Malle thought he wouldn't be honest.

"Or why the sender went to the trouble of sending a copy to the ministry's arch enemy? That was quite clever."

Orla gave the man no answer.

"Back then you were really fucked. The other boys had you by the balls, but we got you shipped off to boarding school and everything got better. We helped you, didn't we?"

"Yes," Orla said. He felt the words diminishing him, demoting him to a schoolboy again, admiring a curly-haired police officer who invited him to sit in his office, to wear his police cap, and to build miniature London buses out of prefabricated wood.

"Of course Ole is nervous. What the hell is all this? He's about to take over the most important job in the nation. The highest office."

Orla said nothing.

"What worries me are the *little* details. They suggest it's a very cunning individual, with precise knowledge. A purposefulness you don't find in fools. *That's* what worries me."

Orla realized he might be under suspicion himself. The former assistant chief of police was known for his own brand of cunning.

"The most damnable thing about all of this is that the TV station has the letter now, too. That or someone whispered the story into Peter Trøst's ear." Malle stared accusatorily at Orla. "Trøst just left a message for Ole, so of course Ole is all worked up now. It's one thing if some scandalized little shit paper prints the story, but it's another matter altogether when Channel DK gets involved."

Orla remained silent.

"Who the hell is John Bjergstrand?" He sounded almost angry.

"I have no idea."

"I think you're lying . . . and I think you have an inkling of what that means."

Orla had not blushed in many years, but he could feel his cheeks growing hot now. He stood. "If I knew anything, I'd tell you." It sounded strangely naive, like a babbling, delirious child.

"I hope so."

"The question is whether or not Ole knows something—since he called *you*."

Malle stared at the man he'd known as a boy. "If he does, I'll find out. And then I'll be back." He stood and then added in a grave voice, "I can promise you that much."

"Is it a coincidence? With Severin, I mean?" Orla asked. The question was apropos of nothing. Although he had left several messages scattered over three days, he'd been unable to reach the only friend he'd ever known—and lost.

Malle stopped abruptly on his way to the door. "With *whom*?"

"Severin, the boy from the yellow tenements? The fact that you know him as well?"

"I have no idea what you're talking about," he said, without turning.

"The boy with the bandage, Søren Severin Nielsen—the one who's now the most sought after refugee advocate in the country. Is that a coincidence?"

The security advisor stood motionless.

"Why don't you ask *him*, Carl, if he got any mail?"

It was clear that his remark had hit its mark. Malle breathed deeply, his back still to Orla, before he replied, "Søren Severin Nielsen isn't exactly on good terms with this ministry. You ought to know that as well as anyone. But you can ask him yourself."

"I already tried, because I believe several former Kongslund children received the same letter. I don't know why, and I don't understand how you and Ole are involved." He sniffled, and an indeterminate fear crept into his voice. "But something's not right." He fell silent, realizing that he sounded like a child again.

Malle ignored the accusation. "If that TV station calls, if Peter Trøst contacts you, don't say anything to him. Not a single word. Enough has already slipped loose."

Orla spread his fingers on the surface of his desk. "Maybe you should investigate whether Peter Trøst is adopted. He's the country's biggest star. Maybe it was the *letter writer* who whispered into his ear."

Without a word, Malle exited the office and closed the door so quietly that all Orla could hear was the sound of the fountain in the courtyard.

9

THE TV STATION

May 8, 2008

Magdalene would say that nothing in life ever goes according to plan, not even in the nation's upper echelons. The little child, whom the governess had compared to Moses in the bulrush cradle, had found her voice in the country's newspapers; the big TV stations would follow suit, and with their reports would come anger and indignation from the country's citizens.

This was, of course, exactly what the ministry feared.

Of all the children I tracked down and kept tabs on after their departure from Kongslund, Peter was the most fragile and peculiar creature—though he didn't appear that way on television. In his adult life, he did exactly as Magna had predicted in her endless song: he marched over the fine web without ever stumbling or even looking to the side.

Everyone watched him, and everyone admired him.

No one ever dreamed that his life contained the kind of secrets that all the children of Kongslund harbored.

* * *

To someone equipped with a strong imagination, the headquarters of Channel DK, a little south of Roskilde, might resemble a stranded spaceship from a distant galaxy, but to more sober minds it was just a modern oval-shaped edifice stretching into the skies. And since the latter held the majority, the building became known as the Big Cigar or simply the Cigar. Critical observers—and there still were quite a few of those among the last Socialists and Progressives whom the station constantly castigated—the nickname seemed fitting for a place that only aspired to increase its viewership and, thus, maximize its revenue.

Every morning, in the mist from Roskilde Fjord, you could see the employees glide from the parking lot, across the lawn, and into the building where they did their daily work. Seen from above, the procession resembled a phalanx of ants marching through a tray of garden cress, leaving only the faintest trail in their wake. No one looked back, and no one doubted the day would be a successful one; everyone showed up on time—bosses, reporters, secretaries, technicians, messengers, and cafeteria ladies—all grateful for their place in the center of the world of television entertainment. Even from his sixth-floor perch, Coordinator of News and Entertainment Peter Trøst sensed the eagerness in the movement of bodies across the lawn.

All the employees of Channel DK were subject to the philosophy outlined by Chairman of the Board Bjørn Meliassen in his proclamation to the Danish people on the day the station was founded: "Television brings us proximity and insight. Television brings us adventure, and it offers us human understanding."

In his civilian life, Meliassen had held the title of lecturer, but this very first television appearance earned him the moniker of the Professor, and his lofty words were drowned out by the applause of more than one thousand employees of the Cigar. Everyone loved the Professor.

In just a few years Channel DK had grown to become Denmark's largest and most advanced television workplace. By the spring of 2008 (a year before its astonishing and catastrophic collapse), it employed its own doctor and nurse, its own psychiatrist, and three psychologists—with a clinic on the sixth floor—as well as half a dozen massage and physical therapists. In addition, there were chefs, cafeteria and janitorial staff, contractors, technicians, messengers, and guards—along with a sea of reporters. On the ninth floor, where the chairman's office was located, there was a movie theater, a concert hall, a large lecture hall, a nightclub, and a cafeteria that was called the Ninth Heaven. This floor also featured a discreet door, hidden to the eyes of visitors, behind which lay the CEO suites, consisting of twelve luxurious sleeping chambers—each with an en suite bathroom, a large oval panorama window, and a balcony with a view of the coast and its many fjords. A spiral staircase wound its way to a beautiful rooftop terrace that featured nine antique benches next to a Jacuzzi and a blue teardrop swimming pool. On the eastern end of the terrace was the employee recreational area, which featured a wild garden with exotic trees, bushes, and flowers, and a small stream with tiny waterfalls. The employees referred to this area as the Garden of Eden—or simply Eden—and the joke was that it was the only Eden anyone ever needed to visit.

God could keep his.

"Maybe we ought to bury our dead up here too!" the union representative had once joked in his lively midsummer-eve speech, only to find himself swiftly relocated to the basement along with the older culture reporters who'd been buried alive down there. Nobody made fun of someone as successful as the Professor.

The editor of the culture department was called Might Have because someone thought he or she might have seen him on the ground floor, where he had no business at all. After all, his department was merely a cover to win the considerable public service funds the station received from the state. In the middle of the culture department was an almost soundproof chamber with a lead-lined steel door that all visitors considered the inner sanctum—the very heart of cultural journalism—but which trusted employees referred to as the Concept Room. In this room, young lions who knew nothing about the world but everything about influencing the masses provided the Professor and Peter Trøst with input for new best-selling programs.

Might Have knew nothing about concepts. He was, however, the only one who read newspapers, and for that reason he was the first to notice the peculiar article in *Independent Weekend* about the anonymous letters and the famous orphanage.

It reminded him of a fable he'd heard in his childhood. Nevertheless, he decided it was important enough to point out to his superiors. He took the elevator to the sunny third floor and put the clipping on the desk of the news editor, Bent Karlsen. But Karlsen, who'd essentially been hired to produce highly dramatic news clips, thought the story would be expensive and inconvenient, one that would require at least half a day of research and a whole day of recording. So he left the story on the oval news desk before he took the elevator to Ninth Heaven to enjoy a green salad. ("We hired him to be a predator, but so help me God he's a vegetarian!" the Professor had once hissed.)

It was there, on the news desk, that Peter Trøst stumbled upon the article, his eyes drawn to the photograph of the old matron.

He recognized her immediately.

He sat on the edge of the desk and began to read, a rare sight for editors at his level.

Then he went looking for Karlsen, who sat in the heavenly cafeteria drinking seltzer, a shred of lettuce clinging to his smooth chin.

"What's up with this story?" He set the article in front of his subordinate.

Karlsen stared at the headline: "The Kongslund Affair: What Is the Orphanage Hiding?" "There's no story. Besides it's in that crap paper, *Independent Weekend*." He bit into a slice of cucumber. "And it's about identity and adoption and so on." He pushed a cherry tomato into his perfectly round mouth as if to underscore the absurdity of the article. "So we shelved it."

"We shelved it?"

"We went over it and decided there was nothing in it. There is nothing there." Karlsen had a habit of speaking almost exclusively in the present tense, because to him the past only existed in boring world history, which rarely made for captivating television.

"But have you *read* it?" Trøst leaned across the table. "Just because it's in a newspaper. None of our viewers read the papers anymore."

"Nah." The news editor speared half an egg with his fork. "But *we* definitely don't have time to do that kind of story. People have already started taking their vacation."

"Then I'll do it myself," Peter said, demonstrating a spirit quite typical for the young TV station. From time to time, the bosses developed a story themselves if it engaged them personally or carried political significance.

Karlsen cut his egg in half and shrugged.

Peter Trøst left Ninth Heaven and took the elevator down to his enormous south-facing executive office where he could be alone. His secretary was on extended sick leave due to stress, and he hadn't asked for another.

He gazed out at the landscape west of Roskilde, across the hills and fringe of woods and the dark-brown spots that signified some sort of constructed environment (as in a half-erased map that no one bothered to update). The shocking part about the article hadn't been in recognizing Kongslund—it was the mother of all other adoption homes and orphanages, after all, and he was far from the only one who knew it. What had shocked him was the description of the envelope: letters cut from the newspaper, the baby socks, and the mysterious form.

He opened and then closed the only desk drawer to which he possessed a key. Hidden in that drawer in the antique birch desk, under an orange spiral notebook, was the very same letter—or an exact copy of it, at any rate. He had received it on May 5—the same date the newspaper and the ministry had received theirs—and in precisely the same type of envelope. He pulled out the mysterious almost fifty-year-old form.

John Bjergstrand, it simply read. Nothing more.

Had he been specially chosen, or was he simply one of many in the media who'd received a copy of the old record?

He hoped it was the latter, though didn't believe that to be the case.

At first he'd simply put the letter in his drawer and tried to forget about it. But the article in *Independent Weekend* had made that impossible. It had brought it, and his entire past, which very few people knew about, to the forefront. His parents and grandparents had told him about the orphanage when they believed it responsible and safe to do so (on his thirteenth birthday), along with what they knew about his mother, which was practically nothing. He had no opportunity to investigate their information and so, ultimately, he had no idea who he really was—a predicament he shared with many other adopted children.

Next to the form were the crocheted baby socks the paper had mentioned. Once they had been white, but now they were gray. He thought of his daughters from his last—failed—marriage. They were now seven and eight years old, and he seldom saw them. He didn't miss them. He smelled the socks; they smelled of dampness and age, but they had a faint, spicy odor too, as though they'd been lying in a flowerbed for some time. He couldn't explain that. His mother had never crocheted anything. He had never seen her near anything remotely resembling yarn or thread. He only remembered her pathological interest in the bushes, trees, and flowers in her garden; she knew more about their growth and daily life than about her husband and son.

Adopted son.

He thought of Knud Taasing, and hesitated. They had grown distant, though they'd often greeted one another (silently) at press meetings over the years (it was easier when they were surrounded by colleagues). They hadn't spoken since the catastrophe at school: the brutal death of Principal Nordal. To Peter it seemed like an eternity ago.

His fingers tapped in the number to the newspaper. He took a deep breath.

The phone rang for close to four minutes. Maybe *Independent Weekend* had cut the switchboard for budgetary reasons, he thought. Then someone picked up.

He asked for Taasing without introducing himself and then waited again. He hadn't used Knud's full name. Very few knew that the reporter was named after a famous explorer of Greenland. Knud *Mylius* Taasing had incited a hell of a lot of teasing at school.

"Taasing," the reporter simply said when he picked up.

"It's Peter Trøst."

"How about that?" Taasing replied.

He always had such composure; with only a second's notice, the once lauded journalist had managed to put just the right dash of irony in his words.

Peter had drawn a large, misshapen question mark on his notepad and now slashed a line through it. The ball was in his court. "I'm sitting here looking at your Kongslund story," he said. "I'm thinking about covering it."

"I figured you might be interested. I am too—since, after all, I know."

Peter was quiet. Taasing had remembered his story and even had it in mind when he wrote his article. He was one of the only people who knew.

"But you didn't write anything about it," he finally said.

"No. In the end, it's merely a single, distant story. How far back does it go? Thirty years?"

"Yes. I told you the day after my thirteenth birthday." It wasn't a response as much as a simple observation.

"Do you think I ought to have mentioned it?"

Carefully, Peter slashed at the question mark again and again, until it was almost black. The present had nothing to do with the event that had once separated them. They'd been boys. "I just wanted to know . . ." He fell silent.

"What else I know about Kongslund. And the matter with the letter." Taasing finished his sentence for him.

"Yes." Peter drew an exclamation point next to the question mark. "I believe there's something to this story, just as you do."

"Did you receive a letter?"

The question was unexpected. Knud was a good journalist, and the pause revealed the truth before Peter had time to deny it. "Yes," he said. Few reporters in the country were at his level. Maybe only a handful.

"Same wording?"

"Yes."

"If you want my help after all these years, you have to be *honest*," Knud said, emphasizing the last word.

Peter sensed his former friend's detachment. It had formed after they parted, like a thin shield against what had happened to him at school—which, in the end, had cost Knud's father his life.

"Would it be possible to find some of the former top leaders of Mother's Aid Society?"

"Maybe," Peter replied without any conviction.

"*Maybe*. What about the old director? What was her name?"

"Mrs. Krantz. She's senile now."

"I've tried to get ahold of Magna Ladegaard. She's somehow involved. But she's terrified. She doesn't want to say anything at all."

"So you believe the story—that the rich were assisted in ridding themselves of the unwanted results of their extramarital affairs? The children of famous men?"

The journalist ignored the question, asking instead, "Who was in the infant room with you? Susanne Ingemann won't tell me. But you visited the orphanage after you . . ." He suddenly stopped.

Peter considered the question for a moment. "I'm pretty sure about three of them," he finally said. "The first is Orla Berntsen, whom we already know, and the second is an attorney you might know—an immigration attorney by the name of Søren Severin Nielsen. It's really quite an amazing coincidence. In one newspaper profile, Søren Severin once revealed that he lived with Orla Berntsen at the Regensen dormitory when he was a young student. Given that they're on opposite sides of the big refugee cases, that's quite striking. Probably no one knows that they also spent time together as infants in an orphanage. They must have had a falling out somewhere along the way."

Knud said nothing, and Peter understood the silence. Friends let each other down.

"And then there's Marie Ladegaard, the girl who was adopted by the matron herself. I believe there was also a guy named Asger, whom Marie once told me about. He was placed with a family in Aarhus on Jutland. I haven't talked to her in many years."

So they all seemed to be afflicted with some kind of fear . . .

"I haven't been able to reach Marie at all. When are you planning to broadcast?"

"Right before the anniversary."

"So, we know about you, Orla, the attorney, Marie, and maybe a boy by the name of Asger. But that leaves two, right?" He was insistent. "Who the hell are the last two . . . a girl and a boy."

"I don't know."

"The boy is the interesting one in this case. If anyone can get it out of Magna or Marie, it would be you. I think there's a great story here. I can feel it." He paused.

Peter could hear his former friend's enthusiasm roaring like an ineluctable wave. Maybe he'd been just as certain when he'd made the mistake of his life.

"Listen. I really need this scoop . . . a genuinely true and revealing story. My dying paper needs it, and it's letting me pursue it as long as it reeks of conspiracy with a pinch of class struggle." Knud coughed. "They'd hate to miss out on the scandal that would emerge if a scaly creature from the past were to suddenly expose a beloved institution that protected scores of respectable citizens who impregnated poor girls who, in turn, put their vulnerable offspring up for adoption. And then in exchange for these protections the institution was protected and rewarded by a powerful government ministry. Christ. And with the party, the self-proclaimed party of solidarity, as the villain."

Peter said nothing. Knud had always been more direct. The working-class kid and the chief medical doctor's son; that's how it had started.

He read the article once more after hanging up, highlighting the most important information with double underscores. Then he decided to make the inevitable phone call. He had the minister's direct number.

"Almind-Enevold," the man said when Peter picked up the phone. Nothing else. The call came through just half an hour later. Peter immediately recognized the characteristically soft, almost feminine voice.

He'd met the party's undisputed ideological hardliner on numerous occasions; he'd interviewed him more than twenty times during his career as an anchor and host at Channel DK. "I'd like to talk to you about Kongslund, the orphanage in Skodsborg that you've supported since the 1960s," he said, getting straight to the point. "This time around, I think an informal talk will be fine, but perhaps later we can do it on camera."

There was a marked pause on the other end, quite uncharacteristic of the powerful man. "Kongslund . . . why?" The minister's voice filtered through some static on the line. Peter shifted the phone in his hands.

"We're developing a profile for the former matron's anniversary," he said. "I'd call it a piece of Danish history."

"I thought Channel DK went after juicier stories."

"We read the articles in *Independent Weekend*."

"Sensationalism, Trøst, in a sensationalist tabloid. It shouldn't have been printed."

Peter narrowed his eyes, searching for just the right words. "The report mentions an anonymous letter," he finally said.

"Listen, Trøst. I'd like to talk about the orphanage and about the at-risk children whom the Ministry of National Affairs has a clear interest in protecting, but—"

It sounded like the beginning of a campaign speech, and Peter interrupted him. "In our portrait, there will be room to talk about the past too."

"Not if you're basing it on the *Independent Weekend* article."

"Can we meet and talk about this, before we record?"

Once again there was a long, uncharacteristic pause. For nearly five seconds he could hear the minister breathing as he considered the proposition. "Listen, Trøst. I'm going to a meeting with my constituency in Vejle tonight. I'll stop by on the way, off the record, around five." He hung up without saying good-bye.

Peter took the elevator to Eden and stood staring to the east, into the mist, until he found the blue shadow he guessed was Øresund, and beyond that, Sweden. A tall, beautiful man on top of the Cigar, a privileged man who could reach the most remote parts of the country with whatever message his superiors wanted to convey. But they would hardly care to disseminate a story that the Ministry of National Affairs opposed. For many years, the Professor had made sure to give exclusive attention to the ministry's stream of releases: new immigration and refugee laws, instructions, and regulations; new rules for the issuing of visas, family reunification, and citizenship; observance of national holidays; and promotion of important debates concerning the country's ailing cultural heritage, education, and—of course—foreigners.

But the Kongslund Affair wasn't about foreigners, unless you classified the tens of thousands of adopted children as foreigners of that era, and Peter had never thought of himself that way. On the contrary, like the other Kongslund children who'd been adopted, he had gotten a new home, a second chance. They had all been helped. He studied the blue shadow in the horizon, and thought that it, in all its remoteness, symbolized the past he'd never been interested in. The child he'd once been had been left, unconditionally, in the care of the people who'd accepted him; he had traveled from an unknown past and was unaware of even his own place of birth.

Some adopted children, he knew, traced their roots when they were older. But he had never felt the urge to do that. Because it would be an act for which he couldn't foresee a conclusion. It would mean losing control, and you didn't do that in his world if you could help it.

He was nevertheless intrigued by how the anonymous letter had spooked the ministry to this extent. And the letter had caused something to stir inside of him too.

Maybe it was spite.

He saw the dead principal in front of him, and he closed his eyes. As always. How much did the anonymous letter writer know about his past?

10

PETER

1961–1973

I think the children in the Elephant Room knew the date of their departure long before they were carried into the arms of strangers. We said our good-byes silently, the way children do, and the message was passed unencumbered from bed to bed.

For some reason I always fell asleep before Magna's song stopped, and I would dream that I was the one being escorted to one of the waiting cars in the driveway, prodded along by Magna's endless chain of verses.

Peter was the next one to go. One morning his bed by the window was empty. In my dreams I saw him walking across the fine web that the governesses had spun for him, and he never stumbled or hesitated in the least.

* * *

At the end of the summer of 1972, I observed Orla intensely for several months, and I was no longer so sure I wanted to leave Kongslund for a family of my own.

I was frightened by his strange life in the row house, among children who scorned him, who treated him like some bothersome element in their midst—and around whom he nonetheless circled with ever-growing rage.

After my excursions, Magdalene often came for a night visit (she spent more and more of my daylight hours with her soul mate, the People's King). On those evenings we would study my notes together and add comments before I hid them away, and it was she who suggested I take a look at another child from the Elephant Room.

Naturally, our eyes were drawn to Peter—Peter the Happy. In the Christmas photo from 1961, he is lying on the rug under the branch from which the drum ornament dangles, and he is smiling directly into the camera. No wonder the chatty governesses thought he looked like the young film star Poul Richardt. Magna's most trusted assistant, Gerda Jensen, later told me how much they adored him.

I took the Strandvej bus through Skodsborg, Vedbæk, and Christiansgave and got off by Rungsted Harbor, which at that time con-sisted only of a pair of wooden piers and some small boats, as well as a little beach where the hippies sometimes sat in their thick Icelandic sweaters in the sun, smoking hash and drinking their homebrew. From there I walked the last stretch to the address I'd found in Magna's secret books. It was a big white villa set within a lush and well-kept garden; there was a small, white bench under a tall elm, and Peter sat inside a ray of sunlight that had miraculously slipped through the foliage. Lying in some bushes, I watched the birds leap from the shadows and flock around him as if he were simply a mirage they didn't need to take notice of. Through the telescope I studied his face. He didn't notice. He never saw me.

For weeks, I hid behind the hedges and bushes that surrounded the magnificent garden that had become his, and in contrast to Orla's world it was like gazing at Paradise itself. Everything was in bloom. If you were inclined to envy, it would sprout and grow and wind its way in and out of your heart, but only at a distance and only until the moment when you looked into the gray-blue eyes that millions of Danes would later see every single night. In his early childhood he possessed a truly mindbog-gling lack of self-assertiveness and an indifference to his own appearance that sharply contrasted with who he later became. Though he was the center of attention from his first day of school, he wasn't spoiled by his popularity; it didn't cause him to brag or boss others around, nor did it make him overlook the weakest in his cohort. On the contrary.

The private school he attended was a low, streamlined preserve for the children of the wealthy. It was adjacent to a small forest where, during recess, older students could go for strolls. A long gravel road led from Strandvejen to a wrought-iron gate that was opened in the morning and closed at night. The principal's dogs—a couple of ferocious but scrawny dobermans that were chained behind a wire fence in a corner of the playground during the day—guarded the gate at night. If anyone came near the gate in the dark, you could hear the dogs barking, like a raging echo through the woods, and the more forbidding sound of hollow thudding when they rammed their lean bodies against the hated barrier. If the two beasts had been even a hair's breadth thinner, they would have squeezed through the bars, and no doubt this was the terrifying image that kept burglars and potential pyromaniacs—indeed, any strangers—off the property.

The ruler of the private school was a man with the most ruthless disposition, feared by his 225 students for his quiet sarcasm and his sudden and explosive displays of wrath. To parents, he was always smiling, always at the ready with a well-chosen compliment about their diligent daughter or bright son—compliments that made the students' descriptions of his roaring, rabid alter ego seem like poor excuses back in their nice homes on Strandvejen. Teary accusations of his sadism frequently resulted in an extra box on the ear and another grounding, and it was especially those parents whose offspring Nordal had complimented for their unstinting honesty who put the most zeal into their punishments.

Peter noted that these were the children Principal Nordal liked the least.

Early in the morning when his dogs were chained up, he sauntered down the path from his private residence with his gaze expectantly fastened on the driveway. In the middle of the courtyard he would pause for a moment under the giant linden tree, the pride of the school, and listen to the roar of the wind in its magnificent crown. Of course, he should have heard its premonition of his imminent death. But he didn't. He had helped nurture the tree, and it had grown so tall that it had become a landmark for the entire area.

That the children continued to be tardy, in spite of the dobermans behind the fence, is a testament to humankind's inherent desire for freedom. With the timidity of rebellion shining in their eyes, these offenders sidled through the big gate and were met with his furious shouts. When he bent over them his breath smelled like sulfur, lightning, and hydrogen chloride, and over time the students feared this nauseating stench more than his most sarcastic digs: "Did his Lordship have trouble getting his fat belly out from under the silk duvet?" he'd scream as he brutally grabbed an ear and yanked. "I'll teach you how to get a move on, you little twit," he'd add, throwing the student down on the gravel. "Goddamnit! I'll teach you!" While the offender lay on his knees in his own vomit, the rector's words would disappear in a foamy lather of cursing.

Parents in the suburban hinterlands of Hørsholm-Usserød rarely considered enrolling their children in the private school; and if they did, Principal Nordal would quickly put an end to it. He would not allow the sons and daughters of secretaries and sanitation workers at *his* school, and no proletarians would tarnish its distinguished reputation with common names like *Olsen* and *Jensen* and *Hansen* and—God forbid— *Pedersen*. A simple workman's name.

Only one person in the entire county prevailed—even threatening to contact the newspaper in Usserød, during a time when it was practically Socialist—until the principal, thin and pale from anger, was forced to give in. The first representative of the world outside the tony towns of Vedbæk, Christiansgave, and Rungsted—where boys wore English blazers and became little patriarchs by the age of eight—entered class with his head bowed against his chest as if in shame. He didn't look like any person—child or adult—that Peter had ever encountered. Ms. Iversen introduced the thin boy with longish hair, wearing a faded T-shirt. He stood by the blackboard, his shoulders slumped, resembling a miniature version of the teenagers the police had just beaten with batons in Copenhagen during the demonstrations against the World Bank and the Vietnam War. She pointed at a chair along the windows, and the boy sank into it, disappearing in an aura of aloofness that seemed to protect him from all the hostile gazes.

He would have been destroyed in any other class; his name alone would have ensured that. He pronounced it in a nearly inaudible whisper: Knud Mylius Taasing. And while his surname came from the Danish island that had been the home of his family for generations, his first and middle names were a result of his father's enthusiastic adoration of the Greenland explorers Knud Rasmussen and Ludvig Mylius-Erichsen.

The latter, Ms. Iversen explained enthusiastically, had been a Danish hero, perhaps the greatest ever. He disappeared into the polar night in March 1907 near the seventy-ninth parallel north; his body was never found. In a loud voice she read from the last journal entry that her hero had made immediately before the expedition fell into the darkness, which made the explorer's namesake redden like the final, desperate light in the polar night: "I turned thirty-five recently. In fifteen years, all my male vigor will be gone."

Ms. Iversen's hero worship incited hatred for the famous name among the other boys, and they resolutely changed the new boy's name to *My*—after the large steam locomotives that pulled enormous carriages out of Copenhagen Central Station and across the country. They made faces and hissed from the sides of their mouths, as if they were letting steam out of overheated boilers, and My collapsed powerlessly between them. His father worked at the garment factory in Usserød, and if rumors were true, his hippie mother had died in Spain as the result of an overdose of pills and hashish.

Nevertheless, one day Peter invited My to his beautiful Rungsted garden, and they sat together on the bench under the elm, where his new friend suddenly asked a question that Peter, to his own surprise, somehow knew he would ask:

"How big was that tree when you were little?"

"Bigger than me at any rate," Peter said with the superb logic that has enabled man to land on the moon and humankind to answer some of life's most complicated questions.

My considered the terse response, but said nothing.

"No," Peter said, before his friend could even voice the next question.

My nodded. He had been wondering whether the tree was ever going to be chopped down.

In the beginning My was a sulky, rather awkward child: a small, narrow-shouldered boy with thin, nervous fingers and dirty nails. Where Peter's father was chief medical doctor with specialties in neurology and heart disease, Knud's father would trundle off to work at 6:00 a.m., return by 4:00 p.m., remove his clothes, shower, and put on a T-shirt emblazoned with a black-and-white illustration of Vladimir Lenin. Then he would sit on the stoop of the apartment buildings on Usserød Kongevej with his newspaper, the Communist Party organ *The People*.

If Peter's father was taciturn, Knud's father, Hjalmar, was silent as the grave. In order to learn about My's family, Peter studied the few details available in the apartment: the portraits of Lenin and Marx over the dining table; the photo of the smiling, departed mother. According to My's whispered account, she wasn't dead at all but had found true revolutionary freedom in a hippie commune that followed a Buddhist way of life in a province in southern Spain; there she meditated in the lotus position within the blue shadow of the mountains. All the while, her likeness gazed wistfully at her son from gilded frames on the television, the stove, the bedside table—even damply smiling down from the shampoo shelf in the shower.

It was a mystery to Peter that this admirer of Lenin, a longtime member of the Communist Party and union representative at the garment factory, had been so adamant about enrolling his only son in the most private of private schools in all of North Zealand's bourgeois idyll—perhaps the most capitalist of all capitalist schools in Denmark.

One day he asked Hjalmar if he'd ever met Principal Nordal. At first My's father didn't react, but simply sat still for a long time. Then he slowly lowered his big head with its bushy brows and opened *The People*.

As if reading it in his paper, he said, "Principal Nordal isn't important."

This assessment would turn out to be a fatal mistake. Knud Mylius Taasing's growing popularity, combined with his unjustified presence at the school, set off Principal Nordal—also known as the Doberman—and sealed his own fate and that of Knud's father. Nordal hated this man who attended political meetings, printed blood-red posters, and incited rebellion against factory owners and their unabashed profits—especially since one such manufacturer was on his board and was one of the county's most solidly conservative eminences. The persecution began in the spring of 1973, and when the opportunity fell in Nordal's lap it seemed a peculiar coincidence (only much later was the story pieced together from the fragments, the way I did, like when you rebuild an airplane that has been blown into a thousand pieces).

Encouraged by My's success, one of Hjalmar's colleagues successfully enrolled his own son at the exclusive school, but this boy didn't have My's charm and brute strength—nor did he become a friend of Peter's—and the skinny boy was overwhelmed with bullying from day one. On the third day he stood in the schoolyard crying, and the mock sobbing of the older students provoked squeals of laughter that made the dobermans bay more loudly behind the wire fence by the principal's office. Knud had learned three virtues from his taciturn father: protect the weak (the foundation of all human community), solidarity (the pillar of change), and pride (the pillar of personal integrity). So Knud, who'd once attended the public school in Usserød and whose mother was a revolutionary in Andalusia in the fourth incarnation, pulled the boy over to a bench and put an arm around his shoulder. During recess they walked into the woods together, their heads held high, as if preparing for a new and united resistance movement.

When they came back, the rich boys lingered around them insecurely, and perhaps at this moment the Doberman sensed the presence of a mightier opponent than the usual parade of tardy rich kids: the very risk that one could become two, and two could become many, and that many would become even more, which is to say that the Pedersens of this world would once and for all knock down the gates to the promised land and flood the domain of the wealthy.

And so he developed an idea to swallow up Knud Taasing's father and solve the problem once and for all. Early the next morning he set his plan in motion. He called five of the older seventh-grade students into his office and kept his door shut for almost an hour; after this meeting, the principal was more pale than usual, his eyes burning. He sent for Knud. During recess, the seventh-grade boys gathered in a circle in the schoolyard and whispered to one another, but Knud didn't return. Instead his father, in work clothes and clogs, picked him up, and together they walked with bowed heads down to his moped, then away through the woods.

He didn't return to school for another week, and when he did, his aura of remoteness was even more powerful, protecting him from the gazes of the other kids for the rest of his school days. A rumor circulated in and out of classrooms and was confirmed by Nordal's bloodshot eyes. In the following weeks, the Doberman treated the students with an abnormal mildness. Even sinners who were five, six, or seven minutes late received only a muted reprimand from his tight-lipped mouth—which issued just a puff of sulfur now—before being sent to their classrooms. Even the dogs were quiet.

Despite the power of his silence, how Knud Mylius Taasing got through the darkest chapter of his young life, stretching over several months, no one knows. A rumor had started—via the seventh-grade boys whom the principal had met with that day—that My and the new boy had walked into the woods locked in an embrace, and that something had occurred between them among the thick trunks. My had forced the smaller boy to do things of a nature that could only be suggested, and this suggestion—which in a way was worse than an admission—sufficed for the principal and the school.

A few nights later, Peter had a nauseating dream: he stood like a shadow in the principal's office waiting for something to happen. My's father arrived with the smell of sweat and cigar smoke that he hadn't had time to wash off clinging to him, the image of his revolutionary hero on his T-shirt. "You have to understand that there's nothing we'd rather do than avoid a scandal and the possible involvement of the police," the Doberman told the laborer, and you could see the antagonism and skepticism and contempt seep—like sand from a torn bag—from men like Nordal for men like Hjalmar.

In that moment, Peter understood that My was innocent. In his eyes there was no trace of shame.

A couple weeks later, Peter's family threw a harvest celebration in their garden. The house was filled with the most distinguished families from Strandvejen, and after the dinner, the garment manufacturer and his close friend, the mayor, settled in a corner of the living room. Peter heard them laughing. Then a word caught his attention: *Communist.* Then another: *scandal.*

Peter edged closer.

"In the end, they always stick in the pipe," the manufacturer said. More laughter.

"Yes. That's one procedure he'll never forget," the mayor agreed, his fat hand raising a glass of cognac.

"So elegantly handled by Principal Nordal," the mayor said admiringly.

The manufacturer studied the glow of his long cigar. He nodded. "Yes, they were both put in their place, the bastard and his little bastard."

A week later, the story was confirmed to Peter: My's father had just announced that he wouldn't be seeking reelection as the factory's union representative. The party had tried to change his mind, wrote the Usserød newspaper, but he hadn't offered any other explanation than that he wanted to be replaced.

Peter immediately realized the devilish ultimatum that Principal Nordal had presented to My's father that day at the school: Hjalmar could stand his ground and let down his son, or he could abandon his cause and save his son. *To justify keeping the police out of this, we have to act with discretion, and act responsibly. Of course, how can you continue your political involvement or continue as union representative when at any minute you might be leading a strike and be fired, perhaps even end up drawing the attention of the police? You're a single parent, and this boy needs you, not least after what has happened.*

Peter could hear, even smell the words as clearly as if Principal Nordal was standing right in front of him. They haunted him when he lay sleepless, listening to the wind blowing through the elm. Whether it was the rustling of the leaves or the nightly visits from Nordal's foul-smelling, triumphant spirit that gave him the idea, no one will ever know.

But early one morning he rose, found a notepad, and started making the preparations that would continue through the fall, as Denmark suffered an oil crisis and the entire nation changed character by welcoming a new right-wing party protesting something the population was barely able to understand.

The chainsaw had been resting, unused, in the garage for years. Peter put it in a big black bag and rode his bicycle deep into Rungsted Woods, where for three weeks he prepared for the execution of his plan: *how to use the throttle, rev it up, how to hold it, apply pressure, and hold the blade steady.* More attentive parents would have noticed the callouses, which had formed over the blisters on his hands, but not Laust and Inge; they read the newspaper and wrote letters, and therefore they sat with their heads bowed much of the time.

Three days before Christmas, the scandal struck the private school like a natural disaster.

That winter morning, the principal was, as usual, headed for the gate to relieve his dobermans of their restless night duty, but for once the air was not torn by their heavy, furious bodies flying at the gate. One lay dead and the other was dying in a corner of the schoolyard, foaming around his pointy lower jaw. And Principal Nordal heard a moaning that might have originated more from inside his head than from the dark, snow-covered schoolyard. The pride of the school, the mighty linden tree, had been chopped down at its base, as if by a giant invisible hand. It had fallen sideways across the water pump, and its longest branches had crushed several sheds and shattered the windows in the south wing of the school. Now the police and firemen who had been called by the shocked man were walking among glass shards, bricks, and branches, as the principal himself stood powerless behind them with clenched fists, trying to comprehend the disaster.

They found only a single piece of evidence, down near the base of the tree: a pair of expensive buffalo skin gloves that were immediately traced to a seventh-grade boy, who without much ado was taken away by two officers. Since no one believed the boy could have done it alone, his four closest friends were brought in as well and driven to the police station. The poisoned dogs were placed on a plastic tarp and taken to the same destination. The principal didn't even look in their direction as they were taken away. For hours he stood motionless, staring at the felled linden tree, and he was still standing there when the last car left the yard. Something alien and powerful had entered the school; perhaps he suspected then what it was. Perhaps he understood that he'd inadvertently challenged a mind much more powerful than his own—one that was more hateful than even he deemed possible.

This was the last time that teachers and students saw the principal.

On Christmas day he suffered a stroke; he died in Usserød hospital at exactly eight in the morning on New Year's Day, without ever having regained consciousness.

One tabloid got wind of the story, and a sharp reporter had no difficulty connecting his sudden death with the brutal felling of the school's pride a few days earlier. In large type on its front page, the paper wrote: "Vandalism Kills Principal."

The murder of the tree had become the murder of the man; a man who, with the same narrow, aggressive appearance as when he was alive, followed his dogs to the grave.

The police interrogated the boys for days. And for weeks the county was embroiled in gossip and rumors, but since the detained perpetrators didn't confess, they couldn't be punished. And since no murder weapon matching the information provided by the arborists was ever discovered, the death of the man and the felling of the tree could not be connected. The principal was buried, and the vandalism was allowed to sink into the place where it served everyone best: oblivion.

The seventh-grade boys were released and returned to suffer punishments that were heard throughout the neighborhood for weeks. They were the very same boys who'd harassed Knud and who'd connived with the principal to create that devastating scandal.

They returned to school with red cheeks and bloodshot eyes.

The suspected ringleader never discovered how his gloves had disappeared from a shelf in the hallway and, much to his terror, turned up by the felled linden.

Despite persistent efforts, the teachers and students at the school never solved the case, never found the real killer of the tree and the dogs and the man.

11

THE MINISTER OF NATIONAL AFFAIRS

May 9, 2008

Once, when I was around twelve or thirteen years old, I asked Magna if she was really sure that the spider's fine web could bear all the feet that marched across it, year after year.

She looked at me impatiently and replied, "Marie, that web can hold all the children in the whole wide world."

Maybe my concern was caused by my deformed limbs, which were slowly getting accustomed to their imprisonment during those very years, or perhaps I already sensed that no one would ever come for me—and that even if such a miracle occurred, my ugliness would trigger the fatal misstep that would cause the threads to rupture, sending my foster mother's herd plummeting into the abyss.

As usual, Magna responded to my fear with booming laughter—the way she always laughed at nonsense—and I closed my eyes and prayed that the Master above wouldn't hear it.

* * *

Peter put the letter and the crocheted socks back into the drawer. He'd discussed the first part of his life with very few people. And thus, his decision to open the door to the past went unnoticed, just like the time he practiced in the woods with the chainsaw.

For thirty years, Peter Trøst had lived in the moment. In his world, the present took the shape of a tunnel stretching from the TV studios in the Cigar to living rooms across the country, where no one, as the Professor put it, wanted his or her evening relaxation ruined by disturbing images that hit too close to home. Television was a way to observe the world *as though* it were close to you without it actually being so, and Kongslund was the most cherished national jewel in this the age of globalization.

In the basement Concept Room, where the young lions snarled and growled out new, folksy ideas for viewers, the Professor had begun the day by shouting: "Nobody has any use for yesterday! Nobody wants to dwell on worries . . . People want to remember, but they don't want to remember problems!"

The young lions gathered around the table nodded until their manes quivered, because, here in television's palace, the Professor's words were law. He was the ruler of heaven, the father of the hardworking ants, and this was the breeding ground of signals.

As a lecturer of Scandinavian Literature at Copenhagen University, he had made his television debut in a debate with a nervous sociologist on the growing influence of the medium on the human soul. That night he uttered the maxim that would alter his rather bland life as an academic-fact retainer: "Television is the world's eighth wonder because it soothes and heals the problems that each and every one of us secretly fears: loneliness, isolation, violence, war—even famine and natural disasters. Television is the only real revolution of our time!"

A few years later, Channel DK made national identity its brand and named the popular professor as its chairman of the board. After that, he said everything that had once been considered inappropriate for television. Unabashedly, he praised the rich and powerful, and he distanced himself from bleeding-heart humanists and their provincial mentality. "We Danes should be allowed to reject everything that is alien to us: customs, foreigners—Poles, Romanians, Slavs, Tamils, Uzbeks, and Turks.

What's coming next?" It was hardly surprising that he'd formed a close bond with the party, and that viewership increased exponentially.

Peter stood before the panoramic window in his oval office studying the stretch of woods near Hejede Overdrev and Gyldeløveshøj. He had visited Kongslund shortly after his parents had revealed their secret to him. They had seemed so relieved, as if they'd killed someone and had now finally found their peace with God. Or perhaps their absolution had come from the old matron, who met them in the driveway and gave Peter a hug, lifting him into her arms as though he still belonged there. He was only thirteen years old at the time.

He had met Magna's foster daughter on the next visit, and they'd sat in her strange bedroom on the first floor, which reminded him of a ship's bridge (she had even attached a kind of telescope to the armrest of an old wheelchair). They'd tried to remember one another from their first year together, but of course they couldn't. At some point, however, she had told him about Asger, who had been adopted during the same period and had begun searching for his biological parents. Even though Asger had moved to Aarhus and lived a life far removed from Kongslund, Marie was somehow able to describe the neighborhood as though she'd been there, had seen him with her own eyes.

From behind his big executive desk, Peter shook his head at the memory, and then began calling the public schools in Aarhus, one by one, asking for a teacher couple with a son named Asger. On his fifth attempt he found them.

"Yes," the principal said, the couple had been employed at Rosenvang School there in Viby for over fifty years, but they had recently retired. Their son was now the director of the Ole Rømer Observatory in Højbjerg, and the students at Rosenvang visited the observatory several times a year to study galactic clouds like Andromeda, the Virgo Cluster, and the Large Magellanic Cloud.

"From a very early age, he stared *up* most of the time," the principal said. "That's the way he is. Like Hawking, he dreams of finding the theory of everything." Then the principal abruptly changed topics. "I hope he's not about to be publically humiliated for something. He has never been extreme politically or—"

The principal stopped short, as if he suddenly considered an even worse possibility.

Before hanging up the phone, Peter reassured him that he was not planning on humiliating him in any way. He found the astronomer's number, lifted the receiver, and then hesitated. From the panoramic window he studied the dark blotches that dotted the hilly North Zealand landscape every mile or so—Skalstrup, Brordrup, and Gøderup—the peculiar names of small towns in a world he practically never visited. He had no idea what people did in places like that.

Then he punched in the number. There was a click at the other end.

You've reached Asger Dan Christoffersen. I'm at the observatory but will be back soon. Please leave a message, and I'll call you back.

The voice was deeper than Peter had expected, about as far from the constellations as you could get. He left a short message without specifying what he was calling about. Then he stood, removed his jacket and shirt, and slipped on a fresh set he had hanging in his office. Lately he'd begun feeling dirty in his clothes after two or three hours, and it was especially bad during these months when the coolness of winter had been replaced by the warmth of spring. It felt as though someone had placed a hot hand on his skin, and he had never really liked being touched. By the end of the day, he was often in his third or fourth suit, and he'd become wary of those colleagues who wore the same shirt and tie all day.

He grabbed the telephone again and this time called Søren Severin Nielsen. Severin's name frequently appeared in the newspapers, Peter knew, and almost always in connection to hopeless asylum applications or distressed refugees' failed appeals for humanitarian stays. Apparently his office was unstaffed, because no one answered the phone—no secretary, no paralegal, just a raw, rugged man's voice practically whispering: *Søren Severin Nielsen is in court. Please leave a message.*

Peter hesitated for a second. He remembered the man from his public appearance in several major cases: thin and ruddy, he looked as though he drowned his many defeats before the Refugee Board and the National Ministry in too many after-work pints. Peter hung up.

For a moment he considered calling Magna, but he faltered without knowing why. Something she'd told him came back to him: "Remember one thing, Peter, illegitimate children come to us like Moses in his basket, and the best orphanages are therefore always by the water!"

It was a strange observation, even in a country surrounded by water.

He stood and looked at the sky over Assendløse and Bregnetved—another pair of oddly named Zealand towns whose residents he'd only caught glimpses of whenever he cruised about in his car postponing his arrival at Østerbro. All those towns with curious names from days gone by. Since the day the letter had arrived, Peter didn't quite recognize himself anymore. The past seemed to be seeping to the surface.

His mother had said, "You were the most beautiful child Kongslund had ever housed. They all wanted to take you home!" And he had understood the curse. The trajectory of many lives is determined by the physical body that God in his irreproachable teamwork with the Devil bequeaths at birth. There are people who are so hideous that they never overcome the setbacks they suffer as children, and there are children who are so beautiful that they never stop craving the attention that has been lavished upon them; this is a tendency that is even stronger among adopted children, he knew. Deep down, Peter carried the knowledge of his own excellence, instilled in him by his adoptive parents, and if he ever tried to evade it—seriously and genuinely tried to evade it—Fate would, with a tired look on its face, lean over the edge of heaven, from where it keeps an eye on both the living and the dead, and slice the nerve that kept all his insecurity and vanity in scant but vital balance.

All stars fear this sudden fall, and with the Kongslund Affair as an open abyss before him, Peter Trøst was on the verge of panic.

His cell phone rang.

The minister was on his way up in the elevator.

* * *

He stood and placed two wineglasses on the oval rosewood conference table, and then opened the door.

Ole Almind-Enevold was smaller than he seemed on TV and, close up, so manicured you might suspect him of being gay. But the hounds in the press had never found any signs of that, quite the contrary. He lived alone with his wife, Lykke, and they had no children. From time to time he was involved with other women, but his wife had no idea.

The minister was accompanied by four guards, probably to illustrate the stories that his press chief regularly told the media about threats and harassment from fundamentalist Muslim groups. The guards, however, stayed outside the office.

Unbidden, the Almighty One sat in the largest and most comfortable armchair in the room holding a glass of red wine in one hand and a thin cheroot in the other. A light smoke ring spiraled toward the ceiling, and the powerful man nodded to the middle-aged journalist.

"There was a time when you didn't mix news and entertainment," he said, as though he were talking to the smoke and not to the man.

Peter struck a relaxed tone. "We have to keep up with the times. And keep up our ratings," he added with a smile. "Just as the administration needs to keep an eye on its own numbers."

For a moment the minister didn't comprehend.

"The polls," Peter said.

The Almighty One expelled a short laugh that sounded like a handful of glass shards falling onto a tile floor. All reporters knew the man had a reputation for being callous—both in his private and professional life—and his coldness had sometimes surprised his opponents. He was a personal friend of the Professor, whom he had known since they occupied the Department of Law back in the years of student protests. Before times had changed.

Peter put his glass on the table. "I know you have a special relationship with the orphanage in Skodsborg. In four days the matron will be celebrating her sixtieth anniversary."

"The *former* matron, yes, that's true." The Almighty One spoke in his usual soft voice.

"Yes. The *real* matron, you might say . . . the one you always supported as the leader of the orphanage you helped bring fame."

The minister didn't react. He had two small rows of teeth and colorless lips, and his high, shiny forehead looked like an impregnable stone wall.

"Was it your idea to throw the anniversary party on May 13?"

"I helped make the arrangements, yes."

"I suppose it generates the right kind of attention—rather than the kind of attention you're getting right now with the anonymous letters. And the ministry's treatment of the orphaned Tamil boy who is about to be expelled?" Peter didn't know why he was suddenly connecting the two cases. Maybe it was the wine. He felt an urge to provoke the man—a feeling no good TV reporter should give in to.

"Yes," his guest said plainly.

Peter opened the top drawer of his desk and pulled out his copy of *Independent Weekend*. He read aloud the headline and a few of the passages he'd underlined:

"Famous Orphanage Accused of Hiding Thousands of Children . . . potentially politicians, officials, or actors who didn't want to risk their reputations and careers because of an extramarital affair . . . They could safely go to Skodsborg Strandvej and talk to the matron who is now celebrating her sixtieth anniversary . . . She would handle their problem discreetly and to their satisfaction."

The minister sipped his wine but didn't react.

"Would you care to comment on that story?"

"Is *that* why you asked me to come here on such short notice? To do a story like *that*? I don't find that dignified."

"But it's your newspaper, in a way . . . the administration's paper. *Independent Weekend* still receives considerable financial support from the party, a holdover from the old days." Peter still didn't quite understand his sudden urge to provoke the man.

"It *was* my paper," the minister said, "before this reporter"—he tapped Knud Taasing's byline—"before this reporter deliberately tried to scandalize the administration with this *muck*." He pronounced the last word as if an earwig had bitten his tongue. His pale skin had developed a rosy hue, like the sky over Såby Church and Tølløse right before sunset.

"*Muck*?" Peter was genuinely surprised at his expression.

"Yes. The kind of thing that gets pulled out of a bog, smelling of rot and brackish water. But don't quote me on that."

"The paper nonetheless says that you've asked an old acquaintance, a former policeman, to dig into the matter, discreetly. So I gather the story is of interest to you?"

The minister leaned toward Peter, his forehead shining. "Listen, Trøst. When something like this gets out—and the letter writer was smart enough to send it to a tabloid—you have to take it seriously. Or rather, *pretend to take it seriously*. And then it's wise to use a private investigation bureau rather than waste taxpayer money by stirring the entire apparatus, the police, and the secret service. Don't you agree? Waste of public money is a favorite theme of Channel DK, isn't it?"

Peter kept quiet. The blue envelope he'd received was in the locked drawer only a few feet away, but he didn't want to reveal his own involvement—which he hadn't even admitted to the Professor.

"According to the newspaper, your right-hand man, Orla Berntsen, was actually placed in that orphanage for a while, long ago. What do you make of that?"

"I assume this is off the record?"

"To the best of my knowledge, there's no recording device here," Peter said, glancing demonstratively about the room.

"I have no idea."

The TV star nearly giggled. *How impertinent,* he thought, staring at the minister, who was still sitting with his hands folded on the table. "You think it's a coincidence that he got that letter," Peter said.

The irony couldn't be missed, but the minister merely shrugged as if he feared an invisible microphone would reveal his foolish ignorance of the subject.

"The article implies that you were aware that covert things were taking place at Kongslund. And that you didn't intervene." Peter let the innuendo hang in the air. He was in dangerous territory now.

The man in the armchair looked as though he was studying a distant fog—a formidable squadron of words that filled the air between his universe and the reporter's—and then he said, "Why don't you tell me why you're so interested in this matter? Why are you so eager to do a program about this muck?"

Peter looked up, a little startled. Did the minister know about his past? No, it wasn't possible. He took a deep breath. "Was Kongslund involved in something of that nature?"

"I know this orphanage well, and I have never heard of anything like that. That's not to say that all kinds of things couldn't have happened—I didn't live there after all. I was just a good friend. I knew Magna—Ms. Ladegaard—during the war."

"Yes, I know."

"I helped her realize her dream, and I am proud to have done that. I think *that's* what Channel DK ought to focus on this week when Kongslund is celebrated by thousands of people, and not just in Denmark. There'll be guests from all over the world." He raised his glass in front of Peter's face.

"Cheers," he said as he drank the last of his wine and began to stand.

Peter considered a final question: *Did she ever help you or someone you know?* But it would trigger the Almighty One's unrestrained fury and no doubt put an end to all further contact with the ministry.

The minister sat back down, as if he'd perceived a shadow of the question in his eyes. "No. I haven't personally been involved in something secretive or stealthy"—he smiled coldly—"and if I had, I imagine that would be of interest only to the sensationalist media." He set his empty glass on the table.

"You're part of an administration that always talks about humane values and honesty and about giving all the nation's children a good upbringing and a good life in a stable Danish family." Again Peter felt an inexplicable, unprofessional anger toward this man. "Naturally, it would be of interest to the public if any members of your party are or were living according to a completely different set of principles and bent all the rules in doing so, like hiding their offspring to protect their own fragile careers. How much could have been under the rug?"

The minister finally stood. He cocked his head. "This conversation verges on offensive. There is nothing to what you're suggesting, and I'm entitled to a certain level of respect, even from the press." He stared angrily at the reporter. "Not suspicion and scandal-mongering."

At that moment the door opened, and the Professor entered without knocking; he walked directly to the minister and took him by the shoulders in an almost jovial manner. "My dear Ole. You know what we reporters are like. We have to uphold some of the old traditions—for the sake of democracy. You yourself praise the independent press because it assures the population of a higher justice, because it's a guard dog, a guarantee that anything and everything is open to debate . . . We need that guard dog."

"Sensational stories don't represent the freedom of speech," the minister said, shaking off the Professor's hands.

"True, and that's why we'll go easy on this matter, I can assure you. We'll treat you right, and with fairness, just as you and your administration have always treated us. We're grateful for that."

Staring south as if he'd suddenly developed an interest in the woods between Borup and Kirke Hvalsø, the minister said, "Yes, we treat one another as we deserve . . . and I would like it very much if we do no harm to the reputation of our finest orphanage." He grabbed his coat. The four bodyguards entered the office and spread out around him.

Peter looked at the Professor, who was still facing the minister. He had the sense that the two men had entered into some sort of pact long ago, and that he might have broken it with a single unasked question.

Perhaps it wouldn't have changed the course of events over the next few months if he had asked it. At that level, men rarely caved to one another—and they almost never yielded.

Even if they'd seen the danger (and perhaps they ought to have), neither would have taken responsibility, and the process would have continued toward absolute zero, where nobody could change anything at all. That's the way it was in the old fairy tales, and in matters of war and love, and that's how it is in the universe of the very powerful, where ambition rules and all other feelings are inconsequential.

But, of course, punishment is meted out.

Three people stood in the sixth-floor executive office that day, and six months later, two of them were dead.

* * *

Later, the Professor approached Peter the way a teacher approaches a student: "You handled that well until you threatened him. That was *stupid*."

Peter realized then that the Professor must have eavesdropped on the whole conversation from the other side of the door.

He walked over to Peter. "I agree with him that you're completely exaggerating the significance of the anonymous letter. Any idiot could have written that drivel."

Peter stared at the chairman of the board. The Kongslund Affair went directly against the Professor's plan to raise ratings in ways that would keep competing stations at bay. Sure, you attacked problems, but the bad guys had to be easily identified individuals: pushers, terrorists, Muslims—not faceless authorities and certainly not the welfare state itself.

"We're *for* everything that is good in life!" Bjørn Meliassen had roared at the strategy convention in January to the other executives, commonly referred to as the Nine Highest. "We have to find happiness on behalf of our viewers. And happiness—that's what we've already got: our families, our kids, our TVs, our social services, and our country. That's what we've got to defend! All those who disagree, all the misfits, they ought to just go back to where they belong. We can't adopt every silly tradition and custom in the whole world."

Now, Bjørn Meliassen took a deep breath. "I know things that you have no idea I know, Trøst. You were at that orphanage as a baby; you lived in Rungsted; you're adopted. I'm aware of Knud, and I also know"—he leaned toward the TV star, whose hand, holding the wineglass, was frozen in midair—"that your principal had a stroke after a case of aggravated vandalism at your school. I know much more than you realize, and I understand that it takes an extraordinarily strong man to go through everything that you've been through."

Peter's face was flushed. Instinctively, he felt the makeup artist's brush on his neck, but it was merely the Professor blowing cold air between his lips.

"What did you expect, Peter? That I hadn't done a background check on my biggest star? Ha-ha. Though many do, you've never sought out your biological parents. You don't even know who they are, and you don't want to know. That's why Kongslund has such a hold on you. It's your own past you're chasing through this ridiculous *John Bjergstrand* character. You ought to go see one of our excellent psychologists and get it all off your chest."

Peter felt the nausea rising from the pit of his stomach. The Professor had mentioned episodes from his past that he, under no circumstances, should know about. The private school, the vandalism, his friendship with Knud Mylius Taasing. How had he gleaned that information?

"Listen, Trøst"—when he lectured, the Professor never addressed Peter by his first name—"even though we are subsidized by a rich uncle in the United States, our future depends not on charity but on hard commercial revenue. That's how it works in our world. We've got no use for stories like this, believe me. And one more thing." The Professor's cruel eyes gleamed like the night he made his first and most brilliant television appearance. "Right after you called me, Carl Malle telephoned on behalf of the ministry. As security advisor, he is very indignant about our involvement. It could harm his investigation."

Peter pictured him—Malle, the surveillance specialist, the hunter—and in that moment he understood where the Professor had gotten his information. Another wave of nausea hit him.

"He was the one who checked out my past," Peter said. "You asked Malle for that information." This truth flickered into the twilight sky and disappeared.

The Professor shifted his glance, but only for a second. Then he shook his head regretfully, and a hissing and rumbling sound seemed to rise from the man's chest. "That story will be the end of you, Trøst."

It sounded like a curse.

With the empty wine bottle in his hand, Peter left the office.

* * *

In the parking lot Peter was again overcome with a feeling of nausea, this time with such a force that he dove between two parked broadcasting vans, expecting to throw up.

For three hours he drove aimlessly through the small towns of Zealand he could see from his office window in the Big Cigar, gazing into the brightly lit windows, studying the shadows of the people who lived there.

Why he did it, he wasn't sure.

Once again he called Søren Severin Nielsen—the lawyer might be able to help. He'd known the ministry's chief of staff back in the day, and he himself had lived at Kongslund. Though he had picked a hopeless legal specialty, he was said to be a good attorney.

The phone rang, but there was still no answer.

12

SEVERIN

1976–1984

I've always considered it a coincidence that Orla and Severin met, even though they were placed in the same area where Carl Malle lived.

During the sixties and seventies, thousands of children grew up in the neighborhood west of the wetlands in this Copenhagen suburb, and the chance that the two boys would run into one another (and lift a corner of the veil covering the peculiar pattern they were both part of) was so miniscule that the invisible puppeteers of the Kongslund Affair probably didn't think it possible.

Severin left Kongslund only a few days after Orla, and, as usual, all the governesses, caregivers, and assistants stood in the driveway and waved, wishing the little traveler a good life. But Severin's home wasn't the kind of home most adopted children grow up in—and in his case, death had, so to speak, traveled ahead of him.

Yet another elephant marched along . . . stepping across the fine web and was gone . . .

And of course I followed.

* * *

Gray and massive, the boulder sat in the clearing like a squatting giant, its chin resting on its knees to study the lawns, the chestnut trees, and the seagulls flying over the rushes. It was here, by the huge boulder in the wetlands, right where Orla fought his last battle against the demons, that Severin—in hiding and from a distance with a big white bandage on his head—first spotted him. Almost seven years would pass from that first sighting until the boy from the yellow tenements made himself known.

In the days following the murder of the Fool in the wetlands, Malle had pulled the many strings he held at the time and found a boarding school on Zealand's Odde, where the goofy, restless, and friendless boy could learn how to succeed in life.

When, almost three years later, Orla returned to the neighborhood to attend high school, the clownish mind—his only defense against boyhood loneliness—was gone, never to return as far as anyone knew. What replaced it, no one in the neighborhood could say—including Severin, who had seen him come back—because the new Orla hid behind vacant eyes that rarely met the gaze of others. He had an ability to practically disappear from his surroundings, so much so that no one even remembered he'd been present in the first place. He avoided people as demonstratively as he'd once sought them out. He kept his hair closely cropped, standing out from the crowd of long-haired, fatigue-clad hippie kids who rode mopeds, wore headbands, and shouted political slogans while demanding their parents be detained and reprogrammed for a just world.

He was alone.

Through some instinct of self-preservation, he graduated—and he even showed up for the official ceremony and subsequent celebration at the high school. It was on this night, donning his mortarboard, that Orla Pil Berntsen met Søren Severin Nielsen. Orla had just entered a pleasant hibernationlike state, an invisibility he'd mastered, when a voice suddenly spoke to him through the music and the clouds of smoke in the great ballroom. He was startled. Normally no one talked to him: Orla the asocial, the boy from the wetlands.

He raised his head and allowed his eyes to emerge from their usual hiding place, and, to his surprise, discovered a boy just across from him staring back. He had to either escape or disappear, or let the thin boy who also wore glasses—black, heavy, and wide-framed—look him over and ask the question that trembled on his thin lips: "Don't you live in the red row houses?"

Orla decided to reply with a single nod. "How do you know?" He said, surprised to hear his own voice, as he hadn't meant to speak.

"I've seen you there. And in the wetlands. My name is Severin. I live in the yellow tenements. Number sixty-one."

Orla went quiet. The boys from the yellow tenements were as numerous as the workers in the gray factories out by the freeway, and that's all he knew about them. An alien race. For ten years the children from the row houses had bombarded them with rocks without ever seeing their faces.

"We threw rocks at you too, without seeing you," Severin said, in response to Orla's silent thoughts.

Orla squinted. Had he spoken without knowing it?

"Once a rock hit my head, and I was taken to the hospital, sirens blaring," Severin continued.

There was no anger or reproach in his voice, no shame or guilt. No tiny invisible toxic deposits between the words. It was remarkable, because the parents in the apartment buildings and row houses had raised their children to despise the community on the other side of the hedge with a force you wouldn't expect to wane over time. Orla was about to sniffle, but no sound emerged. He just barely managed a reply in the three seconds it took for Fate to catch them and push them into the embrace of the God of Friendship and Camaraderie.

"I was the one throwing that rock," Orla laughed. "You got a huge bandage on your head."

His new friend laughed with him.

Orla wanted to say one more thing but didn't have the guts. So he stayed quiet.

They walked home together that night after the party and went their separate ways near the hawthorn hedge shaking hands like real adults.

They were both serious people, and each chose to study law. They moved to Regensen—the big, old student dormitory across from Rundetaarn that had been built for the children from families of limited means who otherwise couldn't afford to live in the city and study at the university. Here the high achievers, the winners, and the students with heavy brass prizes for diligence, along with GPAs higher than the Himalayas, resided. The two friends tested one another in inheritance law, tax law, and criminal law, as well as the names of the hottest girls in the dormitory. They joined a dormitory club, along with the impoverished son of a count from Allerød and a female theology student from Bronshøj who each afternoon walked through Jorck's Passage to the pedestrian street to sing with the Salvation Army. For this reason, she was called the Salvation Girl by her numerous admirers (though no one knew whether they admired her most for her beauty, her mind, or her song).

There was one thing for certain: Severin's room at the dormitory was as neat as Severin himself, simply furnished and plainly decorated except for a rather strange yellow-gray animal skin that hung over the bed, affixed to the wall with large nails.

"It ought to be on the floor," Orla said to him one day. "In front of the fireplace."

There was no fireplace in their dorm room, but that wasn't really the problem with the suggestion.

"It's not a bear," Severin said with a sudden seriousness that seemed to verge on tears. "It's my uncle's dog. It was a golden retriever . . . I played with it as a child. When it died, Uncle Dan had the skin made and gave it to me for my confirmation." He paused, his lips narrow and a little sulky. "Her name's Mille."

Orla stared at Mille—or rather at her pelt—and then at Severin.

Even though the two boys had both been at Kongslund (though they hadn't learned that yet) and had been abandoned by their parents when they were very young, they had developed in significantly different ways. Orla had an unremitting terror that his mother would suddenly vanish into thin air and leave him all alone on the planet (at an abstract level, this fear had fascinated the bearded, pipe-smoking psychologists from Mother's Aid Society). For Severin, neither the recognition nor the love of his adoptive father had eliminated his feeling of not belonging. Whether awake or asleep, the young man struggled with the repercussions of that pitch-dark room he'd been placed alone in right after birth. He both feared and longed for the closeness of other people. That he became an attorney for the weakest, the almost-lost lives, and that over the years he lost case after case and yet kept plodding away, is a fact both understandable and frightening.

In their final year of law school, the two young men got Almind-Enevold as their lecturer. This was in 1982, and the Almighty One had already served as the minister of justice in the previous administration and, for that reason alone, attracted a full house for his monthly lectures at the university. His name invariably inspired quite a few puns—a newspaper cartoonist had by then compared him to the last absolutist monarch who'd surrendered so much power and been such an ordinary man that everyone laughed—though no one dared share those with him. Especially not the remaining Socialists in the department who still defended spectacular armed revolts like those in the Basque region and in Belfast. And these aggressions resurfaced when the last desperate members of the Baader-Meinhof terror cell died in Stammheim Prison in West Germany and the leftists refused to believe the government's claim that they'd killed themselves.

Their teacher, the former minister of justice, had burst into booming laughter: "I was a resistance fighter—a real resistance fighter," he said. "And those pigs down there, they weren't resistance fighters . . . They were nobodies. They took the easy way out, like hares—those cowards had no guts, they couldn't handle it."

His scorn paralyzed the most progressive in the auditorium; they sat petrified in the midst of waves of laughter. One student quit studying law in protest, but he was the only one to take this meaningless stance. The others instinctively realized that the planet had shifted, that the world was changing, and ten years later most of them were incredibly well-fed corporate lawyers, and Stammheim was merely a bad dream, a dark shaft in a youthful mind that had fortunately been covered.

In his third month as lecturer, Almind-Enevold asked the attendees to carefully consider and then list a maximum of seven general traits that they considered irreconcilable with a future career in the legal field.

The seven sins of the lawyer.

Orla's best and only friend, Severin, with his idealistic and principled mind wrote: *Sloth.*

Then he considered a moment and wrote: *Lust for Power.*

Dishonesty.

Greed.

To be on the safe side, he'd shown his list to Orla, who had nodded encouragingly and let him carry on. After all, this was Severin's nature.

Disloyalty.

After that he'd sat quietly for a long time, contemplating his final two words, occasionally glancing at Orla, who sat utterly motionless—like a dead man—with his pen in his mouth and an absentminded expression etched on his face.

Arrogance.

He stole a final glance at Orla, who had yet to write a single letter on the page, then completed his list with an obviously negative character trait that he'd nearly forgotten: *Insensitivity.*

Orla sat sucking on his pen right until Almind-Enevold cleared his throat and asked if everyone was done. With a quick movement of his strong wrist, Orla wrote a single word on his sheet.

When the former minister of justice later looked at the students' lists, he smiled and nodded with satisfaction. His preferred student had written only one word:

Indecisiveness.

Nothing else.

His old pal Carl Malle had been right—he hadn't exaggerated. This was how this boy was put together, just as he had been at that age.

A month later, following a lecture, Ole Almind-Enevold invited his favorite student to dinner at the Ristorante Italiano on Fiolstræde. Orla ate a shrimp pizza while his teacher spooned through a bowl of tomato soup and peppered him with questions about his upbringing and his view of Denmark and the nation's future.

When Orla got back to Regensen that evening, Severin rushed down the stairs from his room and met him in the courtyard where the giant linden tree stood.

Severin grabbed hold of Orla without knowing the world had changed. "What happened?" he almost shouted. "What did he want? Did he offer you a job?"

It was their senior year, and it was a reasonable question, but Orla did not feel like replying. "If he did, you can have it," he said.

"If he *did* . . . ? You must know whether he—"

"He asked me a lot of questions," Orla said abruptly.

Severin's eyes were nearly leaping out of his head behind his eyeglasses. "What kind of questions?"

Orla made a deprecating gesture with his hand, the same that had so calmly written the one character trait that a career lawyer had to renounce: *Indecisiveness.* "They weren't about law or even my studies."

"But you were gone for two and a half hours!" Severin's objection was logical.

Orla put down his bag on the cobblestones and sat on one of the white benches under the linden tree: "All right, then. He asked me whether I knew you'd been in the same orphanage as I when we were little." He glanced up into the crown of the tree, letting each of his words fall like tiny bombs over Severin's head.

"What?" Severin suddenly grew pale.

"He said you were in an orphanage called Kongslund—in Skodsborg—in the early sixties, like me. Is that true?"

Severin's arms fell to his sides. It was a cool fall day, and the breeze made a single leaf dance about his feet before it settled, absurdly, on his shoe.

With an inexplicable intensity, Orla said, "You never told me you're adopted—but you are?"

"Yes."

"You could have told me." The anger. The former justice minister's revelation at the restaurant had shocked him, and it was in that second—sitting across from Almind-Enevold—that decisiveness had actually struck him.

"Yes." Severin's answer hung in the air.

"But you didn't tell me."

"My mother told me before I started school," said Severin, as though that explained his silence many years later. He stopped and shook his left foot, but the leaf stayed put. He stomped the cobblestones.

"Did they pick you up at Kongslund?"

"Yes. But how did he know about you?"

"I told him about it myself . . . that my mother had placed me in Skodsborg the first year after my birth. Then he laughed and said he already knew. And then he told me about you."

"But . . . how?" Severin's eyes were glossy. And he fell silent. The leaf was gone.

"He said he'd known the matron at Kongslund for decades. When he was young he helped out in Mother's Aid Society. They handled the adoptions in the 1960s. The man has a photographic memory . . . He says he remembers every single name he saw there. We were there during the same period."

"That sounds . . ." Severin stalled again, studying the tips of his shoes.

"Like a coincidence . . . that might not have been," Orla said. His anger had returned.

"But what was he doing for Mother's Aid Society?"

"He was an attorney. He worked in the social services, with the weakest members of society. He's known the governesses at Kongslund for many years. He worked with them in the Resistance."

That night they sat under Mille's flattened, outstretched skin, and for the first time, Severin talked about his parents. His adoptive father was a glazier by the name of Erling, and his mother was a Swede named Britt. Before Severin was born, they'd had a little son named Hasse who'd died when he was only six years old.

"He walked onto Gladsaxe Road and was run over by a twenty-ton semi that had swung onto Laugaards Boulevard." Severin looked as though he were about to cry.

The semi had hit the boy who'd stopped in the middle of the road (everyone in Severin's family had a tendency to get lost in their own thoughts), and it had run him over with all four sets of its right-side wheels. The shopping bag Hasse had been carrying lay on the road, all the goods intact. Even a large jar of pickled beets had made it through. Now this bloodstained shopping bag lay in a locked drawer in Britt's bedroom; her husband had never been able to open the drawer and remove the brutal keepsake. Hasse had been their only chance—Britt had suffered from preeclampsia and had almost died delivering the little boy. Since she was sterile, she was unable to remake Hasse, and she withdrew into a cocoon of shock and despair. She just sat quietly by the window facing the playground between the yellow tenement houses, dreaming so intensely of her childhood landscape, the edge of a Swedish forest where foal grazed, that all eyes were drawn to her.

These were the foal the Master of all of life's coincidences had selected as his toys while he constructed the disaster that would later afflict Severin.

For months Britt sat staring, smiling bitterly at God and repeating—slowly again and again—that it wasn't His fault. But of course it was. And then Erling knew what he had to do. They had been approved for adoption relatively quickly, which at that time was about three years, and it was in this way that Severin entered this ghost family—where another boy's spirit continued to wander, lost in thought in the middle of the road, holding a bloodstained shopping bag.

Orla was shocked to hear his friend's story. "You'd think adults would be more . . . adult," he stammered. But Severin just laughed, spilling red wine on his shirt. Again, Orla felt the anger that Almind-Enevold's revelation had triggered.

Erling had picked up little Severin—who at Kongslund was referred to as Buster after a popular actor in *Circus Buster*—and driven him home in his company truck. He had four thick window panes on the truck bed that were to be delivered to a wholesaler in Hellerup. While Severin slept on the back seat, he installed the four panes in the posh villa and drank a beer with the wholesaler. In a field behind the house, four gray horses were galloping around, and this was no doubt how Severin's adoptive father first got the idea for the most important barter of his life.

I think it was his generous mind that decided the matter. In his spare time, he was a bit of a performer: he'd once exchanged two skylight windows for a unicycle that he could ride for a good fifty feet while juggling two blue polka-dotted balls. Despite Severin's arrival, Britt continued to sit by the window, depressed, and there seemed to be nothing that could free her. One day, when Severin was seven years old, his father returned from boozing—a little later than normally—with a real live horse. He wandered down Maglegaards Boulevard and around the corner, pulling a large gray gelding that startled at the cluster of children. Britt stared down at him from the open kitchen window. For once she wasn't the one drawing the attention of the neighbors.

"Look what I got for you," he shouted to her, and the stench of Bavarian beer could have paralyzed anyone close by.

There came no response from the kitchen window.

"No worries, Britt," he continued reassuringly. "I didn't buy it . . . I bartered with the wholesaler."

"And what did you have to give him?" Britt asked, her Swedish vowels trembling as she instinctively clutched Severin, because she couldn't imagine which of their meager possessions could have been offered in exchange for a horse.

"I gave him the truck! What else?" Erling roared in drunken overeagerness, laughing so hard the echo bounced back and forth several times between the apartment buildings. "It wasn't worth anything anyway!"

"You idiot!" For the first time since Hasse's death, Britt raised her voice. "How are you going to run your business now?"

Erling froze—but only for a second—as if, in his rush to acquire the horse, he'd forgotten how fragile and heavy solid glass windows are, how unfit for travel by horse. But that's how Severin's father was: impulsive and brave, especially when beer was involved; never aggressive but soft and tender, reasonable, magnanimous, generous, compassionate, and practical—and above all, spontaneous when it came to people who made good offers.

The moment he'd met the wholesaler and seen the four beautiful gray horses, he'd thought only of Britt, who'd always dreamed of her Swedish home, telling him of the little foals on the field—foals that Hasse would have ridden if he hadn't stopped on the road, hesitating with a jar of beets in his shopping bag. With a lump in his throat—made worse by the beer—he remembered how she'd bought a poster of Pippi Longstocking sitting on a horse's back and hung it over little Hasse's bed, crying as she did so. This had been a year after his death.

"But where are we going to put it?" Britt asked anxiously through the kitchen window. She stood in a floral dress with short sleeves, and her long, curly hair fluttered in the breeze like a Hollywood film star's.

"In the basement," Severin's father whispered at the window, though loud enough that everyone heard. "At night, it'll stay in our storage space. There's plenty of room, and we'll put down grass and peat and warm blankets. Don't you think I've thought it through?"

Britt considered this for a moment and then nodded at her husband. "You have to promise to walk it in the wetlands everyday—otherwise it'll perish from claustrophobia."

Erling smiled. The Swedish lilt in her voice made it clear that the echo from the deep woods had done its job.

Instinctively, Orla gazed up at the walls in Severin's dorm room—but there was nothing resembling a horse head or a hood or a tuft of a mane, so perhaps the animal had survived its strange encounter with the generous family. But, of course, complaints started to pour in, and the janitor, Mr. Johansen, showed up with his half-grown son Kjeld by his side, reciting the many anonymous tips from upset neighbors: complaints about horse droppings and the smell in the basement, stories of children frightened when the nag loped around the playground, and finally, a reminder that it was generally not allowed to keep a horse in an apartment building. This was a few weeks before Kjeld's final ride, which brought the police into it, convincing Erling that he'd lost the battle. After quite a few beers, he persuaded the wholesaler to trade back. A truck for the horse.

Orla sat baffled, listening to the thin boy with the big head. He had a hard time connecting his good manners with the absurd acts of his adoptive father.

"But we aren't really related, you know." Severin read his mind again. "Strictly speaking, we were born into very different families and were just brought together . . . by Hasse."

Orla struggled to comprehend that something so interesting and peculiar had happened on the other side of the hawthorn—in the world he'd only ever known when a scream rose into the red sky at night, the result of his rock finding its target.

"I have a scar right here—where you hit me," Severin said, putting a slender index finger on a small depression above his left eye.

Then he lifted his glass and studied his reflection in it. "Come to think of it, it's strange that they wanted me. With this grimace I was born with."

"Grimace?"

"Yes. I've never been able to smile, really." Severin took a drink of his wine and looked at Orla. "Look for yourself." He smiled sadly. "You see?"

"See what?"

"That my face is made this way. That I can't actually smile."

Orla sat quietly as the God of Friendship and Camaraderie suddenly put a cold finger between the boy's shoulder blades, causing him to tilt his torso forward and stiffen into a nearly impossible position.

"It doesn't matter now. I smile when I want to, even if nobody can tell." He smiled and looked directly into Orla's eyes. Then he lowered his voice. "I had no idea they weren't my real parents for the first six years of my life. When I learned the truth, I was sitting on a small stool in the hallway outside my parents' kitchen, and my mother was putting Carmen curlers in her hair. Suddenly she said, 'By the way, we're not your real parents, Severin. They disappeared right after you were born and then we became your parents.' I remember thinking that she'd done a good job of it"—he looked at himself again in his glass—"in just a few clearly worded sentences."

Orla felt the anger rise up in him again.

"I asked a few questions about minor details," Severin continued, "but I didn't really take it that hard. When my dad got home, I ran to him shouting, 'You aren't even my real dad!' And I'll never forget that because he started crying and said, 'Yes, Severin, I am your father.' But then I said, 'Mom told me I have another father.' And then he cried even more."

After drinking most of the bottle of red wine, Severin's eyes shone. "They lost their real child, and then they got me. They'd had a son, but I was a stranger. It was terribly confusing. My dad put me on his lap and said, 'No, I am not your biological father, but I am still your father, and I love you more than anything in the world. I want you to know that you'll never want for anything.' But already that first night I wondered what my real parents looked like—something had changed, but I wasn't sure what. In reality . . ." Severin sniffled and then paused. Reality would have to wait.

Orla studied him through squinting eyes.

Severin took another gulp of wine.

Again, Orla felt flushed with an anger that he knew would destroy their friendship. "They didn't look like you . . . Britt and Erling?"

"Not at all."

"Neither physically nor psychologically?"

"No. They're tall and big boned. And I'm like this."

Orla thought of his father, whom he couldn't really think about because, like Severin's smile, he existed only in an invisible world.

"Our names are ugly, don't you think? Severin and Orla. They always teased me at the Kennedy public school in Høje Gladsaxe. 'Severin, Severin, you smell like gasoline,' all the boys shouted." He laughed, drooling a little.

Orla nodded. He knew only too well the bullies in Denmark's first concrete ghetto that, curiously enough, had been named after the assassinated American president.

Severin continued, "It was all in Hasse's spirit—finding an orphaned child. They wanted to honor his memory with a good deed." A single red drop resembling blood sat in the corner of his mouth. "I went to a salon with my mother, I remember, and the hairdresser said, 'You have your mother's hair, little buddy.' My mother's fingers grew ice cold, and she said, 'That is not the case.'"

Severin tried to force his red lips into a smile. "The entire family went along with the charade—all of it—for the sake of Hasse's memory." He stood and walked around the table unsteadily, toward Mille, whose skin hung at eye level. He raised his hand and touched the pelt's small gray nails with his thumb and index fingers. "They only got me . . ."—he cupped his hand around a paw, and the nails stuck out between his fingers—". . . they only got me to keep the memory of my damn brother alive. Forever. It's a paradox, isn't it? Like in a courtroom? You have to speak the truth, yet you turn your back on the audience. We're completely insensitive, aren't we? That's our curse. It's not because we're adopted, but because we were there—at Kongslund."

"I'm not adopted," Orla said. "My mother just couldn't take care of me that first year."

"Of course you are."

"Did you ever find your biological parents?"

"I have their names and numbers. We visited the orphanage, and there was a girl named Marie . . . She gave me the names. I've called them, but I always hang up before they answer the phone. I don't have the courage."

Severin suddenly lay down on the bed and fell asleep, the wine doing its job.

After thinking about Severin's story for some time, Orla noticed his friend's black address book on the bedside table. He picked it up and opened it. For reasons not wholly clear to him at the time, he felt no sympathy for the thin boy from the yellow apartment buildings. He knew exactly where Severin would have listed the two most important numbers in his life—under *M* and *F*. How banal.

He went to the dorm pay phone—it was 3:00 a.m.—and looked at the little book with the six-digit number, which, according to Marie, belonged to Severin's biological father. It was strange that the girl seemed to have access to such confidential information. The man lived in the Copenhagen area.

The telephone booth at Regensen was half-concealed behind the green door leading to the courtyard, and Orla saw the linden tree through a narrow window. He dialed the number; it took a long time before someone answered. "Yes?" a drowsy man finally answered.

"Was it a good screw?"

"What?" the voice said, a little more awake. "Who is this?"

"Skodsborg 1961. Was it *nice* to just walk away and forget all about the kid?"

"Who is this?"

"Was it nice to just walk away and become father to another son and another woman's children?"

"What the hell!?"

"Do you ever think about your first born? Would you like his number? No, I guess you don't. We ought to just leave it alone. We need to forget the past, right?" Orla slammed the receiver down. He leaned forward and looked into the courtyard. In a few hours the girls from his dormitory association would begin setting the table for the Sunday lunch under the linden tree. The Salvation Girl would laugh. Her eyes were always clear and wide; she reminded Orla of the Sørensen girl, the one who'd asked him to eat the blue licorice candy.

He had only slept a few hours when he woke late the next morning. He walked down to the pay phone wearing a robe and dialed the other number from Severin's book.

"Hello, this is Pia," said a rather young voice.

"Is Susanne your mother?"

"Yes . . . Who is this?"

"Just tell her I said hello, and that she forgot a child. A long time ago, but nevertheless. In Skodsborg. Just tell her she forgot a little boy far, far away—but that he's still waiting for her. If she's got time, that is."

Orla hung up. He rested his forehead on the window. He saw Severin out there under the linden tree, suffering, hungover. The Salvation Girl leaned over the table as she sliced a hunk of sausage on a thick wooden cutting board; she laughed, putting a hand on Severin's arm. Then they sang a harvest psalm, their voices distant. Orla remained in the booth, listening. He could barely hear the words: *The leaves are falling everywhere.*

But leaves don't just fall. They wilt and fade and no longer protect you from the rain.

Then he dialed a third number, and this time he heard his mother's voice—a little startled, as though she'd had a crazy premonition that something terrible was about to unfold—but Orla let the silence hang in the air, imagining the distance between them: approximately 3 miles, 805 yards, and 23 inches—if none of them moved.

He listened to her breathing. "Hello?" she said.

And then, with trepidation: "Is that you, Orla?"

He put a hand over the receiver and then removed it. A gob of spit seeped from his puckered lips into the shiny, black plastic funnel; he glanced at the water lily, and the eye stared back at him, terrified. He couldn't ask the question. The girl under the linden tree laughed; she sang like an angel. Later that day he invited Severin and the Salvation Girl to his room. She had been raised Catholic, fleeing her home in Søllerød, her only possessions a plastic bag stuffed with Alice Cooper and Black Sabbath albums. It hadn't ruined her good spirit, though. As they walked up the stairs, she sang about Jesus and all the joy he would bring those who asked for forgiveness.

"Let's make a confession booth for all of us guilt-ridden Regensen residents!" Orla shouted.

Severin looked at him with his strange non-smile, and perhaps it was this peculiar idea that prolonged their doomed friendship for a few weeks.

Out of plywood, the three friends built a booth as tall as a man, cut a hole in one side, and covered the opening with a piece of thick black cloth. They took turns sitting on a stool inside the box, listening to each other's confessions.

They were only allowed to respond to the confession with the phrase "I understand." (The exact phrase that idealistic childcare workers and social commentators would've said regardless of the sin committed.)

Severin and the Salvation Girl told anecdotes about their sinful drinking at the dormitory, and Orla intoned, "I understand."

But when his turn came, the atmosphere in the room suddenly changed. With his chunky nose sniffling and his thick lips moving, Orla described sights so strange that both Severin and the Salvation Girl began to find the game frightening. Not even a Catholic runaway had experienced anything like this, and finally they both declined to participate in any more confessions, citing essay writing and headaches. Orla, filled with a rage he couldn't control, knocked late one Friday night on Severin's door. "You need to confess—now!" he growled. Severin saw Orla's red eyes and went along with him. This would be the last time, and he would tell the secret he understood Orla sensed.

"You remember I told you about my father's horse," he said when he'd positioned himself in the box.

The consoler behind the curtain did not reply.

"Something happened to that horse that I didn't tell you, or rather to the boy who rode it. Kjeld, the janitor's son . . ." Severin hesitated for a moment. "He was the ugliest, meanest boy I've ever met, but he was crazy about that horse, and when we took it to the wetlands to graze, he plodded along after us. One day I gave him permission to ride the horse.

I don't know what got into it, but it ran like hell. At full speed. Kjeld clutched the mane, screaming. Right by the rushes in the creek, the horse stopped abruptly, and Kjeld flew into the air, landing on his head on the big boulder. You know the big boulder there. He lay in the grass, his eyes closed, and I remember looking at him. He had blood on his cheeks and forehead, and I just stood there, feeling so much joy. It felt good. He was in the hospital for three weeks before he was discharged, but he wasn't the same person anymore, and a couple of months later, he passed out and was taken away. A few weeks after that we learned he'd died."

He went quiet for a moment. "Like Hasse," he confessed.

Now Orla's voice rose in a sharp, commanding tone as if Severin had placed too heavy a burden on himself. "I understand. It wasn't *your* fault at all."

"I haven't come to the point yet . . . I knew that horse was feral. I knew Kjeld might get hurt. I'd tried to ride it myself, after all. I wanted it to be a real Indian horse, but I too had been thrown off. It was wild and completely unmanageable. I forced it to stand still until he could get on, then I made sure he held the mane tightly, so he would be able to ride for a little bit, and so the horse would have time to speed up before tossing him off. I *hoped* he would get hurt, and I've never wished for anything that strongly." Severin cleared his throat. "At least that he would get hurt. But that he would die . . ."

It sounded as though he was about to start crying.

"You wanted him to die." The consoler did not ask a question.

"I remember . . . he was like . . . just like a little boy lying there," Severin cried.

"I understand," Orla said. His voice through the curtain was clear. "I understand." There was no doubt he understood.

Like Hasse.

"I learned that day that sometimes you feel like killing someone— and that you might do it too," Severin said. "This isn't something you normally tell anyone."

"No."

"Did *you* ever . . . ?"

"No."

The curtain fluttered a little, or maybe it was just the breeze from St. Kannikestræde.

Severin stood and left the homemade confessional. He never returned to it, and a month later, he started dating the Salvation Girl. The confession booth stood unused in a corner of Orla's room.

Or so he thought.

But Orla still had a story, and he no longer had anyone to tell it to. In place of Severin, he put an old Tandberg device behind the curtain. It could record nonstop for three hours. If anyone could have accessed the tapes (they were responsibly locked up in a big oak cabinet), they would have been even more shocked than Severin and the Salvation Girl. Because, alone in the dark, Orla the Weirdo saw no need to reconcile the skepticism of the world or avoid its judgment. Now he was the Father, the Sinner, and the Condemner; and when everyone else in the dormitory was asleep, he glided smoothly from one role to the other as he spoke to the old recorder:

I understand, said the Father. And the Sinner shouted, *Don't forsake me!* But there came no response, and the Condemner sat in the background making sure that the silence was documented.

Forgive me, the Sinner whispered.

The Father remained silent.

Orla heard the silence—recorded onto the spools, where it wound around itself and went deeper and deeper, yard by yard.

No man is an island, the Father said.

Orla answered, *I want to confess that I've asked Almind-Enevold whether he can get me a position in the ministry when I graduate.* Then there was silence for a long time, and you could almost see Orla smile and drink from his wine. *I can start this summer.*

For about a minute the room was quiet, the silence broken only by the muted whirring from the rotating coils of tape. Then the Father's voice: *You have sinned. But you have paid for your sin by losing your friendship with Severin, and one cannot ask for more.*

The following weekend, Orla took his leave without telling Severin or the other residents about his plans. The driver of the moving company had a daughter who loved puppet theater, and Orla gave her the peculiar confessional booth.

Two months later he began working as an official in the ministry then considered the finest and most honorable: the Ministry of Justice at Slotsholm. This was the first step on the career path of any ambitious attorney.

He moved into a room on Østerbrogade with a view of Hotel Østerport and the train tracks. He came home late at night and rose early in the morning. During the weekends, he practiced a new ritual: around midnight he sank into his armchair, relaxing completely. Inch by inch he cleansed his mind of internal disturbances, peeling off first the words, then thoughts, and finally feelings, until he found himself in total darkness under a smooth mother-of-pearl cupola that felt and sounded like the inside of a conch—like the one his mother had once given him when he was a child, which retained the sound of the surf from the sea far out west.

Only at this point would he calmly open the lid to his subconsciousness and let all the images from Glee Court and the wetlands stream into the room. The torn butterfly wings, the eye on the water lily, the black hole in the dead giant's face that disappeared into the darkness. Lighting three candles, he would sit in this state, in the same position, until the last wick had curled up, extinguished. He let the images dance around his lit face while the whistling wind became whispering voices—distant and powerless—and he let them vanish.

Orla often finished the ritual by calling Severin's biological father or mother, and the voices he heard on the other end of the line were sleepy, tinny. He never said a word, simply left the receiver next to the extinguished candles for thirty seconds or so, then hung up.

One night he lost consciousness and slipped into the same invisibility he'd mastered in his high-school days. A puff of wind put out the three candles in front of him, and he suddenly woke and saw himself sitting there, alone in a chair, hunched like an angular black bird. At that moment he turned ice cold inside and couldn't breathe: the terror exploded deep inside him; panic rushed through his nervous system; somebody had left him alone with himself, inside his own body, and, even worse, he couldn't get out. He couldn't live.

He leaped from the chair and ran around, bewildered, touching the walls, his hands shaking, emitting queer little sniffling sounds he'd never heard before. He was two individuals, locked into one—and his head was about to explode: *no, no, no—no-no-no-no-no-no-no-no!* He heard the panicky sound of his own heartbeat and the wings that desperately thumped against the glass.

Slowly, the claustrophobic pressure lifted from his eyes, and he sank to the floor exhausted. He couldn't feel his arms.

The incident repeated itself a couple of weeks later, and this time his reaction scared him so badly that he turned to a more outward-facing ritual. In the beginning he masturbated in the darkness of his room—without moving or touching himself, just on the power of imagination, thinking about the girls working in the department. After a few months he was so good at it that he could do it in the bus on his way home from Slotsholm, sitting by the window with his face turned away, staring at the pedestrians who passed by unaware. He imagined the young law intern bent in an awkward position over a desk, in a powerful embrace, and he would come before the bus had made it past Hotel Østerport, sometimes even before they'd made it halfway down Bredgade.

When the anonymous letter arrived, he hadn't seen Severin in fifteen years.

But the old feelings from his days at Regensen resurfaced: tenderness, longing, anger—and something even deeper that no one dared name, not even the bearded men who had tried to analyze his mind when they'd discovered the one-eyed Fool in the creek.

On the fifth day after the letter's arrival, he sat in the ministry, waiting for Severin's call.

13

THE BLUE ELEPHANTS

May 10, 2008

The anniversary was fast approaching—only three days left now—and I could feel the tension that had gotten hold of the ministry and the press, which was chasing the scandalous story of the possible fall of Kongslund. The entire nation followed along. It looked as though no one could stop the process.

Many years ago, one night before the departure of another Kongslund child, just before the first verses of the old song about the blue elephants would be sung, I asked Magna a question I'd always been curious about: "How many verses are there in that song?"

"How many do you think?" my foster mother replied.

"Two thousand nine hundred and seventy-three," I said without hesitating—and I noticed the startled look in her eyes, as though she thought that little girls like me shouldn't even know such large numbers. Then she said: "Our song will go on forever, Marie. Long after you and I are gone."

I sank under the weight of this tremendous confidence, though it was not an answer that reassured me in the least.

* * *

The follow-up article to the Kongslund story appeared on page three of *Independent Weekend*, and it was so short that one flat hand could hide it, a fact that had not escaped the notice of Knud Taasing's displeased editor.

He knew they risked having the Kongslund Affair fizzle out before it even got going.

It was a cool day. The wind whipped from City Hall Square down Hans Christian Andersen Boulevard, farther down around the corner by Kalvebod Brygge, and along the harbor front, where the newspaper house with all its grandiose ideals about freedom, equality, and tolerance had once, paradoxically enough, marked the end of the hippie encampment in the houseboats along Tågernes Kaj. They'd all been removed by the police without a second thought. The black five-story building that ran along the harbor basin had always reminded Knud of an oversized building block absentmindedly tossed by a child's clumsy hand.

"If you didn't have a reputation, nothing would have ever come of this case," the editor finally said after several long moments of silence. Taasing knew his boss was dissatisfied with the day's lead story: "Former Matron Silent About the Kongslund Affair." While he couldn't deny that Knud had once been a star, he'd never considered his reporter's personal involvement in cases professionally acceptable.

That same morning, Channel DK had aired the first commercial spot, advertising its documentary about Kongslund, to be broadcast May 12 at 8:00 p.m. Just two days from now.

"Have they got anything we don't?" the editor asked.

"I don't know," Taasing said, staring at the empty cigarette pack he'd squashed into a little green-and-white ball. The other journalists were quiet, an expression of the kind of resignation that had recently infused these meeting held around the conference table in the giant editorial office. Maybe the run-off idealists had uttered a vindictive curse on their way out, because nothing seemed to go right for the ailing newspaper. The life force seeped from the editorial staff in small but significant splashes as circulation continued to shrink nearly as quickly as the dwindling staff; the editor of domestic news was only the most recent victim of the paper's hemorrhaging finances.

Nils Jensen entered the room and stood beside one of the green mobile walls that was too unsteady to lean on. His Nikon camera was slung over one shoulder.

"That anniversary party—can we get anything out of that?" the editorial chief asked. "I think the big *revelation* is wishful thinking. We have to acknowledge that it isn't going to happen."

Taasing flicked the crumpled cigarette pack off the edge of the table. "I disagree. But someone *is* putting obstacles in my way." It sounded strangely formal. "I can't get through to the Family Council, what used to be called the Civil Registry. I've put in several requests for access to the old archives, employee contracts, salary payments—anything they have—so I can locate former employees. But someone is blocking it."

"Employees who are probably long since deceased, since no one has contacted us offering to help," said the editor, who hadn't been hired for his talent in story development but on his promise to raise productivity by cutting overhead.

"Or possibly because they're not among the loyal readers of this newspaper, if we've still got any of those," Taasing responded.

The editor's hands tightened into fists. "You can spare us those kinds of remarks, Taasing." He glanced at the photographer, whom everyone knew had developed a kind of friendship with the journalist, but Nils Jensen just stared at the floor.

"We've confirmed that both the form and the baby socks date to that time at Kongslund. And we're going to see two social workers who worked at Mother's Aid Society then. They may be able to throw some light on what went on at Kongslund in the sixties. That's our story for tomorrow," Knud said.

"And what have they got to say, these two ladies . . . the social workers?"

"I haven't pumped them on the phone, of course," Taasing replied, staring at the editor over the rim of his glasses. "That would be extraordinarily foolish."

"Well, it certainly ensures that we have no idea what kind of story we've got for tomorrow—if there even is one."

The twelve journalists around the conference table all smiled nervously at the editor's last quip.

"What it ensures is that they won't be afraid—or talk to anyone who might persuade them to keep quiet." Taasing stood abruptly. "No wonder this newspaper is going under. He cast a glance at the old panoptical boardroom full of former youth activists and union organizers. "Maybe the fine gentlemen up there don't think it's a good idea to bother their old friends in the party and in the administration. Maybe they still want us to be a party newspaper that will do anything to keep its ties to power intact."

The editor rose so quickly that he knocked his chair over. "Our editorial decisions are based on *relevance*. You know that."

"Yes, but relevance has eyes and ears, and it understands, better than anyone, when moving in a certain direction is dangerous."

"You were admired once, Taasing—admired by me too—but then something happened, didn't it? Maybe—and let me make it very clear that I mean *maybe*—you're the one blocking the story you seem to have such high expectations of." The editor paused and took a deep breath before continuing. "Because who the hell dares to believe a story coming from a man who cost two children their lives? Maybe *that's* the message I'm getting from below, above, and in my gut. Who the hell dares stake an entire newspaper on that foundation?"

Taasing had grown pale, and it seemed as though all the oxygen had been sucked from the room. "I see."

The words fell from his lips and were gone in a second.

Then a voice said reassuringly, "We'll get a story out of it for tomorrow." It was the photographer, who was normally silent, especially with so many journalists present.

They all looked up in surprise.

Nils Jensen, a man who typically spoke only in images and who'd called the story sensationalist, continued, "As long as Channel DK is on it, people will retain their interest—until the anniversary—and maybe something will happen that no one anticipates."

Even he seemed surprised by his statement. But it was unclear whether this was the result of his unexpected behavior or because he'd had a revelation.

* * *

The sound technician turned off the engine, opened the van door, climbed out, and looked around.

Peter Trøst stayed in the backseat for a moment. Even though the producers of the competing television stations demanded ever more efficiency on location and assigned fewer and fewer people to each news team, the coordinator of news and entertainment at Channel DK still had a sound technician, a cameraman, and a production assistant, like in the good old days.

Closing his eyes, Peter leaned back. Here in the van, immediately before recording, he'd always felt in his element. He enjoyed the smell of the leather and rubber, the buzzing machines, and the cigarette smoke that hung in the air—the sense that everything was turned on and ready for action. Channel DK's retrofitted Chevrolet was nicer and more expensive than most vans in the business, and it had more technology and transmission power than any other TV van in the country, sponsored as it was by the generous parent station in the United States.

He got out and closed the door—slowly, almost inaudibly, as if he were afraid to awaken a creature sleeping in the bushes under the beech trees, but there was no movement and no one in sight.

He looked up. The house stood as it had the last time he'd visited it, just a few weeks after his sixteenth birthday. As usual, his mother had grabbed his hand and said, in a throaty voice, "This was your very first home, Peter. Don't ever forget that." For much of his life, his parents had tried to do nothing but forget that fact.

The evening before that visit, he'd been sitting in the villa in Rungsted with his mother, following a television report from Rebild Bakker, where a group of activists from a political theater company named Solvognen had dressed up as Indians, donned full war paint, and stormed the bourgeois audience celebrating America's Independence Day. It was his first realization that a simple idea translated into action—and from there to images—could open the television portal wide and reach every nook and cranny of the nation. It wasn't the action itself that was the miracle, but the fact that the world received it so unconditionally. The day he visited Kongslund for the last time was the day he decided to become a television reporter.

He signaled to the sound technician, who put out his cigarette. The production assistant was already knocking on the orphanage's front door, even though there was a doorbell. The pounding echoed through the villa's ivy-clad soul.

According to Magna, Peter had been born at the Rigshospital by an unknown woman who'd delivered him at about 7:00 p.m. and then allowed him to be wheeled immediately away. They'd put him in a bed, in absolute darkness, as though he were a piece of fine clothing too fragile to be touched. They'd left him in a world with neither beginning nor end, where you'd need very good ears to hear the meek workings of Our Lord on the other side of the wall.

Nine months later he'd been adopted, and they gave him the name Peter, the middle name Trøst, and the last name Jochumsen. After he'd completed his journalism degree, he began using down-to-earth names because, at the time, it benefitted one's career to seem like a man of the people, a representative of the working class. Today, most Danes knew him simply by Trøst. Jochumsen had become Jørgensen though he didn't use that name, and it was unlikely that anyone knew of his path from the orphanage to the mansion, because he'd always refused to answer questions about his private life.

Early on, his mother had developed a predilection for the most fragile and delicate plants. Everywhere she planted rare trees and bushes that were supported by a stick or tied with a string to reach the rays of the sun: black poplars, pond cypresses, whitethorn, Japanese cherry trees, a Turkish maple with red summer buds. As a result, his mother banned all common childhood activities like soccer, kite flying, Frisbee, bow and arrow, and even running in the yard, forcing her only son to remain on the bench in the shade of the elm. And this is where he first discussed with My the accusations Principal Nordal had made against him.

Immediately following the scandal, My's father grew more taciturn than ever. Principal Nordal's victory had weighed down his otherwise straight back, and by winter he was curled up like a glazed stalk of bulrush. It had shocked My to witness the transformation; for years he'd thought that his father was invincible, unbreakable. Sitting on the bench, he confided to Peter the most precious experience of his young life.

"When a man . . . like my father . . . dreams of getting ahead in the world, he builds his dream around a few words, and he keeps repeating them in his head. I've heard my father at night, talking in his sleep."

Peter looked at his friend and felt the creeping agitation that arises between people when a problem cannot be resolved.

"Those words are like a spine," My continued. "They run through the body and keep it standing; they keep the bones and muscles in their place, so those words have to be made of the best and strongest material you can find." He spoke almost like an adult. "Hjalmar thought the strongest and best material was stubbornness and pride . . . like in the books." He'd begun calling his father by his first name when he wasn't present.

He shook his head and tried to make sense of this complex train of thought. "The minute he needed those words, he couldn't remember them." He gazed through the elm canopy at the blue sky. "You know what I mean?"

Peter just stared at his friend. He wasn't used to such philosophical insight from My, who had grown up in an almost wordless home. He wanted to ask, "But what is the best material then?" Instead he said nothing.

"The words weren't real," My said. "They just sounded good."

They sat for several minutes in silence.

"'Don't ever give up!' That's what he said. 'Don't ever give up!'" My stared at his hands as though he could see the words right there, between his fingers.

Peter understood. When Hjalmar simply gave up without a struggle, it had been a shock.

"The best material . . ." My hesitated. "The best material is to feel good enough," was all he said, and a tear appeared on his cheek, like a shiny little insect. Now, more than thirty years later, Peter remembered the answer and the fear he felt upon hearing My's very simple description of the gate to any human being's destruction.

He reacted to that simple calling the only way he knew how.

The day the big tabloid reported Principal Nordal's death—a couple of weeks after the linden tree had been sawed down—My's father looked up just once from his copy of *The People*. The two boys were eating Christmas goodies at the table, and he met and held his son's gaze for just a few seconds before slipping back to his crushed world where shame was king.

Peter never revealed his secret to My. The two never spoke about what happened. If their friendship were to continue, it would have to wait.

And as Fate tends to do, it put such postponements off forever.

* * *

The production assistant had called his name out loud, probably a few times, because she now sounded a little worried. A tall woman stood on the front stairs, greeting him with a smile as if they'd known each other for a long time.

Maybe it was just a reaction to his fame.

"Susanne Ingemann," said the woman and curtsied.

It seemed odd to him but also fascinating; she *curtsied* as though they were figures from the nineteenth century, heading upstairs to a ballroom in a fairy-tale castle.

"You've been here before," she said in response to his puzzled look. With her left hand, she waved him into the old house. She wore a green dress and white sandals, and her reddish-brown hair was gathered in a barrette.

He remembered the hallway and the wide white staircase that led to the private chambers—where the matron and her assistants lived—and he remembered the black-and-white photographs by the fireplace, dating all the way back to 1936 and featuring all the children who'd passed through those high-ceilinged rooms at the orphanage.

"When did you last see Kongslund?" Susanne Ingemann asked.

"When I graduated from high school in 1980. As per custom, we drove by horse carriage to Copenhagen. But I didn't come in for a visit."

"Have you spoken with Ms. Ladegaard recently?"

"I've tried calling, but she doesn't answer."

They had tea in the sunroom overlooking the lush green lawn, the beach, and the sound.

"Of course we're not happy about the story in *Independent Weekend*. So if you're interested in a sensational angle, I'm not the right person to ask. I'm concerned with Kongslund the way it is today, and there are no children of famous people here. Quite the contrary."

Her accent was Zealandic, whether from the interior or the western part, he couldn't tell.

"When were you actually adopted?"

"In 1962." He hated that word, *adopted*, which suggested that nothing remained, that nothing could be undone, and that everyone knew it.

"You were born at the Rigshospital, and then you came here shortly after . . . That's how it was for most kids then."

"Yes." For so long Rigshospital had been just a name on a birth certificate that he'd never actually seen. He didn't like to think about it, and he didn't want to be haunted by visions of the darkness that had surrounded him during the first hours of his life. He'd gone back to that hospital more than thirty years later to bring his first child into the world. It was, as far as he knew, the place he'd been born to his unknown mother—and it'd been a fatal act of hubris to return.

Fate woke abruptly. What an opening.

They arrived in the middle of the night and were wheeled into the delivery room. They had access to a tub, body pillows, even a beanbag, which his wife had immediately positioned herself on, moaning. But Peter Trøst had been restless the way journalists are restless when intimacy overshadows the big picture; he wanted to walk around, maybe find a TV broadcasting CNN live from one of the world's hot spots, then return.

He'd met Marianne halfway down the hall, and they'd gone into her office to talk about old days. What an opening. He hadn't expected to see her in this place, as a midwife, and she hadn't expected that he'd be famous (he no longer heard his wife moaning). She laughed. "I was so in love with you in high school," she said with a sudden intimacy that famous people often elicit. The telephone rang, but she ignored it. She was petite and blond and slender under her white smock, and she turned her back to him as she washed some instruments—what an opening. He remembered her dressed as a little white snowball at a Christmas party in high school.

She turned around.

There was a cot in the room where staff could rest. Fate lounged comfortably, almost innocently. And then it happened. It locked the door with one hand and pushed them into each other's field of gravity with the other hand; she looked in surprise at his hands on her, then she gasped deep in her throat, and he knew everything was all right and that she'd entertained the same fantasy he'd had, perhaps the worst fantasy any woman can have (personally and professionally); she wanted to make him forget he was about to become the father of another woman's child.

If he'd had any reservations, they disappeared in the feel of her hot breath as her small body tensed up again and again and her nipples pointed directly at his mouth. She came the second she felt him in her (another result of his fame no doubt), and she screamed—and screamed again—it was as though her screaming went on and on, until she suddenly stiffened in his embrace, pushed him out of her, threw on her white smock, and unlocked the door.

Dazed, he suddenly realized what was happening: a laboring woman was screaming.

Two doctors had been called. They had attempted a cesarean; they tried with oxygen and tubes, and then with threats and prayers and curses, but the child remained dead and limp. It was a boy. He lay on the white sheets, looking exactly like a human being should: innocent, mild, joyful. At the end of its life.

Peter had been full of excuses: he'd just gone to the kiosk; nothing could have been done; we'll try for another.

"I heard another laboring woman scream, and I got scared," his wife said. He didn't respond.

A short while later, they divorced.

"When did they tell you?" Susanne Ingemann said, crossing her legs.

He blinked a few times, brought back to the present. He realized he probably seemed strange to her. He usually hid it so well.

"That you're adopted, I mean," she added.

"They adopted me in 1962, but they didn't tell me until my thirteenth birthday."

"Some people are never told." Susanne looked directly at him. "I sometimes wonder what's best."

He nodded.

"If only parents were better actors. If only they could really identify with the role, then the children would never need to know about the sins of the past. It's the *bad acting* that causes all the crap," she said.

Peter was taken aback by her brutal choice of words. Her voice was muted. She lived alone, his researchers had told him. She used the old matron's apartment upstairs as her private quarters, but she also owned a small row house in Christiansgave.

"How were your parents?" she asked, though he was the one who was supposed to ask the questions.

"Well, we lived in Rungsted," he began a little foolishly, as if he were answering a different question. "That's why we visited Skodsborg so often. Back then, I mean. After they told me."

"No traumas?" she asked.

"No," he said. "None visible."

She smiled.

He relaxed a little. Of course he was damaged. He'd always known that. He saw his daughters from his second marriage approximately twice a year, he had no friends, and he visited his adoptive parents as infrequently as possible. "I was spoiled. My mother was a homemaker.

It was the kind of childhood where the most frightening thing that happened was when my pencil broke during the English composition exam in high school."

"Protected against all external dangers." She pronounced each of the words slowly.

"Yes."

He fell silent. Her openness made him shy, and that was a feeling he rarely encountered. On television, those kinds of reactions were encapsulated in a membrane of light and presence and left behind a buzz of static electricity.

"Of course there are areas of Kongslund where you're not allowed to record." She changed the topic abruptly, standing. "One of those is the infant room, but you've been here before . . . and Kongslund might be able to make an exception for a guest with special qualifications."

He rose as well. Her words made him momentarily dizzy. She'd just given him permission to enter the infant room.

It was a strange declaration of confidence.

With the tip of her fingers, she carefully tapped on a blue door in the corridor. A young woman opened it.

"It's unchanged since the sixties."

He stood in the Elephant Room, where it all began. The ceilings were higher than he remembered. Four beds to the right, four to the left, white curtains fluttering in the breeze from the open window. There was no other movement in the room. The walls were covered with the painted figures that gave the room its name: blue, in the very same bright lines that he remembered; hundreds of plump little elephants that seemed to tower over the little Mowglis sleeping under soft, heavy duvets. He examined a sleeping face, the closed eyes and mouth, the white skin and the dark hair. He swayed slightly over the child, unsure of his footing.

She paused in the middle of the room. "Are you feeling all right?"

"Oh, it's nothing. " Peter smiled his TV smile to show that everything was okay. "It's just strange to be back."

Of course that sounded ridiculous.

There must be at least a thousand elephants around him, as though they'd been cloned from the same source. How had they managed to paint so many of them?

Later he stood in the hall again, looking at the black-and-white photographs, but she managed to stand in his line of vision and shepherd him to the door.

"I just wanted to see if I could recognize myself," he said.

"Few can," she said.

"I assume I'm listed in the records you must have here from that time period?" It was an awkward way to inquire into off-limits territory.

She didn't respond.

"Aren't there any records from those years?"

"I don't know. I think the old records have been filed. I certainly don't use them. I imagine that Magna—Ms. Ladegaard—has thrown them out or taken them with her."

"I gather you've read the article in *Independent Weekend* that you were interviewed for?"

"No. And to be honest, I rarely read the papers."

"You're not interested in what's going on? Whether things have happened here that"—he searched for the right words—"that weren't so fortunate?"

"Fortunate?" She laughed suddenly and with great sincerity. "I don't think fortunate is a word that our children associate with their time here, then or now. Fate is a better word for it . . . the finger that points down from above at *you*, giving you the worst possible start to life. Abandoned by your parents right from the start . . ." She grew serious again. "Surely you understand that better than most?"

Peter thought about the blue envelope with its peculiar contents. He'd removed it from his desk drawer after his spat with the Professor and for a split second considered showing it to Susanne Ingemann. Let distress plant itself in her green eyes. He would have liked to see her reaction.

He shrugged. "No, I just thought you'd be curious. It's strange that a former Kongslund orphan received that kind of letter, isn't it? I'm referring to Orla Berntsen."

"I can't comment on that." Her answer was surprisingly formal.

"*And*, on top of that, he works for a man who has been the primary supporter of Kongslund for decades." *That was clumsy*, Peter thought.

"Do you have had any idea what kinds of coincidences occur in a small country like ours?" Susanne Ingemann said, smiling. "Children from Kongslund have met each other later in life in the most peculiar places—without knowing of their shared pasts and without us being able to tell them on account of confidentiality. In some cases, adoptive parents have lived very close to the biological parents without knowing it. People with connections to the orphanage have run into one another in supermarkets and in department stores without having any idea. They've played in the same badminton clubs; they've greeted one another and thought: what an interesting person, I'd like to get to know him. They've even fallen in love, become engaged, and married one another. And never realized a thing." When she smiled, her green eyes gleamed. "It's fascinating, isn't it? Like in the fairy tales?"

"In the world of media, our job is to *eliminate* coincidences." He heard how stilted he sounded.

She laughed. "Are you serious? Well, in that case it's a big tragedy . . . You probably ought to read more Hans Christian Andersen and not waste so much time arranging your material."

"I don't think the anonymous letters were a coincidence—they were sent to certain people for a reason. Nor do I think it's a coincidence that Kongslund's name came up. We just haven't found the connection." He felt like touching her.

Instinctively, she drew away.

"I understand that Magna's foster daughter still lives here?"

"I don't understand what that's got to do with anything. I don't want her filmed."

"No, we wouldn't do that. But I remember she was . . . disabled. I met her when I visited as a boy, and I wonder if I could say hello to her." It sounded just as wrong as everything else he'd said that day.

"She doesn't speak to people. Unless it's a special occasion. She knows you're here, so she must have determined that this wasn't such an occasion." Susanne Ingemann had closed herself off once more.

He'd filmed a single blue elephant in the infant room with a handheld camera, while his crew stood outside in the fading light, waiting for him. He'd picked one that seemed to march over the headboard beside a sleeping child's patch of dark hair; he'd zoomed in and followed its trunk to its wide mouth, the small tusks, and the black eyes.

That was how he planned to open his segment.

Immediately after that, the camera would pan in an arch downward and to the right, capturing the little child in the bed, a cheek, a pillow, a headboard, the window in the background, before fading into darkness.

He sat in the van reviewing the day's recordings. The crew sat on the stairs, smoking. The production assistant whispered to the others, as though afraid to wake the sleeping creatures in the vicinity.

Peter considered calling his segment "The Children from the Elephant Room," if it didn't sound too much like a Tintin story, and opening with the words: "The room with the blue elephants has housed thousands of children, whose lives didn't start out in the best way."

He stopped, let go of the edit button, and leaned back. It was too trite.

Sitting motionless for a long minute, his hands resting on the audio console, he felt uneasy about his own involvement in the story. His fingers resembled small branches, like the ones from the linden tree that vengefully reached out to him in his dreams for the past thirty years. When he slowly lifted his hands, it felt as though there were blisters on his palms, like he had clutched a piece of glowing iron.

He heard his own desperate cry.

The crew watched him burst from the van and run into the woods, under the cluster of tall beech trees. They heard what sounded like someone throwing up. They didn't understand what was happening, because they couldn't remember their boss ever getting drunk on the job. They stared into the green darkness and imagined they saw the outline of an abandoned, windowless house right where he stood.

One of them thought he saw—he would later say—the silhouette of a hunched figure near the stump of a giant tree. Was that Trøst?

A short time later, he emerged from the trees and nodded at his colleagues without a word. They found their seats in the van and drove off.

During the stretch through the Jægersborg woods, Peter sat halfway turned, staring out the rear window into the darkness. A single set of car lights followed them. "Turn left up here," he finally said. The sound technician signaled, turning off Skodsborgvej and driving onto a side road.

"Take a right here," he ordered. And they made another turn, into an even deeper darkness along Damsvej, a tunnel formed by the enormous beech and chestnut trees that lined the road. Trøst continued to stare out the rear window.

After a minute, headlights appeared in the bend—a couple of hundred yards behind them.

"Damn," he said.

"Do you think we're being followed?" The cameraman asked, trying to keep a light tone, but he fell silent when he saw Peter's expression in the dashboard light. Next to him, the production assistant sank into her seat as if she feared a precision shot through the rear window like in some American television series.

"I didn't think—" Peter stopped in the middle of his sentence.

People working in television often thought they were being followed and wiretapped and surveilled; it had become a bit of a joke in the business, but it was always said with a note of self-importance. Peter was no doubt not the only one to be reminded of the mysterious accident that occurred when a member of the Blekinge Street Gang crashed on a similar deserted forest road after having been shadowed by the secret service. Those with a conspiracy-theory bent claimed the car had been forced off the road.

Not until the pair of headlights blended in with a hundred others, becoming a golden stream on the southbound freeway, did the tension lighten in the van. The production assistant sat up straight and the sounds of measured breathing returned to the cabin. Likely, they were all a little embarrassed by their overreaction.

Southeast of Roskilde, when the oval silhouette of the television tower appeared through the mist, the cameraman, in the same light-hearted tone, said, "There was another house up on that slope, wasn't there?"

"Yes," Peter replied. "But it's been empty for many years and is completely in ruins. I think the owner lives in the US."

"But it looked as though . . . as though a small figure was running around up there."

Trøst sat for a while without speaking. Then he said, "You must have been hallucinating, Jesper."

"A little girl in a white dress . . ."

"In that case, you must have seen a ghost. A little girl did once live in that house—many years ago, people around here say—but she wasn't *running around*. She had cerebral palsy and used a wheelchair!"

They all laughed, and there was a tinge of relief in the laughter.

Under the glow of the Cigar, none of them could comprehend what they might have seen. And, of course, no one had perceived the wordless messages swirling among the gables of the old villa, which, to really discern, you would have to have lived your entire life at Kongslund.

* * *

Peter drove home to his apartment in Østerbro after traveling aimlessly through the Podunk towns, with their strange names, that he could see from his window.

On Holstein Street he parked his blue BMW between a black Jaguar and a white Renault and let himself through the gate. The building was home to a newspaper editor, two well-known social commentators, and a high-ranking attorney from the state administration, whose greatest ambition was to make the acquaintance of a famous TV journalist. But Peter never had the energy for long political discussions about the influence of the People's Party on the immigration debate, the irresponsible salary demands of the leftist electorate, or, even worse, the wars in Iraq and Afghanistan.

He remembered the Professor's advice to his eager employees during his first year: "With us, feelings are described through images, and in the world of television, there are only seven feelings: well-being, Schadenfreude, sentimentality, shock, outrage, disgust, and anger. Nothing else."

He would follow the Professor's recipe point by point for this story as he had for all others. He would describe Magna's difficult upbringing, her heroic efforts during the Occupation, and her struggle against the snooty bourgeoisie, which finally brought victory and nationwide fame to Kongslund. Then he would introduce a nagging doubt in the middle of the triumph, describing the persistent rumors that the finest clientele on Strandvejen had found a use for the orphanage that no one had imagined—and with the help of the party to boot.

It was this dark story that the anonymous letters had revived in a time when even the smallest scandal could destroy a politician in the media.

In the slipstream of the scandal, the television news and tabloids would ask the inescapable questions: *Had Kongslund survived merely because powerful men protected it for immoral and selfish reasons? Were thousands of orphaned children sacrificed on the altar of silence, with the help of the party that had always emphasized solidarity and presented itself as the protector of the weak?*

Hearing voices in the courtyard, he drew the curtain aside. It was a Saturday evening and a young woman was sitting on the lawn, talking to the guys who shared an apartment on the second floor. Her hair was red like Susanne Ingemann's, and she wore three gleaming gold earrings. He opened the window as quietly as possible, but he couldn't make out their words. She really did look like Susanne, the way she appeared in the photo in *Independent Weekend*.

It was unthinkable that he could sit down next to her on the lawn and enjoy the warm summer evening. She would take one look at him and say, *So, what do you do?* And the guys, who looked like him at a younger age, would laugh out loud. *Oh, I know*, and the smile would disappear. *You're the one who makes those news reports that no one watches.* She'd study the wrinkles and furrows in his face. *Your name is Peter Trøst or something like that, isn't it?* And the entire group would burst into laughter with all their youthful vigor, ignoring his genuine grief. He'd respond, *Yes, I'm the one you turn off every night.* And she'd say, *No, you're the one we never even turn on.* She'd laugh like the pictures in the editing room, without sound.

He closed the window, leaned back, and looked at the old Cuban revolution poster that hung over his bed depicting a kneeling guerilla fighter: one knee bored into the dark soil, the left arm pulled back as far as possible. A grenade held steady in one hand, waiting to be hurled.

Peter had had this poster since he was young. He'd never considered what was outside the edge of the frame. He'd never worried about who the enemy was.

14

THE GUARDIAN ANGEL

May 11, 2008

During these days, I think the case about the little Tamil boy and the Kongslund Affair combined to unleash problems that not even the smartest spin doctor could manage. We're a small country, after all, and a people raised on fairy tales about children who have been unhappily chased away: the little match girl, the lonely child down in the darkness, the ugly duckling, and the little mermaid.

Conjuring up such visions was sure to trigger shock, sentimentality, outrage—perhaps even rage—and that's precisely what reporters like Knud Taasing and Peter Trøst sought to do, whether consciously or unconsciously.

Defending the children was time-honored proof that Goodness of Heart still resided somewhere deep in the nation's psyche.

* * *

The prime minister coughed—yet again. His face was so sharply outlined against the windowpane that the minister of national affairs was certain his mere profile could cut right through the glass. Ole Almind-Enevold smiled but immediately covered his mouth with his hand and coughed along with his boss, in solidarity, like in the old days when the party was young and leftist.

The only man in the kingdom with more power than the Almighty One set his white handkerchief on his desk. Where his lips had touched the cloth, there were red spots. Putting the hanky down—both men knew beyond a doubt—was the precursor to the embrace the otherwise shy head of state could not avoid. It would only be a matter of weeks before the red spots became blotches and his barking cough slowly lost its vigor. That's how it would end. The dying man had never named the disease that afflicted him, but it seemed to his second-in-command that there was something immensely old-fashioned about it, from the blood that came from his mouth, to the relentless hollowing out of his chest—and this slow languish was a perfect match with the ruler's view of life, which, behind all the pleasant social democratic slogans, was solely comprised of the patriarch's dream of eternal rule.

"Before we move on, tell me about this, eh, this case about the anonymous letter and all that hullabaloo about the orphanage. What's it called again?"

"Kongslund." The minister of national affairs had called for this meeting, and Kongslund hadn't been on his agenda. It was Pentecost.

"I see," the prime minister said casually. "But why does the press care about it?"

"It's one of our finest orphanages, you know . . . and there's a rather unfortunate accusation that it has run some sort of secret business."

"Is it true?"

"No. But regardless, we're trying to find the person who wrote the letter—and other orphans from back then. We've budgeted funds to Kongslund and set up a special fund."

"Good." The prime minister coughed into his white handkerchief again, leaving another spot of blood. "You have been a supporter of that place for many years, isn't that right?"

Ole Almind-Enevold sat up stiffly. The hint was so subtle and the threat so understated that you'd have to have been the second-in-command for more than a decade to catch it. "I've asked Carl Malle to help us find the letter writer. Malle has helped us before. He's close to making a breakthrough in the case. We're sure it's someone who was at Kongslund either as an employee or as a child up for adoption."

"Good," the head of state said again, putting the bloodstained handkerchief on his blotting pad.

Ole Almind-Enevold stared at it for a second. Then he said: "I wanted to bring you up to speed on the Tamil case."

"The Tamil case?" The prime minister coughed even harder than before. These three words could frighten any politician.

"Yes. I'm referring to the case of the eleven-year-old boy that has been circulating in the press over the last few days. We've got to bury it. Now. According to my sources, a vicious faction is behind it all, and we can't give him residency regardless of what the media say."

"I'm staying out of it. As minister of national affairs, it's entirely your decision." Even in his final days, no prime minister would get involved in the delicate refugee question, especially not when children were involved.

"The boy is the spearhead in a large-scale scheme whereby scores of unaccompanied Tamil children are sent to Denmark to gain asylum as minors; then they demand family reunification with their Sri Lankan parents," Almind-Enevold said. "I've been told that people with insight into these matters are planning to contact the Danish government to stop this abuse of the asylum system."

"Excellent." The nation's leader coughed again and then abruptly changed the subject. "At any minute, I may become too weak to carry on. You'll have to be ready of course."

Almind-Enevold bowed his head like a prince beside the throne. "Naturally. But I'm older than you, and I'd be the oldest sitting head of state in our nation's history."

Between coughs, the prime minister chuckled. He appreciated an honest assessment. "Yes," he said. "But we have to ensure a smooth transition to the next generation, and in a moment of crisis"—he tested the words for a moment before changing them to something more powerful—"in a force majeure situation, we can't be blamed for installing our most experienced man, for a transitional period."

"Maybe you're right."

"Look around, Ole. The world wants strong, aging rulers. Who was more popular than President Reagan or Chairman Deng Xiaoping? Compared to them, you're a spring chicken. You still seem young, and you've never had any children to sap your energy and age you prematurely with worries. Consider that a happy coincidence. You still have your strength . . . On the other hand, look at me." The invitation was followed by another coughing fit. He didn't even have the energy to lift his handkerchief.

This time his successor did not cough along with him.

Red in the face from all the exertion, the prime minister waved at his closest advisor. "Now go, Ole. The next time the two of us meet, we'll have far more important matters to discuss."

He coughed again, and there was blood in the corners of his mouth.

* * *

Peter Trøst had drunk too much wine after editing the footage from his visit to Kongslund.

He left his apartment in Østerbro midmorning, without having slept more than a few hours. Still in his first set of clothes for the day, he sat on the sixth floor of the Big Cigar thinking about Magna, who had once stood in the driveway smiling and hugging him as though he'd never left. Now she didn't dare answer his calls.

The telephone rang just as he reached for it.

"This is Asger Christoffersen." The voice was unusually deep. "From Aarhus. You left a message for me."

The name seemed familiar but he couldn't quite place it.

"From far away . . . hello . . . is this Peter Trøst?" The words had a jokey undertone to them.

"Yes," he stammered. Perhaps it was a symptom of stress that his brain had frozen up, refusing to function.

"You left a message. I'm one of the *small blue elephants.*" He laughed briefly. "Just like you."

Peter returned to his senses then and there. But the man's accusation rendered him speechless.

"Marie told me long ago," the deep voice said reassuringly. "Marie from Kongslund."

"You talked to her?"

"Not since I was a teenager. And if you don't want it publicized, I won't say a thing."

Peter didn't comment on the offer. Instead he said with unintentional stiffness, "I'd like to meet you, Christoffersen . . . as soon as possible."

"I doubt I can be of any assistance in this case, but I'm happy to meet."

"We're filming a segment about Magna Ladegaard's anniversary. I think I'd like to do a follow-up later." He hesitated for a moment. It sounded vague. "It's important."

"No problem. I live at the Ole Rømer Observatory in Højbjerg. You can't miss it—it's in the center of the Milky Way." The astronomer let out the same short laugh as before, like four little grunts. Then he added, "By the way, the man in the ministry isn't the only one who got the letters, but I haven't told anyone else either. And I too found it unsettling."

For the third time, the TV star was speechless. He'd been entirely unprepared for this information. For some reason he'd thought an unknown man in the provinces was beyond reach of the letter writer. Of course he was wrong, but that only deepened the mystery. Who would know how to locate a handful of children who had only one thing in common: that they once, almost fifty years ago, lay side by side in a particular room in a particular orphanage north of Copenhagen? Asger Christoffersen must have registered the surprise on the other end of the line, but he didn't point it out. "A group of students is about to join me. We'll be studying the Andromeda Galaxy." Trøst could almost hear a smile in the man's voice again. "It's far away, so I gotta run. But give me a call in a day or two before you come—if you come."

Peter dialed Magna's number again. She didn't answer. As he waited for the elevator he tried a second time, and then, walking over to the Concept Lions—who, as always, sat hunched and scowling behind their giant cups of Coke—he tried a third time.

In a booming voice, the Professor outlined his plans for the launch of the station's new "Wonder Dane," a philosopher who postulated that he'd solved the puzzle of time and who in the test recordings had leaned into Camera One to say, "Time doesn't really exist at all!" The Wonder adeptly mixed an array of concepts from physics, philosophy, and cosmology; he even tossed in a sprinkle of speaking in tongues for good measure. "This may really catch on!" the Professor exclaimed.

"There is only space!" said the Wonder from the screen behind the conference table. He had an enormous full beard that hid a craterlike harelip, and he was surrounded by a small band of loyal disciples, each and every one of whom were short and stocky like him; three of them maintained full beards, and four of them also had harelips. Peter noted that the one tall man in the group was treated like a dog by the others. Nothing ever changed, Peter thought to himself; television, politics, and religion all share a common denominator: conformity. All that was required was a constant stream of deviants that could be displayed to one's disciples to their horror and rage. Condemnation—and that alone—was the glue.

The Professor jumped from his seat at the end of the table and shouted, "When they were young, the '68ers revolted against everyone and everything—even their own parents—but now they find their greatest satisfaction in saying things they never dreamed they would: *Bomb the Afghans. Deport the refugees. Lock up all the criminals. Eliminate aid to the developing world. Invade Iran!* It's incredibly satisfying to them and gives them an additional benefit . . ." He paused a moment. The lions all craned their necks, ready to shout, in unison, for the answer. The Professor did not disappoint: "It makes them feel young again!"

And with that, the Professor waved his hand, and the meeting was over. Chairs clattered, and the little army retreated from the room. The Professor signaled to Peter to sit down with him. "Have you thought about what I said?"

"About Kongslund?"

"Yes. I'm not trying to hide anything, Trøst. This isn't about my acquaintance with the minister—I couldn't care less about Kongslund. This is about broadcasting stories that are more than forty years old and people don't understand!"

The Professor angled his head toward Peter. He had a strange, sly look in his eyes. "It's really wonderful that you believe in the myth of the free news stream—all these roaring swirls of images and messages—but it's all a lie, and you should know that by now. In reality, the news stream became a new flood that has drowned *us*; we're all just dead divers bobbing in the water, our heads submerged." The Professor smiled, satisfied with his peculiar metaphor. "We're all just dead divers, drifting along the current. It may seem as though we're going someplace, as though we're in control, but it's just an illusion."

Peter felt as though he might throw up, or as though he himself was drowning, belly down, in the Professor's grotesque caricature.

"Let that story go, Peter. It doesn't lead anywhere," the Professor said as he stood up and left the room.

Maybe the Professor was right. He wasn't being rational. How he longed on occasion for the years when his parents had kept him in the dark, so that he would be like all the other children, at least on the surface: a boy without the knowledge that threatened to destroy him.

In the weeks leading up to his thirteenth birthday, he'd recognized a strange atmosphere in the house in Rungsted, and he knew that something terrible was looming. But in reality, he'd sensed the threat since his earliest years. Little children have an intuition that adults don't realize. They sense letdowns before they happen; they predict a departure well before a decision has been made, and they feel the longing even before the separation. Somewhere in his mind as a child was the memory of a world he understood existed even if he couldn't see it; he'd often felt as though another child lived in the house—an invisible child—who followed him into the garden and sat next to him on the bench under the elm, mirroring his every move. But when he dared confess these feelings to his parents, they never said a word. Laust and Inge imagined that they'd shown him nothing but love from the very beginning. They weren't aware of the undercurrent of grief they'd carried with them. To hide, grief will assume any mask: it wears anger and reproach, bitterness and indifference; and, in Inge's case, contempt for families with biological children. Deep inside Inge, though, was a feeling she'd never admit to anyone: an aversion to the child she took care of, caressed, and put to bed each night. Magdalene understood that this was the anger of the unborn child toward the adopted child—the child that proved to Inge that she'd never be able to bear her own.

This anger can reside in the soul for years, and the living child faintly senses the presence of danger. Many adopted children unconsciously try to alleviate this threat by smiling and pleasing others, showing their gratefulness. Many are never told they are adopted, but deep down they know they don't belong, and, without knowing why, they smile at the world around them.

"There's something we'd like to tell you," his mother had said.

He smiled.

There were thirteen birthday candles on the cake and thirteen Danish flags on the table. They'd given him an identical copy of a Tiger tank from the Second World War. When the batteries were installed, its canon tower turned 360 degrees.

His father stood behind her, with his curly brown hair and sunken cheeks. He had a way of walking through the house with a step that made the walls tremble, and Peter thought he resembled the German Panzer

General depicted in the Commando story series set in North Africa. He rarely spoke to his son.

His paternal grandparents sat farther back in the shade, and in the glow of the thirteen candles his mother had pressed into the six-layer cake with custard and whipped cream and tiny pieces of licorice confectionary, he saw an expectant look in their eyes. He closed his eyes, and he could hear the buzz of the disaster as loud and clear as the Panzer driver on the Tiger tank in the desert sands at El Alamein.

"Peter, we know you don't remember your early years," his mother said.

He listened to the sound drawing closer.

"We'd like to tell you a little bit about that time. You were in an orphanage because . . ." Inge stopped. The deep buzzing rose and rose, and he glanced at his grandparents, who leaned across the table so as not to miss a single word: the critical words they'd helped formulate the evening before over a meal of baked eggplant on the patio.

"You see, we're not . . ." Inge began again. She stopped again and drew a deep breath into her small chest.

In that moment the Tiger tank appeared over the sand dune and aimed its long black barrel directly at his chair.

"We are your real parents, but we didn't give *birth* to you . . ."

He saw the message leave her mouth like a little smoke cloud, but he never managed to take cover.

"We didn't give birth to you." She took him by the hand, which lay completely still next to a speck of yellow custard.

Peter waited for the impact. For a moment he stared blindly at her, but nothing happened.

Didn't give birth to you.

Maybe that moment was the most decisive in his life, but the explosions were soundless. There was only a sign that someone must have nailed to the dark over his mother's head and which for all eternity would broadcast the message: *Didn't give birth to you.*

"But we love you."

It was then that he ought to have seen through their perfectly executed maneuver and resisted their attempt to completely encircle him. It was in this moment of despair that he ought to have driven a wedge into the adults' united front and mercilessly destroyed their flanks. He should have thrown himself onto the table among the silver decanter and porcelain cups and cried until his illegitimate heart burst. Instead, he sensed the existence of a being he hadn't known was there—inside of him—a much older being that had mastered the cold and calculated deception, the pretense, the stuff of star material.

Calmly, he observed himself through the thin membrane that separates dream from reality, and he dispassionately witnessed his own reaction to the terrible news. He was aware of the moment of change and understood his universal duty to live up to everyone's expectations. He heard his own voice answering with muted calm; it was the most remarkable sound he'd ever heard: "I kinda had a feeling. Don't worry about it—it doesn't matter. What's important is that I'm with you."

They ought to have wondered about his polite choice of words; they ought to have gotten up from their chairs and asked him to take it back. Those words ought to have terrified them, but instead his words were met with a sigh of relief, the exhalation of which extinguished three candles on his birthday cake and enshrouded the first thirty seconds of his new life in a soft, magical glow.

Tears flowed, tears of pure relief—even the commander in the cannon tower seemed (from a distance) moved. For the first time, Peter demonstrated in public his ability to sense what others felt and expected, and to react accordingly.

Without feeling anything at all.

This talent was the gift that his new life presented him, and from that day forward, it became his alter ego. In that moment, a star was born.

"This is the best day of my life," his mother exclaimed, hugging her son so tightly he could feel her beating heart. "Apart from the day when we picked you up at the orphanage. Oh, it was it such a beautiful spot right by the water."

He smiled. Somehow he'd known she'd say this. *All the best homes are by the water.*

Even his father pulled himself together and came to the table, squeezing Peter's shoulders awkwardly, the way only fathers with military mindsets can. The rest of the day disappeared into the great pretense they had created together, and which he already knew would follow him to the end of his days.

When we picked you up, the sign read.

Later, on the patio that warm summer evening, the adults toasted the family's success, and the voices rose up through the night air to Peter, who lay on his bed, staring into the sky through the windows in the slanted roof. You couldn't tell from his face whether he heard the happy voices below. You couldn't even tell whether he was awake or merely sleeping on top of his duvet with his eyes open, as he'd learned to do in the Elephant Room and had done for so many nights that the alien creature inside had lost count.

But we love you, the sign read.

The next day, he rode his bicycle over to see My, who had decided he no longer wanted to be called this nickname. He wanted to be called Knud. This was a year after Principal Nordal's death.

Knud sat almost buried in his green beanbag chair, his head cocked, considering what Peter had just confided to him.

"That's funny, because I've often wondered whether I was adopted, whether my mother really left for Spain like my father says. I've wondered whether she was my real mother . . . my dad too. I look nothing like him."

Peter said nothing. Except in size, Knud and his father looked exactly alike: the same blond hair, the same freckles across the nose, and the same slightly stooped way of walking with their hands thrust deep into their pockets; though Hjalmar had shrunken significantly since the scandal at the private school, becoming a shadow of his former self.

"We're probably both adopted," Knud said in solidarity.

He still recalled the words his mother said when she woke him the next morning and told him the police had called. Early that morning, Knud had found his father on the living room floor under the Karl Marx poster, and he'd alerted a neighbor. But Hjalmar was dead, and Knud sat all alone at the police station. He had no other living relatives.

"It was heart failure," Laust said.

Peter nodded. His own heart had nearly stopped. Of course it had been Knud's real father. In that moment he felt a rage that frightened him so much that he nearly froze before his father in the hallway.

We love you. The sentence continued to bump about in his head like a little ball bouncing from wall to wall, unable to settle.

"Do you want to come with me to the station?"

Peter didn't respond.

"He can live with us, if he wishes. He's all alone in the world."

It was a moment that shouldn't elicit envy. And yet there it was. Even at his young age, Peter knew he was at a vital turning point; he could run one way or the other, step backward or continue straight ahead as though he hadn't heard a thing.

Peter said nothing.

Laust looked at his son for a long time, and then nodded, having understood the answer. "I've called in sick today. I'm going to drive up there now." He rarely spoke more than a couple of sentences at a time.

Peter got dressed and left the house alone on his bike. When he couldn't be seen from the windows any more, he turned and rode into the woods. He sat in the clearing on one of the tree stumps he'd felled that fall. He hadn't thought about the episode for months—the humiliation of Knud's father, the empty, dark schoolyard, or the snowstorm and the heavy chainsaw that hadn't kicked to life until his third attempt.

He'd never told Knud about what he'd done, and he would never tell anyone about what had passed between him and his father that morning. He barely understood it himself. The letdown was of such enormous proportions that there was no excuse. He'd have to bury that secret even deeper than the one about the linden tree. Knud had an uncle on the island of Ærø, and that's where he'd be living now.

The night Knud left, Peter had dreamed of Principal Nordal. The old principal leaned over his bed, long branches sticking out of his empty shirt sleeves and his breath reeking of soil and rain and rotted leaves (death had not made it smell any better). The next morning, Peter hid his pajamas shirt in the back of his closet, so that his mother wouldn't discover the stench.

He grew up during these days, once and for all, and took up the path that had led him to the sixth floor of the Cigar.

Standing by the panoramic window with his eyes closed, he saw his old friend in his mind: Knud Mylius Taasing, named for the men who'd challenged the polar night and lost their lives to it. For some strange reason, the two boys were thrust together again, more than thirty years later, to solve a mystery found in a child's name, a name neither had heard of before.

Quietly, he reviewed the case yet again. The anonymous letters had been sent to him, to Orla Berntsen, and Asger Christoffersen—and presumably also to the last two boys who, according to the caption in the old magazine, had been in the infant room on Christmas in 1961. The writer had somehow tracked them down as adults and must believe that one of them was John Bjergstrand. The letter was a simple invitation to examine the past: the recipient who couldn't locate his biological parents had to be the mysterious boy.

Peter was not a courageous man, and if it hadn't been for Knud, he might not have gone any further. He opened his eyes and stared west. Magna was the key. Magna, who was so obviously terrified to speak to anyone these days. There must be witnesses from back then—nurses, childcare assistants, midwives, social workers—and Taasing would no doubt find them, one after the other. He had inherited his father's stubbornness.

The thought of the brown villa gave him the shivers, as though an invisible battalion of demons from the past was approaching. Or maybe it was just the wind blowing in from the fjord, arousing his fear as it came around the corner of the Big Cigar. That night in the bushes, when he'd been sick without knowing why, he too had seen a figure between the trunks of the beech trees, a hunched figure that seemed to study him before disappearing.

The guardian angel of Kongslund, a voice had whispered in his dreams. It was absurd.

He gazed toward the small Podunk towns . . . Of course he was damaged . . . He remembered all the nights he lay hiding his hands under the duvets so no one could see what he'd done that night at the private school. The smell of topsoil. The knowledge of the rot and Principal Nordal's gnarled outline framed against the moon glow from the skylight.

The man he'd killed.

15

THE MYSTERY

May 12, 2008

Magna had always represented constancy, calm, and fortitude. All her friends in the Copenhagen chapter of Mother's Aid Society would swear to that until their dying day.

When we expected company I stood, even as an adult, by her side and prepared the flowers that sat in buckets and pitchers of water throughout the house; I would hand her the long, slender green stems, which she resolutely arranged in a row on the kitchen counter, crushing them with a hammer before putting them in vases. Then I placed the vases in the annex, in the playroom, in the turret room, and in the infant room where, in her forty years as matron, there'd never been a single withered or wilted plant.

Anyone who knew my foster mother could swear to it: in her care, plants and people simply did not perish.

* * *

"Drawer babies."

This statement was made authoritatively in a dry, old woman's voice.

And why would the two listeners object? Neither of them knew what the term meant.

"Drawer babies we called them—indeed, we did."

The two aging women sat slumped in their armchairs. Their small but strong bodies resting on seats with large-floral-print covers, colors so bright they almost blinded you. They had to be in their midseventies, and as witnesses of the heyday of Danish adoption, they had a marvelous story to tell.

"By the sixties, things had been put in order," the older one said. "But in the fifties we got these drawer babies—when young women could go into the Rigshospital in the dead of night and put their unwanted newborns into this big piece of furniture we had there."

"A dresser," the younger one added. "With big, wide drawers." She sounded oddly satisfied.

"Yes," said the older one. "They were conceived, delivered, and deposited in a drawer. That is, until the system was abolished."

It seemed completely absurd. But Knud Taasing and Nils Jensen had to trust them. They'd been social workers in Mother's Aid Society during those decades, when the organization welcomed tens of thousands of ill-fated Danish mothers and their unwanted children, when legions of doctors and case workers followed an immense number of adoptions from beginning to end as conscientiously as possible.

In 1961, they had taken care of the young women who gave birth on Obstetric Ward B.

"Thousands were being put up for adoption. We found the best homes for them that we could."

"And when that door closed, the biological mother could never find her child," the older one said, as though delivering a death sentence—but again, in the same oddly contented tone.

"Back then there weren't any birth control pills or IUDs, and if a young girl wanted a measurement for a diaphragm, she needed her parents' permission. The mothers who chose to put their child up for adoption . . . I think it's safe to say . . . never forgot, no matter how hard they might have tried."

"Yes," the other said, glancing first at Knud, then at Nils. "We gave them at least three months to reconsider before we started the adoption process, and even so over half of the women regretted their decision in the end. The others we noted in the diary, as it was then called, and later built paternity cases around in order to finance the orphanage."

Suddenly they both laughed. "If we could find the *chap,* that is!"

"Many of the fathers disappeared then?" Knud asked.

"You can bet your bottom dollar they did, but we gathered information through other sources, and it was all recorded on a green form. And on that form we wrote everything—from the parents' height and weight and eye color, to their criminal records and school references. And if they had a criminal record or other serious social problems, we tried to find a very tolerant adoptive family for the child."

The logic in this seemed perfectly clear to the women.

Knud looked up from his notes. "Who picked up the child and brought it to Kongslund?"

"Oh, that would have been Ms. Ladegaard or Ms. Jensen. They would bring a carry-cot and take a cab back," said the older of the ladies, whose prerogative it was to answer first.

"Do you remember anything about a boy named John Bjergstrand? I know it was a long time ago."

Both social workers smiled tolerantly. "Of course not. We handled thousands of adoptions, thousands . . . But you could try the old church registries at the hospital."

"I've already had a friend look into them. There's nothing there. No one with that name."

"Maybe your friend missed it, since you don't have an exact date."

"You don't happen to have a newspaper from back then lying about?"

Another tolerant look. "If those papers still exist, they'd be put away in the Civil Registry—what is now known as the Family Council."

"But what if the papers and church registries aren't there? Is there any other way to find a child from back then?"

They lowered their heads in thought. "We did have these moral conduct forms," the older one said, and the younger one nodded. "For that form, the adoptive parents needed two personal references to state that they were fit to adopt a child . . . and to raise it." Suddenly they both laughed again, as if they simultaneously knew what was coming. "I remember this pastor—he grew so angry because he felt that he was by definition a good person, and that nobody but *God* could be his reference! Maybe you can find a copy of it somewhere."

"Are there any other ways?" Knud was obviously clutching at any straw he could find.

"Well, later on we'd visit the new family to see how things were going, and we wrote a report about that. But by that point, of course, the child had a new name."

"Do you know where the boy lived?" the younger one asked.

Knud shook his head.

"From time to time, we got Christmas cards from the happy families. We put them on the notice board in the adoption department. But they were removed a long time ago, naturally."

"And besides, many people never told their children that they were adopted. Oh, they wanted to wait until the children were old enough and could understand it, they said. And then they waited forever. We used to say it was too late . . . even after three or four years, it's too late. At that point the children have a sense in their hearts and minds that something isn't right . . . They know instinctively that they don't belong anywhere, and that they've been lied to. It's incredibly dangerous. They need to be told with the mother's milk, so to speak." The two old ladies smiled; they uttered the last sentence nearly in unison.

"But many didn't?" Nils interjected, speaking for the first time.

"Exactly," the older one replied. "They were ashamed that they hadn't been able to bring a child into this world themselves."

"But then when everything worked out—with the application—we pulled out the green form and told the adoptive parents a little bit about the child's biological parents. Only children with visible defects were difficult to place, so they were assigned to foster parents instead."

"Like Magna's foster daughter, Marie?"

The women froze, eyeing Knud disapprovingly—as though he'd suddenly encroached on forbidden territory.

"You knew Marie Ladegaard?" Knud stared intently at the two of them over the rim of his glasses.

"Of course." It was the older woman again. Cautiously.

"How exactly did she come to Kongslund? I've heard she was a foundling?"

Again the two women seemed to silently communicate with one another. The mere mention of Marie Ladegaard's name had charged the atmosphere in the room. Where before they had practically been tripping over one another to speak, now they seemed tentative, quiet.

"She was found on the doorstep—or so legend has it," the younger woman finally said.

"Yes. She was a foundling. And tomorrow it will be forty-seven years," the older woman said.

"It was on the Kongslund's anniversary?" Knud asked.

"Yes, it was the twenty-fifth anniversary of the orphanage's founding, on May 13, 1961. We were there." As if to acknowledge the memory, they nodded in tandem.

"The parents were never located?"

They said nothing.

Knud put his pen down on his pad. "You don't want to talk about Marie Ladegaard, do you?"

For a long time they sat without moving, and then they both leaned gracefully forward. "No," they said in one voice.

* * *

I knew that Knud Taasing would find people from that time—like the two social workers—but it didn't really worry me.

They would tell Magna, and it would no doubt agitate her further as the anniversary approached.

In the days following Knud and Nils's visit to Kongslund, I'd heard Susanne moving restlessly about in the hallways, but she never once came to my door. Perhaps the mystery and controversy swirling around us scared her more than she admitted. We felt the ministry's shadow looming over Kongslund, and she had to know that it incited my anger. She ran the day-to-day matters from the ground floor, while I sat under the eaves in the King's Room and emerged only when I was lonely. Days would pass without us seeing one another, and we never discussed the case.

Nowadays, Magdalene rarely visited anymore, and when she did it was mostly to tell me about the conquest she'd made on the Other Side, which she, like all other lovers, expected would last forever. *We're sitting under the beech tree on a couch made of Italian walnut. His Majesty is telling me about the time he fought for the country at the Battle of Isted, where he lost an arm!* She whispered, and in her excitement she tilted nearly ninety degrees toward the floor. Instinctively, I reached for her. Even though my body was an asymmetrical abnormality, I understood the nature of symmetry and its hold on people. I understood the difference between the life path of the beautiful and that of the ugly.

When I sat with Susanne in the garden facing the sound, she was cloaked in a reddish glow, as though both the rising and setting sun were intent on courting her and inviting her behind the horizon, while I was ungainly and dark, twisted from birth, planted like a broken stick. I had lived in two unequal worlds for as long as I could remember: one harmonic and one grotesque, one for those left behind and one for those who had been taken away. In one I kept my eyes wide open, scrutinizing everything; while in the other, I kept them half-shut, tolerating no light. I made it a habit, when I heard one of the infrequent knocks on my door, to turn my shadow side away before opening it. I didn't want to disappoint my guest, especially not the man Magdalene had promised me would show up.

When I was twelve or thirteen, I had found an old green dress in the attic—almost the same color as the one worn by the beautiful woman in the portrait—and when the orphanage was completely silent and asleep, I would hold it up to me and dance by myself in front of the mirror, ignoring both the mold stains and the tattered material. "You're ugly," the mirror mumbled, but I didn't care because I imagined the dress had belonged to a princess, perhaps even Countess Danner herself.

During my childhood at Kongslund, the orphanage's protector, Ole Almind-Enevold, was already a rising star in the party whose emphasis on inalienable social and democratic rights had become the natural center of the blossoming welfare state. Every time he visited Kongslund, Magdalene resolutely drove off in her wheelchair, disappearing in the direction of the white house on the slope, as though she feared or despised him, or perhaps both. To link up with a man like Ole was an instinctive act on my foster mother's part—I understood that each time he returned—and I sensed, even at that age, that it was about the very survival of the orphanage.

He wasn't as powerful then as he is now, but he was influential enough to sway the conservative neighbors of Kongslund, who didn't care for the home. The young politician slowly changed the public's opinion, and with the help of the *Søllerød Post* and the *Berlingske Evening Times*, he turned Magna's deed into one of genuine Danish heroism, much like his own. He made the foundling a symbol of everything his party had fought for and dreamed about: the very struggle for the weakest members of society. And while it was a cleverly conceived campaign that made me famous across the country for many years to come, it probably condemned me to lifetime incarceration at Kongslund.

During my teenage years, I took comfort in Magdalene's twelve diaries. One section in particular I returned to time and time again. According to the date, she'd begun the entry in February 1966, starting with a reflection that was so mysterious that I was never quite able to interpret its real meaning: *Yet another has been abducted. It happened only twenty-five days after they found the girl. The national news just put out a search for him. It's a little boy. Is that the explanation I've been looking for? Was that how Marie got here?*

Because I didn't understand it, it annoyed me to no end. I sat on my bed and imagined Magdalene bent over the paper, her head fallen onto her chest as she concentrated on each letter. *Who were the two abducted children?*

Five years after my arrival at Kongslund, Magdalene had, for some reason, connected the abduction of a boy from a Copenhagen street with my arrival. And it had clearly disturbed her: *I often wonder about Marie's arrival at Kongslund that morning, when I saw the woman on the slope. Why do it this way when any child can be put up for adoption anonymously? I thought about this again when I learned of the kidnapped boy. Strangely enough, I am just as disturbed to hear about children who disappear without a reason as I am to hear about children who turn up without one.*

That's what she wrote—incomplete and entirely inexplicable—and she didn't let me read it until after her death. When I asked for an explanation, I was met with silence.

* * *

Orla Berntsen was standing by the window when Carl Malle came in and closed the door behind him. Down in the courtyard, the snake in the fountain rose in a giant arch, spewing water so high up into the air that it crossed a ray of sun before atomizing in a blaze of purple and green. People from the ministry hardly ever sat in the courtyard, despite the eight small benches that had been carefully placed there.

"The world does not encroach on your domain," Malle observed with a hint of mockery.

Orla's protector from Søborg had aged; his face had grown more furrowed and his curly hair had nearly turned gray, but his charisma was undiminished. Orla knew the man would not be contradicted, nor would he change his plans for reasons other than those he himself knew and accepted. And naturally he needed a plan. That's what he was paid for.

"How's it going with the Tamil boy?" Malle asked.

"You mean the boy in the detention center in Asylum Center North, the one the papers are writing about?"

"Yes, the eleven-year-old you put in prison?" Malle smiled contemptuously.

"It's what people want. People don't want illegal refugees in Denmark, regardless of how old they are."

"People! You were an eleven-year-old boy once, Orla—and illegal too, you might say. Certainly unwanted."

Orla narrowed his eyes. He couldn't tell Malle that the heavy-handed treatment of the little Tamil boy was in part an attempt to distract the media from the Kongslund Affair. He felt the familiar trembling in his hands and fingertips; he hadn't quite gotten used to Malle's presence over the last few days—or how he went systematically from office to office, questioning everyone, from the youngest, jittery officials to Bog Man and the Witch Doctor.

Every night, Malle had hour-long conversations with the minister behind closed soundproof doors, which only heightened the unease in the hallways and cubbyholes of the ministry. Orla was one of the few who knew how close the minister and the security advisor were. Until the first time he'd seen them together, he'd had no idea that there was a connection between the two men, who had by turns assumed the position as the patron of the otherwise insignificant Berntsen family of Søborg.

When he first made the connection, the two men had been standing together in the room at the ministry that was called the Palace. This was an early morning in the late winter of 2001, and they appeared to be in the middle of a strategy session in connection to the election that everyone expected the party to lose. Of course, that wasn't what happened. The election strategists, led by the Almighty One, managed to seize victory that year by announcing the establishment of an entirely new ministry. The two men were going over a ten-point campaign concerning Muslim dominance in the larger Danish cities—a campaign that was to be executed in collaboration with the newly established Channel DK.

That morning Orla had managed to draw away so quietly that only Malle saw him. Retreating quickly to his office, Orla reclined on the couch and closed his eyes as he tried to discern the implausible connection between the two men. The former assistant chief of police had come to his office a short while later, readily answering the questions the soon-to-be chief of staff had yet to formulate.

"How do we know each other, Ole and I? Oh, since the Resistance. How do you think the little gnome survived the terrors of the war?" Malle said and then laughed out loud.

"But how did you come to live in the same neighborhood as me?" Orla's voice trembled almost uncontrollably.

Malle laughed again, nonchalantly perching on the edge of Orla's desk. "Denmark is a small country, Orla, a very small country. If I remember correctly, Magna recommended a quiet neighborhood to your mother, out of concern for you, and I suppose she named one she knew about—since I lived there. We also knew each other during the Resistance. But no one said anything to me about it. You know Magna. She doesn't ask for permission—and certainly not from a *man!*"

He laughed a third time.

It sounded plausible at the time, and Orla had had so much on his mind during those months. His mother—still living in the row house in Søborg—was terminally ill. The tumor in her stomach continued to grow, as though her accumulated grief suddenly wanted out, no matter the cost. When she would call him, the silence on the line sometimes lasted minutes, and afterward his mouth was often so dry that he couldn't speak to anyone—not even the Fly, who scuttled about in his periphery for upwards of half an hour at a time.

Finally he decided to move back to Søborg to care for his mother. She'd sit wrapped in blankets in the faded blue wingback chair, staring into the abyss. Her hands were white with red and purple blotches; her fingers quivered, but they no longer had the energy to travel across the worn cloth. He had sensed his mother's disapproval when he first decided to move in with a woman. Though she hadn't said a word, the image of her on her blue throne with her lips pursed tightly was seared in his mind. Perhaps that's why Orla hadn't wanted to marry Lucilla as long as his mother was still alive—nor had he taken any steps to bring the two women together. Lucilla, who was born in Cuba and had grown up in the old working-class neighborhood near Havana's harbor, had instinctively understood the danger; she kept silent and allowed Orla to stay with his mother those months.

Every night he helped Gurli to bed and went to his own room, under the photograph of the man and the boy and the orange beach ball that hung immovably between them. He'd often awake with his right hand clutching at the sheets like the talons of a large bird; he'd then stretch his fingers, listening to the reassuring cracks that drove away the powerful visions from his dreams.

One afternoon a message awaited him as he came out of a meeting: Mrs. Berntsen had called. It was March 23, 2001, and she didn't pick up when he returned the call.

He left the ministry immediately, hailing a taxi outside the stock exchange, and rushed to Søborg.

He found her on the patio in the sun, lying on her stomach, as though she were sleeping. If the neighbors had risen even halfway from their lawn chairs and glanced over the hedge in the mild spring sun, they would have seen her, but for years they'd seen no signs of life on her side of the hedge, and now they would not see death there, either. It was completely quiet on Glee Court that day; for once, the man with the grand piano had skipped his afternoon sonata.

Orla carried his mother into the living room and put her on the couch, facing south—the direction she preferred. Something stirred inside him, and he gripped his stomach. He retraced his steps to the patio where he'd found her. A blackbird sat on the garden gate, its eyes set on him. And he was reminded of the Fool on the night he died in the wetlands, the eye staring at him from the water lily as though it would pull him down into the depths. He thought of the blue eddies with the red threads where Death had coughed.

He went back inside and sat in his mother's armchair with its worn armrests. He couldn't recall having sat there before.

The Fly and Lucilla made the funeral arrangements. Orla sat in the first row of pews in an almost empty church and then walked through the cemetery in the rain with the drops running down his umbrella, his nose completely congested from a despair that made him blush from rage. Instinctively, Lucilla understood that there was no way she could help Orla Pil Berntsen, and so she said nothing.

He wandered about his mother's house for days. He went upstairs to stare at the white walls. He sat on the bed and stared at the photo of the boy throwing the orange beach ball into the air, and at the man who raised his arms toward the sky in a never-ending attempt to catch it, the freckles on his nose alighting and flying away, like celestial bodies in the expanding universe. He sneezed and closed his eyes.

A week after the funeral his world remained filled with all the flickering visions she'd left behind. He slept in his mother's bed on the first floor, while Lucilla took care of their daughter in Gentofte.

The next morning he went to Bispebjerg Cemetery and squatted by the little mound of her grave. Seeds fell from the poplar trees. Later that night, Lucilla—who'd grown up in a world much more mysterious than the Danish one she existed in now—had found him lying behind a little hedge near the gravesite. She rescued him with a single sentence. "I'm pregnant," she said. That night they slept together in his mother's bed, and time ran backward until it could go no further. Lucilla screamed in the dark as though she'd seen a ghost. She sat bolt upright in bed staring into Gurli's oval mirror, with its smooth, polished rosewood frame, as though she were looking straight into the Land of the Dead. Orla immediately snapped on the light, but his mother was gone forever. Lucilla pulled him out of the dark and covered his body with her own, sealing the deal that her guardian angel had made with his years ago, when the ships had blown their horns in Havana Harbor and two strangers kissed.

The next morning, he was sitting in the blue armchair when she awoke. Again she instinctively knew how great the danger and how short the road to perdition.

She proposed to him the next day.

They married on April 7, only two weeks after the funeral; the national minister-to-be, Ole Almind-Enevold, was their best man. One newspaper reporter had caught wind of the event and snapped a single, incisive picture of the newlyweds leaving the church, and what a neat story it told: the minister in charge of immigration and deportation walking one step behind his trusted chief of staff and his dark-skinned, exotic bride.

The photo was printed on page nine of one national paper the following day, Palm Sunday; but apart from this single leak, the party succeeded in putting a lid on an episode that might've created confusion among the electorate.

It is the twisted irony of Fate that this very image would later become so destructive—in a very different way—triggering the Kongslund Affair and causing the deaths of so many people.

He left the row house untouched, and that's how it remained when Lucilla gave birth to their little late-comer, and ever since, with only a monthly visit from a cleaning company.

But the last couple of weeks, time moved backward again, almost as though the years had decided to hold on to him, refusing to allow him to let go of the row house or remain with his family.

Orla returns to Glee Court every afternoon and sits in the blue arm-chair that stands in the same place, his hands clutching the soft fabric. He closes his eyes, and far away the pianist begins his Brahms sonata. In strong measures he hears the words he shared with Severin: *Sloth. Lust for power. Dishonesty. Greed. Disloyalty. Arrogance. Insensitivity.*

Indecisiveness.

He hears his own voice like a whisper in the room.

"Nobody has any use for indecisiveness!" Carl Malle has broken into his stream of thoughts.

His soul flies back to the ministry, landing in the swivel chair before Malle realizes that it has traveled seven years back in time.

"If you hear from your old friends, especially Severin, I need to know!"

Orla Berntsen opened his eyes and looked up. Malle had no doubt kept abreast of his whereabouts and knew he'd moved back to the house in Søborg and asked for a divorce. It was his job to know these things.

Only a month after the wedding, Orla had visited Magna and asked her the questions that Malle had answered so plausibly: "How did I wind up living in the same neighborhood as Carl Malle?"

To his astonishment, he'd gotten a completely different response than the one provided by the former assistant chief of police: "Yes, that surprised me too," Magna said. "But I got the impression from Gurli that a close friend had recommended the neighborhood to her. And that she'd received some assistance."

"So you weren't the one who found the place for her?"

"Of course not!" Magna laughed gutturally. "We only took care of the little ones, Orla, my dear. We can't take care of the adults as well. They have to take care of themselves!"

He'd never been able to understand the play he was part of. But fear resided in him for as long as he could remember, finding expression in his fingers, shoulders, and facial muscles. He'd heard his own sniffling become more and more pronounced, and he worried about the nicknames it might trigger within the ministry.

From Glee Court he'd tried to call Magna, but she no longer answered the phone. Then he'd dialed Kongslund's number, but Susanne Ingemann had been quite explicit that Marie Ladegaard did not want to be disturbed—and that she herself had no idea what was happening. "How am I supposed to know about your past, the lot of you? I didn't get here until 1984," she'd said, her voice vibrating slightly. He could tell that she, too, was scared and was lying.

"I've tried to set up a meeting with Marie Ladegaard," Malle said, as though he'd read Orla's thoughts. "She doesn't seem particularly eager, but I'll just have to go up there unannounced. It's not as though she ever goes anywhere."

Orla put his glasses on the desk, reducing the former assistant chief of police to a blurry silhouette. He feared his old childhood ally—whose investigative instincts had never waned—would sense the treason he'd committed only a few hours earlier. He'd broken all trust and every boundary. Orla Berntsen had never thought of himself as courageous. But maybe, when push came to shove, temporary insanity was the most important ally of any traitor.

He feared that sedition was detectable in his voice: that the madness that had made him call Severin and tell him everything clung to him.

* * *

The moment Orla presented his name, he sensed the fear in the attorney's voice. It wasn't a call Søren Severin Nielsen felt comfortable with, to put it mildly.

But at least he'd finally picked up the phone. And despite their longtime enmity, he had agreed to a meeting.

Of course they couldn't meet in Severin's office—Orla's face was far too infamous from the stream of glowing news stories about expelled refugees on Channel DK for that. If anyone spotted the official who had single-handedly designed the administration's staunch immigration policy at one of the few meeting places in the city for despondent refugees, there'd be no reasonable explanation, and Severin's credibility would be forever compromised.

Meeting at Severin's apartment near Dosseringen in Copenhagen was also out of the question, since refugees and their allies tended to show up unannounced, as did journalists seeking a quick human interest story for an otherwise boring Monday paper. Orla therefore chose the neighborhood they both knew so well, and since Severin's adoptive parents still lived there, they ended up meeting in Orla's red row house on Glee Court.

Severin predictably arrived a half hour late—ruddy from stress, thin-haired, and smelling faintly of the beers he'd drowned his usual sorrows in after work. Two or three depending on how many asylum cases he'd lost during the day. Orla held out his hand, but his former friend pretended not to see it, mumbling a barely audible "hello" instead. Both were awkward men, and they walked almost sideways into the house, without looking at one another. They sat on the sofa where, seven years earlier, Orla's dead mother had lain. It was early in the evening and the sun's last rays pierced the half-closed blinds. Small white porcelain figurines stood in the windowsill: angels with wings and farm women in white bonnets.

"Did you also get one of those letters?" Orla finally said, breaking the silence.

Severin nodded, placing his letter on the tiled table.

Hesitantly, they edged closer together to study the paper and, surprisingly, Orla felt no discomfort at their physical proximity, which he generally avoided with the aid of large, polished conference tables. Apart from a few formal handshakes, he had barely touched another human being since he impregnated Lucilla.

"The contents are exactly the same," Severin said. His eyes were as bloodshot as his face, a direct consequence of his knowledge that no rescue team would appear to ensure him and his clients a better world. "The form, the socks . . . the photograph from Kongslund."

Orla went to the kitchen and opened a bottle of white wine. He put the glasses down on the table. "I don't understand what it means, Severin. Or even what *Independent Weekend* thinks has happened."

The attorney continued to stare at the letter. "I don't think the newspaper has presented any evidence that anything has been going on." As always, Severin's assessment was matter-of-fact and sound, something few people associate with an idealistic refugee attorney.

"We don't know whether Kongslund did in fact *ever* facilitate the adoption of rich people's children—or try to irrevocably bury their past." Severin cast another glance at the peculiar letter. "When it comes down to it, it's just Knud Taasing's claim—and it's not the first time he's done something like this . . . as you know."

Orla stretched his fingers, but quickly settled them back on his knees before a single distracting crack could interrupt the conversation. "One coincidence is enough," he said, referring to the form with the scant information about the child with the last name Bjergstrand. "One secret adoption would be more than enough. And I don't care to . . ." He stalled.

"You're wondering whether you yourself have a past you don't know about," Severin observed.

Orla stiffened, almost imperceptibly, but said nothing.

"You're afraid your mother wasn't who she said she was, or that she wasn't your mother at all."

With a single sniffle that he didn't try to hide, Orla stood. "I didn't say that. She's dead. But she was always my mother." He could hear how muddled he sounded.

Severin drank from his glass, as he had at Regensen dormitory before taking his turn in the confessional booth, and before Orla had traded their friendship for access to a career as a top official under Almind-Enevold.

Orla sat back down in the blue chair. "Did you ever call the number you carried around, your real mother's?" The words left Orla's mouth before he had time to stop himself.

Severin set his glass on the table and pushed the puzzle surrounding Orla's mother away. "How do you know about that number?"

"You told me once, at Regensen."

"I've never called, no."

Orla said nothing.

"It was too late. And then I had my own kid."

"You said you got the number from Marie, but where did she get it?"

"I have no idea."

"So you really don't know anything either. About your past."

Severin abruptly changed the subject. "Do you remember when I told you about Kjeld?"

"Yes."

"Besides you, I've only ever . . . confessed . . . to my ex-wife, Bente. And I've never dared tell my daughter." He smiled as though to emphasize the irony of this secrecy. He married in 1988, had a child, and started his own practice during the years when refugee numbers were growing exponentially. He'd practically never been home.

"Maybe it was really Hasse, my dead big brother, who I killed on the lawn that day. For the second time."

In that moment Orla felt an overwhelming urge to tell Severin about the episode that changed his life—the night at the creek with Poul and Karsten and the wounded giant who howled in fear, thrashing senselessly about in the muddy water.

It took Orla less than ten minutes to tell his tale, but he could see it shook even an experienced attorney who'd witnessed many forms of ugliness. "He was dead when we got back," Orla concluded. "It was just lying there . . . the eye . . . on a water lily."

"How do you know that it was your hand that . . ." Severin searched for the words. "Your hand that carried out the misdeed?"

He saw Orla's fingers slide across the armrest in two slow, nervous circles. It was like nothing he'd ever encountered in his own home; his father had reacted to problems by running from room to room, while his mother sat on the balcony dreaming about another child's life. Or her beloved Småland.

"It's what I had inside of me," Orla said, without really understanding what he meant.

"It could have been Poul's hand. You said he was cruel."

Orla's fingers became still. "No, I heard a sound, and it came from inside of me."

"A sound?"

"Like a waterfall—a waterfall that breaks through a . . ." He fell silent.

Severin furrowed his brow and said, "Do you ever think about the people you harm as an official—today?" Suddenly there was anger in his voice.

The chief of staff stood again, sniffling angrily. "What kind of a question is that?"

"Ever since we parted ways—and ever since the first Iranian refugees generated popular support for asylum and residency in 1985—you and I have disagreed about everything, and we're from the same place. It has been more than twenty years now, Orla. In the beginning my side won—but now it's *your* side that runs things."

Orla sniffled.

"*You're* the hand that rushes out of the darkness." In the fading twilight, the attorney's eyes glowed behind his glasses. "And no, *no one* catches sight of your face or grasps why it happens. But you are the blow that kills an eleven-year-old Tamil boy just as surely—why?"

Orla took a step backward, enraged. He could smell the sweet aroma of defeat on the failed attorney. "How melodramatic you are. Because it's what the people want. You know that as well as I do. The people have *chosen* the government that protects them best . . . that safeguards the future by protecting us against the foreigners who threaten our national unity. The people have identified the means themselves. You're simply working against it. Working against democracy."

"That's a lie. Every individual Dane would rise to the defense of such a boy. We want to help people in need. Think about the Jews during the Second World War. We came to their aid."

"The Jews . . ." Orla sensed an uncontrollable anger in his voice. He breathed deeply to avoid sniffling. "All we're doing is taking people away from their roots, from their homelands . . . Did you like being adopted? He could tell how foolish his analogy sounded, but he couldn't stop himself. "They'll wither away, Severin. They'll die . . . like Kjeld!"

Now the attorney rose from the elegant birchwood sofa, and for a moment his face shone in the dim light like a red moon.

He took a couple of long steps through the living room before stopping in the hallway door. "You can keep my letter. Clearly it concerns you more than it does me. I can't help you. You're as thick-skinned in this matter as in all others. It's a mystery to me how we ever lived in the same place, or that we ever became friends. But that was a long time ago, and tomorrow you'll be getting my plea for a humanitarian stay for the Tamil boy. Think about your own past—when you raise your hand, Orla Pil Berntsen."

* * *

"He's just sitting there sniffling, refusing to take part in anything *constructive* whatsoever." These were words that Malle normally didn't use, but he'd clearly been irritated when he left Orla Berntsen, and he had brought his bad temper with him into Ole Almind-Enevold's office at the National Ministry.

"I'm convinced that all five boys from that group have received the damned letter. We overheard a conversation between Asger Christoffersen in Aarhus and Peter Trøst—and it's clear that both got it."

"Are you wiretapping a *television station*?" The minister's voice was tinged with a rare incredulity.

"Yes, and an observatory—which has its own antennae out to the entire universe. Once in a while, it's practical to be able to draw on old connections. You, of all people, have to agree with that." His tone was sarcastic, provoking.

"What have you told Susanne Ingemann?" The minister stood by the window observing the courtyard.

"That we consider the anonymous letter a psychopathic act that may be the precursor for something much more drastic. Possibly an assassination. *Terror.* You can't be too careful in the age of terrorism, when even the Ministry of National Affairs is threatened . . . and Kongslund may be at risk too. Little babies blown to pieces by mad Muslims—the news would travel the globe."

"Yes," said the minister, instantly captivated. "It's a dreadful world we live in now." It was convenient for him to forget the old one.

Malle nodded. "We're trying to track the envelope and the cutout letters, and I'm about to get the names of every family who adopted a child from Kongslund between 1961 and 1962. Susanne Ingemann is assisting us, even though she isn't particularly happy about letting us examine the old records."

"And when you've got the names of all the families?"

"Then we'll find the current addresses of the children. Of course they've all long since left home, but once we know the sender's geographic location we can compare it to the list."

The minister clenched his hands into tight fists, concealing his neatly manicured nails. "Carl, you'll have to go through all the materials from Mother's Aid Society. You'll have to go to the Family Council and see what you can find. Yes, I know we tried it before—without luck—but now Magna's influence is no longer what it was. I want every goddamned box in the archives turned inside out—every single folder and binder. I want you to turn over every stone in this country and abroad, where someone may have written that damn name . . . John Bjergstrand . . . as well as every name that may be similar or derived from it. You'll have to contact the families who adopted children back then and ask whether they were ever approached by a third party who showed more than casual interest in the child they adopted."

Malle smiled faintly. "Yes, sir. But right now the big problem is Severin."

The Almighty One slowly unclenched his fists in front of his chin, and the small gesture seemed to signal disapproval. "Severin," he said. "A rejected little boy who has wasted his potential. A lawyer for all the lost and forlorn and for all the swindlers and frauds who come to Denmark . . . What's the problem?"

"They met last night, Ole. They weren't together for very long, but they met."

The minister's eyes shifted momentarily.

"I've got a man on Severin, and he went directly from his office to Glee Court, where Orla opened the door for him. Like that. . ."—Malle snapped his fingers—"they were reunited."

"Do we know what they talked about?"

"No, but I think we have a pretty good idea, don't we?"

"You'll have to contact him." He paused. The immigration lawyer and the hard-liner in the same boat. It could be a disaster. Malle had been furious when he learned that Ole Almind-Enevold, during his stint at the university, had loosened his tongue enough to tell Orla that he and Severin had been in the same orphanage.

Malle drew a deep breath. "I'll be in touch with them and make sure they have no further contact. I'll also talk to Susanne Ingemann—and Marie Ladegaard—and then I'll go to Aarhus, since Asger Christoffersen has now become involved. I think we'll leave it to the Professor to handle Trøst."

The minister leaned back in his antique chair. A sense of calm descended on his finely drawn, feminine face. Ole had been but a thin boy when they met, a boy whom the other resistance fighters barely noticed—except for the fact that they could use him to run errands and take messages and hairpin triggers from one end of the provincial town to the other. The Germans, they figured, would never suspect such a small boy. Ole had never questioned anything, and he'd never hesitated when he'd been given a task.

Malle hadn't thought he'd amount to anything more than an errand boy.

When he was first appointed minister in 1979, Malle had begun a discreet investigation of his past, because there were rumors that his mother had been a Communist, and during those years, Communism was taken very seriously. The Sandinistas had been victorious in Nicaragua. The Soviet Union kept Eastern Europe in an iron grip, and May Day was celebrated as a national holiday, with large numbers of people in the streets. Malle allied himself with an old friend from PET, the secret service. Working fast, they'd found nothing to be concerned about. Granted, the newly appointed minister had grown up on a small farm south of Vejle, with a father who disciplined his son with whatever tool was close at hand (this was before the somewhat milder era of the clothes hanger) and a mother who had become a Communist soon after the Russian Revolution. But there was nothing to suggest it had rubbed off on her son. She was the one who'd pushed him into the resistance movement (since she figured that the Germans were no more dangerous to her son than her unpredictable husband), and so in effect she had brought him together with Malle.

When Carl and his closest buddies were sent to Copenhagen in September of 1943, Ole came along, and in Skodsborg, he met Magna for the first time when the Resistance began sending Jews to Sweden. Later, in law school, he met Lykke, and then married on his twenty-first birthday. In 1957, he was asked by Prison Services to finish a project on incarcerated females and their experiences of prison life. Early on in the project, the newly minted jurist with the brutal background developed an interesting thesis with a surprising gender perspective: that imprisonment damaged women far more than it damaged men. He claimed it must be on account of their inability to fulfill humankind's oldest and strongest instinct: motherhood.

Malle recorded this particular information about Almind-Enevold's life, and then he put it away, because he saw no reason to share with others these facts. Though, he knew they might serve as his life insurance if Ole ever made him his enemy. The ambitious young jurist with aspirations of a career in politics had a marital issue that was becoming a problem: for three years Ole and Lykke had tried in vain to have children. Despite all their dreams and attempts, Lykke had not conceived.

The young jurist was furious over his wife's perceived lack of commitment to this part of life—no doubt because he'd dreamed of having a son for so long and couldn't imagine a life without one after suffering through his childhood with a wordless, violent father in a low-ceilinged house in the sticks.

Lykke had robbed him of the chance to prove that everything could be made better. That patterns could be broken.

And in this very situation, Fate had risen—lazily, as always, to veil its intentions—and lifted its skinny hand, until it seemed as though it waved at the mortal and the godless down in the inferno. This was April 1960. A single, unforeseen difficulty sufficed. And there are those who say that while both God and the Devil seem to be created in the image of man, Fate, in all its capriciousness, is the feminine counterpart to those two gruff gentlemen.

The Almighty One interrupted Malle's train of thought. "But, Carl, why is it happening now?"

Malle didn't respond.

"It's crucial that we find out."

Malle hesitated a moment, then he said, "There's one last thing that I'm not sure how to tackle." This was an extremely rare admission for a man with his reputation.

He leaned in. "There's a detective out there—or, rather, a retired chief homicide inspector—who has contacted the current head of the homicide department . . . and given him a tip that's connected to the Kongslund Affair."

Almind-Enevold arched his brows, his face suddenly growing pale.

"He has, as far as I am aware, suggested to his former colleague that he look at an older, unsolved case about a dead woman, a mysterious death on the beach near Kongslund. That's all I know. I didn't learn this from the homicide chief but from one of his subordinates . . . who reports to me."

"I see."

"But I'll have to look into it."

"By all means, yes." This was the last explicit order the minister would give his old ally before Fate struck with a force no one could have predicted.

Carl Malle rose without further comment and left the office.

PART III

EVA

16

THE KING'S SKODSBORG

May 12, 2008

Kongslund was built during the very months the Constitution was completed, and it wouldn't have been possible without inspiration from the king who was loved by all the people. According to myth.

And when the orderly rows of ladies from Mother's Aid Society were looking for a fitting home for Denmark's unwanted offspring, what location could have been a better fit than the favorite spot of the People's King? The king himself was the son of a loose woman—from whom he had been separated as a young boy—and as an adult, he'd taken a common woman as his illegitimate wife and so enjoyed the ordinary pleasures of everyday life. When he'd soared to heaven without leaving an heir, his branch of the royal family died, much like the carp in the pond in the Deer Gardens where he'd loved to fish.

Ah yes. He'd loved Kongslund. He'd signed the Constitution absentmindedly, in between two fishing trips.

* * *

I must have missed something. That's what I was thinking during those days when the ministry intensified the hunt for the anonymous letter writer.

Something decisive must have happened before I'd been old enough to understand—something so discreet that it hadn't left a single trace for me to find.

I went through the documents that might shed light on the mystery, scrutinizing even the most minuscule details.

In the months after I was found at Kongslund, there were eight little beds in the infant room—four against the north wall and four against the south wall. That much I knew. When the room was fully occupied, eight little milk bottles hung from a contraption in the ceiling, utilizing an ingenious string and pulley system the woman on the night shift employed to lower a bottle to a fussy child, who could then satisfy its hunger without dropping the bottle in the bed. I've heard Magna deny the use of the bottle device to curious reporters. Later she claimed that my worry about the children being lonely had clouded my outlook and caused me to hallucinate. "My dear little Inger Marie, you've turned elephant trunks to strings!" she laughed. But her voice revealed her deception, and the babies in the infant room shared secrets with one another long before the adults thought it possible.

I kept returning in my mind to the old villa's early years, as I looked for the clues I was sure must have been deposited along the way.

Magdalene's grandfather had only just finished the foundation when the most significant event of his life occurred. The last absolute monarch's favorite place when he visited his summer residence, the nearby Skodsborg Palace, was on the hill above the building site. In mid-March 1847, he stumbled on a tree root and slid down the slippery slope, landing with a thud on top of the only remaining tree stump at the building site.

As fate would have it, the builder who stood at the bottom of the slope, witnessed the king's fall. Terrified, he rushed over and crouched down beside him. The king then opened his eyes and observed the completed foundation of a big villa, and thus was the destiny of the hill sealed with a pure, happy coincidence. The house was move-in ready at the same time that popular democracy replaced absolute monarchy in Denmark; and according to legend, the king was more eagerly involved in the construction of the beautiful villa by the sound than in the drafting of the nation's Constitution. Slightly winded, he trudged through the thicket—relieved to have escaped court life, not to mention the dull meetings in the state council, which he preferred to doze through—announcing his arrival with a cheerful greeting to the workers, "What a lovely spot this is, with beeches all about her." Magdalene's grandfather would later recount the enthusiastic pronouncements the king would make as he puffed on his pipe, singeing the outer strands of his majestic mustache. Sometimes when the last absolute monarch ran out of tobacco, he'd pick up interesting little leaves and twigs and burn them in clouds of bluish-black smoke.

"I see you've done exactly what you said you would do. You built the future owner a small room between the towers, with a view of the sound and the Swedish coast," the majesty puffed through the smoke.

"But that was Your Majesty's own suggestion," the architect protested, with an appropriate measure of humility.

In her journals, Magdalene repeated her grandfather's descriptions of His Majesty sitting under the beeches—often with his long telescope aimed at the sound and Hven. When construction was completed, the king gave this telescope to Kongslund's architect as a token of his appreciation. In the final days before completion, His Royal Majesty appeared in the forest with the great love of his life on his arm. "Here's the palace I've told you about, Louise," he said, the tobacco in his pipe glowing so brightly you could hardly see his mouth behind his goat's beard and the cloud of smoke that enshrouded him.

"When this house is finished, I'll yield all claim to power," he added, almost humbly, as though he were presenting a child to the commoner Miss Louise Rasmussen. She smiled at her plump, lovable husband. "Then I think it'll have been worth all the hard work," she said rather cryptically, as was her habit. A few years earlier, she had—and I view this as proof that women are the ones who weave the chaotic actions of men into a comprehensible pattern—given up a child for adoption in secret following an affair with a chamberlain by the name of Berling.

The People's King died less than twenty years later, near the end of 1863; for some time he'd known it was impossible for him to have children, not even with the passionate Louise Rasmussen in his bed. You might say that the country adopted a new royal family due to the lack of a natural, biological one.

"Marie!" There was a rapping on my door, and I jumped. As I did so often, without knowing why, I'd connected the various stories about Kongslund with the solving of my mystery. Absurd fantasies.

"You'll have to come downstairs right away!" Susanne yelled in the hallway.

I stood, my hand still resting on the old telescope, and opened the door.

It was rare to see Susanne Ingemann in such a state.

Her beautiful face shone as though she'd run up a flight of stairs three times the length of Kongslund.

She'd handled the visits from the newspaper and the TV station with all the composure that Magna had recognized in her, and she hadn't given the reporters any inkling of the fated universe behind Kongslund's walls. If they sensed anything behind the thick doors, Susanne Ingemann had resolutely locked them out, and if they'd still suspected that deep secrets were buried inside the villa, they hadn't come one step closer in the preceding days.

It was different with Carl Malle, and Susanne left me no choice. "You'll have to come downstairs," she said, whispering now, as though she regretted having yelled.

He sat in the sunroom with a cup of oolong tea—Magna's and now also Susanne's favorite—and the delicate porcelain was nearly buried within his giant fist. He'd hardly changed in all the years that had elapsed since he was a regular guest at Kongslund, during Magna's heyday. The smile in his tanned face had retained an openness that convinced most people that he was an honest and good policeman.

Susanne and I knew better.

He rose halfway out of his chair, bowing slightly. "Marie Ladegaard. Thank you for finally allowing me to ask a couple of questions."

I couldn't tell if he was being sarcastic.

Susanne sat on the sofa, her back to the garden and the sound, and I chose the chair directly across from Carl Malle—at a distance but with direct eye contact.

"Marie," Susanne said, "Carl would like to ask you a few things in connection with the anonymous letters."

"I doubt I can be of any assistance." I rebuffed her request crisply and, just to be sure, I delivered my formal statement with a faint lisp.

Malle studied my face for a moment, his brows furrowed. Then he said, "Marie, Susanne is helping me find the children who, as adults, may have had something to do with . . . this matter. The minister wants a thorough investigation. The press is out of control, and the ministry cannot ignore that. Journalists are seeing conspiracies everywhere." He opened his hand and put the teacup down roughly. "The letter writer was so clever as to send their nonsense to several people who are connected to this place . . . I assume you two didn't receive any letter?"

The question seemed to be an afterthought.

I shook my head.

"I see," he said.

"But how can the police help Kongslund?" I asked. "Do you need access to confidential archives? Are you going to ransack the house?" My indignant objections were already on the tip of my tongue.

But my growing anger only caused Malle to smile. His teeth were white, every bit as strong as a young man's. "We're not going to *ransack*, Marie. Susanne is an old friend of the minister's, and this case is of great concern to the children whom Kongslund has aided and protected for decades. A little informal contact and mutual assistance can only be beneficial. And besides, I'm not a policeman anymore."

Susanne sat silently, her pale face framed by the red aureole that men found so attractive.

"Highly confidential records can never become a shared matter," I said.

"The problem is," Malle replied, "there aren't any records here. They're gone with the wind."

I said nothing, but made a concerted effort to hide my satisfaction at seeing Malle so frustrated. They had been certain that Susanne would cooperate. When it all came down to it, however, her commencement as director of Kongslund in 1989 was no more a coincidence than the recipients of the anonymous letters in May 2008 had been.

"We can't find names or addresses of *any* of the biological parents of the seven children who were in the Elephant Room that Christmas in 1961," Malle said. "You're the only one whose origins we know about— because you don't have any." The security advisor paused briefly, as though he'd just delivered an exceptional joke. "But right now it seems like you're all foundlings, and that's what we find really puzzling. *Where are the papers?*" He glanced at Susanne, who of course didn't have an answer.

And he'd never dare ask the questions any more explicitly in my presence. Each of us knew that.

I thought of Magna and permitted myself a little smile. "Nemesis," I said, lisping audibly on each *s*.

Malle allowed my impertinence, surprisingly, to pass unchallenged. Presumably he wouldn't want to risk a confrontation at this stage of the conversation. "There ought to be baptism documents—copies of those—or birth certificates," he said instead.

He was right. The children who weren't baptized because their biological mothers left the minute their babies had been delivered would have at least shown up with a little note that read: *Unnamed child, born this date at the Rigshospital.*

"Where are they?" the big man demanded. For a moment he sounded like an unhappy child at a birthday party treasure hunt.

I didn't reply, because there was nothing to say. I knew better than anyone that those papers no longer existed, that the only trace of them was only a few feet above his head, in the secret compartment of the large cabinet, behind the lemon-tree carvings.

"And there ought to be other documents as well. Mother's Aid Society prepared meticulous certificates of both the biological parents and the adoptive parents . . . The old good-hearted aunties made a point of doing that. *So it must have all been there . . .* once upon a time."

Surprisingly, he knew a great deal about the procedures back then. And he had just revealed a possible explanation for one of the mysteries I had encountered but had never untangled: How had Malle located Orla and Severin when they were kids running about between the hedges in Søborg and didn't even know themselves that they'd been at Kongslund their first year? How was he able to contact those two at a time when nobody but their adoptive parents and the matron at Søborg ought to have known anything about their past and present address? Until Malle's visit, I had thought he'd had another way to access the papers that were kept with the authorities—but his frustration showed very clearly that this had never been the case.

It raised an uncomfortable thought, because the first explanation was that the source of his close contact with Orla and Severin and Peter as children was *Kongslund itself . . .* In other words, *Magna.*

I just couldn't believe it.

I didn't think my foster mother would voluntarily share that information with a man like Malle, who for all these years had been the right-hand man of Ole Almind-Enevold. And that left only one other possibility, which I had to this point eliminated as being too far-fetched: they had simply kept the children in the infant room under surveillance; they'd followed them when they left Kongslund, and followed them to their new homes.

It would be quite easy—but also drastic, it seemed to me.

Of course I'd been naive.

His voice sliced through my thoughts. "In the second half of 1961 and into the spring of 1962, there were only the seven of you in the room . . . and it's those very seven sets of biological parents we can't locate in the files . . . or anywhere else." His summary of the problem was entirely accurate. "Of course, it's the five boys we're interested in."

I looked up. "Tell me, what was so special about the Elephant Room in those months?"

This was a question I'd longed to ask of Magna, and now it paradoxically flew out of my mouth as I sat right across from the man who frightened me most. My question seemed to render him speechless, a silence that lasted several seconds.

"What is all this really about?" I insisted.

Malle found his words again. "You've had access to the records."

I froze. "No, of course not."

My answer was so flat it could suggest anything, and Malle reacted instantly to this provocation. "Fiddling with confidential documents is a criminal offense, Marie Ladegaard."

"And why would I fiddle with those papers? An adopted child who wants to find his or her roots, that makes sense—it sounds quite likely—but I'm the only one from the Elephant Room who we know for sure arrived without papers, and hence without roots."

For a moment he was impressed with the obvious logic of my point, and I exhaled slowly.

Susanne leaned closer, in all her reddish-brown glory. "There's no reason to torment Marie. She has never had any reason to steal anyone's papers," she said.

Nothing could be further from the truth.

Malle was caught in our crossfire; he put his fist on the teacup, and it was a miracle it survived.

"I'm very grateful for the help you gave me once, Carl," Susanne said. "And you know my story as well as anybody. There's nothing in this world that would cause me to accept any activity that could damage Kongslund, if I were able to prevent it . . ."

Her statement was made in a devilish hypothetical subjunctive form. Carl Malle had been played into a checkmate. If he sensed any illogical point, he wasn't able to articulate it.

"Once there was a break-in here at Kongslund," Susanne offered, "way back in Magna's days. The entire second-floor office was ransacked, everything turned upside down. Maybe the papers disappeared then. Maybe you're not the only one interested in them."

Malle stared at her, and for a second I feared that Susanne would take the next step and implicate him directly: *Perhaps you were the one who turned it upside down?*

But thankfully she didn't.

"The only place those names might be is with Magna," she said, thereby passing the buck to her predecessor. But Magna could take care of herself, and Susanne knew that.

I could have named yet another place: many of Kongslund's children would be listed in the files at the National Hospital's church. They would have been baptized in a rush, because they were weak and might die—or their mothers had hesitated and postponed the final separation, insisting on a baptism before they departed. But likely he'd already looked there in vain. Without a name on the birth certificate—and a date of birth—it wouldn't be easy for Malle to find his way around those church records.

Malle nodded. He must have sensed that we were in cahoots without being able to prove how or why. With a visible strain he pulled himself together. The cup lay there like a little white baby bird under his big hand. "I'm in the process of tracing all the adoptive parents from that period," he said slowly. "And through that, the current whereabouts of the children." He paused for at least five seconds before he continued. "The letters to the ministry and the newspaper were mailed from the post office in Østerbro. I've found three stores in all of Zealand that sell the kind of envelopes that were used. One is at Østerbrogade." He paused again. "There are many adopted children in the Copenhagen metro area, of course, but it narrows down the field somewhat."

In other words, he must have cleared Asger Christoffersen from suspicion, since he lived in Aarhus. For now, the tall astronomer had been crossed off Malle's list of suspects.

"But I can't see how that leads anywhere," said Susanne Ingemann, who'd recovered her color and her deep-red glow, holding her head high as usual. "Not until you find a motive that separates the innocent from the guilty." There wasn't a hint of a smile on her face. "Not that I think it's so wrong to write people who have once been in an orphanage—maybe to help them." She gazed at him calmly across the table, across the no-man's-land and the decades that had passed. Then she concluded the conversation with a rare harshness, "But I suppose that's not a sentiment you're too familiar with."

* * *

When he left he had, in spite of his apparent shock, been on the verge of asking to see my room. To search it. Look under the bed and in the closet and in my locked drawers. I could tell from his eyes.

But he kept it to himself.

Again I felt my own fear. He probably considered his next move and wanted to be sure of his decision.

For some reason Asger's acquittal as the letter writer had made me uncomfortable. Malle might change his mind when his Copenhagen trail came to an end. I had followed Asger at a distance; it had been easy, because he was frequently in the papers whenever he offered accessible explanations for the mysteries of the cosmos. I, who'd grown up with a view of Hven and a secret crush on the old, silver-nosed astronomer Tycho Brahe at Uraniborg, had read most of them. Asger had visited Kongslund in the summer of 1975, right before he was to start eighth grade, and a few years after his parents, in a bizarre scene, had revealed his life's secret to him.

I knew that Susanne knew the story; she'd once known him far better than I.

They had arrived at Kongslund around noon. Asger and his parents had traveled halfway across the country, through a heat wave that had Danes gasping at the sun and forcing them to the beach in droves.

He was fourteen and didn't remember anything from his early years—not the house, not the water, not the large woman with the motherly embrace, and not the Japanese pull-along elephant or the young girl who curtsied so nicely, squeezing his hand in greeting that day. I had changed over the course of a few years and become fairer. With silly flattery my foster mother would sometimes call me beautiful.

Nonetheless he asked, "Have we met before?" These were formal words, especially from the mouth of a fourteen-year-old.

I shook my head, and he didn't ask again. Asger's father looked pale and said he would take a walk along the beach. A little later I saw him squatting at the very edge of the water as though he had heat stroke. His mother had drunk green oolong tea with Magna in the sunroom.

I showed Asger to the infant room, letting him stand there and take in the surroundings. The blue elephants trudged along the walls all around us, but he walked directly to the patio door and observed the sound.

"The elephants have always been here," I said to catch his attention.

"Is that Hven—that over there?" he said.

I followed his gaze, but he wasn't looking at Hven at that moment. All the way down by the water's edge, his father continued to crouch with his back to us. Then Asger suddenly pointed to the sky over his father's head, and said, "Tycho Brahe believed the earth was the center of the universe. Throughout history, scientists have believed that they understood everything. But they always discover how little they really know, and how many mistakes they've made—so why would we have complete knowledge today? Someday, even death will be considered nothing more than a limitation of the medieval age."

It was an audacious statement, especially for a fourteen-year-old, even one as smart as Asger. I nodded without knowing what he'd meant; he was the most mysterious person I had ever met.

"Some researchers believe there is no such thing as time," he said. "And if time doesn't exist, maybe space doesn't either. If there's no space, then all movement must be an illusion as well."

They were peculiar words in a place like this (but I wrote them down carefully in my journals when I was alone).

Down on the beach, his father leaned forward all the way to the water as though he were studying his reflection. Asger stepped away from the window, and I remember he had tears in his eyes, though I didn't understand why.

"I wish it was like that," he said dreamily.

"How?" I asked foolishly. Suddenly, I had a feeling he was talking about his parents. But if that was the case, his response was even more distant and peculiar than his other statements.

"That one's *thoughts* were the only force in the world," he said.

Then he ran out of the infant room, leaving me standing alone among the marching blue elephants.

There were 2,973 in all.

17

THE PROFESSOR

May 13, 2008

"Here at Kongslund, we've never needed the help of neither God nor the Devil," I often heard my foster mother tell visitors from abroad, who came to Kongslund to study her impressive work as well as her governesses. One delegation came all the way from Tokyo, bringing the pull-along elephant as a gift, and no one doubted that the entities she was referring to were men—men of the worst kind.

In Magna's world, everything unforeseen and twisted could be straightened out and put in working order, and her own daughter was the embodiment of that belief. For that reason alone, she overlooked the obvious, failing to see the shadow looming above, which Magdalene in her diaries referred to as the Great Master, the king of all of life's seeming coincidences, always on the lookout for human folly, patting your cheek, ingratiating, irresistible, nonchalant, unpredictable—and entirely ruthless.

Naturally, it was from here destruction would come.

* * *

Everyone sensed that it was a very special morning. You could tell from the minister's step, from the chief of staff's sniffling, from Bog Man's huffing, and from the Witch Doctor's unusual silence.

It was Tuesday, May 13, 2008. The sun shone through a cloudless sky, making everyone in the ministry think of wide beeches and green groves, in spite of the growing fear that marked the last few days.

Eight top executives had gathered in the department head's office. Most would attend the anniversary celebration at Kongslund later that morning, because when Kongslund's legendary matron was honored for her sixty years in the service of Goodness of Heart, the ministry wanted to turn out in large numbers, of course.

Half of the group noisily browsed the newspapers that had been set out for them, which included reviews of the in-depth mini-documentary about Kongslund that Channel DK had broadcast the night before.

According to the morning papers, Channel DK's anchorman, Peter Trøst, had criticized the ministry for its "undemocratic inaccessibility" and cast a dark, mysterious sheen over the entire affair with the anonymous letters: *Had Kongslund participated in a secret arrangement to cover up the extramarital affairs of powerful men in order to maintain a good relationship with the authorities in the 1950s and 1960s? Had the home established a secret alternative to the then risky and illegal back-alley abortions, taking children from their mothers at birth and funneling them into a clandestine adoption system that erased all trace of the biological parents?*

Both the TV station and the morning papers had called for the aid of individuals who had been put up for adoption during the period between 1950 and 1970 and who had been unable to find their biological parents. They were reportedly getting a lot of calls. Surprisingly, many had incredible stories about their own mysterious past, even though most could not be verified. Indeed, editors were swamped with fairy-tale-like reports from Danes who thought they might be the offspring of rich and famous people—counts and barons—possibly even the royal family itself, because surely someone had given in to the temptations of the flesh.

At today's briefing the minister had expressly banned his closest staff from publically discussing the story. Nothing, certainly not the tabloids, would prevent him from participating happily in the anniversary at Kongslund. That much was clear. So Bog Man turned instead to the case of the little Tamil boy. The eleven-year-old boy had come to Denmark as an unaccompanied refugee—before his asylum application was determined to be unfounded—and had been routinely dismissed by a caseworker, who knew little about Sri Lanka other than that it was very far away.

On older official had attached to the case file a couple of newspaper stories with headlines that read: "Orphaned Tamil Boy to Be Deported" and "A New Hard Line: Even Young Children Denied Asylum."

Orla Berntsen studied the backs of his hands but kept his fingers calm. "Red Cross protests," he said. His face was pale, aside from a faint belt of freckles across his chubby cheeks and piglike nose. "And Søren Severin Nielsen represents the boy."

The name alone caused involuntary twitches around the table, because this particular attorney always litigated his cases in the press—regardless of how hopeless they were.

"Is there anything for him to return to?" Bog Man asked, gazing out from behind the gray bags under his eyes, and then added uncharacteristically, "After all, he's only a little boy."

Orla Berntsen inhaled deeply before replying. "As we all know the age criteria for an automatic grant of stay has been decreasing over the last couple of years, and now the council and the board have established a new practice according to clear signals from the administration. We will now deport children ages eleven and up." He tapped the file. "This case is a test for the council and therefore also for the ministry and the administration. The deportation will deliver the intended signal."

"Don't send them to Denmark," one clerk said.

There was an awkward silence for a minute, as though something untoward had been said, or at least spoken too loudly.

Bog Man glanced at his watch, which year after year hung more loosely from his bony wrist. His eyes had sunken into a fold as far down his cheek as was physically possible. His face was expressionless.

"I see," he said. "So we're going to have the fight about that principle now?" Bog Man looked at Orla.

The chief of staff held Bog Man's gaze. "Since we haven't taken such a hard line before, an unswerving execution of the deportation may seem . . . unpleasant," he said. "However, it would be most unfortunate if we gave in only to have it used against us in future cases. And that would no doubt happen. Kids from all over the world would suddenly flood Denmark . . ." He let the sentence hang threateningly in the air for a moment. "And that's not what the parliament, or the people, want." This was how even the most irresolute avoided feeling any responsibility for the destinies they handed out. The decisions came from the people and were carried out by parliament, but neither of these groups saw the consequences up close. Nor did the officials in the Ministry of National Affairs. In other words, unpleasant images did not enter the system anywhere. That's how it worked, and it worked exceptionally well.

"Simply put," the chief of staff continued, studying the expressionless faces around the table one by one, "if we deal with the controversy now, it'll have the additional benefit of diverting attention from the ridiculous matter of the anonymous letter that the opposition hopes will discredit the party and, through that, the administration."

He was willing to risk sharing this part of the plan with his tight inner circle, and he did not need to hide the quick, triumphant flash in his eyes.

Everyone instantly understood the position of the chief of staff's office.

"Well, I suppose that's all then," Bog Man said, standing. "We'll continue the casework as we have, including the Sri Lankan ones."

At that, the eight officials rose.

Bog Man remained standing by the window looking down into the courtyard, where the elegantly chiseled snake held its neck back, spewing water into the sky. The Terrarium was what some wise guy in the second immigration services office had called the courtyard. Perhaps he was referring to the entire ministry.

* * *

Peter Trøst had read three of the reviews of the previous night's broadcast while brushing his teeth in the executive suite on the ninth floor and putting on the first suit of the day. And he'd read two more before he stepped out of the elevator on the sixth floor of the Cigar.

The phone lines were buzzing, and he sensed the Professor's presence even before he spoke.

"Trøst?" Bjørn Meliassen's voice emerged from the loudspeaker like a faint buzzing from an electric kettle: nasal, almost whispering. "Trøst, goddamnit . . . Trøst, pick up . . . I need to see you. Immediately."

Three floors up, the chairman of the board would be bent over his large desk with the newspaper coverage of last night's program laid out in front of him. Presumably the minister of national affairs had already called him, furious.

Peter stared at the landscape below, mere shadows in the morning mist: Gadstrup, Viby, Osted, Kike Hvalsø . . . small towns, small people . . . the ordinary life. He hated that phrase.

"*Goddamnit, Trøst!*"

The Professor's voice left no doubt about the subject of his call. The very notion of a follow-up on Kongslund had to be stopped. Any editor with a modicum of sense would follow orders, because it was easier to back down than take on a fight that would inevitably result in a reputation for being a provocateur with a secret political agenda. No one wanted to risk that label anymore. Those battles, which Peter and his fellow reporters had fought in the eighties and nineties, and which they'd referred to as idealism, had become meaningless with the explosion of competing entertainment outlets. Instead, they'd all made an about-face, like an armada that retreats when met by an invincible fortress. Over the years, most of them had come to chastise everything that resembled the views they had once held, and they were merciless in their clashes with anyone who'd not abandoned those same bastions. It had made Channel DK a success, and for seven fat years things had been going well. But now the ratings were dropping inexplicably month by month.

"Trøst, answer the phone . . . now!" Meliassen's voice was now so nasal that his consonants crackled through the intercom.

Peter disconnected his boss and then picked up the phone and called the Ministry of National Affairs instead.

He asked the secretary to be patched through to the minister, and to his surprise he was, without hesitation. At that moment, the May sun broke through a passing cloud and bathed the distant buildings in a blinding light. Peter swung his legs onto the desk and pressed the red "Record" button. The tape started rolling.

"Enevold."

For months, reporters had joked about how the minister no longer gave his full name because *Almind* was too close to the Danish word for *ordinary*, and the boldest among them jested that the future prime minister—at an unheard-of old age—would change the election rules in favor of the party and of himself, so that he could become the first demo-cratically elected dictator on the planet—for life.

"It's Trøst. I'm calling about Kongslund. We're airing a follow-up, with news from the anniversary where you'll be giving the speech. And of course the case itself."

"I would imagine."

"I'd like you on the program. It wouldn't have to take long. We can do the interview in Skodsborg—today—whenever it works for you."

"Have you made these plans with the Professor's blessing?"

Peter sniggered. The conversation sounded like something out of the age of absolute monarchy. "No, of course not," he said. "He's chairman of the board, not an editor."

"Freedom of the press?"

"Yes."

"Well, I'll avail myself of my own personal freedom—to not partici-pate."

"You won't participate?"

"No, and you already know the reason why. And don't call me again about that case. It's filth." The last words were nearly lopped off as he hung up.

Peter took the elevator to Ninth Heaven and prepared for the second inevitable confrontation of the day. For some time, the Professor had considered all critical journalism undesirable because it entailed mental activity no one was capable of any longer: "You can't educate people via TV!" he roared to the Concept Lions. "It's like asking a piano to mow the lawn—it can't be done!" The lions had simply nodded.

The Professor sat behind his desk, aglow from the blue light emitted by the many TV screens. One was on his desk, one was built into the ceiling, one hung above the door, and a couple others rested on two low mahogany tables set on casters in the western portion of the office. The man was crouched forward, and he had a scowl on his face that made him look like the black vulture from the nature film *The Living Desert*—which Peter had seen as a child—as it bent over its prey, a chunk of heart in its beak.

"So now that the freedom of the press has triumphed, I suppose we can put it behind us, Trøst?" The deep vowels made a hissing noise within the Professor's chest.

Peter heard his own voice. "No." Just the one word. Far away he could make out the little town with the peculiar and comforting name of Our Lady.

The Professor visibly held back what was no doubt a brutal reaction, one that any other employee would have felt the full force of. Instead he murmured, "I see no reason whatsoever to pursue this story further . . . so long after something may have happened . . . and we don't even know what that something might have been. And for that reason, I can't see how it would appeal to our viewers. Appeal to *our* viewers, Trøst. The whole story seems completely *unreal*—"

"On the contrary. This story is absolutely real—it's about deception. And the minister of national affairs is involved. His party has had an interest in suppressing the scandal for decades."

"There won't be any more programs." There was an ominous gurgling in the old man's throat.

"If there's any significant development, we have to pursue the story," Peter said. "Everyone expects us to. If we don't, it'll only prove that our— that your—relationship with the minister is too close; you know as well as I do that the papers would love to discredit the biggest TV station in the country."

It was an unmistakable threat. Such a scandal could only be created if someone from the closed world of the Cigar confirmed it. "You think about what you're doing, Trøst. Think very hard about it," he warned. "Our ratings have shit the bed; our shares are terrible."

"That's the reality for all other stations as well," Peter said. "And it's because there's way too many of us . . . Everybody wants to make TV, but there's hardly anyone left to watch it." It sounded like a joke, but neither of the men smiled. Channel DK was about to collapse under the constant pressure to develop new concepts and programs. Stress symptoms had spread like a plague through the building, relegating ever more departments into quarantined zones. Several employees were out sick, while others had gotten into brawls after work at bars in Roskilde and Tølløse. One poor employee had stepped off the train and laid down across the tracks at Lejre Station, while another had tried hanging himself in a hotel bathroom in Gøderup. So far, no one had jumped from the Garden of Eden, but it was a scenario so rife with symbolism that the Professor feared it more than anything else. *Employees at Denmark's largest TV station jump to their deaths.* Channel DK's competitors would have a field day.

Peter stood. "I'll discuss it with the editorial staff, and then I'll bring a team with me to the anniversary this afternoon. It would be conspicuous if we were the only media outlet not to show up." He knew the Professor was invited, along with other members of the press, presumably a request from the minister himself.

The only reply was the sound of a faint gurgle from the Professor's throat.

He left the Professor's office and took the elevator back to his office on the sixth floor. For a few minutes he gazed out the window at the Zealandic landscape, observing the sound and Sweden in the distance.

Then he changed his clothes and prepared for his meeting with Knud Taasing and Nils Jensen at the harbor. The three of them would drive to the old matron's anniversary together.

18

THE ANNIVERSARY

May 13, 2008

Naturally, Fate had decided that none of those implicated in the Kongslund Affair were to be left alone. There were far too many tempting threads flapping about—far too many opportunities. And for that reason, I'd sent my regrets to the anniversary when Kongslund invited the whole nation to celebrate the legendary Magna Ladegaard's sixty years in service of forlorn children. I'd explained that I was suffering a spring cold; after all, during those days of preparation under great, sweet-smelling blankets of newly cut freesia, everyone at Kongslund was sneezing.

If I'd known how silly this last precaution was, I might have acted differently. In any case, the following events struck me just as hard as if the Great Master had found me reckless enough to emerge unprotected on the lawn, among Magna's decorated tables.

* * *

The minister of national affairs sat, his hands folded, next to his chief of staff in the backseat of the service car as they wound their way through Charlottenlund, Skovshoved, and Klampenborg. The chauffeur, a Lars

Laursen from Helgenæs in Jutland, drove at a steady, slow pace on the final stretch from Strandvejen to Skodsborg.

Laursen had been the private chauffeur of the country's second-highest-ranking minister for only a couple of months, but he radiated the unique calm of his home region, and of course that appealed to the minister. It was reassuring to have such a solidly provincial man behind the mahogany steering wheel.

The chief of staff glanced at the minister, who silently stared out the tinted windows. "There's something we need to talk about," Orla said with hesitation.

The minister nodded absentmindedly.

"It's about the Tamil boy who is going to be deported."

The minister didn't reply. It had been quite some time since anyone but the prime minister had been able to demand an immediate answer from him on any matter.

Orla fell silent and leaned back in the seat. Due north, a ways out Bernstorff Road, was the villa where Lucilla lived with their two children. Shortly after he'd started the job at the Ministry of Justice, he'd taken his first vacation ever. He'd chosen Cuba because the country's eternal defiance and its ostracism from world society fascinated him. He was there for the New Year's Eve when the country celebrated the twenty-fifth anniversary of the revolution. In the midst of all the noise at Havana harbor that night, he'd heard a woman's voice greeting him in an American accent: "Happy New Year!" Her greeting was directed at Che in his blood-red sky of course, and not the awkward man standing on the quay beside her—but she noticed that he'd heard her and she laughed along with him. In this way, he came to owe his first and only woman to a Communist revolutionary. Six months later, she came to Denmark and was granted residency almost immediately. It was in 1984, just before the giant waves of refugees began in earnest. They had a baby girl, who was now twenty-three, and after his mother's death, another girl. He was happy they'd avoided a boy.

"I gather that you know what you're doing, you and the department," Ole finally said, interrupting Orla's train of thought.

They drove past Sølyst, Emiliekilde, and Bellevue, where Orla had gone biking with his mother when the other boys' fathers drove by car, their hair slicked back, to Hornbæk and Tisvilde with their well-dressed sons.

"Yes," Orla said. "The boy's deportation will immediately divert attention away from Kongslund. That's all there is to it."

The minister fell silent again.

"Later, we'll reveal his asylum petition as a big lie," Orla added.

The minister didn't react. *Lie* was a dangerous word, whether it came from a friend or foe. And the minister was nothing if not cautious.

"The method is simple. There are many disputes between large and small groups of Sri Lankan refugees—the Tamil and the Sinhalese—and the small cluster of Sinhalese in Denmark will disclose the boy's case as a big sham, charging that all Tamil refugees are involved in a criminal network that defrauds the Danish state by forging documents and creating phony asylum applications."

Still no reaction from the minister. *Tamil* was just as unsettling a word as *lie* these days.

"This revelation will arrive at the ministry from a reliable Sinhalese source—we're already in contact with this man."

"But if the Sinhalese are at war with the Tamil separatists in Sri Lanka, wouldn't such a witness be met with criticism?" Ole asked matter-of-factly.

"Yes . . . if he steps forward."

"Aha."

"But out of concern for his safety, we will only publicize his tip anonymously—perhaps via a letter or a fax he's sent us. Of course, we have to protect his full identity. The press will understand . . . It will even *intensify* the drama. In reality, the press doesn't care about the details—as long as it smells a good story."

The minister nodded.

"Our source will say that a secret network is trying to get as many Tamils into the country as possible, unlawfully, of course, using illegal smugglers and unpleasant methods," Orla said.

Ole did not reply. The lie was now being wrapped in the innocence that signals complete honesty. It already sounded like truth.

"He's going to say that this boy who everyone is bawling for is the very *spearhead* of this nefarious network, that they simply use children to get their parents into the country via the family reunification provision. It doesn't get any more devious than that. Their goal is to create a large Tamil community inside the country, just as they've done in southern India."

"Goddamn!" The minister breathed through his nose.

"When the press and the public learn the truth, I think we'll solve the Tamil problem once and for all," Orla said. No one could eliminate problems the way Orla could.

There was a pause and then the minister said, "And this source . . . he really exists?"

"Yes, I've made contact. We'll be getting a fax." Orla turned toward his superior. "But there's one more thing. I think we should let the Witch Doct . . . the PR director bring the idea to a colleague at the Ministry of State. It'll look better if they receive the information. They're not directly involved in the case—and the boss doesn't have our . . . our reputation . . . for being so brusque with foreigners."

Ole Almind-Enevold stared at the driver's neck through the tinted window that separated the backseat from the front. The boss that the chief of staff referred to was the prime minister himself. This was dangerous territory—very dangerous.

Orla knew what the minister was thinking: his own chief of staff, his favorite official and the best problem solver in all of parliament, was essentially asking him to nudge the dying head of state into the line of fire. If something went wrong, it would cost the PM his job. If things went well, however, the prime minister would thank Ole for a brilliant plan, and Almind-Enevold's boss and mentor would never know the danger he was in. One way or another, the plan would guarantee Ole Almind-Enevold's access to the post he dreamed about all these years as second-in-command. If, at the last minute, the prime minister made a move to pass him by—the sick cannot be counted on to always act rationally after all, and the Kongslund Affair was clearly a worry—the Almighty One could use the Sinhalese plan as blackmail, threatening the damaging revelation that the prime minister had concocted a plan to deceive the public and blame innocent Tamils. It would be the end of his career.

Despite the danger, Orla could see that the minister agreed to the plan, and so they said nothing more to one another on the matter.

It was vital that the minister never formally approve the plan. This way he could deny his participation with genuine indignation.

"It really is a beautiful place," his boss said, gazing out at Strandmølle Inn.

In front of the old inn, which in the king's day was a canteen for the workers at the paper mill, chairs and tables had been set out for the summer season. A man stood on a bench with a view of the water; he was not much larger than a dwarf. On his tippy toes he rose and kissed a tall blond woman on the mouth. Her feet were bare and she smiled, and her hand rested on his shoulder. Neither of the men in the car said a word. So many strange things were happening these days.

The service car crested Skodborg Hill and swung to the right down the wide driveway that opened up between two six-foot-high Chinese stone pillars.

Like a whale in a green ocean, the dark-blue Audi dove into the shade of the beech trees and came to a halt in front of the windows Orla knew so well. Next to him sat one of the few people who knew why.

Chauffeur Lars Laursen stepped out of the car and opened the door for them.

* * *

"Thumbelina and the Giant!" Peter and Knud said almost in unison at the odd scene of the dwarf and the woman kissing on the bench. The journalists had been driving behind the minister's car for part of the trip to Kongslund and had witnessed the same strange scene. Since both covered the bicentennial of Hans Christian Andersen's birthday a few years earlier, they laughed together as they'd done long ago.

Nils Jensen was driving, and he sat alone up front so the two men in the backseat could concentrate on exchanging information and developing a strategy before reaching Skodsborg. As they rolled into Strandvejen, they'd gotten right behind Almind-Enevold's blue Audi.

"I don't think they've spotted us," Nils remarked, putting his hand on his camera as he considered whether to snap a shot through the windshield. No one would imagine that the driver of the big Mercedes had grown up in a small Nørrebro apartment behind Assistens Cemetery, where every Sunday morning he'd visited Andersen's grave with his father, who would always recount the fairy tale of the haughty lad who had renounced his own parents by stepping on the good wheat bread so as not to soil his shoes—after which he'd ended up in the depths with the Marsh Woman, becoming a statue in Hell. The story had both delighted and terrorized the young Nils.

As an adult, photography had given him access to a much wider world, one he'd barely known existed. His talent was in immortalizing the world's seven horrible but visually striking plagues: floods, earthquakes, hurricanes, forest fires, hunger, genocide, and war. Recently, his own father (with the constantly blinking eyes of the night watchman) had stood at Gallery Glasshuset and studied a placard of a dying African (a little girl) without saying anything at all to his son. (He'd retired and very rarely came out into the daylight, which he found to be ever sharper as the years went by.) Nils had been standing right behind him in a leather jacket he'd bought with the exhibition's honorarium, and which had cost more than what it would take to feed ten African families for a year. His father had sniffed the scent of the expensive material and narrowed his nearly blind gray eyes.

"Do you intend to continue covering the case at *Independent Weekend*?" Peter asked. He was referring, of course, to the paper's board of directors with their formerly close ties to the administration.

"Does Channel DK?"

The two journalists stared stubbornly at one another, without replying. Neither of them knew the answer.

Knud Taasing was the first to relent. "I've found something interesting in one of the sources that knew the orphanage back then. During those years, the Elephant Room was simply reserved for certain kids who enjoyed special attention from the matron and her two assistants."

"Wasn't it designated for infants?"

"Yes. All newly arrived children spent their first twenty-four hours in the Elephant Room—where the night nurse could keep a more vigilant eye on them—but most were quickly transferred to either the Giraffe Room or the Hedgehog Room, or to a small bedroom behind the tower that had bunk beds. Only a very few children stayed on and acquired this unique situation."

He didn't have to say that Peter had been one of these few specially chosen children. They both knew this.

"When the room was fully occupied by these favored children, there'd be seven beds in all. They always kept an extra bed ready for acute situations—the assistants referred to this as *the eighth bed*—because it was always prepared to accept a baby on short notice, so that all of the children could spend at least one night in the Elephant Room. One of my sources who worked at the orphanage during the years we're looking at ticked off the nicknames of these kids as though it were yesterday: the Merchant was Orla Berntsen, she knew, because he'd visited the home many times with his mother, who was single and lived in Søborg. And the Wisp—or Buster—that was Søren Severin Nielsen, who also came by a few times. Your friend in Jutland, Nils, went by the name of Viggo, after then Prime Minister Viggo Kampmann. And there was a girl they called Clara after the actress Clara Pontoppidan. As far as I can tell from the photograph, there was another girl in the Elephant Room in 1961 . . ."

"Impressive."

"Yes, but it doesn't bring us any closer to solving the mystery."

* * *

"Orla!"

The name was spoken with the same intensity he remembered, and yet he started. Nobody (except for Almind-Enevold) addressed him by his first name, and in that tone.

The past became the present in that moment. She stands before him, large as life, just like back in the day, and she holds a small, old-fashioned camera in her hand. She takes his picture before anyone manages to respond.

The driver holds the door for them, but the Almighty One has stopped midmotion and sits for a moment, frozen, his upper body half-way emerged from the car. He doesn't care to have his photograph taken.

Then Magna wraps Orla in a bear hug and gives him what she calls a royal squeeze. Orla thinks her eyes are a little duller than usual, but it's hardly surprising given the stress that she and the orphanage have been under lately.

Nonetheless Magna has retained the straightforwardness that is characteristic of her eastern Jutland origins. "You're just about the last guests to arrive," she says, and clutches him as though she wants to comfort him; he lets her squeeze his shoulders and arms but doesn't return the affection. She is wearing a blue, tailor-made suit and has powdered her cheeks as a defense against the hectic hours ahead.

Her successor stands in her shadow. She is tall and slender and for once isn't dressed in flattering green colors, but is wearing a canary-yellow dress. There is a faint smile on her lips, which seems both formal

and ironic. Susanne Ingemann shakes the minister's hand, then Orla's—
and, finally, the chauffeur's, curtsying each time.

The two women lead the guests through the living room with its little
tea pavilion, out a back door on the northern end of the house, where
they turn and walk down a narrow garden path made out of round flagstones.

There are more than two hundred guests on the lawn in front of
the villa and even more under the beech trees by the southern annex. A
light breeze blows in from the sea, and all the guests hold long-stemmed
glasses. A small army of magazine photographers swarm about, taking
advantage of this rare opportunity to be granted access to the famous
orphanage. There are no children among the guests, and none of the
reporters are allowed inside. On the beach itself, a few feet from the
old pier, a crane has been set up, and mounted on it, high up in the air,
is a camera with a long black lens. On each leg of the tripod, it reads
Channel DK.

A group of press people are moving sideways through the crowd and
approaching their prey, the main speaker, Ole Almind-Enevold. Most
are from the "On the Town" section, and to be allowed in, each reporter
has had to pledge to not disturb the joyous occasion with embarrassing
questions. The Witch Doctor has recently arrived by taxi, and his piercing eyes are scanning the crowd; perhaps he is hoping to find the anonymous letter writer in proximity of the minister. A little way off, Malle's
tall figure appears among a cluster of older, white-haired women sitting
on a bench, no doubt representatives from the heyday of the Mother's
Aid Society.

The minister has made it onto the patio, stopping in the shade under
the wide roof between two white pillars. He raises his glass, filled with
sparkling Portuguese white wine, and toasts Magna. "You're still looking
after our little blue elephants?" he asks.

"Yes, of course."

Orla is the only person within earshot, and no one else catches the
words in the sea of voices from the garden.

The guests begin to turn toward the patio, sensing the ceremony is
about to begin. Conversation slowly dies out. Malle joins the group on
the patio, lightly placing a hand on Almind-Enevold's arm. The aging
minister freezes; he does not like to be touched. Then he suddenly smiles,

as though he's received a new cue, and he retrieves a single slip of paper from his pocket. He holds it out at arm's length.

This was how Orla would remember the Almighty One: it took him only a second to ease back into the role of minister, as though he'd never been among mere mortals.

A smooth, momentary, and entirely flawless transformation to being the most celebrated figurehead in the nation.

Susanne Ingemann smiles at the guests. "Thank you all for coming today. Our guest of honor will now address Magna—Ms. Ladegaard—today's honoree," she announces in a clear voice.

Her words are met by loud, spontaneous applause.

Without hesitation, the minister turns toward the former matron and speaks directly to her. You can hear his voice all the way down on the shore, because the patio under the King's Room amplifies every single word. "Time, Magna. Time," he says, raising his gaze toward the twelve beech crowns that tower above them. "Time is invisible, it is unreal, and some say it doesn't even exist, and yet"—he looks at her again—"yet it determines everything in a person's life. In *yours* too. Time and its most faithful companion"—the Almighty One steps closer to the matron—"longing."

A falling leaf would have made more noise than the guests at that moment. This is the kind of atmosphere that the second-most powerful man in the kingdom could create with nothing more than a few trees, a patio, the sky, and a view of the sound.

He glances at the handwritten note, gestures suddenly with his right arm, and says, "Here—under the beeches—a little girl with cerebral palsy was born many years ago. She was the grandchild of the architect who designed this place and whose ideas, according to legend, were supported by King Frederik VII. Here on the slope the king would take his evening walks, here on this very beach." The minister pauses briefly and then turns toward the neighboring house, the white façade just visible behind the foliage, and the absolutist king's story is in full bloom. He raises his right arm again. "Here on this slope he walked . . . the People's King . . . the father of the Constitution . . . and this house"—he gestures toward Kongslund—"was built during the same memorable years when the Constitution became the foundational law of the kingdom of Denmark."

The crowd breaks into spontaneous applause. Even a couple of the magazine photographers lower their cameras and join in.

"At this place she was born," the minister continues, "the little girl whose greeting from the past I've chosen to bring Magna Louise Ladegaard. Spastically paralyzed from birth, unable to walk along the paths and explore the hills, woods, and fields, born to be different . . . ostracized. You could call her ugly or disfigured; you could even call her deformed, and you could call her fate and her physiognomy a burden—but you could also focus on her sunny disposition, her presence, and her appetite for life. She was a child with a strength that we'd all like to see our children bring into the world—children that this country cannot live without. Let me tell you why . . ."

The minister allows himself a smile before continuing: "Instead of grieving and feeling sorry for herself, she taught herself how to write—and indeed she did. Among many other famous people, a man by the name of Hans Christian Andersen called on the house on the slope to visit the little girl's grandfather, and that may explain her singular urge to tell stories and express herself. Maybe he helped and inspired her, maybe he even held her hand, very carefully, when she wrote her first words . . ." The minister has conveniently ignored the fact that Hans Christian Andersen died many years before Magdalene was even born.

He pulls a little notebook from his pocket and holds it so that everyone can see it. "When she passed in 1969, here in this spot, she left her diaries to Magna's daughter, Marie, who is, unfortunately, ill today and unable to attend. I would have asked her to read a particular passage, but I'll do it myself, and the audience will have to ignore the fact that my voice is far from Marie's—and even further from that of the woman who wrote these words."

A mild laughter rises under the beech crowns, and the Almighty One makes another short dramatic pause before continuing: "She wrote this section in the summer of 1945, immediately following the Second World War. As you listen to the words, remember that she was severely disabled. Each sentence took days for her to write. Her name was Ane Marie Magdalene Rasmussen, but she was simply called Magdalene."

He looks at the paper, and if you didn't know any better, you'd think he had a lump in his throat.

" 'Believe me, longing has remained with me all these years. We're like sisters, we've never really been apart, and I don't think I would have lived at all had it not been for the children at Kongslund. They ran about me, they crawled on my lap, they comforted me without knowing it every single day. But I also see the longing in their eyes, and I know their longing is even deeper than mine. One thing I have learned: rather than experience such longing, I'd prefer sitting immobile in my wheelchair knowing my roots.'"

Ole Almind-Enevold lowers the paper. The guests stand still. Even the wind dies down, as if it's holding its breath. A red light blinks from a television camera resting on someone's shoulder, a magazine reporter crouches to the left of the patio (he is probably trying to get the trees into his frame), and even the note-taking reporters silently wait for him to go on.

Slowly he turns toward the honoree. "Longing. Magna, that is the secret of your work here for over sixty years. Nobody has fought against longing like you, with all your presence and being." The minister raises a hand, at once threatening and generous. "These hills, between the sound and the beech forests that have inspired so many Danish poets through the centuries, were home to purebred families with distinguished names like Kaufmann, Nebelong, Ottosen, Damm, Holbek, and Michelsen"— he raises his brows as if to express disapproval—"and then you arrived, Magna, with your little group of children, the offspring of ordinary Danes . . . Jørgensen, Hansen, Svendsen, and Pedersen. Your work reverberated all around Skodsborg and all the way to Copenhagen, and eventually across the entire country. From the beginning, you were part of the Children's Right to Life association, which still exists and is becoming ever more popular by the day—indeed, is at the forefront of the renewed attention on women's access to a so-called free abortion in our country. But what was Kongslund's secret?"

He stuffs his paper in his pocket and looks directly at Magna. "I think your secret was your awareness of this *longing*, Magna. No one knows the nature of longing better than you. It was probably no coincidence that you had the strong blue elephants painted on the walls of the infant room—because in every possible way you've shielded the vulnerable with your whole body, your calm, and a formidable stubbornness that characterizes a female elephant protecting its herd."

A ripple of laughter rolls through the crowd on the lawn. The minister has touched on a dangerous topic—his political hobbyhorse, the restriction of abortion—and left it again. Magna sits with her head bowed. A blush spreads across her neck like a large, torn poppy leaf. She wears a deep green pearl necklace and a purple brooch. Amethyst.

"In this way, you became nothing less than the mistress of longing. For thousands of children, this meant that time could once again move forward. But—and there is always a *but*—as an illustration of this, I'd like to read another passage from Magdalene's diaries. She wrote it shortly before her death, more than sixty years after her first passage."

Ole Almind-Enevold removes the piece of paper from his pocket, opens it, and focuses on the text: "'But no one, and no action, can remove longing entirely. It exists in the darkness around us. It is soothed by daylight, but it returns with darkness. The children play all around me, and they show me clearly and shamelessly that I will die and be forgotten. My questions will never be answered, and when darkness falls, I will have no one to direct them to.'"

He pauses for a moment, as if he wants to underscore a particular point. Then he continues: "'In all of my years, I've hoped for a miracle. Not in the form of physical mobility or more words than those I've been given by Providence. Not in the form of Great Love—others have been able to tell me about that. Instead I dreamed of seeing a sign of the Divine in me, the way the Bible says the Divine resides in every single one of us. A glimpse of the selflessness that reaches beyond the spirit and the body. For many years, I believed such a miracle could only be experienced in a distant place, far from myself, or on a journey I was unable to make—or in books I would never be able to read. But the miracle was right here. Right in front of my eyes, here in the garden under the beeches. I found the miracle in the loneliest person I've ever met.'"

The minister grows silent. The wind doesn't stir. Then he reads the final lines: "'This is what I've always wanted to tell you, Marie, but didn't have the courage to when I was alive. You were the love God gave me. You were the opening in my immobility. You were my light. It's not until you grow old that you see all the simple things clearly. I know the answer now: Every time a human being sits alone in the dark crying for another human being, the miracle comes. And releases us.'"

The powerful minister raises the notebook and turns its handwritten pages toward the audience on the lawn—as if to celebrate an unknown triumph. "A foundling."

The gesture has great effect, and every single guest on the lawn stands frozen—even the youngest photographers, some with tears in their eyes. Being ceremonious is a part of the minister's popular appeal; only Magna's blushing signals another feeling—perhaps anger that her foster daughter has been described, in public, as the loneliest person in the world—but if that thought strikes anyone else, they will tell themselves that he hadn't intended that.

He speaks again: "But how about you, Magna? Have you left souls who now feel the longing? Yes, you would probably say, because all people long for something. And nobody is perfect." He takes a small step back and looks at her. Her lips part as though she is struggling to breathe. From a distance it might appear to be a shy smile, but it isn't.

"I think this is the lesson we can draw from your life, Magna—that longing exists and can never be entirely removed, but it can be soothed. I, too, have a longing. You and I know where it comes from, and that it will take a miracle to soothe it. Magdalene's miracle arrived in the end. Perhaps it will for me too. I hope so."

The words are mysterious, but they are delivered in a deliberately light tone before he raises his voice: "And with that wish, I ask you all to lift your glasses and join me in a toast for Magna—Kongslund's Guardian Angel for sixty years."

One of the ladies on the white bench under the beeches whispers, "He just told her he loves her, and that he has always lived with that longing . . . how beautiful."

The other ladies nod, like sunflowers in a rain shower.

On the patio, Ole Almind-Enevold continues to face the retired matron of Kongslund. Susanne Ingemann now stands between them, as though she intends to split them apart. Orla Berntsen approaches the minister with a glass in one hand, and at that moment, Nils steps onto the patio with his camera. "I'd like a photo of the celebrant with the minister," he says with the self-confidence he's earned after five photography prizes and many more successful installations depicting the world's misery.

Magna stares at the photographer, her hand to her mouth, as if just managing to stop a word from leaking out. Then Orla Berntsen reaches them. "There's a call for the minister, in the office—and it's urgent . . ." He slips his hand under the minister's elbow and takes a soft step away from the photographer.

Behind them the Witch Doctor emerges like the rustling wind, but he pauses on the stairs, and for once leaves things the way they are.

The old matron stares at Susanne Ingemann, who shakes her head almost imperceptibly, signaling to Magna to get back into the house. The catastrophe creeps in slow-motion among the guests, crawling up the patio stairs, and nestling at the epicenter of the quake.

Nils feels a heavy hand on his shoulder. "Put that camera away!" The shutter sounds like a gunshot, and an arm sweeps the camera out of his grip. Then a fist strikes him on the side of the head, and a large hand pulls at both the strap and the camera. Two stumbling steps, another pull, and the heavy digital Nikon crashes against the glass patio door, which smashes to pieces at impact. Two hundred guests stare in shock. Believing they've been shot at, three officials from the ministry dive forward (it is, after all, the age of terror, and they've all attended a survival seminar). A large fist smacks Nils in his gut and forces the air out of his lungs.

Knud Taasing leaps in front of the giant man who holds the camera strap. "What the hell are you doing?" His voice is shaking.

"That damn photographer!" Malle yells.

Susanne Ingemann squeezes between them and calmly says, "Stop!"

Orla Berntsen clutches the minister's elbow, now with both hands, and it seems both comical and awkward. The minister stands isolated on the patio, a stunned look on his face. Five or six feet away, Peter Trøst is momentarily confused because he can't see his cameraman anywhere and doesn't understand what is happening.

"Get them out now!" Malle issues the order like a police officer during a street uprising. Loud cries come from the infant room, and the white patio curtains flap in the wind.

Peter Trøst steps close to Malle. "Those children may have received a shock that'll take months to recover from," he says, and the statement sounds oddly out of place in this bizarre situation. But the security advisor takes a step back; the women and the minister must understand his signal, because a moment later, they disappear through the broken patio door. Orla is still standing there, though the look on his face suggests that he would have rather fled with them than obey whatever silent order was keeping him in his place.

Trøst puts a hand on his arm. "What is going on, Berntsen? Why the hell can't we take a picture of the celebrant with the minister?"

The chief of staff doesn't reply. The Witch Doctor crouches like a shadow behind his left shoulder.

"Why can't the public see them together?"

The minister's protégé stares at the TV journalist: there are small drops of dew or sweat on his large glasses.

"What is happening with the anonymous letter? Have you even reported it to the police?" Knud Taasing asks as he sidles next to Trøst.

Orla stares at his old nemesis and sniffles.

"I've recorded the minister's speech—but, honestly, I didn't understand what he was talking about. Can you clue me in? Did you help write it?"

Orla sniffles again. It is hard to say whether it is out of fear or contempt—or both. He stands completely motionless before his two enemies, as though he was hoping to blend into his surroundings—and for a moment he is almost invisible.

"What are the celebrant and the minister covering up?" Knud says.

The chief of staff sniffles for a third time.

"What was all this talk about *longing*?"

"How the hell am I supposed to know?" Orla takes a step back, awaking the Witch Doctor from his trance, and he floats between Orla and his pests, pulling his boss toward the half-open French doors of the infant room.

"Someone has got some sort of business going on here at Kongslund!" Knud shouts rather theatrically. "And we'll find out what it is!" For a moment he has fallen out of his objective role, Peter thinks, and sounds like an amateur detective in a serial magazine. Nils Jensen is still sitting on the stairs, more shocked than injured by the punches Malle landed.

"Can't we behave like adults?" the Witch Doctor whines. A second later he manages to get his boss to safety behind the fluttering curtains and then closes the patio doors.

At that point, every camera on the lawn is pointed at the last remaining characters in the dramatic scene. They are all members of the press.

Too late, they realize the impact the images will have when they appear in every single newspaper the following day.

* * *

Of course it was called a scandal. A very considerable scandal, even.

Competing media gloated. Mystery was the sensation-hungry companion of the scandal. No one could explain what the clash on the patio had been about, since the security advisor's attack had been completely unexpected—and since he'd quickly disappeared.

No one was able to locate him later.

At *Independent Weekend*, the brawl had one result. "The story is over," Taasing's editor declared, and every single reporter around the long conference table nodded in unison. As was the norm these days, they were in total agreement with their boss. The next day, *Independent Weekend* published a two-column article in section two, page seven. There wasn't even a photograph. The story was as dead as a doornail. Only the scandal—the brawl—remained.

None present, including Nils Jensen, suggested reporting Malle to the police. In the Big Cigar, the Professor moved his jaws as though he'd just finished a big meal, and he felt the same satisfied purring in his stomach. "Exit Kongslund . . . my dear Trøst. That kind of personal involvement is absolutely unacceptable for a reporter, but you know that already." You could hear his laughter rumbling through the high-ceilinged rooms all the way up to Ninth Heaven and the Garden of Eden and down to Counseling Services on the sixth floor. It was clear to everyone that the threat against Channel DK had vanished, and that the outlandish story had gone too far. The evening's coverage of the anniversary celebration had been cut to a very short clip with a terrible recording of the minister's speech on the patio of the orphanage. That night the three reporters met in Peter Trøst's apartment in Østerbro. Taasing studied the poster of the soldier with the hand grenade and teasingly cocked his head but said nothing. Nils Jensen had a small Leica camera strapped around his neck, and he seemed as short of breath as he had after the brawl.

"For my part, I intend to continue my investigation," Taasing announced smugly. It was getting dark outside. Of course he'd continue. If the case ended, he'd be fired soon after. There was already considerable pressure to get rid of him from *Independent Weekend*'s board of directors.

"Regardless of what *you* intend to do, I want you to see the results of my latest investigation." Taasing opened his battered bag.

It was full of magazines.

Peter turned on the lamp above the dining table.

"Look at this . . ." Taasing tossed a magazine on the table. It was a surprisingly well-kept issue of *Out and About*, dated May 25, 1961. The cover featured a little girl in a white lace dress holding a bouquet of yellow freesia in her arms. Surrounded by a smart blue background, the girl smiled playfully from under her long dark tresses. "We Take a Look Inside the World's Best Orphanage—25 Years," the headline read.

"Haven't we read enough magazines?" Peter snapped.

Nils flipped through the first couple of pages, noting that the paper was surprisingly thin. "The photo lottery with prizes of up to half a million Danish kroner continues," one advertisement announced, followed by the coverage of the twenty-fifth anniversary: "Foundling Discovered on Special Day." There was a view of the grounds from the garden—and if it weren't for the women's dresses and hairdos, you might think it was taken just the day before at Magna's anniversary.

"Incredible," Nils said. "I took a photo from almost the same angle."

"Yes. Some things never change," Taasing replied. "But what's interesting here is the text—in particular this bit about the foundling. And one more thing," he said, pausing triumphantly, "this magazine was definitely printed in the same font as the anonymous letters."

The three men fell silent.

Nils and Peter leaned in closer to read the words Taasing had underlined in red pen:

"However, it was no ordinary celebration for Ms. Ladegaard and her staff, because early that morning an unexpected guest announced its arrival. When one of the governesses heard noise by the southern annex and peered out, she saw a small baby cot with the most darling child you can imagine. A little foundling! The governess, Agnes Olsen, tells *Out and About* that no one saw the little boy being dropped off. He was in remarkably good shape, but the police still do not know who his parents are."

"The little boy?" Peter said, puzzled.

Taasing clenched his hand in a fist like the soldier on the poster. "Exactly. Elsewhere the foundling was reported to be a girl, Marie Ladegaard. That's what we've always been told."

"It must be a typo," Nils said.

"That's not a typo," Taasing replied. "But of course, after a little legwork, I located Agnes Olsen, who now, almost five decades later, lives in Brønshøj." He smiled. "I got hold of some old acquaintances from the union I thought she might belong to, and, bam, I found her. She's now retired and living on disability. She has no children. Perhaps she had enough of them at Kongslund."

No one laughed at his joke.

"And now we're getting to the interesting part. To this day, Agnes Olsen remembers that the foundling was a boy. So I asked how the boy had come to be referred to as a girl in all those newspapers and magazines, and she couldn't tell me."

Nils glanced at Knud and then to Peter Trøst and back again, formulating the question that was on both their minds: "So what's the problem?"

Taasing fished a Prince cigarette from the little silver case that he carried only during the summer, when he risked crushing his cigarettes in his pants pocket. Nils was one of few people who knew the date engraved in the bottom of that case. His wedding day: 8.8.88. He'd divorced a year after the scandal that buried his career.

Taasing lit his cigarette and said, "What do you mean, 'what's the problem'?"

Peter said, "You ask us to meet with you, and you tell us you'll continue your investigation. You say it's *possible* that the foundling they found forty-seven years ago was a boy, not a girl." He fanned the smoke away from his eyes. "Why the hell is that so important?"

"Because you're forgetting," Taasing said, "that John Bjergstrand is a boy."

19

DEATH

May 15, 2008

On the second floor of the villa, my foster mother, ever dutiful, is bent over her records and balance sheets. From time to time she opens the top drawer in the beautiful rosewood writing bureau with its bronze mount-ings, retrieves the Kongslund Protocol, *and makes notes in it. It's as thick as a wrestler's arm and bound in dark-green leather; and to the question I once asked in my childish curiosity, she replies without hesitation: "It is my log, Marie. Without it I wouldn't be able to keep my ship on course!"*

Then she laughs so loudly that it sounds like thunder rolling in from the east.

The content of the log was a secret she would take to the grave. The house's foundation would creak and rumble, but she'd bring it with her; not even the greedy curiosity of a foundling could pry open the drawer and reveal its contents. It was solidly constructed, and its lock could not be picked with even the greatest patience—all my attempts were in vain.

Maybe she noticed the fine scratch marks that appeared to have been made by small fingers in the bureau's panels and had drawn her own con-clusions . . . but naturally it hadn't caused her great concern.

Martha Magnolia Louise Ladegaard died two days after the anniversary celebration.

It was a shock to the entire nation that had just seen her—so vivid and splendid—on their television screens. The festivities had nearly overshadowed the serious accusations that had been levied against the orphanage. Again and again over the intervening days, my foster mother was referred to as the one who'd helped thousands of Danish children into the safe homes and thankful arms of tens of thousands of Danish parents.

I remember Magdalene once told me that Magna *"sent all the others into the world, but you she wanted to keep for herself."* And then she added with a strong lisp that underscored her warning: *"The anger, Marie. Anger. That's what you have to watch out for!"*

Before I could ask her to elaborate, she'd turned and had been absorbed by the shadows, leaving me with a faint smell of soil and meerschaum pipe smoke in my earthly quarters. (I think that by now she spent most of her time on the Other Side with her soul mate, the People's King.)

It was Magna's sudden and brutal death that caused the police to reconsider the status of the Kongslund Affair. Thus far, behind closed doors, the leading criminal investigators had practically shrugged their shoulders at the amateurish anonymous letter, agreeing that the ministry was overreacting. They'd been satisfied that a man like Carl Malle had, in effect, taken over the investigation. No one had ever cared for him, and now he might finally do himself in with his recent dealings with those in the elevated circles.

But that was before the case's true main character was found dead in her Skodsborg apartment. Now the homicide investigators came out in full force, and through numerous interviews they examined every detail of her final hours. The Kongslund Affair had been resurrected.

They'd found my foster mother lying on her living-room floor, right beneath the window that faced the funeral home on the opposite side of Strandvejen. They discovered her body several hours after any doctor or miracle from above could have saved her life. She lay in a pool of blood, her head resting on a white scrapbook containing hundreds of newspaper clippings featuring photos of the many cohorts of Kongslund's children.

Several of the articles had been removed from the scrapbook and strewn around her body.

During the next couple of days, the police tried to conjure a kind of phantom image of the homicide. It had occurred at a time when most of those in the building were still asleep, and no one was expecting a visit from Death or anything that looked remotely like it. As a consequence, they had only one witness to work with. He was the only tenant to awaken when a voice spilled through the ceiling from the apartment above. He was the manager of the Oceka Grocery at the corner of Strandvejen and Skodsborgvej, and just two evenings before he had seen the victim on television.

To all appearances, the poor woman had been reading her scrapbooks when she received an unexpected guest. There were several other books, white, red, and brown with letters, pictures, and clippings stacked on the coffee table as well. Two unused coffee cups stood on the table, and the old woman lay on her back near the bookcase. A snuffed cheroot—a Bellman, her favorite brand apparently—rested on the floor next to her. Although the grocery manager downstairs had gone to bed, he had at one point heard some noise in the upstairs apartment. A fretful person, he'd been born—delivered, wrapped in a blanket, and laid in a dresser drawer by his mother—in the very room where he slept, and he hadn't had the courage to get out of bed.

The police figured that Magna had been attempting to pull the big scrapbook off the bookcase when she fell with such force that she conked her forehead on the second-highest shelf, then spun, losing her balance. She'd cried out, and that was another sound the neighbor had heard. This finally forced him out of bed. She appeared to have then dropped sideways into an antique Sheraton chair, which caused a gash in her temple (one of the trademarks of this particular kind of chair were the pointy edges), and when he heard the bang, the neighbor had jumped for a third time.

Her neck snapped the second her head hit the floor. Her right cheek rested on a scrapbook from the years 1961 to 1964 (the dates were written in neat script in the top corner, and it was just about the only spot that wasn't covered in blood).

Finally, the grocery manager flicked on the light and turned to his sleeping wife. He was, as always, struck by a nameless fear of sharing eternity with a person he'd never really known. Maybe it was this fear that, in spite of everything, gave him the courage to get up and call the police. A few minutes later the epicenter of his life was filled with flashing blue lights and sirens and feet stomping up the hallway stairs.

Clearly someone had riffled through the dead matron's possessions. Several drawers had been pulled out of the dressers in the hallway and in her bedroom, the contents spread on the floor. Theoretically, however, this could have happened before she'd died, and she could have been in the process of tidying up, though the police doubted it. The problem was that there was no evidence that her death had been anything but accidental. There were no bruises indicating punches or kicks. All they had to go on was the neighbor's statement concerning noise.

"What was on TV when you heard the guest arrive?" one of the police investigators asked. The grocer looked at him for a long time, and then said rather nonsensically, "I don't remember at all. It's an old Telefunken TV, and I always turn it up loud. My wife snores, you see."

The policeman nodded, though he hadn't understood a word the man said. Morning was breaking, and from the window you could see the Swedish coast like a narrow strip of gray pocket fluff on the horizon. The undertaker stood at the grocer's door staring at the police cars, a blue sheen reflected in his eyes.

Suddenly a light appeared in the grocer's eyes. "The last time I saw Ms. Ladegaard was when she bought stamps a couple days before, right after the anniversary. She got back early. She . . . well, you may not find it easy to believe, but she came in with a letter, or rather a package, she wanted to send to Australia. I remember that . . . Australia . . ." He uttered the last word with undisguised longing.

Then he sank back in his chair and shrugged, as though he wanted to withdraw into the dresser drawer where he'd begun his life.

"To Australia?" the policeman gave his only witness a confused look. He wondered how that could possibly be relevant and decided not to include it in his notes.

But silence had descended on the living room. The cheroot had died out between the old man's fingers. He stared into the darkness, as though he had the power to make the old lady upstairs walk again, to undo everything that had happened.

The policeman let him cry in peace.

* * *

The police drove the few hundred yards from Skodsborg to Kongslund, where I lay sleeping in the King's Room in the early morning hours.

Susanne Ingemann showed them in.

Immediately following the anniversary festivities, we'd tidied up the yard and the house and removed the numerous yellow freesia with their drooping heads, asphyxiated by all the fine guests' cheroot and cigarette smoke. We'd dumped the dead flowers in big garbage bags, and the sweet smell of rot wafted in from the sunroom.

The scent lingered in the hallway outside my room, when Susanne rapped on my door that morning. "It's the police . . . your mother, she . . ." she stammered—and for a moment she looked like she might cry.

"My foster mother," I corrected before she'd even finished the sentence. I had instantly known what she was going to say. Something ought to have collapsed inside me, or at very least a fissure ought to have opened into some deeper layers within. But nothing happened.

I don't remember feeling anything at all.

The few routine questions—and my own brief responses—took less than ten minutes. I had spoken briefly with Magna about an hour before the guests arrived and had then gone to bed—putting orange earplugs in, I told them, because my room faced the lawn where the festivities were still going on. I hadn't heard or seen anything significant.

The policeman gave me his condolences once again and left. I went into the infant room and closed the door. The curtains were drawn. No light whatsoever penetrated the thick folds of cloth. The children were asleep. The song had ceased.

"*Hello,*" the Darkness said. "*You've never been able to stay away for very long.*" If you've known Darkness for a long time, you know that its greetings are not scornful like those of the mirror.

I walked to the window and drew the curtains aside; the blue elephants stepped out of the shadows and threw golden cones of light from their thick trunks, the way they'd always done. I'd once asked Gerda how many blue elephants she had intended to paint in the room, and she'd simply said: "I stopped when there were enough."

I suspected there was a deeper explanation to Gerda's obsession with the blue elephants; one of the assistants claimed that Gerda had painted one for every child that passed through the room. Once, she studied me for a long time (I was only seven or eight then) and said: "Marie, we've had all kinds of children here . . . children of young girls and children of

penniless parents who saw no way to keep them . . . children of professors and politicians and managers, and even children of criminals and
murderers, and that is the hardest of all, because if no one intervenes,
that kind of legacy can follow children through their lives."

Gerda had never doubted the significance of biological inheritance
(this was years before all the clever minds shifted their focus to nurture),
and I later discovered that she feared it more than anything. "A criminal's
mind can live on in the mind of the child—even if they share no physical
proximity," she once told me. "Even if the child grows up under the safest
conditions you can imagine and with the most loving adoptive parents
on Earth, the blood bond will never be torn, Marie. Every single child
contains his or her real father and mother deep inside."

I stood by the window letting my eyes glide with the light toward
the blue elephant above the bed where I myself had lain as an infant. The
elephant's plump body was sliced in two where the wallpaper had peeled,
but it still floated above me on invisible threads; for the first time I sensed
the danger that Gerda had talked about—but without knowing which
direction to look. I was sure she'd been referring to one of the children
who'd been with me in the infant room during that Christmas of 1961. If
my hunch was correct, this child would prove to be the mysterious John
Bjergstrand whom the whole nation had come to see as the symbol of
an unwanted, discarded human being. The kind of being that the well-
intentioned at Kongslund longed to save.

I went upstairs, sat in Magdalene's wheelchair, and stared at Hven.
Still I didn't cry. Out there was the great Stjerneborg Observatory where
Tycho Brahe had made his greatest mistake: "Never will I accept that the
sun is the center of the universe," he'd shouted. "It is an infamous lie. The
earth does not move."

The magnitude of this particular mistake had always appealed to me.

Of course the mirror caught me in this unguarded state of mind and
saw its chance to ask its cruelest question to date: *"My dear little Marie,
who is your mother now?"*

You are, I should have replied mockingly. But I kept quiet. Rococo
mirrors of this very old kind—from the enormous villas on Strandvejen—
do not understand that kind of irony. And during those hours, I had
more important things on my mind.

In the days that followed, the criminal investigators from the
homicide department pursued the mystery of Magna's brutal death

unsuccessfully. They couldn't find motive, or pattern, or a way through the labyrinth, and if she really had been pushed—and if it had anything to do with the anonymous letter as the press conjectured—then there were many possibilities, so many in fact that they only caused more confusion and even more far-fetched theories. Each new theory led to a dead end, and each new dead end increased the frustration.

Then a young policeman suddenly remembered the Oceka grocer mentioning the package Magna sent to Australia. But it had long since left the country, and the sorrowful grocer could not for the life of him remember the name Martha Magnolia Louise Ladegaard had written on the envelope. The package had only been on his counter for a moment. He'd stamped it for more than 200 Danish kroner—that's how far it was going—and Magna had thanked him. Once again the grocer babbled like a child, and the police gave up.

After about a week, the investigation was at a standstill—that much was clear from the papers—and the criminal detectives rolled their eyes when no one was looking.

I understood from the cop who came to Kongslund a few days later and talked to me for a long time about Magna that her death had further startled the prime minister, the minister of national affairs, and their security advisor, Carl Malle. The Danish Security and Intelligence Service had offered its assistance, but the police had declined.

If Magna had any knowledge that might lead to a confrontation in the apartment in Skodsborg, others might be in danger, he said.

Was he referring to me?

Could she have had any dangerous knowledge?

I didn't answer.

If her visitor had gone through all her drawers, what might he have been looking for?

Nobody had an answer. But I noticed that the police had automatically placed both the minister and the security advisor in the category of *nonsuspects*. They had also accepted the shared alibi of everyone at the orphanage: the postcelebration cleanup.

A couple days later, they wanted the names of all the children who'd come to Kongslund between 1961 and 1962, and any who might be connected to the mysterious John Bjergstrand. I gave them only one name: my own.

After that, they seized all of Kongslund's records. They had no way of knowing what I knew: that all evidence of Magna's deeds had been carefully removed from the binders. I thought of Magna again. But no tears came.

Insofar as there were answers to the mysteries of Kongslund, I knew where they were, but it wasn't a knowledge I cared to share then. Everything was recorded in the book that Magna, for as long as I could remember, had kept in her rosewood writing bureau—a book that had always fascinated me but which I had only seen fleetingly a few times. The Kongslund Protocol.

Her precious, secret diary.

I didn't know if Almind-Enevold and Malle knew of the Protocol. The police had gone through all of Magna's belongings, but they hadn't confiscated anything of significance. The Protocol was gone, and it didn't surprise me. After hearing the grocer's description of Magna's last act, I had a pretty good idea where it was.

But it was a secret that I wouldn't share with anyone in the world, not for anything. Since Magna's death, the Protocol belonged to me, and I knew I'd get it back.

At that point, Susanne lost her patience with the investigation and demanded that they release Magna's remains—it had been nearly three weeks—so the old matron could have a dignified burial at Søllerød Church. The police relented. Magna could have been pushed, but she also could have fallen. The case would be dismissed as an accident.

If anyone cared to remember—and at least one person who had become interested in Kongslund could remember—this was exactly what had happened to the woman whose body had been found on the beach between Kongslund and Bellevue seven years earlier. Like Magna, she had died under mysterious circumstances; her case had also reluctantly been classified as an accident. The retired chief homicide inspector who had probed the death and later shared his suspicions with a reporter who had never publicized the story, was now sitting in a summerhouse in Rågeleje reading the newspaper article about the dead matron over and over again.

Finally, he put the newspaper down and stared out the window for a long time.

The dead woman on the beach had carried a picture of Kongslund on her person. And now the former matron of the orphanage had died in equally mystifying circumstances. He couldn't see the connection despite his many years of experience. But he felt the same deep sense of unease.

He sat with his hand on the telephone, weighing his options. His sense of duty told him that someone had to point out these incomprehensible coincidences, yet he feared getting Carl Malle on the line again. Years of experience with police politics told him he wouldn't get further than that, and a former colleague had once warned him not to take any chances: Malle heard everything.

His wife cast a worried look his way. She could always tell when he was tempted to leap into uncertain and hazardous situations.

The distress in her eyes settled the matter for him. He set the telephone receiver back down.

20

THE FUNERAL

June 5, 2008

Perhaps what Magdalene wrote me from the Other Side the evening before we sent my foster mother on her last journey into the Darkness is true: Remember, Marie, adults are just children who have learned to hide their true selves behind beautiful dress and innocent faces; in truth, people react more and more childishly as they age and therefore become ever more dangerous and unpredictable.

Since Magna's death, Magdalene has only addressed me in writing.

I stared at the words and was awake most of the night with an ominous sense that she wasn't just making a general philosophical observation but had a very particular person in mind.

This was a few hours before the journalist Knud Taasing visited me and opened the doors to everything that had been hidden for so long.

* * *

Søllerød Church had aged gracefully. Sitting high above Søllerød Inn, it had white walls, a tower, and choir gable made of large red bricks. The first stones had been laid in the late twelfth century. In the cemetery, which sloped down toward the lake, my foster mother's chosen final resting place commanded a view that no doubt appealed to her lifelong desire to find the best places for herself and those closest to her—not the least of whom were all the children she'd sent into the world.

I glanced at the church ceiling and almost expected to meet Magna's gaze or hear her voice; there was no doubt in my mind that she'd be present at her own departure. Somewhere above us she'd be floating and watching the ceremony, I was sure, and she'd see that I still hadn't cried.

The last time I'd been to church was when I was a little girl and Magdalene, without her wheelchair, had been conveyed to the Other Side. I'd sat on Magna's lap, crying for the loss of my only friend, who'd been so old I'd come to believe she couldn't die. Now Magna herself lay in repose down there in the darkness under a spray of flowers. Beside me sat Gerda Jensen with her eyes narrowed, as though she were counting down to zero in her head. Despite her tiny stature, Gerda loomed large. She was the third most important woman in my life, and the only one still alive.

The scent of freesia pervaded the church, and the congregation sniffled and sneezed in response. It filled me with a childish satisfaction that eternity couldn't meet Magna in dignified silence as was undoubtedly the preference of today's guest of honor, Ole Almind-Enevold. Behind me sat ministers and officials and members of the Resistance; retired doctors, nurses, midwives, and wet nurses; and, at the very back, a small delegation of older ladies from the great years of Mother's Aid Society. The coffin was decorated with white and yellow bouquets, and the God-fearing majority sat with their heads bowed as though in earnest prayer for the dearly departed soul. But I knew this wasn't the case; most of them were thinking thoughts that couldn't be uttered in a church. It wasn't about the dead woman in the coffin, but about their own fragile creep across the field of life. They circled around the fear that Our Lord Jesus Christ had not risen and wouldn't be able to gather them up as they journeyed through the profusion of flowers into Uncertainty. That the Lord might forget the appointment and his promise of eternal life, because He was busy with other matters. Or the unmentionable possibility: that He didn't exist at all, that the body's atoms would fly right up into the stratosphere and become part of a dark and endless universe.

I don't doubt that Magna was excited to meet the Eternal Darkness; her work had equipped her with a ceaselessly curious disposition. She wanted to know all the secrets of life, including the last one. Nevertheless, I know she would have preferred to have remained on Earth for a few more years to fulfill her role in the project that Fate had placed on her path: the Great Repair—that magnanimous task of repairing the defects that the adults of the world in their thoughtlessness had inflicted on God's smallest and most precious creatures. This work has been going on since the days of the Cro-Magnon, of course, and we haven't made much progress. Perhaps we've succeeded in locating (and removing) one one-hundredth of human egotism with each generation (a generous esti-mate), and perhaps we have increased the capacity for compassion by one iota per century (again, a high estimate), and yet this was exactly the kind of hope that Magna carried with her.

Susanne Ingemann is sitting on the bench behind me, next to Carl Malle and the long-since retired director of Mother's Aid Society, Mrs. Krantz. Behind her is Orla Berntsen with Peter Trøst and Søren Severin Nielsen, who are flanked by two elderly couples—their parents—who are sniffling because of the flowers. I recognize them from my childhood trips to Rungsted and Søborg.

The Almighty One is standing by the coffin, distinguished from the impressive profusion of flowers like a small pink tulip with an absurd, genetically modified mop of silvery white hair. He nods because he is—once again—ready to give a speech for my foster mother, the greatest repair woman the nation has ever known. He's wearing a dark suit and stands with folded hands, resembling the undertaker from Strandvejen, who even in this holy moment is sitting triumphantly on a pew in the back of the church in the shadows.

"Magna was a cofounder of Children's Right to Life," Ole Almind-Enevold says, but I am not sure my foster mother approves. Even though she understood the unintended (or at least unconsidered) side effects of abortion—that the living children laughing and singing in front of one's own eyes would never have existed—she also understood the unbearable weight endured by the young women she'd met in such large numbers in her repair shop. And even from the Other Side, she could see her unin-tended role in securing an anti-abortion voting block for the ambitious politician now presiding over her lifeless body.

The minister folded his hands in front of him and raised his voice toward the ceiling. "Magna once told me a story that I never told any-one else, maybe because I wasn't sure how to interpret it . . ." He paused dramatically, and even the scattered sneezing ceased. "She told me of a child who learned that her father, who suffered from tuberculosis, was going to die. The unhappy child prayed to God in Heaven to let her father live, and the father, who heard the despairing entreaties, finally gave his child a promise that went beyond Death: *When I'm gone*, he said, *just wait patiently. I'll come back. And then you'll know I'm still with you, that God exists and watches over you, and that one day we will live together for all eternity.* The sick man died and they buried him, and the child began waiting . . ." The minister paused again, and I thought I saw the hint of a smile on his lips. Behind me, someone sneezed quietly. "Magna stopped her story right there and said nothing until I lost patience and asked, 'But, Magna, when did the child's father return?' She replied, 'Ole, that's the point: he *never* returned.' 'But that can't be right,' I said, 'because if it is, the story is meaningless.' 'Yes,' she said. 'The child waited and waited, year after year; the child grew up and became an adult, but nothing ever happened, and she never stopped waiting, and finally Death came instead, and the father never returned as he'd promised.'"

Now there was no doubt. Almind-Enevold was smiling. I felt the faint unease in the church, as though a little demon were throwing sparks from the ceiling onto people's bare skin.

"It was *her* father," he said. His eyes fell to the coffin. "It was Magna's father."

The congregation became absolutely silent at this revelation.

"As many of you might know," Ole continued, "her father was a minister in Gauerslund, and in Magna's eyes he hadn't broken his promise—and never would—because if eternity exists, you have to possess infinite patience. In her eyes that kind of promise has no limitation—and no end. The father had done the only right thing. He'd both comforted his daughter and proven his case, she said. And she lived according to that principle the rest of her days."

He paused for a moment and then said, "Infinite patience."

I didn't remember the story because my foster mother had never told it to me, and that didn't surprise me because she would have anticipated my rage. I understood better than anyone what Magna had learned from this tragic experience: it was the will to do good that mattered. When that will was properly demonstrated, the good would prove itself in the end. She wasn't one to be distracted by the disappointments this kind of philosophy would trigger along the way, because she never hesitated at the forge in her repair shop. When she was in the process of repairing, sparks flew about her, hitting high and low. In the end, it was this act of sheer will that both defined her and meant the most to her, and I think that's why I didn't cry.

The Almighty One bows his head. The speech is over. This time he has mentioned neither Magdalene nor me, nor quoted from Magdalene's diaries, which I hadn't even known he was aware of.

The church slowly empties.

The white coffin with the golden handles is carried by Carl Malle, Ole Almind-Enevold, Susanne Ingemann, Orla Berntsen, Søren Severin Nielsen, and Peter Trøst. A truly bizarre ensemble. I had refused to participate. I didn't want anyone to see the old matron's foster daughter with her crooked back and inwardly pointing toes collapse under the weight of her dead foster mother's body.

They march outside in small, much too small, steps. Awaiting them are representatives from every type of media: magazines, tabloids, morning papers, TV stations; there are reporters with microphones that stick straight up in the air and tall, gray men with TV cameras on their shoulders.

Knud Taasing stands next to Nils Jensen, who for some reason is making no move to photograph the procession. In the days leading up to the funeral, there had been some speculation in the press: Is the death of Martha Magnolia Louise Ladegaard in any way connected to the case of the anonymous letters? Who'd visited her on the night she died? Who'd received the mysterious package she'd sent a few hours before her death?

Reportedly, the police had made three unsuccessful calls to the Australian authorities, and they had also consulted Danish clubs and associations in Sidney, Melbourne, Brisbane, Adelaide, and Perth—without any results. Apparently, nothing connected the old matron or the orphanage to anyone or anything the Australian police could identify. After three weeks of breathless coverage over whether the death was connected to the Kongslund Affair, it all came to nothing. And I detected a satisfied glint in Ole Almind-Enevold's eyes as he stood beside her grave. In addition, the case of the little Tamil boy had completely disappeared from the front pages after Søren Severin Nielsen had blocked his deportation with a sea of petitions for a humanitarian stay and complaints about violations of laws that protected children. The media didn't have the patience for that.

We stood on the slope facing Søllerød Inn, singing "Beauty Around Us, Glory Above Us"—the way it ought to be sung, without the sentimentality that creeps into the echo of a church space. They lowered Magna into the ground. The reporters stood in uncomfortable silence next to the church's southern wall near a sandstone carving of the Virgin Mary and the Jesus child.

The prominent guests drove to Kongslund, where there were even more flower arrangements. The smell throughout the great villa couldn't have been any stronger than if Magna were still alive, filling the vases with her generous hands. Most of the guests walked onto the patio or stood in the garden, where the sun crocheted patterns on the lawn, and its rays fell through the beech trees, adding a golden sheen to everything. A few weeks ago, many of those present had been gathered to celebrate Magna's anniversary—and now they'd returned to make certain that the grand matron at Kongslund was truly gone.

Ole Almind-Enevold stands in the door to the sunroom, talking to Susanne, when suddenly she calls for me: "Marie, come here a minute!"

Ole stares at me arrogantly, as is his habit. He has never liked me, and perhaps he thinks I know something important about the recent assaults on Kongslund.

"Ole is asking about a diary that he believes Magna kept . . ." Susanne Ingemann says, studying me with a peculiar look in her eyes. I don't think she wants me to answer. But she is also scared of the powerful man.

"A diary?" I sway on my deformed legs. With dry eyes, I imagine Magna's grave. She didn't take it with her. That much I know.

Susanne nods. "Yes. A diary with lists of the children in the home—it may go back all the way to 1936."

"The records are in the office," I say, looking up from the darkness. But not at Ole.

"She might have called it the Protocol or her Log Book. It was about the size of an encyclopedia and bound in green leather."

I shrug and look squarely at Susanne. "Magna didn't confide that kind of thing to me."

Ole stiffens, and I feel his anger like a cold breeze.

Susanne feels it too. "Among other things, it's believed to contain information about Kongslund in the fifties and sixties, which may be able to prove that nothing the newspapers have been suggesting actually happened."

Of course the Almighty One is right. Magna never did anything rash. With the Protocol in a safe place, the powerful people she helped would keep supporting Kongslund.

And then she'd overlooked the real danger.

"Who might she have written in Australia?" the powerful man asks, mutedly. I have a feeling he knows the answer.

Susanne's face is so pale that the shiny halo around her hair is almost gone. I hear the voices in the garden as a distant murmur. Hven lies in the surf, awaiting my visit as always.

I turn and walk away, into the deserted hallway. Nobody follows me, and only the lady in green smiles from her mighty frame on the landing when I pass by. I quickly close the door to my hiding place and flip the key in the lock. Magna put me here more than forty years ago, right here in front of the window, so that I could see the world and the coasts I would never set foot on. She knew what she was doing.

I'd just insulted a king for the second time.

At that moment there came a knock at my door. In all the years Susanne has been the director, she is the only one to come looking for me in the King's Room.

I wasn't a person who went seeking others, and others didn't come seeking me.

There was another knock. Then a third.

"Susanne?" I asked with a thick lisp.

"No. It's Knud Taasing . . . I'm a journalist."

My first thought was illogical: no press had been invited to the private funeral, so how on earth had he gotten in? But it was too late to pretend I wasn't there, and I couldn't stop him anyway. Maybe I didn't want to. I needed to start the next phase of the Kongslund Affair, which would have sunk into oblivion otherwise—just as the administration wanted.

During those days I felt the way Jesus must have felt during his last days on Earth: I knew exactly what had to be done—and how it would all end—but hesitated still (perhaps exactly because I knew) whenever I was about to take another step forward.

I rose and opened the door. The journalist stood alone in the dark corridor. He was lean and surprisingly small in his brown corduroys and green pullover.

I'd never let a man into my room before.

"I just want to ask you one thing, a simple thing, and I'll do it quickly."

I sneezed. There's no such thing as a simple or quick thing. Instead, I pointed at a chair by the window, and he sat down cautiously, as though he was afraid it would collapse under his weight. But it was a Chippendale—the most expensive chair at Kongslund. I was aware that the old mahogany mirror followed the scene with disapproval, but so far it remained silent.

There was no way back now; I sat in Magdalene's wheelchair facing him and gathered my twisted feet on the footrest. This was my preferred position whenever I felt uneasy and needed inspiration from above (I speak of Magdalene, of course). If he found it odd, he didn't show it.

"I would like to offer my condolences . . . Magna Ladegaard was an incredible woman," he began.

I didn't answer but let him study the crooked half of my face, while I waited for his first question. After all, I had called on him myself with the actions I had taken.

"I was hoping I could discuss a few things with you. About Kongslund," he said.

I said nothing.

"Marie, I think you're the one who sent us the anonymous letters." He let the accusation hang in the air between us.

Even though I had expected it, it came as a shock when he said the words so directly. His hand rested on the little brown satchel that he carried with him, and I knew that at any moment he might open it, releasing his demons on whomever did not answer his questions.

I smiled my warped smile. My grimace would have frightened a man less secure than Knud Taasing, but he didn't even blink.

"*You* sent the letters, because you discovered a secret right here at Kongslund—a big secret—isn't that so, Marie?"

I still said nothing.

He opened his bag as I'd predicted and said, "Have a look."

Instantly I recognized the demon he'd brought with him to Kongslund on the very day of Magna's funeral service, and it was true: it would open the floodgates.

"I found this edition at the Royal Library. But I think you've got a magazine just like it . . . and I'd like to see it."

In his hand he held an old magazine, and I didn't need to lean close to know what it was. *Out and About*, May 25, 1961.

He could tell from my reaction that I was caught. "Yes," he said. "I visited the childcare assistant who discovered the foundling on the steps. She'd kept all the magazines—except for one. This one." He threw the forty-seven-year-old edition onto my lap, and in the exact same movement—or so it seemed—another demon flew from his bag, landing, in the form of a small white envelope, on top of the magazine. "Here's the anonymous letter to *Independent Weekly*, the National Ministry, and Channel DK—and to God knows who else. What's interesting . . . Marie Ladegaard . . . is that the letters on the envelope are the same as those in the article about Kongslund's anniversary and the wondrous little foundling . . . the red and black letters, the small and the large . . . *one by one* they were cut from this issue. There's no doubt."

He made a big fuss about his impressive shortcut to the truth.

"And do you know why the childcare assistant who found you doesn't have that particular issue in her collection?" he asked.

I didn't respond.

"Because she gave it to the *foundling*." His eyes lit up. "She left shortly after the episode—and she'd asked Gerda Jensen to give the magazine to the child she'd found on the stairs that day. It was the only magazine she gave away, and that was only because it didn't include a photo of herself."

My movements weren't as agile as his, yet he jumped when I spun the wheelchair around and rolled across the floor to the old bureau that had once belonged to Captain Olbers. I opened the bottom drawer, pushed aside two stacks of old folders and newspaper clippings, and retrieved an exact copy of the magazine he'd brought.

I rolled back to him and handed over the duplicate.

He quickly flipped through the pages until he found the article on Kongslund and then studied it carefully.

The headlines and large chunks of text had been meticulously removed. Letters were missing throughout.

He laughed silently and with a straight face. It was quite a feat.

I closed the drawer and cocked my head. Then, with the lisp that had belonged to the woman in the wheelchair, and which I always used when the world outside Kongslund found cracks in the existence I had constructed, I said, "Yes, that's how it is." I hadn't spoken so strangely since the last of Magna's army of psychologists had visited my room (at her earnest request) and departed a few hours later with his pipe stiff and cold between his pale lips. "But I'll never admit to it in public, so you might as well drop the idea of writing an article about me," I said.

He was puzzled, as was everybody, by my strange way of talking, but only for a moment. For the first time, I sensed an uncertainty in his eyes. "But why not?" he finally asked. "You want the case solved, after all."

I lisped my reply so quietly that he had to lean forward uncomfortably in the Chippendale masterpiece. "It's not important."

"In the article, the foundling is referred to as a boy. How do you explain that?"

I didn't respond.

"Could it be a mistake?"

I remained silent.

"Who is John Bjergstrand?"

I bowed my head all the way to my crooked left shoulder and squinted at him with my drooping left eye. He didn't even blink. The silence between us was like a thick glass door that neither of us wanted to open but through which we could easily see one another. Finally, I said, "John Bjergstrand, who is that?" It was like an echo, a muted, distorted, lisping echo. My *s*'s were a complete disaster that afternoon.

"No, I suppose you don't know. If you did, you wouldn't need anyone's help. You wouldn't have needed to send the letter to the others. But why did you contact me of all people?"

Like all reporters, he was vain, so I decided to tell him the truth.

He was even more shocked than I'd expected.

"You didn't send it to *me*?" For once, Knud Taasing had been pushed off course. If he hadn't been sitting across from such a peculiar creature in such a beautiful room, he would have lit a cigarette. I saw his stiffly arched back like a green mound in the mirror behind him.

I told him who the intended recipient had been, and of course that shook him even more.

"*Nils* . . . ?" he said, incredulous.

"Yes, there were five other boys in the Elephant Room in 1961. Orla, Peter, Severin, Asger, and Nils . . . he was the hardest one for me to locate."

He was thunderstruck. The mirror observed us mockingly.

"Yes, he's adopted—he was just never told. But I've known for a long time," I said, whistling through my *s*'s.

"But why . . . ?" he said.

I didn't respond.

"You wrote all five of them because you wanted to know who John Bjergstrand was, or who he'd become?"

Magdalene looked at him from her hiding place in my soul, but she too was silent. I had a strong sense that I was utterly alone.

"But you don't know yet?"

For a long time he sat with his eyes closed. Then he said, "I found the mother of the boy, or rather, I've discovered who she was when she gave birth to him."

Now I was the one leaning in. The words nearly leaped from my mouth? "Where is she?" I kept the abrupt and somewhat absurd question in the present tense.

"She was a very interesting woman," he said, letting his third demon out of the bag. A notepad filled with dense writing, which he held up. But his handwriting was so illegible that I couldn't decipher it.

"When I saw your letter . . . the one meant for Nils . . . all I had was the name. That was probably the toughest nut to crack of my career: Who was the boy? Who had sent the anonymous information, and *why*? My first step was to go backward in time, and I only had the names of a few people—a family that might not even exist anymore—whose name had been *Bjergstrand*. But I got lucky. Very lucky. A rare name, it appeared in one of the phone company's old directories from the midfifties, and it belonged to a woman who'd lived in Istedgade in Vesterbro. Her name was Ellen Bjergstrand." He paused.

That short pause was almost unbearable. He'd put his hands on some of the most important pieces of the puzzle that I had been struggling with.

"This woman could be a relative of the mysterious John—but none of my inquiries in the different parishes in Vesterbro, or with the Salvation Army or older residents, produced any results whatsoever. Finally I got so desperate I went to the Royal Library and asked to see all the local newspapers from the time, and as is often the case, my persistence finally paid off. The woman with the last name Bjergstrand, the only one with that name I'd been able to find, was killed in her apartment in Vesterbro in 1959.

He sat bolt upright as if witnessing a replay of the killing. "Actually, she was murdered. And not just by anybody, by her own daughter, whose name was"—he looked at me—"Eva Bjergstrand."

I glanced away without a word, my crooked shoulder hiding my expression. Then I decided to ask the only logical question—as he anticipated. With a string of lisping s's, I said: "S-s-s-s-o what happened to this mis-s-s-s-erable girl? This Eva Bjergs-s-trand?"

"There was no information about that. Not in the papers, at any rate. The reporters quickly stopped writing about the case. It was a family tragedy that they didn't want to cover in the first place." He nodded as though to confirm the girl's disappearance to himself. "But I found her in the end. Back then, young girls who'd been sentenced for committing very serious offenses were imprisoned in Horserød State Prison on Zealand, so I got to work looking for her in the library of Prison Services. I went through all of their old annual reviews and records, and discovered that, indeed, she'd been placed at Horserød in 1960. Then I got permission to go through the prison's archives, and finally I found another lead, which was so faint I'd probably have missed it had it not been for—" He fell silent for several seconds, the corners of his mouth turning up in a small, satisfied grin. "It was buried in a sentence scrawled so succinctly in the margins that you'd only be able to find it if you really knew what you were looking for. But I had an idea what I was after."

Now he was unabashedly boasting. I didn't want to reveal my curiosity too obviously at this moment, and it irritated me that he couldn't hide his hunter's pride at having tracked down his quarry.

"In May 1961, a girl by the name of Eva Bjergstrand was pardoned and released from Horserød—in all discretion and likely without the public ever discovering it. And then . . . she vanished."

My shoulders sank, and I sat more crookedly in the wheelchair than Magdalene ever had.

"But why?" he said. "Why was the girl suddenly pardoned?"

I didn't respond.

"Because she got pregnant. Yes. The result of her pregnancy test was actually still in the files. Even competent people make mistakes. And the test was made at Rigshospital. Eva Bjergstrand was imprisoned for murder in 1959, only fifteen years old, and she gave birth to a child in all secrecy at Obstetric Ward B . . . presumably in the spring of 1961 . . . when she was seventeen."

I was impressed. In only a few days, he'd made it as far as I had in years.

Once again, he looked at me triumphantly. "That piece of information correlated with another lead. The midwifery student I'd found in the archives of the Copenhagen union had been a student at Rigshospital in the early sixties. She'd told me the most bizarre story—an almost unbelievable story." Taasing smiled because of course he'd believed it. "It was about a very young woman who'd been brought to the obstetric ward and whose delivery had been arranged using a very special set of rules. She gave birth to a child who was *immediately* removed by hospital authorities, and then she disappeared. It was sheer madness. The midwife, now retired, never forgot that day. She even tried to find the girl to get some explanation for the strange experience, but she never succeeded, because she didn't even know the girl's name—and both the doctor and two older colleagues who were present at the delivery have long since died. There are no records of it anywhere, and she no longer remembers the exact date. Only that it happened in the spring or summer of 1961."

I nodded with reluctant admiration. I could just imagine the former midwife on Kongslund's front steps asking Magna for help—and I could see Magna gesture, using the same hands that had held thousands of infants in their embrace, to express her regret that too many fates had passed her by without a trace.

That of course was a lie. She remembered them all.

Taasing had reached the conclusion of his story: "In other words, around the time the murderer Eva Bjergstrand is pardoned, a girl gives birth under very unusual circumstances at the Rigshospital. It's so remarkable that you can't help but see the two events as related, and I think the result is obvious. The mother of the boy known as John Bjergstrand is the young girl who killed her mother for reasons that she, according to the newspapers, refused to reveal. Somehow she got pregnant when she was serving time, and your foster mother and the governesses at Kongslund helped both her and the man involved out of their predicament. All that remained was the form that you found many years later and which you made sure to pass on to me . . . or rather to Nils."

Taasing stared at me over the rim of his glasses. I could tell he needed both a smoke and a glass of wine. "I'm right, aren't I?" His voice was almost pleading.

I didn't say anything. His puzzle pieces rested on the table, fitting perfectly with mine. There was only one problem: they provided neither one of us with an explanation of the real mystery.

They didn't say anything about who the father was; they didn't reveal his profession or tell us where we might find him today. They gave us no insight into what had happened to the two main characters in the time since. Mother and child.

He knew that of course. "That doesn't tell us who . . . or why your mother died . . ." He breathed through an imaginary cigarette. "Or where the boy is today."

"Was the midwife able to tell you anything about the child?"

The question caught him off guard, but only for a moment. Then he said, "Nothing. She hadn't helped during the delivery. Her task was to assist a nurse in calming Eva down before and after the birth. They had to dress her and wheel her out of the room, the sooner the better. That was the philosophy back then. If you're thinking about any identifiable marks . . . birthmarks—"

"The eyes," was all I said.

He ignored the strange interjection. Perhaps he hadn't even heard me. "What I don't understand is why Carl Malle and the ministry haven't long since made the same discoveries," he said. "Any half-decent detective should be able to find her. After all, Bjergstrand is a fairly uncommon name in Denmark." He looked at me as though he expected an answer.

"Think about it," I said. "They might not need to." My lisp was completely gone.

"Maybe Carl Malle knows all of this already—everything you've just recounted. Maybe that's exactly why that name triggered so much panic in the ministry."

He leaned in so close I could smell the menthol on his breath. "I hear what you're saying," he said. "But how did *you* find the name . . . and the form?"

I wheeled myself to the desk. If he thought I was crazy, his placid gray eyes didn't show it.

In the top drawer was a letter that no one had seen—except for me and of course the woman who'd sent it. Until now I had carefully kept it to myself—and completely out of the Kongslund Affair.

It had originally been addressed to my foster mother, but it had never reached her.

I wheeled around and handed the letter to Taasing. "It's from her."

"From Eva Bjergstrand?" He was flabbergasted.

"Yes."

With a humble gesture, he took the letter and slowly read the single, handwritten sheet carefully, twice, before examining the date. "April 13, 2008," he said.

I held my breath.

Then he read it a third time, as though he wanted to memorize it word for word. "You got this letter, and then you found a form with that name . . . and passed it on to us?"

"Yes."

He looked at me almost admiringly.

I said nothing.

He glanced at his watch. "Today is June 5. This letter was written just over two months ago and was probably en route for a week. We received your anonymous letter on May 5. You acted quickly."

I said nothing. But my heart beat fast. I appreciated that he was shrewd, but I didn't want him to be *too* shrewd.

"Tell me what happened . . ." He sounded like a coconspirator in an old play.

I shook my head. He would only see the pieces of the puzzle that I chose to give him. "There is-s-s-n't much to say. I got the letter. I looked into some things-s. And then I pas-s-s-s-ed on the information."

It was one of the greatest understatements ever articulated at Kongslund, and there'd been quite a few. It was also a lie, and my lisp had returned.

Taasing opened his mouth to speak, but words failed him.

No doubt, at that moment, he wished he could transform into a little worm that could gnaw deep into my brain and explore the secrets it held.

Maybe everything would have turned out differently if he could have.

* * *

The office of the minister of national affairs was as large as a ballroom.

Along one of the wine-red walls stood an enormous cabinet made of Italian walnut and decorated with exotic patterns and engravings. Along another wall, a German interior designer had placed a fake fireplace, with hinges and handles of armored cast iron topped with stained green oak.

In the middle of the room was the minister's giant desk, behind which sat Almind-Enevold on his throne facing Carl Malle. The two resembled a pair of ailing undertakers shaken by the news of Eternal Life on Earth. Orla Berntsen stood by the window.

Ten minutes earlier, the minister's chauffeur had dropped them here after the funeral of the woman each had met during decisive moments in their lives.

"I've been to the Family Council, as we agreed, and something strange has happened," Malle said to the man on the throne.

The minister stared at him for a long time, and then said, "Did you find any trace of that name?"

"No," Malle replied. "But someone had ransacked the place, I could tell. They had carefully combed through the Kongslund files, including those from the Elephant Room. In other words, somebody got there before us—and it has been some time. The dust has grown thick again. It might have been several years ago."

Orla had no problem believing this—Carl Malle had an eye for these kinds of details.

"But that doesn't make any sense. Who the hell knew anything about this so long ago? Before the anonymous letter arrived?" The minister's question lingered as though it demanded an immediate explanation.

Malle turned abruptly to Orla. "Yes . . . who? Who the hell has gone through all the archives from Mother's Aid Society and scattered them about so that it's impossible to make heads or tails of them?"

Orla didn't respond.

"It could have been Severin—but it could also be you, chasing the past . . ." Malle let the peculiar accusation hang in the air. "No one in the council knows anything. But all the boxes have been opened, and the papers have been pulled from the binders. Everything's a mess."

From his spot at the window, Orla said, "It wasn't me."

"Then it might be Severin or Trøst—or Marie." Anger flared in Malle's eyes. Somebody had beaten him to the punch and accessed the sources that might have yielded clues about this John Bjergstrand. He wasn't used to being outpaced.

"Isn't it obvious that someone is accusing the *party* of being involved in all this?" Orla said. "So why don't we concentrate on that? *That's* what's important. Who cares whether anyone has rummaged through the papers in those old boxes?"

"You don't understand a damn thing," Malle said. He stared at the man he'd helped out of a miserable childhood in Søborg. "You have *no idea* that this boy is the key to everything that's happened."

"And what you're saying is *ridiculous* . . ." The minister rose from his mahogany and birch throne. His face had assumed a faintly purple hue, like the glow of the rainbow over the courtyard fountain when the sun was at its zenith.

"But our letter writer must have had a reason to send it to you," Malle said, still glowering at Orla. "Do you have any old items or papers from your time at Kongslund?"

"I don't. My mother would have had to—"

"Your adoptive mother is *dead*." The minister interrupted his chief of staff so brutally that he flinched. The minister had expressly said *adoptive mother*.

"My adoptive mother?" Orla said.

"Your mother, I mean," the minister quickly corrected.

"It's your house now," Malle said. "Maybe there's something in her belongings that could be of service to us."

Orla turned pale, sniffling twice before answering. "I don't think so," he said. "It's such a small house. I would have found it."

"Look again." Malle was fully apprised of the situation and knew that Orla hadn't gotten around to moving a single thing out of his childhood home. He also knew that Orla was living there now, waiting for his divorce to be finalized and for a sign to tell him where to go from there.

"Yes, search the house as fast as possible." The minister gestured toward the door. "Maybe you'll find something you missed."

Orla was dismissed, and he retreated with a look of pure spite on his face, a look that a top official normally would have kept concealed.

Only when the minister was alone with his specialist did he say, "If only I knew who . . ."

Malle didn't respond.

"Who John Bjergstrand was . . . or rather *is*."

"We do have one option . . . We can challenge the person who was closest to Magna, the only one who might have any knowledge of us."

"Marie?"

Malle nodded.

"She's always made my skin crawl. That crazy little shit quoting weird things from the spastic woman's diary."

"You seemed to find those diaries quite useful at the anniversary party."

"I don't think Marie knew her foster mother had made copies."

"Maybe Magna was jealous of her." Malle paused as though he'd expressed a theory too far-fetched.

The minister barely noticed. He was lost in his own thoughts. "What the hell were the contents of that package? Could it have been the Protocol . . . her personal records?"

"Yes," Malle said. "There's no doubt. I think that Magna finally sent her little book, with all her notes, to the child's mother—about us and the child . . . She must have known exactly where to send it."

"We've got to get ahold of it!"

"I've dispatched two men to Australia. We haven't located her yet, but we will. We'll get there first."

"We *have* to get there first."

"Yes. Of course they have to be very discreet—but if she's still alive, we'll find her before anyone else. But there's another matter . . ."

"Yes?" the minister said with bated breath.

"The retired chief inspector that I told you about, the one who called the homicide chief?"

"Yes. You wanted to find him."

"No, I wanted to find out what he called about. I never got along with that man, so I don't want to contact him. But he does constitute a problem."

"Yes?" the minister said, for the third time.

"He was a good investigator. And as I mentioned, he handled a case a few years ago where a woman was found murdered on a beach . . . quite close to Bellevue . . . and to Kongslund. And he's still mulling it over. They were never able to determine whether it was an accident . . . or something much worse. Murder, that is."

"An accident?"

"Maybe she simply fell. She couldn't tell anyone, obviously, since she was dead when investigators arrived. But the circumstances made it a . . . special case." Malle hesitated and then said, "She didn't have any ID on her. They never found out who she was."

"There's hardly anything unusual about that. She was a tourist passing through. Or maybe just a person wanting to commit suicide, who didn't want to be identified."

"They discovered certain things—out there on the beach that morning," Malle said, ignoring the minister's interjection. "And that's what bothered the chief inspector. He sent a list of his findings to the FBI to get some assistance, but this was right after the terror attacks on September 11—and of course the FBI didn't have any background to interpret the clues they found . . . if they even were clues."

"It's not like you to speak in riddles, Carl. What the hell are you talking about . . . clues?" the minister said impatiently.

"Yes. Next to the body was an old science-fiction novel, a branch that had evidently been sawed off a tree and carried to the beach, and a short rope knotted in a noose. But the most peculiar thing they found was a canary with a broken neck. The woman's head had struck a rock when she'd fallen, and it was practically the only rock on the entire beach. One of her eyes had been smashed in."

"And?" The minister's arrogance returned.

"Well, I'm just wondering whether all this is significant in a way I ought to understand . . . I just can't grasp it." Malle stalled and glanced at the ceiling as though for assistance.

The minister leaned back in his antique chair that had been so carefully carved by the famed cabinetmakers, Andreas and Severin Jensen. "You'd have to possess exceptional talent to find the connections in all of that, Carl. Were there other cases?"

"No. I already checked that out."

"So what's it got to do with Kongslund?"

"The final clue was in the woman's pocket."

"Yes?" The minister sounded both captivated and irritated at the same time.

"It was a photograph. A small black-and-white photograph"—Malle leaned in closer—"of Kongslund. And it was exactly the same photo the anonymous letter writer distributed a month ago. That was the photo the inspector recognized in the paper."

This information shook the minister, it was clear. Nevertheless he tried to pass it off. "But numerous adopted children could have found a copy of some random picture of Kongslund."

"Exactly the same?"

"Yes, of course."

"But, eh, there's one more thing . . ."

"Yes?"

"They didn't think the woman was Danish. They examined the clothes." Malle let the comment linger.

The minister went pale. He didn't even have to ask his security advisor to continue.

Malle nodded. "Yes. They thought she might be from New Zealand or"—he paused dramatically—"Australia."

"No!" Almind-Enevold's outburst was genuine.

"That, of course, is what we should really be concerned about."

21

LETTER FROM THE PAST

April 24, 2001

I should have understood Fate's natural aversion to the symmetry that is humankind's defense against uncertainty. I should have seen the signs that it had awoken in its heavenly bed once again to prove to the living and the dead that the world is not ruled by immense chance alone. Of course not.

For more than four decades, Magdalene's words in the small, hand-written journals had served as the sole echo of Kongslund's unknown past, and I thought it would stay like that. But then Fate raised its hand and pointed directly through the clouds—at me—and I knew right away that it was too late to escape.

Eva Bjergstrand's final words reached me on an April morning in 2001. Out of nowhere. The letter lay on the brown doormat in the hallway, under the painting of the woman in the green dress. I should have left it there, but in the most reckless moment of my life, I did exactly what Fate had dreamed about, had waited for.

* * *

One of the stamps on the envelope depicted the Sydney Opera House, the other a leaping kangaroo in a gray-yellow desert landscape. The stamps were large and impressive, just like the country they represented, but I knew from my brief time as a six-year-old stamp collector that Australian stamps were rarely valuable. And the bigger they were, the less value they held.

This absurd thought struck me as I stood there in the hallway.

As I recall the moment, I felt an instinctive discomfort about the letter—but this may have been a later attribution as a result of the catastrophic events it triggered. The address had been hand printed. In a sense it had arrived at the right place, but the mail carrier in his haste had overlooked the difference between my name and the one that was actually on the envelope, Martha Ladegaard. My foster mother had retired in 1989 and had moved from Kongslund to an apartment in Skodsborg farther up Strandvejen. The letter had, of course, been intended for her.

I stood for a long time studying the letter and contemplating its contents. It had been postmarked on the other side of the planet a week earlier, on April 17, 2001.

Most likely, the sender was a former Kongslund child or a thankful adoptive family that was sending a happy greeting from a new continent—but for some reason, I didn't think that was the case.

I took the envelope up to the King's Room and sat on the bed. My deformed fingers trembled faintly, like small pieces of confetti in the breeze, when I finally tore the letter open. Maybe I sensed the fear already at that moment, or maybe it didn't set in until I started reading—it's hard to say now because it feels as though the words have always been with me.

There was a single piece of paper in the envelope, with writing on both sides. The paper had been folded around another envelope, smaller than the first and entirely white. On the front the sender had written in a clumsy hand only two words: *My child.*

I looked at the single piece of paper, which in contrast to the envelope was pretty ordinary, not intended for airmail. I registered this little illogical detail in the right part of my brain for posterity. Perhaps the detail would tell me something about the sender that might be useful in the future.

The letter itself was dated April 13, four days prior to the date on the stamp. On the bottom of the second page, the sender had written her name: *Sincerely yours, Eva Bjergstrand.*

It didn't ring any bells at the time.

Under the name were a few more sentences: *P.S. I hope you do not take offense that I contact you after all these years. I trust that everything can be taken care of to the benefit of all and without too much hassle. I look forward to your response.*

I could have folded up the paper and left it, unread, on my table. I could have taken it to Magna the next time I went to the baker in Skodsborg, but that wasn't the kind of person I was.

Now, with the benefit of hindsight, when time cannot be unspooled, I wish with all my heart that I had never seen the letter. That I'd never read it. That I'd given it to my foster mother, because then no one would have ever found it, and it would have almost surely prevented all the horrible things that have happened since.

On the other hand, the letter offered me insight into a world I didn't know about, but which I was very curious to discover. It was like putting Magdalene's long, royal telescope to my eye and staring straight into an age everyone believed was past and forgotten and therefore didn't want to talk about.

What I saw was my home, four decades ago—and what I heard was a voice that had been silent almost as long.

I couldn't have stopped even if the very guardian of the holy grail of Goodness had climbed onto my crooked shoulder and in a thundering voice had shouted a warning into my ear: *Stop! You're stepping into a world that does not belong to you! Stop! For God's sake!*

I couldn't resist the temptation to wander directly through the open door.

* * *

Dear Ms. Martha Magnolia Ladegaard (Magna),

In the hope that this letter will reach you and will be read in the spirit in which it was written, I now find the courage to write the words that have long been on my mind.

For forty years I've been thinking about Kongslund. Not like a shadow or echo of the past but very much present, as clear as the days back in 1961 when we discussed what was going to happen. About the pardon and the adoption, and that I had to leave the country and start a new life. As I write this, I am looking at your Christmas greeting from 1961, with the photo of the "seven little dwarves." I can only envy them their innocence and their happy eyes under their elf hats. If one of them is mine, and I am certain that is the case, you didn't write to tell me, and of course I know why. They must have all been adopted during the months that followed.

Perhaps it is wrong of me to write you. Perhaps I ought to put my pen down. I'm not writing to try to change anything or to accuse you of making a mistake. On the contrary, I think you did what you did with the best of intentions—hoping to give us all a chance of starting afresh. My child and its adoptive parents. And me.

As you see, I am writing these words on Good Friday, and as you know, this is a very special day for me. Do you remember how we laughed at the strange coincidence that I was born on the day of death commemorated by all Christians! When I was a child, my birthday often fell during Easter when it was still freezing, leaving even the raucous street that I grew up on silent as the grave.

Not a day passes that I don't think about my child. We have to forget everything, you said. That was the promise we made one another for the sake of my child. To this day I have kept my word. I've done my best to forget and almost succeeded at times. I've often asked myself whether we had any other choice, but I never found the answer.

Though time does not heal all wounds, even grief becomes a habit. But as is always the case, it doesn't take much for it to return, and that's why I am writing this letter. Right before Easter, when the past is always closer than otherwise, I happened to walk though Adelaide. Often, Danish tourists sit in front of the old hotel reading the magazines and newspapers that the pilots and stewardesses brought with them from Denmark. One of them had left a paper on the bench, and I gave in to the urge to hear news from my native country. Normally I never do that.

I saw a lengthy article about a wedding in Holmen's Church, and in one of the pictures of the guests I recognized the father of my child. It was taken at Slotsholm on April 7. It was a shock. I could still see, quite vividly, his face in the visitor's room, and I could hear his voice talk to me until I could no longer resist.

God forgive me, Ms. Ladegaard, but on this very day when Jesus was crucified, I ask you: What right does he have to all the happiness he has had? What right does he have to everything I never had?

Can you imagine the loneliness in the room I am sitting in now? A whole life was wasted because of this one awful encounter and one single decision that could not have been different. I fear that he both knows and sees his child while I am sitting here alone. Perhaps it sounds terribly self-pitying? But I cannot react in any other way.

That's why I decided to write you this letter. Not to break my promise of silence but to ask you one last favor: Would you pass on the enclosed letter to my child and confirm my existence? Will you tell my child that not a day passes that I don't wish that things could have been different so that I might make amends for the colossal sin that was committed?

Will you intercede for me now that time is short?

I don't know whether I have been punished enough for my terrible deeds, but I will know soon. Perhaps there is still hope that we may find solace. Maybe even forgiveness.

Yours sincerely, Eva Bjergstrand

P.S. I hope you do not take offense that I contact you after all these years. I trust that everything can be taken care of to the benefit of all and without too much hassle. I look forward to your response.

* * *

But there was no sender's address on the letter, so Magna must have known it already.

The next day I called the Australian embassy in Copenhagen, but it was clear they didn't understand my questions.

The female clerk suggested I call the Danish embassy in Sydney, but I didn't want to involve the Danish authorities.

Perhaps I sensed then that my search for the mysterious sender, Eva Bjergstrand, and her mysterious child would entail a very considerable risk that I hadn't understood in the beginning.

Instead I left Kongslund and took the bus down Strandvejen to Østerbro. The embassy was housed in a surprisingly small building, considering the size of the country it represented.

Face to face with the female clerk, I repeated my request, and she noted the few facts that I presented. Once again she suggested that I contact the Danish representatives in her home country. Finally, however, she promised to investigate the matter.

I went on to the Royal Library on Krystalgade and browsed the three biggest national newspapers, the ones I imagined were most likely to wind up on a bench in Australia—but I didn't find the photograph Eva Bjergstrand had mentioned. Maybe she'd been wrong about the date.

The very next day, the embassy clerk called Kongslund and asked for me. Susanne Ingemann knocked on my door, her curiosity roused. First, no one ever called me; second, the woman on the line had spoken English; third, she had mentioned an embassy. The Australian embassy.

But she knew better than to ask.

I took the liberty of closing the door to the office so Susanne could not hear my conversation, and in those minutes, I was told what I had expected to hear: no woman with that name lived in the region surrounding Adelaide, or in all of Australia for that matter. Either she had moved a long time ago, or I had the wrong name. There was a third possibility, the clerk explained: the woman I was looking for could have assumed a new name upon moving to Australia. Quite a few people did just that. A telling pause followed. Australia was a vast country, and, like America in the previous century, it had swallowed up many black souls, those desperate and troubled individuals who might otherwise have perished. Many of whom had replaced their old identities with new ones.

And this soul was black, I knew that much.

For days, I sat with the letter from Australia; I knew the words by heart.

We have to forget everything, you said. That was the promise we made one another for the sake of my child. To this day I have kept my word.

And then something unexpected happened.

I saw a lengthy article about a wedding in Holmen's Church, and in one of the pictures of the guests I recognized . . .

The child's father.

It was taken at Slotsholm on April 7. It was a shock.

The thought of revenge . . .

What right does he have to everything I never had?

The words hit me with a force I was completely unprepared for. Perhaps it was because I thought I'd known so many children whose fathers had fled from everything others had assumed was dear to them—many early in the morning, and without a trace, to ensure that they weren't found—and then the women would be enveloped in the Great Reproach, which everyone involved conveyed to these unhappy, abandoned women whether they wanted to or not.

For this woman, Magna was the only way to reach the child she'd never met—and she had enclosed a small white envelope with the words: *My child.*

And yet I didn't for a second doubt that my foster mother would deny her wish. She'd never choose to open a door to a past nobody else knew about. This was where her power resided. And I understood that this was why Fate, in the simple body of a mail carrier, had chosen to throw Eva's letter at my feet—and so I sat in the King's Room with the little white envelope in my hands, hour after hour. *My child.* How banal.

This envelope contained Eva's final words to her child, and once again, all the alarm bells went off—just as clearly as Magna's song about the blue elephants—and for days I refrained from opening it as I pondered my chances of fulfilling the woman's wish without committing my final sin. Night after sleepless night I tried to summon Magdalene for counsel, but she rarely left her royal soul mate on the Other Side these days, and I figured that they probably had more important things to do. Her lack of response confirmed my suspicions.

Early on the third morning after receiving the letter, I tiptoed into the Elephant Room, and when the first beam of light pierced the crack between the curtains and struck the eternally marching elephants, I got the answer I'd been waiting for. *Seven elephants go a marching now*, a distant voice sang far above me, and it seemed that the small faces in the beds smiled toward the unknown, for which they had no words yet. The message had never been clear as in Magna's heyday, when the elephants' march across the web resounded like boots stomping on a wooden floor.

I went back to the King's Room and removed the envelope from my desk.

It wasn't even a millimeter thick, and so light you'd think it contained nothing at all. I glanced at the sound and at Hven—the old astronomer had no time for problems as mundane as these, of course—then closed my eyes and slit it open.

There I was in Magdalene's old abandoned wheelchair—where our young and old eyes had studied the world—letter in hand. A letter I should not have read.

Eva's message was printed so delicately on such thin paper that you'd think it'd been spun from spider silk and kept in the dark for a hundred years.

But there remained a faint scent of another person's presence.

My dear child.

That was the first, rather sentimental line.

But not even that warning sign discouraged me from reading further.

* * *

My dear child,

We were never meant to meet. I've long since realized that, and I think it is the best for both of us. But I want you to know that not a single day and not a single hour has passed when I haven't thought of you and wished you all the happiness a person can have.

How much do you know? How much did they tell you? I've asked myself that all these years. You were taken from me when I was still in the delivery room, and I never got to see you. My eyes have never rested on your face, and today that seems like the biggest punishment that a human being can suffer. Ms. Ladegaard wanted to keep both your birth name and the identity of your adoptive family secret out of consideration for us both. I don't know whether she ever told you about your mother and her fate, but if not, I've asked her with this letter to tell you everything and answer all the questions you might have: about my deeds, about my crime, and about the exit I finally accepted because I couldn't live with you after what I'd done to my own mother.

I was seventeen when you were born at the Rigshospital. No one was to know that I was pregnant. My only demand was that you be baptized in my name, and so you were in the hospital's chapel the morning following your birth. That one piece of paper is all that documents our connection. That has been my comfort all these years. You've been in my thoughts ever since and you're as close to me today as the night you were taken away.

Only in the final hours did my courage fail me. I demanded to see Ms. Ladegaard to ask her to find a milder solution, but there was none, she said. You were to be adopted in all secrecy. I begged her to give me the name of your new family so that at least I could assure myself that you'd be safe. That everything would be well where you were going. She refused. It was only when I threatened to cancel my departure and tell my story that she showed me the adoption form that included the name of the woman who was to be your adoptive mother. And I am glad for this today. That knowledge is my evidence that I've never tried to break my promise or do anything that could bring you any harm. I know that the name of your adoptive mother is Dorah Laursen, and that back then she lived in Østerbro. I've never contacted her. It's the hardest thing I've ever done, but I've kept my word.

Life cannot be redone. But you should know that my love lives on regardless of the distance, even if we never meet. There is no drama in my present decision. Only the certainty that I cannot contain the longing anymore. I was born on Good Friday and committed my irredeemable crime on Good Friday. I write my last letter on Good Friday. I live in a world where I've got nothing to do. For me, all that matters is your life. I pray that you can carry on what was good inside of me, not least because you've grown up so far from my terrible influence. I pray that you'll carry me in your memory so that I can live through you like the love you give to your own children. That is all I allow myself to dream of.

Ms. Ladegaard can tell you the rest—she has my blessing to do so.

My love for you will live forever.

—Eva, your mother

* * *

My first reaction wasn't pity for the unknown woman who'd lost everything she loved—her child, her native country, and her family (if she had one)—but a far more egotistical feeling that I didn't understand at first: powerful anger and deep irritation.

I wanted to throw away the letter and forget all about it, forget the fragile handwriting and the clumsy language. Did she hint at suicide toward the end of the letter? That more than anything irritated me.

I turned to the practical side of the matter—the name of the adoptive mother—but I'd never heard of a Dorah Laursen in Østerbro. And I'd seen nothing to suggest that my foster mother knew a woman by that name, neither forty years ago nor more recently.

In the secret compartment behind the lemon-tree carvings, there were the notes from my many years of observing the children whose adoptive families I'd located. From the beginning, my investigation had been logically planned with the help of Magdalene, and Kongslund's records had been as accurate as you'd expect from a matron of Magna's caliber. The only thing that puzzled us—even then—but which didn't seem all that important at the time, was the complete lack of information about the biological parents of these particular children. Normally, family names were meticulously recorded in Mother's Aid Society and Kongslund's documents, but in each of these cases, the files for the biological father and biological mother were empty. I didn't care about them at the time, because all I wanted to know was where the children ended up. And it had been easy to find addresses of adoptive parents.

The first time around, I'd been satisfied to track the families residing closest to Kongslund. I was curious about life outside the orphanage so, at a distance, I studied Peter Trøst and Orla Berntsen, and then later Severin and Asger.

But the fifth boy from the Christmas photo from 1961 was completely absent. There was no record of him in Magna's papers, and regardless of how much I looked, I couldn't figure out what had happened to his file. Or why it might be missing.

This despite the fact that his date of arrival was clearly marked in the Elephant Room's annual calendar from 1961: on May 3, a child arrived at Kongslund and was laid in the bed reserved for new arrivals.

No name was recorded, presumably because there had been no baptism at the Rigshospital, which was quite normal.

Back then, Magdalene and I had reluctantly given up on the mystery. Only Magna could tell me the truth, and she would refuse to do so on the grounds that had always guided her work: the children at Kongslund were under her protection and therefore shouldn't have to fear that anyone would find them—and certainly not the biological parents who had chosen to abandon them in the first place. Besides, I didn't want to admit what I'd been up to.

Years later, the letter from Australia reopened the mystery about this boy. *Here* was the clue that I'd been looking for all along, I was certain.

Once again I studied the name of the woman who, according to Eva Bjergstrand, had adopted her child: Dorah Laursen.

I was surprised my foster mother had run that risk. Despite her brash manner, Magna was an extremely cautious woman.

On the other hand, the alternative was a scandal of enormous proportions, and she must have believed it was her only option. The very young mother had threatened to reveal what had really happened: an upstanding citizen had impregnated a felon, a minor—possibly even in a prison cell of all places. It could hardly get any worse than that. The father might have even been a policeman or a prison warden, a man who had climbed up through the ranks to the point where his face was in the papers—or at least in the newspaper that Eva had picked up on a bench in Adelaide.

In 1961, the consequences of such a revelation must have seemed devastating to both the man and the governesses at Kongslund.

I found a phone directory in Susanne Ingemann's office and looked up Laursen. There was no one by that surname in Copenhagen with the first name Dorah.

Then I called information, but that didn't produce any result either. Unless they had something besides the name to go by, they couldn't help me, and the number might also be registered in a partner's name if she was married or cohabitating.

I was sure she would have been married in 1961, because that was a nonnegotiable condition for adoption at the time. Proper family relations. But of course she could have divorced and remarried and divorced several times since.

My next idea was to confirm that a person or family by that name lived in Østerbro in 1961. It took me a couple of days and a visit to the telephone company. There I borrowed a copy of the telephone directory from 1961 and found, as if by magic, the number for the Laursen family—which peculiarly enough was in Dorah's name. According to the listing, she lived in exactly the part of the city that the Australian woman recalled: Svanemøllevej 31, Østerbro.

By combining street directories from that era with current phone books, I located three persons still living on the same block, two of them even in the same apartment building.

The next day I took the bus to Østerbro, first visiting Dorah's old apartment. Here I talked to a young mother who didn't know anything about the woman who used to live there. I had expected as much. I went down one floor and rang the doorbell of the only family that had lived in the apartment building since the sixties. An elderly man opened the door and stared confusedly at me. A little terrier with a gray beard growled from between the man's feet.

"I'm looking for Dorah Laursen. She used to live in this building forty years ago—on the third floor," I said in a somewhat formal tone. I wasn't used to speaking with strangers.

"Ms. Laursen? But she moved many years ago." Oddly, he remembered her right away. I couldn't believe my luck.

"Did she have a husband?" I asked. Surely he would be easier to track down.

"Married? No, I don't think so. She lived alone."

I was surprised by this information. *Alone?* It would run directly counter to Mother's Aid Society's basic principle that adopted children grow up in whole, healthy families—which is to say, with both a mother *and* a father. "But—she had a child . . . ?" I said, a little flummoxed.

"Ah, yes . . ." The old man hesitated for a second. "There *was* a child right before she moved."

"Right before she moved?"

"Yes. It was the year my wife died . . ." The old man paused again. "In 1966."

"1966?" I was more perplexed than ever. It was like walking through a dark corridor and discovering that all the doors you'd opened led to new, unlit chambers no one knew existed.

"Yes. A little boy." He suddenly smiled. "She took him in his baby carriage to the grocer . . . I think he was adopted—the boy I mean."

"Adopted?"

"Yes."

"Could this have been a few years earlier?" With unease I tried leading him back to the year I was focused on. "1961 or '62?"

"No," he said firmly. "My wife died in 1966."

"But do you know where she moved to, with the boy?"

"Yes. To Jutland. She had grown tired of the city. She sent me a letter after my wife died." He recognized my curiosity at once.

A couple of minutes later, he returned with a small envelope in his hand. Her address was written in neat script on the back of the envelope: *Dorah Laursen, Sletterhagevej 18, Stødov, Helgenæs.*

From between the old man's feet, the dog stared at me as if it understood what was about to happen.

* * *

Though I hated traveling, I had to go. I hadn't gone that far since my secret investigation of Asger Christoffersen and his parents in Jutland when we were kids.

The new date was a complete mystery to me. I simply couldn't understand how the woman who had been selected to adopt Eva's child in 1961 had suddenly been declared childless—until, according to the old man, she adopted a boy in 1966. Five years too late. Maybe they'd given up and found another.

For many hours I thought about my options, but there was no way back. Three days later, I stepped off of bus 361 in the little town of Stødov at Helgenæs and knocked on a small, low door in a whitewashed house with a thatched roof. The door was opened by a small, stout woman with a short, thick neck and stumpy legs, which made me wonder whether her seemingly squashed figure had anything to do with the modest size of the house—if it was actually possible that decades of living in such a low-ceilinged residence had finally compressed this woman's frame, flattening it.

"Hello," I said.

She was about seventy years old, and her living room was rather messy—full of trinkets as well as tiny cobwebs that were visible in the light that filtered through the narrow windows.

The minute I mentioned Kongslund, she interrupted me with a frightened look in her eyes. "You're from Kongslund . . . from the orphanage?"

I kept the crooked side of my face hidden in the shadow so she wouldn't find yet another cause for concern, and said carefully, "Yes. I've lived there all my life."

For a moment she sat completely still. Then she said, "But what's happened at Kongslund after all these years that has anything to do with me?" The question was straightforward, yet peculiar—and her voice trembled.

"How long has it been since you heard from anyone at Kongslund?" I asked.

For some reason she suddenly blushed. "Do you mean when I gave up my child—or later?" Her fear hung like a dark shadow in the pockets of dust under the low ceiling.

"Tell me about the *first* time," I said, trying to conceal my surprise at her strange question.

"It's not easy . . . It's been so long, you see," she said with the immense hesitation characteristic of that hilly region. "I just remember that I contacted them . . . when I became pregnant." She closed her eyes and sank into herself. "I asked them for help . . . because I had no idea who the father was."

"What year did you become pregnant?" I edged farther away from her in the hope that it would help unfold her sunken body just a little bit.

"It was 1961. Today my son is—" She interrupted herself, opened her eyes, and stared up at me. Then she said, "But he was given to somebody else."

"But you have a child today, Dorah, don't you?" I spoke to her as though she were one of the two-year-olds in the Giraffe Room, but she didn't seem to notice.

"Yes. Lars. I got him *the second time around* . . . When I got angry."

"The second time around?"

"Yes. First they came and picked up my . . . son. Early in the morning. It was a woman I didn't know." She sniffled once, quickly and the sound filled the entire room. "They promised me there'd be no trouble. She took the child with her . . . my son . . . It wasn't an official adoption, after all, and that was that." She looked up, a little startled as though it had all just happened. "It was four in the morning."

"Who took him?"

"How would I know?" she said defensively. "I first talked to Mother's Aid Society and then with a lady from Kongslund who said they would take care of it for everyone's benefit. I just had to let in their messenger when she arrived. And afterward, I was to forget all about it."

Messenger. I noted her word choice with a light shiver. She had, without knowing it, used the exact same word that was printed in Magdalene's journal:

It was a messenger, and not a mother. I saw that right away. She simply placed the little one on the steps; there was no farewell, no grief.

"You just had to forget all about it?"

"Yes. We were never to discuss it again."

"But then you got pregnant again?"

She gave me a surprised look. "No. That was the problem. It was as though my deed had . . ." She searched for the words, but couldn't find them. Then she continued in a muted voice, as though she were confiding a big secret to me: "After a while I regretted it . . . that I'd handed over my son. So I called them and demanded to have him back . . . Then I got another visit from the woman from Kongslund—"

"The same woman?" I asked, interrupting her.

"Yes. I don't remember her name, but she was small, petite. This was in the winter of 1965. She said I couldn't have my son back . . . because he'd long since been placed with a family." Dorah sniffled and wiped her nose with her meaty forearm, the way a child does. "That made me really angry, because I was the one who was alone, and they were the ones who'd said it was the best thing for me. But they'd been completely wrong. I should've kept my son." She sniffled again. "Then I told her that they seemed to be living in a world where little babies could be given and taken at will, and that they had to find another boy for me to replace the one they had taken."

I started, and my reaction must have been obvious, because she became nervous and silent and looked like she might just disappear from the face of the earth, right into the sofa cushions.

Finally, she stirred again. "At first they refused. They couldn't do that, she said. But I was serious. And then they got scared." She reemerged from the cushions, as though reborn.

"They got scared?"

She laughed, sniffling at the same time, and said, "Yes. I think they would have liked to have gotten rid of me—handed me to someone who could lock me up—but they didn't dare, and finally they gave in, and I was told to wait."

"To wait?"

"Yes. For the delivery." Dorah's eyes shined bright.

The delivery. I could feel a cold shiver running up my crooked shoulder.

"It was in early February." She glared at me defiantly, as though I was one of them. "In 1966."

I waited for the frightening conclusion.

"Well, then she came . . . one Saturday evening . . . with my child. With my new son. All the paperwork was in order, of course. Everything. They had even baptized him—his name was Lars—and that couldn't be changed. But I didn't care." She smiled up at the clock on the wall; clearly she had traveled back in time.

Her life's triumph.

It was grotesque.

"He could be named Lars for all I cared," she said.

A flood of questions streamed through my mind, and I didn't know where to begin. I couldn't make heads or tails of what she was telling me. How could she have been given a son—*again*—five years later?

And what had happened to the first child?

And who was the woman who gave and took children—Goodness of Heart's very own messenger?

"I don't understand it," I said in a low voice, already resigned to never understanding it.

"No, I've never understood it either," she said. And then she suddenly stood. "I don't want to talk about it anymore. It doesn't matter now. I got Lars, and that's what matters. I've never had any problems with him. And it's been so long."

"Where is he now—your son?"

"He isn't here. He's a chauffeur. He drives for a limousine company in Aarhus. The wealthy hire them for parties and weddings. He's coming to visit me tonight."

"Did you ever tell him . . . that you . . . ?"

"No. What am I supposed to say? I don't know anything about his background . . . and I promised not to say a word to anyone."

I could feel the anger in my twisted bones. I could feel how it forced its way through my stomach and lungs and throat and readied itself to leap, glowing red, into the living room where there was no place for that kind of outburst.

I breathed and checked my emotions—and then stood. "I want to tell you one thing, Ms. Laursen . . . You should *never* keep your child in ignorance about that kind of thing. *Never.*" I almost whispered the last few words. "Because *they can feel it anyway* . . . and that ruins them forever. It ruins their lives because they know that something's wrong, even when no one talks about it. They just know . . . the way every person knows that kind of thing. A lie is an illusion. Deep down you always know the truth."

She stared at me, startled.

"Somebody has played a trick on you, Dorah, and you and I have to figure out who. All we know right now is that Kongslund is involved, and if you don't tell Lars, *I* will, and I mean it . . . You have to tell him the truth. *Now.*"

She had sunken into the gray sofa and was crying.

I never saw Dorah again. I left her late that afternoon, before her son came home. Judging by the light of what happened later, I should have stayed and talked everything through with her. With both of them.

I should have been present when her son received the terrible message. I should have been there to observe his immediate reaction to the shocking story; nobody knows when and in which situations people will react uncontrollably. But confused by the woman's crying, I had imagined a quiet and equally compressed, younger male version of Dorah, which of course was a foolish mistake since they were not blood relatives at all.

I should have known that better than anyone.

When he showed up in Copenhagen, it was too late. And how he tracked down Magna's inner circle, I'll never know.

That day in the hills I overlooked the obvious.

* * *

I returned to Copenhagen determined to do one thing: go through every extant archive that contained the name Bjergstrand, as well as the few painstakingly gathered pieces of information I kept stored in my mind. It would be a long investigation, and I would have to tell Susanne Ingemann about my plans—and therefore also tell her about the letter from Eva Bjergstrand.

That didn't worry me much. She'd be discreet. After all, I had much more in common with her than with any other person—far more than anyone outside Kongslund could know.

She was the one who suggested that I expand the search to include the archives of Mother's Aid Society, which at some point had been moved to the Civil Law Directorate, where they'd been put in boxes and stashed in an attic and presumably were still—unless someone had discarded them, of course. As it turned out, her position as director of Kongslund gained me rather easy access to these archives.

The boxes had not been tossed, and they were piled in enormous stacks under the sloped attic ceiling, representing a seemingly impossible undertaking. Had Magdalene not taught me everything there was to know about patience and persistence—and had my years at Kongslund not taught me to hone these qualities—I would have given up once I discovered that the first three or four contained nothing more than endless case files, a complex, incomprehensible collection of documents, which I, in my quest for the needle in the haystack, nevertheless leafed through page by page, line by line.

Day after day I climbed up to my treasure troves in the attic, opening and closing case files and records from the fifties and sixties, the great adoption years in Denmark. Most astonishing were the comprehensive psychological assessments of the so-called damaged children and their often equally damaged parents, which filled folder after folder. What a display of broken goods and vain repairs, what a ragtag army of ailing, limping, wrecked lives ceaselessly wandering from one defeat to the next until—right at the very edge of the abyss—they met a woman who smelled sweetly of cheroot and freshly plucked freesia and who compensated them for their failed efforts, oblivion, forgiveness: a whole new existence.

My foster mother had really believed that the sons and daughters of the debased could find a new life with the pure and unblemished, and she'd tried to replicate the processes in her shop where God and the Devil, working in tandem, loftily constructed human lives in the hopes of stopping Fate in its tracks. In the vast history of the Great Repair, Magna was the most stubborn mechanic that had ever lived—that was abundantly clear to me.

As the days passed, the air in the loft grew drier—almost as though I'd drained it of its last ounce of moisture with my concentrated anger. I was close to giving up when my quest finally delivered something of interest.

It was at the end of the sixth day when I found it. I had opened one of the very last boxes marked only with the words, "Mother's Aid Society," removing the piece of black plastic that had been placed on top of the contents. In a folder titled "Cases in Progress—1961," I found a divider labeled "Unfinished Cases." Behind the divider were twelve forms that included names of children who had apparently never entered into the regular adoption procedure.

One of the forms contained the name I'd been looking so long for: Bjergstrand.

It was handwritten, and the letters were as legible as if they'd just been scratched in the paper, and in the space before it was a single boy's name: John.

John Bjergstrand.

My hand shook a little.

In the upper right corner of the form, the year 1961 was scrawled in very small letters—and a bit farther down the page was a number of columns to enter name, birth date, place of birth, and residence. Only two of the boxes had been filled out before the case was for some reason shelved and disappeared into the voluminous archives of Mother's Aid Society.

I read it again and again. Puzzled. Following the name, three other words had been added in the same hand: *the Infant Room.*

It would have made sense to take the form to Magna, but of course I couldn't do that. She wouldn't have wanted me snooping around in all this. Instead, the next morning, I wandered up Strandvejen to see Gerda Jensen, who lived in one of the expensive new apartments in Skodsborg with a view of the sound. I had no idea how she was able to afford to retire in such luxurious surroundings—but presumably all the assistants lived on next to nothing during the years they served Mother's Aid Society and had therefore saved up small fortunes.

"Gerda, you have to tell me about the last child from the Elephant Room," I said without preamble, setting the famous photograph of the seven babies on the table before her.

The other clues—the form, the socks, and the letter from Australia—I kept to myself for now.

She didn't even blink. She'd always been formidable and unflaggingly loyal to only one person in this world, Magna Louise Ladegaard. But she'd always had a soft spot for me (I was after all Magna's only relative, albeit an artificial one)—and this was my chance.

"Why dwell on the past?" asked the thin woman who'd once painted blue elephants on the infant room walls. "The past means nothing now."

We sat on the sofa. "To me it does," I replied. I have a knack with old people, the way all adopted children do for some reason. "Where is the seventh child?" I pointed at the picture. "Who is he?"

Gerda stared ahead as though she didn't want to acknowledge my question. Then she sipped carefully from her delicate, light-blue Royal

Porcelain teacup. Her lips were puckered. This was the woman who had once made an entire Gestapo battalion retreat.

"What nickname did the governesses give him?" It was the only logical question to ask.

She hesitated, before suddenly putting her cup down and taking my hand. "Marie, it doesn't matter."

In spite of these words, I felt that she was revealing something. Gerda suffered from a rare affliction: she couldn't lie. In her youth she'd tried a couple of times, Magna once told me, but after a few words, the blood would drain from her lips, her pupils would dilate to double their normal size, and her fine voice would stall, dissolving in the middle of the lie. In short order she would hyperventilate, sway, and—unless anyone intervened—faint on the spot. It was, Magna thought, both a beautiful and disturbing phenomenon. She herself had never had any trouble voicing a lie (white, gray, or black) if it served a good cause.

That morning my knowledge of Gerda's weakness was my strongest weapon: if Gerda was to avoid a lie, she'd have to keep quiet from the beginning, pinch shut her already narrow lips, and stare at a point far beyond any earthly deceitfulness.

She turned her long, almost triangular face toward me, and her unpainted lips formed a single word: "John."

Just that name, with no emphasis.

"John?" I said. My heart beat hard in my chest. "Are you sure?"

"Yes. The governesses called him Little John, because he was no bigger than"—suddenly she smiled—"no bigger than the tobacco you used to be able to buy . . . tobacco for a schilling."

"Little John," I repeated. "His name was *John* then?"

"He was *called* John."

"But—" I stopped, and asked another question instead. "Did we arrive at the same time?"

"It's been a long time, Marie."

"But where did he come from? Who were his parents?"

"His name was John. He was adopted."

I could tell that Gerda was clinging to the only detail she was willing to give. She was eighty now, and hard concentration wore her out. But I was sure she knew more, that she was only evading my questions out of loyalty to Magna.

"Is it the same John who's listed in this form?" I pushed the paper toward her.

She froze. For a moment, her slender fingers rested on the paper like spider legs, then she said, "I don't know, Marie. It was a long time ago."

"Who *was* he, Gerda?"

She slumped in the sofa like a balloon losing air. Then she sat up and began breathing quickly. The blood drained from her face, making it appear paler than you'd think possible. "I . . . don't . . . know . . . where . . . he came . . . from," she whispered. "He . . . was . . . adopted . . . by . . ."

I grabbed her arm, the one that had held me as a baby and painted the blue elephant over my bed. I needed her to finish the sentence before she fainted.

But it was too late. Gerda's body spun halfway around then slipped sideways off the sofa.

Quickly I reached for her, breaking her fall. She hung limply in my arms, which despite the deformations were strong. She moved her lips in an effort to talk. She couldn't lie.

"Yes?" I almost shouted.

"By . . . a . . . night watchman and his family in Nørrebro."

"What was the family's name?"

But Gerda had gone as rigid as a stick, and in a moment she'd be gone.

"What was their name?" I repeated. It could kill her.

"His name . . . was . . . Anker . . . Jensen," she whispered.

"Was he John Bjergstrand's father?" I said, trying with all my might to pull Gerda back into a normal sitting position.

She showed the whites of her eyes. It was a terrifying sight. "It . . . doesn't . . . matter . . ." A little spit had gathered at the corner of her mouth. I recalled how she'd saved Kongslund and hundreds of Jews during the Second World War by keeping silent. But if the German commander had asked the right question and demanded an answer, she would have told them everything.

"Yes, it does—to *me* it does!" I screamed, but I'd nearly given up.

Then she raised her voice as though she'd made a decision that could never be undone. "Marie . . . there is no John Bjergstrand!"

I let her go. She sank to the floor.

This woman's dedication to Magna was so complete that in this sensitive matter she chose to disregard everything she believed in. She who never lied had lied to me.

I exhaled and said for the last time, "It does matter, Gerda . . ." But she was no longer listening.

I left her living room, and I wouldn't see her again until the day we buried Magna, our guiding star.

Of all the mistakes I made, this was the biggest. Not heeding Gerda Jensen's last warning.

* * *

After my visit to Gerda's, I realized I couldn't get any further.

As much as I wanted to, I couldn't see a connection between Eva Bjergstrand's baby and the son Dorah received several years later.

When I told Susanne what Gerda had said, she stared at me, astounded. Then we read the letter from Australia once more. Carefully and slowly.

"It is strange, Marie . . . Eva doesn't even know it's a boy."

"That was the whole idea back then. They weren't allowed to know anything about their own flesh and blood," I replied, sounding as though I was defending the notion.

Other people—besides Magna and Gerda—must've known about it, we decided. To some degree, the doctors and everyone at Kongslund must have been informed, but it would be hard to locate them. Even if we were able to, they would have had good reasons not to tell us anything if something covert had been going on.

"But Magna could have at least told her the child's gender," Susanne said with a peculiar bitterness in her voice.

"But Magna was the one who had to make sure the child disappeared. And then Eva."

"The night watchman's family that Gerda mentioned must be the one that adopted John."

"It's just strange that they didn't change the name. That Magna . . . it doesn't make sense."

Susanne understood my nagging doubts—and my fear. Neither of us wished to go to Magna. If we contacted the night watchman's family, the adoptive parents would almost certainly be ignorant of the boy's past.

And we had no way of proving that the child they'd adopted really was the boy that the convicted murderer Eva Bjergstrand had given birth to and had baptized at the Rigshospital in 1961. If we suggested this was the case, without having even the slightest documentation, we might do serious and needless harm to the family. If I gave him the letter that Eva Bjergstrand had written to her child, it could be a fatal mistake.

In the end, we didn't know whether we were pursuing a false lead or not. Magna would certainly have protected her herd with all the means she had at her disposal, and perhaps Gerda had mastered lying after all—when it really mattered.

The only logical move was to take another stab at finding Eva Bjergstrand. Maybe there was a way to identify the child that only she knew about? There must be some trace of her arrival in Australia; after all, we knew that she had arrived within a specific six- to nine-month period.

Once again I contacted the woman at the Australian embassy, and with renewed insistence, I managed to get her to give it another go. And then the miracle happened. Using the data I provided about the woman's date of arrival, age, and region, she was able to locate a Danish woman who'd become a citizen in 1975—and who had entered the country fourteen years earlier. Her name hadn't been Bjergstrand, but that was no surprise. Her powerful helpers would have no problem issuing her a new identity.

The age fit, however, and her first name too—Eva—and then came the shocker.

The embassy clerk sat staring at her screen for a while, and nearly blushed when she told me what I hadn't believed possible. The woman she'd just tracked down had reentered Denmark only two days earlier. It wasn't a piece of information she ought to have shared, but my Australian friend had been as surprised as I.

Susanne and I became almost hysterical in our triumph. The mystery would surely be solved in days. Good fortune had smiled upon us, and set what seemed like an absurd coincidence at our feet.

Naturally, I wish we'd never pushed forward.

In a way, the next move was simple: a patient campaign walking from one hotel to the other in Copenhagen's inner city, which we began the very next day. I had contrived a touching but entirely false story about an Australian businesswoman whose hotel address I'd forgotten.

Our first day of wandering produced no results, but already the next morning I could report a miraculous discovery to Susanne: at the fifth hotel counter of the day, the receptionist had nodded to me right away and told me they'd had a woman by that name staying there. She'd shown them an Australian passport when she'd arrived a few days earlier—but unfortunately had checked out the day before without leaving any information.

"She went back," I told Susanne.

Susanne agreed, but nonetheless thought we should go to the library on Krystalgade to study their newspapers and investigate whether the woman had been reported missing or been involved in an accident of some sort. It seemed as though she'd had a terrible premonition about this woman's fate.

The next day we sat at the reading room in the main library, and after only half an hour Susanne found the notice in a Copenhagen morning paper.

It is said that shock can paralyze one's motor functions and large parts of both the left and right brains all at once.

That was the effect on Susanne Ingemann.

To this day I remember how she sat bent over her paper, white in the face, and read the notice aloud. It was like thrusting open a door only to find something behind it that surpassed your wildest imagination.

Our investigation had come to an end with the scant but unsettling information in the newspaper.

During the following days, we spoke about the case only in panicked whispers.

I understood that Magna must've had the same information about Eva Bjergstrand that I had. Eva wouldn't have come to Denmark for any other reason than to contact her old ally, the woman who'd placed her child up for adoption telling her everything would be all right.

Instinctively, I knew why Eva was convinced that she needed to return to her homeland, breaking the promise she'd made. She had sent a letter, but she'd never received a response. She had no way of knowing that Magna hadn't received her beseeching plea.

Seen in that light, I, more than anyone else, was responsible for things developing as they did: I had created the prerequisites for a meeting between the two women—and I was certain that Magna, shortly afterward, had discovered that the woman who'd visited her in September of 2001 had disappeared.

No wonder my foster mother had seemed so uncharacteristically nervous when the contents of the anonymous letter were published in *Independent Weekend* seven years later. She was one of the few who understood what demons could be unleashed when you opened up the past. She must have been entirely unprepared to see the hidden and long-since forgotten information about the mysterious boy. Eva was gone forever—the notice left no doubt about that—and yet her past slipped from the shadows and threatened those who tried to forget.

When the reporters contacted Magna to get answers to their prying questions, she finally decided to rid herself of the Kongslund Protocol.

This was the only possible explanation for her package to Australia.

* * *

Naturally, I only told Knud Taasing what was most necessary—and I made sure he retained the mistaken belief that Eva's letter had only just arrived at Kongslund a few weeks earlier.

He read the letter three times without noticing the obvious illogic that could have directed him onto the right track, both in terms of Eva Bjergstrand and my role in the matter. He studied the date without suspecting that something was wrong, and he was galloping full speed ahead down the wrong path. If he hadn't been so farsighted—as so many older reporters are—he would have discovered my clumsy alteration of the number 1 to an 8. Of course I changed the year. No one could know that Eva Bjergstrand was dead.

I smiled at him, without revealing even the tiniest crack through which to glimpse the Darkness inside me. It was an art form all of Magna's little elephants mastered long before they were driven to their new homes by their hopeful new parents.

"What about the letter to the child that she mentions?" he said at long last.

"There was no letter enclosed," I said. "She must have changed her mind at the last minute."

The lie came to me so easily that even the country's most skeptical reporter believed it. But then I'd had a lot of time to practice. Knud Taasing was closed off from all the leads I had followed in my investigation, because I'd told him nothing, not about Dorah and Helgenæs, not about my contact with the embassy or Eva's visit to Denmark—and certainly not about the terrifying discovery that Susanne and I had made in the Krystalgade library seven years earlier.

Then, as expected, he stated the obvious: "The package was for Eva. The package Magna sent before she died?"

I didn't answer.

The next thought clicked into its logical place in his mind. "Maybe in her letter Magna told Eva everything that we don't know. The police should be able to find the woman in Australia—if they have her name."

I had feared this very revelation in my risky decision to involve him. But here again he overlooked the most obvious thing, and my silence only confirmed to him that I accepted his theory.

"Yes, that should be possible," I said. "But it would be unwise to involve the authorities in any of this as long as Malle is in charge of the investigation."

I could tell I'd hit the bull's eye.

After Magna's death, Susanne and I were the only ones who possessed the dangerous knowledge about Eva Bjergstrand's fate. We'd held on to it, too scared to dig into the mystery of her missing child. It simply existed between us, this silent, terrible secret.

In my thoughts, of course, I could never let it go. I'd never been able to forget how she'd judged the child's father. I remembered it all with a rage I couldn't tell was hers or mine. For seven years that anger had lain dormant until I could no longer stand the silence.

I'd made my decision when Magna's anniversary was approaching, and I'd made the decision on my own—in the only way that made sense to me—and sent the scant information I had found to the children involved.

I hadn't told Susanne Ingemann of my decision, because she would have no doubt talked me out of it. I'd sensed the fear that had never loosened its grasp on her. Of course she had to know that I was the most likely sender of the anonymous letters, and I hadn't done anything to make her think otherwise.

But she hadn't said a word.

"This letter"—again Taasing put his hand on Eva's single, handwritten sheet—"this could open up the case again. It connects Magna's death and the mysterious John Bjergstrand with one common denominator: Australia."

"Where the police haven't been able to discover anything," I said.

"As far as we know," he said. "But it ought to be possible to find a woman with such a Danish name in Australia—especially since the search could be limited to Adelaide, the city she mentions." Taasing shrugged. "Certainly I can do that." He was his usual confident self.

A week and a half later, he no doubt realized how overconfident he'd been that day in the King's Room. There was no Eva Bjergstrand anywhere in Australia. He called me one Sunday evening, sounding unusually despondent. If there'd ever been an Eva Bjergstrand in that vast country, she had completely disappeared. She was nowhere to be found, not in the directories, not via the postal service, and not on the Internet. Perhaps she'd taken a name that only Magna knew, he suggested—and I could tell how his failure to locate her disoriented him.

I expressed regret. Luckily, he couldn't see my facial expression.

Even though I'd like to have made use of his talent, I couldn't help but feel relieved. From my and Kongslund's point of view, Eva Bjergstrand was a closed chapter. There were other far more important things that the living should focus on. First and foremost, the father. To me, he was the very embodiment of the arrogance of men, and, day by day, I had become ever more determined to put a name to him—and reveal it. A man who had lived a carefree life after his little "extramarital affair" had been concluded, never gave a thought to either Eva or the child he abandoned. I could never discover my own past—that door was effectively closed—but I swore I'd find John Bjergstrand's. And with that, his father.

That's why I played the final card that Knud Taasing would see. "According to one of the old assistants, the child who was called John could be . . . Nils Jensen. His father was a night watchman in Nørrebro, right? That was the detail she remembered," I told him.

I could almost hear his mind wrestling with the new information.

"But you're not sure?" he finally said, a peculiar hopefulness in his voice.

"No. I'm not sure. I don't know if Nils really *is* the child that Eva Bjergstrand gave up at birth. Magna and whoever else were involved in Mother's Aid Society made everything more complicated than we can even imagine—to confuse pursuers." It was a strange choice of words.

A few days later, he returned to Kongslund and for a long time sat motionless in the Chippendale chair.

Finally he said, "But when it comes down to it, it's not really John that matters, is it? It isn't John that you really care about, right? It's the boy's father that you're looking for with such zeal? The man who'd abandoned his child and let the mother vanish forever?"

I sat back in the wheelchair without responding.

"Only Magna knew who the father really was—and now she's dead—and maybe she was killed for that very reason."

I said nothing.

Then he said what I'd been waiting to hear for many years: "Maybe we should bring all the children from the Elephant Room together again."

I could have sworn that he blushed at that moment. He repeated, "I mean, bring them together to see if they—we—can solve the mystery."

It was the opportunity I'd longed for, and it took every effort to hide my excitement. "We'll never get Orla to show up," I said with painstaking calm. I didn't know why I mentioned him first.

"Maybe so. But Peter Trøst is going to Aarhus on Friday, and I can ask him to bring Asger Christoffersen with him back to Copenhagen." He hadn't mentioned Nils Jensen, and I understood why. In Knud Taasing's universe, the photographer didn't need to know the truth, and I thought that was a strange double standard coming from a reporter who'd always insisted that things be made public.

He had assumed I shared his view.

When he'd left, I studied Hven under the bright sky, and I felt hopeful. That very afternoon, the staff at Søllerød post office had assured me that all letters and packages for Magna would be redirected to me—in my name—at Kongslund, and that was all I needed to know.

Since Eva had been dead for a while, I knew that in due course Magna's package would be returned to its sender, ending up in my hands.

In only a few days, the voice from the past would tell me what everyone wanted to know. And it was vital that I learned it first.

22

THE KONGSLUND PROTOCOL

June 20, 2008

I have always considered fear to be the twin sister of anger. In my case, one rarely appears without the other. But the fear that paralyzed us in the days following the discovery of Eva Bjergstrand's terrible fate could not be overcome by any other feeling.

Susanne Ingemann would never involve herself in the case again. And even I had my reasons to let the years pass.

* * *

The June sky was darkening when the sea-green Bedford Caravan with the royal blue Channel DK logo on the side doors rolled through Aarhus and reached the harbor. It was the last car to board the express ferry to Odden in West Zealand.

The two men had been listening to the ten o'clock news in the van; there was nothing about the Kongslund Affair, but they had expected as much. There *was* a segment on the deportation of the Tamil boy, whom the media had seemed to lose interest in as soon as Søren Severin Nielsen managed to delay the deportation process with myriad legalistic quibbles.

His last complaint had, however, been rejected, and the ministry had reacted swiftly: as soon as possible, according to the news, the boy would be driven to Copenhagen Airport and put on a plane to Calcutta. From there, he'd take a regular routine flight to Colombo, Sri Lanka's capital, accompanied by four Danish police officers.

The national minister had done it again, the approving political commentator cooed. The Almighty One had once more demonstrated his patriotism—so convincingly forged when he helped rescue the Danish Jews during the war—by daring to expel foreigners who had no right to remain in Denmark, regardless of their age; and who, according to a confidential source in the ministry, were part of an extensive network that schemed to bring Tamils into the country. Thousands of them.

In Channel DK's coverage, the boy's fate could be easily (and briefly) slipped between the broadcasts of the weekend's episodes of *Roadshow*, which were set in Denmark's two largest cities, shows that had been arranged by the station itself. Through a series of revivalist town-hall meetings, the TV station would reclaim its leading position on the ever-changing horizon of options, launching a gigantic show in Aarhus University's student union. On Sunday, they would follow up with an even bigger program at Forum Copenhagen.

In Aarhus, Peter Trøst had given the thousands in the audience a taste of what was to come; the seven Concept Lions in attendance had sat in the back row to observe the crowd's reaction. The most controversial concept had been presented when the atmosphere was at its climax, and the lions smiled as a trailer for a show advocating the reinstitution of the death penalty in Denmark streamed across the big screen. The segment was garnished with illustrations of child molestation, terror, and mass murder as irrefutable arguments for capital punishment. Outside, the broadcasting vans, parked one next to the other, captured every single word. At the show's premiere, the audience would sentence real, preselected criminals; everyone expected these sentences to be harsher and more unyielding than the ones currently meted out in Danish courtrooms. Dramatic images of the firebombing of Danish embassies in Syria and Saudi Arabia that followed the publication of caricatures of the Prophet Mohammed were part of the program, with Peter Trøst shouting: "The future isn't free! We have to fight for it—together!"

The floundering TV station was hopeful it had found a winning strategy for its ratings battle. And so afterward, in the makeup room, they'd toasted their victory with vintage wine. It was then that Peter experienced a moment of unease about what had occurred—and his own role in it.

His bad mood hadn't lifted until he'd found Asger Christoffersen in between transmission vans in the parking lot as arranged, tall and lanky and a little confused, with bristly tufts of hair and round glasses. They shook hands, and he hoisted the astronomer's tattered red suitcase into the Bedford.

An awkward silence descended on them as they made their way to the harbor. "We can go to the moon and back for all I care," the tall man said, adjusting his glasses in the manner of an absentminded professor.

"To the moon?" Peter was taken aback by the strange comment.

"Yes. Don't you see the symbolism?"

He shook his head.

"You're Tintin, and I'm"—the strange astronomer suddenly giggled—"I'm Professor Calculus!"

He did actually resemble the distracted professor, albeit a much taller version, and in the midst of his surprise Peter felt a kind of relief—as though his encounter with Asger Christoffersen had been preordained for many, many years.

* * *

On the ferry they stayed in their seats while the rest of the crew went in search of beer and food.

If the distracted comic-book professor had really been reborn in the body of Asger Christoffersen, his puzzled expression was maintained in Asger's long face. He wore thick glasses with slim black frames on his pointy nose, and from this somewhat wild appearance, a surprisingly deep voice emerged. Now he leaned back in the soft leather chair and said, "When I was young, I was very small and skinny, but then I grew and grew and grew . . . toward the stars . . . I wanted to get there before anyone else!"

Peter smiled but didn't respond.

"I began my studies at Aarhus University the year the American physicist Alan Guth discovered the mechanics of the creation in the universe—the inflationary epoch when all matter was shot into space with incredible force—and wrote in his journal: 'Startling realization!'"

The astronomer laughed so suddenly that Peter started. Then Asger changed topic again: "Isn't it peculiar that we used to share a room when we were little—as babies!" Christoffersen pronounced the last word with obvious delight. Then he made yet another quantum leap in his inner universe: "I was married, like you, Peter—and divorced again—and I left behind a child, just as I was left behind. Even those of us who start our lives at Kongslund make the same mistakes that we ourselves were the victims of. Isn't it strange?"

The noise from the ferry engines rose, and the van rocked rhythmically in its luxurious suspension. Peter didn't feel like discussing children—or himself—with anyone.

"My daughter is fifteen now," Asger said. "It's strange. I would have expected that kind of longing to be unchanged throughout life. A father's longing for his only child . . . you wouldn't think it could decrease or disappear. But that's what has happened. After a while it just shrank, as though love demands more than simply flesh and blood . . . and then one day I understood: like the smallest particle of earth, *longing* is influenced by other particles with other composites, and this influence of course depends on the three pillars of life—distance, movement, and time. These are the only three. So if we wait long enough without establishing contact, if we move far enough from one another, those forces are at work. Then the longing disappears, and love becomes nothing. That's what happened to me. The less I saw of her, the less I actually missed her. Don't you think that was the case for our biological fathers?"

Peter felt a little dizzy, as though the pitching ferry were making him seasick.

"I was there at her birth," Christoffersen said, shaking his head in wonder. "You have to be now and back in the nineties as well. I really took it seriously—as though I was chasing after a new planet. I felt every pain that my wife felt, the very same pricking, stabbing, cutting jabs in my stomach and abdomen—like telepathy—and in the end, they had to give me a tranquilizer and place me on a beanbag in a corner of the delivery room to calm me down. They thought I was nuts."

Peter couldn't tell whether Christoffersen was pulling his leg.

"A while later, after my little girl had been born, I started hiccupping and was sick to my stomach. When she became colicky, I began to have pains in my abdomen again. I thought I was going to die." Asger leaned to the left, nearly touching Peter's shoulder. "If this had been in

Steinbeck's novel, the one that ends with a giant flood and characters who take refuge in a barn, I would have started nursing her. But of course I had no milk."

Christoffersen's smile was neither ironic nor challenging. Like Asger, Peter had abandoned his own children. Exiting the ferry, they drove south of Roskilde and into Copenhagen's ocean of light, and Asger resumed his monologue. "Did you know that millions of televisions emit light into the universe and contribute to us being unable to see the night sky—making us blind to all the planets, stars, and galaxies? It's almost symbolic, don't you think?"

Again Peter glanced at the man with whom he'd once shared a room in a famous orphanage. Was he joking? It didn't seem so. On the contrary, he seemed utterly solemn.

Peter's own innocence was irretrievably lost during his second year as an apprentice, when he seduced a female secretary in his pursuit of information on her boss's abuse of public funds—for travels, hotels, restaurants, even mistresses—and this heartless method had become part of the Peter Trøst Jørgensen legend. He had met her, a seeming coincidence, in a public swimming pool in Gentofte, and after three weeks of lovemaking, she told him everything he wanted to know about the minister. After that, she didn't see him again until he appeared on television breaking the big exposé. It had been his debut; he was only twenty years old. He hadn't thought much about it; the editor's expectations had been all that mattered to him. She, on the other hand, left her job and colleagues and friends—in shame—and five months later they found her drowned, not in the warm pool at Kildeskov Sports Center, but in a bathtub filled with ice-cold water. To be on the safe side, she had swallowed three packs of sleeping pills and sliced both her ulnar and radial arteries.

The legendary episode continued to evoke the admiration of young reporters, who thought that such methods were part of the game—and that such unfortunate outcomes shouldn't affect a real reporter. He himself had pushed the experience aside—during his waking hours—because of late she'd returned to haunt his dreams: she sat in the night sky staring down at him, her wet hair dripping on his duvet. She might as well have been holding the hand of Principal Nordal—and he would awaken, in sweat-soaked sheets, to the sound of water gushing from a sluice in a dam somewhere close by.

They parked in front of the SAS Hotel on Hammerichgade, where Peter had booked Christoffersen a small but luxurious room on the top floor, far from all earthly interruption and with a view of the sound and the Swedish coast.

Here Asger Christoffersen stood by the window for a long time, trying to make out Hven in the distance—but his famous predecessor's island was hidden in the darkness.

* * *

It was the third Friday in June, and we'd followed Channel DK's broadcast of *Roadshow* in the Aarhus student union all night. The program had just ended with the playing of the national hymn, when a sixth sense compelled me to stand and look out the window. A dark-blue Audi drove down the gravel road from Strandvejen, and I recognized it right away.

Carl Malle was behind the wheel.

We hadn't expected another visit from the security advisor so soon after his first, and it suggested a mounting desperation in the ministry he was hired to protect. He couldn't seriously think we would tell him more than what we'd already revealed.

We sat, as we had the first time, by the small glass table in the sunroom, with a view of the garden and the beach. You could just see the outline of the Barsebäck nuclear power plant to the southeast, and Malle relaxed for a moment as though enjoying the dusk—which anyone who'd followed him over the years would know was unthinkable. Malle was not a daydreamer. He had come solely to find the truth he thought Kongslund was hiding. He reacted logically, with determination, to the signals being sent from this very place, and fear lounged—ready to pounce—on the sofa right next to him, fixed on us.

Malle furrowed his brow, and said, "I've spoken to the national minister. He still believes you know something that is of use to us." He looked directly at me. "For the sake of your foster mother."

It was an uncharacteristically sentimental appeal.

"For her sake I am to produce information I don't have," I said contemptuously. Momentary anger caused me to forget my fear.

His enormous hand squeezed the teacup, hard. It could break at any moment. "What did Magna know . . . about the boy?" he said.

"She never mentioned any John Bjergstrand," I said. It was true.

"Who sent the anonymous letters?"

"Which one?"

He stared at me for a long time. "The letters that were sent to the boys from the Elephant Room. To Orla Berntsen and the press."

"How would I know?"

"You've lived here a long time." He gestured with his hand and the cup. "You must have a sense—"

"A sense of the past?" I said.

Susanne hadn't bothered to serve cookies or any other finger foods. Perhaps as an expression of her disapproval over this unwelcome visit.

"Yes," he said.

"What connection do you and the minister have to all of this?" A sudden and very direct question.

The hand that held the cup fell abruptly to the table, and he sat motionless for a minute. "We've known Magna almost since Kongslund's founding."

"Yes. I saw you in Søborg."

He narrowed his eyes. It was an awfully nervous gesture coming from a man like Malle.

"Yes, I saw you with Orla and Severin—when they were children."

"I lived there." His voice was low.

"You kept up with the others too, didn't you?"

He turned his head toward Susanne, who sat as usual with her back to the sound against a square patch of sunlight that rested on the little sofa, which was carved of dark mahogany and upholstered in gray-blue silk. It seemed to me he'd become paler.

"What was so interesting about the children from the Elephant Room . . . about those of us who were there in 1961?" I asked.

I could hear his breathing across the table. "Marie, I've followed this place for over fifty years. I've known your mother just as long."

"My *foster mother*," I corrected without hesitation.

"What did Magna tell you? That's all we need to know."

"You didn't answer my question." Now I sounded like the police officer.

"You're smart. You always were." There was an odd, admiring tone in his voice that I hadn't expected. "But your silly questions have nothing to do with this case. I knew from Magna that two of her children grew up in my neighborhood. It was natural that I would take an interest. There were other children she asked me to check up on—both out of curiosity and love." That word sounded completely wrong out of his mouth. "Or because they were in trouble. You know as much." That sounded a bit more plausible. "In a way, I was her guardian angel." He tried to smile, but failed, and the last word faded to a near whisper. I could tell he was annoyed that he had to explain himself—as though he were the one being interrogated.

"What do you know about Asger Christoffersen?" I asked, while I still had the upper hand.

"You expect me to know who that is."

"I have a feeling you do."

"Yes, I know him." His admission came sooner than I'd expected, and was accompanied by a challenging look in his cold, gray eyes.

"Yes. Because his parents were about to mess everything up, weren't they?"

His eyes darted, and that was a rare sight. In all the years I'd spied on him in Søborg, I'd never seen anything like it.

"They brought Susanne and Asger together, didn't they?"

I could tell that Susanne was startled. But Malle kept silent.

"We weren't supposed to talk, were we? We weren't supposed to discover that none of us knew a damn thing about our parents, or that we'd all been in exactly the same place, with exactly the same dark hole in our knowledge of the past? Indeed, completely against Kongslund's normal protocol, Magna had encouraged these particular parents to not reveal anything to their children about their past, right? They didn't need to know they were adopted, or that they came from an orphanage . . . because then she . . . and you . . . could hide the scandal that would have destroyed Kongslund and everyone else involved . . . Isn't that so? Do I have it right?"

He sat still for a moment—then simply shook his head.

"What was the scandal?" I was amazed at my own outburst and my surprisingly formal word choice. "Who is John Bjergstrand?"

He sighed and then found his tongue again. "Listen, Marie. Help us find the boy, since Magna no longer can—and because someone might have killed her because of those letters . . . and, not least, because of that name. For crying out loud, she was your mother."

"My *foster* mother."

"Yes. And someone may have killed her in order to prevent us from finding him."

"Or in order to find him." The accusation lingered. I didn't even dare glance at Susanne.

"You've never been easy to talk to, Marie."

"You've never shown any interest."

Again he became silent as he struggled to control his anger. His large hands remained motionless around the cup he'd barely drunk from. Then he said, "We're also looking for her personal diary, the Kongslund Protocol."

I was surprised that he knew of the journal but ignored his comment. "What was it about us, Carl? What *is* it about the kids from the Elephant Room that worries you? What is it that makes us so interesting?"

Abruptly he stood, letting go of his cup. He'd lost his patience. "We think, Marie, that she passed on the Protocol to someone before she died. And you are the most obvious choice."

He tossed his business card on the table. "Call me if you want to talk. I'm sure you grasp what all this is about," he said, regaining his composure before making his exit.

"Ah, yes. Marie's sense for murder . . ." I said, and I could hear how it sounded like a growl, but I couldn't restrain my anger.

"Yes. Straight out of a potboiler, isn't it?" This was as close as Malle got to sarcasm.

Then he exited the room, and we heard the front door slam. His teacup remained on the table, practically full.

Susanne Ingemann, an enigma to most—outside of Kongslund— hadn't said a word during the confrontation.

* * *

Of course she'd have to reveal the secret very few people knew, which Malle and I had just shared in her living room.

One of the few others who knew, of course, had been Magna.

Susanne's position as the director of the famous orphanage (the title of matron was no longer used) was as much a coincidence as all the other events that bound the children of the Elephant Room.

Magna had hired her as a trusted assistant in 1984; five years later, Susanne had replaced her as the director. When we had tea in the sunroom a few weeks after her appointment, I was struck by how beautiful she'd become over the years, and like everyone else, I wondered why she'd never married and had children. There must have been literally hundreds of suitors, but of course I didn't dare ask her about something so private.

To my astonishment, she visited me a few days later in my room, where no one but me ever set foot. Because I'd never had any guests other than Gerda and my foster mother (and of course Magdalene before she was wooed by a king on the Other Side), I was instantly shy.

Feeling insecure, I offered her the Chippendale chair while I sat on the bed, unable to speak. Even the mirror fell quiet that day and seemed to withdraw into the wall, which it had never done before. I think it was as overwhelmed by her radiance as I was.

During her first visits she asked about the children and about the home's routines over the years I had lived here. I answered to the best of my ability—and perhaps offered more details than I needed—telling her about Magna's pedagogical methods, which no one had ever questioned; about her relationship with Gerda; and about her battles with all those powerful, haughty men who over the years had meddled in Kongslund's affairs even though they knew it was Magna's absolute domain—and that she'd pushed back with the same force she displayed when she crushed flower stems on the kitchen table. This long explanation made me short of breath, because I wasn't used to speaking louder than what Magdalene could hear, but after a while I relaxed. Susanne listened so attentively and never asked any personal questions.

But that changed.

"You're a very beautiful woman, Marie," she suddenly said one Saturday evening when I had just described Gerda's famous face-off with the German Gestapo commander during the war.

Then she added the unthinkable: "Why didn't you ever find a man?"

The blood instantly flowed to my neck and into my deformed cheekbones, making my slouching left shoulder burn like it was on fire. I'd never shared my ugliness with anyone but the big mahogany mirror that hung on my wall. Already, as a child, I had grown used to its mean character and its prying questions (which I knew were due to the insistent nature of the magic mirror), and our nightly conversations that revolved around my deformities. Throughout my childhood, Magna had tried to soften my bizarre appearance in the eyes of others by telling them the story of the amazing design of the little foundling, a design that had captivated a host of orthopedic surgeons and specialists.

But Susanne wasn't smiling. Instead she moved her chair closer to the bed, where I sat at the edge, near the headboard.

"You don't know it yourself, Marie. Because you only look at yourself in a broken, old mirror that can't contain you. You don't see the whole picture." Her lips were parted slightly, and the light from the setting sun over the sound caressed her neck and shoulders. I can't describe it any other way today. Not even Magdalene had touched my soul like that—boldly—and I was completely overwhelmed. Behind her the mirror hung dark and frozen in a deep shadow; and I sensed jealousy, which even a magic mirror can't hide from. For the first time in its hundred-year reign, it was quiet.

Yet I dared not reply to her words—in this magical moment—because I feared that the lisp I shared with my disabled friend would return, and Susanne would not be able to understand me. But I needn't have worried.

She leaned in, and in the glow of the seven lit candles in the gilded candleholder Gerda Jensen had given me, she kissed me—and I was so shocked that I couldn't move my body an inch from hers. In the sunlight, her red halo enveloped us, and I disappeared into it. To my own wonder, I embraced, for the first time, a person my own age—and I basked in the moment in a way I never had before.

When I lay in bed several hours later—after she'd departed—I laughed so loudly that I imagined it could be heard all the way to Hven, making the old, silver-nosed stargazer turn his eyes to the Big Dipper and Ursa Major and wonder which demons the night sky had released.

All of them, my dear Tycho! Every single one of them!

And a voice that had to be mine shouted: *Now I understand!*

Susanne returned every evening, and all winter long we spent our nights together in the King's Room while the children slept and the assistants were on nightshift on the ground floor; and, one night, when the wind whipped icily around the seven chimneys, she told me who she really was.

She closed her eyes and transported us back to the little peninsula and the small farmhouse with its garden of thorns and blackberry bramble. Her story was more ominous and incomprehensible than any other I'd heard, including those of Orla, Peter, and Severin—all of which I had studied with a wariness that bordered on fear. It was a declaration of confidence she'd never made to anyone else, and behind her back the mirror still hung dark, invisible, and mute; that night, I think its magic was finally broken once and for all.

No one hid her past better than Susanne Ingemann, and she had no way of knowing that I already knew her deepest secret. She'd arrived at Kongslund in 1961 and was put in the infant room, where she spent Christmas with me—she was the other girl in the room—and five boys.

I never would have dared tell her what I know about her. Maybe I was embarrassed by my childhood longing to get to know the children who'd left, and embarrassed by my unique talent for tracing them down and spying on them without being noticed. There were other reasons I'd refrained from telling her. Her upbringing was, without a doubt, the most peculiar of the five I had painstakingly pieced together, and, of course, it was due to her parents' decision—already from the beginning—to ignore the difference between biological and adopted children. An adopted child is born into a strange, upside-down world, in which its biological parents have rejected it and complete strangers have given it their love instead—and that is a peculiar, fragile balance that doesn't take many unforeseen events to disturb.

But, of course, the most important reason for my silence was the one that could cost her everything, and which I think, deep down, made her—in spite of her remarkable beauty—the same as the old governesses.

She had killed someone in a way that no one could explain.

23

SUSANNE

1961–1978

Susanne was an adult the second time she came to Kongslund. She walked into the villa with the special blend of caution and defiance that children of Kongslund seem to embody.

I think she gave in to her curiosity; I think she let herself be persuaded by Magna when she was hired as her trusted assistant and, later, her successor. And of course no one was better suited for the job.

To me she had always personified the fairy-tale character Thumbelina, who made herself comfortable on the giant green leaf to paddle down the wide waterways to the Kingdom of the Mole. I had loved her since I first sought her out, back when I squatted behind elder and hawthorn bushes to watch her in secret, imagining what her life was like—way out there on the cape.

* * *

She arrived as a stranger, and she left as a stranger.

The beginning and end of Susanne's childhood can be described that simply.

Five years had already passed since Magdalene's death, when I turned my attention to the girl who left us in March 1962. My endeavor was somewhat complicated by the fact that her family lived in a region that wasn't easy for me to reach.

The first time I took the train from Copenhagen Central Station I was thirteen years old. Magna was at a conference that weekend at a summer guesthouse in Hornbæk with all her friends from Goodness of Heart. I remember Gerda gave me the look that had frightened the German battalion away from Kongslund, but finally she let me go—and even promised to keep my trip a secret. I think she remembered her own desire to travel—which over the years had been replaced by her love for Magna—and perhaps she understood subconsciously that I was going to see one of the children I had once known. Susanne.

I spent a whole day on the cape, where she lived in the shade of a big maple. She didn't see me, and I didn't reveal myself; though perhaps I should have, in light of what happened later. She was the most beautiful, innocent creature the Elephant Room had ever let go of—and no one who saw her could imagine that anything had ever happened to her. It was a delusion I would fall prey to many times. Susanne Ingemann had moved to a home that contained powerful demons, the likes of which I'd never seen, and that was the reason I didn't recognize them the first few months I watched her from a distance, concealed behind a thicket of hazel. Like so many children preceding her, she became the victim of a force that lives on in many adults—not least women—and which Magdalene once described to me as the dream of everything that *could* have been: the love they *could* have found; and the places they *could* have visited, but for which they never found the courage. And who knew better of this than Magdalene?

Susanne arrived at the little farmhouse on the cape in the cool, early spring of 1962. The farm was well maintained and solidly built; it had been connected to the Ingemann family for four generations. Seen from the main road, between Våghøj and Kalundborg, the main house seemed like a flattened pastry box that a creative child had equipped with windows and doors and a steep roof and then jammed between two hills where it was sheltered from curious glances and the powerful gusts of wind from the fjord. Next to the main building was a small barn, and at the end of the field a little marsh and a lake where the kids from the village skated during the winter and swam during the summer. The lake was gray-blue at midsummer and a rich green in November when the winter storms took over. Susanne's first memory was from a fall day when she walked to the lake and waded a bit into the water. Staring into the depths, she suddenly glimpsed a strange face swaying back and forth, disappearing and reappearing among lily pads and dock leaves. That's how she once described it to me.

From the darkness under the water's surface a little girl stared despairingly at her, and Susanne felt a strong urge to sink down among the lily pads and share the cold and silence with her. Much later, I think that she realized whom she'd seen down there, but she never acknowledged it to anyone, perhaps not even to herself. Her father's shouting on the bank saved her, and she was never willing to say more about it than that.

Four generations ago there had been many boys at Hill Farm, but Susanne's grandparents had raised three children, all girls. So when their oldest daughter, Josefine, chose to marry the foreman on the neighboring farm, it brought relief to their hearts: the farm would stay in the family for another generation.

I think Fate must have heard their sigh of relief and taken some precautionary measures. A single mistake would be enough, a naive dream—a love that would never amount to anything anyway. And Josefine Ingemann stepped over the edge herself. A few months before she decided to accept the foreman's marriage proposal, she flirted with a summer visitor from Copenhagen named Ulrik; he had impressed the provincial girl with his exotic, cosmopolitan manner. She'd met the tall, handsome man on a market day in town, caught his eye, and shared his dreams of everything that could be. First he wanted to go out into the world to gather material for his epic travel novel—and the following year he would return and publish it, earning his fame and fortune. Then he would marry her and make her the queen of his dream castle.

That's what he said.

And one day he did in fact leave, but even though she wrote him letters for months—so many she lost count—and mailed them to his general delivery addresses around the globe, she never heard a word from him.

After sending one last letter, she gave up and married the foreman from the neighboring farm, who had always loved her—and thereby added her name to the endless list of women who'd married a devoted husband while secretly dreaming of another.

* * *

The farm at Våghøj would have satisfied Magna's notions of the ideal home, that much I understood, because to the south and east was water as far as the eye could see.

The oldest residents of the cape would tell anyone who bothered to listen that the windswept landscape bore secrets from the early days of the kingdom. According to legend, King Valdemar the Victorious's son was struck in the heart by a stray arrow, and thus, in his powerless grief, the king lit a fire so large it consumed every tree, branch, and leaf on the cape—and then he swore in the glow of that fire that all of the cape's residents were to be whipped by storms and winds every day for a thousand years, never again finding shelter.

But, as is the way of things, the trees returned, taking root in damp clay and rising into the sky. Across the hills and valleys and meadows, white, yellow, and orange butterflies flapped their colorful wings, and squadrons of buzzing insects engulfed the land.

Within this burst of color stood Anton Jørgensen—Josefine's preternaturally modest husband. And perhaps it was this modesty that prevented his loins from producing an heir—as though some force denied him fertility and the realization of the greatest dream at Våghøj.

The idea of adoption arose when Josefine's youngest sister happened upon a magazine article that, in eight pages, featured beautiful black-and-white photos from an orphanage in Skodsborg. One photo showed the matron standing on a lawn with her arms open wide in a grand gesture under a heading that read: "Let All the Small Children Come to Me."

They waited for approval for almost two years, receiving notification the very week that Susanne was born and transported by cab the few kilometers from the Rigshospital to Kongslund, where the governesses placed this tiny being on her fateful path. By chance, in the days when I observed her from my hiding place in the thicket at Våghøj—discovering the hardship that had only just begun—I learned that during our first months of life, she had lain in the bed right next to mine; and this fact fascinated me.

Whether it was Anton's humility in the face of the formidable women at Kongslund that prevented him from adopting the preferred boy (another fact learned later, this time by Susanne), no one ever knew;

perhaps they had merely been promised a second child, as was sometimes the case. When Susanne confronted her father about this detail many years later, he looked at her in surprise, then stuck his hands in his pockets and pretended he wasn't there. When faced with one of life's few but difficult questions, that's just what he did: disappeared abruptly from his body, returning only after the problem or pest had gone away. Susanne knew as soon as she asked it that it wasn't a question he was ever going to answer.

Despite the child Anton may have desired, when the couple arrived at Skodsborg on March 9, 1962, in their brand new Volvo the color of vanilla custard, Josefine immediately fell for the little beauty sitting on the floor before them. Not until many years later did I discover that Magna had told them about the little girl's background, a story that could be true or not, but which probably caused one person's death: Susanne's biological mother had gone directly from the delivery bed to Copenhagen Central Station where she met with a number of men, did what she needed, and afterward bought a first-class ticket to Hamburg—and that's where the trail went cold. (After that description the couple agreed to the matron's suggestion that she destroy all existing papers concerning the child's mother, an act that ran expressly against the principles of Mother's Aid Society.)

They drove the 120 kilometers back to the cape on icy roads without stopping once. They were filled to brimming with the desire to put their new baby to sleep in her new home and see her wake up to a new life when the sun rose over the fjord the next morning.

Late that night they made love, as if they wanted to symbolize the conception of the new life in a shared embrace. And in this act, Josefine released all the grief she'd accumulated over many years at the cape, crying out under Anton's muscular body.

When day broke, the snowstorm had driven north, and the sun shone down on Våghøj and Hill Farm, wending its way through the branches of the trees that had once been cursed by old King Valdemar. In a ray of light from the window, the little girl sat in her white crib, like Thumbelina on her leaf, and listened to a calling only she could hear.

* * *

In those very days the globe-trotting Ulrik, after one his many journeys around the world, reappeared in Josefine's life. Discreet and courteous just as she remembered him.

She spotted him on Storegade in Kalundborg where she was doing her Friday shopping, and of course there was no saving her. If she heard a powerful crack from above, she paid no heed. No woman has ever let such a faint warning prevent her from giving her heart—and more—to her one and only.

He invited her for lunch at the Sømandshotel. Afterward she followed him to his room and listened to his stories from all the countries he'd traveled to (without giving her the least thought), and it was as though the traveler had never gone away; it was as though her body had never longed for any other.

Anton was the kind of man who didn't wonder why his wife came home so late that day, and Josefine carried her memory of the adventure so deep inside that not even her best friend noticed anything amiss. Yet, from that day on, a shelf in her bookcase held binders containing clippings of his articles from various ladies' magazines.

In the years that followed, she resumed sending unanswered letters to the far corners of the world, and he published ever thicker books recounting ever greater adventures from continents farther and farther from Denmark and the little cape where Josefine Ingemann was destined to live until her death. She dutifully bought all his books, but never saw him again.

In the summer of 1962, exactly four months after Susanne's arrival, Josefine discovered that she was, miraculously, pregnant. She kept the news to herself for six days.

On the seventh day, she pulled Anton aside and relayed to him the astonishing fact. The miracle happened on the night they had made love after returning from Kongslund, she said. This, at least, was her carefully crafted story and, with a little hopeful stretch of imagination, the time frame was plausible.

A man like Anton wasn't capable of imagining a deceit of that magnitude. So there he was, in the middle of the driveway in his fluttering red-checkered shirt, trying to find words to express his happiness. At that very instant Josefine spoke impulsively, without considering the consequences: "But how are we going to return Susanne?"

"What do you mean . . . *return Susanne*?" Anton uttered, almost breathlessly.

Josefine's blue-green eyes were the color of the lake during the winter months, and she spoke to him as though he were a child: "Anton. This is how it should have been—from the beginning, right? We should have had our own child. Now that I am pregnant with *our* child, there are other childless couples that can love Susanne. We don't need *two*, do we?"

This kind of logic normally silenced Anton immediately, making him vacate his body, rising gracefully upward—especially when he was in the company of women—but not this time. And that alone should have served as a warning to Josefine.

For several seconds he swayed back and forth as he searched for words. "You're saying that you want to hand her over . . . to someone else . . . to complete strang—" He couldn't complete the word.

Josefine nodded, opening her mouth in a smile. "*We* were complete strangers to Susanne too, until we met her."

Anton's long arms dangled at his side, and he looked like the scarecrow in the vegetable garden, which his mother-in-law dressed in his old, faded flannel shirts winter after winter. He struggled to find the words before the wind carried him away.

"Listen," Josefine said. Swaying gently from side to side, as if she were already rocking the newborn baby that was her own flesh and blood. "We'll call Mother's Aid Society in Copenhagen and explain the problem. They'll find another family for Susanne—a family that can give her everything we no longer can."

As an adult, Susanne Ingemann often speculated on this one crucial moment, when Anton stood before his wife, silently and suddenly understanding her intentions, when he left his body and rose to the skies, looking down upon what he had never thought possible. From one second to the next, his proud, unconditional love was transformed into black despair. In the old world, his tall, industrious body stood beside the tractor, blissfully unaware, waiting for the mother with the child—in the new world, he looked into Josefine's blue-green eyes, and the image of her dissolved before him.

How can anyone prepare for such a catastrophe? Should he have swallowed his fear and anger? Anton was unable to answer such complicated questions, but his soul had already found the answers. I'm sure

Josefine saw him disappear right then, and I think they both knew that Susanne was staying on the farm, but that they would never again live together as husband and wife.

Of course they didn't separate—not physically—for as Susanne later told me, they had no place to go. It was just their souls that floated separately into the twilight, much like a couple of torn leaves.

Josefine turned and walked back to the house, stooped as though carrying the invisible child in her arms. Anton remained standing, like a tree trunk in the middle of the driveway, not moving until dusk began to settle.

The following winter Josefine gave birth to a girl, whom she named after a school friend who had married an American and left to explore the big wide world. The friend's name was Amanda, and they changed it a little so that Susanne's new sister was named Samanda, because already before her birth, Josefine had decided the two would have names that shared the same first letter. Perhaps she was trying to cover up the fact that the girls had very different origins—that Samanda was her own flesh and blood, while Susanne was a stranger, born to a woman Magna had described as a whore in Hamburg.

A fact that, with Samanda's birth, became even more important to hide.

In those first years together, the girls appeared to be growing up in harmony, but in reality they were surrounded by the peculiar silence of the place. Most people carry their childhood impressions with them through life, wrapped up tightly and shoved into the lower levels of their consciousness, but once in a while the impressions fall from a shelf and land in the present with a bang; a hinge breaks, and odd sights and sentences pour out. Thus, it was only much later that Susanne remembered the tension she felt sitting in the kitchen with her mother, as though she was in the company of a stranger. She could smell the freshly baked bread, could hear Samanda's babble, could see her mother pick her sister up, put her on the kitchen table, and gaze into her eyes as she stroked her hair—and in that moment she sensed the difference she had no way of understanding.

She felt her father's love when he picked her up and brought her out to the fields, telling her about all the wonders that exist above and below ground, but she also detected pity in his voice—a pity Anton couldn't hide because he didn't realize it was there. When she was older, her parents could have told her why things had been this way, but in the white pastry-box house it had long since been decided that the truth would be kept hidden. Over the years, Josefine bonded more and more with Samanda, increasingly ignoring Susanne—consumed with her real daughter and her tall, narrow bookcases, where Ulrik's thick tomes described the big wide world she would never see for herself: white mountaintops in Tibet, deep gorges in the Himalayas, narrow and rocky Inca trails in the Andes. Through Ulrik's words, the conquistadors slipped unseen past Anton and the girls and into Josefine's room. Susanne heard them whispering through mundane phone conversations about groceries, card-game nights, dentist appointments, and preparations for the Christmas bazaar—and she stood by herself, looking out over the fjord.

Josefine never tried to run away. Where would she go? She'd read about the liberation of younger women in Copenhagen—this was around 1970—but instinctively she understood there was no room for her there. They didn't even know she existed. Instead she disappeared into herself, capsized, and sank to the bottom of the life she'd been dealt. Every night she sat on the bench in a sea of shadows, under the hazel branches where I lay hidden, facing south. She greeted her unseen visitors with a faint shake of the head, as though silently denying a message that only she heard. I saw her shoulders sink toward the ground where they would finally disappear. Her mouth hung half-open, protesting an immense, chronic hunger that no one could satisfy.

I've never seen so deep a longing. Not even in Magdalene, who was an expert on the subject. I recognized it strongly, perhaps because I myself was becoming a woman, and because I feared that Magna's favorite message to the children at Kongslund had been a lie. *All the best homes are by the water*. It wasn't true. I learned that at the cape.

The homes by the water are the ones no one escapes from.

* * *

"If she had only answered their call," Susanne once said of her mother. But there was no real conviction in her voice.

If only her mother had followed their murmurs to the rainbow's end, instead of letting the conquerors' words become whispered messages about a world so far removed from the garden and the hazel bushes on the cape.

Seen from the outside, she was a happy mother with two beautiful daughters—daughters who were very different from one another and hardly ever played together. But that's how it is with some siblings. No stranger would have ever dreamed that Josefine didn't have the same maternal feelings for both of her children.

No one noticed the strain on Josefine's face whenever she detected small signs of the stranger in Susanne. To most parents, innate differences between their children are inconsequential, because their love is so endless that it envelops idiosyncrasies and weaknesses and inexplicable variation. They don't fear that their love is weighed, filling too much or too little, because it is everywhere. But it wasn't like that for Josefine. When she sat with her daughters at bedtime, the subtle differentiation that shouldn't have been there surfaced. In her voice there was an undertone so faint you wouldn't think a human ear could hear it, but the illegitimate child did—and knew right away that she was a guest, a stranger. That a connection hadn't been made.

Instinctively, Susanne drew closer to her stoic father, who didn't seem to make the same differentiation, though he wasn't able to express his feelings in words at all, neither love nor anger. With men like him, those kinds of sentiments had to find other outlets.

One day he sat on a tree stump in the woods holding a small frog toward his daughter. He closed his hands around it tenderly and said, "This is one of life's biggest miracles . . ." And then he pinched the frog's neck with two fingers until his nails turned white. "This is the portal between life and death . . ." It was dead before it hit the grass.

Back then Susanne hadn't understood him, but she did understand the look in his eyes that made hers burn. Rubbing them, she felt the tears on her fingers.

Brutality takes many forms. In the fifth grade, Susanne began complaining of stomach pains. First there was a rumble in her gut, then a prickling, as though she'd swallowed a wasp. The principal and the homeroom teacher initially wrote it off as an upset tummy, but she displayed textbook ulcer symptoms and was finally put on a strict diet of oatmeal and crackers. People were compassionate toward her, and at appropriate intervals, she would remember to clench her teeth as though bravely enduring a particularly painful episode. Then she would sigh from deep within—but she never exaggerated her performance, because she already understood that genuine compassion makes people feel good, but it doesn't tolerate total despair or hopelessness, let alone complicity.

For her twelfth birthday, Susanne was given a blue bike with shiny mudguards. Two weeks later, a teacher found it in the gravel under a lean-to, broken and battered. It appeared as though someone had, in a rage, flung it to the ground and stomped all over it. When the teacher showed Susanne the wreck, she simply stared silently at it. Then when the indignant principal and the janitor announced their plans to launch an investigation into the incident to find whoever was responsible for the vandalism, she still said nothing. Perhaps her silence made the two men uneasy, because they abandoned their interrogations of the students, and the investigation was dropped. No one mentioned the episode again, even the teachers fell silent about it, as though they realized there was something unmentionable behind the inexplicable occurrence.

Around this time, all energy seemed to leave Josefine's body. Her eyes crept back into their sockets, and her whole person acquired a faintly shiny aura, as though she were gliding through a ghost world. The carpets crackled when she walked over them, and the heavy curtains fluttered in the living room whenever she walked past, even during the long periods when the windows were kept closed at her express order. Silence was everywhere, in every room she entered.

Just a few weeks after the bike incident, the vandalism began once more, violent and random. Again, Susanne was the only target: her clothes, her backpack, her pencil case—even her math books—were taken and later found in a bush or puddle, tattered and broken. The episodes occurred at least a couple of times a week, and no one managed to stop them, but strangely enough, the bizarre incidents only seemed to strengthen Susanne's patient calm—she never cried and never blamed anyone—and for that very reason she was the object of growing admiration.

Shortly before the summer holidays, the vandalism ceased. It was as though the maliciousness had left the county, letting all aggressions seep into the ground from where they'd come. Nobody could explain why, but most people were relieved—a feeling that would later turn out to be entirely misguided.

That year, the harvest festival was held four short months after Susanne's twelfth birthday. It was a relatively warm evening, and when Anton, in a rare tipsy state, fell into bed still wearing his clothes, Josefine crept through the rooms—the curtains fluttering—and sat on the floor with her back to her bookcase. She pulled one of Ulrik's exotic books from the shelf and began reading. And that's how Samanda found her at 5:15 a.m. Without turning, Josefine whispered to her daughter, "Look, it's the man mommy used to know." She pointed at the book cover and the little photograph of the author wearing a white safari shirt and wide-brimmed hat. He smiled under a neatly trimmed, blond mustache. His teeth were strong and white.

"Mom?" Samanda said.

Josefine looked into the man's blue eyes.

"Mom?"

Josefine remembered how he'd put a finger on his lips and kissed her good-bye, the taxi door half-open, before he disappeared into the world.

"Mom," Samanda said. "Tell me the story!"

So Josefine closed her hands around the book and read aloud from the chapter about the Spanish Armada, which brought back shiploads of "living gold" that the conquistadors had found in the Canary Islands— the small golden birds that sang more beautifully than any prince or king in Europe had ever heard in their deep, dark woods.

"Let's buy one of those!" Samanda shouted joyfully. No one could know then that this innocent desire was simply a continuation of what Fate had planned years ago—and would bring about her own demise.

By the time Josefine and her daughter left for Copenhagen on Monday morning, they had decided on getting two birds. As they stood in the pet shop, the number doubled to four and even the largest cage was too small, so Josefine burrowed holes into a big cardboard box from the store before hurrying home. At the behest of his enthusiastic wife and youngest daughter, Anton built a giant aviary in less than a day, using heavy wire—the kind found on mink farms—stretched across a floor of birch tree planks and stained Masonite. Following Josefine's direction, he placed the aviary right inside the kitchen by the south-facing window. Within a month, the four new lodgers were given two new friends; and soon the beautifully carved oak, birch, elm, and ash sticks in the cage held eight vigorous, loudly chirping bright-yellow canaries with their eager beaks turned straight up to the sky. They chirped so loudly that Susanne felt like covering her ears, but she didn't dare to, because she sensed her mother's peculiar excitement about her new allies. Before the end of the year, eight had become twelve, because that was the very number Josefine had always dreamed of—and she named each bird after a Greek god or philosopher she'd discovered in Ulrik's book about Olympus, written the year she gave birth to Samanda. Hera, Aphrodite, Amphitrite, Aeolus, Athena, Hermes, Dionysius, Prometheus, Poseidon, Zeus, Socrates, Plato: the ten females were gods or goddesses, the two males were philosophers.

Josefine spent hours in front of the aviary, sitting on a stool and staring through the screen until her eyes went red from concentration—as though she were waiting for an event she couldn't yet see. One morning she went to Kalundborg; late that afternoon she returned, set her shopping bag on the sofa, and pulled out a little wooden cage covered with a green blanket. The cage stood next to her bed all night, and in the morning the house awoke to a whistling, warbling singing. Susanne heard her mother laugh exuberantly. "That one will be my most beautiful darling," she said.

She called the fateful, thirteenth bird Aphrodite—her favorite name—renaming the first Aphrodite Aristotheles; granted, it was neither a god's name nor a philosopher's, but one she invented, and in her exalted mood she had no time to worry about that.

The new Aphrodite had been born with a unique color mutation: a white chest with only a few narrow stripes of yellow. For two days the bird sat in the aviary, glancing nervously at her twelve companions. On the third day there came a strange coughing sound from the floor of the giant cage, and the remaining twelve birds cocked their heads and stopped chirping. Josefine screamed. Aphrodite, with her fine golden markings, sat hunched over, the center of the other birds' undivided attention, breathing heavily as if the beautifully arched chest might at any moment burst. Another two days passed. The forlorn Aphrodite lost all of her splendor and many of her feathers, looking more and more like the aging Socrates than the exquisite goddess of love: straggly, bloated, and nearly bald.

The following morning she laid her egg. A big, greenish thing with brown spots. Josefine for once held Anton's hand tightly as she watched the shell first appear; it seemed an impossible size—bigger than the cherry plums they picked at the cape each summer—and Josefine let out a despairing whimper, as if she were the one giving birth. Then the arched shell protruded further, and the bird's eyes opened wide as its chest heaved in terrible angst. Josefine moaned at the sight. The rest of the egg followed, and Susanne, who had been standing behind her mother, hurried to the bathroom and vomited—spitting and rattling and practically drowning out the grotesque birth. The remaining birds sat petrified, and Samanda wailed.

They watched in horror as Josefine's favorite collapsed next to the large, formidable egg. Her chest rose and sank—and she tried to climb atop the egg to brood, but kept slipping over the side. No one intervened, and Susanne found herself completely devoid of compassion—both for Aphrodite and for Josefine. Finally, Anton reached into the cage and removed the egg. He studied it carefully. It looked cracked, dead. "She's broody," he said. "She'll keep laying eggs until we have her put down."

Josefine looked at him, her eyes wet. She stood and took the egg from him. She placed it in a blue Tupperware container, which she carefully carried into her room. The next day she absurdly patched up the shell with a bandage and candle wax, but it looked every bit as lifeless as before.

Two days later the egg remained in its shell of candle wax. Josefine replaced the bandage every morning, and the shell assumed a brownish color as though a still-living creature was pushing against the inside of the shell with all its might.

On the sixth day Josefine gave up. The following morning, Anton took the feeble Aphrodite and the cracked egg and went into the forest. Susanne hesitated in the kitchen doorway, recalling the frog her father had killed before her.

"Come with me!" he said, and she ran after him.

Father and daughter stomped through the thicket until they came to a suitable spot behind a juniper, its bare branches poking out in every direction. Here they laid Aphrodite on the ground, and the bird sat shaking in the little wooden cage it had arrived in, as though it understood what was about to occur. Susanne studied her father's strong hands, and, to her surprise, she felt goose bumps spread across her entire body, down to her very fingertips, like thousands of little needles pricking her skin.

Anton squatted with the terrified bird in his hand, and he looked at Susanne for a long time. Slowly he held the bird out to her, and she accepted it and did exactly what he'd shown her with the frog. A moment later, Aphrodite lay in her box, her elegant neck snapped and her head dangling at an impossible angle. The beak that should have sung so beautifully was half-open, and the bird's eyes had already glazed over. They dug a hole in the forest and put the box in it. They covered it and patted the ground firmly, erasing all traces of the grave so no one would ever find it again. At last Anton crushed the egg with his boot, until there wasn't a chip of shell left. He kicked it into the dirt, the last few pieces blowing away in the wind.

It was a dreadful winter. Josefine had taken the death of her beloved golden bird as an unusually bad omen, refusing to enter the surface of ordinary life. She floated about the rooms like a faintly gleaming ghost, her mouth a thin white line under black eyes that focused on nothing earthly. Never had the house at Våghøj been so filled with a heavy, invisible mass; it tore at the curtains and the walls and tried to suck them into its vacuum. Even Josefine's friends stayed away, and the quiet chirping of the remaining birds could barely be heard through the vast silence.

Then Fate sneaked unseen though the rooms one night when they were all asleep—completing the catastrophe, which Susanne had known would happen ever since Aphrodite's arrival and subsequent death. (I was the first person she told the story to, and it is the most bizarre story I've ever heard.)

Early one morning all sounds were suddenly gone; the little raps against the sticks, the familiar tinkle and rustle from the kitchen—silent now. And the door to the aviary was open. So too was the front door. The birds had flown off, each and every one. With a noise that didn't seem to belong in this world, a woman's voice broke the silence that had lasted for nearly two months since Aphrodite's death. It was a Sunday morning, and the scream spread across the hills, causing people several miles away to glance into the sky, puzzled. What living creature could make such a sound?

When Anton arrived from the fields, Josefine was sitting by the kitchen table, rocking her pale but still beautiful face between her two fists. Her mouth was half-open and a strange wail emerged from her throat. Then there was the patter of quick-moving feet across the floor. Anton turned and blocked the doorway, holding his daughters at bay. "No, no, no!" he shouted loudly, and the tone in his voice made the two girls back off, frightened.

Any reasonable person would have understood that somebody had let the birds out on purpose. A cage door might have come open by accident, but a front door does not unlock itself—only a pair of purposeful hands could do that, and they would have had to do so quietly when everyone was asleep.

Maybe a vagrant, Anton suggested.

But Josefine stared into the void and did not respond.

Then he too fell silent. Only a fool would run off with twelve canaries and leave the silverware.

A couple of months later, Samanda and Susanne finished the tenth and eleventh grades of high school. The first shock seemed to have blown over, and everyone must have assumed that the bad luck that had plagued Hill Farm had finally ended—at least for that year. Susanne considered the door that had been opened while everyone slept, and the sun that had risen over the fjord, shining like the conquistador's gold and tempting the little birds toward it. She thought of the frog and of Aphrodite, lifeless, in the cold soil.

In the months that followed, Josefine's skin became dry as parchment. It practically crackled under the gray light that enveloped her. Her walk grew hesitant; her joints seemed stiff and tense, as though struggling to turn on their hinges when the brain ordered them to do so. Twice, Susanne had seen her stand in the middle of the room for nearly half an hour as if she'd forgotten where she was or how to move her limbs. They didn't buy any more birds; the aviary stood empty and only rattled faintly whenever Susanne or her father walked past. They ate dinner in silence. She hated the empty wire cage because it reminded her of a giant mausoleum. She couldn't understand how its bars remained so shiny, without a trace of rust. It was as though Josefine's dust cloth continued to polish it when no one was looking.

One night at dinner, Susanne took a deep breath and said, "I'm going to move away when I start twelfth grade."

Josefine looked up for the first time in a long while. Very slowly Anton guided a forkful of goulash into his mouth. Almost as though he hadn't heard her. Maybe he'd already floated up under the ceiling in order to withdraw from the scene.

Samanda sat strangely frozen.

"I can rent an apartment in town," she said. She meant Kalundborg.

Josefine didn't move.

Susanne stared at her. "If I have to stay in this house, I'll drop out and get a job as a cashier." She wasn't sure why she said this.

Anton stared at his plate. Josefine's mouth was half-open. Samanda remained frozen, pale, without the smile Susanne had expected.

"There's something sick in this house," she said.

At that moment, Josefine's chest expanded to the breaking point, and her body filled with energy, as if all the accumulated pressure that had for months caused her skin to shine and her limbs to tremble were suddenly released.

Samanda reached for her, but it was too late.

"*You* . . . !" Josefine pointed directly at Susanne. "You've never belonged here!"

Out of the corner of her eye, Susanne saw Samanda's wide eyes, and in the background she heard a faint rattle in the aviary, as though all its contents had been shaken loose and were bumping against the cage. Or perhaps the birds had miraculously returned and taken their seats for the final showdown.

"Don't you . . . bother to come back, ever! Don't ever set foot here again!"

Anton awoke at these words and tried to reach out for his wife's raised arm, but all the pent-up air was forced from her hunched body and swept him aside like a tumbleweed in the wind.

The blast of anger struck Susanne, practically lifting her from her chair. "You know what you are . . . Do you even know what you are . . . ? Do you know where you come from . . . ? You were born to a whore in Hamburg . . . !" Josefine stretched the last vowel out, before it was torn apart by a moan emanating from deep within her belly. Susanne jumped up from the table and ran out of the kitchen with Anton in pursuit. She made it to her bicycle, which was still scratched up, and was gone before he could catch her. That's how abruptly her life at the pastry-box house at Våghøj came to an end.

Just as abruptly as it had begun.

She had arrived at Hill Farm in the vanilla-custard Volvo sixteen years earlier, a stranger. And she had remained a stranger. The orphanage suitcase with the little blue elephants on it still sat in her closet, a memory of the short period when she had been Anton and Josefine's dream come true: the girl from Kongslund with the golden halo.

* * *

"Did she really yell that . . . ? 'A whore from Hamburg'?"

This was my astonished question to Susanne the night she told me the story for the first time. She put a finger to her beautiful lips. "Marie, promise me you'll never—" And then she paused. Behind her the mirror hung black and silent, horrified at what had been disclosed, that something like this had actually happened to a human being as radiant as Susanne.

"It's not like I have anyone to tell it to," I said.

"But yes . . . that's how it ended."

"So suddenly?"

"Yes. But I always knew it would happen. It was in the air. When she got the birds—" She paused again.

"The birds?"

"Yes, when Aphrodite died."

But I was too impatient to dwell on the peculiar tone in her voice, and that was a mistake I discovered only much later. Instead, I asked the most obvious question. "Then what happened?"

"I lived with a friend and her parents in Kalundborg—and of course I started thinking about being adopted . . . wondering where I was from. But what was most shocking to me was that I was no longer my father's daughter. That just kept hitting me. I couldn't care less about my mother and Samanda. I hated them."

I noticed she said *mother*, though.

"My father hushed it up, and I brushed it off. After all, he'd taught me how to float away until things calm down again." Her reference to Anton's angst was accompanied by a little smile. "Later I took a room on the fifth floor in an apartment building in Kalundborg."

"You never spoke about it again?"

She shook her head. "Not even at the funeral."

"The funeral?" I sat up and saw her straight, immovable back like a dark shadow in the magic mirror behind her.

She nodded without changing her facial expression. "Yes. Samanda's funeral. She died. It wasn't long after."

"Died?" It was such a strange statement that I wasn't sure I'd heard it right.

"Yes. She died a year later. In the lake. Where we caught frogs." She looked at me with her bright-green eyes, and there was a peculiar calm in her features. I was shaken. "After I left, she grew feeble in a way that no one could explain . . . She never moved away from home. No one could figure out what was wrong with her."

A shiver ran down my spine. I cursed myself for not seeing the danger that lurked for Samanda—back when I had observed the two girls at Våghøj. I had only paid attention to Susanne.

"She couldn't breathe, and finally she couldn't move," Susanne said, still oddly calm. She leaned forward so I no longer saw her outline in the old mirror, which had long since withdrawn into the fairy-tale world where both mirrors and human beings have some control over their terrors. "Her legs grew very thin and wobbly, as though they didn't want to walk anymore."

I opened my mouth to ask the next question, but she answered before she even heard it.

"They couldn't figure it out, the doctors. Every part of her just seemed to give in. And one morning they found her in the lake. She'd probably gone out to swim. She did that in the mornings from time to time. When it was warm enough. I imagine she didn't have the energy to get back out again."

She described Samanda's demise in short, flat sentences; and, in that moment, I wished more than ever that I'd had Magdalene with me—but she never visited me when Susanne was there.

"She drowned?" I said slowly.

"Yes."

All the best homes are by the water, I thought.

"We buried her. It was the first time I'd returned to the farm."

"But did that have anything to do with—?" I didn't know how to formulate my grotesque question, but Susanne cut me off before I could finish my sentence.

"No. She was almost always with my mother," she said. "With *her* mother, I mean. It gets confusing, doesn't it?" She got up and looked into the darkness, which at that time of night swallowed up the Swedish coast and the old stargazer's fairy-tale castle on Hven.

"I don't know what my mother's conception was . . . about a *happy* family life, I mean," she said. "Maybe it was just to see her daughters move away from home when they were ready to marry—like she had. But then I suddenly broke the mold. And everything changed. The life she'd lived . . . suddenly there was a stranger in the room."

I nodded almost mechanically, without understanding her strange, fragmented observations. I could only think of Samanda.

"Don't you think that's it? Mothers want their children to be like them. They want us to be exactly like them, even when they ought to help us make everything better . . . avoid all the mistakes they made. Josefine *wanted* me to be like her. She didn't want to accept that she'd had to take another's child as her own."

I didn't agree with her—and in any case, there was another explanation that I thought was much more plausible. "She could have been incredibly angry that you let her canaries out," I said. "That might be why she lost control. After all, those birds meant everything to her."

Susanne put two fingers to her well-formed lips. She was a very beautiful woman, even in the gloaming and at some remove in the antique chair. No wonder men behaved like shy boys in her presence—or that I loved her.

"But, Marie," she finally said softly and with a cheerfulness in her voice that struck me as odd. She cocked her head, as if to imitate one of the twelve golden birds. "You don't understand at all, Marie. I didn't do that . . . Do you really believe I had?" Then she laughed, and everything lit up around her; even the mirror was, for a moment, blinded, reflecting her radiance like ordinary window glass.

I slumped in my bed, more deformed and darker than ever, unmoving.

"Marie, listen to me. It wasn't *me* who let the birds out!" She laughed again, then turned serious. "And I'm sure she knew that."

I couldn't respond at all.

"But that's what you thought? Like when my things were vandalized. Everyone thought it was Samanda. But it wasn't."

Now I understood the anger that had filled one of the children at the cape; it was a revelation that almost toppled me.

"I really hated her, Marie . . . I have to admit that, even now. You have no idea how much you can hate someone when you feel . . . like that . . . like an interloper . . . like someone who has no right to be anywhere." Shrugging, she said, in a peculiarly light tone, "Of course I shouldn't have left . . . because after all, it wasn't Samanda's fault . . . but I didn't care. I didn't care about her longing, because I hated her so much. Or maybe . . . maybe I knew exactly what I was doing . . ." She shrugged again. "And she did die."

At that moment I had a terrible sensation that another person was in the room with us. I've always had an aspect of melodrama about me. But it was only me and Susanne, and she sat motionless before me, practically invisible. Maybe she was about to float away like Anton. I remembered her description of the face she'd seen in the depths of the lake at Våghøj. Had it been a mere vision? I suddenly felt so cold, like I might freeze to death right there.

Then she said, "Marie, you've always lived in a place where everything was destined to be in harmony—always; in the most beautiful house here by the water, under the twelve beeches, in the nation's most famous orphanage. You have no idea how much hate you can feel . . . how the anger . . . it can make you kill . . . and sometimes you do in the end."

Once again I glanced into the mirror to establish contact with the creature that I was sure lived in there—but the glass was completely black, and in that instant, it became clear to me that I'd never speak to the creature again.

"Who do you really think opened the door to that cage?" Smiling, Susanne cocked her head teasingly. "Who do you think, Marie? Until you figure that out, you don't know anything."

At that point I'd been sitting in front of her for so long that my mouth was dry, and I felt dizzy. *Maybe there are human acts one really doesn't want to understand,* I thought, keeping my silence.

"You'll have to figure it out for yourself, Marie."

I didn't reply.

She shrugged again and said, "When you understand that, you will understand everything."

* * *

Later that night, when we lay in bed with the lights off and I had settled down a little, I heard her voice in the darkness—though I don't think she could hear me crying. I knew that some kind of barrier had been raised between us that night, but back then I didn't understand why.

"While we sat there singing psalms in the church located at the very tip of the cape," she said, "the pastor spoke of eternal life and Samanda's mother just cried and cried, and I decided to find my real parents."

I felt panicky for a moment and kept my eyes shut. "But you never found them," I whispered. I knew the answer better than anyone.

"No," she said.

"Nothing at all . . . ?" It was a silly question. My voice trembled, but she didn't notice.

"No," she said. "There was nothing to go on at all. No adoption form, no dramatic *King's letter* as it was called then, no papers. Not at Mother's Aid Society, either. There weren't even any records at Kongslund . . . everything was gone . . . or had been misplaced, as Magna put it. Maybe that's why she hired me to be the deputy director. I guess she felt sorry for me."

That night, I remembered how she'd once done something strange that I'd never dared ask about. She had installed a beautiful birdcage with four egg-yolk-yellow canaries that chirped to their heart's content, delighting the children who were big enough to be on the second floor. She marched up the stairs to the governesses' lounge and Magna's old office and put the cage in the tall windowsill facing west, so that all day the birds could look at the twelve beeches they would never be able to reach.

Three of the birds lived for nearly fifteen years—an unheard of age for the species—and when the last one died, she didn't get another one; she just left the cage standing untouched. It was like the room a deceased person leaves behind, because the grieving cannot bring themselves to clean it.

The fourth canary had died suddenly a few years earlier, and that had been an incident as curious as the one Susanne had experienced as a child. One morning the bird was just gone.

Susanne stood in a ray of morning sunlight trying to understand the simple, indisputable fact that no one could explain.

The window was open, but the door to the cage was closed, as it should have been—its hinges apparently untouched. Every indicator suggested that it had been opened during the night and then closed again.

As Gerda entered the room, she said, loudly and a little more frightened than anyone had heard her in years, "Canaries don't open cage doors and then close them again." She didn't have to finish her thought.

Before they fly away. . .

No one responded.

24

NILS

June 21, 2008

Of course Magna had pulled the strings and dispatched her loyal envoy, Carl Malle, to talk to Susanne Ingemann while she was still attending the teachers college.

That's how the most powerful woman in my life operated and planned things, because she had never put her trust in God or the Devil.

Susanne was offered a job at the home, and in addition, was promised to succeed Magna after she retired. Who was better suited after all? And how could the girl from the cape decline that offer, especially after she came to understand her universal duty: to become the next repair woman in the workshop Magna had perfected, and which could never come to an end?

Everything had been arranged exactly the way my foster mother wanted it.

* * *

After a dreamless night I woke early, though our guests weren't due till noontime.

It had been almost six weeks since my foster mother's death.

This was the day I had been dreaming of my entire life, the day old Magdalene had promised would come since the day we met.

Patience, she had whispered in her lisping voice. *Patience is the only ally of the ostracized and the deformed.* Then she'd giggled in the usual way, as she'd done during all the years that she was my only friend. It was the day I would be reunited with the five boys from the Elephant Room.

I looked over the sound toward Hven. But for once I left the telescope in its holder. According to Kongslund's calendar, it was the longest day of the year; and I was sure that was more than a coincidence, as usual.

A little before noon, I heard two cars pull up on the other side of the house. I waited for almost five minutes before I slowly rose from the wheelchair, glanced into the mirror, which stared back at me silently, and slunk down the stairs past N. V. Dorph's large painting of the woman in green.

I remember that my eyes met hers for a moment expectantly, as though she had something to do with the imminent ceremony—or could tell me something about it—but she too answered with silence. Then I walked through the hallway and opened the door to the infant room, where all of Gerda's blue elephants immediately surrounded me with their raised trunks, hundreds of them. The smallest children had been taken outdoors to nap in the pavilion, and there was no one else in the room. For a long time, I stood behind the curtain observing the four guests on the patio. My heart beat so hard and so fast that I clenched my teeth out of fear that they'd hear it through my mouth.

This is it, Marie, my life's ally whispered to me. *It's* now. Magdalene had a weakness for pomp, which I think she shared with her distinguished host on the Other Side.

Four men stood beside Susanne Ingemann. I couldn't hear what they were saying, but judging from their facial expressions, they were making the first awkward introductions. Asger Christoffersen smiled faintly. His glasses were as thick as telescope lenses, and he was almost a head taller than the others—as if his study of the stars had pulled his bones and tendons toward the sky. Nils Jensen stood to his left, weighed down by the collection of cameras around his neck—a Nikon mirror reflex, a small Leica, and a large flash that made him look like the man in the photo the newspapers had published when he won the Press Photo of the Year prize for his picture of a dead Iraqi boy. Peter Trøst stood at a slight remove with his hands in his pockets, staring at the sound. Maybe he'd read about the history of the place and knew that the little wooden pier down below had a glorious past: this was where *The Falcon*, a royal ship, had called at Skodsborg during the months leading up to the adoption of the Constitution, when the People's King and Countess Danner needed to discuss the slope of the roof and the placement of the external walls with the architect of Kongslund. Peter very slowly turned to face the others on the patio, as though he yearned to escape.

And finally, Knud Taasing, who had accompanied Nils and who was uncharacteristically quiet, his brow furrowed. Two childcare assistants had put sun-yellow freesia in four blue vases under a blue sunshade and set a white table with crystal glasses and shiny silverware on the patio. Susanne Ingemann leaned in and nudged one of the vases a half an inch more toward the center of the table.

I could tell she sensed my presence, and suddenly she turned toward the fluttering curtains in the half-open patio door and said something to the others. Everyone glanced toward the door to the infant room.

I stepped into the sunlight, joining them.

They froze almost as if they'd seen a ghost or a human being they thought had been dead for years. And in a way that was true. I had put on a black dress and buttoned it all the way up my neck, like an aging Magdalene would have done. It seemed to me an appropriate gesture, but it no doubt made me appear as though I'd arrived from a bygone era.

"This is Marie." Susanne quickly gave me a glass of elderflower juice, no doubt to break the tension.

Surprisingly, my hands weren't shaking, but I sensed their curiosity like little birds in the air around me. Throughout the Kongslund Affair, I had been a mystery, just as I had in all the years before that; and now here I was, very much alive—the deformed little girl who had once played in the attic, the famous matron's strange, invisible foster daughter. Susanne introduced me to them one by one, but none of the four men made a move to shake my hand. Touch didn't come easy to any of us—not even to Knud Taasing who hadn't been born to unknown parents. I knew he'd told the others about the letter from Eva, making me the anonymous letter writer, but there was no hostility in their faces. I assumed that they, like Taasing, thought her letter was very recent, and of course I didn't do anything to change that perception—just as they had to trust my assurance that there'd never been a letter to Eva's child enclosed.

Susanne explained that both Taasing and Peter Trøst had tried to get ahold of Søren Severin Nielsen, but that he hadn't returned their calls. No one had tried to contact Orla. The TV star greeted me with a subtle bow; the friendly gesture made my squinting left eye water, and I wiped away a silly tear. No doubt he ascribed my odd reaction to his fame and his beauty; he had no way of knowing that I had studied every one of those features up close for many more years than most, and therefore remembered them much better than anyone else today, now that his handsomeness had begun to fade.

"Thanks for having us." Asger bowed politely and a little stiffly. Despite the summer warmth, he wore a wool crewneck sweater. At that moment, he cocked his head as though he recognized a distant creature in my asymmetrical appearance—or maybe he remembered the assistance I had given him when he wanted to find his biological parents. I'd had to act fast, giving him the most logical answer I could find.

He suspected nothing.

Strangely enough, the conversation began with that very topic. "Asger says you once helped him get the name of his biological mother," Peter Trøst said casually.

I looked away, shocked. My heart was now beating harder than when I first made my entrance. As a child I had loved Peter—at a distance. How could you not?

"How did you find her name?" He gestured toward Asger, as though it was the astronomer's question to begin with.

Knud Taasing stood a few feet away, giving me an inscrutable look. He hadn't even mentioned my involvement with the anonymous letters in his articles, and while I understood the problem of proving it if I denied it, I couldn't help but wonder why he'd refrained from doing so. Maybe he was hoping I'd provide more fragments of the answer to the riddle concerning the adopted child—or maybe he just feared that the next revelation would involve his only remaining friend. I understood that in order to preserve his friendship, Knud had chosen not to tell the photographer what he knew. For that reason, Nils was now standing only a few feet from where he'd spent his first year in Magna's care—without knowing the least about it.

"In the records," I finally said, breathing deeply to keep my voice steady. "I found the name in the official papers in Magna's office." I emphasized the word *official* and retained my lisp so that Magdalene wouldn't feel she'd been kept out of the conversation, but made sure I was fully intelligible to my long-awaited guests.

Susanne was the only person present who knew this was a complete lie. Presumably, she was rather shocked at what I might have said to the fifteen-year-old Asger that had satisfied his curiosity. But she hid her surprise perfectly, as always. I could tell that all four men were affected by her beauty just like I had been—and I assumed they knew the main events in her life, since they'd been described in the articles about Kongslund.

Taasing turned to the tall astronomer. "Who was your biological mother then, Asger?" I detected some skepticism in his voice.

"Her name wasn't Bjergstrand, I can tell you that much." Asger's voice remained cheerful.

"Did you ever visit her?"

"Yes and no. I saw her." His answer was both contradictory and peculiar, and his cheerfulness evaporated.

Susanne came to his rescue. "Let's have lunch, shall we?" She turned to the infant room door, clapping her hands authoritatively.

"Did anyone else go see their parents?" Taasing asked, fixing Peter Trøst in his gaze.

Peter did not reply.

"Where are those records now?" Taasing asked, turning to Susanne.

"I'll go to the attic and search for them as soon as possible," Susanne said.

"Maybe then you'll find your own form—*from back then*," Taasing said.

Everyone on the patio froze.

The glass I held in my hand began to shake. There was no way he could have known that.

In the doorway to the infant room a childcare assistant stood with dishes of cured herring and a bread basket. Out on the water, white sails glided inland toward Tårbæk and Tuborg Harbor.

Susanne didn't succeed in hiding her surprise, which for a second marred her otherwise beautiful face.

"You weren't going to tell us?" Taasing stood directly in front of her. He was wearing the same green sweater and brown corduroys he'd had on during his last visit. "I had been so blinded by my focus on the five boys that I never, until now—right now—took an interest in the last girl from the Elephant Room . . . the last child in the photo."

Susanne sank into the chair at the end of the table. And we all followed suit, as if spurred by a shared impulse—except for Asger. With trembling hands, the childcare assistant placed the herring dishes next to Susanne. Taasing continued to stare at her.

Then Asger cleared his throat. "Actually, I was the one who discovered it . . ." he said. "A long time ago." His glasses had slipped down the bridge of his nose and seemed to be plotting their departure, the black frames flapping away over the sea. "This morning I told Peter and Knud—and Nils—after we heard that it was Inger Marie who had sent the anonymous letters. I didn't think it was necessary to share this information before—because the whole case is about a boy—but I think we have to understand everything in order to figure out what happened." More than ever, this researcher of the galactic gas clouds seemed as though he was trying to see across the light years to the other side of the universe, slightly afraid of what he might find.

He was afraid, no doubt, of Susanne's reaction.

She gestured for the assistant to leave the patio, already regaining her composure. It was impressive.

"How do you know about that?" she said.

Asger put a hand on her shoulder, in an oddly intimate and comforting way. "My parents met your adoptive mother, at Kongslund, back in 1962 while they were waiting to adopt. Then they met her again ten years later in Kalundborg when I was admitted to the Coastal Sanatorium. Your mother had the idea to visit the poor sick boy . . . She felt she knew me, and she wanted to take care of others, as you know. But we didn't know we came from the same place, because they hadn't told us at that point."

Asger nodded almost defiantly to Taasing, who sat with his back to the sea, and then he turned back to face Susanne again. "After I'd been at the sanatorium for a while, my parents decided I ought to know, and so they told me I was adopted. My illness was genetic, and they had to tell the doctors that I wasn't their biological child. That's why. A few years later they told me about you."

Susanne Ingemann sat with her head bowed.

"I have no idea why you stopped coming to see me." Now Asger addressed only her.

"My mother forbade me," she said and fell silent.

"She forbade it?"

"Yes."

"That's why you stopped coming? Your mother didn't want to risk that I might tell you about my past and then you might become suspicious of your own? You weren't to know?"

"Exactly."

It looked as though the tall astronomer wanted to ask another question, but then he sank down on the last vacant chair, practically disappearing from the party, like a sunspot flickering on a wall.

"But how did you end up *here*?" It was Nils Jensen who asked the question, looking more and more confused.

"I met Carl Malle." Susanne shrugged by way of an explanation. "He visited me at the teachers college and told me about Magna. They were old friends from the war. She offered me a job at Kongslund. I thought about it for a while, and then I decided to accept. I wanted to see the place that my parents had kept from me all those years . . ." She blushed, a rare sight. "So I came back, yes."

"Yes," said Taasing. "You've all been under surveillance by a very powerful guardian angel with dark curly hair." If this was an attempt at lifting the mood, it failed.

"I haven't seen Malle around, until now," Peter said.

"Or maybe you just haven't noticed." Everyone looked at me. The words sprang to my lips before I could stop them. The others had no idea how well-informed I was. Just as Peter had failed to notice how quickly the episode with the dead principal had been hushed up when he'd avenged his friend's humiliation. Or just as Orla had never realized how quickly and easily he'd been dispatched to the boarding school after the murder of the Fool in the wetlands. But I had. The police had shelved the case of the felled linden tree despite the stir caused by a single article in a morning newspaper—one that posited that the chopping down of the tree had been an attempt to destroy the despised principal.

"They didn't want us to compare our pasts," Asger said. "They kept watch over us, and it wasn't with the intention that we were one day to meet." He looked around at everyone seated at the table. "Neither Susanne, Marie, Peter, nor—" He paused, as though an unknown celestial body had plumped down among us.

"*Nils*," I said mercilessly.

It was one of my talents.

All but one instantly knew what I meant.

But they sat in their chairs like statues.

Nils was the first to react, and he stared at me. "What?" He breathed deeply. "Why am I here?" The words fell to the flagstones like a brood of chicks that had been kicked out of the nest too soon. You could barely hear them. He turned to Taasing then Peter, then Asger, and finally Susanne Ingemann. Fear was in his eyes. The black cameras hung from their leather straps, immobile, around his thin neck.

I didn't dare look at Taasing, or Peter—and certainly not at Asger. They didn't know what I knew about perdition. They only saw my intransigence, and the personal victim I had decided upon was Nils Jensen.

"I was here . . . ?" In despair he fixed Susanne with his gaze. If everything was to remain as it were, she had to say no.

"Yes," she said.

"But I have parents. This can't be right." He was as white as a sheet.

"Yes."

"No. My parents would have told me." Flatly, he refused to hear.

She didn't respond.

For a long time, we sat in silence, the way people do when either death or grief has emerged between them and no one dares break the silence. Nils's eyes were moist, and I saw a fury stir in him, its wildness growing as the ongoing silence confirmed that this was not a dream.

I saw it lift its head and break out of the Darkness they'd left him in.

He stood. "I have to go home now."

No one stopped him. We heard him start his Mercedes and drive up to Strandvejen.

No one said a word.

"Would you have let him live in ignorance for the rest of his life?" I finally said. Instantly, I felt the same rage I'd directed at Dorah Laursen.

"Would it have mattered?" Taasing said. "You do whatever you want anyway."

"Doesn't the truth matter at all?"

Asger cleared his throat. "I have to admit that when my parents . . . when Ingolf and Kristine told me I was adopted, I would have rather not known."

Susanne gave him a look that would have pleased him had he not been staring at the tablecloth as though heaven and earth had shifted places. I had admired Asger all the years I had followed him at a distance.

His longing for the stars reminded me of my own longing whenever I gazed through the telescope at Hven.

"Of course you don't know my story," Asger said—almost formally—and everyone shook their heads, as if glad to have a reason to erase Nils from their minds.

"If Marie hadn't helped me find my real mother, I would have—" He stopped.

I didn't dare look at him.

"They hadn't intended to tell me," he said. "My parents . . . they didn't tell me until circumstances forced them to." He folded his hands, as though praying to the god with the best seat in the heavens, shoulder to shoulder with all the celestial bodies Asger admired. I knew every detail of his terrible story. I knew the prelude, the beginning, and the continuation—by heart. He didn't know that.

But for the first time I spoke without a lisp. "You lived at Kongslund for exactly one year and nine weeks before you left."

He looked up, surprised.

"They came in a blue Volkswagen, picked you up, and drove to Aarhus."

Everyone was staring at me intensely now.

"You arrived at Atlasvej in the summer of 1962."

Asger seemed as though he'd seen a ghost. And in a way he had. Only the ghost was of this world, one who carefully recorded observations made in secret and later memorized the recordings.

"You were adopted to a teacher couple in Højbjerg, and as a kid you were the direct cause of your best friend's suicide."

Now everyone was frozen in place. If the moon crashed onto the lawn, no one would notice. I lowered my head and went quiet.

Our little reunion had fallen apart in just a few minutes, and I wasn't surprised. People who've lived in a closed room for as long as I have don't expect things to work themselves out in a couple of hours, not even on a sunny patio with a view of the shimmering water.

Even if Magna had been right when she swore to me that nobody grew up in a better home than I, there would have been no other way to solve the mystery of Kongslund.

25

ASGER

1961–1972

If any of my old kinsmen in the Elephant Room had been selected for Fate's small, teasing raps from above—and of course they had—you'd have to say that the whack that bowled over Asger for the second time in his life was so malicious that no earthly power could have planned it.

I still see him in my mind's eye—at Kongslund, and in the room with a view of the sea where I found him much later, and at the sanatorium where he met Susanne. His misfortune was of the kind that the Master loves, because they really do seem like coincidences placed in random order.

It wasn't until Asger, with a good deal of cynicism that I otherwise hadn't associated with him, caused his friend's death that I understood the other side of him. And how limitless his love of the stars and galaxies had always been.

* * *

He was wheeled away from his mother's bed at Obstetric Ward B one early morning in 1961.

Three days later, a pair of strong arms lifted him from his bassinet, and Magna left the hospital with the little boy in her protective embrace.

No doubt he glanced over her shoulder as she carried him to the taxi, and I imagine how his round, inquisitive eyes gleamed, fascinated by space and all the blue that framed the planet they would soon be capable of seeing.

Asger couldn't have been born at a more fortuitous time. Mighty telescopes explored ever more distant star clusters, and ingenious scientists were discovering the blinking quasars billions of light years away. By age five, Asger had found his life's calling in an illustrated magazine teeming with stories of flying saucers and alien civilizations. When Asger was seven, two American scientists discovered the extraordinary traces of the universe's beginning; they heard a faint crackle in a radio telescope in New Jersey. At first they thought the equipment was faulty and tried to wipe away the creation of the world from their equipment using soap and water. As we know they weren't successful, for what they'd heard was the sound of the Big Bang—the very birth of the universe—and it was a true and wonderful story that once and for all directed Asger's eyes upward—high above the physical tediousness of life on earth.

When he was six, he was so obsessed with the sky and all its luminous, blinking, flaming, and flying objects that night after night his parents found him wide awake, crouched in the windowsill of his little room, completely absorbed in the glimmering silver trail of the Milky Way. Again and again, Ingolf and Kristine awoke to discover their son studying the moon, bright eyed and focused.

Like so many practical women, his mother, Kristine, believed on the one hand that the night sky was entirely mapped out—and therefore unimportant—yet on the other, she sensed that it represented a mysterious abyss that no human being under normal circumstances could ever explore. An uncommonly witty higher power had even managed to organize things so that their house was located in a neighborhood where the streets were named after celestial bodies: Neptune, Atlas, and Jupiter. The symmetrical streets were on the northeast side of Observatory Hill, where the city's famous observatory—with its two giant cupolas—had been built and named after Ole Rømer.

The two young teachers who were his parents worked at the local public school at Fredensvang, only a few minutes' walk from the white one-story villa in Højbjerg they called home. In every way, they embodied dependable care—the vanguard of Denmark's new middle class—and to complete the image, every night when they tucked their son in, they discussed countercultural ideas about freedom and uprising: the Vietnam War, nuclear test bombings, the Franco dictatorship, the Berlin Wall, and civil rights in America.

At some point, their stimulating conversations would be silenced by the one topic they could no longer ignore—and Ingolf would nervously pull at his pipe, while Kristine's voice grew shrill: "I found him at the windowsill *again!*"

Her husband folded his legs and looked nervously toward Asger's bedroom. They sat like this for a while. They were both painfully aware that the boy in the other room wasn't theirs and therefore contained traces of people they'd never met.

"I wonder whether it's *our* fault?" she whispered, casting a sidelong glance at the two cupolas visible from the window. She didn't understand how something as vast as the universe had found a crack into her life. Finally she answered her own question: "It was *you*," she said categorically one evening when her fears had come creeping back. "You were the one who told your friends he was born the same day they sent that *man* into space," placing a particularly reproachful emphasis on the word *man*.

Ingolf trembled a little. She was right; he had bragged how the birth of their son had coincided with the first major triumph of space exploration. The very moment Asger's small, long body was being washed and weighed and measured at the Rigshospital in Copenhagen, the world learned that the Soviet cosmonaut Yuri Gagarin had made it precisely three hundred kilometers into nothingness—in the spacecraft *Vostok*.

"One brave man went into space—and one brave little guy came down to earth," Ingolf had playfully told everyone. But he'd only done it to give the impression that he and Kristine had attended the birth—and that Asger was their own child.

Was he supposed to regret that now?

On that April day it had taken Gagarin exactly 108 minutes to reach his distant target in space, only a few more minutes than Asger's biological mother needed to deliver her perfect boy. Both fearless travelers, the man and the infant then received a healthy dose of liquid food; the infant fell asleep, while the space traveler wrote a couple of sentences about his weightless condition. What Ingolf omitted from the story was the terrible fact that, just as the man in the space capsule returned to his Russian embrace (this was in the middle of the Cold War), the woman rose from her bed and walked out the door to a waiting taxi, disappearing from her child's life forever. That's how Magna had described it. Asger's mother had been a harlot, she'd said.

"But he had no idea what was going on," Ingolf would say, irritated, whenever Kristine referred to the harmful effects of the Gagarin story on their little boy.

But Kristine would only look at him with empty eyes. "There's more to this life than what meets the eye, Ingolf!" she would say and then burst into tears again.

Whatever the reason, the boy's irresistible urge to study everything that moved in the sky grew: stars, comets, planets, galaxies, supernovas, jet planes, even gulls, song birds, ladybugs, wasps, bees, and butterflies. When he was seven, he had a larger head than other boys his age and wore glasses as thick as binocular lenses. He looked like a pensive professor of theoretical physics.

When he was eight, the two American astronauts Neil Armstrong and Buzz Aldrin landed in the Sea of Tranquility. Armstrong wandered about in the alien moon dust for two hours and fifteen minutes and then uttered the words that Asger had pinned to the wall above his bed: "One small step for man, one giant leap for mankind."

The following day, Asger began limping on his right leg for the first time—and that was another peculiar coincidence: that his own steps in the months after the moon landing became smaller and smaller, until he could barely take a step. This strange defect continued for over a year, until one day he sat with his back to the sky and looked down. He took off his glasses, studied his right leg for a moment, closed his eyes, and cried. It was then that Ingolf and Kristine finally took him to the hospital. The doctors examined him for a long time, before finally agreeing that their young patient had contracted the rare and hard to pronounce Legg-Calvé-Perthes disease. The illness was named after the doctors who'd first described its disabling appearance in the human body: his right femoral head had collapsed due to insufficient calcium absorption—in the illustration it looked like a broken clay ball rattling in the hip socket. This breakdown of the machinery was due to a defect in the boy's genes, the doctors said—in the very building block of the human organism, which at that time was the obsession of all scientists who weren't studying space.

One week later, they drove Asger to a hospital at the cape near Kalundborg, where his sick leg was to be treated with traction so he could fight the disease with a hundred other children in the same condition. He was to remain in his hospital bed for a full year and a half—and just to be sure they did, all the children at the Coastal Sanatorium were cinched into their beds with three sturdy canvas straps on each side. The boy who'd always dreamed of flying into space was now tied to his earthly bed as tightly as possible. The irony was rich. But, I wasn't surprised. I knew Fate could be banal when its mood was foul. I took three long trips to the Coastal Sanatorium while Asger was lying on his back there.

Nothing could surprise me anymore. At least, that's what I thought in the beginning.

The first day at the hospital, Kristine broke down completely. She cried inconsolably—and Asger heard her all the way down the hall, until the heavy hospital gate slammed behind her. His father stood frozen and white in the doorframe and couldn't manage a single word. For the first time, Asger really examined his parents, and he was shocked at what he saw. He was alone in the world. Any illusion about salvation was dwarfed by the scope of the catastrophe. He was like an astronaut who'd fallen out of his space shuttle into nothingness. Granted, he could see other points of lights in the dome of the sky, but he would never reach them in his lifetime. Back then Asger had no idea that he was already an experienced child in that regard—much more prepared for the darkness and loneliness than any of the other children in the big sanatorium.

On his first night he awoke screaming—it was as though the hospital room was filled with people he couldn't see—and at one point he heard a voice that seemed familiar.

"Whose child is it?" it asked.

In Aarhus, Kristine awoke suddenly in her bed and shouted: "It's mine!" And she wondered why she had answered a question she hadn't been asked. She thought of Asger lying in the dark with his sick leg and the genetic defect that had betrayed them all. That's what struck Kristine with more force than anything else—the little piece of information that the doctors had given her when the diagnosis was made: the defect was inherited on the maternal side; it was intrinsically connected to the female chromosome. The biological mother who'd abandoned her boy had left an illness inside him.

To the doctors, then, she'd had to confess that Asger wasn't her biological son.

When they pressed her hoping to include this interesting aspect in their research, she gave them the name and address of the matron at Kongslund, but afterward she was left with a deep fear that the secret she had revealed might cause her to lose her son to an unknown adversary.

Ingolf stroked her hair and said, "No one can take him from us, Kristine, and nobody wants to, either . . . But we probably have to tell him the truth now that all the doctors know."

She felt like a trapped animal.

In order not to lose him, she'd have to tell him the very thing that assured she'd lose him.

* * *

For the first Christmas at the hospital his parents gave him a small telescope with lenses so powerful that even at night he could study the sailors going up and down the ladders on the big oil tankers anchored in the fjord's inlet.

In his room there were kids from all over the country—from the island of Møn, Copenhagen, Elsinore, and Vejle, indeed, even from Thorshavn on the Faroe Islands, from where two twins had arrived with the almost identically sounding names—Høgni and Regni. There was even a little boy from a small town in Greenland with a distant, alien name. Daniel never had a single visitor and after nine months forgot the faces of his mother, father, and sister. Month by month his brown skin grew paler, his face rigid, and his black eyes ever distant. No one knew what went on inside his head—he simply lay on top of his duvet, clutching a coarse-haired seal hide that he'd brought with him.

Early one morning before the sun rose above the fjord, Daniel reconnected with his ancestor's soul; curling his fingers like claws, he tore at his belt and straps and jerked his outstretched legs with all his might as he screamed and groaned and foamed at the mouth. Finally, the belts and straps flew across the room, and it took four nurses and an orderly to hold down the limbs that now threatened to jump from his imprisoned body. He was pacified with pills and even stronger straps and was no longer allowed to clutch the seal hide that had triggered his revolt. He never spoke to anyone again.

A couple of days later, the broad-shouldered, working-class lad, Benny, from Copenhagen, continued the revolt, loosening his straps and unraveling the bandages from his legs. With a peculiar, contemptuous laugh that rose from his belly like a growl, he pushed down the bedrail and edged triumphantly to the floor. Here he stood a little unsteadily for a few seconds, squeezing a chair before letting go and trying to walk on his frail legs. Surprised at his own lack of strength, he fell to the floor and lay moaning. In the beds around him, his buddies watched with wide-open eyes, petrified by the looming and unbearable catastrophe. As with all newly formed rebellions, they held back cautiously and let the leader take the first (and often also the last) steps alone. But then Benny suddenly stood and made the walk of his life from one wall to the other—with no muscles in his legs. And then on the return (the twelve feet or so to his bed) his painstakingly rebuilt femoral head snapped in its hip socket, causing him to fall sideways into hell and an extra two years in bed.

There were other terrifying stories from the Coastal Sanatorium—like the awful one of Karsten, the truck driver's son, who ran errands for Asger on his crutches the summer he was discharged. He went back to his father, who promptly made him carry boxes and big sacks day in and day out as his assistant until the fragile hip finally gave in. He never made it back to the sanatorium. A few days before he was supposed to return, he hobbled through the darkness into the adjacent forest and hanged himself. He was twelve years and two days old, and this terrifying story spread like a whisper among the nurses and frightened the kids out of their wits.

From his bed with a view of the fjord, Asger realized that Fate does not spare those already afflicted—on the contrary. He understood that it had a particular aversion to boys like Daniel and Benny and Karsten, those from families who didn't understand, who had learned nothing, who stupidly ignored or resisted the inevitable. It seemed to take a particular pleasure in knocking down the poorest and most desperate families. Asger got the message though. He held his breadth and made no hasty movements during those days. He knew better than anyone how clearly even the smallest movement could be seen from as far away as outer space.

They took the belts and bandages off in July 1972, on the very day the robotic space probe *Pioneer 10* became the first spacecraft to enter the asteroid belt. At the request of American scientist Carl Sagan it carried humankind's first message to alien civilization: an aluminum plaque depicting the figures of a man and woman and including directions to planet Earth, just in case anyone wanted to stop by for a visit.

It was anything but a coincidence to Asger; it simply foretold the freedom awaiting him. Suddenly he could bend his legs again and sit up in bed—and for a couple of hours a day, he was allowed to unfasten the six straps that tied him to the mattress.

On the first day he sat up in bed, a little girl with long reddish-brown hair falling over her shoulders—like a halo—appeared in the doorway. He'd almost forgotten what a girl's voice sounded like.

"Can I come in?"

His heart beat hard.

"I live close by," she said. "My name is Susanne." Her voice nestled under the skin of his chest.

"I just wanted to see how you're doing," she said. "My mother said you were here."

He didn't want to frighten her off and therefore didn't question the peculiar statement.

"What's that you've got there?" she asked, nodding toward the telescope.

"Do you know they sent a spacecraft to look for life in the universe?" he said. And then something incredible happened: she didn't laugh at him. She simply said, "Did they find any?"

Love washed over him right then and there. It was that easy. The two children had no idea that they'd met before, but I believe their subconscious identified unmistakable signs: a scent, a color, a way of moving—perhaps the tone of voice—everything they'd shared in the Elephant Room, but which neither of them knew at the time.

In August 1972 she appeared again, one Thursday afternoon, as the sun was shining from a deep blue sky and an enormous supertanker had dropped anchor in the fjord right outside Asger's window; there it lay like a silvery whale, on that wonderful day, and Asger smiled to the whole world.

"Did you know our parents knew one another a really long time ago?" she asked.

He thought about the question a bit. "No," he said. "They've never said anything about that. When was that?" But he was cheered by the thought, because it gave him a special position none of the other boys in the ward could trump.

"When we were born . . . when we were born in Copenhagen," she said merrily.

A promising thought. The two of them had somehow been together from the beginning.

"I've never heard anything about that," he nevertheless said in all honesty.

"It was at the Rigshospital."

"All I know is that I was born the day Gagarin launched into space."

"Parents don't tell us everything," she said, precociously. He felt like reaching out and stroking her hair.

In her Aarhus living room, Kristine sat up straighter in her chair and put her hands to her temples as though warding off a sudden headache. "It worries me that Ms. Ingemann Jørgensen has asked her daughter to visit Asger," she suddenly said.

"But we already talked about this . . . and neither knows their past," her husband said calmly. "We'll have to tell him soon. All the doctors know."

"Maybe she really wants the truth to come out," Kristine said.

"Why on earth would she want that?"

"We have to tell him." Kristine shook her head. "Otherwise the doctors will. And then . . ." Her eyes were fearful.

Far away in Ingolf's mind a shadow moved, taking the shape of the son he loved, before disappearing again. "Well, then *I'll* do it," he said, standing.

That night they made love with a passion they hadn't felt since their college years. It was as though something had suddenly fallen out of their relationship—perhaps their hopes of becoming pregnant—leaving them playful and lighter than they'd ever been before.

* * *

There was complete silence on Kongslund's front patio. I could tell that this was the toughest part of the story for Asger.

With some difficulty I'd managed to put together parts of his story (Susanne knew some important pieces but not all of them), but this was no doubt the first time he talked about it so coherently and under such special circumstances.

He seemed to understand that the past would reveal a connection to the riddle we'd gathered to solve. The adults around us had made a pact that bound them together in silence, and both the orphanage and the adoptive parents would have had strong motives to keep it.

"My father . . . my adoptive father, I mean," he added, blinking behind the glasses, "took the ferry to Kalundborg as he'd done so many times before. But this time on his own."

Everyone around the table listened. Everyone knew that this moment was crucial.

Yes, Ingolf had been alone. He was determined to complete the assignment his wife had entrusted him with. The cab ride from the town to the hospital took fifteen minutes. A nurse's assistant wheeled Asger's bed into the waiting room where they could speak.

"Perhaps you're wondering why I'm here," Ingolf said.

"Yes," said Asger, who had been busy making a list of the most important events in space exploration since 1890, and his brain was only slowly returning to planet Earth.

"Your mom and I have been thinking things over. And there's something we'd like to tell you—and—well, maybe we should have told you, eh, earlier."

Asger's blue eyes were alert. Fear had not yet sent the first little pulsar into his consciousness.

"Your mom and I couldn't have children," Ingolf said.

Asger's eyes didn't seem to react, but inside his brain a little beam of light shot through the frontal lobe and pierced his skull with a white-hot heat. The seconds that followed his father's peculiar statement could have contained the entire life of the Milky Way from dust particles to a midsize spiral galaxy over a span of billions of years.

"That's why your mother and I decided to adopt a child." It sounded strange and was uttered in a much-too-loud and decisive voice. Ingolf smiled. "It's the best decision we ever made."

Your mother and I. His father said, "*Your mother and I*"—not Mom and me and you—the only sense of security he'd known.

He wanted to return the smile. But a noise traveled from deep within his chest and exited his mouth; something broke in him, and he grew dizzy. The floor of his gut slipped free and hurtled through the mattress, the bed frame, the floor, and finally the basement—all the way under the hospital. Fluids streamed from every orifice; he was like a cracked jug that had split open from top to bottom.

His father's smile disappeared. "But, Asger, we are your parents . . . Your mother and I will always be with you."

Your mother and I.

The head nurse, Ms. Müller, appeared by his bedside and held his hand; she asked Ingolf to wait in the hallway while they changed the sheets.

When he returned, he smiled apologetically at his son, but shock was still etched in the boy's face. They sat for long moments in silence, until Ingolf finally stirred. It was late and he had to teach the following day. He couldn't stay, and besides, he had to get back to Kristine; no doubt worry would be overtaking her by now.

"I have to leave now," Ingolf said gently. "I have school in the morning." In his long, uninterrupted teaching career he'd never played hooky. "As I said, your mother sends all her regards. She wanted us to talk this through, man to man, and we did. You've taken it really well . . . really well."

Asger hadn't said a word.

Ingolf shook his head, a little impatiently. "Your mother wrote you a long letter that you'll get in the morning, and then we'll call you Tuesday or Wednesday." Of course they didn't want Asger to lie there grappling with this new reality without hearing from them for several days, he told nurse Müller. "We'll come see you on Sunday, as usual. With all the new magazines—*Akim, Captain Mickey, Speed and Pace, Battler Britton . . .*"

He kissed his son's forehead—where fathers prefer to plant their kisses—and said good-bye.

Many years later, Asger would understand what his father had been thinking after his visit to his broken son as he rode the ferry back to his wife and their newfound tenderness: *It's no sin to tell the truth. It was the right decision. Maybe they should have done so earlier, but they'd had a lot on their minds—and they'd done nothing wrong.*

His mother's letter never arrived, but she did call him three days later. The staff wheeled him out to the telephone in the hallway, and he told her he was doing well. "Your *father* was tired when he came home," emphasizing the word *father*.

Asger didn't reply.

"We'll get you some magazines for our next visit, and we'll call you on Thursday," she said before hanging up.

All of Thursday he waited for them to call, but they never did.

He spent the following night half-asleep until the chief medical doctor made his rounds. Doctor Bohr, son of the famous atomic physicist Niels Bohr (whom Asger greatly admired for his immense contributions to quantum mechanics), entered the room, flanked as usual by Ms. Müller and a small train of nurses. "And how are we feeling today?" he asked. For once Asger seemed completely focused on the external world.

Again, fluids gushed from the boy—just as powerfully as earlier—and everyone stood puzzled. Later he would remember the smell of Ms. Müller's powder and her freshly ironed uniform. She looked at him and said, "I'm going to give your parents a call. They'll come see you. They'll stay at the chief doctor's guesthouse tonight."

He understood that her prophecy would come true.

An hour later, Susanne showed up. Normally, she didn't come on Saturdays. It was as though she could tell something was wrong. In his bed under the blue duvet, Asger's little body sank back in despair. She put her arms around him quite unexpectedly and cried. He told her everything. "They should have stayed with you," she said, ice-cold anger in her voice. "I'll tell my mother and father. They know them. They can talk to them. I'll be back."

He should have never let her go. It was the biggest mistake of his life. She never returned. Not at 3:00 p.m., 4:00 p.m., or 5:00 p.m. He didn't have her phone number or address, and when he screwed up his courage to ask Ms. Müller where Susanne lived, the tall head nurse looked at him for a long time and finally said, "I think we'll have to leave it up to her to come back." Seeing the magnitude of this situation for Asger, Ms. Müller seated herself on his bed and said gently, "Maybe her parents decided that they want her at home tonight." Her eyes shone with the same luminous gray as the water in the fjord.

When he awoke, his mother was at his bedside, and his father stood behind her. Farther back was Ms. Müller with her white nurse's cap sitting atop her silver hair.

That night—and the following night and the night after that, and for a thousand more nights—he tried to understand the events that had changed his life in only a few minutes, but he couldn't organize them logically, couldn't identify quantifiable phases the way he was accustomed to doing when he studied the origin of stars and planets. No formula could explain the forces that had been unleashed by an unknown power.

In less than a second, he'd been cut off from the people who'd been his parents.

And then, a few days later, from Susanne.

October, November, and December came and went, and finally he gave up waiting for her. He had no doubt that the girl he'd loved—loved the way only an eleven-year-old boy can love—was gone forever. She'd been a fairy tale, a fable, a dream made manifest by his own longing. The strangest dream he'd ever had.

* * *

Susanne Ingemann had tears in her eyes, and that was a rare sight—because in her experience sentimentality had quite literally proven deadly.

Asger put his hand on her arm, and I imagined, a little absurdly, that this was how they'd sat as children. When he touched her, it seemed to contain the comforting weight of forgiveness.

Knud Taasing, who in his profession had learned to distance his emotions, said, "But that gives us no new knowledge of Eva . . . or Eva's child. I told you about Marie being the letter writer, and she doesn't know any more than we do." It was a question without a question mark.

Peter Trøst sat silently on the other side of the table, his eyes glazed as if he'd just woken from a long sleep.

"I've tried to locate Eva Bjergstrand," Taasing said. "It's impossible."

I bent my head and tried to hide my relief. My left eye began to water again.

Asger spoke, his deep voice was almost soothing. "If anyone else is looking, they haven't succeeded either."

"Of course not," Taasing said sharply. "Because they are looking for a ghost."

I held my breath. *How could he have learned what no one but me knew? What no one but me could have known?* Desperately, I looked down at the table again, then closed my eyes.

Then, mercilessly, he dropped the bomb: "Because as far as I can figure, the person who wrote the letter Marie snatched up died"—he paused and smiled faintly—"seven years before that letter was written." And then he spoke directly to me: "Can I have another look at that letter, Marie?"

I had tears in my eyes, and I didn't dare raise my head to meet his gaze.

"Why do you want to see the letter?" Susanne asked.

"Because either the dead have started writing letters . . . or this letter was written when the person was alive." His voiced dripped with sarcasm. "According to the date, the letter Marie showed me was written only a few days before Marie sent the anonymous letters—in April of this year—but of course that would be impossible."

I stood, both eyes still closed, and left the group. It was an odd retreat, but no one moved.

A moment later, I stood by the desk in the King's Room, drying the tears from my face. I made a decision. This time I left Eva's petition to Magna in the blue airmail envelope, the one I hadn't shown Taasing the first time he'd visited.

When I returned, everyone was silent and in the same position.

Asger's hand still lay on Susanne's arm.

Without a word I threw the letter on the patio table in front of the shrewd journalist.

"The missing envelope!" he said in a lighter tone and smiled. "Yes, I had it quite right—postmarked in Adelaide where the mysterious woman lived and died. And look at the date . . . It's actually postmarked in April of 2001 . . . seven years ago."

Everyone looked at him, mystified.

He removed the first sheet and held it against the sunlight. "And the date . . . that Eva wrote . . . in this light it's very obvious . . ." He turned to me, and now I felt the insistent stares of Asger and Peter as well. "The date has been almost undetectably changed. You changed the 1 in 2001 to an 8, simply by adding a couple of curls on each side of the 1. It's not particularly pretty, but I fell for it. So Eva's seven-year-old letter was dated to the present. But why . . . ?"

Susanne pushed Asger's hand away. I hadn't confided in her about this part of my enterprise, and she wouldn't be able to understand why.

"You're right. The letter did arrive then," I said. "I tried to find Eva, but I wasn't able to." I kept Susanne out of it. She sat motionless, and I could tell that she was mystified. But I also knew that she wouldn't correct me as long as she didn't know what was going on.

"Instead," I said, "I found a trace of the child in Mother's Aid Society's old archives. That's where I found the form with John Bjergstrand's name." I raised my head, trying to ignore that my deformed left shoulder had almost sunk to the level of the table, and that my left cheek was flushed and streaked with tears. If my heavy lisp had them puzzled, they didn't say so—and no one tried to interrupt me.

"But after that, I got no further. That was seven years ago."

Asger wrinkled his forehead, as though he'd caught sight of a mysterious supernova but couldn't quite believe the phenomenon existed. I understood why. Because, of course, I still had to leave the most important pieces lying in the dark. At that moment, I was balancing at the edge of the abyss, just like the elephants in Magna's song, and could only hope for a certain amount of luck and the strength of Magdalene's advice from the Other Side: *the finest web, the most cautious gait.*

No one spoke for a long time, and then Taasing broke the silence. "You waited for seven years. But finally you decided to send anonymous letters to the people you knew would understand, who would publish them—in the hope that something would come to light?"

I nodded. A few teardrops fell onto my plate, but no one noticed.

"But why did you change the *year*?"

"Because I wanted it to look current, newsworthy." I had carefully prepared my answer. The journalists nodded thoughtfully. Asger's eyebrows were raised even farther toward the sky. I couldn't read Susanne's expression, but it didn't matter as long as she kept quiet.

"But why did you wait?" the insistent Knud Taasing asked.

"I wasn't sure what to do. I spent seven years trying to find my way forward, and I didn't want to risk having the case dismissed because it was an *old* letter," I said, dodging his actual question completely.

The journalists nodded again, and I was astonished at their naïveté, even though in a certain sense I'd expected it. Everything in their world needed to be *present* and *current* so it could be connected to reality—and for that reason alone they were duped by my blatant lie.

"But the first time around you didn't send anyone the letter itself, only the form." Asger said.

"I changed the date in case anyone saw it someday. After all, it wouldn't be hard to figure out who sent the anonymous letters." I stared directly at Asger, looking for the support my ridiculous story didn't deserve.

Finally he too nodded, and I could tell he found me interesting—and for the first time not only because of my mental quirks and cracked bones. People like Asger have a hard time with lies; they sense their presence much like they sense the mysterious black holes deep in the universe; they sense their presence (even when they are nearly as invisible or camouflaged as mine) and try to approach them without being sucked in by their power. "But that was foolish," he said. "It could have brought the credibility of the entire matter into question. If Knud had published it . . ."

He didn't need to finish the sentence.

Taasing looked at the untouched bread basket and then said, "I should've seen Marie's little deceit right way. Because Eva Bjergstrand explicitly stated that she was writing on Good Friday—and that she'd just read about a wedding in a Danish newspaper from April 7. But in 2008, Easter fell in March—almost three weeks *before* the wedding was to have taken place. I should have seen it—but I've always passed by Easter in silence." He smiled ironically. "In the first line she also writes that she'd departed Denmark forty years earlier, but in 2008 it would have been forty-seven years later, and she'd hardly be that imprecise." He lowered his head as though shamed. "The signs were there, but I didn't see them. I contacted the Australian embassy in Copenhagen, thinking that the letter had just been mailed, but I was lucky . . . I spoke to a secretary who several years earlier had fielded a similar question."

Taasing grabbed a piece of bread and broke it in half. "Another person had asked about Eva Bjergstrand, and the inquiry was not recent, but several years ago . . . a *woman*, and I got the description of this woman." He turned toward me. "And then it clicked . . . Could the letter be much older than I realized? Had I been deceived? A single glance at the calendar was enough. In 2001, Good Friday fell in April—on April 13 to be exact."

My heart pounded hard in my chest as I awaited his next, decisive words.

He raised the bread to his mouth but didn't eat. "The embassy secretary also recalled that no one named Eva Bjergstrand existed—presumably because she'd changed her name. After going through a list of all the Danish women who'd received Australian citizenship in the Adelaide region over the years, she'd come up with one whose age fit, but that woman had—at the beginning of September in 2001—left Australia." He took a bite of the bread. "And traveled to Denmark."

I didn't dare look at any of the others. This was what the embassy clerk had told me when I contacted her the second time. But she had likely not told Knud Taasing that she'd given me the same information, or he hadn't ascribed any significance to it.

I sent her a silent thanks.

"She had of course forgotten everything about it, but I asked her to find out where the woman was now. And the answer surprised me. Because she had apparently never returned to Australia. At any rate, they had erased her as a citizen in all their records. As far as they could tell, she had remained in Denmark."

"In Denmark?" Asger expressed the astonishment everyone felt.

"Yes. But then came the next shock—when I actually found her . . ." He hesitated.

"What?" they all seemed to say in unison.

"She was dead."

"*Dead?*" Asger repeated.

"Yes. Right here in Copenhagen. Very close by."

Asger's glow faded as though he'd seen a ghost. And in a way he had. "But how?"

"I sat and read all the big morning papers from the fall of 2001—from front page to back. Maybe something had happened in Denmark that I could connect to her. Like an annual meeting of the Danish-Australian Friendship Association, a conference . . . or maybe she'd been in an accident. Maybe the purpose for her trip was to repatriate. This was a complete shot in the dark, of course, but Denmark is a small country after all. When you're shooting in a barnyard, even random shots sometimes strike the target."

Taasing looked pleased with himself. Then he put his bread down and delivered the final blow: "The police found an unknown woman on the beach between Kongslund and Bellevue on the morning of September

11, 2001—dead, possibly murdered. Possibly from Australia—judging from her garments."

He was met with only silence. It was a rather old-fashioned word, *garments*, Marie thought.

Taasing stood. "Does the date ring any bells?"

No one said a word. It was a superfluous question.

"Right. A few hours later, two passenger planes flew into the World Trade Center in New York City. So as a result I only found a few lines in the two small dailies about the woman and her death. They had other things to write about, of course. But I found enough. Because now I knew what had happened to Eva Bjergstrand . . . Now I knew why she hadn't returned to Australia."

Despite my horror at his revelations, I couldn't help but be irritated by his histrionics and his word choice. Still the man had, quite exceptionally, hit the bull's eye. He'd found Eva Bjergstrand's final resting place in the sands of the sound—as well as the noteworthy date of her death. I didn't dare look at Susanne, afraid we might give away our mutual complicity.

"But why did they think it might be a homicide?" Asger asked.

"She was lying at the water's edge. She had lesions on her head from a sharp stone. There were no evidence and no technical leads to go on. She could have fallen. She didn't carry any identification, and the style of her clothes suggested that she wasn't Danish. One of the countries the newspapers suggested as a possibility was Australia, but no one came forward. The police shelved the case. And the media dropped it."

And then the knowledge I'd carried for seven years (and had only dared share with Susanne) arrived at Kongslund for the second time. This time with Taasing as the messenger.

The three remaining men at the table had no idea what had happened since, but each understood what forces my anonymous letters had in all probability released. Someone had made the connection to the dead woman at Bellevue, and someone had known where she was from and why she'd come.

Even brave Magna had feared the danger she sensed during those days after the anonymous letters had been received—and had tried to rid herself of her secret Protocol just days before she was found dead.

"It has to be connected to the Ministry," Peter said. "It has to be connected to Enevold or Malle, who are both so eager to find that boy."

"Or Orla Berntsen," Susanne said. And then she blushed, as though she'd transgressed an invisible line the rest of us couldn't see.

"If Orla is under suspicion, then we all are." Asger's glasses had slid down his nose, and for once the tall astronomer had forgotten all about the sky and didn't even notice the airplanes that were circling over Kastrup Airport in the distance. "Eva could *only* have come to Denmark to look for her child." He looked pleadingly at each of us, one by one.

No one contradicted him.

"Eva would have revealed to her child that it had been born under strange circumstances . . . and revealed the scandal . . . that its mother was a murderer," Asger continued. "The child may have unleashed a great fury. A least that's how I would have reacted. I would have detested being told that. And then maybe the murderer's child became a murderer, and that throws suspicion on all of us who were in the Elephant Room that Christmas 1961. Me. You, Peter. Susanne. Severin. Marie. Orla. Nils . . . Eva could have contacted any one of us, and the reaction could have been very brutal."

"The biological inheritance?" Susanne said. "The murderous mind?" It sounded like mockery.

Asger turned toward his childhood love, returning her gaze from behind his thick glasses. "Yes, Susanne . . . the murderous mind . . . it's possible."

"Then what—what about Magna—do you think she was murdered too?"

"Maybe the murderer tried to destroy the evidence," Asger replied. "And Magna got in the way. With all her knowledge. The anonymous letters set off a chain reaction."

"*If* she was murdered—they couldn't prove it," Peter said.

I closed my eyes.

"But then Marie can't be under suspicion. She was trying to rake things up," Taasing offered.

"Yes . . . maybe," Asger said, a bit absentmindedly.

I would have preferred a firmer response.

Then Taasing abruptly changed the subject. "You haven't asked me what was in the paper I told you about—the paper that Eva Bjergstrand mentioned in her letter, which she'd found on a bench in Adelaide, and that made her so angry she wrote Magna."

I opened my eyes again.

He was enjoying this, like a hunter lording fresh kill over his empty-handed hunting party. I'd tried to locate the article Eva had referred to by looking through all the major newspapers that might've made it to Adelaide, but without success.

Everyone waited in silence for Taasing to continue.

"Only one paper ran a story that could fit the bill," he finally said. "And that happens to be my own—what was then the party organ, which isn't so strange, because in a way it was a party matter." He practically smacked his lips from the satisfaction of this discovery. "How such a small paper winds up on a bench in Adelaide is beyond me—but miracles do happen," he said with a smirk. "On April 7, 2001, a discreet wedding took place in Copenhagen—more specifically, at Holmen's Church. The most powerful official in what was then the Ministry of the Interior—which later became the Ministry of National Affairs—was wedded to his cohabitant of many years." Knud paused again and didn't continue until it became almost unbearable for his audience. "Chief of Staff Orla Pil Berntsen married Lucilla Morales of Havana, Cuba"—he smiled at the obvious irony and incongruity of the match—"and by his side was the then minister of the interior, our old friend and benefactor, and protector of Kongslund, Ole Almind-Enevold."

Taasing waited a few seconds, coughed once, and then played his trump card. "They were all there, shoulder by shoulder, in a big photograph. There were no other wedding photos in the paper that day."

I could feel the shock wave travel around the table.

Each of those present knew what this meant. If you took Eva Bjergstrand's furious letter at face value, the only interpretation was the one that Knud Taasing's excellent detective work led to: The shadow in the young woman's life, the man who'd fathered her child and then made her disappear and in doing so destroyed her, wasn't some dime-a-dozen former celebrity who might produce a little fertile gossip for a few weeks. No, it was a citizen who in every context advocated high morals, loving thy neighbor, and not least the inalienable rights of little children before and after birth.

The minister of national affairs, himself. Ole Almind-Enevold.

If the young woman's words from the past could be trusted, the nation's most popular minister had in the early days of his career made a very young girl pregnant—in prison of all places—and then pulled all the strings he could to bury the scandal. When she had her child, a little boy, he was removed immediately, and she was secretly exiled. All traces of the unfortunate episode expunged. Only one minor trace remained—hidden in a box at Mother's Aid Society for decades—the name . . . John Bjergstrand.

No wonder Almind-Enevold—if the story were true—was taking such desperate measures to cover things up. Without any witnesses—and without the boy himself—the story could be written off as pure fabrication, the result of sick media frenzy and a bloodthirsty opposition. But if the boy materialized, a simple DNA test (which a man of his moral and political standing could not easily decline) would reveal the truth faster than the Witch Doctor could utter "no comment." Imagine the scandal: one of Kongslund's little elephants had a mother who'd been imprisoned for murder, and a father who at that time had begun his long journey toward the nation's highest position. If a story like that rose from the crypt of the past—if Knud Taasing or some other reporter were able to verify it—it would cost the minister everything, and in particular the title of prime minister. He would be disgraced to a degree that no Danish politician had ever been, and if degradation were all he got, then he'd be lucky. A criminal investigation could ensue—not least because of Magna's death—if anything suggested a motive for murder.

No wonder Taasing refrained from articulating that part of the story. It was, at this moment, just a treacherous theory, but one that could endanger anyone who knew it, let alone acted on it. There were still too many loose ends, and Taasing, who had already once in his career made such a fatal mistake, knew this better than anyone. I felt fear circle the room again. There was more at stake than anyone had imagined only a few minutes ago.

"It's a damn shame we don't have the letter that Eva wanted to send her child."

I looked down.

In a muted voice, Susanne tried to articulate what most of us were thinking but had no words for: "If Ole really is the father, then that gives him a motive as well . . ." She stalled as if the thought contained demons she was afraid to unleash. "I mean . . . the woman on the beach . . ." She paused once more, growing oddly pale. It looked as though she might at any moment be sick. "Almind-Enevold and Carl Malle—"

Taasing shook his head. "Maybe. Maybe not," he said, cutting her off. "I discovered something else at the embassy. Two men from Carl

Malle's security firm obtained a visa to travel to Australia a few days after Magna's death. Of course the embassy clerk had no right to disclose this information, but she did. The next day I called Malle's office and pretended to be a clerk from the ministry. I asked the secretary whether the two men had returned from Adelaide." He glanced toward the sound as though the answer was to be found in the waves off the Swedish coast. "She said no."

"But if Ole or Malle knew . . . or were behind . . ."—Peter let the obvious omission in his sentence linger—"they'd know that Eva Bjergstrand was already dead."

Asger nodded. "What you're saying is that if they knew she had come to Denmark in 2001—and never left again—they'd have no reason to go to Australia now. So why would Malle send two men there? It's a damn good question. And I think the answer is obvious."

"Yes," said Peter. "They didn't know."

"But maybe they're just looking for the package Magna sent," Taasing suggested. "That might be reason enough, so it doesn't tell us anything."

Asger didn't respond. His eyes rested on Susanne, who remained motionless. No doubt she'd been just as beautiful when they were children.

"Or," Asger finally said, stretching out his words, "maybe there's more between heaven and earth than we realize. One thing is for certain. We all have to gather information about our biological mothers—who they were, where they came from—to find out whether one of them might have been Eva Bjergstrand." He paused for a moment. "That goes for Orla and Severin and Nils too, of course. We each have to ask our adoptive parents what they really know. What Magna told them. We must demand to see the documents they were given when they adopted us, if these papers still exist."

As Asger spoke, I could tell what Peter and Susanne were thinking. For Asger it would be no problem—because he already knew where to look. It was easy to incite an unpleasant and risky offensive when you had nothing at stake.

* * *

That night I dreamed of Nils Jensen.

He was standing in the moonlight next to his father, the night watchman, at Assistens Cemetery, and they were listening to the Great Poet's strange and fantastic fable of the child who must live in the darkness underground after having trampled on his parent's loaves of bread so that he might reach home with dry feet. Because of his arrogance, this child had lost forever his right to the light of this world and the sight of the birds in the sky—and this was a lesson to all the children who followed him.

The old night watchman had told his son nothing about his past, or the miracle that had given the poor tenement family such a desired adoption, of the kind that was otherwise reserved for much wealthier families; that part of the story had been kept hidden until today. Nils Jensen had never suspected anything. He'd never had a little, snickering devil on his shoulder whispering truths into his ear—and his father, who in his work forsook the light, had preferred to leave it unsaid. He'd never thought the lie would be uncovered.

Now in the living room right off the cemetery of my dream, his eyes darted.

Nils Jensen repeated the question: "Who are my biological parents?"

The truth lit up first in the old night watchman's eyes, then the entire room. His wife slipped quietly behind the two men and out the door of the room, closing it behind her.

The night watchman and his son were alone in my dream. They sat for a long time without speaking.

"Who are my parents?" Nils said for the second time.

I could just make out what the old man said: "I've kept your birth papers for all these years. They told me to burn them, but I kept them." He sounded apologetic and defiant at once—and he extended his hand toward his boy.

For a moment there was no movement in the room, and for a terrifying second, I thought that was the way it would always be.

But then Nils Jensen took his father's hand, and I cried because I knew it meant that the child in the darkness wouldn't be lost forever. The fairy-tale poet might change his ending.

For once I let Fate hang over the edge of the sky, disgruntled, staring down at us furiously—the living and the dead, the newly arrived, the rejected, the barely repaired, the deformed, the pathetic—without jumping up and humbly asking permission to seek cover. It was a rare moment in my life. And of course it was a provocation that—even in dreams—would be punished.

* * *

Later that night I lie awake in the darkness listening to the sounds of children in the house, and I cannot help but think of the many children who've slept in these rooms for over seventy years. Sometimes I imagine that I remember all the faces that have turned toward mine, that I'm able to distinguish every single facial feature from a thousand others. But I know that only Magna possessed that skill.

In Gerda Jensen's old apartment in the southern tower, Asger has settled in. Susanne is sleeping a little farther down the corridor on the second floor—and their presence stirs a faint feeling of triumph in me.

Ever since Magna put me in the King's Room—an eternal reminder of the unfinished and imperfect in her otherwise symmetrical home—I have waited for this moment.

I think of those who now return, and a rare smile crosses my lips.

I wonder whether Asger possesses a heavenly innocence that so few adults retain. Certainly not Orla, or Susanne, or Nils, or Peter, not even Severin—who chose the path of Goodness, helping so many in distress—and certainly not I. We've never had such innocence.

But Asger?

"Is it possible to trust anyone at all?" I asked Susanne, as we made his bed in the tower room, when we were finally alone.

"I've never thought about that," she said.

"But you used to know him . . . once?"

"When I was a child. But do you really know anyone when you're a child?"

"Do you think he suspects us . . . or anyone in particular?"

Susanne stopped outside the King's Room. "How did you find his parents back then?" she asked. She too had mastered the art of changing topics.

I withdrew into the doorframe until we could barely see one another in the darkness. Only the lamp from the stairwell gave off some light. We must have looked like two apparitions from a ghost story set in a larger house than this. It had been a long time since she'd followed me into the King's Room.

"I thought the names of all the biological parents had been removed from the binder . . . from the records of the children in the Elephant Room," she said.

I didn't reply.

"But the papers still exist?"

I fled into my room and pushed the door closed. "I don't remember anymore," I said. My deceitful words lingered in the dark behind me like tiny, glowing orbs.

The words rolled like an echo down the hall and disappeared.

In that moment I knew of only one thing that had always been true at Kongslund. Always. I had always loved her. Susanne Ingemann possessed that rare quality that both men and women love. She was unobtainable.

26

THE BLIND GIRL

June 22, 2008

You can kill a person in many ways. And, of course, you can do it in ways that make it look like an accident, nearly undetectable. The small blows, the ones that can only be the work of a cruel fate, have always interested me. But to a boy like Asger, I think the hand that did the deed was merely a shadow in his soul. And that's why he didn't see it coming.

* * *

The prime minister's eyes had acquired the sheen of surprise that people get when Death steps into their path—even though this encounter is the only sure thing in life.

All the signs of imminent departure were there. There could only be a few days left of his term, and Almind-Enevold no longer tried to hide that fact.

"Everything is ready—and everything will be the way you want it," he said to his dying boss, rather formally.

He was talking about the arrival of Death as well as his own rise to the highest post in the land.

"Good."

In the presence of Death, the prime minister had put his hand-kerchief away to deliver the final cough—without cover—right into its face. It was an impressive, unparalleled provocation that the minister of national affairs couldn't help but admire, even though the sight of those blood-red threads of spittle running from the corners of his mouth was disconcerting on such a sunny Sunday morning, when the ministry was peaceful and nearly devoid of people.

He would have liked to push for a quick transition of power but didn't want to risk challenging a man who so flagrantly defied his own fate for so long.

"Is the Tamil case . . . under control?" The use of the banned word alone was a testimony to how far on the edge of the abyss the boss was.

"Yes," the minister replied, though it was the Kongslund Affair that worried him now.

* * *

Malle had visited Asger Christoffersen's adoptive parents in Aarhus and had spent a long evening asking them about their son's past and their contact with Magna. Had the matron ever given them information that suggested anything about the boy's background or his biological parents? Had she given them any adoption papers that they could show him? Had anyone contacted them with a mysterious purpose?

They'd answered no to all of these questions.

As expected, Asger was a child without a past—or rather, the past seemed to have been carefully erased. Magna had advised them to raise the boy as their own. There was no reason for him to know that he was adopted, she'd said, when there was no way of discovering his past.

Malle told the minister and his chief of staff about his lack of results, while in the background the snake fountain spewed its yellow and green crystals so high in the air that even the Fly who brought them coffee was uncharacteristically distracted by it.

"What about the doctors from the Coastal Sanatorium . . . any clues there? They must have discovered all the biological data that's scientifically possible to determine?" The minister's questions were logical enough.

Malle waited until the Fly had buzzed away and then said, "There's nothing. I've already been there. They never found his biological mother. But there was something else . . ." Malle shifted uneasily in his seat. "His father once told me that Asger disappeared from home for four days. He told them he was going to a festival on Zealand, but one of his friends later revealed, accidentally, that he'd never shown up. And shortly before that he'd talked to Marie." Malle shook his head as if to emphasize an almost astounding revelation. "His father overheard their conversation . . ."

He paused dramatically and the minister leaned toward him.

"He thinks Asger visited his biological parents during those days—without telling anyone."

* * *

The best orphanages are always by the water, Magna would have said. And I think you could say the same about hospitals. The majority of them are in the interior or in the center of the biggest cities—but the Coastal Sanatorium was right on the water with an undisturbed view of the fjord.

In December 1972, Susanne had been gone from Asger's life for three months, and in those days newspaper editors filled their pages with reports from the American bombing of Vietnam. The new prime minister at the time, who had once been a regular laborer but now had to bring Denmark into the European community, made regular, fervent speeches about peace and hope. As the world burned, Europe needed to form a tight bond. "Why do we have to be a part of that?" the nurses grumbled. They wore white caps as symbols of their altruistic work among forlorn children. Like other self-sacrificing people, they believed first and foremost in their will—and often feared the will of others.

A couple days before Christmas, Asger heard steps in the hallway and reluctantly turned his eyes from the sky and the fjord to the door. He had grown accustomed to the sounds of the sanatorium and could identify every single shoe by its thump on the floor. For months he'd listened for the sound that would bring Susanne back—but of course he never heard it—and he knew that it wasn't her steps he was hearing, unless she'd become severely handicapped and had begun walking with a cane.

Tock-tock-tock.

He sat halfway up in bed and looked toward the door.

A little girl his own age entered his room—*tock-tock-tock*—and felt her way carefully with the cane until she found the chair next to Asger's bed. It was quite a feat. For a moment she sat immovable, staring straight ahead. She had a soup-bowl haircut and rather exotic features. Her one shoulder slumped (maybe it was because of her grasp on the cane), and her face was a little out of focus, as though he saw her through two sets of misaligned lenses.

But Asger was so astonished by her blind march practically into his arms that he held his breath for five long seconds before he finally asked, "Who are you?"

Before the words had barely left his mouth, she answered—as though she'd known he would ask and had prepared a response, "I attend the School for the Blind here on the cape, and that's where I live as well." Her little mouth formed into a perfect flower, sucking the juice out of the words. She looked directly at him as though seeing him, but he knew that was impossible.

Most likely one of the nurses had taken pity on her and invited her in.

"Are you really blind?" he said.

She didn't answer.

"What's your name" he asked, staring curiously into her eyes.

"Inger," she said. It sounded like *Ing-ger* because she lisped a little.

"Do you want to hear a story?" he asked.

Her left hand suddenly awoke and began groping for something to hold. Soon he felt five fingers around his lower arm, and she huddled like a little bird in Susanne's chair.

He read aloud the first chapter of Carl Sagan's book on the exploration of life in outer space. When he was done she stood, rapped a couple times with her cane, and left.

Some weeks later she returned, and Asger risked sharing even more advanced theories: "Scientists like Niels Bohr demonstrated how it isn't possible to predict the way electrons move within the tiny atom. Each time you get close they invariably shrink back at random, and that means that nothing in the world will ever reveal its true self under observation."

She sat listening, her little cane resting between her legs; she was wearing tights. It struck him that they were a good fit: the cane, the leg, the body—all as slender as a willow branch.

In January, he began rehabilitating his healthy leg, walking with crutches for an hour a day. Once in a while they went for a walk together, and afterward he read aloud to her while she listened, always in silence.

"Where is your real home?" he asked.

"By the water," she said after a long pause.

"Is it nice there . . . by the water?"

"Yes," she said. "All the best homes are by the water."

He thought it a strange response, and the words startled him a bit. Even by a stretch, you couldn't say that his home in Aarhus was by the water.

"I'll be going home soon," he said.

She didn't respond.

Three days before he was discharged from the sanatorium he heard her *tock-tock-tock* a little earlier than normal. In the hand not holding the cane, she carried a small package, which she gave to him once she sat down.

He unwrapped it and stared at the contents for a long time. In a little white box lay a dried frog with protruding eyes; it was stuffed with wilted straw and leaves, and its neck seemed to have been broken. There was a brief pricking in his sick leg, and he felt goose bumps rise on his arms. But she couldn't see them, thankfully.

"A frog . . ." he stammered. "Thank you!"

He considered how long it would take a blind girl to catch a frog and then how she'd killed it with a brutal clutch of its throat. An astonishing accomplishment. He looked at her thin brown fingers.

She didn't speak or move.

"Have you ever heard of the Andromeda Galaxy?"

She appeared not to have heard his question.

But Asger kept talking, because he loved the Andromeda Galaxy, even the very sound of the name thrilled him. "Andromeda is the closest galaxy to the Milky Way, and at night you can see it quite clearly," he said, impulsively taking her hand. Her skin felt as cold and dry as the frog's, but he didn't want to let go of her. "At night I see Andromeda in my telescope—it's a fantastic sight."

Her hand remained in his.

"There's an observatory where I live, and I can show you if you'd like."

She withdrew her hand, slowly, and straightened up. As before, her hand lay on the knob of the cane, and her knuckles shone white in the twilight. Then she stood and walked to the door. She'd never left him like that. Almost as though she were in a rush.

At the last moment, she turned and looked at him, and he waited for her good-bye; he understood that they wouldn't see each other again. "I have seen Venus over Hven," she said. And then she was gone.

Perhaps it was like the sun and the moon, he thought during the days that followed. He had loved Susanne's warmth, but the moon crossed mercilessly in and out of the clouds, telling stories that were darker, older, and more mysterious than any other in the universe. While the other children slept, he cried for three nights in a row without knowing why. The creatures he attracted were even stranger and lonelier than he himself. It was one of Fate's tricks. Often, he'd had the feeling he was living in an endless number of parallel universes, the way the eccentric physicist David Deutsch described it: with no singular, fixed reality. If he could only learn the art of stepping to the side and disappearing into a new universe, even the wickedest blow couldn't affect him.

Of course, that was a dream as unattainable as the love he'd just encountered—and overlooked—the way people do.

* * *

In December 1973, the American space probe *Pioneer 10* passed the largest planet in the solar system, Jupiter, carrying humankind's message out into the universe.

"It was Carl Sagan's idea," Asger said at the dinner table in the house in Højbjerg.

His parents nodded. To avoid making eye contact with each other, they looked away.

Asger's long hospital stay apparently hadn't significantly changed anything—but he was no longer alone in his interest in the universe. He had a new friend, Ejnar, who lived at the Ole Rømer Observatory, which was located on a small, grassy berm at the end of Asger's street. Ejnar's mother had died during labor, and his father, the director of the observatory, had, for the sake of science, married one of his students, who could then care for his son while he examined the stars. The western half of the grounds was dominated by two Cassegrain reflector telescopes, and during the day, the two cupolas resembled a pair of shining silver helmets a giant had left behind under the blue sky.

Asger's friend was a descendent—not directly but still—of the astronomer Peder Horrebow, who had studied astronomy with Ole Rømer himself and who, according to the know-it-all Ejnar, had feuded with playwright Ludvig Holberg, no less, about an old debt. Out of sheer irritation, Holberg had stuffed his play *Erasmus Montanus* with astronomical allusions to Horrebow's enthusiasm for Copernicus's Heliocentric Theory—which in Holberg's version simply became a question of whether the earth is round or flat. Ejnar sniffled contemptuously at this demonstration of art's banality.

As Fate would have it, it was his father's scientific mistake that had such a terrible impact on Ejnar's own short life. Like so many scientists, Ejnar's father adored the British astronomer Fred Hoyle, who had placed outer space in sublime, static equilibrium by suggesting that the universe existed in a steady state, with neither beginning nor end. It led Hoyle and his disciples to the inevitable conclusion that the Big Bang—which according to rival scientists was the start of everything—was nothing but hot air. The turning point came when two American researchers discovered the sound of the universe's birth, and with that, the evidence that it wasn't static and never had been. The way I see it, that was the beginning of the end for Ejnar and his father, and indirectly for Asger.

In the years that followed that disappointing discovery, Ejnar's father sat hunched in stubbornness under the cupolas, scowling into the darkness in the hope that a new momentous answer would burst out of nothingness, saving him and Hoyle by recasting the question to one of eternal constancy. During those years, Ejnar became his father's most faithful disciple, and that was what really connected the two boys: how they continually circled around this topic, on which they disagreed vehemently. *Was there a beginning to the universe or not?*

"It began with the Big Bang!" Asger said excitedly.

"No," said Ejnar stubbornly. "The universe has always existed, and it's in a steady state."

Even for a neighborhood with streets named after stars, it was a remarkable discussion between two thirteen-year-olds, and their disagreement grew more vehement month by month.

"Do you believe in UFOs?" Asger asked one day, hoping to find a topic that might rescue their friendship from the abyss.

"If they're here, they always were—but then, where are they?" Ejnar said, glancing about tentatively and offering the kind of matter-of-factness common to generations of astronomers.

"Maybe they only appear at night," Asger suggested gamely.

Horrebow's descendant gave his friend a skeptical look. First Asger defended a complicated scientific hypothesis that reduced the universe to a single point of origin, and the next minute he was fantasizing about aliens; but Ejnar possessed a longing and a love that Asger wouldn't recognize until it was too late, and like Hoyle's universe, Ejnar's feelings were limitless, without beginning or end. So, to put an end to the alien question once and for all, the two boys—like the astronomer James Craig Watson, who one hundred years earlier had dug a deep trench in the ground to observe, in complete darkness, events in the sky as clearly as possible—dug a deep, pitch-black hole in the forest near Moesgaard Beach, a little south of the city. When it was done, together they climbed down a homemade rope ladder without noticing that Fate had climbed in with them.

"Scientists have always believed that pretty much all knowledge has been mapped out," Asger said thoughtlessly to Ejnar their first night in the hole under the stars. "Like how your father and Hoyle believed in the steady state theory . . . it's nothing new."

Ejnar shifted in the darkness. "Are you saying my father is ignorant?"

"No, but he *believes* in something that's ignorant . . . You don't have to."

Ejnar's love for his father was immense, and Asger felt a strange anger roil in his chest.

"But what if he's right?" Ejnar said.

"But he isn't. He's wrong. The universe is expanding because of the Big Bang. Just about everybody knows that by now," Asger said dismissively.

A terrible, sad expression spread across Ejnar's small oval face, but in the darkness of the hole, Asger didn't notice, so he continued along this trajectory: "Your father simply dreams of turning back the clock . . ." He paused, and the words articulated themselves in the silence . . . *to the time before you were born.*

And the painful truth of those words lingered between them. Before Ejnar's birth, the universe had been in perfect balance wherever his professor father had looked: his theory was still valid, his wife remained by his side, and he felt a kind of freedom and a boldness that Ejnar's appearance—coinciding with the new theory of the universe—had robbed him of.

"I don't want to sit in this damn hole with you anymore," Ejnar growled. And, a moment later, he crawled out and disappeared.

Scientific dissent can be articulated that simply in a funnel-shaped hole some twelve feet below the surface. From that day on they didn't see each other. It is a peculiar fact that the strongest bonds can sometimes break from a series of even the lightest blows. The boys had zero chance of understanding the force that, time and time again, leads people to the point of no return. The hole in the forest fell into disrepair, and the alien spaceships—if they'd ever been there—opened their cosmic afterburners and disappeared.

After their quarrel, Asger was alone for months, and he grew ever more restless, as though his thoughts were occupied by something much larger and much more mysterious than the movement of galaxies in the sky. That was when his parents decided to take him to the orphanage on Zealand to see the place he'd come from, a visit that ultimately didn't seem to make any impression on him.

Then one Saturday morning, when the dining room of his parents' house was empty, he went to the phone in the windowsill and dialed the number he'd long kept on a piece of paper stuffed in his pocket.

"This is Inger Marie Ladegaard."

The answer was muted but clear, as though the call had been expected. "Hello . . . ?" she said.

"This is Asger Dan Christoffersen," he said.

"Yes . . . You were here with your father and mother. Your adoptive parents."

"Yes, that was me." He didn't know what to say. Marie's gentle voice made him shy. "I was just wondering . . ."

She breathed calmly but didn't say anything.

He cleared his throat and took a deep breath. "Don't tell anyone . . . anyone at all. But I'd like to contact my real parents. I'd like to know where they live and what they do."

"So soon."

"Soon?"

"Yes. Most people don't call them until they've reached their twenties or thirties."

He heard her muted voice deliver the strange statement and didn't know how to respond.

"Many adults have that urge," she said by way of explanation.

He still didn't reply.

"I'll see what I can do," she said.

In the background, he heard someone shout her name.

"Give me your parents' names and telephone number and I'll call you back."

He did so and then said his good-byes, already mentally preparing himself for a long wait, but the phone rang just an hour later.

"Hi. I just needed to be alone," she said. "You aren't the first."

His heart pounded.

"Do you have a pen?" Her voice was calm, as though she delivered these messages regularly. He thought he detected a faint lisp.

He put the receiver down on the table. Through the window he saw his parents moving about the yard; his father was repairing the bird-house that Kristine filled with breadcrumbs and sunflower seeds each morning. With his shirt half-open, his father stood there breathing heavily, as though he'd biked fast all the way up Jylland's Boulevard. In his mind's eye, Asger imagined his father at his bedside at the sanatorium, and he heard the voice uttering the crucial message . . . *Your mother and I.* He watched him pound nails into a piece of wood that held up the roof of the little birdhouse, shielding the platform from rain, and he saw him smile with satisfaction.

Such care.

"Yes, I'm ready," he said into the receiver.

"Your mother . . . your *real* mother . . . we only have her name . . . is Else Margrethe Jensen. When you were born, she lived at Nørrebro in Copenhagen . . . in Fiskergade 5. You'll have to do the rest yourself."

"The rest?"

"Yes. Go to the Civil Registry. They'll find her for you in a second. If she's still alive, that is."

Asger closed his eyes and envisioned the young, beautiful woman with the name Else Margrethe.

"Who are you talking to?" his father said suddenly, from just behind his right shoulder.

"Nobody," he replied with a start, and then quickly reached for the pad on which he'd written his biological mother's name.

"I think you're the one being interrupted now," Marie said playfully. "Tell your parents they ought to pay more attention to you than to their *garden.*" And then she hung up.

He'd been too shocked at Ingolf's sudden appearance to inquire about her peculiar knowledge of his parents' obsessive gardening. It struck him later, but by then he had more important things on his mind.

"Else Margrethe, who is that?" His father stood behind him with a hammer in his hand, reading the name on the pad. A second later, Asger heard the hammer hit the floor. "Come out in the garden with us," his father said. "You can help me patch up the holes in the garden hose. It's leaking like a sieve. I've repaired the bird feeder so your mother can spoil all her winged friends again." He laughed merrily and then marched thunderously across the room.

Asger followed, feeling a sudden, unrestrained joy that the man in the garden wasn't his real father.

* * *

He told them he was going with two friends to a music festival in Roskilde—and Kristine and Ingolf were happy to see him displaying more normal interests.

Alone, he sailed on the ferry from Aarhus to Kalundborg and then took the train toward Tølløse.

From the station he wandered westward down the main road, walking through small towns with peculiar names like Gammel Tølløse and Tjørnede; he made no attempt to hitchhike because he wanted to arrive at his destination discreetly. Oddly enough, he passed through the same town that Peter Trøst, many years later, would view from his office window in the months when his television career was falling apart—but back then no one dreamed of such media palaces or a world teeming with TV signals.

According to the Civil Registry, his mother had moved to the town of Brorfelde in the middle of Zealand and lived on a farm less than three miles from a famous observatory that shared the town's name. For the fifteen-year-old boy, all the pieces of the puzzle came together: if his biological mother had been working at the observatory, it would explain his lifelong, and clearly innate, passion for astronomy. (It didn't occur to him how scientifically contentious this explanation was.)

From his hiding spot behind a low branch, he pulled his telescope from his bag. On each side of the ditch, wheat fields stretched to the east and the west, and with his naked eye he could make out several details of the farm: an old, covered well; a red wheelbarrow lying on its side; a little blue bench next to the green front door.

It wasn't long before a woman came out into the barnyard, her face filling most of his lens, a dark oval in a deep shadow; it could have been anyone, but Asger didn't for a second doubt that this was his mother. His real mother. It was one of the strangest and most intimate moments he'd ever experienced, and he sent a grateful thought to Marie. He studied the figure standing in the driveway. He looked at his glow-in-the-dark watch, then pressed a button, marking the moment he first saw her. She remained in the middle of the frame. No one else in the world existed, just her. Did she feel his presence? He blinked again, and it seemed to him there was dew on his lens.

The shadow moved. The door closed, and the sound of the latch clicking reached him after a second's delay.

Asger settled into his perch and soon fell asleep, as children often do, with the sky in a perfect arch above. Tears ran down his temples and dried at the edge of his hair.

When he awoke, he cleaned the lenses of his telescope, carefully rubbing the fine glass with a piece of leather. It was then that it struck him like a fist in the chest, knocking all air out of his fifteen-year-old body: he was still a stranger. His real mother no longer felt him. And his current parents had dreamed of another child. He might as well be dead. In a way, he *was* dead.

His head was swimming. *The most remarkable realization . . .* then everything went black and he fell and fell and fell . . . An eternity later mission control reached him in the calm tone of voice he knew so well . . . *do you copy?* He felt like he was in water and thought he heard the oxygen tanks sputter, and then big gulps of air streaming into his lungs. A couple of minutes later, the horizon came back into view, rising through a shower of gleaming lights to fall into its place in the blue stripe that held his world in balance. He spat out a couple chunks of gravel and removed a little chip off the tip of his tongue.

It was white like porcelain.

A few days later, he stood at the railing of the ferry *Princess Elizabeth*, watching the Coastal Sanatorium slide by on the starboard side. He still felt strangely alone in the world, but the red twilight over the cape gave him a sense of freedom that he'd never experienced before. He'd studied the little house for three days; the woman who was his mother came and went. Finally NASA brought his capsule safely through the atmosphere and dipped it into the ocean, where it floated. He fixed his eyes on the dark shadow to the right of the cape hospital, the small cluster of trees he knew so well, and tried to get another peek at her face. Susanne. But she wasn't the one who stepped from the shadows. It was the blind girl whose name he'd long since forgotten. In the wind from the fjord it sounded as though she was shouting a warning to him—but he knew it was a silly thought. His exhaustion from Brorfelde was causing him to hallucinate.

Out of the blue, Ejnar came to his mind, and that was the first time he'd thought of him in the two years since their friendship dissolved in the darkness of the hole at Moesgaard.

He turned and headed into the ferry's cafeteria.

* * *

The next day, at Atlasvej, he sat by the window studying the two people who'd been his parents for fifteen years. As always, they circled around the bird feeder, seemingly satisfied with their repairs. The window was ajar, and he heard Kristine say to Ingolf, "Asger can't even remember what music they played at that festival!" He knew his mother knew that she'd lost him—and that she had no idea why.

He sneezed and glanced up at the sky.

* * *

A few days later, a group of young Danes strode into the crowds, disturbing the annual Fourth of July celebration at Rebild Bakker in Jutland, one of the largest of its kind outside the United States, and the strange televised photos of Indians on horseback brought his attention back to the planet on which he was born.

The following day, the boy whom his friends had given the nickname UFO-Ejnar—because he was always going on about alien spaceships—tried to call him. Same thing the following day, but now that earthly matters had interfered so significantly in his life, Asger didn't have the energy to revive the drawn-out discussions about the character of the universe.

He had to think about his relationship with his biological mother, and there was no room for Ejnar in his life anymore.

When they each began studying astronomy at college in 1980, they were put in the same class, but Asger saw that as a mere coincidence; he had, at any rate, put their shared, youthful fascination with UFOs behind him.

"You wanna go to Moesgaard and see if the UFOs are still there?" Ejnar asked, standing awkwardly in front of Asger in the university cafeteria. Like the time they'd argued about the universe, his face was flushed.

Asger shook his head.

Ejnar tried to play his only trump card: "But the hole in the ground might still be there!"

It didn't work. Asger wasn't interested in Ejnar anymore.

You wouldn't think it was possible that Fate could weave its thread so invisibly and masterfully, given its reputation for laziness and improvisation—but it's a fact that Asger's thoughtless rejections during that first semester at college taught him a lesson he'd never forget. Week by week, these rebuffs sapped his old friend of the will to live. Ejnar was made of something special, something that usually disappears with boyhood. He didn't contain that magical elixir that allows for sorrows and worries to be broken down and dissolved, instead they were carefully preserved and stored, and that was the problem. Around the New Year he suddenly disappeared, like dew in the sunlight. Rumors circulated that he'd gone to Copenhagen with a girl, but no one had ever seen him with one, and given his aura of loneliness, that theory seemed implausible. Some of his old school chums still called him UFO-Ejnar, but now it was more of a reference to his restless nocturnal roaming than to his fascination with other worlds.

They found him at the beginning of March, deep in the woods.

A jogger had just turned inland from the beach so that he could run on the narrow forest path leading to the main road near Bellehage, when he suddenly spotted some old wooden construction that blocked his way. It looked like a tower sticking up from the ground, resting against a thick tree. But it was a rickety ladder. The jogger squatted to catch his breath, and through the early dawn light he recognized a hat under the ladder, but it wasn't a hat: it was a half-covered hole. He walked a little closer.

The smell made him stop—and take a few steps back. Shocked, he called the police.

They retrieved the body a couple of hours later. It was partially decomposed, with white knuckles jutting out of what had once been skin and flesh. At the astronomy department all conversation came to a halt. In the planetarium, the stars were turned off. Classes were cancelled. Nobody knew exactly what to say. Asger was the one who'd known him the best. But Asger didn't speak to anyone on that day, or later for that matter.

According to the police, Ejnar had crawled into the hole to stare at the sky the way children do, displaying his remarkable patience one last time. He never crawled out again. Next to him lay a book by an author named Fred Hoyle—the officers found its title quite fitting, even though they didn't know what it was about. The book was called *The Black Cloud*.

The police confiscated the book, unsure of whether it had any significance to their investigation. Perhaps some yawning deputy read the 238 pages for the sake of procedure, and then the case was dismissed.

In the church, UFO-Ejnar lay in a casket surrounded by white, yellow, and red flowers; and Asger, who was there along with the entire college, imagined with terror the nameless silence of that darkness. He imagined how the hollowed-out eyeballs touched the underside of the coffin lid just as they had touched the dome of the sky, but this time in blindness. He saw Ejnar's father, the professor, in the front row crying over his only son, and he didn't dare look into those red-rimmed eyes for fear he'd display the sense of triumph that he, to his horror, had brought with him into God's house. In this moment, the old man had to know that the universe wasn't in a steady state, and that it never had been; and deep within himself, Asger heard his own voice lecturing Hoyle's disciples, both the professor and his son, who in reality he'd always envied and nearly hated for their faith and loyalty.

You wanted the universe to be static, the voice said, *so that it could last forever with neither beginning nor end. But that's not how it's constructed. I tried to explain this to Ejnar, but I failed before he could crawl out of that hole. He didn't have the patience required.* Subtly, he allowed his dead friend to take some of the guilt. And in the first row, UFO-Ejnar's father raised his head as though he'd heard a very faint sound he couldn't place.

The police had found a dirty sheet of paper with Ejnar's body. It was addressed to Asger. Only a few of the detectives, the lead investigator, and Asger himself had read it.

You were right. From this position, you can see the Andromeda cloud very clearly. Without a telescope. It's always been yours. And it is more luminous than ever.

Outside the church, Asger slid around the long line that wound its way to Ejnar's father. He didn't want to look into those eyes that had stared so defiantly at the white coffin inside, as if even in that moment, when they'd lost everything, they wanted to maintain that immobility was a mystery, not a scientific gravesite.

Asger shouldn't have gone to Brorfelde that summer. Even if he didn't know why, he knew it was true because everything is connected. That is the knowledge astronomers share with the very old. Ejnar had loved him with all the love found in the universe—it was that simple.

I think that Fate was more than a little satisfied that day, because the living have to fulfill the minimal requirements of thoughtfulness and consideration if they hope to avoid its reprisal.

The finest web, the most cautious gait, Magna would have hummed.

* * *

"You'll have to find her again." Knud Taasing said firmly.

The journalist had arrived without Nils Jensen, and Peter Trøst had sent his regrets after having hosted the second episode of Channel DK's *Roadshow* in three days. And like the day before, the late brunch sat untouched on the table, until finally the two assistants removed the dishes.

If Asger Christoffersen's story of Brorfelde, death, and disappointment had any impact on Taasing, he didn't show it. Instead, he turned to the astronomer and said, "You have to ask her whether she really gave up a child for adoption in 1961—you, that is."

Gone was any pretense of journalistic objectivity. "I'm really surprised that you—alone—had no trouble finding your biological mother," he said.

I held my breath and hoped that Asger had forgotten the important details, now so many years later. We were in the sunroom. Outside it was raining, and Susanne had lit the three lamps on the sideboard.

"Like I told you the other day, it was Marie who found the name for me," Asger said. "There's nothing to doubt."

I froze at this disclosure—but thankfully Taasing directed all his attention toward Asger and didn't notice me. Asger didn't look like a man who wanted to return to Brorfelde and his dark memories. "For me it's enough to know who she was," he said categorically. "She wasn't Eva Bjergstrand."

"But something happened here that both Kongslund and the National Ministry have sought to keep under wraps for decades," Taasing said insistently. His lean face had the same yellowish tint as the smoke from his ever-present cigarette. Asger didn't respond.

As usual, Susanne Ingemann sat on the dark mahogany sofa with her back to the window and the sound. She pulled her legs up under her like a teenage girl and turned to Taasing. "Maybe both Eva's and Magna's deaths were accidents?"

"It's remarkable the way people die the minute they get involved in the Kongslund Affair," Taasing said dryly.

"Yes, and you're famous for never being wrong."

This sarcastic jab at Taasing was delivered in a malicious tone that I didn't normally associate with Susanne. It was also unfair. For as far as I could tell, he'd put every bit of his energy into the case. The Kongslund Affair was his last shot at reviving his career. He'd spent the first hour going over his investigations into the prison system, and even if they didn't bring us any further along, his discoveries were impressive. He'd been able to confirm that Eva Bjergstrand had been incarcerated in Horserød State Prison, and he'd found a retired correctional officer who'd led him to another and yet another. All in all, he'd been able to find five guards who remembered the young girl. Unfortunately, their recollections were scant and didn't lead him any deeper. The events occurred, after all, nearly fifty years ago.

But the fifth guard believed he remembered the girl because she was so young—and had been pardoned so suddenly. But he didn't remember that she'd been pregnant, nor did he recall any visitors who'd shown particular interest in the convicted murderer. Taasing had sought further access to the records of Prison Services, and he'd combed through all the documents that had anything to do with Horserød; he'd read every single word and every single syllable but still hadn't found anything useful. If there was any relevant information, it had either been discarded or removed by the individuals who'd desperately wanted to keep the pregnancy and birth a secret.

With a long, thin finger, Asger made a deprecating gesture. "Were there any episodes here at Kongslund that . . . ?"

"Anything strange you mean?" Susanne Ingemann nodded. She'd kept an eye on me during Asger's narration the day before, discreet but persistent. I was probably the most mysterious thing that had ever happened below the slope—since the King's tumble, that is—and her visible nervousness made me uneasy. I hadn't been in the company of strangers since the clandestine voyages I'd made so long ago to Glee Court, Rungsted, the cape, and a couple of times to Asger's in Aarhus—and of course the Coastal Sanatorium.

"Once there was a break-in at Magna's office," she said. "*Everything* was turned inside out, and nobody ever found out what the thieves were after. Nothing was stolen. Gerda once told me it was an example of one of the few things that could ruin Magna's mood. A break-in."

"If anyone came looking for something here at Kongslund, we have to find out what it was," Taasing said.

My eyes blinked and a few tears dropped onto my hands, but no one noticed, luckily. Of course they'd come looking—and Gerda had apparently only mentioned one of around a dozen break-ins we'd had at Kongslund. Everyone knew that it was Magna's express wish that we pretend nothing had happened, that we ignore these mysterious visits.

The same pattern repeated itself every time: no sign of broken windows, no sign of picked locks—the uninvited guests had apparently just walked right in. They always came when we were away on a trip or on Sundays when we traveled to the city; in Magna's heyday we paraded up and down the main pedestrian street, because she wanted to show the world that we had nothing to be ashamed of. After the *guests* visited Kongslund, we'd find all the records and files pulled from the shelves and lying in a big mess on the floor. There was something almost demonstrative about the persistent repetition of the exact same, curious procedure. Magna was equally upset each time it happened. But she never reported it. She said she was afraid of what the authorities would think of the orphanage's security if they found out. And then it all stopped in the summer of 1985.

"It takes a lot to ruin Magna's mood," Asger said, as though she were still alive. I huddled on the sofa, trying to make myself invisible. The last break-in had occurred during the first large Pentecost Carnival in Copenhagen, and as usual it had pushed Kongslund into a state of silent unease, like it had been under the Occupation. Gerda had by no means exaggerated her description of Magna's reaction. Every time it happened, she'd hammer away at her flower stems, clattering her vases for days in a silent rage, and I think the assistants interpreted it to be pure fear. But I sensed something else in her vigorous antics—something that was, for me, just as clear as what the assistants saw.

Pure triumph.

Instinctively I knew why. The tireless thieves had never found what they were looking for. And Magna crushed the stems with a force that revealed both anger and stubbornness. And Schadenfreude.

They couldn't find it.

"What could they have been looking for?" Asger formulated the banal question in a voice so reverent you'd think he was asking about the creation of the universe. I held my breath and kept quiet.

"Papers . . . documents . . ." Susanne said rather vaguely. "If they were looking for the child—if anyone was on the track already then—then they'd be looking for records and forms from Mother's Aid Society, just as we're are doing now."

"Did Gerda have any idea who might have been doing it?" Asger asked Susanne.

"No," she replied.

There was such blind trust for this woman who'd bullied the German commandants and booted an entire Gestapo battalion out of the orphanage.

Asger sat for a while staring at his fingers, which should have never touched anything but hollow-ground lenses or the fine mechanics of far-reaching space telescopes. "But *Magna* must have had an idea," he said stubbornly.

"No. She didn't even report it to the police." Categorically, Susanne cut off any access to Magna's thoughts and motives.

"But why haven't there been any break-ins since?"

"I gather he gave up."

Everyone looked at me. After several hours of silence, I had interrupted their contemplations. My contribution came quite unexpectedly, even to myself.

"Isn't it obvious?" I said, trying to backpedal from my idiotic blunder by hiding behind something even more naive. "If they didn't come back, it must have been because they gave up."

Of course it sounded foolish. Like describing UFOs that never returned—because they'd never existed.

I didn't say anything else. My outburst had ended the conversation.

27

KONGSLUND'S CHILDREN

June 24, 2008

It was during those days that the collapse accelerated, spreading from the ministry to the newspaper house to the TV station—all the way to Kongslund, of course. There was no way back for any of us.

Magdalene once said that, even as infants, the children in the Elephant Room spoke a language that no adults could hear because it existed in a space where thoughts and words had not yet been formed. It was an ability that was conditioned by absolute darkness, she told me: Being abandoned was the first feeling you shared—and this knowledge moved easily from bed to bed. Later you talked about the angst and how to combat it—and maybe one day you let anger pass back and forth in the darkness, even though of course that might be risky in such a small room.

Then she laughed at my bewilderment and said, Marie, remember that within little children is everything that they later lose as adults—the total acceptance of Darkness and of all the creatures that live in it.

* * *

"The living cling to life. The unborn aren't allowed to live."

In one breath, the minister referred both to the prime minister and to the project he'd been passionate about for his entire life.

The remark might have been perceived as a cynical statement, but the only two persons present knew his style too well.

This bluntness had captivated the Danish people and had therefore characterized the Almighty One since the historic election of 2001.

On this Saint John's Day, the minister of national affairs glimpsed the only true ambition of his adult life: ruling of the nation. In his drawer was the agenda he'd prepared for his first term, and at the top lay the proposal that would mark the Grand New Departure: *Proposal to define women's access to abortion.*

The core components of the bill had long since been crafted and could be found, word for word, in the founding principles of the Children's Right to Life organization, which the minister and a large number of the top advocates for Goodness had founded based on inalienable humanitarian principles: all Danish children were to have the best possible beginning in life, and no child was to be barred from the greatest possible happiness. Naturally, these principles needed to also include unborn children, because in a Christian country like Denmark, the protection of life had to extend to the voiceless fetuses, and any proponent of human rights would have to concede that point in the end.

The barbarism would end once and for all.

Magna had become a member of the organization out of concern for Kongslund's relationship with the powerful politician, and she had even agreed to become a board member. But I think she knew how strongly Almind-Enevold despised his wife's infertility, the supreme tragedy of his life. And it was the reason he made it the centerpiece of his political agenda; if it was his tragedy, it would be the nation's.

Concerned about the more rebellious women in the party, he had, over the years, articulated his intentions in appropriately vague terms; and in his political life he had only gradually intensified his tone as his power grew. First, he recommended lowering the abortion limit from twelve to ten weeks into pregnancy, then from ten weeks to eight. In the secret bill he kept in his drawer, he proposed that it be lowered from eight to six weeks. And when the prime minister's handkerchief had become chronically bloodied, he'd crossed out the six and written four. That too would be corrected as the country moved toward the complete ban that would only exclude the few women who could prove a clear and irrefutable threat to their lives. As with most asylum cases, the vast majority of such claims could be dispelled due to lack of concrete evidence.

This morning, the national minister had read an article about the morning-after pill aimed at slutty teenage girls, and it made him furious. "When the time is right, we'll grant life to every Danish child—without exception," he said. "And we'll ban all drugs that kill fetuses." He stood by the window with his back to his guests, as was his habit, and studied two young female assistants who were having lunch on the granite bench in the courtyard.

"Are we going to ban condoms too?" Malle asked.

The unexpected question from the security advisor left the sanctimonious minister speechless. Then he turned and said, "If it helps."

"If it *helps* . . . ?" This was Malle again.

"Yes. If it helps increase the birthrate. The birthrate goes hand in hand with our welfare project. We can promise Danes who have children, no matter how many, that they'll never be humiliated like the women who gave up their children to—"

"To Kongslund," Orla Berntsen offered from his seat on the minister's sofa. For some reason, he'd put his expensive designer glasses in an empty ashtray before him. Maybe he didn't want to see anything more than what was strictly necessary this morning.

Malle shrugged and changed the topic. "As you know, I sent a couple of guys to Australia to track down the package and Eva. And it has proved difficult . . . Actually, impossible," he admitted.

The Almighty One walked around the birch table and then said slowly, "Is that so?"

"She isn't there. At least not under any of the names we know of. Or maybe she just isn't there . . . anymore. Every clue we have suggests that she left the country—long ago," Malle said.

He didn't have to say anything else, and regardless, the two men wanted to keep the significance of this disturbing piece of information from Orla. He didn't know about the busybody chief inspector who'd long ago found a mysterious woman dead on a beach near Kongslund and just couldn't forget about it.

Ole Almind-Enevold bowed his head, in what appeared to be a gesture of humbleness, but Malle knew the Almighty One was never humble. Instead it was simply a desperate, unarticulated question.

"Yes . . . yes," Malle replied. "She might have died . . . as we've discussed."

Malle sent a subtle warning in Orla's direction, and the minister took the hint. He stood and walked to the sofa.

"Congratulations," he told his chief of staff.

"Congratulations?"

"Yes. On kicking out that little Tamil boy, returning him to Sri Lanka. He's been completely smeared in the press. We're *home free.*" This was the kind of American expression the Witch Doctor had popularized throughout the ministry.

Orla said nothing.

"According to Channel DK, the boy was at the center of a Tamil gangster network that used him to deceive public opinion by claiming that his life was in *danger . . .*" The minister savored his last word. "They wanted to affect public opinion so that people would demand compassion for the boy. From then on, every asylum seeker would be the subject of that compassion, the sluices would be opened wide . . . but that plan was thwarted. The press caught wind of an anonymous fax sent to the Ministry of State by a resident Sri Lankan who described the plan." The Almighty One raised his voice: "It's exactly the kind of fraud we have to put a stop to, and where even our administration has been too soft. It's just the type of thing that demonstrates the legitimacy of this ministry!"

Neither of the other men replied. The plan was all Orla's, and it had no basis in reality, but that was a detail the minister had practically eliminated from his consciousness.

"We'll only need a couple of such examples a year, then—" The Almighty One searched for the words to finish his sentence but was interrupted before he could continue.

"But it's all a lie," Orla Berntsen said. His outburst was so abrupt and naive that they all froze for a second. Even Orla.

"I met with him," Orla said, now in a more controlled tone (but of course it was too late). He reached for his glasses.

The two older men looked at him, saying nothing.

"I went and *met* him, and there wasn't anything wrong with him, and he was never a part of any criminal network." He put on his glasses.

"No, I suppose you'd know that better than anyone." For a brief moment the minister strayed from his role and seemed about to laugh hysterically.

"We just needed to kick him out, right? He was an insignificant card we played—we just needed him out."

"Out?" the minister said in mock innocence.

"Yes. That's our philosophy, isn't it? Your philosophy." Orla shook his head. "But there's no difference, not really." He stood.

"No difference between what?" The minister was clearly dumbfounded at this.

"Between them . . . the boy from Sri Lanka . . . and the adopted boy John Bjergstrand."

Almind-Enevold shook his head.

Malle smiled as though he'd understood Orla's foggy statement in his own way: "Because you are his *father*, right?"

The Almighty One stared in disbelief at the boy who'd never had a father of his own. He opened his mouth to speak. But there was no sound.

"*Lower your voices*," Malle spat as he rose from his seat. "Sit down, Orla!" It sounded as though he were speaking to a dog.

But for the first time in his life, Orla ignored the big man. "You are his father, and that means something very special to you—but the others can just go to hell, and so they do . . . as they have their entire life." He hurried across the room and opened the door.

Malle made no move to stop him.

"I'm leaving," Orla said with the last remnant of formality, superfluous by now.

The air in the room barely stirred when the door closed behind him. Orla Berntsen left the office, the ministry, and his secure life for the final time.

* * *

"It is *really* disconcerting." The Professor's forehead was cast in an ice-blue hue, disproportionally wide and blank like a plasma screen just before the picture breaks through. "It's as though everything is breaking down—as though *everyone* is questioning *everything*. But to what end?"

To forestall any silly suggestions, he answered his own question: "To no good."

"But he intends to reveal a *conspiracy* right in the heart of the state's mouthpiece," Peter Trøst said. The word *conspiracy* felt good in his mouth. You could shoot vultures with a word like that. The Professor must have heard the danger whizz past his head, because he sank stiffly into his chair.

"Orla Berntsen was ordered to manipulate us—and he did—but now he regrets doing it," Trøst said.

"You're a fool, Trøst. He's manipulating us even now."

"Why would he do that? What's his motive?"

"If he's lied once, he might as well do it again—and how do you know when he is speaking the truth anyway?"

At this reasonable interpretation, the vulture craned its neck triumphantly from the chairman's seat on the ninth floor of the Big Cigar. "Of course he has a right to give us a call. And it's fine if you want to listen to him—though I think you should have asked the minister straight off if this guy is even sane . . . But we're not putting him on TV with that nonsense when it is clear that he's full of lies. One of the two versions must be a lie, that's self-evident—so you can't trust either one of them. With your background, surely you see that."

Peter felt a pleasant warmth spreading through his belly. It was a strange sensation to have at the very moment he realized he had no future with Channel DK. He was defenseless before the old man who'd given him his career and taken everything else from him. He should have left a long time ago. But he no longer knew what anyone was thinking or how life was lived outside the Big Cigar. He didn't even know how people talked outside a TV studio; how people expressed themselves without a teleprompter to rely on.

After his third divorce, he hadn't had the energy to go home but had driven around aimlessly on Zealand's roads. These small towns normally filled him with the kind of dread of the everyday life that he and many of his colleagues feared. *Gøderup. Assendløse. Svenstrup. Rorup. Osage. Ørninge.* What a parade of absurd, antiquated names. *Lejre. Osted. Borup. Højelse. Manderup. Kløvested.* It was his awareness of these enclaves of life, in living rooms and kitchen nooks, that had finally shaken his self-confidence. What did people *do* when they weren't watching television?

Peter Trøst had no idea.

Today they'd concluded the morning meeting in the Concept Room by singing *On your way! Be brave and true!*, the standard funeral hymn, and the five hotheaded lions had mumbled their verses over their enormous coke bottles without protest, the way no one opposed even the most bizarre ideas now. The Professor had presented the frame concept for a new program that would advocate for the disenfranchisement of all unproductive members of society—the unemployed, welfare recipients. "But isn't the right to vote the very pillar of democracy?" the youngest of them had objected in a moment of boldness. "Isn't it more undemocratic to repress the debate and keep up the taboo?" the Professor had hissed. And the young lion was quieted.

"There'll be no denial of the Tamil story, Trøst," the Professor said. "And Orla Berntsen is finished."

"I see." Peter turned and left.

A couple minutes later, Channel DK's chairman of the board stood by himself at the south-facing window gazing out at the Zealand landscape. He didn't see what Peter had glimpsed there. He couldn't find it. All he saw were a cluster of homes set against a dull backdrop—and his own close reflection in the glass.

Finally he shook his head in resignation, and the ice-blue luminance of his forehead seemed to fill the entire room.

* * *

Asger Christoffersen spent his fourth night in Gerda Jensen's old room on the second floor. The room was sparsely furnished, because Gerda had taken almost all her furniture with her when she retired. All that was left were a couple of chairs, a small sofa, and a bed. And, at first, Asger had felt nervous in the nearly vacant room. Maybe he felt the mighty ceiling, with its substantial beams, pressing hard against his forehead with all its symmetrical might—or maybe the house made him claustrophobic, the way astronomers often feel when they can't see the night sky and its hundred million galaxies.

I said good-night to Susanne in the room that had been Magna's for sixty years.

Magna's old rosewood sleeper sofa was newly made, as though she'd used it as recently as the previous night and still lay in it, staring at me. Many nights, as a child, I'd stood at this very door for just a few moments longer, eyeing with fascination Magna's thick, green leather-bound book and all its precious secrets that she'd cast onto her duvet. But throughout my foster mother's lifetime—and now after her death—she'd kept the Kongslund Protocol out of my reach. I had never imagined that there'd be any other motive for the break-ins than this very book. And to my mind, there was no doubt about the reason the burglars had given up and left the orphanage, their business unfinished. Magna had been too clever and too patient. They'd never even been close to what they were looking for.

That night, as I thought about the child we couldn't find, I sat in the window in the King's Room and stared at the calm waters of the sound.

Marie, there is no John Bjergstrand, Gerda had said. But she'd lied. Of that I was certain.

With the moon casting its silver arrows over Hven, I felt a sudden urge to cry, but just as I rose to go to bed, a knock came at the door.

Of all the people in the world, Asger was the only one I would have let in, and the one I least expected to find when I opened the door.

For a long time he stood silently just inside the room staring at the empty wheelchair next to the bureau. Cautiously, he sat in my Chippendale chair, his legs folding around the elegant piece of furniture.

I remained standing. Even then, I was only slightly taller than he, and he met my gaze over his aquiline nose. "You shouldn't have sent those letters," he said.

"You're right," I admitted.

"You started something that should have been left to Fate."

Now Asger, too, was talking about Fate. It'd taken him a long time to discover that there's a force stronger than both God and science.

"Yes," I said obediently. The last time I'd been this close to him was during the weeks at the Coastal Sanatorium, when his parents had let him down and he'd seen me—and yet not seen me—because he'd fallen in love with Susanne. He'd thought I was a blind girl, but he'd been the blind one. That was a truth he had yet to discover.

"We have to look forward," he said. He'd almost said *up*.

"Why did you become an astronomer?" I've always had the ability to ask questions that were light years away from the topic.

But apparently it didn't bother him. He had the same ability. "You have a telescope yourself," he said, pointing at the king's telescope that was aimed at the sky. "And I can see you're studying Stephen Hawking's interpretation of the event horizon of black holes." He'd turned his attention to the few books in my bookcase. "Perhaps you support the *Theory of Everything*?" He wasn't being ironic.

I would have liked to respond, but the words were stuck in my throat.

I stood and blocked his view of my bookcase. On the shelf right above my astronomy books and the ones on Tycho Brahe were a couple of Agatha Christie's most famous crime novels in their English editions—*Evil Under the Sun* and *The Murder of Roger Ackroyd*—which had always fascinated me. I didn't want him to see them.

"Wouldn't it be fascinating if Bohr and Einstein could be looped together in the end . . . their theories, I mean?"

He'd posed the question as though I possessed some special knowledge of these dead scientists.

" 'God does not play dice,' Einstein said, as you know—he believed in a rational, predetermined fate for all living creatures. But that was an incredible paradox—because if everything is predetermined, what do we need a god for . . . ? God would be bored to death."

I searched for a smile on his face, but there wasn't one.

"According to Bohr's model of quantum mechanics, all future events are unpredictable—and we don't even know where the dice are. Humankind has no access to a rational world in which everything can be planned and steered, even though we think we do. Bohr opened our door to freedom. He gave us the opportunity to choose, and not only that . . . he gave us the opportunity to make any number of choices—which would forever separate us from machines, computers, and robots. This is the most important realization in the history of humankind."

Asger confided this precious piece of information in such a firm tone of voice that his glasses nearly fogged up. I sat in the wheelchair without speaking, but he didn't notice. "If Einstein's worldview is correct, free will would be an illusion since everything would be predetermined, and the fate of all human beings would derive from a particular order of events, which in the end would be set and unchangeable . . ." He spoke like a textbook, and I didn't normally care to speak about Fate with anyone except myself. "But if *Bohr's* worldview is correct, then there's a force that no human being can explain and that is beyond human reach—forever."

"Amen," I said, trying to bring God back into the picture and Asger back down to earth. Had Asger come to lecture me on eternity?

He stood—abruptly—and pulled the antique chair closer to me; his eyes were lit with a clarity that made me close mine; no man had come this close to me since the psychologist with the unlit pipe, who'd ultimately made a startled beeline from my room. However, I could still detect the smell of wool and scented soap that I've always connected with men of great knowledge—because that's how all of Kongslund's army of scribes and psychologists smelled.

"Hence, the unpredictability of the world isn't just an illusion in a machine we don't understand," Asger said. I considered the choice I'd made on his behalf when I gave him the address of the couple in Brorfelde, and suddenly I was ashamed. He had, with no inkling of the truth, followed the path I'd laid out for him—from one observatory to the next, and finally all the way back to Kongslund, where I'd waited for him. Here, at the end of the journey, he still sincerely believed that his path was merely the result of a quantum-mechanic coincidence that no one could have predicted.

"But we'll never comprehend the system," I said, as if to punish him for my own shady dealings.

He sat for a moment with his head bowed and then once again changed the topic. "Imagine if you were the last human being who could appreciate a beautiful painting or a beautiful story while everyone else merely saw doodles on a canvas or page, having no concept of what they meant. That's what's always been my greatest fear—that our wealth will suffocate us some day . . . that we'll only elect the politicians that promise us more and more wealth, until finally we'll forget the grand scheme we're a part of."

Suddenly Asger sounded immensely sad—but also a little grandiose, I thought. He must have sensed it because he said nothing more.

* * *

The next day we went for a walk in the garden. We ambled up the slope under the twelve beeches and sat on the very bench where the People's King had rested.

I pointed through the green foliage to the white villa whose southern-facing wall seemed to float toward us in a sea of trees. "That's where my friend lived when I was a child," I said, and felt a longing that I hadn't in years. "Her name was Magdalene."

"Magdalene." He repeated the name in the same dreamy tone he would have said Andromeda or the Virgo Cluster. And that pleased me.

"Yes," I said. "She had cerebral palsy and was confined to her wheelchair. Yet she taught herself how to write. She wrote twelve diaries writing *one* line a day."

He studied the sails out on the sound.

"In her diary she describes how Kongslund was built. She knew the story from her father's father. The first owner was a sea captain and his wife. The Olberses. They were childless," I said.

Asger looked searchingly toward Hven just as Magdalene and I had in clear weather.

"They spread joy and happiness wherever they went. Magdalene described them as the most lovable couple on Strandvejen."

He didn't reply. Maybe he'd forgotten I was there.

"The Olberses continued to develop new ways of improving the growth of their plants. Magdalene met them for the first time down on the beach where they were harvesting seaweed, which they used as a fertilizer." I laughed and put a hand on his arm for a second, as I repeated the words Magdalene had written in her first journal (I knew them by heart). "*One morning I saw the marine captain on the slope eagerly digging holes. 'You're busy, Mr. Olbers?' 'Yes,' he said. 'I'm planting verbena; this is the Queen Victoria breed.' 'But tell me, what're those peculiar chunks there?' 'It's butter,' he said. 'Butter?' 'Yes,' he said. 'The soil here is so poor I give every plant a little chunk of butter down by the root.'*"

I laughed again. But Asger still hadn't taken his eyes off the sky over Hven.

"I think Magdalene loved them so much precisely because they were childless but never showed any grief or regret over their fate."

To my best friend there'd never been any hope of reproducing. Even if her shrunken body had been able to produce a strong, viable child, no suitor would have ever taken the turn into her driveway to meet her. I fell silent. It was as though Asger didn't want to recognize Magdalene's existence.

Suddenly he put his long arm around my deformed shoulder, which sank so low to the ground that we almost lost our balance and toppled down the slope like the People's King that memorable March day in 1847. "Magdalene isn't here anymore," he said.

I grew so shy that I felt like one of the hedgehogs curled up in the thicket in the woods. "That's why *we're* sitting here," he said. "We're both looking for things that aren't here anymore—or things that are too far away for anyone to remember. You remind me of someone I once met."

Instinctively I drew away a little.

"All of us from the Elephant Room are alone today, just as we were then. Maybe we're afraid to get close to anyone. I think many adopted children have that fear."

I didn't answer. I wasn't an adopted child.

"I was married. Peter was married. Orla and Severin were married. We've had kids. Yet everything fell apart for us."

"It isn't because you're adopted; it's because you're men," I said, despite my lack of experience in such matters.

He smiled.

"All relationships fall apart," I said.

"Not all."

"All parents are selfish. They disappear in the end. Even though they ought to stay."

"But at least I know where my real mother is, thanks to you," he said.

I drew back further. I didn't want him to hear my heart pounding.

"Maybe it's true that Orla wasn't adopted," he said. "He did live alone with his mother."

"There are so many stories," I said.

"Stories?"

"Orla Berntsen is a strange man." I stared toward the sound in order not to meet his gaze.

"It almost sounds as though you're afraid of him, Marie."

I was silent.

"Good God, don't be afraid of a career official who is so dry that dust falls off him when he walks. A law careerist from Slotsholmen whose daily life is so dull and gray you could sew a mouse pelt out of it," he said with a short laugh. "Orla Berntsen is only dangerous to those he perceives of as alien elements . . . and of course, in his case too, you might say he's bringing a lot of baggage from home." He laughed again.

But I could feel the unease creep into the long body next to mine, and his laughter reminded me of Magna's when, as a child, I told her about the visions that haunted me in my dreams, and which not even the psychologists knew about.

For that reason, I understood without a doubt that Asger's merriment was for my sake only. He wasn't looking at the water or the sky anymore, but into his own soul, and I knew long before he did. Asger was just as scared as I was. Like me, he recognized that there was something unknown and inexplicable in the past we were about to unearth without grasping where it would lead.

And like me, he cursed the force that pulled us closer and closer to the ministry and the men who ruled it.

* * *

He bicycles from Slotsholmen to Grønnemose Allé, cutting through the wetlands from east to west.

By the big lawn he turns in between the trees and follows the creek where, one summer evening, the spirits flew through the treetops and marked the end of his childhood. It's as though the Fool's scream lingers in the air along with the laughter that belongs to the Devil himself. The wounded giant is splashing about in the middle of the creek—and the eye that has been torn from its socket lies close to the bank in a porridge of half-rotten dock lily pads and leaves. The giant spins around again and again, splashing and roaring toward the bank, as though a final death protest could heal his mortal wound. Blindly, he staggers toward the bank but falls over halfway up the slope. He stretches an arm up into the world he has left behind then grows quiet. The hole in his face stares into the sky, the other eye is closed tightly, and Orla feels the fear that has never left him. Again and again, he feels the hand rush forward at the Fool's grinning face and the white dot that arches high into the twilight, but he has never caught a glimpse of the face behind the hand, neither in his dreams nor in the trancelike states he more and more frequently disappears into. The crucial moment is shrouded in darkness.

As he did back then, he disappears into the woods and finds the bridge over the creek and then bikes the last four hundred or so feet to Glee Court. Using the key he has carried since childhood, he lets himself into the house and at once smells the scent of his mother, as if she were awaiting his visit in the living room. Even though he regularly tidies up, he hasn't felt the need to really clean the place since she died. Now there are cobwebs under the ceiling and along the walls, and festoons of fine, gray-white threads vibrate in the draft from the patio door, which has never closed properly. The dust in the windowsill is several millimeters thick, and there's a thin film on the dining table where he hasn't sat for years. He eats his meals standing in the kitchen and then sits in the sofa where he can study his mother in hiding (diagonally from the side), so she can't see his gaze and can't guess what he is thinking. Of course she can't see him in the real world because she has been dead and buried for seven years, but nonetheless he still feels most comfortable in the corner behind her where he always sits. He lowers his head and tucks his limbs close to his body, disappearing the way his mother taught him so long ago.

"Are you hiding something from me like Carl Malle says?" he asks her. The sound of a voice, even his own, is comforting after the flight through the wetlands. He knows his question is in vain; she'd never wanted to discuss the past.

"I've promised to find out the truth," he says, leaning in. He speaks a little louder and a little more defiantly.

But the shadow in the blue chair doesn't react.

"I'll search the house," he announces. He has never spoken to her this angrily before. Then he stands and resolutely walks up the stairs to his room. He sits on his bed. The curtain is faded and stained with mold and age. Over his bed is the magazine photo of the boy throwing an orange beach ball into the air to his father; it's frozen in the air between them, arrested in the moment, never changing. Orla the Happy leans back in bed under the picture and thinks of all the years when he longed for the father who never materialized. It wasn't until the day he found the giant boulder in the wetlands that he understood what must have happened—and it was a solution that he, as an adult, admitted belonged in fairy tales.

"I don't look like you," he'd told his mother. She'd remained silent as though he hadn't spoken at all.

Orla the Adult opens the door to her bedroom, and the smell of her skin and nightgown—which is still lying on a chair—nearly makes him regret his decision. He hasn't been here since the night Lucilla found him and lifted him out of the darkness.

He stands in the room. He can hear the wind in the treetops above the roof, but as hard as he tries, he can no longer hear the sound of his mother's breathing; it's gone forever.

A little later he turns off the light and walks back downstairs to the living room. She is sitting there as though she never left—between the two blue armrests that enclose their world.

You're persecuting me Orla, even after Death, she says.

He stares at her from behind. "It's *Carl* who asked me to look for evidence," he says.

Her thumbs touch the armrests carefully. *Tell him I am no longer here.* Her hands are young again, as though they've never caressed or sinned, and nausea makes Orla breathe fast. Now her thumbs slide side to side, making small neat circles in the upholstery before they stop and transform; he falls to his knees as though he is going to pray right there on the floor in front of his mother, and at that moment the blue cocoon inside him must have burst because words gush up through his chest and exit his mouth with a sound he has never heard the likes of.

He asks the question that Carl Malle demanded of him only a few days ago: *Are you really my mother?*

She turns to him on her blue throne.

Then he shouts to drown out her response and something warm slides over his tongue and down his chin as he lies there on his knees next to the blue chair. To his surprise he still hears a voice inside his head, and he thinks it sounds like Poul calling his name after the murder of the Fool in the wetlands. He looks up, but it isn't him.

In his mother's chair sits a boy, eleven or twelve years old, with his arms on the blue armrests, and there is a long red scratch from his wrists to his elbows. *He certainly knew how to make that cut, but they learn that from one another!* The guard at the asylum center had shaken his head, giving the chief of staff a cautionary look. *We can't pity them, though, because then it'll spread!* The exhausted boy had only been found alive because a psychologist from the Red Cross had chosen to visit the ward just as his life was ebbing out. (The remaining asylum seekers were terror-stricken, hunched over, with expressions that seemed to convey their approval for the boy's means of escape, though none had yet worked up sufficient courage to make the same decision.) Orla had stared down at the bloody cuts in the boy's arms as though he'd never seen that kind of thing before. *This is just their way of blaming us!* The guard had shrugged—but here, in Orla's living room, the boy's eyes are no longer brown like his parents' but blue like Poul's the day they killed the man in the wetlands, and it seemed absurd given the dark, almost black skin that Tamil children are born with. Orla is close to laughing out loud. *There—now he'll sit still.* The guard had tied a couple of white plastic strips around the disfigured wrists, and they'd taken him to the airport and put him on a plane to Sri Lanka. *Now he can't do any more harm to himself or anyone else!* The guard had clicked his tongue, and another voice had said: *We only do what we have to do!* It had been his voice. And normally that conclusion would have seemed fundamentally reassuring, but this time some invisible creature had stayed inside him to tear up everything and destroy him.

He jumps up with the reflex that is as old as humankind and flees into the basement. For many hours he lies huddled in the darkness, and it's not until he dares turn on the ceiling light around midnight that he sees the heavy oak dresser where his mother kept her old scarves, nylon stockings, brooches, and earrings. He opens the top drawer, and, under two packets of stockings, he finds a small, rectangular case with a golden lock that he has no key for. He has never seen it before.

He carries it into the kitchen and finds a bread knife, which he uses to pick the lock. Under a pair of blue earrings and a collar with shiny blue gems is a photograph of a smiling man. The picture is no larger than a stamp.

Orla studies it through his thick glasses. He smells it, and it is his mother's scent that lingers on the stiff paper. The man, who has curly hair, seems vaguely familiar, but he can't remember where he's seen him before. As far as he knows, no man ever visited his mother. He feels the familiar buzzing in his finger and behind his eyes as he slowly sinks to the center of Darkness, tucking his limbs in and disappearing from the visible world. It is crucial that no one touches him, that no one sees him.

Orla's hands lie on the blue armrests. Soft and indistinct, without the least hint of the bones he's become a master of pulling and cracking since childhood. His fingers glide silently back and forth over the upholstery, but something disturbs him and causes him to turn his head. There's a dead bird on the patio. He can see its dark outline on the flagstone, and it looks as though it has been dead for some time. The beak is open and points straight at the sky. It must have flown into the window. He can imagine hearing its wings give a final flap against the glass . . .

There comes a knocking on the door, and the light returns just then.

It's Severin hammering on the big window. Orla looks around, confused. The case is on the floor bottom-up in between broken chairs and torn pillows; farther into the room, the curtains have been pulled down and lamps knocked over, and his mother's paintings of fjords, forests, and windmills have been yanked from their frames, slashed, and torn at the corners. It looks as though a raging wind has swept through.

Severin stands for a bit in the middle of the room, staring at the destruction. Orla can't see the little photograph of the man anywhere.

Severin opens and closes his mouth as though he's the one who flew into the window and is now paralyzed on the flagstone.

"Christ . . . I must have been so angry." Orla hears his own whispering voice, but he can't believe he is saying something so stupid.

The lawyer stares at him in surprise and then starts to laugh. It reminds Orla of the young Severin at the Regensen dormitory long ago—and for several minutes the two men stand there, laughing hysterically, until there's no more air in their lungs.

Later, Orla sits among the wet stains of blood and gall that he's spewed during the night. The water collects it all into a thick stream that runs toward the patio door, and the two legal specialists sit next to one another between islands of blue upholstery that have been torn up with a bread knife. Severin holds his friend awkwardly.

He is the first to speak. "I've just told my parents I'm leaving the law profession. I no longer have the energy to make money out of other people's misery, so I'll be going away." He laughs again. "If I could become a missionary, I'd be happy—because it's true what they've always said. It's in my nature. I'm so damn virtuous . . . but until I leave, I'll be staying with them."

"But what about Hasse . . . ?" The question leaves Orla's lips before he can stop it. Hasse has always lived there, before, during, and after Severin's arrival. They both know that.

Severin doesn't seem to mind. "I told them I'd be staying in his room—so they had to clear out his stuff. It's hardly an unreasonable demand after forty-seven years." For a moment he looks as though he might start laughing again.

In his mind's eye Orla sees the bloodstained shopping bag with the groceries spilled out on Gladsaxe Road. Hasse's last purchases.

"And after that I told them about Kjeld, because I didn't think anything needed to be kept secret anymore. I told them it wasn't until Kjeld died that Hasse disappeared from my life. Presumably because he was scared of me even in death. Though they'd rather not, they remembered the day Kjeld rode the horse in the wetlands."

Orla observed the man who'd been his opponent in the refugee and immigration courts for two decades. To his own surprise, he put an arm around Severin's shoulder. If the Fly had seen her boss at that moment, her black cupola eyes would have sprung from their sockets and rolled onto the floor. Orla Berntsen had no feelings; the entire nation knew that.

"Finally my mother said that I sounded a little tired, but that no one was going to use Hasse's room anyway, so I could certainly have it—and set it up the way I wanted. But what, she asked, was so wrong about commemorating him? Of course Hasse had been dead for many years, but they still loved him and they always had—and with or without the room, he'd be with them. I shouldn't blame myself for anything when it came to Kjeld, my mother said; he'd simply fallen from a horse because he didn't know how to ride, and that could happen to anybody. My father agreed. He'd simply fallen—stupid little Kjeld. And in that way everything was smoothed over. The way it always has been."

Yes, that's what mothers are like, Orla wanted to say. But in truth he didn't know how mothers were. His mother had never said anything to him of any significance. All her communications had focused on the practicalities of everyday life.

Or maybe he'd forgotten.

Severin turned his head. "That's what mothers are like," he said. The God of Friendship whirled into the room and, once again, made them laugh. Their faces were so close together that one might for a second mistake them for lovers.

The chief of staff at the Ministry of National Affairs sat on a floor in Søborg with his old adversary and laughed like a lunatic. So peculiar are humans, created out of a strange and fragile material that at a distance seems impenetrable, but suddenly a hand swoops in from above and sweeps it all to the ground—their guard, their common sense, their delusions. *Crack*, it's gone—and the wise ones laugh.

Søren Severin Nielsen sat in the midst of the smashed chair with its blue upholstery in tatters. "I asked Erling and Britt if they even knew who I was—and you know what they said . . . no . . . they didn't even have a piece of paper with my name on it . . . or the name of my biological mother. The matron had said it didn't matter. So even if someday I really wanted to know . . . no one would be able to help me. That's how things stand. We don't know who we are—and that's probably how we prefer it."

"I know who I am," Orla said. "I'm not adopted."

Severin ignored him as though he hadn't spoken and said, "You mean the best and plan everything accordingly, but then you forget to do the right thing when it really counts. That's how we've been as parents too. You're divorced. I'm divorced. Peter is divorced. Asger is divorced . . ."

"I'm not divorced," Orla said with a resolve in his voice that he couldn't quite explain.

"And everything that we ought to have learned from our own upbringing—things that we've had more opportunity to learn than most—we didn't. Not at all." He sniffled. "Britt and Erling adopted me, but they only did so because Hasse died . . . In reality, I was Hasse, newly repaired."

Orla let go of his friend's shoulder. Orla had never been so close to someone crying. His mother had never shed a single tear even though she'd had more reason than most, and Lucilla had always taken care of their daughters' tears.

Severin shook his head and rose from the ruins. He wasn't wearing any shoes, and his socks had holes in them, Orla noticed.

"Let's get going," Severin muttered through his tears.

They left Orla's home and drove to Bispebjerg Cemetery, where Orla had arranged to meet Peter Trøst and a camera crew.

The three boys from the Elephant Room stood together under the poplars. It was late, and it had started to rain again. My letter about the past had finally gathered the Fates.

Peter recorded the segment on Orla's story, his mother's gravestone forming a foggy rectangle in the film's background.

* * *

"There are no homes other than this," Inge Troest Jochumsen said with a resolve that characterized the doctor's wife who had once dreamed of becoming a doctor herself.

The huge elm was silhouetted against the sky, and the last rays of sunlight colored the clouds over the sound in a perfect rose-pink. The three of them sat under the electric heaters on the patio, and Peter hadn't broached the subject until dessert was served and everything had gone quiet in the spacious Rungsted garden.

Laust moved his legs nervously under the elegant oak table that had been built for a much larger family. It was the same table where thirty-four years ago Peter's grandparents and parents had decided to reveal the truth about Peter's origins. Afterward the family had celebrated their beloved boy's thirteenth birthday, satisfied in the belief that everything once hidden had now been revealed in the most perfect way.

Peter recalled the disastrous event in details that never lost their lucidity: The Tiger tank that had appeared over the sand dune without warning. His father sitting in the turret hatch behind the armor, with the fear-inspiring invincibility that surrounds both fathers and tank commandants. His mother uttering the words everyone had been waiting for with just the right measure of joy in her voice that the family deemed appropriate. "We are your real parents, but we didn't give *birth* to you . . ."

"Who did give birth to me then?" he now asked in the Rungsted garden, thirty-four years later.

She looked as though he'd just kicked her in the face. Behind her bloomed cypress, Japanese cherry, black poplars, willows, hawthorn, mountain ash, and elderberry trees. Everything was the way it had always been.

He'd just filmed Orla in front of his mother's grave, giving the statement that would end his career and trigger a crisis in the administration. The gravestone read *Gurli* in swirly, gold lettering. Outside the frame, Severin had sat like a little boy with his legs folded under an especially large poplar, smiling and nodding as though it were all just a big joke. Both the tape and the camera now lay in a bag in his parent's garage, next to the chainsaw that had once felled the linden tree, changing Peter's life forever. In the morning, he would edit it and make it the most sensational segment in the history of Channel DK.

"But they never told us about your parents," Laust said cautiously. "Magna said it was best to just forget about it."

The threads had been tied up remarkably well.

"But what little they said gave us the impression that she was a . . . loose woman." Laust smiled apologetically and then blushed.

And they hadn't wanted to know any more. *For crying out loud.*

"We didn't think it mattered," Laust said.

His mother, dressed all in black, sat hunched like one of the fisherman's wives Peter had photographed on the Portuguese coast on his first InterRail trip at the age of nineteen. Frozen in time and by the wind from the sea.

"I think someone *killed* Magna because of that information," he said.

The old woman who was his mother lifted her head with a jerk. And as was his habit, Laust climbed onto the armored skirt of his tank and opened the hatch. "Why in the world would anyone do that?" he said from his perch high above. They'd returned to El Alamein, as though time had stood still since his thirteenth birthday. Whenever the enemy approached, Laust Troest Jochumsen would crawl into his steel armored tank and become unassailable once again.

"Because she hid it," Peter said. "And because she wouldn't tell it to the person who killed her."

"But they're not even sure it was murder."

"We're all under suspicion. Especially those of us who've killed before."

The hatch was just above his father's head. "I don't understand what you're saying . . . killed before?"

"Yes, people like us."

"Nonsense . . ." Laust crept into the black hole and prepared to close the hatch.

"Yes, Dad. I killed Principal Nordal."

His father froze midmovement and, in a brief, flickering second, forgot both his armor and his escape route.

"I got our chainsaw and felled his damn linden tree—and that killed him. I felt gleeful afterward, for months, even years, because it was exactly what I had hoped for!"

"But we were at his funeral . . ." Laust's absurd objection faded into silence.

To his left Inge sat speechless, her mouth agape.

"He ruined Knud's father's life," Peter said. "He killed that man, even if he himself died first."

"But how on earth was that any of your business?" The argument sounded like a polite interjection in a televised debate.

"No," Peter replied. "It's never anyone's business, is it?"

There was fear in Laust's eyes.

At long last Inge reacted. "We don't believe a word of that." She put a gentle hand on her son's arm. "You've always had a vivid imagination, Peter."

A mother does not need an entire armored division to eschew the truth about her child.

"I can tell you in detail what happened," he said.

"Of course you can." Her eyes gleamed, as though they were parrying a mild taunt.

"It's been so many years ago that no one remembers anything anyway," Laust said. "What's fiction, what's real . . . ?" He nodded eagerly to himself, and the polite justification kept him standing in the light a little longer.

"I know what's real . . . I listened in on you in the living room and on the patio . . . I heard everything you said about me . . . and I remember *all* of it . . ." His voice was trembling.

The hatch slammed shut. Inge was alone with her adopted son. She let go of his arm.

"Do you remember the tape recorder that you gave me for my birthday, Mom? The old B&O recorder . . . there was a cord that ran from a microphone in the living room through the ceiling and into my room. I could wiretap you for eight hours on four tracks, so thirty-two tracks on each of the four large reels . . . I had hundreds of hours of recordings of you . . . I heard everything you said when you thought you were alone."

The desert heat roiled around them, and everything was deathly quiet.

"You always talked about me . . . and about yourselves as parents. How good you were. How well you handled it—when you told me that I was adopted. How mature I had been in my reaction to being told. Grandpa said, 'That maturity can take him far—maybe even to a Nobel Prize in medicine.' Do you remember that?"

Silence descended on the patio, and the sun's rays finally disappeared. Peter was drunk by now and cornered his parents (the goal of which wasn't even clear to him). He had nothing else to say.

His mother stood. She gathered the empty glasses on the elegant silver tray that they'd used for fifty years.

"Why did you never have a career?" he asked.

She didn't respond.

"Why did you just putter about in the yard, planting cypresses and flowers and writing letters—that you signed as a doctor even though you weren't?"

She edged past him with the tray, and the glasses rattled; he felt like shoving it but didn't.

"Why did you let me sit in that yard, surrounded by all your bushes and trees saying nothing for all those years?"

She'd made it to the patio door.

"What were you waiting for?"

The door slid closed behind her.

He got up and went upstairs to his room. The bed was, as always, freshly made, and his mother had put a selection of newspapers and magazines on the bedside table. The B&O recorder sat on a platform in a corner, and the two large eighteen-inch reels reflected faintly in the darkness, as if they needed only a simple command to start turning again.

* * *

Maybe he was sleepwalking. But, if so, it was peculiar that a sleepwalker could enter the garage, lift the large chainsaw from the shelf, sharpen its rusty teeth, and manage to fill it with oil and gasoline without spilling a drop.

His parents awoke when the saw roared to life, and they clutched one another in the darkness as if they knew what was about to happen. But neither got out of bed.

The next morning, they cautiously tiptoed downstairs and out into the garden. They could see that their son had been sitting on the white bench under the elm. The way he had as a boy.

The chainsaw lay in the grass next to the bench, and not a single twig or branch had been sliced from the old tree. The elderly couple nearly cried in relief.

Then they turned around.

Inge screamed as though she'd tripped on the edge of an abyss and would never find a foothold again. Perhaps she thought that the black branches stretching toward her were the skeletal arms of some terrible creature—or maybe she just immediately understood what her boy had done. The neat little cypresses and the Japanese cherry trees—which she'd nurtured to the great admiration of numerous guests, and at the expense of her son's childhood—lay slashed on the lawn, each and every one of them. It looked as though a tornado had ravaged the garden.

Laust stood frozen behind her, and it was lucky that Inge didn't turn around and glance at her husband just then, because in his eyes was neither anger nor compassion.

That morning, in that yard, they had the answers to all of their son's questions.

For a moment everyone had been struck dumb.

"I won't ask again," was Peter Trøst's ultimatum.

The wind carried his voice up over the rooftop terrace and into the breeze that, in just a few seconds, would reach the small towns of Brordrop, Salløv, and Havdrup as it moved toward the sound.

There was a storm moving in from the northwest.

"Are you going to support me, or are you going to support the chairman?" The question was simple and to the point. The Professor was standing a little ways apart, leaning against the east-facing balustrade. There hadn't been a station-wide meeting in Eden since the Saint Hans dinner, when a careless but spirited union representative had shouted, "Maybe we ought to bury our dead up here too!" After that outburst, he ended up dragging out his existence as a culture researcher, buried deeply in the basement.

Most of the station's employees stood or sat in the park among little waterfalls and exotic trees, and the general mood had turned decidedly against the Professor. If the surroundings hadn't been so idyllic, you would have thought a mutiny was under way. Peter Trøst had arrived early in the morning, and a few hours later, he circulated an e-mail describing the segment he'd just finished editing. In the segment, the Ministry of National Affairs chief of staff, Orla Pil Berntsen, revealed how Minister Almind-Enevold and the prime minister had colluded to turn public opinion against the eleven-year-old Tamil boy who'd been deported to Sri Lanka. If the segment didn't air, Peter Trøst would resign that day and take a job at a competing station—one that was willing to air the story. He had filmed it himself. And he had a copy.

The message had sent shock waves rippling through the TV station. No one had ever experienced anything like this. In the staff's eyes, mutiny was evident and the outcome certain. Trøst's story was the biggest of the year; it should air during the morning news.

As soon as the ultimatum left Trøst's lips, a forest of arms shot into the air, and no count was necessary to conclude that the Professor, for the first time in his career, had been outmaneuvered. And by his own employees, at that. "On behalf of my colleagues, I want to ask whether even *contemplating* another decision wouldn't require immediate intervention from the counseling office," yelled the union representative who'd emerged from the basement for the occasion, no doubt smelling revenge. "How can we trust a leader who demonstrates such an odd assessment of a piece of credible journalism?"

All eyes turned toward the balustrade.

"I only asked that you consider the man's motives and current state of mind!" the Professor shouted in response to the muted growl that had been triggered by the union representative's words. And even though the mutineers were emboldened by their numbers, the vulture looked so terrifying at that moment that most took an instinctive step back. No one knew if he was referring to the man in the segment—Orla Pil Berntsen—or to their colleague Peter Trøst.

With a well-honed sense of even the most microscopic shifts in mood, the Professor took the floor. "But this manipulation is too much—simply too much. We're talking about a man who points to a defenseless, eleven-year-old boy and says: this boy didn't do what we thought he did . . . he lied to us . . . his parents lied to us . . . his family and friends lied to us . . . and then what's left?" The Professor gestured appealingly to the crowd, and to his horror, Peter noticed that this nonsense statement—which had no rhyme or reason—had somehow hurtled his colleagues back into the fog of doubt. They had become so accustomed to words without content that they simply reacted to the presentation of the words, to the tone, the rhythm, and the intonation.

"If you're hesitating, you might as well all jump right now!" Trøst shouted to drown out the Professor's nonsense. He stepped toward the railing. Something about his posture sent a shiver through every single person in Eden. Even the Professor appeared worried. Just the thought of the scandal that would ensue was paralyzing. Not to mention the immense Schadenfreude among competing stations if entire columns of deranged employees jumped like lemmings to their death in protest over the Professor's dictatorial reign. Maybe the powerful leader even imagined being clutched by willing hands, carried to his last, dizzying media platform, and given one last sensational push into eternity.

"That segment is going to ruin us—it will ruin everything we've created!" the Professor cried, playing his last card, because of course it would be difficult to betray an employer that for so many years had offered so many benefits.

But the decreasing ratings and increasing number of nervous break-downs over the past months had greatly diminished the influence of the Professor's final argument. Now for the first time, he found himself powerless, and his opponent took advantage of his vulnerability.

"Who do you prefer? Who ought to jump straight to Hell—us or him?" Trøst said.

The Professor already knew the answer. He turned on his heels and fled from Eden and from the Abyss.

* * *

The Witch Doctor snapped off the television and turned to the gathered crowd, his back taut.

Orla Berntsen had stared directly into the camera without blinking and said, "Using a Sri Lankan residing in Denmark, we made up a story about a complex network that would frighten the press from writing about the eleven-year-old Tamil boy." No one in the ministry pressroom doubted that he was speaking the truth. He hadn't even sniffled.

"Yes, the prime minister knew about it too. But it was the National Ministry that concocted the plan," he'd said.

"Concocted . . . that was *him* doing that," the Almighty One whispered furiously, sinking into a white plastic chair intended for visiting reporters. "First we would deport the boy to distract the media's attention from the Kongslund Affair—and then it would be justified with a false story . . . That was all *his* idea."

Bog Man turned to the window, his red-rimmed eyes fixed on the gleaming fountain. The little garden he'd so looked forward to growing, with his full pension safely secured, evaporated in the water's mist.

"Ever since that damned anonymous letter arrived, everything's changed," Ole Almind-Enevold said. "Even Orla Berntsen . . . that stupid letter turned him against me. He set me up." For the first time ever, the minister appeared to be on the verge of tears.

"As far as I can tell, it all falls back on the prime minister—and he's practically dead already," Malle said, his muted cynicism eliciting a stifled bark from Bog Man. "You just have to deny any knowledge of the plan," Malle continued. "Anyone can see that Berntsen must be deranged if he gets in front of the cameras like that—and if there even is a case here, it's the Ministry of State that has deceived the public . . . Nothing has been leaked from us."

The Witch Doctor lowered his shoulder a bit and whispered, "Carl is absolutely right. *Nothing* has been leaked from our office."

The minister nodded as though his mind was elsewhere. It wasn't. He was thinking about the office he'd aspired to occupy for so long and how the prime minister now must know that his closest ally and appointed successor had betrayed him in a most unforgivable way.

"Where is Orla?" Ole Almind-Enevold asked.

"I came here straight from Søborg," Malle said. "He isn't there any-more."

He'd rung the doorbell in Glee Court—as he'd done a very long time ago—and then entered the little row house. No locks had barred him, and even in the foyer he sensed that the house had been vacated once and for all. When he'd stepped into the living room he'd paused, dumb-struck, despite his many years in the force. Furniture and paintings were strewn about the floor, curtains, pillows, vases, glasses, and bureau draw-ers lay scattered, everything had been smashed in what was clearly an unrestrained rage. If this had been Orla's work, Malle now had evidence that Berntsen had gone stark raving mad.

"He'd ravaged the entire living room. He'd smashed to smithereens the corner where his mother used to sit," Malle told the others, and the Witch Doctor, whose own childhood had been entirely streamlined and free of melodrama of any kind, smiled spontaneously.

Malle had found a small passport-sized photo under chunks of the blue lounge chair, and he remembered the day it had been taken. Orla's mother had insisted on holding it as a keepsake when she realized he would never leave his wife and daughter. She'd never revealed that they had been anything more than distant neighbors. Malle had torn the pic-ture into a thousand pieces. Afterward he stood in the backyard looking at the dead blackbird on the flagstones. The bird lay on its side, its beak open toward the sky. Above the hedges that separated the backyards— where the nosy neighbors had always stood on tiptoes to listen—you could hear musical notes from the pianist in No. 14 dancing in and out of the open patio doors.

"It sounded as though he broke something," a neighbor, who stood on the other side of the hedge craning his neck, had reported. "Are you here as a police officer?" There was a faint hope in the man's voice, a suggestion that he wanted to be close to one of life's rare tragedies. Then his voice was drowned out by the sound of the piano, as always, when the pianist beat his strong fingers on the keys and let the bass tone linger in the sunshine longer than you'd think possible. But the neighbor didn't seem to mind. After all, the man played on the radio at least once a week, in between news from Iraq and Afghanistan and street uprisings in Copenhagen and Paris. The residents of Glee Court appreciated his efforts to blow away the gloom of evil from the aging neighborhood, despite the infinite number of Brahms sonatas they'd endured.

"He shouted something indecipherable—and then there was the sound of things breaking." The neighbor's voice had trembled in cadence with the piano.

"Yes, but he isn't there anymore," Malle assured him.

"He's not there anymore?"

"No. He left. There's no one there."

"But I didn't see him leave . . ." Disappointment registered in the man's voice like someone who'd missed a miracle.

"Well, he's certainly gone."

"Then it's obvious. He's gone completely crazy!" the Witch Doctor said. He stood with his legs spread, like a gladiator. "We've got him now!"

Malle studied the little wizard who spun his web around everything and everyone. "I've already put out a search bulletin for him, but I'm pretty certain we won't find him."

That statement caused the minister to stir uneasily in the plastic chair, but he didn't comment.

"In the meantime you can use the bulletin to discredit his *truthful* description of your absurd treatment of the case of the eleven-year-old Tamil boy," Malle said.

The Witch Doctor ignored his sarcasm. "That's to put it mildly," he said. "We're talking about an unpredictable and very dangerous man who has gone berserk—in a row house in a nice neighborhood— someone who has lost his mind . . . Don't try to apprehend him on your own but immediately contact your local police . . . What a card he's dealing us."

Nobody replied to the little man. The Witch Doctor's drawn-out giggle lingered in the room for a moment. Then he too fell silent.

Finally Malle spoke again, "I need full access to everyone involved. Wiretaps, mail, Internet surveillance . . . the terror law gives us warrants for all of that . . . and I need *all of it.*"

Again the minister nodded almost imperceptibly.

At this stage, Malle would get whatever he wanted.

Part IV

DARKNESS

28

ESCAPE

June 27, 2008

I don't believe the Professor or the national minister ever imagined that such a random event—an anonymous letter with some name on an old form—would shake their houses so fatally and in such a short time.

I remember Magdalene once described the People's King's delight in knowing that the construction of Kongslund would be completed just as he was signing the Danish Constitution. "This magnificent villa will be a symbol of everything that is," he'd said. But the monarch's prediction didn't bear out, because three days before he was to sign the law, the wind shifted to the east and Skodsborg was hit by a forceful storm. First it knocked over the northernmost of the seven chimneys, and then, just as the crew began repairing the damage, the strangest thing happened: despite an absence of wind, the southernmost chimney crumbled and landed in the driveway in the exact same spot as the first.

All seven chimneys had to be rebuilt from scratch.

That was Fate's decree, and not even a king could change that.

* * *

Orla had arrived at Kongslund late in the evening.

He'd taken a cab with Severin and sat in the backseat, his face in the shadow like a refugee being shuttled off to the detainment center—and in reality, that's what he was.

The Ministry of National Affairs had discreetly alerted all police units in the Copenhagen metropolitan area to keep an eye out for the missing chief of staff, without offering any explanation. There was no official APB, but vigilant officers nevertheless sensed that apprehending him would be properly appreciated.

I heard Susanne greet the men but didn't bother to open my door. She put them in the room that had belonged to one of Magna's senior assistants, Ms. Nielsen.

The next morning I rose early and even changed a couple of the infants before joining our guests and Susanne in the living room.

It was no doubt the most peculiar breakfast party in the history of Kongslund. Across from us sat the national ministry's scandalized chief of staff and the country's most famous immigration lawyer, his diametric opposite.

Orla looked as though he was still startled by his own deeds—broadcast on TV the evening before—and didn't utter a word. Severin, on the other hand, seemed strangely exhilarated, as though he'd finally escaped a prison where he'd spent the last hundred years. The Kongslund Affair had somehow liberated him from the merciless idealism that deprived him of any praise, except for the measured nod of morality. Even when some of the most miserable fates in his care obtained asylum, even these lucky few, they often left only a nominal fee as thanks (some even reacted with hatred because he had, with his act of salvation, stripped the last thing they possessed: their pride).

The fifth person to join the table was Asger, who stepped into the living room and paused a moment. His big professor glasses sat at the very tip of his long nose as he stared at the strange group. He sat down at the end of the table. "Have you been filled in on the case?" he asked the two newcomers.

Severin shook his head, but Orla didn't move.

While buttering a roll, Asger went over the revelations of the last few days, not least of which was *my* responsibility for the anonymous letters. He told them about Susanne's connection to Kongslund and about Eva Bjergstrand's letter to Magna—which I had intercepted—and which

Knud Taasing and I had investigated while Malle chased the anonymous letter writer.

During Asger's monologue, Orla sat with hunched shoulders and two pieces of half-eaten bread on his plate, and I couldn't read in his facial expression anything but the astonishment that had befallen him. I listened for a sniffle but heard none.

By his side, Severin nodded almost cheerfully as he listened to Asger's explanation. "If only we had the letter that Eva wrote to her child," he said.

"The letter she *intended* to send but never did," I corrected. It was crucial that I maintain my version of this particular point.

"Yes. She must have changed her mind at the very last minute," Asger said.

Susanne bowed her head. I knew what she was thinking. She had her own suspicions. And unfortunately, I was at the center of them.

Asger smiled suddenly and exclaimed, "We're an odd bunch, aren't we?"

Orla started as though he'd reached the same conclusion that very moment. And then the characteristic sniffle finally appeared.

"There's five of us here . . . at the table"—Asger stole a glance at the far wall, behind which was the infant room—"and we all spent the first months of our lives in this place. Now we're here again, and I suppose no one had ever imagined that." Once again he looked as though he were studying a newly discovered constellation that shouldn't have existed— equal parts excitement and scientific caution.

I noticed a deep blush in Severin's cheeks as he listened to Asger. For a second he seemed like a man who took a personal responsibility for an entirely unexpected event. Perhaps his savior's soul was ready to be filled with fresh feelings of guilt.

Susanne poured Asger a cup of coffee. She glanced at me over the coffeepot as though she were asking me a question, and I halfway expected that she'd ask me to explain why we were all here, despite the fact no one wanted to be.

Thankfully Asger began speaking again. "According to Knud Taasing's source in the Australian embassy, the Danish woman was granted residence in her new country in December 1961. But she could have easily arrived earlier, and I think that must have been the case. Eva Bjergstrand gave birth to her mysterious child in the spring or early summer of that year, and then someone who could pull some pretty powerful strings made sure that she got an entirely new passport—new name, new identity." He raised his coffee cup. "And bam, an incredibly embarrassing problem solved."

"Embarrassing to whom?" I asked, even though I knew the answer.

"To *them*." It was Orla Berntsen who, to our surprise, spoke for the first time. "To Almind-Enevold and his henchmen, Carl Malle and Magna."

"We don't know that yet," Asger said. "We have to confirm the theory."

After breakfast Asger retrieved his duffel from the room, and Susanne called for a cab. Her blue suitcase rested in the hallway—under the painting of the woman in the green dress whom Magna had called the Guardian Angel of Kongslund—already packed and ready to go.

I'd spent the evening with Asger in the sunroom, and he'd revealed their joint plan: "I'll go with Susanne to Kalundborg. She's going to visit her parents on the cape, while I go to Aarhus to see mine." He stood without looking at me and said, "We'll have to see if they know anything besides what you've told me. There are dark areas in every person's life, but it should be possible to find the truth."

For my part, there was no one alive to confront. I hadn't revealed anything at all about my spying on my former roommates—it would come as a terrible shock, and I wasn't ready for that reaction—but I could hardly tolerate the thought of missing the final scenes of my fairy tale. Once again I longed for the excitement of crouching behind the bird feeder in Asger's garden; squeezing unseen through the thicket near the white, pastry-box house, and watching the final confrontation, jotting down my notes—for my sake and for Magna's. But mostly for Magdalene's.

Asger had rejected my subtle hint, however, and insisted that I stay with Orla and Severin, who had nowhere else to go. For now, they were to be kept hidden at Kongslund.

Susanne and Asger carried their bags to the cab, and I walked to the pier, as I had so many times before. I stood with my back to the wind—at the very spot where I'd met the best friend I'd ever known—and listened to them drive away.

It was a warm day, and I put out patio loungers for the three of us who remained.

Orla and Severin dozed in the sunshine, their faces turned toward the sound. I pulled a lounger into the shade and closed my eyes too.

* * *

The telephone rang around dinnertime. I'd just fallen asleep. The youngest childcare assistant signaled to me from the patio door, a hand to her ear. It was Knud Taasing. He spoke, loudly and nasally.

"I'm with Susanne and Asger on our way to Kalundborg," he said. "Asger will go on to Aarhus where he'll be meeting his parents. I'll be going to Mols—or rather Helgenæs."

I didn't answer. I didn't want him to hear the distress that would surely surface in my voice.

Taasing misunderstood my silence. "Did the police stop by . . . ?" For a second he actually sounded worried, but perhaps more worried about the story that would save his career than about the two officials on the lam and the strange woman who harbored them.

"No one was here," I said. A helicopter had actually circled over Vedbæk and Skodsborg for a few minutes late in the afternoon, but I doubted my slumbering guests would have been recognized: both men had been sitting, immobile, with their chins drooped on their chests. They looked like vacationers after a long swim and a lunch with generous amounts of alcohol.

"Did you hear the evening news?" Knud asked. "Our little Tamil friend is the top story now—coming in ahead of both Iraq and Afghanistan. Two reporters from my paper went to Sri Lanka to find him."

Taasing sounded excited—even though he was heading in a different direction—and out of the corner of my eye, I stole a glance at the man who, by all accounts, had driven the eleven-year-old asylum seeker back to a life of imprisonment or worse. His regrets had come too late. Next to Orla, Severin grunted in a kind of subconscious agreement, but he didn't wake. His exhaustion had to be immense after twenty-five years of working in the thankless service of foreigners.

"And another anonymous letter has arrived," Taasing said even louder into my ear. I nearly dropped the receiver.

He sensed my reaction. "No, no, Marie." It sounded as though he were smiling. "I know you didn't send *this* one . . . it's an ordinary letter. But it's still extraordinary."

I waited for him to continue.

"The sender encourages me to visit a woman at Helgenæs—hence this emergency trip," he said. "It looks like a serious letter."

"A woman at Helgenæs?" I asked the question as innocently as I could. But I already knew the name—and could have echoed him.

"Her name is Dorah . . . Dorah Laursen. According to the letter, she knows something about the Kongslund Affair, and about our mystery . . ."

The word *mystery* sounded a little naive coming from him—as though we were children looking for a little excitement. I wanted to warn him but couldn't find the right words. And I couldn't think clearly. I didn't understand Dorah's role in everything that we'd uncovered, and I had no idea who'd sent the anonymous letter. But I hadn't mistaken the fear that had trudged through the rooms at Helgenæs the day I'd threatened to tell the truth to her son—about herself and about Kongslund.

And I understood at that moment with more clarity than ever that I should have been there when she did.

I should have tried to uncover the pattern that connected the lives of these three peculiar women: Eva Bjergstrand, Dorah Laursen, and my foster mother.

* * *

"I warned him . . ."

The old lady sat hunched over, her trembling hands folded in her lap, as if she was praying for an irresolute God to redo everything done on earth. Not least this, his latest deed.

"I warned him . . . but now . . ." She fell silent. "Now he's . . ."

The young police officer reacted to this last, unspoken word. Not because of misplaced sentimentality—they taught you to avoid that at the Police Academy—but because the dead man was a former colleague.

"We don't know for sure . . ." he began hesitantly. He wasn't referring to the irreversibility of death but to the widow's claim that someone had pushed the man over the railing at the quay.

The police car had been sent to her address, and they'd identified him immediately—the very moment they pulled his body from the water and flipped him over on his back. The deceased had, when he was chief inspector of the homicide department, supervised several of the men who now stood silently by the railing; they were shocked to see their former boss like this.

They'd found him in the black water below the Quay of Fog and the newspaper house, where the ailing *Independent Weekend* was located, among other presses. "He wouldn't let go of that case," his widow cried. "And now he's *dead*." This time she said the word out loud.

The police officer raised his brows. "What case?"

The widow would have liked to explain everything to the sympathetic police officer, but she was crying too much to do so. And she was afraid, as well.

She didn't want to tell the officer about the case that the newspapers kept writing about and that her husband had decided to solve, even though she'd told him it was much too dangerous. Or about the clues he'd seen—a rock, a rope shaped like a noose, a bird, and a linden branch. The last thing he'd done was to call someone and arrange a meeting.

"Who is it that you're going to meet?" she'd asked her husband fearfully.

"I can take care of myself," he'd growled. They had loved one another over a lifetime. And yet in their last exchange, they'd completely talked past one another.

The young officer shrugged. He feared other people's tears almost as much as his own. Besides, there wasn't much to add, and he wanted to spare the old woman the details. They had found a single laceration on the nape of the victim's neck, but it had probably occurred as he bopped senselessly around the quay; from the water they had retrieved an empty liquor bottle. His old colleagues had sniffed the dripping body carefully. The odor of liquor penetrated the brackish water; it appeared their former boss had spent a considerable portion of his retirement at the bottom of a bottle of aquavit.

Quite a few of the department's retirees did that.

And no beat cop wanted to explain that to a crying widow who was babbling on about some old, unsolved case.

* * *

If unpleasant days could be returned to their Creator, Friday, June 27 would have been erased from the national minister's memory and put to rest in the cemetery of unwanted days. But as things were, he could only complain about it to his two guests, and they didn't look like people who were good at chasing away the unpleasant visions of others.

The three men were sitting on the large patio that wrapped around Ole Almind-Enevold's luxurious hacienda at Gilbjerg Head in North Zealand; on a better day, they would have enjoyed the magnificent view of Kattegat. They let the group's only woman serve their drinks, and Lykke Almind-Enevold didn't have to ask her husband's two guests their preferred brand, because they'd both visited the summer residence at least twenty times since the foundation of the Ministry on National Affairs in 2001.

As always, she played the part of the smiling minister's wife to perfection, providing a comfortable environment for the important conversations the men were having. At the right moment, she would quietly withdraw without anyone noticing. If invisible creatures had a kingdom, she'd be their uncontested queen. She'd spent fifty-four years on her throne, in a marriage that consisted solely of routines, and she had long since learned to think of her name, Lykke, which meant joy, as one of Fate's cruelest jokes. If the joy that had inspired her name had ever been within reach, she'd never noticed it, neither had she earned it. Because Lykke Almind-Enevold had committed the sin of denying her husband the child he had always dreamed of—and for that failure, she had assumed full responsibility, even though in reality no one knew whether the cause for their unhappiness was hers or his. She viewed infertility as her gender's most unforgivable shame, and she had stayed with him because he had stayed with her in spite of this.

The three men sat in silence for several minutes, and their silence underscored the ominous nature of the meeting. Nobody spoke until Lykke had poured their drinks and disappeared. Then the national minister raised his glass. "Let's toast to a god-awful day," he said vehemently, emptying his elixir in one gulp.

The Professor, Bjørn Meliassen, followed his host's example. His own life's work was now beset by catastrophic ratings, which several editorials gleefully noted would mark the end of Channel DK, and he had no idea how to ensure, let alone finance, the survival of the Big Cigar. None of his miracle cures—the sensational concepts—worked any longer. People had become downright apathetic.

The national minister filled their glasses with the amber-colored malt whisky from the banks of Loch Lomond. He'd built this house immediately after the legendary election of 2001 and hadn't skimped on any part of it. He'd managed to get the minister of the environment to rescind a problematic section of the conservation law that had been in place since 1950, and with that little trick it became possible to build the villa on the most beautiful lookout point at the very top of a one-hundred-foot cliff.

Below them the beach was littered with rocks, but that didn't matter, because none of the powerful man's visitors would ever dream of interrupting important conversations and meals to climb down a steep set of stairs to take a refreshing swim. To the west of the minister's private stairs was a memorial stone to the philosopher Søren Kierkegaard, whose work the minister had never read but whom he frequently quoted in the speeches the Witch Doctor wrote for him. The stone read: *What is truth but to live for an idea?* Kierkegaard had composed that aphorism thirteen years before the People's King had slid down the slope near Kongslund and found a way out of his gloomy involvement with the democracy question.

Although ministerial summer residences were rarely mentioned in the press—there was, after all, no reason to tempt madmen or anarchists—Almind-Enevold's place had become nationally known. Below the house, on the cliff, there had once been a small fishing village by the name of Krogskilde. When the fishing grew meager and was abandoned, the residents, in typical Danish entrepreneurial fashion, made a living by luring unsuspecting ships too close to the coast during nightly storms and then robbing them. One can almost imagine those industrious and energetic Krogskilde people, shoulder to shoulder, waving their storm lights—come closer—before pulling in the marooned crew with ropes, assaulting them, robbing them, and murdering them. For that reason the area was commonly referred to, for centuries, as Hell—and the national minister's many political opponents had always considered it an apt term for the powerful man's refuge.

The day had been derailed barely before it had even started. The prime minister had sent for him at eight o'clock in the morning, and the tone of the order was vexing. The Almighty One had rushed off without waiting for the Witch Doctor, and everything had gone wrong from there. The faces of the secretaries in the ante-office already reflected the trouble ahead for the minister. Their gazes expressed both grief and disbelief, and the most senior secretary, Mrs. Mortensen, was red-eyed from weeping. The officials who greeted him were expressionless, their movements stiff and awkward. They had no idea how to handle what had just become the country's biggest problem.

And who would explain it to the foreign delegations scheduled to be in audience with the nation's leader later that day?

The national minister entered his boss's office but stopped abruptly in the doorway, studying the scene with an astonishment he couldn't hide.

During the night, the prime minister's official chamber had been transformed into a hospital room, fully equipped with all kinds of modern electronics and medical aids. There were tables on wheels and rattling trays, but first and foremost, there was a giant bed standing like a rampart in the middle of the room.

With a physical unease that bordered on disgust, Ole Almind-Enevold observed the transformation of the state's epicenter. The once stately room was now littered with stands, tubes, bottles, and scanners. This was *his* office, which now, only a few days before the transfer of power, had been degraded to a sick room. This was *his* future dragged through the dirt.

The nation's ruler was reclined in his bed with the clenched face of someone who had boiled his hardships down to one single, stubborn wish before the curtain fell. In this case, after his death, the patient wanted to be carried away from his life's work—in full public view and with direct TV transmission from the Ministry of State, complete with helicopter shots of the hearse rolling through the main gate. No historian could ever charge that he'd abandoned ship at a crucial moment. At the sight of the Almighty One, the prime minister grabbed a small black remote and tapped a button that fired the hydraulics in his state-of-the-art bed. His body rose majestically into a sitting position. The sight was terrifying: the shriveled-up man looked like a long-deceased Pharaoh who'd suddenly emerged from his sarcophagus to issue his subjects a final, determined order.

"Enter," the Pharaoh whispered mercifully.

In a prone position, the prime minister could see out the west-facing windows over Christiansborg and the roofs and spires of the city, and now he sat erect in his alabaster-white shirt with wide, short sleeves and the monogram of the Ministry of State stitched on the chest pocket. He nodded to his right-hand man without smiling.

"It is a beautiful place to die," he said. Only those seven words—like a breath about to stop.

Ole Almind-Enevold didn't have any idea how to respond, so he said nothing.

"That longing will come to you too someday. I believe it's the mark of a real statesman."

The Almighty One couldn't decide whether the Boss was joking or whether Death had once and for all settled into his soul.

"I saw the interview with Orla Berntsen on Channel DK . . ." the dying man continued, whispering hoarsely and in a suddenly ominous tone that belied any weakness of mind. "About how you supposedly planted a deceitful story and let this ministry take the blame, but of course that is purely a falsehood."

The national minister saw the condemnation in the dying man's eyes.

"Of course," he said.

"You'll have to tell the Professor that those kinds of lies are unacceptable. And on *television* to boot . . ."

Ole Almind-Enevold nodded. His treachery couldn't be explained, he realized. He bowed his head, as if in prayer, but was filled with a rage he didn't dare express.

As if to demonstrate his last, stubborn vitality, the prime minister then said, "But what happens now . . . with that boy? Will you be saddled with another Tamil case?"

"No, no, no, that case is completely dead," the national minister said, immediately regretting his choice of words.

"The Tamil situation . . . and the Kongslund Affair . . . are those two cases connected?"

The question was so poisonous that it could have been the precursor to a final strategic maneuver: *For personal reasons, the national minister has decided to decline an appointment as my successor . . .*

And Ole Almind-Enevold felt his desperation like a fiery tongue in a hot, dry mouth. "Absolutely not," he said, a cough escaping his throat. "They are merely coinciding crises."

The prime minister winked at him, and it could almost be construed as a cheerful gesture but for the sinister darkness in his eyes. Then he pressed the remote with the four buttons again, allowing the hydraulics to lower his headrest to a horizontal position. A thin stream of blood seeped from the corner of his mouth toward his neck, as though something inside of him had dissolved when he spoke, and the red stripe made it seem that he was smiling faintly.

Afterward, they held a crisis meeting in the Palace.

Bog Man and the Witch Doctor sat across from the Almighty One—their muscles coiled to flee at a moment's notice—as they stared into the light drizzle that fell outside. Never before had the rainbow over the snake's head looked more beautiful, and never had the minister's two advisors been so stymied.

A couple of bulletins had arrived from Sri Lanka. Danish reporters had gone to Colombo to track down the little Tamil boy, who'd no doubt be discovered in a torture chamber in some state facility. So when the minister returned from his visit with the prime minister, who had barricaded himself in the office he had waited so long to occupy, he was furious.

The Witch Doctor, who was now in line to become the next chief of staff after Orla Berntsen's sudden fall, attempted a concise, reassuring analysis: "No news holds people's attention for more than two days, three max. It won't take long before other stories take center stage." Nobody knew if he was talking about the Kongslund Affair or the Tamil boy—or both topics in one breath.

A faint, raspy mumble could be heard from the other side of the table. It was Bog Man thinking out loud in the final moments of his career. "Yes, of course . . . we had to make our decisions in accordance with our political directions and the signals we were given." He sounded as though he were already practicing his defense at an imaginary inquiry as visions of his retirement receded behind the rainbow.

"Calm down now," the Witch Doctor said, a little too loudly. "No one here has done anything wrong, and there are very clear limits to the story's popular appeal . . . a boy no one knows"—he burst into laughter—"and no one knows where he's from . . . it doesn't offer much fodder for the media!"

"Fodder?" The department head tasted the word, growing even paler as he did so. He didn't understand the lingo the powerful but young advisors had introduced in the ministry.

Late that afternoon, the minister's favorite chauffer, Lars Laursen, had driven Almind-Enevold to North Zealand in a mere forty minutes, then carried his briefcase into the summer residence, before leaving Gilbjerg Head to spend the night at Gilleleje Inn. Now the minister sat on the patio with his guests, studying the sun's blood-red path down into the waters of Kattegat, and for some reason the sight made him think of the hydraulics in the prime minister's enormous hospital bed. The officials had already begun gossiping about the grotesque situation, which could leak to the press in no time. But it would hardly lead to a crisis, because the reporters would no doubt give in to the temptation to celebrate the man's historical steadfastness: the stout-hearted father of the nation who'd remained in his post until his dying day. That was the kind of stuff that legends are made of. What he actually did while in office meant very little by comparison. At the end of the day, Danish politics was not powered by boring intellectualism. On the contrary, it was all about brief flashes of action and resolve.

The national minister summarized for his guests the absurd scene in the makeshift hospital room, and they'd been shocked on behalf of the nation, but also on their own behalf—the triumvirate was forced to consider a new direction. The dying man could easily become a threat.

But there were other signs of danger their host insisted they consider.

"I've just read about the drowned chief inspector on *Independent Weekend*'s website," Almind-Enevold said. "It seems to be *somewhat* . . ." He would have said "troubling" but was immediately interrupted by Carl Malle.

"There's no reason to worry, Ole. Nobody can connect him to anything . . . or anyone. An old drunk who falls into the water and drowns. *Splash*—exit." Cynicism skipped across his statement like a stone over water.

"But he was the one who discovered the clues that you mentioned . . . during the investigation of the dead woman on the beach. Could he have told someone?"

The question could have hardly been phrased any more vaguely, and it immediately stirred the interest of the Professor. "Clues?" he said. "Who is this dead woman you're talking about?" He'd been pecking at the venison Lykke Almind-Enevold had served in a spicy sauce with cowberry and red-currant jelly. Lykke had eaten with them in silence for five or six minutes before leaving the table unnoticed.

Malle threw a cautionary glance at the man who'd run dangerous errands for his older resistance buddies during the war, but the minister didn't stop. He ignored the Professor and spoke directly to his old ally:

"There was something about those . . . those clues . . . something that I don't like, Carl. They symbolized something . . . something *disturbed*." Drinking his Burgundy, he stared into the twilight sullenly.

"Yes, Ole, *disturbed* is the right word," Malle said. "Or perhaps just coincidental . . . an old science-fiction novel . . . a rope . . . a woman with a smashed face . . ." He looked out toward the dark sea, where in the olden days distressed sailors headed for the coast of Hell. "I can't for the life of me figure out the connection."

"You're forgetting the canary," the minister said. For a moment he looked as though he'd eaten one himself.

Then, with a significant though nearly invisible effort, he shook off the unpleasant visions and turned to the Professor, who was listening to the peculiar conversation, mouth agape. It was a rare sight. He still reigned supreme over his television empire, but that position could very quickly come to an end if the American owners decided to pull the plug on their failed Danish experiment.

"Why didn't you squelch that story about Kongslund a long time ago?" the minister asked. "Peter Trøst and all his idiotic exposés?"

"Because Peter Trøst threatened to take the story, and Orla Berntsen, to a competing station, and that would have been an even bigger disaster—for all of us. It would have crushed Channel DK, and none of us would have benefitted from that." The Professor spoke in an unusually soft voice, as though someone had turned down the volume. "This case has made everyone *sick* . . . *everyone* . . . it's as though everybody's just doing what they want."

"Yes. Let's toast to that," Malle said, raising his empty glass. "Isn't that everyone's dream? And isn't that what you preach on prime time?"

The Professor scowled at the obvious sarcasm, but allowed the faint rattle in his throat to stand as his only response.

"Release your prejudices," Malle said, referring to a new Saturday evening show, which the Professor referred to down in the Concept Room as "bleeding-heart humanism." All the country's prejudices would be exposed and then turned unabashedly against those one had previously felt the need to defend: the unproductive, the outcasts, the nonconformists, the dissenters, the avant-garde, the provocateurs—and, of course, the foreigners. Everyone for whom the citizenry, for various reasons, harbored special gripes. These groups would be confronted boldly—in the television studio—live. "We will liberate tolerance," the

Professor had shouted to his Concept Lions before adding, "We will be witnesses to a whole new understanding of the world, a whole new world order, a whole new human type!" Only the youngest lion dared question his decree: "But isn't tolerance one of the pillars of democracy?"

The Professor hissed back, "Isn't it more undemocratic to repress the debate and maintain a taboo because no one dares talk about what is really going on?" The younger man had no rebuttal.

The national minister poured more wine into the three men's glasses. During the popular wars (far from the nation's own borders) and during the big debates on terror, Islam, and globalization, the Professor and the administration had maintained complete control of public opinion, and it had brought them votes and high ratings. But things had slowly changed. Granted, people still responded to lots of quick and often extreme fixes—both in television and in politics—but at the same time, they'd become restless. And many zapped impatiently between an ever-increasing number of quickly designed discount products—in television and politics—and it drove the Concept Lions and the Witch Doctor crazy. In the end they'd promoted ambition as the nation's driving force in a globalizing world, and for thousands of former hippies and democratic socialists it had been a tremendous relief to slough off their distorted visions of the past—visions about equality and generosity. Channel DK had given them the courage to embrace their hidden urges.

Yet the ratings continued to drop.

"You, Ole, you're the only one who can solve the problem in this country, as prime minister," the Professor offered. The future of Channel DK depended on the favors it could cash in. "I'll make sure that my reporters direct all their criticism at that *abomination*," he added, referring to the nation's ruler propped up in the hydraulic bed inside the parliament building.

Malle leaned over the table. He'd never cared for the cocky television man. "It's strange, Bjørn, your TV station is so obsessed with eternal youth and beauty, yet when it comes to the top post in the country, you prefer an . . ." He paused before uttering the words *old man*—but it was in the air, and his impudence was a testimony to how important he'd become over the last few days.

The Professor's head dropped. "That's different, Carl. The young celebrate *dreams* . . . and modern young people try to buy them. Without them, we wouldn't be selling any commercials. But *power is never young*.

It can never be conquered by dreamers." The Professor glanced up. "Power is as old as we like it to be, and the people don't care as long as we keep boredom and fear of the future at bay. My tools are seduction and inspiration; yours are surveillance and control, but our ends are the same."

He stood, signaling he was ready to leave. The minister called his driver at the inn in Gilleleje, and even though it was late—almost midnight—Lars arrived in the royal-blue vehicle to take the Professor back to the Big Cigar.

When he'd left, Almind-Enevold said urgently to his remaining guest, "We *have to* talk more to those adoptive parents, Carl."

Malle sat like an immovable shadow in the light of the oil lamp, which Lykke had soundlessly placed on the table. He shook his head. "As you know, I got nothing out of the Christoffersens, nothing at all. They don't know a damn thing about Asger's origins. I don't think any of them know anything about their origins, and it could be risky to ask . . . we'll just draw attention. We've got another problem to worry about." Malle paused as though searching for the right words to deliver his message.

Even in the faint starlight over Kattegat, you could see the national minister lose his color.

Again Malle leaned across the wide table. "There's a woman at Helgenæs who claims she knows something about Kongslund. Apparently, she adopted a son under very mysterious circumstances: a boy who was delivered to her discreetly, outside of official channels."

"A *boy*?"

"Yes, but five years after the one we're focused on," Malle replied. The time difference meant that he didn't think it necessary to mention the name of the woman or her adopted son. He found the incident mysterious, but on that night, perched above the coast of Hell, he couldn't see how it might connect to the national minister.

When you consider Malle's unparalleled reputation as his country's primary problem solver, Fate must have single-handedly leaned over the beautiful patio railing and put its fingers on Malle's lips. He should have reacted to its touch, tasted the treachery, and sensed the danger. That was a crucial mistake, and in the Kongslund Affair those kinds of silences had thus far proven fatal.

"Is she dangerous to us?" the minister asked. He was an experienced politician, and as such wanted no further details about yet another mystery that might later burden him, so he cut to the chase.

"She contacted Knud Taasing."

"Oh . . ." the minister muttered. A confrontation was, apparently, unavoidable. Again.

"How do you know?"

Malle shrugged. "Wiretap," he said indifferently.

29

LOOSE ENDS

June 27, 2008

They must have known how dangerous their position was, how close to the abyss they were, even though the weeks after the anniversary had passed without any significant revelations.

With a dying prime minister clinging to his last days of life, they couldn't risk even the least bit of worry or doubt among the populous. The Almighty One had never been closer to attaining his dream; the only thing that stood in his way was a madman lying on his back at the Ministry of State.

It didn't occur to him, or to Carl Malle, to fear the confrontations between the children from the Elephant Room and their adoptive parents.

They must have thought that door had closed a long time ago.

* * *

Asger's mother stood in her usual spot by the panoramic window, pointing at the bird feeder that hadn't budged an inch since they'd moved into the house on Atlasvej fifty years earlier. It had been repaired—and varnished—every single summer.

"Look," she said to her son. "There's a wagtail."

She identified the bird in the characteristic singsong Funen dialect she'd never abandoned, and which made his parents' increasingly rare visitors feel like they'd fallen into a time warp, transported to the 1960s where everything remained dreamlike and innocent.

Every single piece of furniture was from that era; everything stood as it had on that summer Sunday when Asger had arrived in the subdivision where the streets were named after stars in the sky.

In one corner of the living room sat the two red lounge chairs in which Asger's parents had spent roughly 18,250 evenings in each other's company, and where they'd engaged in at least 36,500 hours of profound conversation about the collapse of basic morality and the egotism of people, which could only be rectified by the guidance of conscientious teachers. They'd replaced the old telephone with a newer model, but it stood in the same spot in the windowsill as always. This is where he'd received the call from Marie Ladegaard back when she'd given him the name of his biological mother.

On that afternoon in the distant past, his father had hammered nails deep in the bird feeder's triangular roof, and afterward Kristine had filled the little sheltered platform with breadcrumbs and sunflower seeds; she appeared as content as ever. Such care. Then Asger had realized that his father was suddenly behind him. *Had he caught the tail end of his conversation with Marie?* He could easily have read the name his son had jotted down.

Asger remembered the somewhat worried tone in his voice, and he'd followed him with his eyes, feeling the peculiar joy that this man wasn't his real father anymore.

That was more than thirty years ago.

Out in the yard the wagtail flew from the bird feeder, and his mother watched it depart. He'd arrived in the late afternoon without calling, which was not unusual.

A little uneasily, they asked how things were going, and he answered evasively. They sat at the dinner table, and both Kristine and Ingolf ate their oven-roasted eggplant, in a slightly hunched position—as though they wanted to protect themselves against a puff of wind, or perhaps because they were better able to sense their son's strange mood in this crouch. All the birds had flown to the treetops. Kristine glanced nervously toward the feeder, then back at her son.

There was a feeling of unease in the house, which she didn't understand.

"You've read about the crisis at Kongslund," Asger said suddenly, only two mouthfuls into the main course. His parents flinched in unison.

Ingolf sat up straight and nodded.

Kristine's eyes were wide open; for weeks she'd feared that the Kongslund Affair would find a door they'd failed to lock or a window they hadn't fastened, and would gain access to the rooms that she, for so many years, had managed to keep clear of the world's bustle.

"That case has a special meaning to me," Asger said, setting his knife and fork down on his plate. "Because . . . I received one of the anonymous letters the papers are writing about."

Ingolf put a hand on Kristine's arm.

She was wearing her Sunday dress with yellow and blue flowers. Fear was now evident in her eyes.

Asger carefully arranged his knife and fork diagonally, side by side, the way they'd taught him as a kid. "The boy they are looking for could be me," he said.

Kristine's eyes met his but without the measure of infinite terror he'd expected, and he immediately understood why: she already realized this.

"Who . . . ?" he began. But he didn't need to complete the sentence.

"There was a detective here . . . a security specialist," Ingolf said. He blushed because he and his wife had kept this visit a secret from their son.

"Carl Malle?"

Ingolf coughed, then swallowed two mouthfuls of water from a tall, thin glass he'd gotten when Asger was still a boy. "Yes, I believe that was his name . . . he told us about the case. He works for the ministry, and he wanted to know if we knew anything about . . . the woman who was your biological . . . I mean, your . . . It was very important, he said." In this breakneck fashion, he managed to avoid the word *mother*.

"But we didn't know anything," Kristine whispered, interrupting her husband for once. "They never told us anything." She reached for her son's hand, but Asger leaned back to avoid her touch.

"If we'd known anything, we would have told you."

"Told me what?"

They were both silent.

"But that isn't the issue anyway," he said. "I know who my biological mother is—and where she lives."

Now their shock was genuine. Tears appeared in his mother's eyes.

"She lives in Brorfelde—if she's still alive. I haven't checked for over twenty years." He turned to his father. "But you knew that, right? You knew that I'd found her . . . ?"

Ingolf sank lower in his chair. Half a minute passed before he spoke, and he didn't look at his wife when he did. "Yes. I was aware of that. The day you called . . . there was a woman's name on your note, and that was a little while after we'd informed you that you were adopted. I heard the conversation . . . you called Kongslund."

"Why did you tell me about the adoption?"

The question came out of nowhere, and Ingolf seemed surprised. "You know why. It was the right thing to do. You needed to know your life story."

"But why did you tell me there, at the Coastal Sanatorium?"

Ingolf fell silent, staring at his glass.

Kristine interrupted again: "The doctors said that they . . . they knew everything about it . . . that your illness was hereditary. We couldn't . . . I mean, your father and I, we wanted to . . ."

"You sent a man whom I thought was my father to see me, but he said he wasn't, and then he returned home. From that point on, I was a stranger. And *you* stayed home hiding."

To his surprise, Asger felt tears streaming down his cheeks. He removed his glasses and placed them parallel with the knife and fork, one fogged-up lens resting on a half-eaten hunk of eggplant.

His adoptive parents sat frozen. Through the fog, he saw Kristine's face like a little yellow sun, while Ingolf's scrawny torso had become a blurry outline that nearly blended into the chair.

"Your mom and I couldn't have children . . ." Asger's voice reiterated Ingolf's words that day at the sanatorium, muted, but clearly.

Neither of them reacted. They looked like two people who'd seen a ghost, and perhaps they had.

"That's what you said: That's why your mother and I decided to adopt a child. It's the best decision we ever made . . ."

Now the foggy outline rose from the chair and moved deeper into Asger's field of vision.

"Your mother and I will always be with you . . ."

He could make out a hand lifting his glasses off the plate.

"She wanted us to talk this through, man to man . . . we'll call you Tuesday or Wednesday."

The shadow pressed the glasses back on his nose; it was a strange, intimate act, and once again the room became clear inside the bubbles of his tears. His mother's face floated above the half-eaten eggplant, and the black craters that must have been her eyes and mouth resembled knife-sharp edges. He sensed her dread.

From her side of the table, Kristine pulled her husband back and held him there, as she slowly closed her mouth tightly to trap any words that might escape. The most important moment in their son's life would never be explained at this table.

For a long time Asger sat silent, absorbing this truth. "The anger I felt made me kill Ejnar," he finally said. "My longing for a . . . I knew you hated him because he helped me explore space and because he lived at the observatory. You hated him, didn't you?"

They huddled close to one another, still hunched over. They didn't respond.

"He loved me. I knew what would happen—and I let it happen."

"But Ejnar died in the *hole*," Ingolf said sharply with a strikingly brutal emphasis on the last word.

The objection was so mundane and bizarre that Asger felt an urge to throw himself onto the table for a moment and pummel the blurry face, until his resolve weakened. "No," he said. *"He died of longing."*

Ingolf and Kristine had to know that Asger's gravest accusation was targeted at them—and against the home where they'd lived together.

"You didn't want me to see him. You didn't want me to go with him. You didn't want me to be like him." Even to his own ears, it sounded as though some strange creature was speaking through his mouth.

Kristine let go of her husband's hand and yelled, "No! But you had to go find the only one, the only kid who . . . with all of his . . . whose whole head was filled with flying saucers . . . and all those goddamned planets . . . ! I wasn't going to let him . . . he wasn't going to . . ." The last stutter ended in a loud fit of coughing, and Ingolf grabbed his water glass and held it toward her. But she pushed it to the side and it fell on the floor, where, strangely enough, it landed without breaking.

Then she threw herself onto the floor next to the glass, halfway under the table, and began to cry hysterically.

A second later, Ingolf was beside her, stroking her hair. One of the untouched eggplants had somehow landed next to them.

"Look what you've done," he whispered between gasps.

Asger stood. He left them on the living room floor, and he packed a few of his things in his duffel.

As he opened the front door and departed the place where he'd been raised, he heard Kristine weeping and Ingolf trying to console her.

* * *

Taasing studied the little woman in the low-hung living room. He'd arrived in Aarhus around noon and then had taken the bus from there to the town of Rønde. He'd caught another bus early in the afternoon, bumping through the hills at Stødov on the Helgenæs peninsula, and then finally walking the last hundred yards to the little cottage as the bus driver had directed.

By the time he arrived, it was almost evening.

He banged on the low door—and then on a nearby kitchen window—before he sensed any movement in the house.

A small woman reluctantly opened the door and let him in. There were figurines and knickknacks in all the windowsills and a thick layer of dust on the furniture, which even a hermit like himself noticed. He had the feeling he'd stepped into a world where nothing had been touched in decades. Dorah Laursen's discomfort at meeting him was so evident that for the first few minutes he was at an unusual loss for words. She sat curled up in a big green lounge chair, looking as though she both expected—and feared—him.

Briefly, he explained the reason for his visit: the anonymous letter. Then he handed it to her.

She held it motionless. There was no signature on the letter, and its only purpose had been to lead Taasing to Dorah Laursen.

"Who might have sent that to me, Mrs. Laursen?" he asked.

She shook her head, but he could see yet another layer of fear on her face.

"But did you *know* that it would be sent?"

"No, of course not." Her voice was barely audible.

He leaned toward her. "Did you know . . . that I'd come?"

For another moment she sat motionless. Then she nodded, and to his surprise a large tear rolled down her fleshy cheek, coming to a stop in the corner of her mouth, where strangely enough it remained like a clear glass bubble.

"But how?" He let the question hang in the air; she wasn't the kind of person that an experienced journalist would have trouble eliciting information from, but for some reason the tear distracted him.

"He . . . called, you know . . ."

Taasing nodded encouragingly. She took a deep breath and another crystal-clear tear followed. Then she said, "A man called. He told me it would be very dangerous to talk to anyone about this secr . . . eh, about . . ."

"The secret?"

"Yes . . . Because it was . . . a state . . ."

"A state matter?"

She nodded.

"Dangerous to whom?"

"For me . . . or . . ."

"But what is it that you know?" The question was more direct than he'd intended.

"Or for my son," she said.

"Your son . . . ?"

"He's from there too," she sniffled.

"From Kongslund?"

"Yes. Yes. They helped me before."

And then she described the events that she'd only ever shared with two people—first with the visitor who'd called herself Marie Ladegaard, and then with her son, because Marie Ladegaard had insisted she do so.

She told Taasing the strange story of how her little boy had been picked up early one morning in May 1961 by an unknown messenger from the famous Infant Orphanage Kongslund—and how she'd regretted her decision and threatened the matron to get her another child, which she finally did in February 1966.

It sounded like a fairy tale—or the babblings of a confused old woman—but she nodded the entire time as if to underscore the veracity of what she was telling him.

"But . . . it doesn't make any sense." Taasing was as mystified as the old woman herself, just as her first visitor had been.

"Was *she* the one who . . . did she reveal it?" Dorah asked. "She'd promised me she would never say anything if only I told my son what had happened. And I did. But even so, she . . ." Tears streamed now from both her eyes.

Taasing was transfixed for a moment by the shiny teardrops that had been triggered by his presence. Then he said, "Who is *she* . . . ?"

The old lady pulled out a handkerchief; it was very small and had tiny, red crocheted roses in the corners. "Marie Ladegaard. The matron's daughter."

"She's been here?"

"Yes, she came. She was the first one that I talked to about Lars . . . about my son." She sniffled into the handkerchief. "That was in . . ."

"2001?"

"Yes." She held his gaze through her tears and then blew her nose. "That was seven years ago, but she'd promised. Forever." Her tears pooled in lagoons at the corners of her mouth.

"Then where's your child now . . . the child you gave up for adoption . . . the one you say was picked up that morning?"

"They never told me. But I was given a new one." She set her handkerchief in her lap. "They told me to forget about the whole thing."

"Because you got Lars?"

"Yes—all I had to do was wait for the delivery." She sniffled.

"The delivery?"

"Yes."

"Where is Lars now?" Taasing asked offhandedly. He couldn't see how Dorah's adopted son could be connected to the Kongslund Affair. Probably, she had simply forgotten the specific circumstances surrounding what was, in reality, an ordinary adoption.

"He's a chauffeur."

"But I suppose he can't remember anything . . . about back then?"

For the first time, she seemed relieved. "No, he was too young."

It was then that the nation's most skeptical journalist made exactly the same mistake that the experienced investigator and security specialist Carl Malle had made. He didn't ask any more questions about the matter.

He couldn't see how there'd be anything of interest in the answers.

Before making his departure, he asked one last question. "And you're absolutely certain that it was Marie Ladegaard who came here that day . . . back in 2001?"

She nodded again. That much she remembered.

Taasing stood, trying to conceal his anger in front of the old woman. It was yet another secret—a small but notable one—that Marie had kept from them.

And that was the matter that occupied his thoughts on his trip back to Copenhagen.

* * *

I was prepared for his anger and his questions.

He'd used the long journey back to contemplate my role. And I'd prepared every single response and every possible maneuver, so it would just have to run its course. Either he accepted my answers, or the real reason I'd kept Dorah's existence a secret would be revealed. That thought was the reason I'd spent most of my time waiting in Magdalene's old wheelchair, slumped down, eyes closed, the way she'd often done. I needed her help more than ever.

Taasing arrived around noon. A startled childcare assistant came to get me right away.

Orla and Severin had once again chosen to be idle; they'd spent most of the morning sprawled on lounge chairs on the lawn. They'd barely spoken to one another and hadn't even asked me how the case was developing. That morning I'd told them there was no news. They were hiding from the world, and I understood why.

Taasing stood by the window in the sunroom, looking at the two sleeping men outside. When I stepped closer, he sat without a word on the dark mahogany sofa with the gray-blue silk cover and got straight to the point. "What's going on, Marie? Why did you keep your visit to Dorah's seven years ago a secret?"

He was so angry that his usual, objective journalistic manner had vanished after only a few seconds. If Magdalene really was nearby—or was watching me from her seat on the Other Side—I didn't feel it. This was a battle I had to fight alone.

"Why did you keep it from us?"

I sat cautiously in one of the antique chairs, letting my shoulder hang all the way down to the armrest before delivering the first of my carefully prepared responses: "If I'd told you that from the beginning, you would have gone to see Dorah. And I'd promised to protect her."

It was a plausible explanation, and I took care to keep my lisp at a moderate level so that it wouldn't annoy him, but where it might be enough to disrupt his legendary concentration.

"But you could have told us without giving us the name of the source," he said. "I would have respected that." His objection was just as logical as I'd expected.

"Yes," I said after a brief hesitation, the intentionality of which I hoped he wouldn't detect. "But back then you thought this case was current, and there's no way I could have tracked down Dorah so quickly. So it was way too risky."

Now I connected the first lie to another.

It was yet another logical, carefully prepared explanation.

"But later . . . later, when you admitted that the letter from Eva wasn't new?" he asked.

"At that point I wasn't even thinking about Dorah. I don't know why she matters anymore." I made my lisp worse, knowing it was at this point that my explanation would be put to the test.

For an instant I thought I'd succeeded. Then he asked the question I'd feared.

"But how did you actually find Dorah's name to begin with?" He'd waited for just the right moment.

I said nothing.

He leaned closer, battle-ready, studying, over the rim of his glasses, a bizarre but interesting creature. "*There was another letter,* wasn't there?"

Reluctantly, I had to admire his acuity and intuition.

"You've lied to us about everything, Marie, and you've been clever about it. But on the way back from Helgenæs, I realized that"—he hesitated for a moment—"that almost nothing of what you say is true. You've lived here too long." He looked around the place. "It's no wonder you've started mixing up fiction and reality." He shook his head. "You're living in a fairy tale, maybe even an ancient fable."

I didn't respond.

"You told us Eva hadn't enclosed the letter for her child, which she'd asked Magna to pass on. She probably regretted it at the last minute, you said. But she didn't, did she?"

I reached under my shawl and retrieved a single sheet of paper, then put it on the table. He hadn't expected it, and I got the pleasure of seeing the dumbstruck look on his face.

For a third time, I'd been exposed, but this time I'd anticipated it.

Slowly, he removed the paper from the table and spun it around. The writing was dense on both sides, and the paper was so thin that the ink seeped through. I had kept it hidden for seven years, and there was not a speck of dust on it.

And in a peculiar way it was beautiful to hear Taasing's voice, raw from tobacco, read the opening words that I'd read numerous times.

"My dear child. We were never meant to meet. I've long since realized that, and I think it is the best for both of us . . ."

I could tell that he needed a glass of red wine badly and probably also one of his menthol cigarettes. Although in her time Magna had filled the sunroom with clouds of smoke from her Bellman cheroots, Susanne would never allow it now.

"Ms. Ladegaard wanted to keep both your birth name and the name of your adoptive family a secret out of consideration for us both . . ."

And then he learned about the little woman—Dorah Laursen from Helgenæs—information that he'd demanded from me.

"It was only when I threatened to cancel my departure and tell my story that she showed me the adoption form that included the name of the woman who was to be your adoptive mother . . ."

He glanced up. "Dorah Laursen."

I nodded.

"That's why you kept Eva's letter to the child from us. You didn't want me to see Dorah's name." Taasing read the whole letter again. Then he said, "But it says nothing about the child. It was removed before she could catch a glimpse of it. And Dorah didn't adopt her son, Lars, until five years later. I don't think she's lying . . . she's not the type. I don't see the connection."

I took the paper from him. "I think Magna took us—and Eva—on a wild goose chase," I said. "Dorah has nothing to do with all this. And that's why I didn't tell you about her. It doesn't mean anything."

"Of course it means something." He pushed his glasses up on his nose and shook his head. "She gave up her little boy at the exact same time that Eva gave birth to her child. It might even be the same . . ."

"The same? You mean Eva might be *Dorah* . . . ?" I mocked.

"No, of course not," he said. He wouldn't be provoked. "But the *boy* . . . the boy could be John Bjergstrand, right?"

"Yes," I said. "But how would Eva's son end up in an apartment by Svanemøllen with a mother who was certain she'd given birth to the child herself?" The sarcasm brought my lisp to the tip of my tongue.

He stood and walked to the window. Again he stared at the lawyers sleeping on the lawn. I saw the hunter's frustration in his twitchy shoulder, but kept quiet to reassure him.

I'd given my final answer.

"I don't understand it." His shoulders sank. It was over.

"Nobody does," I said. My lisp was back to normal. And I breathed calmly.

"I'll have to borrow the letter and make a copy . . . there must be some lead."

I handed him Eva's letter for the second time.

"Dorah," he said vaguely. "She knew I was coming . . . she'd received a call from a man who'd threatened her." He turned to me. "Have you mentioned her to anyone?"

I shook my head. "Not even Orla and Severin."

He sat on the couch opposite me. "But Marie, I called *here* when I'd gotten the anonymous tip about Dorah and was on my way to Helgenæs." He slammed his palms on the table. "We're being wiretapped," he said, a surprisingly nervous tone in his voice.

I'd never seen Taasing so out of sorts.

He leapt to his feet. "We have to warn the others." He grabbed his brown schoolteacher's bag and exited the sunroom, in a near run—just about as melodramatically as he'd once thought the whole affair with the anonymous letters was.

* * *

I called Dorah. She was the only person I felt an urge to warn.

After nearly a minute she answered the phone.

There was no doubt she feared another threatening voice from the unknown—but she was also thinking of her son, who'd become involved in a game that she, sitting in her small house in Stødov, had no way of understanding.

Her disappointment was as evident as her fear had been the first time I'd talked to her.

"Yes," she said simply.

I got straight to the point. "Dorah, go to your son and talk to him. He's seen the coverage from Kongslund too. It's the best thing you can do now."

She could tell I was lying. I was talking to her about her safety, but the message was *get out while you can*.

"Dorah?"

But she didn't respond. I imagined her hunched up in the darkness beneath plumes of dust.

"Go to your son now, Dorah."

"I never should have told him." Her voice was a whisper.

I didn't know what to say.

"I never should have told *anyone*."

"But somebody knows, Dorah . . . and they've always known!" The old lady didn't realize the caliber of secrets she'd seen a glimpse of. Now I was seriously scared.

"Go to your son!"

"But . . ."

"What?"

"He moved to Copenhagen."

I opened my mouth to urge her one final time, but I couldn't manage it. She hung up.

I sat with the phone in my hand for a moment, until I finally hung up the receiver.

Maybe I was waiting for some guidance from above, but that didn't come. Of course not: Magdalene had left the stage to her successor. The games people play almost always end up spinning out of control. And now I knew that better than anyone.

* * *

We were sitting on the patio in front of the door to the infant room, and one of the assistants served tea with vanilla cookies, Magna's favorite dessert.

Peter Trøst had arrived right after Knud Taasing's warning. For a long time, the two journalists stood together at the foot of the slope, under the twelve beeches.

I'd watched them from a distance, in the Giraffe Room where the older kids lived, and I could see how frustrated they were. There was nothing they could do; I could see it in their faces as they ambled back to the house.

I let my guests sip the fine tea. Even though the sun was shining in a clear blue sky, the feeling of being a hostess (something I'd never been before) gave me goose bumps along both arms and a strange swishing sound in my ears. I felt like I had back when I'd dragged my Japanese pull-along elephant about on its rusty chain in the corridors, and the childcare assistant who'd found me on the stairs had shouted: "Look! Marie is taking off to see the world with her friend the elephant!" It wasn't meant to be mean-spirited, but of course it had been thoughtless and incredibly stupid. "Remember to come back home tonight!"

I pulled a bright-green woolen shawl—a gift from Gerda Jensen on my eighteenth birthday—around my shoulders and waited for someone to speak. I wouldn't get up from the table or walk away, and that gave me an odd thrill that nearly paralyzed my ability to think. I desperately needed Susanne or Asger to intervene and end the silence; it didn't help that Orla Berntsen, for the first time, sat across from the two journalists who for years had been a thorn in his side.

His mumbled hello had merged with a sniffle and was followed by complete silence. Now he sat nervously sipping his tea, spilling precious drops on his chin.

"Is the ministry really wiretapping people?" It was Taasing who finally spoke, asking Orla Berntsen directly, and accusatorily.

Søren Severin Nielsen quickly came to the aid of his old friend. "Of course they aren't, certainly not with Orla's or any other official's approval. I can vouch for that. It must be Carl Malle's methods . . . and right now they're desperately trying to find Orla."

Severin had rediscovered his old battle spirit after two days of uninterrupted rest. He'd even chatted amiably with a couple of two-year-old boys making figure eights with their three-wheelers around the driveway.

"As far as I know, there is no search for Orla . . . not officially," Peter said, a note of cheerfulness in his voice. "But on the other hand, they're saying that they'd like to hear from anyone who knows of his where-abouts. Discreetly." He smiled, as if to underscore the absurdity of the request.

"If there is a search for me—well, I'll of course turn myself in to the authorities . . . I have nothing to hide," Orla said quietly. Nevertheless, he sniffled, and the sound of the fear that had always followed him contra-dicted the last part of his statement.

"Let's summarize this whole mess we're in—not the least thanks to Marie," Taasing said, pulling an orange spiral-bound notepad from his brown bag, which rested on the flagstones at his feet. His glasses bal-anced on the tip of his nose. The first three or four pages were scribbled with illegible notes, and he flicked back and forth as though the words had fallen onto the different pages, disappearing from his view. Finally he found the right place, and in a somewhat official tone of voice began his recap.

"In short, the facts of the Kongslund Affair are as follows: In 2001, Marie mistakenly received a letter intended for Magna. A woman named Eva Bjergstrand wrote the letter. Shortly after sending it, she came to Denmark, where she died suddenly. She was found on the beach just north of Bellevue, quite close to Kongslund. Her death coincided with the terrorist attacks on September 11, and for that reason few people ever heard of it. In the meantime, Marie tracked down part of the story of Eva's life, including her son, John, who'd been adopted under very strange circumstances and has since disappeared."

He turned to the next page in his notepad. Neither he nor Peter had touched their tea. The breeze from the sound carried with it the faint odor of cheap wine.

"After that, Marie postponed her inquiry," he went on, pausing briefly in reproach. "For no less than seven years." He made an irritated noise with his tongue. "As Magna's sixtieth anniversary approached, she retrieved the old letter and resumed her investigation. Maybe you thought you owed Eva another go at it, since, after all, it was your fault that the letter never reached Magna. Or anyone else." Again he looked at me reproachfully over the rim of his glasses.

"I just wanted to know," I said, instantly realizing how silly that sounded.

"Since you knew the names of the seven children in the infant room in 1961—and you yourself were one of them—you sent the five boys an anonymous letter a few days before the big anniversary party, when you knew there'd be maximum focus on the nation's finest refuge for distressed children. With each letter, you enclosed four prompts that were at your disposal: a photo of Kongslund, a photo of the seven orphans from Christmas 1961, a copy of the adoption form with John Bjergstrand's name, and finally a pair of baby socks that you'd found in the attic . . . here at Kongslund." Taasing gestured by nodding his head in the direction of the towering black roof. "You made it as dramatic and sensational as you possibly could by cutting hundreds of multicolored letters from a magazine that had announced your own arrival to Kongslund, and you glued those to the envelopes . . . it was like something lifted from an Agatha Christie novel. So melodramatic." Taasing was getting his verbal revenge on me.

"I don't have a computer or typewriter," I said. "And I didn't dare write it by hand. I felt the anger driving forth a forceful lisp between my teeth. He really wanted to cast me as an amateur, so he could cast himself as Hercule Poirot.

Severin, who, unlike Taasing, was highly skilled in the field of foreign entities, stared intensely at me, as though I were yet another lost creature in one of his long columns of failed missions. I sensed his skepticism.

Taasing shook his head and resumed his monologue. "So, Marie, you knew that at least two journalists would receive your strange and melodramatic message—and just to be certain, you mentioned in the letter to the *Independent Weekend* that Orla Berntsen had already received a copy. You knew without a doubt that when I saw that, I'd react—you knew of my history and my clash with Berntsen and Almind-Enevold."

I bowed my head and settled my dark and guarded gaze at the bottom of the deep green fluid in my cup. For a second Orla looked up from his mug, but then sank back down in silence.

"And then everything started going wrong—or it went well, depending on your point of view. Because the ministry panicked. We have to assume that it was the very name—John Bjergstrand—that made someone in the ministry call a crisis meeting to order and even bring in Mr. Fix It, Carl Malle. Your throw hit the mark, Marie. And at that moment, both Peter and I knew there was a story worth pursuing."

Against my will, I blushed like a ten-year-old girl and felt the blood rush up my neck, spreading from my twisted shoulders all the way to my forehead. It startled me that I—after all my years with two remarkable women, who neither praised nor condemned anyone—would react with so little control.

But Taasing didn't notice, he just continued his recounting. "And somewhere—Marie—that fear triggered a reaction with fatal consequences. At any rate, your foster mother is now dead—after receiving a visit from an unknown guest—and yet another mystery has been handed to us with the woman from Helgenæs. She really shouldn't have anything to do with this case, but somehow she is connected. Finally, at long last, I think Marie has gotten a load off her mind . . . case in point is the final document that none of you have seen. I didn't see it until an hour ago."

He shifted a little to the right. And then very slowly—and I couldn't help but think with a good deal of drama, mastered in his professional life—retrieved a yellow folder from his tattered bag.

The yellow folder contained four copies of Eva's letter to the child she'd never met. Rather ceremonially, he pushed three copies across the table toward Peter, Orla, and Severin, kept one for himself, and handed me back the original.

Casually, he set his copy on his untouched teacup. "This is the paper it's all about, the epicenter of the case . . . these are the words that never made it, and which caused Eva to travel back to the country she hadn't set foot in for forty years. Something she clearly shouldn't have done."

He raised the two sheets closer to his face. "This letter was no doubt written to one of you—the Kongslund children—here at this table, or to one of the other three who aren't here right now but who'll be back tonight or early tomorrow. Susanne and Asger are with their parents at the cape and in Jutland. I've tried to get ahold of Nils these past few days, but he's not picking up. I'll get ahold of him, though. I'm sure he's talking to his parents—for good reason."

He emphasized the last word as if to once again protest my brutal revelation of Nils's adoption.

"But why do you include *Susanne*?" said Peter Trøst. "We've got the adoption form that shows that the child was a boy . . . John Bjergstrand is a boy's name," he continued somewhat naively.

"That's true," Taasing said. "I just don't want to rule out anyone from the Elephant Room at this point, anyone from this completely mysterious and bizarre place." He half turned toward the patio doors a few meters away. "Magna had full control of the information that accompanied the children who came from the Rigshospital—the names they went by, their arrival dates—and maybe even more than that. I just can't rule out the possibility that she . . ."

He stalled, leaving us to draw our own conclusions about Magna's possible dark deeds, even darker than we'd ever imagined. Orla Berntsen put one hand over the other, as though he were trying to keep his fingers nailed to the table as he concentrated on Taasing's information.

"There's no reason to think that my mother isn't my real mother," he said. His voice sounded like a child's, defiant and sad at the same time, and I could see both of his hands trembling, while one thumb was bent backward at an almost impossible angle.

"You don't know a damn thing, not about your own mother either," Taasing said brutally, and the old aggression against his former adversary flared up. Orla grew considerably paler at the remark. His left hand was half-hidden under a blue cloth napkin with Kongslund's monogram, but I could tell, even in the dark, how his fingers grew stiff and heavy in anger.

Søren Severin Nielsen, who'd been a buffer between scores of asylum seekers and the Danish immigration authorities, rose to defend the man who'd laid the foundation for most of his numerous defeats. It was a strange and extraordinary gesture, born from both pride and humility. I'm sure none of the aging, pipe-smoking psychologists from my childhood would have been able to explain it.

But Severin didn't manage to speak before Orla spoke for himself. "Single mothers in difficult circumstances often placed their children at Kongslund for a while." His tone was surprisingly calm, and you could almost hear his mother's endlessly repeated explanation in his words.

"Yes . . . maybe," Taasing said. "My apologies. I'm sorry for my outburst, Berntsen. It's just that we can't be sure about anything at all."

"I *am* sure." Orla Berntsen leaned back, pulling his napkin onto his lap. You could hear his joints cracking.

If the others heard, they pretended not to have.

"In any case," Taasing continued, "the minister's reaction to Marie's letters showed that he was somehow involved—as confirmed by Eva's letter. The other day I took the trouble to go to Copenhagen University to search for information about that time period, and listen to this: Ole

Almind-Enevold was in law school, as we know, but there was remarkably little about that period in the archives. Nonetheless, I found a small note from the juridical faculty, dated in 1959, about a collaboration between Copenhagen University and Criminal Services that was supervised by a young student. He was only in his midtwenties. He wanted to write a thesis about the problems associated with incarcerated women and their right to motherhood. It must have been a rather strange topic at the time—well before women's issues were on the agenda. It's a testament to the tenacity and good connections of the Almighty One that it was even approved. According to a note that I didn't find under Ole's name but in a yearbook composed by the faculty's director, the young Enevold developed the bold hypothesis that extended periods in prison damaged women more than men. Though back then, of course, women generally weren't given sentences as long as men for committing the same crime. In short, Enevold believed that this deeper damage was due to the fact that incarceration prevented women from realizing the instinct of their sex: motherhood. The incarceration of women was completely destructive, he thought, and for that reason truly anti-society and gender discriminatory. Remember that he was already then a member of the big social party, and apparently he saw a link between his somewhat manic theory—which was no doubt rooted in his own childless marriage—and a politically compelling topic that would make him interesting to half the electorate, namely women."

For a long time there was silence around the table. No doubt, we were all contemplating the powerful man who, from his earliest days in politics, had mastered the modern amalgam of cynicism and social engagement, where the ideals also served his own career.

After about a minute, Taasing resumed, "In other words, I think I know what happened. Ole Almind-Enevold had always been childless; it's often mentioned in newspaper profiles of him, and it's clear this wasn't what he wanted. On the contrary. He is protector of the nation's most famous orphanage, and yes, it is evident that his commitment is due to his wife's infertility. So, there he is in 1960, young and successful, a rising star in both politics and legal scholarship, married to a beautiful and admired woman; but . . . she can't give him the one thing he wants more than anything else: a child, a son, specifically. The young, frustrated student then becomes obsessed with motherhood and designs his legal thesis in that spirit; and in prison he meets Eva, the guilty young woman who at that time was practically a child, and a virgin, and therefore somewhat innocent in his eyes, and so we have to assume . . ."

Taasing paused dramatically, and then said, "She was only seventeen when she conceived their child."

I could tell that Taasing's story had everyone in the sunroom spellbound—even Orla Berntsen, who was now leaning back in his chair, his hands folded behind his neck. He had known the accused man for decades. He wasn't sniffling anymore.

"He impregnates her, and that is both a catastrophe and a blessing for him. Of course he wants the child . . . I think that's his first thought. Remember that he has dreamed of a child for several years—just like today, he is the chairman of Children's Right to Life after all. The *accident* is, in a strange way, his big chance. Now he can have the child he has dreamed of, through a discreet and hidden passageway—if only Magna will help him. That of course is absolutely crucial. And that's why Eva ends up on Obstetric Ward B at the Rigshospital, where late one night she gives birth. The only witnesses are all dead today. The midwifery student I talked to wasn't in the delivery room itself, and she knows almost nothing. The baby disappears from Eva's life in the arms of Magna—we know that much from the midwifery student—and then Enevold arranges for the girl's clemency by funding her relocation to the most distant place on earth: Australia. As in the gruesome fairy tale, she is sentenced to one hundred years of exile."

Taasing paused for a moment.

And despite his sense of melodrama, no one even blinked.

Everyone believed his story.

"And the boy . . . ?" In the end, Orla Berntsen couldn't help but put the difficult but crucial question to his former adversary.

"Indeed . . . what can we make of it? What do *you* think? I know what I think."

Everyone leaned toward the journalist, utterly confident in him despite his rather ruinous professional history.

"I think," said Taasing, "that Enevold got in his car, drove to Kongslund, and sought to adopt his son. He wanted the boy. Eva was gone. The door was open."

Something resembling a collective sigh rose in the warm summer breeze and was carried across the sound.

It was followed by Severin's dry, lawyerly voice: "But there's one problem. He doesn't have *any* children—today."

"No. Because something must have gone wrong," Taasing said.

"So, let's see. Magna helps him in the beginning and the child disappears discreetly from Rigshospital to Kongslund without anyone having done anything illegal," Peter Trøst spoke up, putting his hands on Eva's final letter as though it were a sacred object that needed to be protected. "The only unusual thing is that the mother isn't some young, relatively innocent girl—but something quite different. Isn't that what you're saying? She's a murderer. But Enevold's helpers pull some strings and they make a deal. They take the child from her and send her as far away as possible. But why the hell don't they finish it, so Enevold can adopt his son?"

"Because either we're wrong—he didn't actually want the boy—or, and this is the explanation that gets my vote, his *wife* didn't want the child," Taasing replies. "She didn't want to adopt. It takes *two*, after all. And then perhaps we can speculate on what happened . . . Because in that case Magna would have been terrified that even the least evidence of her illegal and scandalous actions might at some point leak out. For that reason, she cuts Enevold off from the child and erases all evidence of the boy, hiding him effectively among the other children at Kongslund. And then finally an unknown family—somewhere in Denmark—adopts him."

Taasing glanced at the three men one by one. "Søborg . . . Rungsted . . . or maybe Aarhus . . . who knows?"

"And then she forgets about the form that Marie found in the archives of Mother's Aid Society?" Severin added.

"Yes. It's her only mistake. Everyone commits one, after all. But aside from that, Enevold is now prevented from revealing anything or finding his son, and that interpretation of events matches what we saw at the anniversary. His peculiar and sentimental speech about *longing*." Taasing nodded almost formally at Severin. "He referred to Magna as the mistress of longing, and right before he raised a toast to her, he said something like, *Magna, I have a longing that only you know the origins of . . . which only you can alleviate.* Everyone believed it was a declaration of love—that they'd been lovers when they were young—but perhaps we were wrong. Maybe what he expressed was genuine anger."

Severin cleared his throat the way he presumably did in the Immigration Court. "But, who visited Magna after the anniversary party . . . the day she died? Was that *Enevold*?" He sounded slightly mocking, as though such accusations against the nation's second-in-command were entirely far-fetched.

"Maybe. Or maybe someone else." Taasing shook his head, changing the topic. "I'd hoped to limit our search by asking you to come back with the names of your biological mothers. I'd hoped that some of your adoptive parents had kept the information they were given during the adoption process. But now I think that Magna destroyed all of it. She knew that Enevold would try to track down the seven children from the infant room. Seven children who couldn't be tracked—not one of them—was foolproof camouflage. Of course, we can still hope that Susanne or Asger learns something, or Nils—" Abruptly he turned to me. "Because he is *your* bet, isn't he?"

"I only know that—" I began, but Taasing cut me off.

"Tell us what Gerda told you . . . about Nils," he said.

My shoulders sank even lower than ever, if that was possible. But I had to continue the story I'd started so long ago. "I went to see Gerda in 2001," I said without looking at any of them. "This was after I got the letter from Eva." I was astounded that I spoke so clearly. "She told me there was a boy in the Elephant Room whom the nurses referred to as Little John." I smiled, and that must have seemed entirely misplaced to them. "Because he was just a little shrimp. That was the only child I couldn't track down during those years when I . . ." My voice slipped far down my throat, and I stopped, only a hair's breadth away from revealing my childhood obsession: the tracking and spying of the only roommates I've ever had. I considered the carefully kept records of their comings and goings, which were hidden in the secret compartment of the cabinet— the descriptions of their adoptive parents, their friends, their new lives, and clippings of all kinds chronicling their adult achievements: Asger as the new director of the Ole Rømer Observatory, Peter as the star of a new TV station, Orla as the feared chief of staff at the Ministry of National Affairs, Nils as a war photographer, and Susanne as Magna's illustrious successor.

I blushed for the second time.

"During those years when *what* . . . ?" Peter Trøst asked. A logical question. He had a curious but surprisingly kind look in his eyes. He was the most beautiful man I'd ever seen.

"When I wanted to find John Bjergstrand," I said vaguely. My explanation almost sounded like a lisp, but strangely enough, that seemed to reassure them. My oddness satisfied their curiosity.

"I put a lot of pressure on Gerda," I said. "She's a woman who has a hard time lying—and that day, she finally told me that the boy they'd named Little John, after the character in *Robin Hood*, had been adopted by a night watchman and his family. They lived in a tenement in Nørrebro, in Copenhagen. It was very unusual. Normally that kind of family would *never* be approved by Mother's Aid Society. They would have ranked as too poor, their living conditions too squalid: the kind of life considered too risky for a child." I raised my voice to underscore my final, crucial point: "John's new father was a man by the name of Anker Jensen."

Taasing leaned over, clumsily knocking over a cup. But he didn't pay any attention to that.

All he needed were three words: "Nils Jensen's father." And he whispered the name so everyone could hear it. "The night watchman in Nørrebro."

"Yes," I confirmed.

* * *

On the patio high above Hell's coast, the national minister slowly cocked his head to look at Carl Malle, who had spent the night in the guesthouse and was now savoring a grand brunch served by their silent hostess. Malle was responsible for the plan that had failed so disastrously that they now were both in danger.

He'd been married to Lykke for five years when they realized she'd never conceive. Then the girl in the prison became pregnant, and he'd proposed to his wife that they adopt a child from Kongslund, with the simple idea that, if she agreed, they'd get Eva's child—Lykke would never find out that her husband was actually the biological father.

It was diabolical, and diabolically logical.

But Lykke hesitated—she intuitively knew that men deceive—and met his suggestion with silence. That had been the most terrible time in his life, because the child was already born. The famous orphanage at Strandvejen was only waiting for their decision. The convicted murderer's child had been delivered in secret at Rigshospital and brought to Kongslund by Magna, and Malle's plan for Enevold to convince Lykke to adopt had seemed utterly simple, as well as the right thing to do for the child, morally speaking.

On Christmas Eve 1961, he asked her again, and at that moment, Lykke flew into a fit of rage like he'd never seen before. She announced her decision without glancing up, her gaze fastened to the seasonal tablecloth that she'd embroidered herself with little reindeer, and made it clear that she never wanted to hear the word adoption again. If he pressured her further, she'd leave him and tell everyone who asked that the man all Danes admired as the youngest resistance fighter—and the most promising politician of his generation—had sacrificed his life's companion because she hadn't been able to bear him a son.

He'd known then it was over, that there was nothing he could do; she'd checkmated him. It would be the end of his career if she did what she threatened, and he couldn't produce the conclusive piece of evidence that *she* was to blame for their shared, childless misery.

Later that night, while they mechanically sang Christmas hymns (she in perfect pitch as always), he'd been on the verge of saying the one thing that couldn't be rescinded: *You're the one who is infertile!* He'd known for a year and a half—since Eva's pregnancy. But that judgment would be accompanied by a revelation he feared more than anything—and of course he couldn't tell her the rest of the story, neither the part about the girl in the prison nor about the boy now in Magna's care. It was a story that would trigger a scandal of enormous proportions, and he'd probably be arrested.

"If only we had—" he began, but he was unable to complete his sentence.

"Yes. If only you'd been able to . . . talk some sense into Magna," said Malle, who knew what his old resistance buddy was thinking. "But no one ever succeeded in doing that. God himself must be tired of her . . . organizational talents . . . if he was stupid enough to let her in . . ."

The national minister didn't respond to Malle's cutting joke. He'd told Magna about Lykke's irrevocable decision three days after the fatal Christmas dinner. They'd been sitting in her second-floor office behind a closed door, and he'd sensed the ambitious matron's instant terror at the danger Lykke's decision had exposed them to. Magna had stared into the dark night sky above the sound with a look that left no doubt about her decision. She would cover up all evidence of their brazen maneuver as thoroughly as she possibly could; the child would have to leave Kongslund shrouded in as much secrecy as it had entered, and any remnants of its identity would be erased with the meticulousness that characterized Magna. If this were revealed, her life's work would be over—and thousands of destinies would no longer benefit from her enthusiastic repairs. Of course, she'd never let that happen.

Magna had predicted the worst possible scenario, he realized, and she'd had an emergency plan prepared before Eva gave birth. Not once had she given in to Enevold's pleading to see the baby. She wouldn't have allowed it until the adoption was cleared, and she'd been as relentless with him as with any other biological parents who begged her for mercy when they regretted their decision to relinquish their child. What was best for the child always came first, and from the beginning, Magna had sensed Lykke's resistance, even though Enevold had tried to dismiss it. "If you don't manage to persuade her, I am going to protect this child," she'd said. "This is the indispensable condition of this orphanage. No adopted child will ever be put in the situation where it is sought out by its biological parents—unless the child wishes it. And only when they've grown to adulthood."

It sounded like a tenet of the Mother's Aid Society. But she'd never let Ole see the child. The second Lykke refused, she became even more stubborn.

He'd had no means by which to persuade Magna. He couldn't lure her or threaten her, since any hint of the scandal they were both involved in would pull him down into the depths. And then he'd never see his son.

That night at Kongslund, he'd walked downstairs; and in his grief, he understood that his plan was doomed to fail, or she would have stopped him. Yet he'd continued down the stairs, past the woman in green who more than one hundred years earlier had fallen in love with another bastard child—King Frederik VII—and followed him to his grave.

He opened the door to the infant room as carefully as he could so as not to awaken the sleeping children (the "elephant children," he sentimentally called them), and stepped inside. A green night-light illuminated the room, and he stood for a bit as his eyes adjusted to the dim light. He looked around: there were four beds along one wall, four along another, and he edged closer as his heart beat at a pace that would have worried an older man. He knew so little about infants that he couldn't even tell their sex as he stared at their tiny faces. In despair he leaned over them, one after another, examining them for any trait that might reflect his own: the shape of the eyes, the curve of the nose. But he found nothing convincing. One of the children had long black hair, most likely a girl, and he'd continued to the next bed. There, yet another blue elephant tossed its trunk toward a sleeping face, as though wanting to protect the child from the man who leaned in. In all, there were seven babies in the room that night; the eighth bed, the one by the window, stood vacant, as he would recall many years later. To him, the babies seemed practically identical, aside from slightly different hair length and color; and he felt a powerful anger toward the woman who controlled their lives, and whose will he could not budge.

Magna had been standing in the doorway for some time before he noticed her presence. "Just go away," she'd said, like an exorcism from the age when superstition had ruled the world.

It was a muted death knell to any hope he may have harbored—and at that moment he had actually felt like killing her. Probably the only thing that kept him from doing so was that it would eliminate his last chance of ever finding his child.

That night he'd believed that analysis and planning would, in the end, give him what he wanted. But for some reason that he never understood, Magna would not ever come close to succumbing to his pressure.

As the morning mist perched on his Hell's cove, he sat at the table brooding over the plan that not even Malle knew about. Once he became prime minister, he'd order DNA tests of the boys he'd been looking at that night: Asger, Severin, Orla, Peter, and Nils. Back then, the technique didn't exist, even if it had been possible to persuade Magna to do such a thing. The first time he'd ordered Malle to do the tests as best he could—back when Malle was still in the police force—there'd been no conclusive result. The technique was too new and untested, the specialists said. Later, Malle had refused to make another go at it—it was simply too risky, he insisted. He was no longer in the force, and too many others would be involved; they'd begin to wonder about the inquiry and the whole investigation, and the risk was simply too great.

But no one would be able to refuse the prime minister's order. It could be done in secret, as a state matter, and only he and the medical doctor would know. It would be safe then for him to do it.

And then he'd finally find the child he'd lost. His son.

In a way, life itself—the continuation of his lineage—had entered into a furious race with death.

It was crucial that the man in the most powerful office in the nation die before he could issue the fatal order to fire his minister of national affairs over that silly business with the Tamil boy.

* * *

There was a knock on the door in the southern annex a couple of minutes after midnight. This was the very back door that Agnes had opened the morning when the foundling was discovered.

The night-shift attendant opened the door this time to find Asger Christoffersen standing there. He'd arrived by taxi all the way from Central Station. He didn't look like someone who'd enjoyed a peaceful trip after a pleasant day. Presumably, he'd been thinking about the confrontation in his parents' living room ever since leaving Aarhus.

When the others had gone to bed, I made a pot of tea and carried it into the sunroom, where he sat with his eyes closed and his hands folded as if in prayer.

He told me about his visit to his childhood home. About the failure that he'd asked them to admit to, and about how they'd reacted. It sounded as though he was asking for forgiveness.

I was flabbergasted. "You've carried that rage for all these years—then it's over in only a few minutes, and you just walk away, even feeling guilty about the ones who caused it all? Something else must have happened. Things can't just end like that, over a stupid dinner conversation—with *eggplant*." I wasn't sure why I used the last word as an accusation.

"I don't know why it ended up like that, Marie. But now I've said it, and maybe they'll think about it. My father was a great teacher, especially to the most challenged students." Asger looked at me almost defiantly. It was absurd. "He had an amazing ability to understand all kinds of problems. He created courses for other teachers about how to handle the difficult kids—the ones no one wanted to teach. He was Goodness itself." Asger paused. "I'm sorry . . . I'm babbling," he said.

After we finished our tea, he followed me up to the King's Room.

He hesitated in the doorway. I waited for him, standing by the window until he decided to enter. For a little while, we stood together in the darkness without touching, studying the sky over Hven. He was taller than me by almost two feet.

Maybe it was the grief he felt following his visit with his adoptive parents, whom he'd left on the dining-room floor; or maybe it was simply his physical proximity that made me uneasy; but I asked him to sit in my wheelchair and use the telescope.

His long legs curled up on the footrest, and he had to bend down a ways to be at the right level to see into the ocular. He stared into the darkness. "It's very beautiful, Marie," he said.

It sounded as though he said, "*You* are very beautiful, Marie." But of course that would be a delusion of the worst kind, as Magdalene would have reminded me.

Then he angled the telescope up a little bit. "I see the Big Dipper and the fog . . ." He'd never been closer to me. "I've always longed . . . longed for—"

I froze.

"Andromeda," he said.

I slowly exhaled.

"Actually, I don't think we humans are meant to get too close to the final truths," he said. "Throughout the ages, science has always thought that it knew everything—everything worth knowing on earth—but it's never been the case, has it? Maybe someday, death itself will prove to be the door to eternal life just like the believers claim—we just can't measure it with our scientific instruments. Maybe someday it'll turn out that the priests and the believers held the long end of the stick—and not the scientists." Asger smiled again. "But nonetheless, I'm grateful you led me to my biological mother. Did you have the file?" His change of topic was so sudden that he caught me off guard, and I instantly decided to tell the truth, a rarity for me.

I could tell Asger sensed the presence of the ghost in the King's Room, and he turned to face me. His intuition was impressive.

I took a deep breath—just one—as I waited for the words to come. Then I said, "I removed all the files from Magna's office . . . when I was only ten or eleven. They are in a secret place, but it makes no difference . . . because there was nothing whatsoever in them about biological parents . . . about your biological parents . . . nothing at all. All of that was missing."

I'd leaped into uncertainty.

He stood, and the wheelchair rolled backward a few inches. "Nothing?"

"No."

"But . . . my *mother* . . ." He paused at that word, and I could see panic appear in his eyes.

"No," I said, mercilessly. "She wasn't your mother. I just found a woman who'd put her child up for adoption at Kongslund—a boy—but it wasn't you." The swift confession made me lisp so strongly that Magdalene must have heard it high up in the celestial space among the clouds. But she didn't come to my rescue as she had in the old days. "I also gave Severin a telephone number when he called Kongslund to find his parents. That, too, was fake."

"But for all those years I've . . ."

"Yes, I made sure she lived in Brorfelde, close to the old observatory so you'd understand everything. I knew you'd appreciate that."

Behind his thick lenses, Asger's eyes still contained no anger—just a deep astonishment.

"You offered me everything when I visited you . . . without reservation. Why wouldn't I want to give you a biological mother who was better than any other, and one who even lived next to Denmark's most famous observatory?"

"When you visited me?"

"Yes," I said. Now there was no turning back. "At the Coastal Sanatorium. You offered me the galaxy—and the neighboring galaxy—and all the stories you told me. Said I could visit you in Aarhus sometime. But of course I never did."

Asger slowly removed his glasses. They weren't of use now anyway, now that he'd begun to understand what I was saying. At the last minute, he sought refuge in a fog as deep as the Milky Way—or as distant as his beloved Andromeda—but it was too late.

"You're *the blind girl*?" he said. For some reason he used the present tense.

"Yes . . . well . . . of course I wasn't blind—it was just a disguise. It was an excuse I could use with the nurses so they'd let me in. What was the harm if I was one of the kids from the School for the Blind up the road, a poor lonely girl?" I bowed my head. My lisp returned, so strong *I* barely understood what I was saying. "I was probably insane already then—maybe crazy to meet someone . . . some of the ones I'd known. The only ones I'd known."

"But how did you know where I was? How did you know to find me there?" Asger again looked stunned. Probably, he already understood, but he was more reluctant than ever to acknowledge the truth.

I didn't answer. My lisp would have rendered even words not containing *s*'s incomprehensible anyway.

"Good God," he finally said. "Did you track down all of us? Did you . . ."—he couldn't find the right words for what I'd done—"*spy on us*?"

"Susanne visited you too," I said, dodging the accusation. It was a skill that came easily to me.

"What about her?" The mention of her name disoriented him.

"Wouldn't you have done anything for her back then?" I could tell he'd already lost the thread. That was the effect mentioning Susanne's name had on him. "She left you—but I was there when you were in need. You were an upset little boy. You weren't a scientist in control of everything. You lay there staring out over the water and the sky, and finally someone brought you comfort. Isn't that what matters?"

"Good God," he repeated—as though he really didn't believe in anything but measureable and visible particles.

"What she did was very dangerous," I said.

"What she did . . . ?"

"Yes. Susanne. That morning she let all the birds out. She never should have done that. She claims she didn't, but there's no other logical explanation."

Asger didn't reply.

"Before she left the day before yesterday—to see her adoptive parents at the cape—she told me about her mother," I explained. "She said, 'Even though she wasn't my biological mother, we were very alike in important ways, the uncompromising mind, the rage. Samanda needed to be protected from someone as strong as me. That's why she bonded with my mother. My father was much too weak. I think all three of them feared what was going on inside me—and they just waited for the catastrophe to happen. And then the birds flew away.' Those were her words."

It was all true. Susanne had been standing beside me on the doorstep, waiting for a cab. She'd whispered so only I could hear, her face close to mine. "I knew," she said. "Back when I left Våghøj, I knew who it would hurt the most. Not Josefine, not Anton, but Samanda. She was already guilty. She was the real daughter, and I was the illegitimate child, the pariah. I'd spent my childhood making her feel that guilt because I sensed it unconsciously the way kids do. When the truth finally came out, it didn't destroy me—it destroyed her. And by the time Josefine recognized this, it was too late. That day, in that room, when she called my biological mother a whore in Hamburg, she didn't destroy me—or herself or her husband—but her own daughter."

I stiffened then, having no doubt that she was right. And then she made her final point—one that I couldn't bring myself to tell Asger—about Samanda drowning in the lake. She said, "I had often talked about that lake when we were really little—about how it would be our way out if things got too hard—and that that's where I once saw a little girl's face in the darkness . . . far down in the depths, in the peace and tranquility that exists only there. I had even described the two of us together there, like two little Thumbelinas who would paddle out into the world on a lily pad . . . she'd given me a strange, gleaming look and said: 'But a lily pad can't hold us both, can it? That's the point of the fairy tale, isn't it? The fake Thumbelina sinks to the bottom while the real one floats?' I knew the ending, but Samanda had never been anywhere except her home. She didn't understand the ferociousness that exists . . . or the evil that rules the world. So she drowned in the lake—as I always knew she would."

* * *

The pastry-box house stood between the hills at Våghøj as it had for the five generations it had been owned by the Ingemann family—the family that was now called, ever since Anton had married Josefine, the Ingemann Jørgensens.

The two old people sat quietly at the solid oak table behind the house, as was their habit. They mainly communicated about practical matters and could easily pass an hour in silence, as they ate the open-faced sandwiches that constituted their lunch. It was as though they'd made a pact to stay together for reasons that no one knew but them.

Their daughter had arrived two days earlier, unannounced, in a cab from Kalundborg. Though Anton and Josefine sensed that there was something Susanne wanted to tell them, they said nothing. It was as though the prolonged silence was in preparation for an event neither dared consider. If they knew about the newspaper and television coverage of the Kongslund Affair, they didn't say.

Since Samanda's funeral more than three decades ago, their other daughter had only visited them a few times. Typically every three or four years, and probably only because she still loved her father, whom she didn't resemble but with whom she'd nonetheless felt secure as a child during the years Josefine and Samanda grew close. She'd never stayed for more than one night.

On the third day, they had lunch on the patio together; and from where they sat, they could see the thin white cross that marked Samanda's grave on a dark-green knoll behind the house.

The cross was about three feet tall, no more. As always, it had been Anton's practical hands that had fastened the two narrow boards with a twist of white steel wire—just like when he'd built the aviary that had housed Josefine's and Samanda's twelve singing canaries, as well as the thirteenth.

Susanne lifted her napkin from her lap and set it down on the table. Then she pointed at the cross, finally breaking the long silence. "She wasn't the one who broke all my things."

Anton put his fork down, and then his knife, but didn't reply. Josefine seemed to have frozen in midmovement. Every day, since she was very young and first made lunch for herself and her husband, Josefine ate two half slices of rye bread with salami, another with liver pâté, and one piece of white bread with cheese. Now, all four slices sat untouched on her plate.

"Everyone thought she did it, but she didn't."

"She wasn't the one who . . . what?" Anton hesitated.

"I did it myself. The vandalism . . . back in school . . . I was the one who kicked the bicycle—I was the one who made you all feel sorry for me. I made sure everyone blamed Samanda, even though no one dared say it out loud because it couldn't be proved. Even you, who were closest to her, you thought she did it. Everyone did."

Josefine put her hands on the table, palms down, and looked away from Susanne, shaking her head faintly. She gazed at the lonely cross on the knoll as if expecting some sort of contradiction of this story to issue forth. But all that could be heard was the wind from the fjord whistling in the oak trees that surrounded the little lake where Samanda had drowned.

"We don't know what you're talking about," Anton said. It was very rare that he used the plural form to include his wife, and it seemed to take enormous effort.

"Who are my real parents?" Susanne said.

"What do you mean?" Josefine said.

"Who is my mother—my real mother—the one you called a whore from Hamburg?" Susanne now looked directly at Josefine, who was studying the sky over the cross with great intensity. Again she shook her head so subtly that a casual observer of their little gathering would not have noticed.

"I tried to locate my real parents when Samanda died, but I didn't find them—because all the papers were gone." Susanne spun toward her father. "Where are they?"

"We never had any papers. All we know is what the matron told us, and that was next to nothing."

Susanne believed him. He'd never lied to her.

"It's *your* fault," Josefine said, still without turning. It was hard to tell whether the accusation was directed at Susanne or her husband of half a century.

"Is it *my* fault?" Susanne said. "Look at me, Mom. Is it *my* fault?"

"I don't think this is the right time—" Anton began, but it was too late.

Josefine finally turned to her daughter, and the words resounded so clearly from her mouth that rarely spoke. "You took her from me."

"Do you mean . . . Samanda . . . or Aphrodite . . . that stupid bird? You remember the time it laid that monstrous egg . . . I laughed for three weeks afterward. *That's* when it all started."

Josefine whimpered and closed her eyes. Her husband sat silently at her side, his mouth agape.

"That's when it started, Mom—with those birds—and you were the one who brought them. I know what they symbolized."

"But you still shouldn't have let them out!" Anton suddenly caught his tongue as he put his large hand on Susanne's arm. "But it's all right. We forgave you a long time ago."

"You forgave me?" An astonished expression washed over Susanne's face. "Forgave me—for what?"

"For the birds." The large man hesitated. "It must have been you . . . it couldn't have been Samanda . . ." He stopped, confused. To his right, Josefine sat motionless.

Susanne leaned toward her. "Do *you* want to tell him the truth, Mom—or should I?"

Josefine didn't move.

"The truth . . ." his father's voice trembled a little. He should have long ago escaped into the air above Våghøj.

With a sudden movement of her left arm, Josefine swept her plate off the table, and a hunk of thin toast thinly smeared with liver pâté landed in Anton's lap. He picked it up in a strangely mechanical way and set it back on the table.

"You're the one who let them out!" Josefine yelled. "You who . . . if you hadn't hated your sister so much, it would have never happened!"

"In a way that's true, Mom. I let them out. But you were really the one who did it. And you know it. That morning . . . I saw you. I heard you walk down the stairs, and I followed you. I watched you open the cage door and the kitchen door and then go back to bed. It was you—and all these years I've been wondering why."

"*You* let the birds out?" At that moment, Anton seemed as helpless as the day his wife had told him she was pregnant, and that they should return Susanne. But instead of exiting his body, until the person talking had disappeared along with the dreadful message, he clutched his wife's wrists. "*You let the birds out?*"

"Yes," Susanne said. "When her favorite, Aphrodite, died, she took an awful revenge on the rest of us—and punished herself as well. Any first-year psychology student could deduce that."

Josefine stared at the tablecloth where her plate had been.

"I think Samanda discovered that it was you who released the birds . . . she sensed it. And then she got really scared. I think she also discovered your other secret, Mom, the one I've always known."

"Secret?" Anton said.

"That Samanda's not *your* child—she's only Mom's. Isn't that true, Mom?"

A moment of absolute silence followed, and you could hear the wind in the oak trees. Then Josefine screamed, wresting free of Anton's grip; the sudden movement knocked all the glasses over.

Anton didn't react at this horrible moment. Maybe he'd already left his wife and daughter and was floating in the air above the yard, calmly observing the scene below. Or maybe he simply couldn't find his words before his wife spoke.

"Yes," Josefine said, and her voice was more powerful that it had been for years. "Yes . . . Samanda discovered who let the birds out. And then I told her everything. How her father and sister had taken pleasure in Aphrodite's illness, how they'd taken her into the woods to break her neck and throw her in a hole where nobody would ever find her again. And then I had to calm her down, by telling her she wasn't really related to either of you."

"So you told Samanda why you loved her—and not me?"

Josefine bowed her head at this statement—delivered in such a calm and matter-of-fact way. "I would have gone with him," she replied, her voice surprisingly loud and clear.

"You would have gone with him, but you didn't."

"I told Samanda all of it . . . that she probably wasn't even . . . that she wasn't who she thought she was. And that I would have gone with her real father if . . . if we . . ."

"If you'd had any courage," Susanne said.

Josefine began to cry.

Anton sat unmoving, his face expressionless.

Susanne stood. "What a life. First you conceive Samanda dishonestly, your secret love child, then I frighten her out of her wits with my vandalism and stories about sailing out on the lake, and then you tell her she isn't even the daughter of the man she loves and believes to be her father, but the bastard child of a charlatan and a globetrotter who has long since abandoned you. You didn't even dare follow him to the garden gate . . ."

Josefine whimpered again.

"And this man, her father, didn't even know what was going on?" Anton said. Miraculously, he'd remained grounded here with us, and now faced his wife with a coldness I didn't know he had within him.

"I would have gone with him," Josefine whispered.

Susanne took one step closer and lowered herself to her seated mother. "Did you get pregnant on purpose, Mom?"

Before anyone could answer, Anton stood. "I can't stay here." These words came slowly, as if he hesitated on each syllable, yet it was clear to anyone who might have been listening that he meant them. Never again would he sit across from his wife, in silence or otherwise.

Josefine never answered her final question, Susanne later told me. She remained seated at the table where, like always, she gazed at the horizon. From what I heard, I don't think she saw her daughter or husband leave; and anyway, I don't think it meant anything to her, deep down. She sat just as she had the first time I'd laid eyes on her: sunken in a sea of shadows on the bench under the hazel branches, facing south, listening to a message only she could hear, and which she acknowledged with a peculiar nodding of her head.

And that's how she remained as the sun set over the cape that had once been cursed by a king.

30

BREAKDOWN

June 29, 2008

Somehow I'd always thought that Susanne would be the first of us to break under the pressure, after which she'd reveal all of her secrets.

I should have known that her past had long since hardened her for far greater burdens than the ones we now faced. What I should have realized was that the breakdown would come from a very different place—and much too quickly for anyone to react.

* * *

Everyone in the room was smiling, and most of the smiles were bigger than ever, even if they should have turned to grimaces—or worse.

More than a thousand people—board members, managers, technicians, reporters, and celebrities—stood shoulder to shoulder in Channel DK's enormous ballroom on the lowest level of the Big Cigar. The space was so tightly packed there was barely room to raise a glass in response to the many toasts being offered. Everyone was in especially high spirits, and more than a few celebrants had spilled champagne on their neighbors, but that hadn't dampened the mood. The Professor started off the festivities by reading a telegram that he'd received directly from the Ministry of State just a few minutes earlier.

"I wish all the best for Channel DK in the years ahead," the dying but indomitable prime minister had written from his sick bed. The words were a little pedestrian perhaps, lacking conviction, but that hadn't affected the atmosphere.

The Professor had insisted on celebrating the successful *Roadshow*, which he contended had united Danes around the station's new visionary concepts; now everyone could see with their own eyes how well the station was doing.

Peter Trøst Jørgensen had receded to the far back of the ballroom, trying to block out the euphoric cheers being given for the man on the podium. He nodded politely to those who flocked around him offering their congratulations; in one cluster of celebrity guests stood his former wife—his second—who after only three months of marriage had formed the group "Famous Men's Wives." He didn't know if she was still a member or even if it still existed.

Peter surveyed his boss on the podium; there was no doubt the Professor was in high spirits tonight, just as there was no doubt he was planning to sack him on account of the Kongslund Affair scandal. Of course, he'd wait a few months, until the successful conclusion of *Roadshow*, whose main star was Peter, but there was no doubt that he would do it. He would start by gradually removing him from the screen and from his executive functions and press contacts, and then he would launch a new star with much fanfare to replace him. Before the audience could even think to object, let alone protest the change, Peter would be gone and soon forgotten. That's how the world was designed—on both sides of the screen.

Despite what the Professor and the other members of the board wanted everyone to think, Channel DK was on the verge of bankruptcy— yet here they were, in the ballroom, drinking champagne and cheering— and in a short while they'd be dancing and singing until midnight to the station's own big band, as though all was well.

The Professor stepped onto the podium—grasping his beloved pipe in his right hand—and gave the most peculiar speech in the station's history: "*Doubt*," he said. "Doubt kills people and television stations. It's the only significant crack in the armor of evolution. The damage that most people suffer, through the process we refer to as childhood, is from a lack of self-esteem. It's by far the most dangerous epidemic among us." People were already beginning to wonder what he was talking about. The pipe stuck out from under his beard, bobbing up and down as he spoke. "We've given the most important years of our lives to random and often unpredictable people: our parents—who are victims of an uncontrollable inferno of emotional outbursts and traumas precipitated from their own childhoods—and that's why we grow up to become crippled, ill-adapted, half-complete individuals haunted by doubt."

At the end of this monologue, he coughed, and the sound system crackled. Trøst wondered whether the Professor was drunk. This was far from his usual diatribe.

God knows he had every reason to get wasted.

He spat a glob of pipe juice onto the marble floor—he'd never done that before—and this act, so out of character in its disregard for appearances, made the entire crowd shift uneasily on their feet.

"That's why we who control the media images and who select the information must master an ability no one needs to be ashamed of"—the Professor put his hand to his narrow, striped tie, which ended halfway down his belly—"namely, the ability to love ourselves. It's the only kind of love that truly matters. The elimination of all doubt."

Scattered applause, clearly a beat off, met these words. To Peter, the chairman sounded as though he'd eaten a handful of psilocybin mushrooms.

Then the Professor began to shout: "If that love wilts, well, then we're back with the parents who gave us all the fucking psychoses to begin with!"

The audience stared at him, dumbstruck.

Without noticing it, the Professor placed one newly polished shoe in the glob of his pipe spit. By now, several of the distinguished guests had already left the room.

"That's all there is to it!" the Professor boomed.

He staggered off the podium, and to everyone's relief, exited the ballroom. A few minutes later, a couple of Trøst's executive colleagues started whooping—and soon the exuberant crowd members were once again smiling and enjoying themselves, the strange speech nearly forgotten.

The following morning, when the employees of Channel DK arrived at work, hungover and sluggish, they learned of the sudden illness of the TV star.

Early that morning, Peter Trøst had called for help from his ninth-floor executive suite. He couldn't stand up; his legs had gone numb.

The Cigar's own physical therapists had called in a team of orthopedic specialists from Rigshospital, but no one could explain the bizarre phenomenon. Finally, the senior doctor on the team posited that it could be a mysterious virus and transferred Trøst to a special unit for unknown and potentially fatal infections.

For the sake of appearances, the Professor, who had only barely recovered from his drunken stupor (the strange speech was nearly forgotten), took the Cigar's limousine to the hospital on Belgdamsvej. It would be exceptionally convenient if he could rid himself of the celebrated reporter for something as dire, and understandable, as a health emergency, poor fellow.

"Trøst, what the hell did you step on?" he ebulliently cried, mostly for the benefit of the attending nurses, as he entered the star's hospital room.

It was meant as a cheerful greeting between men, but the supine patient didn't respond. For lack of any better ideas, the doctors had given him a shot of morphine, and he had slipped into a deep darkness several hours before.

* * *

Once again I dreamed of Nils Jensen, and I knew in my dreams that he still hadn't worked up the courage to ask his parents the terrifying question—even though it was crucial to solving the Kongslund Affair. I envisioned him at the Assistens Cemetery, where he'd played as a child. This was where, using his little Kodak Instamatic, he'd developed his skill—evident even in his first black-and-white photographs of birds and squirrels between flowers and gravestones—of how to combine light and dark.

Nils Jensen could find the Great Poet's grave with his eyes closed—and without stumbling once. He'd sat silently in the living room with his parents much of the afternoon, trying to formulate the question he knew he must ask—although he feared the answer more than the Darkness his father had described so often when he was little.

The purgatory that no soul escapes.

The poet's grave was the place he'd always gone with his father, on the rare occasions when the man ventured out in the daylight. There they'd sit and his father would tell him stories so fantastic that Nils Jensen knew them by heart to this day. *Our life on earth is the seed of eternity / Our body dies but the soul cannot perish!* the gravestone read—written for posterity in the poet's own words—and Nils hoped with all his might that it was true. He had a crucial question to ask the man whose earthly life had long since ended.

In my dream, he sat for a few minutes studying the grave as he tried to sort the words marching around in his head. He was searching for a suitable opener that wouldn't offend the old man with the fantastic stories. As an adult, the stories Nils remembered best were the ones about lonely children like *Thumbelina*, *The Ugly Duckling*, and *The Boy Who Trod on the Loaf*. It was the last one that compelled him to seek out the Great Poet today. As he saw it, the answer to his question would help him decide what to do with Marie's revelation.

As he had as a child, he closed his eyes and imagined the Great Poet slowly rising from the grave. He envisioned a skinny, black-clad man, as you see in old photographs, bowing politely and greeting Nils kindly. *What a lovely surprise that is bestowed upon me to see you again. To what do I owe this honor?*

"I want you to tell me a story. A very special story." That's what he'd always said to his father when they came here. It was a ritual all three of them knew.

You mean—a real story—one of those that begin with 'once upon a time,' which has become my finest trademark?

"Tell me the story that I loved the best, old poet . . . the one about the boy who trod on the loaf."

The one about the boy *who trod on a loaf . . . ?* There was a puzzled tone in the poet's vibrant voice.

"Yes, that one . . . ! Why did you write that story . . . ? That's what I'd like to know."

Listen, my little friend, you need to understand that I can't just explain everything. And the fairy tale you mention isn't about a boy like you, you know, but about a girl *who came to such grief. That's the whole point.*

A small squirrel darted across the path.

I trust you've heard of the girl who trod on the loaf so as not to soil her shoes, and what terrible things befell her. It has been written and it has been published. The poet's voice rose up, flowing like wind rustling in the poplars, and then fell to a whisper just as the little squirrel ran across a thick trunk. He began recounting the shortest version Nils had ever heard: *She was a poor child, proud and arrogant. Lacking character, as they say. As a very young child she liked catching flies, pulling their wings off, and turning them into reptiles. She grabbed a cockchafer and a dung beetle and pinned them down, then put a green leaf or a small piece of paper at their feet, and the poor creatures held on, turned and bent it to try to get off the needle. "Now the cockchafer is reading!" said little Inge. "Look how it turns the leaf!" As she grew older she got worse rather than better, but pretty she was, and that was her misfortune . . .*

Nils interrupted, even though he could tell how delighted the old poet was to tell the story again after such a long time: "Listen, old poet—I don't need to hear the story again, because I know it by heart. After all, it was my father's favorite fairy tale. And it wasn't a girl who trod on the loaf but a boy, and I know that because my father told me. The boy was condemned to eternal life down in the Darkness deep underground—alone. Just tell me the ending, because that's the part I don't understand. Tell me about how the boy ascends from Darkness—how he finally becomes a little bird that flies high up in the sky."

A little bird zigzagged up to the world of humans . . . the poet began spontaneously, his voice light and flowing, his hat bobbing cheerfully as he spoke such wonderful words—but Nils interrupted once again.

"Yeah, yeah, but tell me what it all means."

What it means? For a moment, the poet sat pensively, forlorn, under his top hat. Then he said, *I can only say the words that are already written, that are already in the story. They cannot be changed.*

After hearing this, Nils sat for a long time with his head lowered, until finally the poet took pity on him. He said, in a whisper as fine as the squirrel's fur against the tree bark above his hat, reiterating what the photographer thought was so important: *But one day the little girl down in the Darkness heard her story told to an innocent child, who broke into tears upon hearing it. "But won't she ever come back up?" the child asked, and the answer was "No, she'll never come back up!" Then much time passed, long and bitter, and the child grew old and was about to die, and in that very second it imagined the poor girl again and cried inconsolably for her. Its tears and prayers resounded like an echo under the ground, down in the hollow, empty shell that surrounded the imprisoned and tormented soul.*

That very instant a ray of sunlight reached into the abyss and melted the little girl's petrified form. An angel from God was crying over her, and a little bird swung zigzag up to the world of humans . . . she was free. You could tell that the poet himself was choked up.

Nils interrupted him for the third time, and this time almost angrily: "It's no use, old poet, because I don't understand it. You'll have to interpret it for me."

Interpret it? Maybe it was the poet's voice, or maybe a muddled whisper in the leaves. There was a long pause; the squirrel darted around the gravestone and disappeared. It sounded as though it had been received with a heavy breath from inside the earth, but then everything grew quiet again. The cemetery was empty.

For a long time, Nils stood listening to the wind rustle in the trees. Finally, he realized that both the wonderful words and the poet were gone. He hadn't wanted to put up with Nils's insistence that he break the etiquette of fairy tales—and now Nils would never get his answer.

He'd have to ask his parents without having any idea how they might respond.

* * *

"That's what happened. There's no doubt about it, and it'll be returned to sender."

The words were uttered without the least hesitation, and the national minister knew right away that Carl Malle, his ally for half a century, was right.

They had been discussing the latest development in the Kongslund Affair for more than an hour. After the discovery of the retired chief inspector's body in the harbor, Malle had written the main points of the case on a slip of paper, which he had shown only to the minister before burning it in a giant porcelain ashtray that bore the party monogram.

In his last years as homicide chief inspector—and later in his retirement—the dead inspector had been obsessed with the mysterious death of a woman on a deserted stretch of Bellevue Beach in 2001. His widow had confirmed as much to Malle. The logical connection to the Kongslund Affair could no longer be denied. The dead woman had carried a photo of Kongslund in her pocket, and according to the homicide chief inspector's widow, this picture was what had prompted him to make the fatal decision to resume the case after the Kongslund stories began appearing in the media.

There was no longer any doubt. The dead woman had to be Eva Bjergstrand. She'd come to Denmark no less than seven years earlier and had probably gone to see Magna. Whether she'd been able to do so, Malle didn't know. Magna might very well have discovered her fate, because Malle's investigation suggested that Eva Bjergstrand's death had been mentioned in the local paper, the *Søllerød Post*, a few days later.

If Magna's letter package had really been sent to Australia—as the unstable Oceka grocer swore it had—then to whom did she send it?

Of course, it was possible that Eva had a secret ally in Australia, but they had no way of knowing about that, so the other possibility was far simpler—and more disturbing. Malle explained, "If she sent the Protocol in a package to Australia . . . addressed to Eva . . . to Eva's old address in Australia—which she knew no longer existed—then that would be very cunning. And that's how Magna was. The package would be returned to sender, to *her* that is. Because Australia is such a distant and vast country, it would take a while before the mail service would give up on delivering the package to the addressee, and at that point the Kongslund Affair would have long since blown over. Nobody would be able to find the Protocol. Not even if we'd been given permission to search her home— which might have been what she feared. The Protocol just needed to be gone—as quickly as possible—but it also needed to be returned!"

"But what the hell is in that damn . . . ?" The minister broke off in the middle of his question, as though he didn't want to utter the book's name.

"*Everything*," Malle said. "*Everything* is in it."

"*Everything* . . . ? Damn, Carl, where the hell *is* that package? It's been a long time . . ."

"It might take some time yet. First it had to be sent across the globe. Then the Australian mail service would have to search for the addressee . . . it might take months before they give up . . . and return the package."

"At which point—"

"Yes, at which point it'll end up with Marie, since she is Magna's heir." Malle came to his ominous conclusion without hesitation.

"But that can't happen." The national minister leaned closer and whispered, "Can't we get INTERPOL to . . . ?"

"Under no circumstances. We can't risk anyone else opening that package and finding the Protocol. And if any police authority finds the package and officially returns it to Denmark, it won't go to us but to investigators at police headquarters."

His point was abundantly clear to the minister.

"Could we find it at the postal service before they expedite it?" Ole Almind-Enevold asked, having grown considerably paler over the course of their conversation, which was something of a common occurrence in the past few weeks. "They might have it already."

Malle stood and leaned against the fake fireplace the ministry's interior decorators had affixed to the northern wall, complete with brass hinges and a stained green oak mantle. "I'll see what I can do, Ole. But this can't get out. That's absolutely crucial . . . *None* of this can get out."

"If that package ends up with Marie . . . she's completely unhinged. For God's sake, Carl. If she opens that book and reads the truth . . . Magna's truth . . . that loony woman . . ." Even the nation's second most powerful man didn't dare finish the thought.

And as usual, his old war buddy didn't try to reassure him. "You're right, Ole. You're entirely right. If she reads what's in the Protocol—we'll all go down—the whole gang."

A strange choice of words, the minister thought.

31

FINAL ATTEMPT

June 30, 2008

I think the People's King would have been happy to see the seven of us together at Kongslund. As a child, the old monarch had been brutally separated from his mother, the loose Princess Charlotte Frederikke, whom his father exiled to Horsens, forbidding her from ever seeing her son.

There is really no doubt that his motherless childhood had a significant impact on his later decision to abandon absolute monarchy, listen to the people, and accept the introduction of democracy. I think that as a king he let his childhood grief manifest itself in his body, which then refused to plant the seed to allow the continuation of the royal Oldenborg family. And in this way he exacted a gruesome revenge on his father and all his ancestors. He left no heir. Increasingly, he sank into a state of mental darkness that only his life's companion during his final years was witness to. He never saw the completed Kongslund.

The last absolute monarch sat for long days, one after the other, fishing for carp at the Deer Garden.

* * *

I happened to hear the doorbell before anyone else because I was sitting in Susanne's office with the door open.

The chrome bust of Sir Winston Churchill, given to the orphanage for its effort during the Resistance, was still standing on Magna's old desk, shiny as new. This was where I was when I gave Asger the name of his "biological mother"—and this was where Magna sat when she talked to the adoptive parents she so discreetly controlled and followed in the years following their adoption. For the sake of the children, of course.

I went down and opened the door, and in front of me stood a short, stocky man.

"My mother is dead." The message was astonishingly simple—and impossible to misinterpret.

He was around fifty, I guessed, and his voice seemed familiar to me. Or maybe it was just the tone and the faint Jutland accent, the origins of which I couldn't determine.

"I'm Marie Ladegaard. Maybe you've come to the wrong address," I said as politely as I could.

"No, no . . ." For a second the voice sounded almost panicky. "I'm sorry, it isn't . . . I'm talking about Dorah . . . about Dorah Laursen from Helgenæs."

I held my breath.

Then he added: "I'm her son."

Now it clicked, and I had to go to great pains not to show my surprise. The man on the doorstep was the mysterious son whom the governesses at Kongslund, according to Dorah, had given her to replace the one they'd taken from her five years earlier. This was the son I had mercilessly ordered Dorah to explain everything to—what little she knew—about both his background and his incomprehensible and mysterious arrival in her home.

I didn't know what it meant. The only thing that really interested me at this point, two months after the Kongslund Affair had begun, was the answer to the question: *Who was Eva's lost son?*

Clearly it couldn't be this man.

I summed up my confusion about everything in a brief and not particularly clever reply. "Dead?"

He responded immediately. "Yes, her neighbor found her. She'd fallen down the cellar stairs."

I hadn't seen any cellar stairs when I visited, and I hadn't imagined that such a small and low-ceilinged house even had a cellar.

"Her neck was broken."

I didn't say anything, but in my mind's eye I saw the scared, hunched woman and imagined her lying there at the bottom of the stairs with her short, thick neck broken, bent at a sharp angle, her dead eyes staring into the nothingness.

I closed my own eyes.

"The police think it was an accident."

"That's what they think?"

"Yes. But I'm not so sure." His voice had grown deeper and contained a strange mixture of anger and peace.

"But why are you coming to see me?" I said, rather more coldly than I meant to.

"Because my mother told me all about you . . . and Kongslund. She told me about everything that happened. Now I wish she'd never done that."

I stood dumbstruck for a moment. "You had a *right* to know," I said.

"That's not the same thing."

"The same thing as what?"

"As what I've been thinking about since. That piece of information changes everything."

"Children have a right to know their origins, and that knowledge must never be kept from them." I realized my tone was too earnest for the situation at hand, but it was crucial not to give in on this very point.

I think he sensed my stubbornness, because he abandoned the topic abruptly. "I'm afraid . . . I just wanted to know if you've heard anything."

"If I've heard anything?"

"Yes—did something happen? Might someone have . . . maybe what she knew somehow . . . ?" He stopped in the middle of his fragmented inquiry.

"I don't see how the information she told you, because it was her motherly duty to do so, could be connected to her death today," I said.

"Yesterday," he said.

"I see, yesterday. Nothing has happened here that might be connected." I hoped my tone was convincing. Because of course something had happened. Knud Taasing had visited Dorah three days earlier.

We talked for another couple of minutes, but I didn't reveal any more information. The last thing I needed was this naive man interfering.

"All right . . ." he finally said.

"My condolences," the trite phrase dropped from my mouth despite my intention to avoid such phony sentiment.

"Thank you," he said flatly before taking his leave.

As soon as I closed the door, I began calling the others to tell them about Dorah's death. I didn't say anything about her son. First I called Knud, who said he would tell Nils. After the brutal scene the other day, he clearly didn't like the idea of me calling his friend.

Then I called Peter, who didn't pick up, and finally Susanne, who grew quiet when she heard the news. She was at her house in Christiansgave and hung up without saying good-bye. Orla, Severin, and Asger were already here, and now Susanne was on her way.

Despite my apprehension about Dorah's mysterious fall, I was in high spirits in a way I hadn't been for years.

This was the day I'd been waiting for all my life, however banal that may sound.

Tonight, for the first time, all seven children would be reunited at Kongslund. The way I'd planned ever since writing the anonymous letters to my old companions. We would be sitting in the sunroom, here in Magna's house, each in our own body but with our special, shared consciousness—just like when we sat under the Christmas tree and were immortalized in an almost fifty-year-old photo.

Today, we were just as connected by fate as we'd been that Christmas day in 1961.

* * *

We're sitting around the old glass-topped table in the sunroom. A strong wind blows from the sound. The wind lashes against the roof, making the wood creak.

At first there's an awkward silence, and everything feels at once natural and ceremonial; an embarrassing sentimentality has snuck up on each of us, causing us to avoid eye contact for a few minutes.

Somehow, despite his sudden and strange illness, Peter Trøst is present—supported by the crutches he needs to support his weakened legs. He had insisted to his doctors that he could not stay in the hospital, and, reluctantly, they let him go. He intends to return to the TV palace and the desperate Professor immediately, probably to observe the station's total breakdown at close range.

Severin and Orla sit next to him on the sofa, both with their heads bowed, while Asger—not surprisingly—leans back and stares at the ceiling as if it were made of glass, giving his eyes access to the darkness and the universe above.

Nils Jensen sits stiffly in one of the antique, high-backed mahogany chairs that Susanne has put out for him, and I think he is trying to show us that my revelation hasn't knocked him off his feet. Not anymore. Susanne seems withdrawn; from her perch in a deep, plush lounge chair, she sips her exquisite oolong tea with half-closed eyes.

I study the small party from a semi-dark spot between the sofa and Asger's chair and recall the words in Eva's letter that started it all: *I can only envy them their innocence and their happy eyes under their elf hats. If one of them is mine, and I am certain that is the case, you didn't write to tell me, and of course I know why. They must have all been adopted during the months that followed.*

Of course, an eighth person is present—Taasing—and he's the one who breaks the uncomfortable silence with a little speech that is at once self-important and consciously practical.

"There's something I need to mention right off," he says, "before we go into the details of the Kongslund Affair. My sources in the ministry suggest that the police will visit your families either today or tomorrow . . . the five remaining adoptive families, Asger's, Peter's, Susanne's, Severin's—and then of course yours, Nils."

Nils looks alarmed, and instantly I know why. His parents still don't know what I told their son. He hasn't dared to confront them with the truth they've kept from him—and now he realizes that he will have to, very soon.

I can tell that Taasing has reached the same conclusion, and that's why he emphasizes Nils's name. I don't think Nils has forgiven me the knowledge I passed on to him. None of the others would have told him, I realize.

"As for the public, well, everyone thinks the Kongslund Affair is over and done with," Taasing continues. "But there are some who are pursuing the case—and we know why. The ministry—and not least Almind-Enevold—wants to find Eva's child, which is also his child. And it wants to erase any evidence of what they've done; it was all very illegal and completely immoral, even by today's standards. At best they tried to steal a child from a pardoned murderer whom they then deported to the other side of the planet; at worst they were involved in a more comprehensive business for many, many years, one that all but guaranteed Kongslund's very existence. The business essentially helped certain wealthy and powerful men who'd given in to their desires and were facing unwanted consequences. *That* is a really neat story."

"If it is true." Strangely enough it is my own voice—and in that moment I immediately feel Susanne's eyes look up from the rim of the cup and study me. She must possess the same skepticism as I do when it comes to rushed judgments about the past. But she doesn't say anything.

"Those who've yet to ask their adoptive parents the crucial question will have to do so tonight, before the police beat them to it. I understand that Susanne, Asger, and Peter have all received negative responses. Severin too." This is Taasing's way of discreetly pointing out that he only needs Nils Jensen to complete this part of our private investigation.

Nils remains stiffly seated, the way an unjustly accused man would in front of his jury. But he can't hide, and he knows what he needs to do. He's the last possible candidate—and by far the most likely.

* * *

Later, I sat with Asger on the dark mahogany sofa. The wind had picked up from the northeast, and the gusts made the villa creak and shake as though an underground demon were pushing its shoulders against the very foundation of the house.

I got the sense that there was something he wanted to tell me—or ask me—and I didn't feel at ease in my own narrow section of the small sofa.

"You were born with a physical handicap, limping, almost a cripple, yet you had the courage and strength to . . . travel about . . . and visit all of us, though we didn't know it," he said.

I couldn't tell where he was going with this, so I kept quiet.

"We've shared it all, the light, the darkness, everything . . . back when we were in the infant room, exchanging little particles of life. Of course we were too young to understand."

He almost sounded like Magdalene.

"You know what, Marie . . . none of us will ever find our real parents; they've been erased from our lives forever. In a strange way that's a good thing. It's precisely how it ought to be."

He reached out and put his hand on my left arm; he had to crane his long body toward me to do so. Maybe Magdalene was right after all: if you were patient enough, a determined man would someday dare to walk past the two Chinese stone pillars and up the driveway to ask for even the most insecure and crippled hand, like a miracle.

I pulled my arm back.

That night I dreamed that I made love to a man, and that was in and of itself quite a feat, because I had no experience with that. A fate I shared with Magdalene.

In my dreams, it wasn't Asger that I desired—as I would have expected—but a man whom I never would have imagined. I moaned his name again and again, and I screamed it in my sleep louder and louder each time, until finally I awoke with a jerk. Everything under me was wet, the sheet, my skin, my fingers, and that shook me more than anything else I'd ever encountered.

I sat up in bed and cried in the darkness, like an abandoned child.

I, who had lived so invisibly for so long, had—when given the opportunity, in my dreams—chosen to make love to a man who was the very embodiment of visibility. In that moment I clung to the delusion that the most unknown person would be desired by the most known, and that in this way dark and light would meet.

Everyone knows those kinds of things don't happen.

But perhaps that's how it had been with Josefine from the cape. Susanne had been quiet for most of the evening, and I knew her well enough to know what that meant. Her visit with her parents had been a disaster. Final and irreparable. The grief in her eyes told me as much. Her mother had lived a secret life of longing, which Anton had completely overlooked in his efforts to perform his daily chores. In reality, he'd let her down immensely, because it had been his duty to free her from despair.

It struck me that all the women who'd adopted the children with whom I'd shared the first months of my life had been married to this kind of man: men who never discovered what was really going on around them and who, for that reason, were unable to help.

In the darkness, I pictured the seventh child sitting on the bench at Våghøj, beside Josefine. Both gazed toward the south. I understood why: south is the ordinal from which all longing originates.

32

THE THREAT

July 1, 2008

Susanne Ingemann understood that the Kongslund Affair had deep layers she'd never been able to access before. With the sixth sense she'd developed growing up on the cape, she knew that even the smallest obstacle could trigger an entire series of events that seemed coincidental but weren't.

When Dorah died in the low-slung house in Stødov, the mystery of her role in the Kongslund Affair deepened; we couldn't explain the mysterious boy who'd arrived in her home.

Sitting alone in the King's Room, I had no doubt as to who was responsible for her death: Almind-Enevold and Malle. I just couldn't answer the simple question: Why?

* * *

When a story has been blown up and then suddenly collapses, it affects everyone at a place like *Independent Weekend*.

The entire newspaper building trembled under the weight of what could only be described as a collective sense of guilt, mixed with copious amounts of aggression, confusion, and fear. Doors slammed, feet stomped, voices shouted: these sounds merged, becoming a continual hum that encircled the main editorial conference table, where a desperate crisis-management plan was quickly being put together in a final attempt to stave off disaster.

That morning, it wasn't the Kongslund Affair that prompted the middle managers and the editorial chiefs to rush about frantically, holding short confabs every five or six minutes; no, it was the story of the deported eleven-year-old Tamil boy that suddenly exploded, ricocheting back on everyone who'd touched it, and in a way that no one could have predicted.

The paper's two apprentices had just returned from Sri Lanka, where they'd searched for the infamous boy. They had received financial support for their trip from an array of charities hoping to dig up information that could deliver a fatal blow to the anti-immigrant administration. Everyone had expected big things from the trip, most of all *Independent Weekend*, which hoped for information that would lead to a sensational exposé—once and for all placing the newspaper square in the middle of the new media landscape.

The first report they'd called in—from the airport in Colombo—had sent waves of excitement through the newsroom. "He's dead," they'd said. No explanation.

The editor in chief had stretched his arms into the air and screamed, "Yes! Yes! Yes!" It may have seemed rather cynical to an outsider, but everyone present understood their boss's reaction: nothing could salvage this administration now, and the most prestigious journalism prize would land here, on this news desk, at this paper everyone had written off.

That joy couldn't be dampened even by the news of the boy's passing—and it was too late to do anything about that anyway.

Then one of the apprentices added a word that no one understood, and of which the editor in chief hadn't managed to get an explanation before the connection was lost.

"But . . ."

But? No one could fathom what this might mean. So the journalists looked at each other reassuringly: they were only apprentices, after all, the only ones the editor could spare for a case that might linger for weeks.

This little mystery only heightened the enthusiasm for the apprentices' arrival at Kastrup Airport. The two young heroes would be brought swiftly back to the exalted editorial bureau that awaited them.

"It's a *fantastic* story," the editor in chief shouted as he welcomed the two apprentices home. "Fantastic: *'Danish Government Drives Eleven-Year-Old to His Death. Despite All the Warnings and Critical Reportage, Including by This Paper!'*" He was yelling in headlines.

Oddly, however, one of the apprentices looked as though he were about to cry—an unanticipated reaction to such unreserved and effusive praise. A shudder passed though the editorial offices, where almost fifty staff members, including Knud Taasing and Nils Jensen, had gathered.

Bravely, the second apprentice came to his colleague's rescue. "It wasn't quite like . . . that."

"What do you mean it wasn't like that? He's not *dead* . . . ?" The editor in chief tried to ward off the disastrous revelations that were sure to follow.

"Yes, but . . ." That terrible word *but* lingered again, trembling, in the silent newsroom.

The first apprentice spoke again. "Yes, but the thing is . . . he was killed by soldiers . . . government soldiers. Because he'd joined the Tamil Tigers, the separatist movement."

"Ah," the editor in chief said, eyeing the miraculous save ahead. "But so what? The Tigers force everyone to fight for them, children especially—the boy can't be blamed."

A wave of relief washed over the room; clearly the two apprentices didn't understand half of the reality of what they'd been sent to cover.

"But it didn't happen like that . . ." the first apprentice began and then stalled.

The second apprentice picked up where the other left off. "He was killed . . . because he tried to blow up a school—as a suicide bomber."

A long silence ensued—perhaps the longest silence ever to take place in that particular room. And Knud Taasing understood why: shock. Suicide attacks weren't forced on anyone. Only the most trusted, hardcore Tigers were allowed the "honor" of carrying one out. That kind of thing was voluntary—and fanatical.

The braver of the two apprentices said, "His father was one of the leaders of the movement, and he was recently killed. The son volunteered for the mission."

His voice trembled as he spoke. The last vestiges of hope drained from the room.

The other apprentice added, "They'd sent him to Denmark to spy on the Tamil refugees at the asylum centers here—the Tigers considered them traitors."

"No, no, no!" the editor in chief screamed. He collapsed in his chair, as pale as a corpse.

"He wasn't part of the network in the way the administration claimed," the braver of the two apprentices said, no doubt aware of its irony. "Yet because he was a full member of the Tamil Tigers and was able to operate in that network here, he nevertheless was."

"No, no!" the editor in chief repeated.

The international editor leaned forward. "But are you absolutely sure about this . . . bizarre information, boys?"

"Yes," they said in unison. And the braver one continued, "We have sources for everything, cross-checked sources—documents, confirmations from the Sri Lankan police, and from UNHCR in Colombo, the UN's own department of refugees, that is."

"No," the editor in chief whispered.

A collective sigh of dread passed through the room. This case would be the end of them. For weeks the paper had run a smear campaign against the administration and the national minister in the firm conviction that all the rumors and undocumented claims would, in the end, be confirmed. No one had doubted that.

"But . . . we can't write *that*, for Christ's sake," the editor in chief whispered. He hadn't been hired to handle controversial situations. His specialty was streamlining business, organization, efficiency, cuts—the very demands that caused the paper to launch a high-profile exposé on the Tamil boy without much research, long before it had been investigated and confirmed in Sri Lanka.

"It's absolutely void of concrete evidence . . . !" The editor in chief grasped at the only straw that he could see from his seat at the conference table: the story was too improbable for anyone to believe.

Several of those present nodded eagerly. If the story were too far-fetched and unspecific, with many loose ends, it would be entirely unprofessional and rash to publish it. Naturally.

"But it's all right there—in the documents," the first apprentice said. "In the documents . . ." He rummaged in his bag, and Knud Taasing shook his head in pity. The apprentice had no idea what was about to happen.

"*You!*" the editor in chief cried. "Don't try to teach us anything, you little *moron . . .* !" He leaped from his chair and pointed threateningly at the young man who, just a few minutes earlier, had been celebrated as a hero by the grateful newspaper.

The unfortunate man slumped to the ground and looked as though he were about to cry.

"This is such a serious case that we simply have to delve into the specifics, before we commit to one thing or another," the editor in chief said. "If one interpretation has proved wrong, so might another." Without knowing it, he used exactly the same logic as the Professor when he'd shot down Channel DK's coverage of the Kongslund Affair.

But it worked. All the assembled journalists mumbled approvingly. The paper was on the verge of collapse, and this kind of scandal would send them all to the end of the unemployment line. The whole story would backfire terribly, and they'd be the subjects of ridicule among their colleagues at other newspapers.

"Are you suggesting that we just suppress the fact that the Tamil boy is in fact *dead*?" It was Knud Taasing's voice that sliced through the room.

"No, Taasing." The editor in chief turned to face the reporter. "Of course not. Naturally we'll report that he is dead, because that is true. But we'll also write that there are so many conflicting details in this bizarre story—which the administration itself was the first to mess up so awfully—that we now have to make a concerted effort to unravel all the threads: Was he forced into the Tamil Tigers movement? Had he volunteered? And, if so, why? How did he actually get to Denmark, and so on and so on . . . We don't know anything about any of that yet. It could take months to find out. But *Independent Weekend* will not relent until the truth is brought to light."

Everyone knew what those words meant. The story would slowly peter out. In time, readers would forget the paper's promise to pursue the matter.

"But that means we're no better than those we accuse of such behavior—the administration and anyone else who suppress information." Taasing had made his way to the conference table and now stood directly in front of the editor.

"But, Taasing, do you think we should write a story as complex and important as this one—*before we're completely sure?*" This dig at the former star journalist's fatal mistake in the case of the murderous Palestinian was so tangible you could have sliced it into chunks and stacked it in piles on the conference table.

Once again an approving mumble arose from the crowd. Everyone understood the editor in chief's reasoning. This was exactly the kind of rationality and accountability he was paid to maintain.

Taasing knew the battle was over. He could return to his desk like the others and accept the new reality, or he could choose a more heroic and dramatic course, such as leaping from the triple-thermo window directly into the harbor basin (he had a feeling his colleagues would relish the latter, such a glorious and sensational action).

He did neither. Instead he uttered the words he never thought he'd have the courage to say: "I quit."

He packed his things in silence and exited the building without another word. He didn't see Nils Jensen anywhere.

When he stepped into the fog on the quay, he expected to hear the photographer's steps behind him. Yet he heard nothing but his own footsteps.

He stopped and listened for a moment. Then he shrugged and continued toward the city.

* * *

The nation's leader lay exactly where his little army of doctors and nurses had been ordered to position him, which is to say right in the center of the Ministry of State—a position that satisfied all his dreams of a final, glorious send-off.

Once again the national minister had been summoned to the Lazaretto, as the cleverest among the lower-ranking officials had dubbed the office, and once again the summons had come before eight in the morning.

His boss's explanation was concise and crystal clear: *Meeting about the future. Present: just you and me.*

Like an omen, the rain, now in its third straight hour, poured down from the skies on yet another dismal day. When the national minister arrived, his black umbrella—the one with the party monogram stitched into the waterproof material—was sopping wet.

The dying man lay, as he had the last time Enevold had seen him, in the grotesquely large bed that took up half of the room. His shrunken body was elevated to a sitting position, and he greeted his guest with a faint wave of his right hand.

Even though his death seemed imminent, he still held the power to rule the kingdom and to reduce each and every one his subordinates to nothing if he saw fit; thus the otherwise confident national minister hardly dared breathe for fear of triggering the man's wrath. The treachery with the Tamil boy, he realized—for which the Ministry of State was now liable—had worsened with the latest development of the boy's death. That he had yet to be sacked could only be explained by the appearance of guilt, and the resulting scandal it was likely to create. The prime minister had no intention of being carried out of his office as a leader of the opposition.

"Have you read the *Independent Weekend*?" The prime minister cut straight to the issue at hand.

"Yes."

"They're already calling."

"Yes." Ole Almind-Enevold had no idea what to add to that. He was afraid to strike the wrong tone, or say the wrong thing.

"The little Tamil boy . . . is dead."

"Yes," Almind-Enevold said for the third time, confirming the dreadful news.

"Can you do nothing more than affirm what I say?" The prime minister grabbed the small remote that controlled the enormous bed's hydraulics and pressed the red button that lowered the bed to a horizontal position.

He almost said *no*, but caught himself in time. "There are rumors that he'd joined the Tamil Tigers."

A muted buzzing filled the office, and, along with the bed, the prime minister once again rose like an Egyptian Pharaoh in a 1970s horror movie. "Yes, Ole. Rumors . . . and that's exactly the problem. The only thing people will pay attention to is that the boy is *dead*—and then they'll say that we killed him."

"No, I certainly don't think . . ." Almind-Enevold paused at the worst moment—before the crucial denial. After all, they'd had the boy deported.

"*Deported to His Certain Death*," the prime minister said. "That will be the headline . . . for weeks to come."

The prime minister sat up straighter; in his mighty bed he was a foot and a half taller than Almind-Enevold, who stood at the foot of the bed. He hadn't been asked to sit.

"I once had a canary," the prime minister said.

"A what?" Ole Almind-Enevold's mouth fell open in surprise.

"A *canary*. Are you deaf? As a child," the dying man whispered. "It died just like this . . . in a straw bed . . . drained of energy, wings clipped and unable to fly. But it could still sing. And it *sang* to me until the very last moment."

Almind-Enevold understood the point his superior was making. The prime minister was dying, but even his weakest call would be heard everywhere, and obeyed.

"First you concoct a plan—which you carry out without my express approval, even though it all seems entirely unnecessary—and then . . ." Furious, the prime minister paused, and Almind-Enevold remained at the foot of his bed, breathless, awaiting the fatal words that would mark the end of his career.

But they didn't come. Or rather, the prime minister gave the death sentence a new spin: "I intend to call a special press conference tomorrow. It will take place right here, and I plan to make a very special announcement." A small trail of blood dribbled from the corner of his mouth, down his chin. "Think about it until then, Ole. You can make your decision—*your decision*—before that. For your sake, and the sake of the party."

There was no mistaking it. Being sacked in disgrace could be avoided if the Almighty One—as a result of the Tamil boy's death—resigned.

Better today than tomorrow.

For Almind-Enevold, the remainder of the visit occurred in a fog. When he returned to the Ministry of National Affairs, the Witch Doctor, Bog Man, and Carl Malle were all waiting for him.

"Everyone is calling . . . all the media . . ." the Witch Doctor began. There were red splotches high on his sunken cheeks.

"Shut up!" the Almighty One shouted.

The scheming assistant recoiled as though he'd been whipped.

"You're fired!"

A look of relief crossed his face, and—with the same swift movement as a cockroach dashing for a lifesaving crack in a thick concrete wall— the former top advisor scuttled out of the room.

Bog Man collapsed in one of the minister's fine antique chairs, his skin blue from the bridge of his nose to his temples. To the dismay of the two remaining men, he started giggling, his stiff upper body rocking from side to side. "Isn't it marvelous?" he sniggered, spit forming peculiar bubbles in the corners of his mouth. "A Danish administration has been ripped to shreds by a Tamil case . . . by an eleven-year-old boy . . . isn't it just . . ." He collapsed into another snigger, foamy bubbles running down his chin.

"Shut up!" Malle snapped.

Bog Man began to cry, and Malle escorted him roughly to the door. Outside, the rain was pouring from the darkened skies. If the broken department head had wanted one final glimpse of the rainbow he'd always longed for—and his well-deserved retirement in his little Harewood garden—then the moment had now passed forever.

"You'll have to go back," Malle whispered to Almind-Enevold.

"Go back?"

"Yes. To the prime minister. What you have to tell him will be the most important thing in your career. For both you and the nation. Ever."

The minister stared in befuddlement at his last and oldest advisor (there really hadn't been any others). Malle leaned toward his friend and longtime ally—the man they'd nicknamed the Runner so many years ago, and who in the last days of the war had shot an informant in an alley near Svanemøllen—and he saw that he still had it in him.

The security advisor whispered his next words so close to the national minister's ear that, even if the room had been wiretapped, no one could have heard what he said. In times like these, and with a government like this, you could never be too certain.

* * *

"Dead?" The Professor wrung his hands like a theatrical emcee at a provincial flea market (and perhaps that was what he was becoming now, as his life's ambition loomed near), but Peter Trøst wasn't fooled by his reaction.

Trøst had limped into the lion's cage on his crutches and had just sat at the table in the front of the Concept Room with the Professor and the Concept Boss when Bent Karlsen, the news editor, rushed in, the usual remnants of egg salad on his unshaven chin.

"He's dead!" Karlsen shouted. "They've just reported from the Ministry of State that the prime minister is *dead*! They've declared three days of national mourning."

"Yes! Yes! Yes!" the Professor cried at the top of his lungs. Peter had enough presence of mind to use one of his crutches to push the sound-proof door closed. These days, no outsiders were granted access to the Concept Room, which the waning television-station staff sardonically referred to as the Führer's Bunker. Here, the Professor and his remaining executives spent their time leaning over plans for glorious new concepts and hitherto unknown program formats—which in one stroke would turn defeat to victory and save Channel DK from the brink of bankruptcy. Given the prospect of a global financial crisis, the American mother station was busy saving itself and had decided to cut all ties with its loss-making Danish experiment. A message that had been delivered the previous evening.

"This is a *sign* . . . !" the Professor exclaimed. "I knew it would happen . . . We'll get through this crisis after all. When Almind-Enevold becomes the mightiest man in the nation, everything will work out." The Professor paused as though he'd said too much.

"Yes, and he was present," Bent Karlsen said as he gobbled up a piece of lettuce stuck to his chin.

"Who was present?" the Concept Boss asked.

"The minister of national affairs was there when it happened. They were discussing his future rule when the prime minister had a heart attack—and died in less than a minute. They'll bring him out of the ministry tonight. With the honor guard and—"

"Thank you, Karlsen. You may return to work," the Professor said, interrupting his subordinate in midsentence and summarily dismissing him.

The news chief made his retreat to the door, half bowing, the way people do at the moment of defeat. Then the Professor drew a breath so deep that his throat rattled for several seconds. "This is truly amazing . . . It is so grand . . . so grand I almost can't believe it is happening in our time. What an *incredible, indomitable* mind . . ." His voice brimmed with air. *"What courage!"*

Nobody replied. But they knew who he was talking about.

"Now it will be clear to everyone . . . all my critics. With Ole at the helm, everything will work out. We'll get state subsidies, we'll have good-will—we'll get all our viewers back . . . and we'll expand our audience!"

Trøst noticed that the Professor had, for the first time ever, genuine and sincere tears in his bloodshot eyes.

"Everyone who has left the sinking ship these last months . . . all these traitors . . . media careerists, good-for-nothings, whore reporters, all the ones who let us down . . . now they'll all see that we won in the end."

Trøst studied his boss without replying. His leg prickled. Doctors didn't know what was wrong with him. He could walk, but only with difficulty, and the undiagnosed illness had postponed his departure from Channel DK indeterminately. With so much compassion pouring forth for the beloved star reporter, the Professor could hardly fire him yet.

"We won!" the Professor said again.

Trøst stood—strangely, since he hadn't ordered his legs to go any-where—and left the Concept Room. He just managed to hear the Professor's objection before the heavy door slammed behind him. He took the elevator to the lobby where the last loyal receptionists greeted the Cigar's ever fewer guests and employees.

Walking outside, he felt as though he'd finally entered the Light after an eternity in Darkness. He turned his gaze toward the southwest and blinked.

* * *

Throughout his life, Nils Jensen avoided situations that were embarrass-ing or uncomfortable—situations in which others became self-conscious or in which he was forced to say things that might hurt them. So, he'd decided to wait until his mother had gone grocery shopping and he could be alone with his father.

"There's something I need to ask you and Mom about . . ."

From behind his thin glasses, the old night watchman looked at his son mildly. He'd been reading the Sunday paper, an activity that tended to take the better part of a week.

Nils tried the simple sentence again—this time directed only at his father: "There's something I have to ask you about, Dad."

"Yes?" said the man who'd guarded the Black Square against burglars and shady individuals for fifty-four years before his retirement.

"Why did you say the *boy* . . . ?" The question came out of the blue—even to Nils—and for a moment there was total silence in the living room. It was a bizarre question.

"The *boy*?" the old man said.

"Yes. You said, the boy . . . you always said, the boy who trod on the loaf—but it wasn't a boy. It was a girl."

"Oh. That's possible"—his father shrugged—"but that doesn't change the story."

"Yes, it does. Because I've always thought it was *me* who . . ." Nils could say no more.

"You, who what . . . ?" His father's eyes became inquisitive, as though once again inspecting a deep, dark alley for shadows.

"That it was me who'd end up down there in the darkness, underground . . . if I were ever mean to . . . my parents."

His father closed his eyes but didn't speak.

"Who is my real father?"

The old man slowly leaned forward.

"Who is my mother?"

No answer.

"They say I was adopted from Kongslund."

The old man raised his head and looked at his son. Tears formed in his eyes. "We did what the matron told us to do."

Nils considered his father's significant admission.

"You're not my real father then?"

"Yes, Nils. I'm your father. There's never been anyone else."

"What did she tell you . . . the matron?"

Nils could see a trace of fear cross the old man's face. "There was a reason," he said.

"A reason?"

"That's all you need to know."

"You've lied to me my whole life. Tell me."

"It isn't important anymore . . . It doesn't mean anything."

Nils waited.

"We couldn't adopt. We were too poor. We lived in a slum tenement at Nørrebro. They would have never given us a child. And that's what she told us, Ms. Ladegaard, I mean. But then . . ."

Nils thought of all the fairy tales—and then his father—the man he'd thought was his father. Magna had allowed him to grow up in this way, in darkness and in back alleys, never knowing the truth.

"They'd gotten a child . . . a child that she couldn't place with one of the approved families . . ." He stopped; twilight had descended on the room.

"Yes?"

"It all happened so fast. Suddenly we were approved. In just a few days we had clearance, and you arrived and we loved you from the minute we saw you. But because it happened in such a strange way, I was suspicious. So I demanded to see the documents. I wanted proof that you were a healthy child, and to see your biological parents' records."

The old man rose and walked to the oak bureau that had been standing in the corner next to the window for as long as Nils could remember.

"Yes. There's an explanation that no one knows. Except for me and your mother." He pulled out the top drawer, and Nils saw him carefully flip it over, pulling the veneer bottom up and retrieving a large brown envelope. Even at a distance he could see his father's name handwritten on the envelope: *Anker Jensen.*

"It's all in here." He held the envelope toward his son.

For a moment Nils was frozen in place. In an instant his expectation of a shameful and humiliating confession—one that would be embarrassing but tolerable—had transformed into something much more terrifying. Now it was about him—and him alone. There was no escape. The old man held the envelope in an outstretched hand. Nils couldn't let it fall. He couldn't reject its contents. Just as he had when he'd heard the story of the child under the ground, he felt something akin to panic.

"She said that your biological mother was incarcerated indefinitely—in a prison—and that your father was unknown. He might be another convict."

Nils took the envelope from his father's hand.

"She gave us the papers—so we could see for ourselves—and we promised her we would burn them afterward. 'There are some things,' she said, 'that children don't need to know.'"

The envelope contained only one sheet of paper.

"I told her that all we wanted was to give that kind of child a good life, but that I would keep the documents—especially the birth certificate—until I was completely sure that my son was healthy. And *then* I'd burn them."

Nils looked at the paper.

"But I never did."

It was a birth certificate, with just a single line written on it.

"It's probably because in my line of work, I was the one who made sure that everything . . . that everything was handled properly."

John Bjergstrand, DOB 04/30/1961. Mother: Eva Bjergstrand. Father: unknown.

"Yes. It's you."

Nils closed his eyes, and a wave of nausea followed. He managed to throw the form on the table before falling to his knees and vomiting. His father grabbed him by his quivering shoulders and held him close. "Nils, Nils, Nils, we love you. I'm sorry, so sorry . . . I thought it was best for you . . . for us. I'm sorry."

"They say I am the son of a murderer." Nils cried. And his father cried with him.

When the crying stopped, Anker described the first years to him: How they'd changed his name from John to Nils; how he'd burned all the papers except for the birth certificate—just as the powerful matron had wanted. There had been a declaration from Prison Services documenting that the girl was incarcerated, but that she was otherwise entirely normal. She was neither physically nor mentally ill. In addition, there'd been a notebook containing the most important information about Little John's arrival at Kongslund and his stay in the Elephant Room.

Everything seemed to confirm what the matron had told them, his father had said.

"To us, that was a closed chapter. We loved you and never thought it would come to mean anything. We've been so scared these last few months."

His parents had seen the article in *Independent Weekend*, and of course they'd recognized the name. They had agreed that it must have been a mistake or a misunderstanding that had nothing to do with them and certainly not with the old adoption form that no one knew existed. They'd tossed out the subsequent newspapers, unread, and carefully turned off the television when the case was discussed on Channel DK and other stations.

They had literally shut their eyes—the way parents often do—as they waited for the entire ordeal to blow over.

And to their immense relief it suddenly seemed to have blown over, when Channel DK and *Independent Weekend* stopped covering the case, in favor of the story of the eleven-year-old Tamil boy and other matters. They'd been certain that their grotesque secret was once again safe.

Nils would have never been told the truth if I hadn't told him he was adopted.

33

ANDROMEDA

July 2, 2008

We'd reached the end. That's what it looked like to all of us who'd been implicated in the Kongslund Affair. We'd found John Bjergstrand.

Personally, I had awaited a sign from Magdalene during those days—because if she still harbored the least bit of curiosity about the living, the resolution should have triggered some kind of reaction.

But there was none, and that worried me more than I'd imagined.

* * *

"I just don't get it."

It was Knud Taasing who once again went straight to the heart of the matter. Like the last time we'd gathered, we were sitting in the bright sunroom with a view of the sound.

"I just don't understand why she'd run the risk."

I could tell that Nils had been crying—even these many hours later—and I could feel how his presence affected us. Not just because we'd finally found the one we'd searched for, but also because he'd been transformed overnight. His normal, absentminded expression, a characteristic trait of his, had been replaced by something dark and vigilant that he couldn't hide. The faintly dreamy look I'd always seen in his eyes had been replaced by a kind of emptiness. I wasn't too concerned. I knew relief would eventually replace this fear. He would come to appreciate the certainty I had given him access to, and which I myself had never experienced: the knowledge of his own origins. I had made a necessary repair, and it had hurt, but there was no other way.

"Why?" Taasing repeated. "*Why* would Magna hand out those papers to a Nørrebro tenement family who, when viewed from her much more fashionable place in society, must have seemed rather wanting? I understand that she was in a pinch and couldn't afford to be picky—but *why* would she run the risk of letting them keep the papers without ensuring that they would destroy them as they had promised?"

This was the fourth time he'd said the word *why*, and for some reason it annoyed me. Beyond this living room, no one had heard of our discovery, and Taasing had often underscored the importance of keeping it a secret.

"But nothing *happened* as a result. They didn't reveal the truth to anyone," Peter Trøst said. Right after his arrival, he'd told us he no longer worked for Channel DK. Something had occurred that he didn't wish to discuss, and no one had asked any further questions.

"No," said Taasing. "But Magna had no way of knowing that." He turned to me. "Does it fit with your knowledge of her character, Marie?"

I considered his question for a moment. "She might have been under pressure—or felt forced . . ." I looked at Nils, whose entire existence I'd completely altered. "Your father might have been a tough customer when he was younger, and, of course, he'd held the long end of the stick. What she'd done was clearly illegal."

Nils—John Bjergstrand—said nothing. I assumed he agreed with me.

"But why wouldn't she safeguard herself against that very thing? Why not find a family that was easier to manipulate?" Taasing objected.

Nobody had an answer.

"He actually did keep the birth certificate. Why?"

For a long time everyone was silent. Then, because the others ought to know whether they understood it or not, I said, "Because instinctively he understood that erasing the last shred of information about a child's roots is the one of the greatest sins any human being can commit."

All eyes were on me, though nobody spoke.

Finally Asger turned to Nils. "In any case, you're the son of a minister. Who is now the mightiest man in the country!"

This remark was delivered with an uncharacteristic lack of empathy, and I could tell it stung Nils, who had just discovered a past he had no idea existed. For once he was unencumbered by his beloved equipment, and his hands lay balled in his lap. "Yes," he said. "But I don't want that to go public. I don't want to be known as *her* son—or *his*."

Taasing nodded. He seemed confident and satisfied, the way we'd all grown used to seeing him over the last few days. "That's certainly understandable. We didn't expect you would. And that's why I have a plan."

He told us what he had in mind. And without exception, we agreed, because if we were to face the real villain of the Kongslund Affair—and live through it—we'd have to do it as a group. That was the only possibility. One for all, and all for one.

* * *

Once again Asger remained after the others had left, and once again we decided to end the day in the King's Room.

As usual his presence made me a little nervous, but he didn't seem to notice.

"He *didn't* believe in a major coincidence," he said pensively, "and he didn't believe for a second that God was playing dice."

I understood that he was speaking about Einstein again and his famous dispute with the Danish atomic scientist Niels Bohr. Still, I felt there was something he wanted to say, without being able to articulate it.

"Marie, if the most brilliant scientist in the world can be wrong, then all scientists can be wrong—and in the end, it might be that Einstein was right. That's a pretty amazing thought, isn't it? The possibility of perfect symmetry, a completely flawless puzzle where every single piece can be calculated, explained, and predicted."

Thankfully he didn't try to touch me again.

"Andromeda." The nine-letter word was spoken in a rather darker tone than his earlier outburst. Perhaps he was unconsciously thinking about UFO-Ejnar at the bottom of the black hole in the woods near Moesgaard. "Why is it that the wounds we are afflicted with early in life don't disappear? Whether they are caused by abuse or humiliation or loneliness?"

His sudden change of topic reminded me of my own ability to talk past people, but I didn't understand the connection that Andromeda had with early childhood and his own parents letting him down.

"It's because those events never really become wounds or scars on the surface, but parts of you deep down inside," he said, answering his own question. "You can't see them with the naked eye, but they nevertheless shape the way you move and everything you say and do—until the day you die."

"Like my deformed feet. Even though the doctors have long since declared them healed and you can certainly see them?" I replied teasingly.

"Yes." Asger laughed without noticing the sarcasm. "And like my hip that healed a long time ago but which nonetheless makes me limp whenever I'm a little tired."

He sat next to me on the bed, and like the previous times, I edged away from him, toward the end of my bed. My fear of touch was like an electrical engine that fired of its own accord.

"It's the loneliness that really matters," he said. He was hunched over.

For a moment I dreaded him wrapping his arms around me, but he didn't.

I saw him smile, from the front and from the side, in the mirror across from the bed, and even though the old mirror no longer intruded in my private affairs, I easily heard the taunt from the Darkness inside it.

Kiss him, Marie!

I moved a little farther away from him.

"Isn't it, Marie?"

I sensed what was happening and reacted instantly—I stood. "It's important that I get some sleep," I said and opened the door. "As you know, I've been asked to go to the most important meeting in all of Kongslund's history early tomorrow morning."

The remark was so matter-of-fact that it instantly brought him back to reality. But after I closed the door behind him, his words about loneliness—and about all of Einstein's practical calculations—lingered in my room for the rest of the night. I wondered whether he'd really told me what I thought he'd told me—or whether it was my own hopeless, distorted imagination that caused me to dream when I was awake.

34

THE PRIME MINISTER

July 4, 2008

Every newspaper and television station declared the Almighty One the most celebrated father of the nation the people had ever chosen for the top job—and he hadn't even been elected.

But in their exhilaration, the editors and commentators considered that a special distinction, because it meant something important had happened, namely that Providence had placed him where the Danes most needed him—right now—in a world that seemed to grow larger and more frightening by the minute. Responsibility for the terrible fate of the Tamil boy was attributed solely to the unbalanced chief of staff, whom the police were searching for.

At long last, Ole Almind-Enevold's desire had been fulfilled: he had become the absolute ruler of the kingdom, and no one in his right mind would ever think he would abdicate of his own free will.

* * *

With a small army of aids, officials had converted the prime minister's office from a sick bay to its proper place as the beating heart of the nation.

They had done so in record time, because Ole Almind-Enevold wanted to assume leadership immediately.

They had brought his most important papers and personal property from the Ministry of National Affairs to the Ministry of State in four brass wheelbarrows that rumbled along the fine hallways, up and down elevators, and across manicured courtyards laden with their precious cargo. The wheelbarrows were a somewhat unconventional mode of transportation, but they'd been close at hand; a construction crew was working on yet another expansion of immigration services in the west wing of the National Ministry (paradoxically, as the actual number of immigrants declined, the services afforded them had increased), and the Almighty One wanted to get going right away. He had his reasons.

The last wheelbarrow had just been emptied when the newly crowned ruler held his first meeting. There would probably never be a more important one.

Nor would there ever be another meeting whose participants he'd be less reluctant to receive. All Knud Taasing had needed to say on the phone to secure the coveted appointment was: "*We've found him.*"

Almind-Enevold had immediately cleared his calendar for that morning, including the rescheduling of an important meeting to review his plan to remove the current female director of the Ministry of Gender Equality and replace her with a younger man of his choosing who would swiftly implement the Children's Right to Life law and its new restrictions on abortions.

That too would have to wait.

When we arrived, broad-shouldered Carl Malle appeared surprisingly calm at his boss's side. I'd been hoping to glimpse a nervous—or even outright fearful—expression in his brown eyes, but as always he was unflappable. And that worried me even though I couldn't identify any flaw in the plan that Taasing had outlined, and which we'd quickly agreed to.

The formal greetings were dispensed with as quickly and perfunctorily as possible. I saw the astonishment in Almind-Enevold's eyes when he shook Nils Jensen's hand. Taasing and I were well-known troublemakers, but Jensen's presence completely baffled him.

Malle didn't even bother to shake hands. He simply nodded at each of us once, a look I couldn't decipher on his face.

Then the Almighty One took his seat—the one he'd waited so many years to occupy—behind the prime minister's desk; it was actually much smaller than his old desk at the National Ministry. Malle sat in a chair to his right, and we sank into a couch several feet away, the position of which had been deliberately determined to instill a sense of vulnerability in guests.

Nonetheless, Taasing clucked his tongue, and the loud noise seemed especially vulgar in such a posh office. It was certainly a gesture no one had expected, and Nils Jensen (who was sitting between us on the sofa) flinched. The lanky photographer was by far the most nervous one in our small crowd, and that was hardly surprising.

"We found John Bjergstrand," Taasing said, confirming his earlier statement on the phone.

No one moved, but Ole Almind-Enevold studied his old adversary with narrowed eyes. The clear but unspoken question was: *Who?*

"He's sitting right in front of you."

I felt Nils's slender shoulders tremble.

Malle raised his brows and turned his gaze on the man who was the only possibility—since I was a woman and Taasing was clearly just the messenger.

The prime minister sat silently for a moment. Then he said, without raising his voice, "That's impossible."

"It is possible." Now Taasing did his usual trick, retrieving the damning evidence—seemingly from nowhere—and slapping it down in front of his prey. The birth certificate from the old night watchman's drawer now lay on the nation's highest desk.

"We found this . . . at Nils Jensen's father's house. Anker Jensen has confirmed that it's genuine, and that Magna Ladegaard gave it to him. That means," Taasing said, "that his son, Nils Jensen, was adopted—from Kongslund—under the name"—he tapped the birth certificate—"*John Bjergstrand.*"

At that moment, I could've sworn that the mightiest man in the nation was about to slide off his throne. He made a concerted effort to stay upright and seated, leaning close and studying the document while holding his marble-gray forehead in his hands. Was he going to faint?

Malle must've had the same thought, because he stood—ostensibly to read the document, but also to be at the ready if his boss lost his balance.

A full minute of silence ensued, and I had to admire the old man's self-control. He blinked several times but finally straightened his back and said in a whisper, "I need . . . proof." This was the kind of thing power afforded. Making demands from an untenable position. "A DNA test," he said. He still looked as though he'd been punched in the gut. The Black Square photographer was probably the child he was least willing to recognize as his own. He had dreamt of Orla—or perhaps Peter, whom he respected after all—he could have even lived with Asger.

He'd ruled out Severin from the get-go—and had never seriously considered Nils, the poor boy from the tenements, even though he too had been in the Elephant Room during Christmas 1961, and Malle had kept his eye on him from a distance in the years that followed.

Now it looked like he'd gotten a son who was the best friend and colleague of his nemesis and whose only professional accomplishment was capturing light and dark in small squares and selling the results to glossy magazines and sensationalist papers. His disappointment was palpable.

"There will be no DNA test. The evidence is here—right in front of you." Taasing shook his head as if to underscore his refusal. "We're the ones holding the power in this matter. You can't run the risk of any negative publicity, and to avoid that, you need to accept three unyielding conditions."

It was clear that Taasing had prepared his ultimatum down to the last detail, and that he was reveling in the presentation of it. "And I *only* make this offer because Nils has expressly asked me to. He is just as shocked as you are. He doesn't want anyone else in the world to know the connection you two share."

The Almighty One fixed such a hateful gaze on Taasing that I couldn't believe he kept his composure. But he did.

"I've told Nils that there's only one way to realize his wish, and which will enable me to look myself in the eyes as a journalist when I *don't* write about the story. That is for you to fulfill all three of these conditions. If you refuse, I will go public with all of it. And I'll be delighted to do it."

"And what are the three conditions?" Malle said. For some reason he looked at me, not Taasing, and the old fear settled in my belly; I felt my left shoulder sink even more. If I'd attempted to speak, no one would have understood a word, and Magdalene, by comparison, would have sounded like a speech therapist. Even in utter defeat, Malle could scare the wits out of me.

"The first condition is that Ole explains to Nils exactly what happened when he met Eva Bjergstrand."

"And the others?" Malle asked, ignoring the obvious disrespect Taasing was showing the prime minister by addressing him by his first name.

"We'll get to that. First the explanation."

Finally Almind-Enevold spoke, and it was as though the enormous shock had purged the arrogant and aloof tone from his voice. "But Taasing—if it remains a secret, all of it—then you'll *never* get your big scoop. The one that would give you the honor and dignity you've never possessed."

It was a strangely bold statement to make in his position, and I imagined the chaotic thoughts swirling through his sharp politician's mind: Not twenty-four hours in the office he's coveted for so long, and he's already in jeopardy of losing it all and becoming the center of a scandal that would destroy him—even, presumably, being sent to prison. Now, offered a way out, he examines all corners for any possible trap, while insulting his executioner as he does so. Reluctantly, I had to admire his audacity.

His son sat across from him, but neither paid any attention to the other. In mere seconds, a whole life's worth of longing for a child he never knew was all erased by something as utterly mundane as fatherly disappointment.

"I'm not working for the paper anymore," Taasing said. "And you know what, Ole?"

No reaction.

"I don't give a shit. Tell us your story. It won't go beyond this room. If you keep your end of the bargain, that is."

"What are the other two conditions?" Malle asked.

"They're things you can fulfill with a wave of your hand, I promise you. The boy's origins are the most important thing. Nils is entitled to hear the story."

I couldn't agree more.

Even Malle nodded—slowly, but unambiguously. No doubt he imagined the other conditions had to do with special favors, maybe even money—perhaps a generous allocation to Kongslund in the next budget.

I practically smiled when I thought of the surprise Taasing's last two demands, diabolic as they were, would trigger.

"Okay."

It was a word Malle rarely used, a word indicating acknowledgment. Defeat. He hated it.

Then he turned to his ally from the resistance movement and said, "Tell them, Ole. All that's left are the details anyway."

* * *

At first he spoke hesitatingly, traces of shock still in his voice, but then it was as though telling the story steadied him and even afforded some relief, which I couldn't bear for him to feel—because the details were so grotesque that he should have broken down long ago. He didn't deserve redemption, didn't deserve the bittersweet sensation that revived his old passion to find his son.

The room was square, and it had been provided by the prison warden: about ten feet one way and ten the other. There was a low, plank bed with a narrow blue mattress, a yellow-lacquered wooden table, and two chairs. There'd been a sink with a rusty faucet that worked reluctantly, producing a thin, irregular stream of water. That's what he remembered in broad outline.

The girl in the room had—the day his nightmare began—seemed a little sadder than usual, but sadness was in any event the emotion he'd always associated with her. And she'd had plenty of reason for it.

It would be an exaggeration for him to call her beautiful. And to think of her as the love of his life would be ridiculous; no man in his position—and as young as he was then—would allow himself that conceit.

He remembered her the way she actually looked: not beautiful, not striking, but nearly as transparent as a Hans Christian Andersen papercut. She carried a silence about her, which was a paradox when he considered her violent past. She'd never denied committing the crime she'd been sentenced for—she'd never justified or explained it either—and he'd never before met a girl like her. He didn't say that, but I could tell that was true from his voice as he recollected events.

He'd tried to escape her sad eyes by sinking into the chair and opening the report he'd looked forward to showing her. It was his crowning achievement—his thesis about female inmates and their especially difficult situation—and it had brought them together in the strangest of ways. "Read this, Eva. It's about you."

"I'm with child," she said—as though it were an irreparable situation or a place where time stood still and nothing could ever be redone.

Shocked, Ole Almind-Enevold scrutinized her face for signs that she might be teasing. He heard one of the guards walk past on the other side of the door, but he couldn't see him because the window was covered with a piece of dark cloth.

"I'm with child," she repeated and waited for a response.

For a moment the guard stopped outside the door, clanging a chair about. But then his steps grew more distant again and disappeared.

"It's *your* . . ." But she didn't complete the sentence. Instead her mouth shrank until it looked like a little red flower that had folded in on itself. This was the mouth that had greedily received him on those occasions when he'd succumb to his lust. They'd had sex on the low, plank bed with the blue mattress—that much he remembered. Each time the room had been locked and the window covered—theirs alone for the two hours his visit would last. Their affair had gone on for months.

He had just turned twenty-seven, and his political career had been described as extremely promising in both the *Social-Democrat* and, after the Party Congress that year, in the *Berlingske Evening Times.*

"Answer me," she'd said, sitting slightly curled up and staring at him through her troubled eyes.

He thought of her naked (because she had been incarcerated for nearly two years, her paleness was perhaps the most fascinating thing about her body). He thought of how sweat ran down her skin and onto the blanket he'd spread out beneath them, of how it stormed and rained as she pressed her mouth to his ear and whispered words that only girls from her neighborhood would ever use; she'd convulsed under him as though cramping up, before she opened her eyes wide without seeing anyone or anything, and she'd completely entwined him.

He put the papers on the table: the official report that was to advance his career. "It's almost complete," he said. "This is my last draft." He was very proud of his work

"You're *insane* . . ." She shook her head. "I'm telling you we're going to have a *child* . . . and all you talk about is that *report.*"

"But this might help . . . your case. Maybe get you out of here," he said. But he really didn't want her to get out. He was already married.

He had written the introduction to the report himself. *Prison Services and Copenhagen University 1960. Female inmate. DOB April 7, 1944—ex. 01.*

The entire first chapter was about her, and he considered it a crucial document that would advance the cause for both women and the marginalized: *I talked to 01 about her mother. She gave the impression that her mother's past was a determining factor in what occurred.*

After that came all the necessary observations, and then it was on to plain facts: *The child of an unknown German soldier, 01 killed her mother with a single shove—she fell down a steep rear stairwell in the apartment building where they lived. This after an argument about that relationship. The episode occurred on the girl's fifteenth birthday. At first she called it an accident, but later she rescinded her denial and declared such an intense hatred toward her mother that she was taken into custody.*

The treatment described in the following sections had been more successful, however, judging by the standard at the time: *After three visits, 01 speaks more openly about herself and her incarceration. Using the questions 16–23 (section 01C), I am trying to find a pattern in her impression of the criminally preventative effect of the sentence. But the questions seem to exhaust the girl. She just turned sixteen.*

After that third visit they'd had sex for the first time. He could still hear her shouting, "Yes! Yes! Yes!" And at the moment he wasn't sure whether she was responding to her own primitive force as a woman—her back had tensed and she'd been assailed by tremors he'd never before seen, which kept her raised in a high arch above the blue mattress for nearly a minute—or whether her words were a confession, emanating from deep within her conscience.

"They'll have to let me out now!" She put her hands on her stomach.

"They'll never let you out," he answered without hesitation, the relief in his voice audible.

She sat looking at him.

I thought of the girl staring at the cockchafer she had pinned down, and then much later her freedom from Darkness in the form of a white bird disappearing into the sky.

"You'll have to abort it." The words had just tumbled out. Because it was Ole Almind-Enevold's only solution. "They won't let you out just because you're . . ." At that moment, her name (the same as the mother of all women) seemed absurd to him, yet he repeated it as a last resort. "Eva, you'll have to abort."

"A monstrosity, is it?"

He felt the chill in the room. If she ever spoke to anyone about the baby's father, or if the prison staff failed to maintain their discretion (of course they'd easily figure out the connection, but prison management could be persuaded to silence), they'd simply lock him up.

Associating with a woman convicted of murder. Abusing a professional client relationship. Abusing a minor in the custody of the criminal services.

Every newspaper in the country would print it on the front page. He'd be convicted and lose his license—and the party that had promised to support his run for parliament would abandon him.

The girl before him began to cry. "I'm not going to kill my child too."

He understood that she'd made up her mind, and his thoughts rushed through his head at breakneck speed. Then he made the decision. "Eva, there's another way. But it requires a big sacrifice that I don't know if you can handle," he said. "In that way you can atone for everything that has happened."

She dried her eyes and stared at him.

He felt her presence in his head, that she was looking for the deceit. But she wouldn't be able to find it, because sometimes reality is just so bizarre that it's all the liar needs. He saw the pattern in his mind's eye, the whole plan, and he knew exactly how to execute it—and who to ask for help.

He held her shoulders for a long time; she'd have to listen if she were to save herself and her child, and that was one thing he'd learned in his time as a consultant for Prison Services: working-class girls would save themselves and their children at any cost. It was perhaps the only thing they'd learned from their mothers.

"We have just this one shot," he said, holding her narrow shoulders.

Later, he'd thought of the situation as an accident—one born of other accidents. Isn't that the origin of most lives, if you really examine matters? Isn't that how it's been in the mansions of the wealthy in Klampenborg and at large country estates in Jutland—and even at the King's Palace—hasn't it been proved again and again through centuries that children are born into the world accidentally, they drift to shore like Moses in the basket, and are loved by the person who happens to walk by and hear their cry?

By the person who picks them up.

Yes, he thought to himself.

And there would have been no room for any other thoughts in Visitation Room 4 in Horserød State Prison that autumn day.

* * *

"That was in 1960. She gave birth nine months later—on April 30, 1961."

"In Obstetric Ward B at Rigshospital," Taasing added.

"Yes. That's true," Ole said. "We wielded a certain influence after all. We pulled the necessary strings. And we succeeded. With Magna's help . . . and her personal contacts with the chief medical doctor at the prison. A cash gift to the prison warden . . ."

"And an alternative scenario in which the warden would be fired for failing to protect his female inmates properly." Malle allowed himself a little smile.

No doubt that threat had been Malle's contribution to the plan.

"Magna picked up the child—and she spoke with Eva," Ole said. "We persuaded her to do the right thing, and finally she left. And then . . ."

"And then everything went wrong," Taasing said.

The Almighty One replied with a nod. It felt as though the peculiar story had established a historic—and no doubt temporary—armistice between the two men. "Yes . . . then everything went wrong. My wife . . . my wife, Lykke . . . she didn't want to adopt. And then Magna got scared. She'd been an accomplice in a crime, even though she claimed she did it for the sake of the child."

"And of course because she knew that it would secure her orphanage for all the years to come." Again Malle added his cynical take to the story.

Irritated by the comment, Almind-Enevold shrugged and went on, "Carl and I didn't know which of the boys was the right one . . ."

I noticed that Eva had already conveniently disappeared from their story.

"We didn't know how to determine which one it was. And then Magna succeeded in getting him out of the way before we could do anything." At that moment, he looked almost as sad as the young woman he'd just described. "For all these years, she refused to tell me anything about that time. She had a duty, she said, to offer all her adopted children protection. And that's how she atoned for her crime. She'd broken all of

Mother's Aid Society's rules when she helped us with Eva's child, and she was determined never to break another one."

"So we tracked the seven orphans down." Malle's tone suggested there was nothing unusual about shadowing an infant on its journey into the world. "Whenever a child was adopted, there was a farewell ceremony at Kongslund. All the staff would stand in the driveway waving at the little one and their new parents as they made their departure. We simply followed them."

Malle smiled, and I don't believe I've ever found him more unsympathetic than at that moment.

"Later we visited the orphanage from time to time—whenever possible—to see whether Magna had kept something we could use or something that indicated she still kept contact with the child or the mother," Malle said.

"You burglarized the house," Taasing said.

"I do recall that the first couple of times had been at night." Again Malle smiled at us, defiantly.

"But finally we gave up." Almind-Enevold was clearly uncomfortable with the more felonious part of the story. The burglaries hadn't produced any results anyway. "Through the years, we tracked down the seven children from the Elephant Room and followed them at a distance, but we never figured out who . . ."

"John Bjergstrand was." There was an unmistakably triumph in Taasing's voice. The armistice between the two was over.

"No. We realized that the adoptive parents weren't told the truth, and we couldn't find any other clues," Almind-Enevold said.

"But genetic science has advanced quite a bit," Taasing said. "Couldn't you have gotten samples . . . ?"

"We tried that once, but it didn't yield any result, so we gave up," Malle interjected. "It was too risky. Which doctor and lab would we approach and what explanation could we give them? We'd risk exposing evidence that could be used against us."

"It *also* meant you could retain your power over Ole—as custodian of the invisible child—which must have suited you very well," Taasing said, cocking his head like a gigantic bird. "When—strangely enough—the first test didn't give you anything, maybe you started to feel that Ole wasn't the father after all, and then you'd lose your hold on him. *Of course* you could have found a way if you wanted to."

For once Malle didn't respond. His eyes remained expressionless, and I couldn't tell whether Taasing had hit the bull's eye or not.

Taasing changed the topic. "Did you have anything to do with Eva's death in 2001?"

Almind-Enevold narrowed his eyes and appeared genuinely shocked. "No . . . we didn't even know she was here."

"And Magna . . . hers was just another mysterious death?" Taasing's accusation hung in the air.

"Think about it." The new prime minister stared angrily at his inquisitor. "We had no reason to kill Magna. She was the *only one* who could tell us . . . tell me about my son—if she ever decided to."

Not once during the conversation had he looked at Nils. He'd received a son and denied a son—all in less than a minute.

"And Dorah . . . the old woman at Helgenæs?"

The Almighty One looked almost perplexed. "Dorah . . . ?" he said.

Malle waved his hand dismissively. "I know who you're talking about. What about her?"

"She was the third . . . inexplicable . . . death. And we know you talked to her, Malle, right before she died—trying to intimidate her and prevent her from talking to us. She told me."

"Think, Taasing. I didn't even know she was dead. What threat would she provide anyway? She couldn't even find her own shadow if she tried. But she was causing confusion, and it messed up the investigation, and that's why I told her to shut up. *Nicely.* Not by shoving her down her basement stairs."

Taasing sat for a moment considering Malle's statement, and I could tell he didn't know how to respond. Of course the old lady could have simply fallen down the stairs after losing her balance. Even compact, earthbound types like her might do that.

"What's the second condition?" Malle was impatient to get to the more practical part of the meeting.

"You're going to put a stop to the Children's Right to Life legislation," he said. "In no way should this insane affair result in an absurd limitation on women's rights to make decisions about their own lives."

Apparently Taasing decided to let the deaths go for the moment.

"The lives of *others* . . ." the Almighty One practically shouted.

"Put an end to that bill, Ole, or we'll end your career. And you know we're capable. It's quite a nice office you've got for yourself, by the way."

I saw Almind-Enevold slump down in shock; he now faced a choice he never imagined having to make. In these few seconds, the very reason for his lifelong ambition to take the nation's highest office was being denied him.

"Okay." Malle had now used the expression of defeat for a second time, and for some reason, I didn't dare look at the Almighty One. It was almost as if I feared feeling sorry for him—but of course that was absurd.

Taasing presented his final condition, contained in a short imperative.

This one wasn't met with hesitation either. "Okay," Malle once again replied. I sensed that this condition pleased him, though of course he tried to hide it.

We left the ministry in single file, like the three members of the Olsen Gang—a trio of scoundrels from old Nordic films. Taasing was only missing a chewed-up cigar, but he lit a menthol cigarette instead.

"How did Carl know Dorah fell down the basement stairs?" I said.

For a second the other two stared at me, puzzled—clearly they'd been thinking of other things. They didn't have an answer, and I let it go.

Along the canals they were building shiny, tall silver and gold tribunes. The late prime minister, who'd been laid out in a fancy cedar coffin—not exactly a mighty Egyptian sarcophagus—would be driven around the small island of Slotsholmen seven times before the final memorial service was held in Prins Jørgen's Courtyard.

It would be a celebration the likes of which no one had ever witnessed.

We hailed a cab outside the stock exchange and rode back, along Strandvejen, to Kongslund.

* * *

Newspaper Files for Bankruptcy.

Those blinking words lit up the screen above the Professor's head. Alone in the Concept Room in the Big Cigar, he probably didn't realize how just that one message buried the former party organ.

Independent Weekend had stopped making its payments. The few remaining investors—including one major union—had given up on it.

"The newspaper's last two major stories, which were supposed to blow new wind in its sails, went unresolved," said one of the Professor's last remaining reporters up on the screen, but the Professor paid no heed. "I refer to the Kongslund Affair and the Tamil boy scandal," the reporter continued. "Now, probably no one will ever know what actually happened in those cases."

Only ten minutes earlier, the Professor had been accompanied by his right-hand man, the Concept Boss. Together they'd tried to impose some order on the many stacks of printed plans and program proposals arrayed on the giant conference table. Other piles had fallen to the floor, and no one had bothered to pick them up; many even had footprints on them from employees who'd thoughtlessly trampled them in their haste to exit the room.

The final, awful message arrived by telephone—a direct call from the ministry—and it was Malle himself who'd uttered the simple, terrifying word.

No.

No? All the color drained from the Professor's face, down to the last blue glow on the crown of his head. It all just seeped away.

And no, the Professor couldn't talk to the prime minister—and, in fact, he should make no further attempts to contact him. A prime minister was also the minister of the press, and as such, he couldn't discriminate between the various actors in the media world. He couldn't selectively intervene to save a particular outlet—it wouldn't look good.

Without a word, the Professor hung up. No, there wasn't any more to discuss. It had sounded like a snigger from Hell. His chest pounded so hard it felt as though his heart had worked itself free and now beat against his ribcage.

"The prime minister isn't going to help us . . . ?" the Concept Boss surmised, staring hopelessly at the chairman.

Shaking his head, the Professor breathed deeply until the hollow rattle in his chest ceased. He straightened up. "We haven't tried this proposal yet." He pulled a green folder from an enormous pile. But he didn't get any further than that.

"I'm leaving," the Concept Boss announced, observing with pity the broken-down old man.

And with that, the Professor was alone. Some force had pulled the very foundation out from under Channel DK, and the bunker closed in around him.

The Professor, hunched over, locked the door to the world.

35

FAREWELL

September 2, 2008

In the photos the magazines published about Kongslund during the great adoption years, the entire nation could see for itself that it was a home populated with flocks of smiling children animated by a shared will to live that no human hardship could break.

That's not how it was in reality, of course.

I think most Kongslund children kept their acquaintance with Darkness in a little chamber of their soul, where no one could enter. Nobody wants to show wounds that are so deep not even the land's finest mechanic could heal them.

For some of us, the outer façade collapsed, suddenly and without explanation, and there was no longer any protection against what we had hidden.

* * *

I'm standing on the edge of the grave, quite literally, and without tenderness I observe the mound of soil beside the black hole at Hørsholm Cemetery.

Fittingly, there is also no mildness in my assessment of the act that has brought us here.

At last I turn and follow the others into the impressive church, which stands on the spot where kings and queens spent their decadent lives in a grand palace that King Frederik the VII finally tore down to protest his terrible childhood.

I'm the last to arrive. Predictably, I slide unnoticed into the very last pew. Here no one can study me with barely concealed glances.

The smell in this church reminds me of the one in Søllerød the day we buried my foster mother.

Maybe not quite as powerful, but it's strong enough to trigger scattered allergic reactions among the many hundreds of guests. An abundance of freesia has been arranged in small, white vases along the pews, and there are even more sprays of freesia atop the coffin, which rests on a platform before the altar. You'd almost think Magna herself had a hand in it—and if anyone asked me, I wouldn't rule it out. This was an occasion she'd hate to miss.

To the right of the altar is a small tree in a beautiful, rust-colored flowerpot, and of course I recognize it from the most beautiful garden I've ever seen. It's a Japanese cherry, and I know who has put it so carefully at the place of honor in this grand ceremony.

On the coffin lid, half-hidden beneath a white and yellow bouquet, those sitting close by can see a long, gnarled branch with a few green twigs. Those with a good understanding of trees may recognize it as a linden—but no one can explain its presence there.

One of the distinguished guests in the first row sneezes powerfully several times. And then complete silence follows as we await the pastor to turn toward the congregation. I can't help but imagine the man in the casket, who, in one way, I've known all my life. If they sat him up straight and powdered his pallid cheeks, he could probably appear on the screen without anyone at first noticing any real difference. I have no doubt that the conscientious undertakers from the city's choicest establishment have spent hours prepping his body—as is appropriate for a man of such stature—even dressing him in one of his most expensive suits. Maybe they've even put an extra suit in the casket so that he can change his clothes for a journey of who knows how long.

Now the pastor steps to the altar, and again there are a few scattered sneezes. For a moment, he waits for an especially loud one to end. I can tell from his posture that he's irritated by the repeated interruptions.

To my surprise, I'm suddenly the one who's sneezing—a very loud series of them—I, who grew up amid a cornucopia of flowers.

My eyes are watering heavily, and my rather macabre vision of the adult man in the casket bobs under a stream of tears, disappearing in a whirlpool before resurfacing as a very different image: a beautiful young boy sitting on a white bench under a very tall elm in a shady garden—Paradise itself, you might think. I close my eyes and wait for the visions—and the tears on my cheeks—to disappear, and hope that no one turns around to discover the foundling from Kongslund in such a state of despair.

Finally the pastor steps forward and takes command. "We have gathered here to bury Peter Trøst Jørgensen, born Peter Troest Jochumsen," he says. "We have come to share the grief, but also to rejoice in a rich life."

His parents occupy the left front row; after their last meeting, they never reconciled with their son—and this time the tank commander cannot hide behind his armor, leaving the world's agonizing interruptions to his wife.

Behind the immediate family, the church is packed with people from the upper echelons of society: ministers, executives, chief doctors, media stars, prize-winning journalists; only the Professor, the once celebrated chairman of Channel DK, Bjørn Meliassen, is absent, and that has many wondering. Whispers passed between the pews, both before and during the tolling of the funeral bells, about how he's locked himself inside a special command center deep within the Big Cigar, refusing to open the door to anyone. No one knows exactly what he is doing there, but the Roskilde Fire Squad has not yet been able to break down the steel door with its three lead-encapsulated locks.

Personally, I am more curious as to why Gerda Jensen is nowhere to be seen. Even though the Kongslund Affair has frightened her (and I know almost beyond a doubt that she possesses knowledge she hasn't divulged), she should be in attendance when one of her beloved children marches over the last, dizzying chasm, stepping away from the fine web—falling, falling, falling. Down into Darkness.

"Let us have a moment of silence," the pastor says solemnly. And everyone is quiet for an entire minute before he turns toward the casket and breaks the silence. "All honor to your memory."

As is my habit, I glance at the high ceiling, the way I know others do when they're wrestling with unmentionable thoughts. *Is He even here? Is He keeping an eye on us? Will He discover that at this moment, despite all our pious and timely precautions, our own dread dwarfs the compassion we feel for the deceased and their next of kin?*

For my part, I make a little addendum to the notion of heavenly surveillance that has terrified generations: if Principal Nordal has gained access to this memorial service, he must be smiling cruelly about what has, at long last, happened to his slayer—not to mention *how* it happened.

The long since decomposed principal was interred in the very same cemetery.

Now the pastor is reading from the book of Psalms, reciting the Song of David with a surprisingly light voice, as though trying to exorcize all the demons that for the past few days have surrounded the TV star's mysterious death—including the nearly unmentionable possibility of suicide itself.

O Lord, you have searched me and you know me . . .

For good reason, I'd been the first at the site of the accident, along with Asger, while Orla and Severin had stayed behind to call for the ambulance. The car was at the bottom of the slope. We'd recognized it immediately.

If I go up to the heavens, you are there; if I make my bed in the depths, you are there . . .

The preliminary investigation indicated that Peter had been driving down Kongslund's driveway, as he had so often before, when he suddenly—for whatever reason—had taken a sharp turn to the right, driving along the edge of the slope at an insane angle. When the car's point of gravity changed, the whole vehicle rolled to the left and down the steep drop. It had literally tumbled the same way the People's King had when he fell from the top of the hill in 1847; the car slammed against the same tree stump that had stopped the king, and with such a force that Peter was flung through the windshield.

If I say, "Surely the darkness will hide me and the light become night around me," even the darkness will not be dark to you; the night will shine like the day, for darkness is as light to you . . .

Maybe he'd suffered a sudden attack of numbness in his weakened legs and hadn't realized how hard he was accelerating—after which he'd frantically angled onto the slope. That was the most plausible theory I could come up with, but I could tell from their eyes that the police didn't entirely buy it.

The Apostle writes in his Letter to the Romans: "For none of us lives to himself, and no one dies to himself . . ."

Peter Trøst Jørgensen's body had been caught between the strong branches of one of the twelve beeches, and he'd dangled there, grotesquely, head down as though someone had dropped him to Earth from Heaven itself. A terrifying sight. Apart from the paramedics, Asger and I were the only ones to see the macabre scene up close (they cut him down and covered him up before the police arrived), and now we must live with the image for the rest of our lives: both of Peter's legs had been cut by the smashed windshield glass, nearly slicing them in half.

As surely as I live, every knee shall bow to me . . .

I threw up among the butter-fertilized plants the navy captain had planted so lovingly in the ground. Through my tears, it seemed to me, I saw a small girl between the trees, standing still, observing me. When I moved she disappeared in the direction of the empty white house, where my best friend had lived, and that was a detail I shared with neither the police nor the paramedics. Or anyone else.

Amen . . .

They found a receipt from an inn located in a town no one had ever heard of before, Gøderup. No one could explain what Peter had been doing there on the last night of his life. It didn't make any sense.

All rise . . .

The pastor had returned to a more earthly plane.

They carry out the casket; Asger is in the left front, Susanne the right. In the middle are Knud and Nils, and at the back, the two lawyers, Orla and Severin. They bear the coffin to the edge of the grave. There's a green iron fence with narrow bars encircling the gravesite.

The gate is open.

Praise to the Lord, the Father of our Lord, Jesus Christ . . .

They lower the casket. Asger blinks back tears, like many of the guests and the three wives who stand among the mourners, all giving in to the pathos of the moment. None of them really knew Peter, though; I know that better than anyone.

Who according to his abundant mercy has begotten us again unto a living hope by the resurrection of Jesus Christ from the dead . . . for dust thou art, and unto dust shalt thou return.

Accompanying his words are the dry, hollow thumps of three shovelfuls of dirt, and it occurs to me that all interment throughout the history of humankind has aimed for only one thing: the dream of never dying, never ever . . . *for Heaven's sake.* The ritual seems to be a signal to all the magazine photographers who have, until now, kept their distance. The swarm approaches the grave, surrounds us, and snaps pictures of the celebrities and the mourners from every possible angle.

Let us sing "On your way! Be brave and true."

We stand and sing beside the grave. Some of the photographers even sing along as they snap close-ups of the tall white marble headstone.

Peter Troest Jochumsen.

Around us in the enormous enclosure lie men and women with extremely distinguished family names like Lehman, Spreckelsen, Federspiel, Hasfeldt, Hinzpeter, Falkenskiold, Warburg, and Wedell-Wedelsborg. There's not a Jensen to be spotted for miles around—nor a Jørgensen.

* * *

As soon as we returned to the villa, the two lawyers went up to pack their belongings. Orla Berntsen and Søren Severin Nielsen had slept in the same room—Ms. Nielsen's old room in the southern tower—and that was a source of humor for the rest of us: the two former enemies who'd been cut off from one another's lives for decades over a nation's handling of the immigration question had, in only a few weeks, practically become as close as when they were children. It seemed both banal and fantastic. Even Asger Christoffersen gave up trying to explain the new bond between them.

The two clearly considered the Kongslund Affair to be a closed chapter, and after Peter's shocking death, they announced that they were planning to start a legal practice together under the name *Nielsen & Berntsen.*

It sounded immensely respectable, and we toasted them with a glass of champagne. The only cases the company wouldn't touch, they said, not with a ten-foot pole, were those dealing with immigration and asylum (neither man smiled as they told us this). The irony of it all made me smile.

"The Kongslund Protocol is at the heart of everything," Asger said later that evening, when the two lawyers had said their farewells and departed.

"It's the missing Protocol that keeps this case alive—regardless of what Malle and Almind-Enevold want us to think. And regardless of whether or not Severin and Orla run away with their tails between their legs, the way lawyers do when push comes to shove."

Nils had also gone home after telling us of his decision not to share with his parents his real origins. They'd lied to him for half a century, so now they'd have to live without the truth in their remaining years. In a strange way, it satisfied him to possess this unspoken knowledge—perhaps it was a form of revenge.

Susanne, serving green tea in the sunroom, agreed with Asger. Taasing, who had both legs propped up on an antique footstool of African antelope leather, nodded as well.

"Maybe there's nothing to it but what we already know," I said. "And then it isn't that interesting anymore . . ." Lisping only slightly, I could feel my left shoulder sink toward the floor.

It wasn't a topic I wanted to make more of than I had to.

"That kind of personal log detailing secret events would be extremely dangerous to many . . ." Taasing seemed to almost swoon at the thought of all the scandals he'd be able to unleash with that kind of weapon in his hands. "I imagine it contains the names of the most respected dignitaries, many of whom are probably still alive and holding very fancy titles, extremely upstanding citizens in Danish society—just imagine, there might be people from the royal family on that list!" His eyes gleamed at the thought. I understood Taasing's interest in a story he hadn't promised the Almighty One he would suppress—if it could be substantiated, that is.

I chose to say good-night and walked alone to my room—leaving only Asger and Susanne in the sunroom. And to my surprise, I didn't feel a thing at leaving them in each other's company—nothing like jealousy.

36

EVIL

November 2, 2008

The fable of Kongslund and the seven children from the Elephant Room could have ended right there—with the brightest star among them extinguished in the sky. But as Magdalene said the very last time she visited me, rolling her old wheelchair to my bed, there's always some rustling about upstairs, which people only hear when they think they've come to the end. Dear Marie, for seven years, you've been looking for the truth—and you've challenged three kings: the earthly king, the heavenly king, and— most dangerous of all—the king of all life's coincidences . . .

Then, cackling from equal parts satisfaction and effort, she leaned toward me, and I could hear the deep rattle in her throat when she lisped her very last message to me. No one does that without being punished.

* * *

Knud Taasing rang at the old woman's door, pressing the doorbell again when he got no response. For a long time he listened for a sound, the scraping of a chair or a cough that might reveal the presence of someone inside. He waited. He had time.

In a way, he'd returned to the starting point—to the very source of the mystery, even though that might not be an entirely logical way of looking at it—because at a subconscious level, he still connected the thousands of blue elephants that Gerda Jensen had painted on the infant room's walls with the seven people he'd followed ever since the anonymous letter arrived.

For months he'd analyzed the seven children involved in the Kongslund Affair, and he'd connected the seven pieces that seemed to form a clear and logical picture, which most would accept if they knew it—seven small children who were now adults, one of whom had had a strange prehistory: Nils Jensen. From beginning to end it looked plausible.

And yet there was something that didn't fit.

In spite of his strong faith that he'd found the answer in Nils, he could feel that something was amiss. Strange things had happened— such as when the firemen from Roskilde had finally broken down the steel-plated doors in the basement under Channel DK and found the dead Professor hanging from a rope (you wouldn't think a man that old had the energy for such a difficult undertaking).

He rang the doorbell again and heard a sound this time. Now he knew she would open the door.

Right away he saw the fear in her eyes. All the strength she'd once mustered when the Gestapo confronted her at Kongslund had vanished.

"I have only one question," he said.

Nothing else. It wasn't necessary.

She didn't respond. But she did finally invite him into her apartment, simply by leaving the door ajar when she turned and walked back to her high-ceilinged living room. It was furnished with a large mahogany dining table, four upholstered mahogany dining chairs, and a blue sofa. There were no bookcases, no books, and Taasing thought that was strange; he'd pictured her as a knowledgeable, well-read woman.

In the windowsill were three small porcelain figurines, a giraffe, a hedgehog, and a blue elephant. The three animals had a panoramic view of the sound and Hven. She sat on the sofa.

Taasing pulled one of her four dining chairs nearer the sofa and sat down. Without further ado, he asked the one question that had kept him awake for many nights since the old night watchman opened the bureau drawer that held the secret form. "Is Nils Jensen . . . is he John Bjergstrand?"

For a long time she didn't reply, and he began to think she hadn't heard his question, until she suddenly said, "It doesn't matter."

Her voice was muted, practically a whisper, but those three words were crystal clear.

"He isn't the one, then? Not the *real* John Bjergstrand?" A slight reformulation of the critical question.

Her long, triangular face with its pointy nose had taken on a grayish tint, as though the blood had slowly drained from the upper part of her body. He recalled Marie telling him that this woman couldn't lie, even when she most wanted to.

"Who *is* John Bjergstrand?" he said bluntly. "The *real* John . . . who is he?" His eagerness caused him to lean so close that there remained less than a foot or two between them.

Her skin was now the same color as the porcelain hedgehog on the windowsill.

"Answer me, Gerda. *Who* is he?"

She began to slide off the sofa; he reached for her, startled, and clutched at her thin white arm. At that moment he heard a whisper that seemed to arise out of the depths of her chest. "There is no John Bjergstrand." She stared at the ceiling and fainted.

Afraid that she would die in his arms, he didn't dare ask the final, crucial question again.

As he lifted her from the floor and placed her upon the sofa cushions, she babbled incoherently. "Magna . . . she never helped anyone but herself . . . and me . . . and the children . . . She was here for the sake of the children *alone* . . . She never helped others . . . never helped wealthy people that way . . . covering things up . . . like they're saying."

Taasing nodded, but mostly to reassure the old woman, because he couldn't quite tell what she was blathering on about.

"I was the one who took him . . . it wasn't Magna, it was *me* . . . I took him, for Magna's sake . . . but she couldn't know about it . . . She'd done everything for me."

The old woman wasn't making any sense. Taasing nodded again, reassuringly, and waited for the incoherent stream of words to cease. Then he heard a name that surprised him—the name of the person whose role they'd never understood.

"*Dorah* . . . she promised . . . she promised . . . if we delivered . . . if we . . . oh, my God, what have I done?" Her small body trembled, and to Knud's surprise she began to cry.

She was still crying when he left the apartment. Her tears appeared to originate from somewhere deep within her, from an inexhaustible source you wouldn't think could be contained in such a diminutive frame.

He wondered about that name for hours afterward.

Dorah Laursen.

What was her role in all of this?

She'd adopted a child who couldn't possibly be John Bjergstrand—and now she was dead. As so often before, he gave up trying to find the connection. There didn't appear to be one.

But he'd gotten the most important answer he could from the woman who couldn't lie—and he understood what it meant. Something was completely wrong with the Kongslund Affair. Some invisible hand had shuffled the deck so ingeniously that everyone had come to think they saw patterns where there were none. The electron had never been located at the point in the atom where everyone thought it was. When you touched what seemed to be real and established, it disappeared. He decided not to share this knowledge with any of the others. And, in this, Taasing committed his third mistake in the investigation of the Kongslund Affair. Naturally, it wouldn't go unnoticed by Fate.

* * *

"Yes, *I killed him,*" Orla Berntsen told Søren Severin Nielsen.

The two men were seated in a couple of patio chairs at Glee Court, and the former top official's admission came abruptly, halfway through their evening meal together after their departure from Kongslund.

During the day, movers had gradually emptied the living room, basement, and the bedrooms on the second floor of his mother's home; most of the furniture had been driven to a storage facility until Orla could decide what to do with it. He was planning to move back in with Lucilla and his daughters in Gentofte—as he'd told Severin—but didn't know if he wanted to stay with his family very long. His guardian angel hadn't commented on these plans because she understood the dangers that lurked; she had merely said he was welcome to come back and stay for as long as he wished.

By midafternoon, the movers had removed the last piece of furniture from the small living room, and without comment, had eased the remains of the blue lounge chair onto a dolly and wheeled it out to the moving truck. Now it was gone—and with it all the old images of the woman who kept an eye, from the shadows, on Orla the Lonely. The picture of the boy and the man with the orange beach ball still hung in the second floor bedroom, because Orla had asked the movers to leave it—and he didn't know why. That evening he noticed another change: the tones of the Brahms sonata emanating from the pianist's living room were gone, as though all the reports of urban uprisings and international skirmishes on the evening news broadcasts had to be endured without his calming accompaniment. A few days later, he learned that the pianist had actually died in the middle of a bass chord on the most beautiful summer day anyone could remember.

"You're saying you killed Benny the Fool," Søren summarized in law-yerly fashion, nodding to his friend.

"Yes, I killed him." It was a pure confession.

"But the *hand* you saw . . ."

There was a moment's pause. Then Orla said in almost the same voice: *"My hand . . ."*

"Yes. But Orla, if you tore out a human eye that brutally—with bloody sinews and veins and nerves and all the rest—you'd have had blood everywhere . . . at the very least on the hand that threw the eye into the creek."

Orla closed his eyes and tried to recall the night that changed his life.

"Did you?"

"I could have just washed it off."

"Did you do that?"

"I don't remember . . ." He hesitated as he recognized this, as though under cross-examination in a courtroom where the accused has not yet understood the ulterior motives of the prosecutor.

"But was there blood on your hands—or on your clothes—later on?"

"Not as far as . . ." Orla stopped.

"The police would have seen it if you had."

"Yes."

"And then you would have ended up in the slammer—regardless of Malle's intervention."

"Yes."

"But there was someone else who went and washed up that day, wasn't there . . . ? Someone who went and washed in the creek?"

"Yes," he said for the third time. Orla sat with his eyes closed. "I thought he was going to help him . . . the Fool, that is . . . but he just stood there . . . his hands motionless in the water."

"Poul."

"Yes."

"Orla, I saw the whole thing, from the bushes under the elm trees."

"You did what?" The voice came out practically as a whisper, the confidence detonating like a bomb on the small patio.

Severin blushed in a way grown men rarely do, and certainly not a lawyer in the middle of a cross-examination. "Yes. I was hiding in the bushes that night. I'd heard the shots, and I followed you. I tried to shout, but he was much too fast, and afterward I was terrified. I was scared stiff that he'd see me, and that I'd end up in the creek along with the Fool. That boy . . . Poul . . . he was crazy."

"But why haven't you told me before?" It was a logical question.

"Because . . ." Severin fell silent, blushing even more.

Orla opened his mouth—presumably to repeat his question in a more demanding tone, as lawyers tend to do. In just a few seconds they'd swapped roles. Now Orla was the accuser, and Severin was the guilty one.

But at that moment it was as though an angel passed through Glee Court—perhaps not a guardian angel, but nonetheless some creature with the power to ward off evil—and let the God of Friendship drown out the answer, if there even was one. If friendships are to last, you ought never to demand answers to certain questions.

"So you're *not* a murderer," Severin said finally. "You might even be the only one of the seven of us who isn't. You're neither an adopted child, nor a murderer." He tried to smile.

For the first time in many years, sitting alone in his mother's empty living room, Orla cried.

37

THE ASSASSINATION ATTEMPT

February 5, 2009

When I contacted Dorah's son it wasn't to comfort him or to teach him the art of reconciliation, but to tell him a story I had no doubt would have a certain effect on him.

Naturally he would believe me, as he had before, and he would gather courage and confront the person I'd identified as responsible. That's what I had in mind.

To this day, I don't know if, deep down, I truly realized what was going to happen. I could easily claim that I thought he'd move in the only possible direction—by peaceful means—and that no one could have known he'd change course at the last minute. How was I to know the violent temper I'd provoked?

* * *

It happened early in the evening on February 5, 2009.

Quite a few pedestrians heard the faint sound of a gunshot—though some thought it was just a midsize firecracker exploding—and for that reason they could help the police determine the time.

The guard at the National Ministry raised his head from a crossword puzzle and listened more attentively. It sounded as though the noise came from somewhere underneath his feet; he instinctively shuffled his shoes and stared at the wooden floor, as though his eyes were able to penetrate the floorboards and uncover a secret hidden in the very core of the earth. Leaning forward, he glanced up at the windows. Behind one of them, the former minister of national affairs was in the process of sorting through old files, a good many of which he believed were better off destroyed. The guard had let him in earlier that evening.

The guard's feet settled down, and he dozed off. In any other country, there would have been a team with dogs and walkie-talkies and machine guns at the entrance to such an important ministry, but here people still had faith that others wouldn't resort to violence even if they had obvious reasons to do so. The minister's chauffeur was the one who rapped on the guard's office window, calling his attention to the fact that something was amiss.

At 6:32 p.m., the chauffeur from Helgenæs, who had gotten the job about a year earlier, had been watching the first evening news on the little dashboard TV in the minister's car. A tag on his breast pocket read "Lars Laursen," a solid Jut name; his job was to be ready around the clock, in full uniform, and he accomplished that with the inherited discipline of his forebears. His mother's name was Dorah, and it had been almost eight years since she told him the shocking truth. Seven months had passed since he'd buried her at Helgenæs Church, right outside the little town of Stødov, where farms and small holdings were scattered across the hills.

Together, the chauffeur and the guard ascended the wide stairs to the ministerial floor and stepped into the section known as the Palace. It was faintly illuminated by the numerous electronic lights from the clerical desks. As he was accustomed to doing, the Almighty One had asked his secret service detail to wait at a discreet distance—in a car outside the entrance—because he absolutely didn't want to risk the impression that the hero from the resistance movement was afraid to move about his kingdom alone.

The two knocked on the minister's heavy office door. A new minister of national affairs had not been named, and there were rumors the ministry would be shut down, the Ministry of State would swallow up all its functions, and state and nation would become one. They knocked a second time, then opened the door. For a moment they stood indecisively in the empty office. Finally they tapped on the door to the adjacent suite, the minister's lounge area, where their lord and master often napped when the day grew too long.

This room too was empty. The bed, with a beautiful embroidered blanket atop a wine-red silk duvet, was untouched.

Then they came to the third door, which was held in place by solid steel hinges. The few people who knew of the existence of this door referred to it, half-jokingly, as the Escape Route—and that was its intent in the olden days. In case of war or attacks or other threats to the nation's safety or administration, the ministry could be evacuated discreetly through this exit. It led to a staircase that wound down under Slotsholmen, to an extensive cellar system networked underground like a series of giant mole tunnels. From here, the most important ministers could cross beneath the square and up through another staircase—to safety.

After hesitating for about ten seconds, the two men opened the door; they noticed the light was off, and that the ceiling lamp wasn't working. They fetched flashlights from the storage room.

They descended into the depths, which hadn't been properly ventilated for centuries. The tunnel sloped downward and came to a bend before resuming its incline. The chauffeur aimed his flashlight at the ceiling, as though inspecting for stalactites or clusters of bats, and therefore nearly stumbled over the nation's premier, who lay in the middle of the corridor, his legs pulled to his chest, as though he were asleep. Like a small child.

Leaning closer, the guard caught sight of the prime minister's face, and then proceeded to shower the chauffeur's shoes with the contents of his stomach. Blood oozed from the premier's mouth, glowing purple-red in the beam of the flashlight.

Lars Laursen stood like a stone pillar, intransigent just like his stalwart ancestors who'd once found a mysterious ticking pocket watch on an East Jutland main road and considered it the work of the Devil. Quickly he flipped the unconscious prime minister onto his back, revealing the bullet's entry point. Blood seeped from the hole and down the white dress shirt and breast pocket, with its gold-leaf cigar clipper, and onto the chauffeur's large hands. To his surprise, the prime minister was still alive, cursing under his breath.

The guard sat up, pulled out his gun, and called 911 on his cell phone.

During the following hours, it was believed the perpetrator had been identified—a Tamil refugee who worked for the company that cleaned the ministry. Considering the fate of the deported Tamil boy, it seemed a plausible motive to the police. The assassination could have been an act of revenge.

What clued them in was the fact that the janitorial staff, which consisted entirely of underpaid foreigners, had their locker room and break room in the same part of the basement where the minister was found. They had—quite literally as some of the officials liked to joke—created their very own subculture in the ministerial cellars.

But a couple of days later, further investigation revealed that the suspect had been on his way home, sitting in bus number 6 in Vanløse, when the prime minister was shot.

No new theory about the assassination attempt was formed. Investigators scrutinized the backgrounds and family relations of bell-hops, security guards, secretaries—even department heads and administrative bosses. Alibi upon alibi was established and together formed an almost impenetrable wall around the man who'd been shot. For all intents and purposes, it should never have happened.

Miraculously, he had been revived twice in the ambulance to Rigshospital, and the entire nation celebrated the old resistance fighter's resurrection as though it were yet another heroic feat.

"It was a bull's eye shot," the chauffeur from Helgenæs had told the TV cameras as he ascended from the dark, adding, "but he's alive." No one had taken notice of the slight change of tone, when the man uttered the word *but*—even though it was transmitted and replayed over and over again across the entire nation. Everyone called the chauffeur a hero and attributed his peculiarly gloomy expression to shock. Not even the police thought of checking this man's past; to suspect him of anything shady would have seemed to the public absurd and insulting.

I could have told them about Lars Laursen. And about his mother, Dorah, who sat in her low-ceilinged home in Helgenæs and who, after many years, finally told her son the gruesome truth about his life. I could have told them about the feeling of not knowing your roots, and about the angst you suffer when you discover you will be forever denied access to it. It's a feeling we know better than anyone else.

Lars Laursen and I.

I studied his expressionless face on the TV screen and thought of the piece of information I'd given him, which had released the blind, merciless rage I knew only too well. He had reacted even more violently than I'd thought possible. But they wouldn't catch him, I was sure.

The king was still alive, however, and in a few months he would resume his wrongful place on the throne—now an even bigger hero in the eyes of the people.

38

RESURRECTION

September 11, 2009

In a way, they are still there—the proud governesses who brought us light and who taught us to walk and curtsy and bow, as they observed the other children romping about on the grass a stone's throw from the beach.

Smiling, they followed us with their eyes, lifting their teacups and controlling life in the beautiful garden down to the last detail.

On this particular day, there is a storm brewing from the northeast, and the wind cuts, as it always has, at the cornices and gables of Kongslund, and I wouldn't be surprised if one of the seven white chimneys pulled loose and slid down the roof, into the depths.

I am sitting by the window, a little hunched over; my left shoulder hangs a tad lower than the rest of my body, as it always has. I am living proof that Kongslund's symmetry has always been an illusion.

* * *

The Protocol lies in my lap.

It's bigger than I remembered.

Perhaps in my child eyes, it seemed smaller than it actually was, cradled in my foster mother's immense arms.

There are brown spots on the green leather binding, maybe remnants of her fingerprints, or just the usual signs of age.

It contains outlines of the lives Magna found particularly interesting. Patient descriptions of the children she invited into the Elephant Room, because they had a very special need for care. There are details about harrowing fates and developments, which she would never have divulged in official journals and psychological reports for fear that these failures and weaknesses would one day return from their archival hiding spots and be used against the people she protected.

I hide it in the cabinet, next to my own binders filled with notes about the children in the Elephant Room in 1961: the carefully recorded observations of my visits and the newspaper clippings from their adult lives.

Now I open it to find the sections I need to destroy a king.

From the beginning, it was obvious to me that there was more than enough evidence. Magna was a methodical woman, after all.

When the following lines are read, it will be too late to undo my last and biggest decision.

It's already too late for the Almighty One on his glorious throne, too late for the ascended monarch who built Kongslund dreaming of perfect symmetry, and too late for the Master himself, who never in His mocking hubris would discover the obstacle that was intended to trigger the last fatal fall . . .

And, of course, it was too late for me.

* * *

On the morning the prime minister rose from the dead, I received my very last, almost inaudible message from Magdalene. The whisper was so muted that if I hadn't known her for as long as I had, I would have mistaken it for the wind sweeping around the gable.

I realized that there was one thing left to do.

Ole Almind-Enevold had finally risen from his hospital bed and was driven the short distance to Slotsholmen in a cortege whose length dwarfed even that of an American presidential inaugural motorcade along Pennsylvania Avenue. It had taken a left turn down Blegdamsvej, then a right onto Østerbrogade; had driven down St. Kongensgade to Kongens Nytorv, over the bridge at the stock exchange, and through the gate to his rightful domicile.

He assumed the Ministry of State, while seated in a silk-upholstered wheelchair that had been provided free of charge by the country's biggest manufacturer of medical equipment (and whose logo was strategically imprinted on both silver-plated wheel hubs). The wheelchair featured a small, red handle that allowed him to maneuver it majestically to and from his desk. It goes without saying that the chair bore no resemblance whatsoever to the ramshackle vehicle I'd inherited from Magdalene.

Cameras from at least twenty TV stations followed the process (absent of course was the bankrupt Channel DK), and the joy in his recovery reached across the nation; it leaped from house to house, from street to street, and from town to town—just like in a fairy tale.

I turned off the television in the sunroom and walked angrily up to the King's Room.

I won't pretend that it didn't give me personal satisfaction that I, a mere amateur, had outmaneuvered the journalist and the security advisor, as well as the police, who had searched so hard for Magna's last package.

Of course I succeeded in figuring out my foster mother's last move. I had lived in her house, as her chosen one, for three decades before she retired. In contrast to the professional hunters, Taasing and Malle, I knew what she was thinking when she decided to send the precious book out of the country, beyond the reach of her pursuers. Given all her experience with the reparation of abandoned children, she would take pains to consider what her own death might mean. And that was the understanding that my two competitors could not quite grasp.

My foster mother would have planned for even the most improbable and undesirable turn of events.

The ministry and the police had no doubt kept the relevant post offices under surveillance as they searched for the package that everyone was sure would eventually return from the other side of the planet. But, all these months, they'd looked at the wrong address of the foreign packages they examined; and even more crucially, they'd focused on the wrong name. I was the only one who understood who Magna would have listed as a sender as she shipped it out of the country.

It was her only chance, the only person in the world she could trust.

Gerda Jensen.

The rest of my investigation was simple. After exactly three months, I sought out Gerda. That would definitely be enough time for the Australian postal authorities to determine that the address didn't exist and to return the package to the sender.

She opened the door only after I'd waited outside for a while, and I felt her nervousness just like I had the last time I'd visited her.

"You received a package containing the Kongslund Protocol," I said, still standing on her doormat.

The thin woman nodded, a quicker admission than I would have expected, even from the most honest human being alive.

"It's legally mine," I said. "I am Magna's heir." I stepped into the hallway, and she began shaking even before I mentioned my foster mother's name. At first it was just a little tremble, then more and more—until finally she was quaking uncontrollably.

I helped her into the living room and to the blue sofa where we'd sat the last time I visited her. "It means everything to me," I said, and though my tone was meant to be reassuring, it had the exact opposite effect. In her renewed trembling, I felt the peculiar fear spreading from her body to mine.

I didn't quite understand it. *How could the prospect of handing over the book with descriptions of Magna's impressive life be that frightening? What did it contain?*

But I was stubborn. "I have a right to know what's in that book," I said.

That message didn't produce anything but renewed shaking. I stood up and left her alone in the living room.

The Protocol was on her nightstand. I brought it into the living room and asked the only question on my mind in that moment, "Did you read it?"

"Yes."

The most loyal and upstanding person, who struggled to lie even when her life was at stake, had—for the oldest reason in the world—broken Magna's trust. I almost laughed, but that would have probably frightened her even more, and I didn't want her to faint on me again. Gerda had simply been too curious not to read it.

"I knew it would arrive . . . but I'd decided to burn it," she whispered. "But . . . I didn't dare . . . Magna . . ."

"That's what Magna would have wanted," I said mercilessly. Brutally.

Without forewarning, Gerda Jensen fainted, but I knew she would regain consciousness the minute I left. She was both tougher and wiser than she let on.

Later that night, Knud Taasing called Kongslund. It was almost a ritual. He'd called every other day for months to ask if there had been any "new developments" in the case.

What he meant, of course, was: *Has the Protocol surfaced?*

I had had a feeling that he no longer unconditionally believed in his own prediction that the Protocol would end up in my hands—and then with him. He had begun to think that his theory about Magna's cunning plan might be wrong after all, and that she had never sent the secret book to a deceased woman on a distant continent, in the hope that it would be returned when the storm had cleared.

Or maybe he thought that somehow Malle and Almind-Enevold had succeeded in intercepting the package when it returned to Denmark, even though Taasing with his experience and extensive network of sources couldn't tell how or when that could have happened.

On the telephone he told me that Orla and Severin had received several death threats at their new office—and paradoxically, they came from both ends of the heated debate about refugees and immigrants. Their new partnership had opened them up to accusations of ideological treachery by their own. A threatening letter had arrived in which Orla's round face had been glued onto the body of the executed Che Guevara lying on a cot in a Bolivian cabin. The juxtaposition was a bit confusing, but much to Knud's amusement, the police had provided Orla with a bodyguard from the secret service. The former chief of staff once again resided with his wife, Lucilla, in Gentofte, while Severin lived in Søborg—in Hasse's old room.

For a long time, nobody had seen Nils Jensen, not even Taasing. He'd gone on a work trip to "another continent" as his father put it, without offering further details.

Taasing, for his part, had no doubts. "He went to Australia," he said. "He's trying to find a trace of his mother—of Eva Bjergstrand. He wants to find a nicer story than the one Almind-Enevold offered him."

I could tell it rankled Taasing that he'd been unable to topple a prime minister—deep down, that's what all reporters wish to do—when he'd had such a unique opportunity. And no doubt this regret grew as the days passed. I knew that the possible retrieval of the Protocol had been his backup plan when he let the Almighty One off the hook the first time around. The contents of those notes were not necessarily covered by the promise he'd made so honorably to his old enemy—and to Nils Jensen. Over the past months, no media outlets had offered the former top journalist a job. An exposé of the scandal at Kongslund, supported by the notes in the Protocol, was presumably his last chance at redemption.

He asked how Asger was doing, and I chose to lie so as not to reveal the grief I'd felt when I talked to him for the last time. After all, he'd been my secret love for most of my childhood and youth.

But I'll admit that he visits Susanne once a week, from Saturday to Sunday, and that from time to time, he visits me in the King's Room.

He comes not as a suitor but as a consoler—always during the daytime—and he always leaves before darkness falls.

I still feel the caution that arose during the first days after my lies were revealed—both my lies about the letter's real date and about my meeting with Dorah Laursen at Helgenæs. Asger never believed a word of what I said—I sensed that very clearly—but I also knew that he would never reveal his suspicion to the others. But I think it was this unpleasant knowledge about my deceit that finally drove him out of my room, despite our shared fascination for God and Fate and the stars.

From the beginning, he must have thought that all these shared interests had arisen in happy parallel tracks that aligned almost miraculously, and that he'd found a soul mate of rare caliber. But my deceits suggested another possibility. They suggested a pattern that would make any scientific observer uncomfortable, because it was *too* perfect; and the way I see it, he chose beauty and safety instead of the asymmetrical and the uncertain—the queen of Kongslund instead of the girl in the tower—and what man wouldn't have?

When he visits me, we don't talk about Susanne Ingemann—or about what happened between them as children. Nor has he said a single word about our meeting at the Coastal Sanatorium when I played the blind girl, and I sense that he thinks of that as another deceit. My first. He no longer sits in my wheelchair or uses my telescope, and he takes care not to look out the window where his gaze might be sucked in by the light over the sound and Hven.

"People like us, we'll always have that feeling inside of us," he said when he visited me for the last time (though he himself was unaware that it would be our final meeting). Like always, he smelled of soap and wool, the way wise men do. "We lay in the darkness without knowing who we were, or where we were going, but we were together, Marie. Even though it shouldn't be possible for children that young, we understood each other. Even though we didn't have a language yet, we spoke, and that's the miracle: we proved that *no* human being is ever completely alone."

He stood in the doorway before taking his leave, as though struck by a premonition about the final good-bye, and said, "To people like us, any human being we meet is one of the blue elephants, and for that reason we can't hate anyone, can't judge anyone, can't reject anyone. Because once they lay there too—right next to us—speaking to us in the darkness. Nobody can ever change that feeling."

When he was halfway out the door, he stopped again, and said his very last words: "Marie, the only problem in the world, between left and right and light and darkness and intelligent and stupid and parents and children, is that we all forget the capacity for empathy that we are born with." He took a step backward into the darkness, but I still heard his voice: "The Elephant Room proves that human beings do not from the beginning contain that judgment"—for a second he sounded as though he were going to cry—"and it proves that Niels Bohr was right: electrons never rest in the same condition if you don't want them to. It's not possible—*nothing* is predetermined."

That was his last farewell, and I might have been naive enough to believe him if it hadn't been for the book I'd just wrested from Gerda and my foster mother's arms.

It was no longer some starry-eyed orphanage protocol full of old women's tales about long-forgotten adopted children and their adoptive parents: it was a weapon, an especially brutal weapon, because it contained the description of a reality that had been hidden for so long.

It told the story of a fairy-tale-like deceit. Of the father of our nation's real sin, of the cynical plans of three individuals—Carl, Ole, and Magna—for the fates of seven children: Peter, Asger, Severin, Susanne, Orla, Nils, and myself.

It told the story of a murderer.

And it would take down everyone who'd been involved along the way.

39

NEMESIS

September 12, 2009

There are headstones carved like an open book of fairy tales where the dead person's name is chiseled in golden brass on the left page. I would have preferred that Magdalene had been buried under such a stone rather than lie in an unmarked grave under the twelve beeches up there on the slope; after all, the Great Poet had been a guest in the white villa shortly before she was born—and she could have had a spot next to him, I was sure.

If I had proposed that kind of arrangement to my foster mother, she would have laughed at me with that deep rumble that was meant to reassure the children under her care. She would have put her hand on my left shoulder and said, "Marie, in truth there is no God or Devil. There is only this reality. We live and we die—and in between, we have to do things as best we can."

Needless to say, it had never been like that in my world.

* * *

The old leather-bound book literally drifted in from the ocean. Had there been rushes between Skodsborg and Bellevue (as there had been on the stretch of the Nile where Moses had arrived), Magna would have definitely found it there.

It was in the water and quite dissolved, with no name on the cover or any other indication of who'd lost it or where it had come from.

These were her notes on the first page.

It's three-fingers thick and contains at least 4,000 or 5,000 pages, she wrote. *My first thought was that it was a ship's log, and that for some reason it had fallen into the water. Nothing had ever been written on its pages, or maybe the saltwater had erased the ink—but I don't think so.*

My practical foster mother brought the book to Copenhagen to a retired bookbinder, whose adopted child had once been in her care, and he restored the beautiful keepsake for her, affixing new pages and engraving her full name on the cover in gold lettering that had barely faded over the years: Martha Magnolia Louise Ladegaard. Here she acknowledged her full identity, and that suggested to me the book's importance to her.

Already as a child, I imagined that my foster mother was writing in the log from a sunken submarine or some beached vessel from one of the great wars, or maybe from a Spanish frigate that had long since sunk to the bottom of the ocean. But Magna wasn't inclined to such far-fetched thoughts. She was just satisfied that the book had come to Kongslund—since in the future it was to contain the most important details about the home whose location near the water had always been crucial to her. And it had been her intent that it would follow her into the grave.

This book is never to be read by anyone, not even after my death, she wrote in the Protocol's introduction.

I ignored that.

The thoughts that Magna at first confided in her new keepsake were not particularly spectacular. They revolved around the children who spent the first part of their lives in her care, and she described the everyday routines—an afternoon by the beach or an outing to the Deer Garden—and more serious problems such as the adoption of an especially damaged or ailing child.

As the notes progressed, her descriptions increasingly centered on the weakest and most poorly adapted, the fragile ones: their flaws, defects, and the slow progress that was owed to her careful repair work (although she herself never used that expression), and which made up the content of her life.

It seemed to me that the Protocol contained a life's quest for the answers to the misfortunes that are ceaselessly passed from one generation to the next—as though a higher power wanted humankind to never learn from its mistakes and therefore never correct the previous generation's blunders.

The specially chosen children, the ones in the most need, were the ones she let stay the longest in the Elephant Room, where they received the special protection and care of herself and Gerda Jensen. She described her selection criteria, what kind of negligence they had suffered, and which correctives she intended to hammer in to help them transform into a more usable shape.

One little boy's parents were both alcoholics, and one little girl (who never spoke a word) had been pried with forceps before the authorities delivered her in a hospital (her mother died). A third child had become so emaciated that no one thought it would live—and like this, onward they marched: the stooped, miserable beings across the pages of the Protocol just like the elephants in Magna's song—in apparently endless rows.

But then things changed. From the spring of 1961 to the summer of 1962, she deviated from the pattern: she let the Elephant Room serve as the setting for the lives of seven children—of which only one could be said to really need her ingenuity and special care, namely me, the little foundling.

None of the other six are described in the pages of the old log as being especially damaged or as having a particular need for protection and care. Nothing like that is ever mentioned, and that would probably strike readers as peculiar.

What was her motive for letting us remain together for so long in the most important room in the house? I leaned over the book, crookedly. I would finally know the answer.

In the Protocol, Magna's careful notes transformed into some of the most shocking I have ever read. Her notes revolved almost exclusively around me—and they told me a story I'd never imagined possible.

Page by page, I realized what had made Gerda Jensen so terrified of handing over the book to me.

The fear had nothing to do with protecting the children described within, nor about Magna's activities. To the contrary.

It was all about me.

She knew this book would destroy the child they loved.

* * *

What worries me most are her fantasies. More and more frequently, I catch myself fearing what is going on inside her. Some of what I see and sense is so peculiar and different that I cannot find the words to describe it: The wheelchair. The telescope. The mirror. Not to mention the palsied woman she has begun to dream of night and day. God knows that I've come close to taking that chair from her at least a hundred times and driving it to the landfill in Klampenborg, but I fear her wrath, and something tells me to heed this fear.

So wrote Magna, who otherwise feared no one.

And I should have stopped reading—right there at the beginning of her narration—but of course that was impossible.

I am the daughter of a pastor, and from time to time I get the sense that Evil has come to reside at Kongslund in a creature I don't know, my foster mother wrote in an even more mystifying note on one of the following pages. I didn't understand the connection, even though her tone left a sinking feeling in the pit of my stomach. For a woman like Magna, who never had any time for artificial drama, these kinds of incantations were shocking.

In the following pages she writes of Eva Bjergstrand—and the child—and everything that should have never happened but did. And she does it in a way that shows that she slowly realized what she'd initiated—with the help of her faithful assistant, Gerda Jensen.

Her first encounter with the newborn child is described in the Protocol as a revelation: *Never during all my years at Kongslund have I seen a creature so fragile as Eva's child. And I have, after all, seen quite a bit.*

This is in the beginning of May 1961, three days after the arrival of the mysterious woman to Obstetric Ward B, where her baby was delivered and since disappeared.

The crucial event is not the birth itself, because it was, as Magna elaborates, planned to the last detail by powerful men and therefore followed to the letter. The determining event that changed everything about the fastidious plans was Magna Louise Ladegaard's own encounter with the child that was to be offered up for adoption—as had been arranged with the very young mother.

When Ole Almind-Enevold and Carl Malle had first told her the incredible story about the prison affair, Magna had refused to help them. Kongslund did not want to get involved in such a deceitful and dangerous game.

But when the two men outlined the plan that would cover up the affair and spare the mother—and enable Ole to adopt his own child— she'd finally agreed. For the sake of the child, of course. Even if the last part of the plan was to be kept secret from the unhappy woman.

Eva Bjergstrand had agreed to her own pardon in return for the child, the two men told Magna—and they didn't dwell on this. The justification for her pardon would be her age and that she was a new mother.

From their time in the Resistance, Ole and Carl had close contacts at the Ministry of Justice. Party members registered the contours of a scandal that had to be avoided at all costs, and they were more than happy to turn a blind eye. Well-placed officials pulled the right strings and cashed in some favors. The girl would begin a new life in Australia, and that was the best scenario she could hope for. In any case, as a felon and a single woman, she'd never gain custody of the child anyway. No matter what, the child would be put up for adoption.

In that situation it was better for the child to live with its biological father than to end up with complete strangers, Ole and Carl argued. Of course they had not told Eva the last part of the plan—that Ole would adopt the child—because, they said, it might trigger an even more profound longing in the mother. (It was like putting a white-cloth diaper over the young mother's eyes, I thought to myself upon reading it.)

Magna, having finally talked to Eva herself, agreed to the plan. For the child's sake.

But then the unpredictable happened—as it does so often when bold people proceed without heeding the old Master up in his heavenly bed. It's a strange truth that even the mightiest constructions are blown away by what appear to be simply mere coincidences.

In this case, it was Magna's encounter with Eva's child.

Kongslund's great matron regretted her participation in the plan the minute she leaned over the crib at Rigshospital. During those minutes in the obstetric ward, there had been no doubt in her mind: never before had she seen such a lonely and damaged child as this—never. And she'd seen it all.

In Kongslund's Protocol, she described it like this:

While the child's mother slept, I spoke to the head nurse to make sure she was not more exhausted than normal. Then I let them show me the way to the child, which lay by itself, and it was like a revelation. Although I have never believed in God or any higher power, I can't describe it any other way. Not even I, who have seen so many abandoned fates, could help being affected by the sight: a little girl with black hair, her back and one shoulder deformed, her feet at an odd angle as though a giant hand had grabbed them and turned them round and round. It was a heartbreaking sight, and I knew instantly that this creature couldn't be protected by anyone but me and Gerda. Under no circumstances could I leave this child to a man like Ole Almind-Enevold and his wife, Lykke, whom I was sure had no interest in adopting to begin with.

I believe I read this section three times before I understood what the words meant.

The shock came like a kind of slow-motion replay. It rolled in, as though from the earth's core, and burst the very foundation of Kongslund, up through the infant room ceiling to strike me in my chair by the desk. I slid sideways onto the floor and lost consciousness.

I awoke in a pool of water—just like that time long ago when I'd let myself be carried away in Magdalene's arms, when I thought I was drowning—and the water was everywhere around me. *A little girl.* Maybe I'd always known . . .

With trembling fingers and sapped of all energy, I undressed, crawled onto my bed, and lay on top of my duvet. Apparently no one had heard me fall, because no one came to my rescue. The fatal Protocol lay open on the desk under the window.

During the hours that followed, darkness fell, and I began to slowly understand everything: the child that Magna had described as so immensely damaged that it would take years—maybe a whole lifetime— to repair, could only be one person . . . and I understood it with all of the horror that a human soul can harbor . . .

It was me.

Eva's child had been a girl—not a boy as everyone had thought— there was no other possibility.

The deformed shoulders, the black hair (which became lighter as I grew older) and the deformed feet; all of that only described one body in the whole country—a body that had once drawn specialists from near and far to admire its unique design.

I lay there for a couple of hours, I think, staring out the window at the sound, and then I forced myself to get up and continue reading Magna's grotesque story.

I loved her from the very first moment, she wrote.

This disclosure revealed with more clarity than you could ask for that the repair woman's expectation of this tremendous new challenge acquired an even stronger partner the moment she peered into the bassinet: a sudden and deep maternal feeling that had lain dormant for decades.

Together the two positions must have been invincible: *Mother and Repair Woman.*

I remembered how Gerda had once told me (presumably in response to one of my strange but insistent questions) that my foster mother had refused to start a family of her own because it wasn't reconcilable with her activities as the protector of *all* children at Kongslund. And of course, as a single woman at the time—as Orla's story abundantly shows—she would be seen as irresponsible and, to put it mildly, tarnished if she were to choose to have a child. Of course Kongslund's matron could not be subject to that kind of judgment.

The notes that followed were clearly written a few weeks after the events that had been rendered in detail—and I wasn't surprised. Anyone would have needed time to collect herself.

It was Gerda's plan that we carried out during the following days. Without her sense of detail it never would have worked. It was clear to us that if we wanted to save this child we had to hide her from Ole and his ever eager helper, Carl. It was difficult because we knew all about their craftiness and cynicism from our time working with them in the Resistance.

I leaned back in Magdalene's chair and envisioned the two women: determined and convinced of their objective.

First, we baptized the child in the hospital chapel—in part because the staff thought the girl was so afflicted that she might die, and in part because Eva had demanded it. But above all we did it because the birth certificate became the most important part of the cover-up that would hide Eva's child from its biological father forever. It was Gerda's resourcefulness that saved us.

At this point, I made an effort to read the text extra slowly and carefully—in order not to miss anything important and because I feared the discoveries that each new sentence might reveal about my life story. At times my heart pounded so hard that I could barely hold on to the old book's pages. With terrifying clarity I sensed where things were heading.

Eva had expressly made me promise that her child would be baptized Jonna if it were a girl and John if it were a boy. She had already agreed that she herself would be told nothing whatsoever about the child, not even its gender, because it would then be even harder for her to leave; her longing would be stronger. And of course that's how Gerda got the idea for the switch.

I stopped reading again and closed my eyes. The Protocol was shaking in my hands as though the book was equipped with a small, invisible motor. Now, after half a lifetime, the final, unavoidable truth would finally reach Kongslund. It would bang the front door wide open, trudge purposefully through the hall past the lady in green, and sweep into the King's Room where I sat alone.

I opened the book again and turned to a new page. To my surprise (and horror), I saw that my foster mother described the two women's shrewd plan with a pride she could barely contain.

We baptized her Jonna Bjergstrand, as we had promised, and the name was entered into the church registry at the hospital chapel. A few days later we got the birth certificate, and for Gerda, whose artistic talents had brought joy to generations of Kongslund children, it was an easy matter to complete the transformation. First she extended the first n in Jonna to an h, and then she erased the a with her pastel paste. Finally she made a copy and threw away the original.

It was that easy. Jonna had become John. I still remember how satisfied Gerda looked when she showed me the final result: John Bjergstrand. It was like magic. We had erased a little girl and replaced her with a boy. The line in the h resembled a little elephant trunk.

I was shocked. I stood and retrieved my copy of the forged birth certificate and scrutinized it. There was no doubt. There was indeed a double space between the first name and the last name (where the *a* had been), but it was barely noticeable—less than a millimeter—and had never been detected, neither by the night watchman, nor by the rest of us who'd been so pleased with ourselves for finding the birth certificate that we hadn't looked too closely at it.

I had arrived at Kongslund on a Friday, and Magna and Gerda had let off the governesses early for the weekend. For the first few days they'd put me in Magna's living room on the second floor and merely told the staff that it was a little boy in need of special care, one who needed absolute quiet.

But my journey into the nightmare that the Protocol revealed hadn't reached its end yet. The women still had two important things to do.

Of course there was still a problem we had to solve, and we had taken that into account: we needed to get hold of a boy no one knew of who could fit the name John on the birth certificate, the boy that Ole was to adopt.

To my horror I saw where the story was going—and how the two women's maternal instincts and desire to protect had clouded their judgment. These two ladies, who more than any other at that time embodied national morals, were in the process of fabricating a deceit that they would never be able to divulge to anyone—and from which they would never escape.

First, Jonna had to disappear completely, Magna wrote.

And then she continued in an almost conversant tone: *A few days later, Gerda discreetly gained access to the church registry at the hospital chapel. She removed all traces of the name Jonna Bjergstrand.*

Yes, she tore out an entire page, I thought to myself.

The next day I persuaded a woman who lived near Svanemøllen and desperately wanted to put her child up for adoption—a little boy—to participate in a much faster and more discreet arrangement than was typical. And then we launched the final part of Gerda's plan.

Again I paused in my reading. *The woman at Svanemøllen?* This could only be Dorah Laursen, whom I had traced to Helgenæs so many years later. That was how the fragile woman had become part of the mysterious drama.

Gerda went and retrieved the boy early in the morning. It was May 13, the anniversary of Kongslund. She dressed him in a jacket and set him in the carry-cot she'd brought under a pink blanket, as we had planned; when we revealed the find, the color would make everyone assume we'd found a girl. I drove Gerda to Kongslund and stopped the car, letting her out on the slope, which she climbed to place the carry-cot at the doorstep by the southern annex. No one saw her come or go.

I took a deep breath. No, no one except for the invalid woman in the neighboring villa, who saw everything and had tried to tell me about the scene right before she died.

And yet a problem had occurred, as Magna notes: *Unfortunately Agnes noticed the carry-cot before I made it there. Good thing she found it, and not one of the brighter students. She suspected nothing and, thankfully, didn't pick up the baby. Instead she screamed out loud and called for help. She's a very naive girl, and she'd never seen a foundling.*

I closed my eyes. There was no longer any doubt. The two mad women—whom the entire nation knew as the emissaries of Goodness—had deceived everyone into thinking that they had found a little *girl* on the doorstep—me, that is—and that I was a foundling, placed there by an unhappy and irresponsible mother. It had all been one big lie. I saw the genius of their strategy. It would keep me hidden forever. No one would even consider looking for a foundling's origins. They were simply untraceable.

As soon as the boy from Svanemøllen had been brought into the house, everything moved swiftly. Magna carried the cot past the Giraffe Room and into the bathroom, where Gerda was at the ready with my deformed body, which she immediately placed in the cot instead of the boy. I stayed there for the rest of the day so I could be photographed again and again—the miraculous foundling—by the many magazine photographers who buzzed about Kongslund for its anniversary.

The timing hadn't been a coincidence, either. Magna's assistant had carefully selected May 13—the day of the anniversary—because then the story would break through all the country's media and be confirmed by hundreds of witnesses. Even with a photo. Not even the most skeptical reader would see through this deceit. Fortunately, Agnes's unintentional remarks to one magazine—about it being a boy—hadn't been paid attention to by anyone.

Magna had yet another reason to make me a foundling—as she later noted in the Protocol: *Marie's identity as a child without a past means we don't have to provide her with a fabricated history, which could be easily revealed as such. We needed a foundling, so we created one.*

In this way Eva's little daughter gained her own (thoroughly false) prehistory, and I was exhibited as the famous foundling who had come to Kongslund from nowhere and had been rescued on the very day of the great orphanage's twenty-fifth anniversary. It was so mysterious and compelling a story that, much like an actual fairy tale, it enchanted everyone. The lie could have lived for a hundred years.

A few days later, when Eva Bjergstrand suddenly refused to fulfill her part of the agreement and leave the country, the two women were forced to overcome a final crisis.

Maybe she sensed that something fishy was going on—maybe even that the child's father was involved, the way Magna suggested in the Protocol: *Girls from the social class that Eva grew up in have a sixth sense for that kind of thing.*

Eva had been furious, Magna wrote. She insisted they tell her about the adoptive family—and during the final hours before her departure, she threatened to demand the child and reveal everything if Magna didn't comply.

In desperation, my foster mother showed her the only official document available—and here, the ruler of all apparent coincidences must have shrieked so loudly that it could almost be heard on planet Earth. But of course it couldn't. On the form was the name that Eva would never forget—the name of the woman whom she would come to believe was her child's adoptive mother: *Dorah Laursen.*

After the name came the address that she'd remember fifty years later: *Svanemøllen, Østerbro.*

Magna must have been convinced that she'd forget the name. But even if she didn't, it wouldn't matter because Eva Bjergstrand was going away as far as possible, never to return.

After that, grieving deeply, Eva left Denmark. To find a new life and atone for her crimes—both the one for which she was pardoned and the one she had committed when she became pregnant with the young law student and career politician's baby in Visitation Room 4.

* * *

In Gerda's and Magna's eyes, all their efforts had been motivated by the honorable need to save the little creature who required such extensive repairs. In one move, they had achieved a number of advantages, which they felt was more than sufficient justification for their deceit.

Eva Bjergstrand had been pardoned and was setting out for a new life; she would no doubt meet an Australian man and have children of her own. Ole Almind-Enevold got the son he'd always wanted—add to the bargain a child who was not deformed like his real child. In addition, the boy from Svanemøllen would get a wealthier and better home than the one he would have had with a mother who didn't want him.

Finally—and most importantly—Eva's child would receive crucial care with Magna. Kongslund's matron saw herself as the only person capable of protecting a child with such a terrible mental ballast and unusual physical shape.

From the two women's point of view, this was a scheme that worked in everyone's favor, and which was therefore in line with the principles of Goodness. In the Protocol, Magna even described how they congratulated one another when the project was completed, toasting with a glass of port in the King's Room.

And yet it all went wrong.

Lykke Almind-Enevold refused once and for all to adopt and then had a nervous breakdown. The young lawyer dared neither press her on the issue nor leave her because it would make him seem callous and lacking in the moral fiber necessary for public office.

It was during the days between Christmas and New Year's that Ole Almind-Enevold told Magna about his wife's decision.

My foster mother's shock is evident from the Protocol: *As I always feared deep down, Lykke has declined, and that puts us in a terrible pinch. Ole is begging me to see his son, but I refuse, as always. Now it's clear how wise it was of us to never show him the real child. The boy named "John Bjergstrand" must be hidden from everyone, forever.*

She put the name in quotation marks, of course. Because no John Bjergstrand ever existed, not then, and not now.

During those days, the most difficult and dangerous of their lives, the two women had a boy child at Kongslund who—if they were to expose their own forged papers—was the son of a murderer. Of course Ole already knew that, and after the adoption, he would have tossed away the certificate and, through his contacts in the state administration, gotten a new one—with a new name. But an entirely new and responsible adoptive family would no doubt require more information and would attempt to dig into the child's background. That couldn't happen. Magna and Gerda could never risk that.

A night watchman's family has applied to adopt, even though we have told them their social rank does not qualify them for approval, Magna wrote under the heading March 1962 (though she rarely dated her entries).

Gerda thinks this is our big chance.

A few weeks later, she described the solution Gerda came up with: *Everything has gone as she predicted. The family has agreed to go about things quietly, both for their own sake and the sake of their son. When the man asked me for the child's papers and birth certificate, I wanted to deny him access, but Gerda convinced me otherwise. I told him to burn the certificate as soon as they're sure there's nothing wrong with the boy, and he promised to do that. But Gerda says he will no doubt keep the birth certificate because that's how people of his kind are. It could be to our advantage, she says. If someday anyone is clever enough to track down Eva's child, this is where they'll wind up—and the birth certificate will, as it was originally intended, identify the boy as Eva's, thus keeping her real child hidden.*

A final, deeply buried assurance.

Gerda's cunning and her ability to predict even the most bizarre patterns filled me with both consternation and admiration. How could a woman who'd never been able to lie make such deceitful plans?

One page later in the book, Magna writes: *They've said they'll call the boy Nils, and that they'll forget everything about his background. Gerda is satisfied. "John Bjergstrand" has finally disappeared once and for all, as though he never existed.*

And then she added: *And, of course, he never did.*

* * *

Already in January of 1962, the young lawyer Ole Almind-Enevold began to investigate the five boys from the Elephant Room in order to identify his son. He must have been desperate as a consequence of Magna's stubborn rejections.

I can imagine the considerations he and Carl Malle made, which were confirmed by later events—and by Almind-Enevold's admission in the ministry when he was finally presented to his son, Nils Jensen.

Convinced Magna would never put Eva's vulnerable child with a working-class family in the slums, the two old comrades must have instantly ruled out Nils. They completely missed the significance of this cover-up.

They were also inclined to rule out Peter because his adoptive parents came from the other end of the social spectrum and, as a distinguished and intellectual family, would no doubt be dismissed as victims of such duplicity.

They ruled out Asger because they didn't think that Magna, with her heavy burden of responsibility for this adoption, would send Eva's son to a family that lived as far away as Aarhus, since the distance would leave her very little control.

That's why they focused on the two boys in Søborg: Severin and Orla—and especially Orla, who'd ended up with a single parent in Glee Court. With their illicit scheming and tactical planning, they concluded that it might have been an ingenious move on Magna's part—to construct the story of a single, biological mother—to divert their attention. Orla was often at the orphanage, and, besides, the stocky boy looked like the successful politician.

Toward the end of 1962, Almind-Enevold therefore promised his friend, Malle, his full support for the duration of his career if, in return, he would do him the favor of moving into one of the newly built brownstones in Søborg where the two boys lived.

In that way the two men were able to discreetly follow the comings and goings of the boys.

Time passed, and they got no closer to answering the riddle, and no one discovered the injustice inflicted upon Eva and her child. When they obtained, a few years later, blood samples of all five boys and the results proved inconclusive, Malle advised against further testing—no doubt because he feared that Almind-Enevold's son was not one of the five, which would mean Malle would lose his hold on him completely. I couldn't help but smile at the real reason for the failure . . . that the two men never thought to test a girl.

The three conspirators—Magna, Ole, and Carl—are locked into an uneasy alliance. If one falls, they all fall.

Eva remains in Australia and thus fulfills her part of the pact. She changes her name and finds a job as a secretary at an oil company but never marries.

I'm guessing that her longing—and her profound self-reproach—was a major obstacle.

During the following years, according to Magna's narration, Ole's career falters. The prime minister who assumes office in the fall of 1962 passes him over for a ministerial appointment, because there are still rumors in the party about a scandal having something to do with his time in Prison Services and, perhaps a young, incarcerated woman.

No politician wants to dig any deeper.

In the meantime the country's best doctors fix, to the best of their ability, my deformed body, and I slowly straighten out and have a life of my own, albeit a hidden one, at Kongslund.

I've named her Inger Marie, because they are two beautiful old Danish names derived from the words for Beauty and She Who Comes from the Sea—and what could be a better fit? Magna writes in the spring of 1963. *She is still going through some procedures, but the doctors have succeeded in straightening her feet a bit, so she is now able to walk, almost like the other children. I take great joy in that development. Two years after we discovered the foundling, several magazines once again wrote about the fairy-tale-like story, and once again reporters complained how no one had been able to find the child's father and mother. The police continue to receive calls about the case whenever it's discussed publicly, but most calls are from disturbed people who are invariably attracted to such stories.*

A couple of years later she writes: *At my request, Mother's Aid Society has now recognized that our little Inger Marie will be very difficult, if not impossible, to place with an adoptive family. She still looks very odd, and she is still so fragile that she isn't able to live in a normal family. Mrs. Krantz is sympathetic to my suggestion that Mother's Aid Society grant me official status as Inger Marie's foster mother.*

There is no mistaking her joy at becoming a *real* mother in these pages: *Marie loves to wear dresses in light colors. She often picks yellow ones, like the color of the freesia that are in full bloom in the beds outside the Elephant Room's window. Her favorite thing is to walk with me in the garden and pick newly blossoming freesia for special occasions at Kongslund or for when we receive visits from distinguished people who have learned of our work—sometimes from as far away as Japan.*

I furrow my brow, because I don't remember it like that. To the contrary, I have a clear image of an energetic, determined woman who picked the flowers by herself, in solitary majesty, and who then stood beside the kitchen counter, a huge presence, crushing the stems until they were flat—as though they were small people who needed to be shaped into a viable form.

In one passage, Magna observes, almost with a sense of relief: *After all, it is fortunate that Marie was so deformed at birth. She resembles neither parent.*

A few years later, she confides in the Protocol the role Gerda had taken in my upbringing: *We've decided to homeschool little Inger Marie, because the psychologists believe that she is still too weak to be sent to school with the other children. It is important that she has calm surroundings. I've decided to give her the King's Room. I've told her about the room's history and its place in the exact center of Kongslund, right between north and south. The other day, Gerda read aloud to her from an old article in the Søllerød Post, which told the history of the area. Inger Marie was most interested in the story about the little invalid girl who grew up in the white villa on the slope behind Kongslund. The newspaper printed some of the girl's journal entries about sea captain Olbers, the first owner of Kongslund. Inger Marie loves the journals, even though she has never met the author.*

The last remark surprises me. Magdalene had been with me again and again, up on the slope and down on the beach—especially when she sat on the pier in her old wheelchair studying the sound through the king's telescope.

Magna must have seen that.

Gerda tells me that it was no doubt Magdalene's story that caused Marie to write at such an early age, and to everyone's surprise. Gerda gave her a stack of sky-blue notebooks, which she writes in and guards as though they were her most prized possession. So far no one has been allowed to look at what she has written, but I'm very excited to, of course. She will probably show me some day.

This is the last passage in which Magna's descriptions of my life and actions are narrated in a light, cheerful tone.

The transformation is abrupt. Page by page the mood seems to darken, and it becomes more and more evident that Magna is worried about her foster daughter, and that her concern increases as the months go by. It culminates the morning they find my friend dead.

The old invalid died last night. They found her at the foot of the slope next to the wheelchair she used whenever she risked going out. She was brash enough to leave the house while it was still dark, the police believe, because it was the night after the American moon landing. An old telescope lay crushed at her feet. The police think she wanted to study the moon but had flipped over in her chair.

I feel a growing rage at reading Magna's description. At this point in the Protocol she was talking about something very crucial in my life, and I no longer wanted her presence. I didn't want her to come any closer.

I should never have brought Marie along to the old woman's funeral. It's as though since the woman's death Marie has become obsessed with her. In the shed, she's found the wheelchair the governesses used to spin her around in when her feet were in bandages. And the other day she found an old telescope that someone had thrown on the beach. She has affixed the telescope to the armrest of the wheelchair. Some days she carries the chair down to the beach and sits there for hours studying Hven through the old rusty instrument, which you probably can't even see through. I'm not sure what she is looking for, but I know from the librarian that she checked out three books about the astronomer Tycho Brahe. Maybe it's the moon landing that has inspired her. Gerda tells me not to worry so much, but I am not so sure. Gerda always believes the best in people.

Month by month she turns it over in her mind—this growing problem she has understanding her daughter, and my interest in the place I would never escape from.

Now Gerda worries too. And for good reason. Yesterday Marie told her that her telescope belonged to a king, the monarch who built Kongslund, and that it has been passed down to her by the invalid woman. Where do kids get such crazy ideas? Gerda has tried to make her put the wheelchair back in the shed, because she doesn't need it at all. But Marie maintains that it belonged to the old lady in the neighboring villa—and it is this persistent delusion that worries us the most.

Again I felt my anger stirring as I read this, because Magna had followed my relationship with Magdalene much more carefully, and in much more detail, than I'd ever imagined. I didn't understand why she had never shared her observations with the child she claimed to love—not a word—so I could have reassured her and corrected all these misunderstandings.

Maybe some of what happened later could have been avoided, I thought. But my foster mother chose to remain silent, leaving her descriptions in her beloved Protocol to stand as distant whispers for posterity, even on pages she didn't intend for anyone to see. Least of all me.

During those years—when I was ten or eleven—she kept a close eye on me, and her concern sent her looking for the journals, which Gerda had given me to write in, when I wasn't in my room. She wanted to know what I was inventing, as she put it, but she didn't find them the first time around because I'd hidden them as well as I possibly could. It was during this period that I made my secret trips to see the children I was shadowing, while she was at meetings or at conferences in the name of Goodness of Heart—and Gerda chose, for reasons I don't understand, to cover for me.

In the beginning of 1973, there came a breakthrough in Magna's surveillance of me: *Yesterday, when Marie sat as usual in her chair on the pier, studying Hven in the telescope that had long since lost its lenses, a thought occurred to me that really ought to have come a long time ago. I hurried into her room, and my hunch proved right: in a drawer with a fake bottom in the captain's old bureau, I found the blue notebooks that Gerda had given her.*

That afternoon Magna opened my notebooks one by one, studying all the secret thoughts and observations I'd entered onto the pages—and it infuriated me. But at the same time, I noted to my satisfaction how deeply she regretted doing it.

Today I wish I had never read those notebooks, but what has been done cannot be undone, she wrote. There were things she didn't understand and which she questioned: *Is it normal for an eleven-year-old to write in such a way that it resembles the diaries of a dead woman? Not just as though she knew the dead woman, but as though she is that woman? Could that be considered a natural element of a child's fantasy life? I hardly dare write this, not even in this book that no one will ever see. And I certainly don't dare ask the psychologists at Mother's Aid Society.*

She skipped a line and then wrote: *I am more distraught than ever.*

My anger grew to a point where I was about to suffocate. I felt tears, which always gave me away, running down my left cheek. Magna had crossed all boundaries. She didn't just read my notebooks, she'd copied them too, and she had considered showing them to Kongslund's bearded gang of pipe-smoking oracles to ask their advice. She had come dangerously close to revealing my and Magdalene's innermost thoughts to everyone in the world. She'd read about our first meeting—when the water flowed and nearly drowned us both. She had had access to my most intimate memories, and all she'd thought to do was to pass them on to the men who would destroy the children they didn't understand.

It was Gerda who'd pleaded for her to let it go.

Gerda is afraid of the risk involved. That in the end, they'll take Marie from me. Maybe it is normal to live in that kind of fantasy world, but if it isn't, then I risk losing my daughter, Gerda says. Of course that would be a catastrophe to all of us, because if she really is as sick as I fear, no one can help her better than I.

The logic was as sound as Gerda herself, but how typical of my foster mother to make up an illness for another person that she could then work on for another couple of decades in the service of Goodness—but in this case, of course, I was relieved at her decision. Nevertheless she continues: *I've talked to Gerda about the problem again, and for once she is as much at a loss as I am, as though she is confronted with something she had never before experienced. I'd never thought I'd see Gerda like this. Inger Marie has always made up a lot of stories, so maybe that is the explanation for Magdalene's diary. Even when she was little she told the naive governesses that Kongslund was full of famous people's children, suggesting that Kongslund had a hidden purpose as the protector of the wealthy. I suppose it comes from seeing all the wealthy families taking their kids out for walks on Strandvejen. As Gerda says, maybe she combined it with the funny nicknames we derived from famous people and gave to the children while they were at Kongslund. At the time, we just let her make up things. It seemed innocent, after all. We didn't think anyone could take such tall tales seriously. Maybe that was a mistake.*

Again, it's typical of my foster mother to blur the reality that no one is supposed to see. I myself am living proof of that. I was—or rather am—actually the daughter of a famous man, however much I'd like to be blissfully ignorant of that fact.

In the months that followed, Magna continued her investigation of what she now referred to as Inger Marie's secret life. In addition to the twelve notebooks that contained Magdalene's journals, she found some of my old diary entries—the ones about my conversations with Magdalene in the years after her death. Magna read those, too, one day while Gerda was tutoring me in the sunroom.

My fear is now entirely indescribable. She writes that the old woman died peacefully in her sleep on her patio the very night the Americans landed on the moon, and that she therefore died happy. Perhaps, she has simply repressed how it really happened. Yet, there is something about her distortion of reality that I find disturbing. I don't know what to make of her account, but I don't dare ask anyone for advice. Not even Gerda.

In the years that follow she often visits my room when I am out, the Protocol reveals, but she never finds my oldest and most secret hiding place—in the compartment of the old cabinet, behind the lemon-tree carvings—where I keep my accounts of Orla, Peter, and the others. She never finds my descriptions of my cohorts from the Elephant Room—the ones who left me one by one but have now returned.

At one point it appears as though she relaxes, assured that I must have stopped writing and fantasizing, as she calls it, and it seems to lessen her jealousy of my friend.

I think Magdalene is finally a completed chapter, she writes in the beginning of 1974.

That's how naive the repair woman of the world's lost souls was.

At that time, Gerda is still tutoring me. Once in a while, she's assisted by a teacher from Søllerød School (who herself has adopted a child from Kongslund), and on weekends I help take care of the older children in the Giraffe Room and the Hedgehog Room. Everything seems almost normal.

Magna's worries now focus on more practical matters, and when I become a teenager and later approach twenty, she writes in the Protocol: *I think we've succeeded at Kongslund in doing the work we were put on earth to do. But, of course, I am still worried that she has no other interests than drawing moons and planets, which she copies from her astronomy books—and then studying Hven through the broken telescope she loves so much. It is clear to me that she is going to spend the rest of her life here at Kongslund. And that is the only comfort I have to offer her.*

From her notes in the Protocol, I can tell that it's important for her to keep me at Kongslund and to prevent any plans for my adoption by repeatedly underscoring to Mother's Aid Society that I was too fragile and different to be around other people.

She's not going anywhere.

In order to prevent her colossal deceit from being revealed, she had—I realize—let me live in the awareness that I'd never go anywhere.

During the following years, it appears that Magna thought my flaws disappeared one by one—until the day she viewed me in an almost magical light: as a beautiful, shapely woman who looks more and more like her *mother.* Of course that's a distortion of her immense, unfulfilled maternal love, but it causes her to keep me away from other people—as energetically as possible. She writes how she fears that Almind-Enevold, on one of his visits to Kongslund, will discover my likeness to his young lover from Visitation Room 4—but of course he doesn't. I'm dark as a stick and have been planted crookedly in the ground; nothing but a mother's imagination could change that.

Only once in the Protocol do I find any indications of enchantment in regards to what has happened, the fate she has given me. This at the very end: *In this book, which was swept in on the ocean waves, I have described everything as it really happened. Not out of consideration for those involved or anyone else, because Gerda has promised to burn the Protocol in the event of my death, but because I myself have to try to understand what happened. It pains me that I have to keep such a big secret from my little girl, and that I have to keep it all her life, but there is no other way. My only fear is that she will one day ask Gerda the wrong question: Who is my mother? Because Gerda has never been able to lie. Thankfully, Marie doesn't even know that this question could be answered, and therefore she has no reason to think to ask it.*

With their silence they'd locked all the doors to the world around me. I sat in Darkness and tried to comprehend the vastness of their deceit.

I felt my tears drop onto the old paper in Magna's log. I wanted to close the book, but I couldn't move my hands or my crooked shoulders. I remembered all too clearly my visit with Gerda the day I'd asked about the mysterious John Bjergstrand, and how before fainting she'd whispered, "Marie . . . there is no John Bjergstrand!"

I'd thought she lied for the first time in her life, and I'd despised her for it. But I was wrong, because her response was entirely truthful. Five small words, like wreckage in the sand.

I am nearing the end of the Protocol; there aren't many pages left. Even though the anger hasn't completely left me, my breathing has grown somewhat calmer.

Then things take a bad turn again, because Magna mentions something that disturbs her. Now her worries are focused on the rococo mirror hanging on the wall over my bed. According to her notes, Magna first became aware of my special relationship with the mirror when I was a teenager and had found an old dress in a wooden chest in the attic. *It was green like beech leaves*, she writes, *but worn with age.* I put it on anyway, the way children will do, and one day when Magda entered my room unannounced, I was standing in front of the mirror turning around and around, my arms raised above my head.

A grotesque sight, she wrote.

And because she only saw me dancing, she didn't hear me ask the mirror the question the only logical reinterpretation I knew of the fairy-tale question, Who is the fairest of them all? *Who is the ugliest of them all?*

So she didn't hear the answer either. Because she saw me in such a romanticized light—the way mothers do—the experience made her even more desperate: *I don't know what to do, and no one can help me. Inger Marie tells me she's incredibly ugly. She still thinks she's the little black-haired girl with a deformed back and funny feet that walks about Kongslund toting a rusty old Japanese pull-along elephant. I've tried to tell her how much she has changed. I've tried to tell her how beautiful she has become, but I don't think she wants to hear of it. The mirror has been her most cherished possession over the years, even after it fell and fractured so badly that no one could see her reflection in it anymore. I don't understand what she sees. And when she turns to face me, I'm nearly in tears.*

I was tempted, once again, to turn to the old mirror right behind me, but I didn't. I was sure it would immediately take advantage of my weakness and jump at the chance of getting out of its Darkness—once again. I didn't dare risk that.

In a month, I will retire, Magna wrote. *I bought a condo in Skodsborg. But Inger Marie will stay at Kongslund. This is her decision. I understand it and accept it. This is where she belongs.*

I am reassured by the fact that Susanne Ingemann will replace me. Susanne loves her as much as I think it is possible for anyone besides me to love Marie.

* * *

There are only a few, dramatic entries left in Magna's Protocol, namely those that reveal the truth about the Kongslund Affair.

No doubt they will topple the Almighty One—I'm sure of that—and that's why I intend to reveal the Protocol in the only way I can imagine. But the very last notes could also be used against people, especially me, the child she raised as her own. And there's nothing to be done about that.

For forty years, Magna and Gerda were certain that no one could uncover their secret about my real identity, and then things went wrong.

Not because of sloppiness or carelessness, but because Fate allowed a Danish tourist to rise from a bench in Adelaide and leave behind a newspaper that had traveled halfway around the globe. That's all it took.

By accident, Eva Bjergstrand noticed it on the bench in front of the Australian hotel where the Danes always stayed. *Independent Weekend*: what an odd name, she no doubt, thought. On impulse she picked it up, perhaps because it was published April 8, 2001, Palm Sunday, and therefore reminded her of Easter celebrations from her childhood.

She'd been born on Good Friday—April 7, 1944.

Inside its pages, she noticed the wedding in Holmen's Church, which even occurred on her birthday. There's no doubt that with these few, casual details, Fate deliberately drew her further into the game that no one understood at the time. The man who had been the cause of all her misery smiled at her from one of the photos taken outside the church—and everything that she had sought to forget returned, as though it had never been gone.

Five days later—on Good Friday, April 13, 2001—she writes two letters: one to Magna and one to the child she has never seen.

She mails them on April 17, 2001. This is the first business day after Easter, and they are addressed to Martha Ladegaard at Infant Orphanage Kongslund.

But the letter ends up in my hands because Magna has retired and moved away, and the mail carrier fails to recognize that my name is not on the envelope.

At its bedside that morning, Fate must have danced in heavenly glee.

After Eva waited in vain all summer to hear back from Magna, she takes the only course of action that can put an end to it all: she ends her exile and decides to visit her past.

She arrives at Copenhagen's Kastrup Airport on a direct flight from Australia. It's early September. From the arrival lounge she calls Kongslund, and an assistant tells her that Magna has long since moved away and now lives in Skodsborg. Without warning she turns up at Magna's apartment in the early evening of September 10, 2001. Coincidences are falling into a miraculous pattern now, just the kind that the Master finds most delightful.

It was a shock, Magna writes. *It was a shock to see the woman I had never thought I'd see again, on my doorstep. She had aged, but in her way she was as beautiful as she had been when we helped her win her pardon and her freedom. Of course I could have wished for a more conciliatory reunion, but that was not to happen. She wanted to see her child, and this time she wouldn't accept any rejection. She was furious, I sensed.*

And now something happens—maybe it's triggered by Magna's guilt, or maybe just by an intuitive fear of the woman she knows to be a convicted murderer.

Her fury and determination frightened me terribly. Not least because once again she threatened to break her promise of keeping quiet if I didn't relent. In my fear and confusion, I told her she could find all the answers at Kongslund, because that was true. I didn't dare tell the truth to her face even if she had a right to know. I think she decided to go directly there, despite it being late at night. But I never had the courage to ask Marie. I don't know what happened after that.

Deep in her soul, Eva must have sensed the betrayal she'd been the victim of.

When she knocked on the door by the southern annex, it was I who opened it, just as Fate had devised.

It was late and dark, Susanne had gone back to her house in Christiansgave, the night-shift assistant was watching television in the sunroom, and the rest of the orphanage had long since settled in for the night.

"My name is Eva Bjergstrand."

She stood on the doorstep, in the shadows, but I could tell it was an older woman—and my astonishment could hardly have been any less than Magna's. The woman I'd tried to find for several days with Susanne was here, miraculously.

For a few seconds I said nothing. If I hadn't had so much practice carrying out conversations with the magic mirror in my room, my facial expression would have immediately revealed my surprise.

Before I could stop her, she lunged desperately into the hallway of the villa that had once housed her child—and had then separated her from it forever. I remember noticing blond strands in her gray, wavy hair—the strangest details from that night.

She stood staring at me for a long time. After that I only remember her one whispering question: "What is your name?"

I didn't answer.

"Magna told me to look for my child here." Her voice was surprisingly light and earnest.

"Your child?" I hid my nervousness behind formality, something I rarely did in a world that I wasn't a part of.

"What's your name?"

On impulse, I pushed her back out into the darkness on the front steps and asked her to wait while I got my coat. It wasn't so warm in early September, after all.

"The children are sleeping," I said. I remember this idiotic rationale quite well.

We'd barely made it to the sound before she repeated the question that she was so dead set on getting an answer to: "What's your name?" Then she added, even more insistently: "Who are you?"

The wind was howling in the crowns of the twelve beech trees behind us. "My name is Marie," I said. "I'm Magna's daughter." For once I didn't mention my status as a foster child, and I was uneasy about this, without quite understanding why.

For the next few minutes we walked side by side along the beach, heading toward Bellevue in silence. She seemed to be contemplating something. Suddenly she stopped and shook her head. "No," she said.

And stood still.

With my face turned away from her, I gazed toward Hven. But I heard what she said, and in some way understood what it meant, though I had no idea *then* of what I know now.

"Your name is *Jonna* . . . your name is *Jonna* Bjergstrand. That's your birth name, regardless of what they call you now."

"No, my name is Marie. Your *son* might be *John* Bjergstrand," I said without expression. "Not *Jonna*." I figured the woman had lost her mind looking for her lost child.

"Come on, look at us," she said strangely, which irritated me as much as the wind in the trees behind us. "There's no doubt. Look at our *eyes* . . . I'd recognize that expression and that color anywhere. We have exactly the same eyes."

"Your son's name is *John*," I repeated. "Not *Jonna*. You had a son. I am Kongslund's foundling."

Though I had turned to face the sea and had my back to her, I could tell she was shaking her head.

"No. *Jonna*," she said.

"No," I said insistently, turning to the water and the darkness.

At that very moment she reached for me. Without turning my head, I felt her right hand draw near to my shoulder. I didn't let anyone touch me. Not Gerda. Not even my foster mother.

There is no John Bjergstrand. Suddenly, it was as though I'd heard Gerda's voice, even though those words hadn't been spoken yet.

Her hand touched my left, sloping shoulder, and I spun around. Startled, she took a step backward. To make her let go of me, I shoved her hard with my eyes closed.

I don't remember anything else. Not the waves crashing against the beach. Not the sound of the storm across the sound. Nothing.

Everything seems so oddly familiar in the Darkness: we listen, we are invisible, we walk along the edge as one verse catches another. The song is the only sound we hear.

Maybe at some point I am singing in the wind—or maybe I mimic the words with my eyes closed the way I used to in the infant room.

I don't remember anymore.

When I awoke from this dream, she lay at my feet. She'd fallen in the sand. I could tell that her head had struck a rock. One eye was closed, and the other was wide open. When I kneeled down there was no doubt, just as the Fool's eye had stared into the sky above the wetlands, Eva's remaining eye stared into the darkness over the sound. Her head was smashed upon the only rock on the beach. She must have been terribly unlucky. And right then I saw something else: a length of rope that was twisted like a little noose.

When time stands still, you notice the strangest things.

Presumably it was those three things—the eye, the boulder, the rope—that inspired me to take the only logical step imaginable, and which I have to explain here in order to finish the story. For the first time ever, Fate showed me its hand. Eva lay as has always been intended: right next to her children. Or better, the symbols they'd left behind: the rock that Kjeld had struck when he was thrown off Severin's horse in the wetlands; the rope the police officer hanged himself with when Nils Jensen photographed him beating up a demonstrator in a back alley on Blaagaardsgade; the eye that stared straight into the sky the way the Fool in the wetlands had when Orla's brutal attack had maimed him. Like all the stories in my secret notes.

For a long time I stood in the darkness studying the three objects. Here was the dead woman only a few hundred yards from the place where the seven children in the Elephant Room began their lives, alone. She had died trying to find her child.

She had been frighteningly close, but she hadn't made it before Fate stopped her with a single, powerful shove.

With that in mind, I emptied the contents of her pockets of all her personal papers, money, passport, tickets, and other possessions. I didn't want her to be identified or named, because she belonged to none of us.

She belonged to no one.

I only missed one thing, the photo that Knud Taasing later heard about from his source in the police: the picture of my childhood home.

That cost him his life. I am sure it was Malle's work, but like so much else in the Kongslund Affair, it could never be proven.

Even the best hunters make mistakes.

* * *

After that I walked north as fast and quietly as I could.

At Kongslund I slipped silently from room to room in order not wake anyone.

First I retrieved the old linden branch that I'd picked up at the private school when I read about Principal Nordal's death in the *Søllerød Post*. I had instantly understood what had happened and who was responsible—of course I had, because more than once I'd seen Peter bike off toward the woods with his black bag on his bike rack.

Next I got the old book that UFO-Ejnar had read during his final hours in the hole, where he had sat down to die because of his love for Asger. *The Black Cloud.* I'd found it on Asger's patio table one of the last times I'd visited him. I had kept these two tokens in the King's Room for all these years—not even explaining to Magdalene their significance to me.

Finally I opened the birdcage in Kongslund's office and grabbed the smallest of the four slumbering canaries—the one that reminded me most of Aphrodite—and snatched it before it could escape. It was twelve years old, but still beautiful. Then I closed the cage door. I only needed one bird to underscore the symbolic meaning of my act.

Without making a sound, I closed the front door behind me and walked back to the dead woman on the beach, my gifts in my arms. I made sure to tread on the edge of the water so that I would leave no trace behind. About halfway there, I kneeled down and pressed the head of Susanne's canary into the sand until it suffocated and was still.

When I reached the dead woman, I arranged my offerings around her the way I thought was most beautiful and appropriate.

For once, the symmetry preferred by kings and gods was mine, as I made sure that all of my offerings to the dead woman were in the right spot; as I saw it, they formed a perfect pattern, symbolizing what had happened. Eva Bjergstrand herself lay with her face to the sound on which abandoned children had been borne, to meet their savior in the form of a magnificent woman in an old villa.

That was all I could do for the dead woman.

Of course there was another offering on the beach that night, a sign the police never considered because it was long gone by the time they arrived. My own personal gift to Eva. The one thing that the very few people who know me would always associate with me: the Darkness . . .

And when I left that spot the Darkness hid me as it always had.

Later I felt a peculiar sense of relief. It was the same sensation as the morning I'd met Magdalene at the pier and cried in her arms for hours. The meeting with Eva had the same effect on me. When Fate puts obstacles in your path, it doesn't put a lot of thought into it. It's pure reflex. Like when a doctor taps a little child on its knee with a small hammer. And when Fate lands its final blow, it doesn't care about motives or states of mind.

I knew beyond any shadow of doubt that the police wouldn't either.

They would just pick me up and remove me from Kongslund forever—and I couldn't let that happen.

* * *

Two days later, my foster mother found a small notice in the *Søllerød Post* that changed her whole world.

From that day on, I knew she lived in fear.

An unidentified woman was found dead on the beach between Kongslund and Bellevue, she wrote in the Protocol.

To Magna's eyes, the description fit Eva Bjergstrand perfectly. *I'm more afraid than ever,* she wrote.

The day after Eva's death, I began erasing the last possible traces that might connect me to the body on the beach. During the previous days I had—along with Susanne Ingemann—searched for Eva, and an employee at the Australian embassy had told us she'd come to Denmark. After that we'd tried locating her in hotels, and now I told Susanne that I'd miraculously trailed her to a small Copenhagen hotel at Frederiksberg Allé, but that she'd left without paying her bill and without leaving a single clue.

She was irrevocably gone, I said.

But she insisted on going to the main library to read the newspapers. Maybe she'd been in an accident, she suggested.

I was relieved that her discovery of Eva Bjergstrand's death compelled her to demand that we immediately stop investigating the case. And I was grateful for what seemed like a rare, friendly gesture from my old adversary up there in the beyond. Fate had chosen to overshadow that unfortunate push with the greatest act of terrorism the world had ever seen.

Hardly any attention was paid to a mysterious death of an unknown woman on a Danish beach.

I hid the letters from Eva in my secret compartment in the old cabinet and began patiently waiting for it all to blow over. During the following years, I often looked at the letters and read her words to Magna and the unknown child whom I realized had to be one of my companions from the Elephant Room. Every time I read them, I felt the same anger as the first time—and every time my fear of being exposed outweighed my urge to find the man who'd destroyed Eva's and her child's life.

For the next seven years my hatred directed itself against this unknown man, but I had no idea how to proceed in my investigation. Not until Magna's sixtieth anniversary approached was I stirred from my trance, which might have lasted my whole life otherwise.

When the newspapers began covering the impending anniversary of Kongslund on May 13, 2008, I understood it would be irresponsible of me to wait any longer. I owed it to Eva and especially her child to locate the man who'd ruined their lives. There would be a lot of focus on Kongslund and my foster mother, and therefore never a better opportunity to garner publicity on the case without getting involved myself.

That's what I was thinking.

On Ascension Day—May 1—I completed the painstaking work of gluing letters on five envelopes addressed to the five boys from the

Elephant Room. There was no reason to involve Susanne, who was afraid to do anything.

Since Nils Jensen did not know that he was adopted, I followed a sudden impulse and, out of tenderness, I put Knud Taasing's name on an envelope, informing him that a letter had been sent to Orla Berntsen, chief of staff in the Ministry of National Affairs as well. I was thoroughly aware of the deep enmity between the two after having followed Orla's career over the years.

The ramifications of my maneuver were much greater than I'd anticipated, especially since *Independent Weekend* was, at the time, desperate to find a scandal that could rescue the paper from its death spiral. The story immediately became front-page material.

From the beginning it must have been clear to Ole, Magna, and Carl that something had gone completely wrong. Someone had come into possession of this dangerous knowledge and was now trying—in full public view—to open up the dark passageway back to the secret they'd managed to keep for nearly five decades. The minister's panicky reaction only confirmed the case's significance to those demanding answers, and it was motivated of course by his position as heir to the kingdom, since the prime minister was terminally ill.

Any suggestion that he was connected to a murderer—and that there was a secret pact concerning the adoption of famous people's children—would cost him dearly.

For that reason alone, Malle was called in and given a single, urgent task: find the letter writer.

That was followed by yet another task: find John Bjergstrand.

Before anyone else.

As is evident from the Protocol, Magna also panicked; it wasn't just that she feared the damage to Kongslund's reputation or her own involvement; she had another worry that, in many ways, overshadowed the others because it was highly personal: me.

The unease I'd sensed in Magna after Eva's death had been unimaginable, but I'd never understood why it continued unabated over the years. It was as though she no longer dared look me in the eyes and never truly relaxed in my company.

Now, I knew why. She described the reasons for that in the Protocol, and I should have guessed it long ago:

Could this be connected to Inger Marie?

When she read about the mysterious woman who was found dead on the beach, whom she knew *had* to be Eva, she'd first believed it was Carl Malle's doing (along with Almind-Enevold, who had a clear motive), but then a much more logical and eerie possibility dawned on her: the last person to have seen Eva alive might very well have been her own foster daughter—indeed, it was the most likely scenario.

I fear the truth more than ever, she wrote.

Despite all her well-meaning repair work, I had perhaps inherited my biological mother's temperament after all. A temperament that Gerda had warned me against, though I'd never understood why.

On the other hand, Magna's fear also contained all her natural, maternal anxiety if I had indeed committed such deeds: like most mothers, she couldn't bear to see her child exposed, disgraced, humiliated, and imprisoned.

* * *

There are only four more entries in the old book. The first of these is from May 2008—in the midst of the hectic press coverage:

I think the anonymous letter mentioned by Independent Weekend *frightens Carl and Ole as much as it does me. They don't know that Eva is dead; no one else knows, because the woman on the beach was never identified.*

In one of the following pages—in one of her few dated entries, on May 12, 2008—she writes:

These days I don't dare read the papers or listen to the radio because I'm afraid to hear confirmation that what cannot happen is happening. I don't dare leave the house, but stay at home and turn away all attempts at contact. I just pray that no one else will come to harm, and I no longer have the nerve to think about what we started so long ago. I cannot bear to acknowledge what my own pride and vanity has led to. It cannot be true. I really fear for the deeds that my love for Inger Marie has led to.

In desperation she visits Gerda, and here she absorbs another shock. I can tell from her writing that her hand was shaking when she made the entry:

I visited Gerda this morning to tell her about Eva Bjergstrand's death. I asked her if there was something she hadn't told me about Eva and what had happened. She immediately began to hyperventilate, and I know what that means.

I had to give her two large glasses of port before she told me the story—and this is the most shocking thing I've ever heard. Her story was about Dorah Laursen from Svanemøllen, whose boy had become "John Bjergstrand" when we made the exchange. Five years later, in February of 1966, Dorah called Kongslund saying she regretted that we "took her child." She spoke to Gerda and her demand was grotesque. She wanted us to provide her with a "new child," or she would reveal everything. Gerda then decided to act on her own without involving me. To protect me.

It is the most dreadful thing I have ever heard a person say, but I know it is true because Gerda cannot tell a lie. Two days after Dorah's call, she kidnapped a boy from a baby carriage on a street in Copenhagen and gave the boy to Dorah. She forged a birth certificate and gave it to her as well; she has always been the great artist of this place. I've always admired her strength and determination, but I never knew she was capable of doing something like this.

And then my foster mother adds: In a way she was right. I would have never agreed to commit such an act; it would have meant the end of Kongslund and everything we had built together. Gerda could not let that happen.

At that moment I heard Fate laugh with a rare human tenor, because nothing is more entertaining or grotesque than to see the great advocates of Goodness of Heart sink under the weight of pure, unadulterated brutality—their own.

The very last entry in the Protocol is an angry outburst following the sixtieth anniversary celebration: Ole had the impertinence to read from a text he referred to as the diary of the old invalid Magdalene. That text constituted the main part of his celebratory speech, and he must have known how I would react.

It confirms what I've always known deep down: that he and Malle were behind all the break-ins at Kongslund. They found my copies of Marie's journals and stupidly thought they were actually the life wisdom of that woman!

That kind of man won't stop. He won't give up. Not until I give him the name of his child.

But I can't. And at this very moment I am honestly happy about that.

* * *

That was the last thing she wrote. A few hours later after the anniversary.

The next evening I went to see her. This was after the fight between Malle and the reporters had capsized the whole case, and I knew the battle was lost because the ensuing scandal would drive the Kongslund Affair from the front pages, the TV news on Channel DK, and elsewhere.

I've never suffered the illusion that Magna would reveal Kongslund's potential dark sides to me, but at that point I was desperate. I knew the media coverage over the last few weeks had shaken her. Maybe she would finally talk—if I begged her.

During those weeks, I had no idea about what she described in the Protocol. I didn't know who John Bjergstrand was; I had no proof that could trap a biological father; and my enemies, Almind-Enevold and Malle, seemed invincible.

When darkness was about to fall, I rang Magna's doorbell. Her surprise was evident. I never came unannounced. I wanted to say something angry to her, but as usual not a word passed my lips. It was as it had always been in our relationship: she crushed the stems, and the flowers yielded—exactly the way they were supposed to. The scent of freesia clung to Magna.

She set out the coffee cups, placing them soundlessly as always in their saucers, and just when she was about to pour, Fate made another move of the kind that is irrevocable. The question came without warning. I heard my own voice asking: "Who is he, Mother?"

And then I repeated it in a slightly different way: "Who is John Bjergstrand?"

And then a third time, differently still: "Who is John Bjergstrand's father?"

Slowly, she put the coffeepot down and gave me a strange, almost fearful look. She waited for a long time. Then she said, emphasizing every word and syllable: "Marie, there is no John Bjergstrand."

These were the exact same words that Gerda Jensen had uttered—and the same words I'd heard in the night air before Eva Bjergstrand fell and died.

"It's too late to lie now," I said. "Seven years ago a letter arrived at Kongslund from Eva Bjergstrand, and I *know* Eva is the boy's mother."

She looked at me with a tenderness that I didn't understand. "Yes, Marie. Eva was the mother." It came out almost dreamily, and that wasn't like her. "And she had her child at the Rigshospital, in Obstetric Ward B, that's true—a spring night many years ago."

Then she told me about Eva's pregnancy in prison and how she, Magna, had tried to devise a good solution following all the principles of altruism.

She told me about meeting Eva in 2001, and she described her fear of what I might have done that night. Abruptly, she paused in her monologue to ask a question in a voice so anxious that she no longer sounded like my mother: "Did she visit you at Kongslund . . . before she died?"

I ignored her. "Who is the father?" I asked. "Where is Eva's child now?"

These were the only questions that mattered.

She rose and made her way to the bookshelf. Once again I felt she was evading the most important questions of my life.

"Marie, I'd like to show you my scrapbook on the foundling's arrival—and then I'll tell you the story of . . . everything." She said this as though it were the most natural thing in the world, as though she didn't sense my desperation at all. To my surprise, there were tears in her eyes. As usual, I had no right to pressure her. She had always taken care of both of us in our shared world.

She raised her right hand to pull the white scrapbook from the shelf . . .

It was the last movement I registered.

She fell hard against the shelves, spun around, and collapsed in front of me. She lay on the floor beneath the window with its view of Strandvejen and the undertaker business across the street, and it didn't take me long to understand that she was gone. Not just for a little while, but forever.

That's how shockingly fast it happened, and with an ease that contradicted her aura, not to mention the tremendous work she'd left behind. That's how easily she left life—her life, my life, everybody's life—and the world she'd been repairing for her whole existence. It seemed almost absurd.

The scene reminded me of the only two other deaths I'd witnessed at close hand: Magdalene, who lay grotesquely crumpled at the foot of the slope with the broken wheelchair beside her; and Eva, who'd fallen on the beach and lay with one eye staring at the sky.

I hadn't felt a fear that intense since the night Eva reached for me and in a moment of insanity called me *Jonna*—perhaps not since the morning the invalid woman in the neighboring house called me over and told me I was old enough to hear the truth only she could tell me. A secret that would have an immense impact on me.

The babbling of an idiotic old woman.

As deformed as she was, she'd leaned halfway over the armrest— misshapen as I myself—and had tried to smile reassuringly, but of course she'd failed because of her grotesque lisp. At that moment I hated her with all my heart.

It is not fair that you die, Marie, without knowing the truth, she'd said in a voice that would have scared any child.

Since Gerda showed me the articles about Magdalene in the *Søllerød Post*, she'd become my best friend, even though I'd never—until then— actually met her. It sufficed that she lived in the house next door and was as deformed, unwanted, and chained to that slope as I was: an elderly version of myself. She was a person I could talk to and ask for advice, and she would answer in ways only I would understand.

She'd seen the person who arrived at Kongslund with the carry-cot, she told me, lisping—*the messenger*; she'd been awake that morning when the foundling was placed outside the backdoor by the southern annex; and she'd seen something so bizarre that she had never revealed it to anyone. But she wanted me to know before she died.

It was almost prophetic. She only had a few seconds to live.

It wasn't a stranger who brought the carry-cot, she said, staring at me with her one ailing eye—and at that moment her peculiarly corroded, old-fashioned wheelchair tipped over the edge and tumbled down the same way the king had back when he'd challenged the future of an entire nation. I don't remember whether she screamed or not.

Do people who can only lisp through the roof of their mouth even scream?

* * *

She never completed her sentence. And of course I didn't tell the police I was there.

Magna was the only one who might have felt it. But naturally, she was silent.

According to the officers who later searched the slope—spiking batons into the soil that old Captain Olbers had fertilized so generously (to their surprise they found old parchment paper with remnants of butter)—there was a plausible reason for the accident: it was, as mentioned, the day after the moon landing and the invalid had probably had an accident while pursuing adventure, looking for miracles in the sky. After all, there was a telescope affixed to the wheelchair's armrest—completely smashed when found, as though someone had stomped it into the soil.

"The poor old loony," the supervising officer sighed.

I'd found a single piece of paper in the living-room hutch—on which the old invalid had written some almost illegible sentences about what she'd seen the morning of the foundling's arrival, plus a few other scribbles about the Olbers family. I could just decipher it. She'd never written anything else. I took the paper with me and later entered the words into the blue notebooks I called Magdalene's diaries, and hid them in my bureau.

In Magna's case, the police also found the circumstances of her death suspicious, but impossible to explain or prove.

To be on the safe side, I went through Magna's apartment before I left. Mainly I was hoping to find the Protocol—but of course that was already on its way to Australia. The day after the police discovered that Magna had sent a package out of the country, I brought out Eva's letter from the desk and changed the date from 2001 to 2008, using the same technique that Gerda had used.

The number 8 looked a little flat, but no one would notice it with a cursory glance, I thought. Magna's fear that her apartment would be ransacked had rubbed off on me, yet I couldn't make myself destroy the final words Eva had written to her child.

This was the alteration that threw off Knud Taasing, much to my satisfaction. At first he'd believed that Eva was still alive—since the letter had been sent in April of 2008—and in that way I had erased any trace of an unknown woman's death on a beach near Kongslund in 2001.

It was that simple.

At the same time, I made sure that if either Carl Malle or Knud Taasing figured out that Magna had sent the Protocol to Eva in Australia, which was quite likely, they would never assume it would be returned.

They would think Eva was alive and well somewhere, and would receive the package.

Since the Protocol could contain a detailed description of Magna's unmistakable suspicion that I was responsible for Eva's death—I was sure that was a possibility—this illusion was absolutely crucial.

It was only Knud Taasing's shrewdness that later ruined this part of my plan. And it was only because Magna had listed Gerda as the sender that I avoided exposure.

* * *

It would be hypocritical—and that's not my inclination, at least not any longer—if I ended this account claiming that I regret everything that has happened.

Naturally I don't.

I can't think of anything that could have been done differently. As I see it, the fatal flaws in my plan were unintentional—and impossible to anticipate.

It's not until now that I see the overall pattern clearly: Eva, Magna, and Dorah in that order—and the bizarre course of events surrounding Dorah's son, which mystified us for such a long time.

When I found Dorah in 2001 and demanded that she tell her son how he'd come from Kongslund, I ought to have predicted her son's reaction. I acknowledge that now. That day he called Magna and demanded to know what went on back then. And he'd been furious.

Of course my foster mother, who at the time knew nothing about Gerda's monumental gesture to save Kongslund's honor and existence, denied any involvement when she talked to him on the phone—but her voice must have revealed a measure of panic, even though in this instance she was actually innocent.

Because even though Magna didn't know what had happened, she did remember the name of the woman from Svanemøllen: Dorah. *He didn't believe a word I was saying*, she wrote in the Protocol.

Lars Laursen, Dorah's son, had immediately realized that all answers would be found at Kongslund, and he'd spent the following year investigating its history including the bizarre circle of powerful people who orbited it. He'd talked to all the former employees he was able to track down, and he'd used just about every hour of his free time to synthesize and analyze his findings, which revealed the myths and rumors about Kongslund's secret activities in collusion with powerful men—and with that the party's involvement in what was being kept secret.

He was obsessed, and when he told me much later about his rage and ill-fated determination, I recognized it completely. He'd concluded that the national minister must be the central figure in the orphanage's shady past—aside from Magna, whom he had no way of getting close to—and he had a plan that seemed logical and feasible, if also time-consuming: Ministers need chauffeurs. He was a chauffeur. At the time he worked for a limousine service in Aarhus. Kongslund's protector for fifty years was a minister, and ministers frequently hired new drivers. Lars Laursen was hired on his third attempt. It took him another five years to become a driver for the national minister, and this immense patience can only be ascribed to the doggedness that pervaded his people in the East Jutland hills.

When Lars began working for the Ministry of National Affairs, he was putting the finishing touches on his plan. That was immediately before the Kongslund Affair erupted. These are the kind of coincidences—however great and seemingly accidental—that Fate finds most intriguing.

And when he came to see me after Dorah's death, he told me everything that had happened since I'd entered his mother's life: he'd tried to get as close to Almind-Enevold as possible, and he was now his chauffeur. Maybe he would find more information, he said; maybe, over the next few weeks, we could be of use to one another. Even before his mother's death, he'd sent Knud Taasing an anonymous letter after reading his articles in *Independent Weekend*.

Naturally I was terrified at the thought of having this strange, naive man digging around in the Kongslund Affair and finding out things I didn't want leaked to the public; for that reason I rather impolitely declined his offer, solemnly warning him about proceeding in the matter. The Kongslund Affair was both dangerous and impossible to penetrate, I told him.

Everything changed when I found the Protocol at Gerda's and discovered my own role as Magna had described it.

It was at that time that I decided to commit homicide, and I have to emphasize that this decision has been my only fully intentional plan to murder, though perhaps my cohorts from the Elephant Room will find that hard to believe.

I'd been sitting in my bed in the King's Room for hours, thinking about Magna's revelation concerning my actual arrival at Kongslund. On the third day I walked to the only remaining phone booth in Søllerød and called Lars Laursen, who sat alone in his apartment in Frederiksberg.

He listened to the shocking information I shared with him.

I told him of the *delivery*—his delivery—and about the duplicity that implicated him, without apologizing for my previous refusal to cooperate. I think he was too upset to scold me anyway.

In words that could not be misinterpreted, I explained to him that Almind-Enevold had been behind all these mysterious *deliveries* that Kongslund secretly facilitated, and that he, Lars, was presumably the son of a wealthy and powerful man but that every trace of his biological parents was effectively and irrevocably erased.

I emphasized—brutally—that he would never be able to find his roots because the Almighty One had destroyed every piece of information regarding his origins. It was exactly the same thing that had happened in the case of John Bjergstrand, I said.

I was aware that Fate, at this moment, could pick one of two paths: either the predictable one or the interesting one; and of course I had no doubt as to which my old buddy would choose. It would be very unlike the Master of Life's Coincidences to let that kind of chance slip away.

I, myself, would be nowhere near the scene of the crime and would make sure to appear to have no motive whatsoever.

I simply never imagined that such a determined murderer might miss his target. The bullet had entered half an inch from his hated boss's heart, and that was yet another one of Fate's insane ideas, which probably had the old Master dancing the polka up there in his heavenly bed. When *I*—without a weapon and without wanting to—could cause the death of three people with a simple unintended push, how could a deliberate shot miss its target by a fraction? The man from Helgenæs had the steadiest hands that have ever held the steering wheel of a car, and yet he must have trembled when he fired at the heart of the Almighty One. He'd carried him into the basement of the parliament building assuming that he was as dead as a doornail.

40

THE KING'S ROOM

April 30, 2010

When I lean forward, I see directly into Kongslund's garden, and if I stand on my toes and open the window, I still see the white-clad authoritative governesses who ruled the orphanage for a generation, almost as though they are still sitting on the patio.

It is as Magdalene always said, When Fate knits its careful patterns, it doesn't do so with grand ceremony but as simply and unassumingly as if playing a child's game. And that's why we never discover what's going on until it is too late.

Even the smartest minds believe that their lives follow a chronological but ultimately accidental course, and we regard even the largest and most precise obstacles as coincidences. This is a delusion that is shared by the believers as well, even though outwardly they claim to follow a course plotted by God. Because no God could have deliberately arranged for this much chaos.

* * *

The story doesn't have a happy ending, the way Magna would have preferred.

I have laid the Kongslund Protocol and my own diaries on the beach near Kongslund, where I know the person I have selected will find them. In the exact spot where Magdalene sat the first time we met.

The papers are under a pink blanket in the carry-cot the foundling arrived in. I think this is the right way to do it, and one thing is for certain: this time no one escapes, and certainly not Ole Almind-Enevold.

It will be up to others to determine whether those involved in the Kongslund Affair will be doled out their share of the blame, or whether it will have to fall on the individuals who started it all: Ole and Carl, Magna, and maybe Gerda, who painted the blue elephants in their apparent innocence, then concocted a deceit that fooled us all. And, of course, the child that couldn't let go of finding a way to a world outside Kongslund's walls. Down and down and down to the point where I killed my own mother, just as she had killed hers.

In my dreams, the sky over Hven is still full of blue elephants that swarm with clouds and sunspots the way they always did. They march from south to north upward and onward—toward the stars where UFO-Ejnar has finally found his place and is engrossed in a profound conversation with the silver-nosed king of astronomy on the very character of the firmament.

I imagine Magdalene and her chosen one watching them from their heavenly abode.

Here at the end of the story, I'm at my desk alone, as always, and I remember the words that were read at the anniversary that was to be my foster mother's last: "Every time a human being sits alone in the dark crying for another human being, the miracle comes . . ." It's hardly a masterful use of language, but once in a while I think it's true.

I'm sitting in Magdalene's old chair with the telescope in my lap, staring into the old magic mirror, but of course I no longer get an answer—no more mocking challenges, or hints at my ugliness.

Is it really broken?

I can't believe it. My right side is quite normal, as it always was, while the left side hangs as it always has; I cannot be imagining it.

I turn my attention a little to the side, and suddenly it's as though I see the lake where Samanda died. And I spot her mother in the shade under the hazel branches.

Right beside her, in the Søborg living room, Orla's mother sits in the blue chair, from which she studies her son without a word; and in Rungsted, Peter darts through the bright green garden that was his mother's paradise.

I even see Hasse's bloodied shopping bag. I reach for my telescope. But it isn't there. Or maybe my fingers can't locate it. I grope to find it, but it really isn't there. I lean toward the old mirror, but there is no movement, not anymore. Then I hear my own voice calling for Magdalene, but there is no response. It's as though she were never here—with me, in the King's Room.

Who is the fairest of them all? I jump, startled.

It's the ancient question we have always asked, but it sounds oddly distorted.

At that moment I sense who is speaking to me as well as why I no longer hear anyone respond. I understand Susanne's teasing words about occurrences that are more fantastic and incomprehensible than a human mind can grasp . . .

Until you understand that, you understand nothing.

I know that Magna was right when she held me in her arms—on the patio in front of the Elephant Room so long ago—and taught me what I would always remember.

All the best homes are by the water.

She forgot to add one detail, something that no child can grasp, so no adult would reveal. The worst thing a child can discover: there are houses where, in the end, you're left all alone.

Epilogue

MARIE'S SONG

Her home lies where it always has, near the sound, with a view of the Swedish coast and Hven.

That is, of course, how Marie found me, even though we never met face to face, and even though I never got to know her.

Like the main character of this book, I spent the first part of my life at Infant Orphanage Kongslund, and like so many others I often returned there as an adult, driven by an urge I've never been able to understand. Nor have I wanted to.

Each spring (the time of year when I was cleared for adoption), I would ride the bus up Strandvejen, pass Bellevue and Fortunen, and disembark right before Skodsborg Hill, where I would scale a small fence and find a narrow path that only I and a few others knew about (this was where the king and his beloved had walked during the months precipitating the abolishment of absolute monarchy in Denmark). Then I would trudge over the slope, past the abandoned white villa where the Fairy Tale Poet had once visited the king's architect, and head down to the beach, where I would walk north a little way—perhaps just a few hundred feet—the way Marie had done the night Eva Bjergstrand's soul flew up to God.

Finally, I would stand as Marie had once stood even longer ago, on the old pier below Kongslund, right where the People's King's ship, *The Falcon*, had once berthed.

Often I would stand there for quite some time, motionless—for an hour or two—looking toward the old house, and once in a while an assistant or childcare worker would come down to the beach inquiring about my business.

I always said the same thing, which was the truth: I once lived here.

I found the carry-cot in the sand, precisely where she'd said.

Under the pink blanket were the book, the Protocol, and the notes Marie had left behind; among them were the careful entries by a person she'd loved and whom she'd given the biblical name Magdalene.

In Magdalene's books I looked up the famous date, May 13, 1961, and I shook out the one piece of paper that Marie had jammed between the pages. It fell onto the sand.

The old song.

A moment later it was carried out to the sound like a beech leaf in the sunset, but I'd read what I needed to read . . .

Seven elephants go a marching now.

Inger Marie Ladegaard from Kongslund had reached the final verse.

About the Author

Copenhagen native Erik Valeur has been an award-winning journalist for Denmark's most influential media outlets for the past twenty-five years. Like many of the characters in this, his first novel, he too was orphaned as a child, and the plight of adopted children has been of perennial interest to him. *The Seventh Child* was released in Denmark in 2011 and has since been published in twelve other countries. This international bestseller has garnered numerous awards across Europe, including the prestigious Glass Key award given by the members of the Crime Writers of Scandinavia, as it makes its debut in the United States.

About the Translator

© Eric Druxman

K. E. Semmel is a writer and translator whose work has appeared in *Ontario Review*, the *Washington Post*, the *Writer's Chronicle*, *Redivider*, *Hayden's Ferry Review*, *World Literature Today*, *Best European Fiction 2011*, and elsewhere. His translations include Norwegian crime novelist Karin Fossum's *The Caller*; Danish novelist Jussi Adler-Olsen's *The Absent One*, selected by *Publishers Weekly* as a *PW* Pick; and Danish novelist Simon Fruelund's *Civil Twilight* and *Milk & Other Stories*. He has received translation grants from the Danish Arts Council.